THE
CAMBRIDGE EDITION OF
THE LETTERS AND WORKS OF
D. H. LAWRENCE

THE WORKS OF D. H. LAWRENCE

EDITORIAL BOARD

THE RAINBOW

D. H. LAWRENCE

EDITED BY
MARK KINKEAD-WEEKES

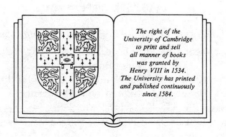

The right of the
University of Cambridge
to print and sell
all manner of books
was granted by
Henry VIII in 1534.
The University has printed
and published continuously
since 1584.

CAMBRIDGE UNIVERSITY PRESS

CAMBRIDGE
NEW YORK   NEW ROCHELLE
MELBOURNE   SYDNEY

Published by the Press Syndicate of the University of Cambridge
The Pitt Building, Trumpington Street, Cambridge CB2 1RP
32 East 57th Street, New York, NY 10022, USA
10 Stamford Road, Oakleigh, Melbourne 3166, Australia

Printed in Great Britain at the University Press, Cambridge

British Library cataloguing in publication data
Lawrence, D. H.
The rainbow. – (The Cambridge edition of the letters and
works of D. H. Lawrence)
I. Title   II. Kinkead-Weekes, Mark
823'.912[F]   PR6023.A93

Library of Congress cataloguing in publication data
Lawrence, D. H. (David Herbert), 1885–1930.
The rainbow.
p.   cm. – (The Cambridge edition of the
letters and works of D. H. Lawrence)
Kinkead-Weekes, Mark.   II. Title.   III. Series:
Lawrence, D. H. (David Herbert), 1885–1930. Works. 1979.
PR6023.A93R3   1989   823'.912 – dc19   87-36838

ISBN 0 521 22869 7 hard covers
ISBN 0 521 29689 7 paperback

CE

CONTENTS

GENERAL EDITORS' PREFACE

D. H. Lawrence is one of the great writers of the twentieth century – yet the texts of his writings, whether published during his lifetime or since, are, for the most part, textually corrupt. The extent of the corruption is remarkable; it can derive from every stage of composition and publication. We know from study of his MSS that Lawrence was a careful writer, though not rigidly consistent in matters of minor convention. We know also that he revised at every possible stage. Yet he rarely if ever compared one stage with the previous one, and overlooked the errors of typists or copyists. He was forced to accept, as most authors are, the often stringent house-styling of his printers, which overrode his punctuation and even his sentence-structure and paragraphing. He sometimes overlooked plausible printing errors. More important, as a professional author living by his pen, he had to accept, with more or less good will, stringent editing by a publisher's reader in his early days, and at all times the results of his publishers' timidity. So the fear of Grundyish disapproval, or actual legal action, led to bowdlerisation or censorship from the very beginning of his career. Threats of libel suits produced other changes. Sometimes a publisher made more changes than he admitted to Lawrence. On a number of occasions in dealing with American and British publishers Lawrence produced texts for both which were not identical. Then there were extraordinary lapses like the occasion when a compositor turned over two pages of MS at once, and the result happened to make sense. This whole story can be reconstructed from the introductions to the volumes in this edition; cumulatively they will form a history of Lawrence's writing career.

The Cambridge edition aims to provide texts which are as close as can now be determined to those he would have wished to see printed. They have been established by a rigorous collation of extant manuscripts and typescripts, proofs and early printed versions; they restore the words, sentences, even whole pages omitted or falsified by editors or compositors; they are freed from printing-house conventions which were imposed on Lawrence's style; and interference on the part of frightened publishers has been eliminated. Far from doing violence to the texts Lawrence would have wished to see published, editorial intervention is essential to recover them. Though we have to accept that some cannot now be recovered in their entirety because early states have not survived, we must be glad that so much evidence remains. Paradoxical as it may seem, the outcome of this recension will be texts which differ, often radically and certainly frequently, from those seen by the author himself.

Editors have adopted the principle that the most authoritative form of the text is to be followed, even if this leads sometimes to a 'spoken' or a 'manuscript' rather than a 'printed' style. We have not wanted to strip off one house-styling in order to impose another. Editorial discretion has been allowed in order to regularise Lawrence's sometimes wayward spelling and punctuation in accordance with his most frequent practice in a particular text. A detailed record of these and other decisions on textual matters, together with the evidence on which they are based, will be found in the textual apparatus or an occasional explanatory note. These give significant deleted readings in manuscripts, typescripts and proofs; and printed variants in forms of the text published in Lawrence's lifetime. We do not record posthumous corruptions, except where first publication was posthumous.

In each volume, the editor's introduction relates the contents to Lawrence's life and to his other writings; it gives the history of composition of the text in some detail, for its intrinsic interest, and because this history is essential to the statement of editorial principles followed. It provides an account of publication and reception which will be found to contain a good deal of hitherto unknown information. Where appropriate, appendixes make available extended draft manuscript readings of significance, or important material, sometimes unpublished, associated with a particular work.

Though Lawrence is a twentieth-century writer and in many respects remains our contemporary, the idiom of his day is not invariably intelligible now, especially to the many readers who are not native speakers of British English. His use of dialect is another difficulty, and further barriers to full understanding are created by now obscure literary, historical, political or other references and allusions. On these occasions explanatory notes are supplied by the editor; it is assumed that the reader has access to a good general dictionary and that the editor need not gloss words or expressions that may be found in it. Where Lawrence's letters are quoted in editorial matter, the reader should assume that his manuscript is alone the source of eccentricities of phrase or spelling. An edition of the letters is still in course of publication: for this reason only the date and recipient of a letter will be given if it has not so far been printed in the Cambridge edition.

ACKNOWLEDGEMENTS

I am deeply indebted to Michael Black, James Boulton, Lindeth Vasey and John Worthen for scrutinising text and notes, and for so many helpful suggestions that mere gratitude seems hardly enough. For valuable help in particular matters my thanks go also to Warren Roberts, Carl and Helen Baron, Keith Cushman, Ron Draper, Paul Eggert, David Farmer, Mara Kalnins, John Littlewood, Charles Ross, Claire Tomalin and my Kent colleagues David Ellis, Ian Gregor and Howard Mills. For aid with local history I must thank Michael Brook and Alec Cameron of the Nottingham University Library, Stephen Best of the Nottingham County Library and Michael Jopling of the Ilkeston Library, together with their staff; and for questions of economic history I turned to Theo Barker and Gordon Mingay. Ann Morton guided me to the Home Office files in the Public Record Office; and Janice Price of Methuen kindly hunted for misplaced records. To Nora Haselden, youngest sister of Louie Burrows, and Mary Saleeby Fisher and Elizabeth Hawkins of Greatham, my warm thanks for their kindness and for sharing their memories. I am grateful to the Harry Ransom Humanities Research Center of the University of Texas for access to the manuscript and typescript of *The Rainbow*, and the fragments of earlier versions; and I would like to express personal thanks, also, to Mary Hirst, Ellen Dunlap, Lois Garcia, Cathy Henderson and Ken Craven. Marilyn Celeste Atkins did some Hinmann collation for me on the Center's first editions. I am grateful to the Library of Congress for access to the Huebsch papers and Kuttner's report on 'The Wedding Ring'; to the New York Public Library for letters of Doran, Methuen and Pinker in the Berg Collection; and to Sylvia Secker and the University of Illinois at Urbana-Champaign for the Secker Letter-Books. I owe particular thanks to Stephen Holland, Special Collections librarian of the University of Kent at Canterbury, for trusting me with a first edition on extended loan.

My work was greatly helped by a grant from the British Academy.

My wife Joan gives thanks, that we have got somewhere (somehow) over *The Rainbow* – and I give mine to her, for bearing with me, and it, throughout.

November 1987   M.K.-W.

CHRONOLOGY

11 September 1885	Born in Eastwood, Nottinghamshire
September 1898–July 1901	Pupil at Nottingham High School
1902–1908	Pupil teacher; student at University College, Nottingham
7 December 1907	First publication: 'A Prelude', in *Nottinghamshire Guardian*
October 1908	Appointed as teacher at Davidson Road School, Croydon
November 1909	Publishes five poems in *English Review*
3 December 1910	Engagement to Louie Burrows; broken off on 4 February 1912
9 December 1910	Death of his mother, Lydia Lawrence
19 January 1911	*The White Peacock* published in New York (20 January in London)
19 November 1911	Ill with pneumonia; resigns his teaching post on 28 February 1912
March 1912	Meets Frieda Weekley; they elope to Germany on 3 May
23 May 1912	*The Trespasser*
September 1912–30 March 1913	At Gargnano, Lago di Garda, Italy
February 1913	*Love Poems and Others*
mid-March 1913	Begins 'The Sisters'
22 March 1913	'The Sisters' – 46 pages
30 March–11 April 1913	At San Gaudenzio
5 April 1913	'The Sisters' – 110 pages
19 April–17 June 1913	At Irschenhausen, Germany
23 April 1913	'The Sisters' – 145 pages
c. 2 May 1913	'The Sisters' – 180 pages
17 May 1913	'The Sisters' – 256 pages
29 May 1913	*Sons and Lovers*
1 June 1913	'The Sisters' – 283 pages: 'nearly finished'
June–August 1913	In England
9 August 1913–17 September 1913	At Irschenhausen
24 August 1913	'The Sisters II' – 'two false starts already'
4 September 1913	'The Sisters II' – 'has quite a new beginning'

15 September 1913	'The Sisters II' – 100 pages
18 September–4 October 1913	Travels from Germany through Switzerland to Lerici, Gulf of Spezia
November 1913	Begins to work on 'The Sisters II' again
4 October 1913–8 June 1914	At Fiascherino, Italy
2 December 1913	'The Sisters II' – 'writing . . . slowly'
6 January 1914	'The Sisters II' – first half sent to Edward Garnett
19 January 1914	'The Sisters II' – 340 pages
30 January 1914	'The Sisters II' – 150 pages of second half to Garnett
by 7 February 1914	'The Wedding Ring' – 'begun it again'
7 March 1914	'The Wedding Ring' – 'going strong'
3 April 1914	'The Wedding Ring' – 'done two-thirds'
22 April 1914	'The Wedding Ring' – '80 pages more to write'
by 16 May 1914	Finishes 'The Wedding Ring'
8–24 June 1914	Walking tour to Germany
24 June–15 August 1914	In England and, mainly, in London
27 June 1914	Duckworth agree to publish short-story volume in place of the novel
c. 29 June 1914	Signs contract with Methuen for the novel
Late June–mid-July 1914	Revising stories extensively
c. 7 July 1914	Invited to write book on Thomas Hardy
13 July 1914	Marries Frieda Weekley in London
31 July–8 August 1914	Walking tour in Westmorland
4 August 1914	Great Britain declares war on Germany
c. 8 August 1914	Methuen return 'The Wedding Ring'
15? August 1914–2 January 1915	At Chesham, Buckinghamshire
c. 5 September 1914	Begins 'Study of Thomas Hardy'
c. 3–20 October 1914	Revises page proofs of short-story volume intensively
18 November 1914	'Just finishing' with 'Hardy'
26 November 1914	*The Prussian Officer*
Late November 1914	Begins rewriting 'The Wedding Ring' which will create *The Rainbow* and leave material for *Women in Love*
5 December 1914	Sends last of 'Hardy' to be typed
	The Rainbow – 100 pages
18 December 1914	*The Rainbow* – 200 pages
5 January 1915	*The Rainbow* – 300 pages

7 January 1915	Divides the novel into two volumes: *Women in Love* material laid aside until 1916
21 January–30 July 1915	At Greatham, Pulborough, Sussex
1 February 1915	*The Rainbow* – 450 pages
24 February 1915	*The Rainbow* 'very, very near the end'
2 March 1915	Finishes *The Rainbow*, which Viola Meynell and friend will type
mid-March–May 1915	Revises *The Rainbow* extensively as batches of typescript arrive
6 March 1915	Visits Bertrand Russell in Cambridge: 'hated it beyond expression'. . .'one of the crises of my life'
29 May 1915	*The Rainbow* typing to be finished 'this very day'
31 May 1915	Sends last of revised typescript of *The Rainbow* to J. B. Pinker
9 July–mid-August 1915	Revising proofs of *The Rainbow*
30 July–21 December 1915	To Littlehampton, then in London
29 July–19 October 1915	Revising Italian sketches for *Twilight in Italy*
5 September 1915	Plan for *The Signature* announced
20 September–10 October 1915	'6 papers' completed ('The Crown')
30 September 1915	*The Rainbow*
3 and 5 November 1915	Police call at Methuen and take copies of *The Rainbow*
1 November 1915	Third and last of projected six issues of *The Signature*
13 November 1915	*The Rainbow* suppressed by Court order
30 November 1915	B. W. Huebsch registers copyright of American first edition of *The Rainbow* but does not 'publish'
c. 17 December 1915	Receives a copy of American edition and discovers it is expurgated
30 December 1915–15 October 1917	At St Merryn and Zennor, Cornwall
18 April–c. 27 June 1916	'The Sisters III'
June 1916	*Twilight in Italy*
July 1916	*Amores*
July–November 1916	'The Sisters III' rewritten as *Women in Love*
December 1916–January 1917	*Women in Love* rejected by Methuen, Secker, Duckworth and Constable
15 October 1917	After twenty-one months' residence in Cornwall, ordered to leave by military authorities

October 1917–November 1919	In London, Berkshire and Derbyshire
26 November 1917	*Look! We Have Come Through!*
October 1918	*New Poems*
November 1919–February 1922	To Italy, then Capri and Sicily
20 November 1919	*Bay*
1920	Huebsch publishes further 'limited' edition of *The Rainbow*
9 November 1920	Private publication of *Women in Love* (New York)
25 November 1920	*The Lost Girl*
10 May 1921	*Psychoanalysis and the Unconscious* (New York)
12 December 1921	*Sea and Sardinia* (New York)
March–August 1922	In Ceylon and Australia
14 April 1922	*Aaron's Rod* (New York)
September 1922–March 1923	In New Mexico
23 October 1922	*Fantasia of the Unconscious* (New York)
24 October 1922	*England, My England* (New York)
March 1923	*The Ladybird, The Fox, The Captain's Doll*
March–November 1923	In Mexico and USA
27 August 1923	*Studies in Classic American Literature* (New York)
September 1923	*Kangaroo*
9 October 1923	*Birds, Beasts and Flowers* (New York)
December 1923–March 1924	In England, France and Germany
March 1924–September 1925	In New Mexico and Mexico
August 1924	*The Boy in the Bush* (with Mollie Skinner)
10 September 1924	Death of his father, John Arthur Lawrence
November 1924	Thomas Seltzer publishes *The Rainbow* with Huebsch text
14 May 1925	*St. Mawr together with The Princess*
September 1925–June 1928	In England and, mainly, in Italy
7 December 1925	*Reflections on the Death of a Porcupine* (Philadelphia)
21 January 1926	*The Plumed Serpent*
February 1926	Secker republishes *The Rainbow* in England (sheets purchased from Seltzer)
June 1927	*Mornings in Mexico*
24 May 1928	*The Woman Who Rode Away and Other Stories*
June 1928–March 1930	In Switzerland and, principally, in France

CUE-TITLES

A. Manuscript locations

LC   Library of Congress
NYPL   New York Public Library
UIll   University of Illinois
UInd   University of Indiana
UN   University of Nottingham
UT   University of Texas

B. Printed works

(The place of publication, here and throughout, is London unless otherwise stated.)

Carter, *TLS*   John Carter, 'The Rainbow Prosecution', *The Times Literary Supplement* (27 February 1969), 216.
Draper   R. P. Draper, ed. *D. H. Lawrence: The Critical Heritage*. Routledge & Kegan Paul, 1970.
'Hardy'   D. H. Lawrence. *Study of Thomas Hardy and Other Essays*, ed. Bruce Steele. Cambridge: Cambridge University Press, 1985.
Letters, i.   James T. Boulton, ed. *The Letters of D. H. Lawrence*. Volume I. Cambridge: Cambridge University Press, 1979.
Letters, ii.   George J. Zytaruk and James T. Boulton, eds. *The Letters of D. H. Lawrence*. Volume II. Cambridge: Cambridge University Press, 1982.
Letters, iii. James T. Boulton and Andrew Robertson, eds. *The Letters of D. H. Lawrence*. Volume III. Cambridge: Cambridge University Press, 1984.
Letters, iv.   Warren Roberts, James T. Boulton and Elizabeth Mansfield, eds. *The Letters of D. H. Lawrence*. Volume IV. Cambridge: Cambridge University Press, 1987.

OED	Sir James A. H. Murray and others, eds. *A New English Dictionary on Historical Principles*. 10 volumes. Oxford University Press, 1884–1928.
Roberts	Warren Roberts. *A Bibliography of D. H. Lawrence*. 2nd edn. Cambridge: Cambridge University Press, 1982.

INTRODUCTION

INTRODUCTION

The Composition of *The Rainbow*: New beginnings

Both *The Rainbow* and *Women in Love* were to grow out of a flippant little 'pot-boiler'[1] which Lawrence began in mid-March 1913, at Gargnano on Lake Garda in Italy, as a distraction from a more serious work which was getting out of hand.

After posting the manuscript of *Sons and Lovers* the previous November to Edward Garnett, his literary mentor and reader for Duckworth, he conceived and discarded several ideas for a new novel: 'Scargill Street',[2] suggesting a setting in Eastwood that might be connected with the novel 'purely of the common people' he had thought of in August (i. 431); the 'Burns' novel whose opening fragment is set in the familiar wooded landscape near The Haggs;[3] and, in late December, a novel with a plot, 'further off from me' (i. 496–7), of which the first-person fragment by 'Elsa Culverwell' is probably a survival.[4] In 'Elsa', at least, were a promising new heroine and situation; a way of fulfilling his promise to 'do a novel about Love Triumphant. . .my work for women, better than the suffrage' (i. 490), and also of finding that combination of nearness to his concerns and distance from himself, after his prolonged struggle with *Sons and Lovers*, which the earlier notions had suggested but not sustained. By 17 January 1913, having probably dropped the idea of first-person narration as well as changing the names, he had written eighty pages of what was now called 'The Insurrection of Miss Houghton', 'a most curious work, which gives me great joy to write' (i. 505). The Cullen family of Eastwood had been the models for the household in which Muriel/Miriam

---

[1] *Letters*, i. 536. (Subsequent references to *Letters* will be given in brackets in the text.)

[2] See *Letters*, i. 466. In 'Nottingham and the Mining Countryside', written September 1929, DHL locates Scargill Street as 'the steep street between the squares' in Eastwood, built as housing for miners, just below 'the little corner shop' in Victoria Street where he was born (*Phoenix: The Posthumous Papers of D. H. Lawrence*, ed. Edward D. McDonald, New York, 1936, p. 134). In *Sons and Lovers*, however, he had used the name for a fictive recreation of Walker Street, where the Lawrences lived 1891–1903.

[3] See *Letters*, i. 487, 489. The surviving fragments (Roberts E59.3) are printed in *Love Among the Haystacks and Other Stories*, ed. John Worthen (Cambridge, 1987), pp. 201–11.

[4] See *The Lost Girl*, ed. John Worthen (Cambridge, 1981), pp. 343–58, and xx–xxii.

had originally been placed in 'Paul Morel', the early version of *Sons and Lovers*.[5] He now turned to them again for 'Elsa Culverwell' and for the new work, (and eventually for the Houghtons of *The Lost Girl*, though that did not simply complete 'The Insurrection', but was newly conceived and rewritten at Taormina in 1920).[6] 'The Insurrection' began in almost 'venomous' pleasure (i. 501) which sounds like satire against Eastwood, in keeping with Lawrence's feelings about England from the vantage-point of his new life in Italy.[7] It was over a hundred pages by 1 February (i. 511), but was already becoming 'a bit outspoken' by 18 February (i. 517); and though more than half-finished by 11 March (i. 526), was then regretfully laid aside after two hundred pages (i. 546). As Lawrence told Edward Garnett it was 'most cumbersome and floundering' but also 'great – so new, so really a stratum deeper than I think anybody has ever gone, in a novel. . .all analytical – quite unlike *Sons and Lovers*, not a bit visualised' (i. 526). Even after he had set it aside it still lay 'next my heart' (i. 546). But it was '*too* improper' (i. 536). Anna Houghton's rebellion (Lawrence's answer to the 'acceptance' of Bennett's heroine of the Five Towns)[8] had clearly deepened through the social to the sexual, and the response to be feared was not merely the 'extreme annoyance' he had cheerfully predicted at the start (i. 505). This was no time to go on with unpublishable work, or what was he 'going to live on, and keep Frieda on withal' (i. 526)?

So he began instead, between 11 and 22 March, a determinedly 'lighter' piece which would be 'quite decent' (i. 530), indeed 'absolutely impeccable' (i. 526).

'The Sisters' (first version, March–June 1913)

'The Sisters' began as 'flippant' (ii. 68), because 'it was meant to be for the "jeunes filles"' (i. 546), and 'jeering' (ii. 165), because both sisters hit at Frieda, '*me*, these beastly, superior arrogant females! Lawrence *hated* me just over the children. . .so he wrote this!' (i. 549). But though it did Lawrence 'good to theorise [himself] out, and to depict Friedas God Almightiness in all its glory', releasing rebellious feelings about her

---

[5] Roberts E373d, in *Sons and Lovers: A Facsimile of the Manuscript*, ed. Mark Schorer (Berkeley and London, 1977).

[6] *The Lost Girl*, ed. Worthen, pp. xxvii–xxviii.

[7] See *Letters*, i. 459–60, 504, 515; and *Twilight in Italy* (1916), which grew out of the experiences recorded in the letters of early 1913.

[8] 'I hate England and its hopelessness. I hate Bennett's resignation. Tragedy ought really to be a great kick at misery. But *Anna of the Five Towns* seems like an acceptance. . .I want to wash again quick, wash off England, the oldness and grubbiness and despair' (*Letters*, i. 459).

combination of the Prussian aristocrat and Pallas Athene in plaits, this was only 'the first crude fermenting of the book', as he wrote when it was well advanced; 'I'll make it into art now' (i. 550). But the 'theorising' may also have had something of the 'great religion', the 'belief in the blood. . .the mystery of the flame forever flowing. . .and being *itself*', about which he had written to Ernest Collings (artist and illustrator) while at work on 'The Insurrection' (i. 503); and also something of the new religious sense of selfhood, born out of sexual relationship, that informs the 'Foreword' to *Sons and Lovers*, which he had also written in January.[9] The 'impeccable' novelette (i. 526) had soon not only 'fallen from grace' (i. 546), but had begun to recover some of the seriousness of the abandoned work, without its satire. At quite an early stage, by page 110 on 5 April, the pot-boiler had become 'earnest and painful' (i. 536), changing and deepening as he wrote, and as the fiction came closer to his deepest preoccupations. He took it with him to Germany in April, and letters from Irschenhausen show both the effect and the cause of a new dimension of exploration. 'I am doing a novel which I have never grasped. Damn its eyes, there I am at page 145, and I've no notion what it's about. I hate it. F[rieda] says it is good. But it's like a novel in a foreign language I don't know very well –' (i. 544). It had grown out of flippancy and jeering because 'I can only write what I feel pretty strongly about; and that, at present, is the relations between men and women' (i. 546). By now, early in May, he was at page 180; by 17 May at page 256 'but still can't see the end very clear' (i. 550); and by Sunday 1 June it was 'nearly finished' at page 283 (ii. 20). The following week (ii. 20) he posted the second half to Edward Garnett (who had apparently not cared much for the first half[10]), and set off for a visit to England on 19 June.

The novel had been planned at three hundred pages (i. 546), and what was probably its ending has survived as a fragment numbered 291–6, printed as Appendix I.[11] It is an early version of what would eventually

---

[9] The 'Foreword' – actually, of course, an afterword, and not meant for publication (see *Letters*, i. 510) – is reprinted in *The Letters of D. H. Lawrence*, ed. Aldous Huxley (1932), pp. 95–102.

[10] 'I was glad of your letter about the Sisters. Don't schimpf, I shall make it all right when I re-write it. I shall put it in the third person. All along I knew what ailed the book. . .I'll make it into art now' (*Letters*, i. 550).

[11] Roberts E441a, in the possession of UT. The pagination is right, and the paper is very like that used in other writings of the Gargnano period, especially the 'Foreword' to *Sons and Lovers* of January 1913. If the paper is continental, the fragment cannot belong to the *Women in Love* material of 1916, which is unlikely in any case, on stylistic grounds. Nor could it (in that case) relate to the equally unlikely possibility that an early version of *The Rainbow* existed in Spring 1912, when George Neville claims to have discussed 'the

develop into *Women in Love*, beginning with a portrait of Gerald's mother. Then Gudrun, pregnant with Gerald's child, confronts both Gerald and Loerke in England. Gerald now wants to marry her, but though she suspects that this may be only because of the baby, she takes him back. The theme, in the Gerald/Gudrun story, seems to have been the conventional Englishman's inability to submit himself to love, but at the end Gerald has become 'something he had feared he never could be: he had got something he had pretended to disbelieve in'. Only, he is forced to measure and accept the damage that his inability to love has caused. The sister story, of the other 'superior flounder', was, however, to become the more immediately compelling, though Frieda saw herself in both (i. 549). Presumably the mockery was directed through Ella's lover; the letters twice suggest first-person narration (i. 550, ii. 20), though the surviving fragment is told in the third. The difficulty is more apparent than real however, since much of the story of Gerald and Gudrun would have to be third-person narrative in any case, as in *The White Peacock*, where it is easy enough to find sections which would give no hint of first-person narration if they survived as fragments, such as the scene between George and Lettie in chapter VII.[12] It is also possible, if unlikely, that the fragment comes from a revised version. Lawrence was 'rather keen to re-write it in the third person' (ii. 20); but it is not easy to see where he could have found the time, since he was soon very busy creating new stories and revising old ones. Ella must have been a positive character, not to say opinionated, since Frieda refers to one of her own sweeping generalisations as 'Ellaing' (i. 550). But the portrait seems to have become more and more significant to Lawrence, and the problem of understanding how Ella came to be as she was, through some past hurt, would constitute the growing-point towards *The Rainbow*.

bedroom scene' with DHL before his elopement with Frieda, see *D. H. Lawrence: A Composite Biography*, ed. Edward Nehls (Madison, 1957), i. 154, and G. H. Neville's *A Memoir of D. H. Lawrence*, ed. Carl Baron (Cambridge, 1981), p. 44–5 and Appendix A, pp. 167–71. Little reliance should be placed on DHL's statement in April 1915 that *The Rainbow* was 'nearly three years of hard work' – see footnote 30 below. It remains possible that the lost portion of 'Paul Morel' may have contained some scene that DHL removed, but later worked into *The Rainbow*, as he removed the Cullen family and used them again; yet it seems more likely that the scene which Neville thought would cause trouble – as indeed it did – was the bedroom scene in *Sons and Lovers*, and that his memory deceived him about its location, and what book DHL was finally 'bringing into shape' in March 1912.

12 Ed. Andrew Robertson (Cambridge, 1983), pp. 208–16.

'The Sisters II' (second version, August 1913–January 1914)

Having written three stories in Germany[13] which have a new kind of inwardness, Lawrence busied himself in England assembling and revising a number of stories, sketches and poems, and having them typed for submission to periodicals. On 13 August, a week after his return to Germany, he was promising Garnett 'As soon as possible I begin The Sisters' (ii. 58); but by 24 August he was calling it 'the devil – I've made two false starts already' (ii. 66). At the end of the month, complaining that he was writing things 'about which I know nothing – like a somnambulist', he had clearly made yet another new start. 'I've begun a novel on the same principle: it's like working in a dream, rather uncomfortable – as if you can't get solid hold of yourself. "Hello my lad, are you there!" I say to myself, when I see the sentences stalking by.'[14] But by 4 September confidence had returned: 'The Sisters has quite a new beginning – a new basis altogether. . .It is much more interesting in its new form – not so damned flippant' (ii. 67–8). Eleven days later, before he left on a walking tour to Switzerland and Italy, he had done a hundred pages and hoped to finish in a month (ii. 74–5). But though he took up 'The Sisters' again in the new home in Fiascherino – 'It is *so* different, so different from anything I have yet written' (ii. 82) – the move had clearly broken the flow, and October went by with little progress (ii. 99). At the beginning of November he began to work on the novel again (ii. 99); a month later he was 'writing. . .slowly' (ii. 118); and on 21 December he promised to send Garnett the first half in a few days (ii. 127) – presumably the two hundred pages he had suggested earlier (ii. 82) – but on 30 December he was still promising (ii. 132). Whereas the first 'Sisters' seemed 'to have come by itself' (i. 546), the second had proved much more recalcitrant. The difficulty went deeper however than the unsettling effect of the move back to Italy and a disinclination to work, for the new novel was demanding a new kind of art. 'It is *very* different from *Sons and Lovers*: written in another language almost. . .I shan't write in the same manner as *Sons and Lovers* again, I think: in that hard, violent style full of sensation and presentation' (ii. 132). He had already thought of a new title, 'The Wedding Ring'; and told Garnett, when he did send the first half on 6 January 1914, how not only the name but 'the whole scheme of the book is

[13] See *Letters*, ii. 26 and n. 8. The stories were 'Honour and Arms' (later 'The Prussian Officer'), 'Vin Ordinaire' (later 'The Thorn in the Flesh') and 'New Eve and Old Adam'; see *The Prussian Officer and Other Stories*, ed. John Worthen (Cambridge, 1983), p. xxv and n. 33.
[14] Letter to John Middleton Murry, 30 August 1913.

changed – widened and deepened' (ii. 134). Having reached page 340 he explained:

The Laocoon writing and shrieking have gone from my new work, and I think there is a bit of stillness, like the wide, still, unseeing eyes of a Venus of Melos. . .There is something in the Greek sculpture that my soul is hungry for – something of the eternal stillness that lies under all movement, under all life, like a source, incorruptible and inexhaustible. It is deeper than change, and struggling. So long I have acknowledged only the struggle, the stream, the change. And now I begin to feel something of the source, the great impersonal which never changes and out of which all change comes. (ii. 137–8)

On 29 January he meant to send a second batch of a hundred and fifty pages the next day (ii. 142), but Garnett's criticisms of the first half seem to have brought his own dissatisfaction to a head, and by 7 February he had laid the work aside, unfinished, and had begun all over again (ii. 144).

This second version of 'The Sisters' appears to have been the original of *The Rainbow*. Again, only a fragment has survived, numbered 373–80,[15] and probably therefore the point at which Lawrence abandoned the work near its end – though it is early in the relationship of Ella and Birkin (if we think in terms of *Women in Love*). The second 'Sisters' was not, then, a rewriting of the first, but rather an attempt to get back behind it, into the past of Ella, the prototype of Ursula, in order to discover how she came to be as she was through some deep bruise to her inner being, in an earlier love-affair with Ben Templeman – mentioned at the close of the fragment, which is printed as Appendix II. The 'new basis' can also be detected in the style. The writing, at crucial points (such as Ella's collapse into grief, 475:31ff.) has developed a new rhythmic quality, a new mode of cumulative interior exploration of the psyche, very different from the overtly dramatic and symbolic modes of *Sons and Lovers* which Frieda had criticised as lacking any 'Hinterland der Seele' ('inner reaches of the soul', ii. 151). Garnett's criticisms, however, were that the character of Ella had become 'incoherent'; that the previous affair with Templeman was 'wrong'; and that what Lawrence called his new 'exhaustive method' meant that 'the artistic side' was 'in the background', and that the scenes were not 'incorporated' enough. Lawrence agreed with the first point, explaining that 'it came of trying to graft on to the character of Louie [Burrows] the character, more or less, of Frieda'. For the young Ella he had used the rather different personality of the young woman to whom he had been

---

[15] Roberts E441a, in the possession of UT. The paper is watermarked A.BINDA & C=MILANO, and the identification as 'Sisters II' is rendered certain by the girls' encounter with 'Ben Templeman' at the end.

engaged, and whose father and family were to serve as models for the middle generation of Brangwens[16] – but, clearly, the joins were showing. He also agreed with Garnett's second point, while insisting that Ella could not be what she became 'unless she had some experience of love and of men. . .Then she must have a love episode, a significant one. But it must not be a Templeman episode.' He refused however to accept the criticism of the new imaginative mode. 'I have no longer the joy in creating vivid scenes, that I had in *Sons and Lovers*. I don't care much more about accumulating objects in the powerful light of emotion, and making a scene of them.' He felt that his new style, even if its 'flowers' were 'frail or shadowy', was true to himself in a period of transition: 'I prefer the permeating beauty. . .It is not so easy for one to be married. In marriage one must become something else. And I am changing, one way or the other' (ii. 142–3). The new style had to feel, like the new man, for the hidden forces behind the surface drama, in a novel whose end was to be Ella and Birkin finding their true selves, 'the eternal and unchangeable that they are', and ceasing to be 'strange forms half-uttered' (ii. 138).

Nevertheless, Garnett's criticisms confirmed his own sense that the novel 'wasn't *quite* there', so he wrote on 7 February to Mitchell Kennerley, who he hoped would publish it in America,[17] that he had begun all over again (ii. 144). As he explained two days later:

It was full of beautiful things, but it missed – I knew that it just missed being itself. So here I am, must sit down and write it out again. I know it is quite a lovely novel really – you know that the perfect statue is in the marble, the kernel of it. But the thing is the getting it out clean. (ii. 146)

'The Wedding Ring' (third version, February–May 1914)

Lawrence was obviously intending now to combine 'The Sisters' I and II, but once again he made several false starts. On 9 February he complained of beginning 'for about the seventh time' (ii. 146), and a month later, 'for about the eleventh time' (ii. 153) – amounting, together with the false starts of the previous stage, and the two 'Sisters', to 'quite a thousand pages that I shall burn' (ii. 161) – but by 7 March the book was once more 'on its legs and. . .going strong' (ii. 153). Thomas Dunlop, the British Consul at La

[16] See Explanatory notes on 108:36 and 122:3.
[17] Kennerley became DHL's American publisher with *The Trespasser*, and subsequently published *Sons and Lovers* and *The Widowing of Mrs. Holroyd*, before DHL broke with him over 'The Wedding Ring' and a defective cheque for *Sons and Lovers*, never replaced. See *Letters*, ii. 246 and *The Letters of D. H. Lawrence and Amy Lowell 1914–25*, ed. E. Claire Healey and Keith Cushman (Santa Barbara, 1985), pp. 28–9.

Spezia, offered to type it, though on Moore's evidence the work was probably done mostly by his wife Madge.[18] By 3 April Lawrence had 'done two-thirds' (ii. 161), and by 22 April only some eighty pages remained to be written. He was now certain that both 'The Wedding Ring' and his relationship with Frieda had finally come right, and that there was the closest connection between the one and the other. 'I am sure of this now, this novel. . .Before, I could not get my soul into it. That was because of the struggle and the resistance between Frieda and me. Now you will find her and me in the novel, I think, and the work is of both of us.' He sent Garnett what had been typed, at a point from which, as it happened, 'follows on the original "Sisters" – the School inspector, and so on' (ii. 164). Having the novel typed was itself a mark of confidence that it was ready to be published. On 9 May he was 'about three thousand' words from the end, and Frieda had suggested a change of title to *The Rainbow* (ii. 173), though this was not adopted. On 16 May he told Garnett 'The novel is finished, and I have gone through the sheets' (ii. 174). In fact Frieda had helped him transcribe corrections into the duplicate typescript (see below p. lii), putting herself into the novel literally, as well as with the full backing and inspiration she had promised this version, for the first time (ii. 151).

Though the story still went on into what became *Women in Love*, 'The Wedding Ring' brought the second 'Sisters' much nearer to *The Rainbow* as we have it now. Indeed, Lawrence thought well enough of one section to preserve it later, in the manuscript of *The Rainbow* itself (two portions of typescript running from Ella's first day as a school-teacher to the family's removal to their new house); and though Lawrence heightened it thematically in his revision for *The Rainbow*, he did not change it basically (see below p. lii, and Textual apparatus). Unfortunately, since the episode lies outside Ella's relationships with both her lovers (though 'Charles' Skrebensky is mentioned and has clearly taken the place of Ben Templeman) it reveals nothing of the nature or development of those relationships. It does however show that the affair with Winifred Inger and her later marriage with the younger Tom Brangwen were *not* in 'The Wedding Ring', since references to Winifred had to be put in for the later recension. We also know, from the MS and TS of *The Rainbow* (see below p. xxxviii) how the Cathedral scene was first developed there; and from the typescript that the later relationship of Anna and Will, after the episode with the girl in Nottingham, was an even later development in revision (see below p. lii),

---

[18] See *Letters*, ii. 152; Harry T. Moore, *The Priest of Love* (New York, 1974), p. 198.

probably arising out of *The Rainbow*'s new conception of the affair between Ursula and Skrebensky after his return from Africa. Even so, 'The Wedding Ring' was 'a magnum opus with a vengeance' (ii. 173), not only because it combined the first with the second 'Sisters'; but also, as the surviving pagination shows, because nearly three hundred of its typed pages (which are unusually long) had been taken up with matters prior to Ella's twentieth year, and her relationship with 'the School Inspector'. The most likely explanation is that Lawrence, seeking to extend the concern with marriage which had suggested 'The Wedding Ring' as a title towards the end of the second 'Sisters' (ii. 132), had gone further and further back into the marriages of Ella's parents, and her grandparents – which might also help to explain his difficulties in deciding how, and where, to begin both the second 'Sisters' and 'The Wedding Ring'.

This is confirmed by a reader's report (for Mitchell Kennerley to whom the second typescript had been sent, ii. 190), by Alfred Kuttner, who had also written a 'psychoanalytic' review of *Sons and Lovers* for *New Republic*.[19] The report – which possibly Lawrence saw – is printed below as Appendix III, with a letter opining that a 'painful' deterioration was going on in Lawrence, but that a 'rigorous Freudian analysis would make Mr. Lawrence both a happier man and a greater artist'. Even though Kuttner found little advance on *Sons and Lovers*, and 'chunks of psychological motivation almost literally transferred' from the earlier novel, he also found 'some very fine writing and in parts a more mature character delineation (Birkin)', and he clearly responded to Ella and Gudrun, feeling that the book did not 'strike its best pace until we deal with them'. Hence 'it must be condensed and foreshortened and it must also be expurgated, not for moral reasons but for artistic effect'. (He instances a sentence from a scene where Gerald is 'raping Gudrun in the boathouse' – perhaps his way of describing an early version of the scene in chapter xxiv of *Women in Love*.) But the real significance of the report lies less in its opinions than in its evidence of what was in 'The Wedding Ring'. He complains that Lawrence 'takes us through practically three generations' though the real interest lies in the sisters, whose story does not come until 'almost half way through'.

The story of Anna's childhood, charming as it is, acts as a kind of false start because she is dropped so sharply as soon as she is converted into a baby machine. . .the whole story of Tom Brangwen's courtship of the Polish woman as well as Anna's marriage could be told in retrospect in much less space if the novel began with Ella's childhood.

[19] 10 April 1915 (Draper 76–80).

So the new novel contained all three generations, though the earlier stories must have been considerably attenuated, and also without the definition that was to come from the 'Study of Thomas Hardy', since the development up to Ella's school-teaching in 'The Wedding Ring' was still a great deal shorter than the comparable section of *The Rainbow*, probably not much more than half the size. In the typescript of 'The Wedding Ring' Ella begins as a teacher on p. 219, and a typed sheet corresponds to about a page and a third of *The Rainbow*'s typescript, so that the 219 pages should have produced about 292; but the corresponding moment in *The Rainbow* comes on p. 552. The calculations can only be approximate, but it is clear that a very substantial expansion has taken place. It would take Lawrence as long to rewrite 'The Wedding Ring' into *The Rainbow* as it had done to write it.

He now thought of his novel as complete, however, and received a lucrative offer for it through J. B. Pinker (ii. 174), who had been agent for Conrad, James, Bennett and Ford Madox Ford. Though he had accepted some of Garnett's criticisms of the second 'Sisters', the criticism of its style seems to have rankled; and the letter of 22 April which expressed his new certainty about 'The Wedding Ring', as he sent off the first batch of typescript, also reproached his mentor for a failure to believe in what he was trying to do, and took him up short on a remark that Lawrence was at liberty to go to another publisher (ii. 164–6). On 5 June, having received Garnett's reaction to 'The Wedding Ring', he tried in a famous letter to formulate the new attitude to 'psychology' and to 'character' which he had been struggling towards, and to which he felt Garnett had been quite unwilling to adjust. The shadow of a coming break is clear; but so is the sense of alignment with the future – though he is also critical of the intellectualism of the Futurists:

I don't agree with you about the Wedding Ring. You will find that in a while you will like the book as a whole. I don't think the psychology is wrong: it is only that I have a different attitude to my characters, and that necessitates a different attitude in you, which you are not as yet prepared to give. . .somehow – that which is physic – non-human, in humanity, is more interesting to me than the old-fashioned human element – which causes one to conceive a character in a certain moral scheme and make him consistent. The certain moral scheme is what I object to. . .You mustn't look in my novel for the old stable ego of the character. There is another ego, according to whose action the individual is unrecognisable, and passes through, as it were, allotropic states which it needs a deeper sense than any we've been used to exercise, to discover are states of the same single radically-unchanged element. (Like as diamond and coal are the same pure single element of carbon. The ordinary novel would trace the history of the diamond – but I say 'diamond, what! This is carbon.' And my diamond might be coal or soot, and my theme is carbon.)

You must not say my novel is shaky – It is not perfect, because I am not expert in what I want to do. But it is the real thing, say what you like. And I shall get my reception, if not now, then before long. Again I say, don't look for the development of the novel to follow the lines of certain characters; the characters fall into the form of some other rhythmic form, like when one draws a fiddle-bow across a fine tray delicately sanded, the sand takes lines unknown. (ii. 182–4)

Three days later he left Fiascherino on his way to England, via Switzerland and Germany, and arrived in London on 24 June. Around 29 June he decided to accept Pinker's agency and the offer which Pinker had arranged with Methuen;[20] signed a contract which would give him £300 (£150 on the receipt of the manuscript and £150 on publication); and opened a bank-account. He had been annoyed by Duckworth's 'peremptory' tone when he saw him to discuss Methuen's offer (ii. 189); and the decision made more overt the parting of the ways with Duckworth and with Garnett, though this was temporarily disguised by giving them a collection of stories instead of the novel.

The Prussian Officer and 'Study of Thomas Hardy' (June–November 1914)

Lawrence then set to work assembling, and revising once more, the stories which would become *The Prussian Officer*.[21] On 8 July he mentioned to Pinker another, apparently minor project. Bertram Christian, a director of the publisher Nisbet's, had asked him to 'do a little book for him – a sort of interpretative essay on Thomas Hardy, of about 15,000 words. It will be published at 1/– net. My payment is to be 1½d per copy, £15 advance on royalties, half profits in America. It isn't very much, but then the work won't be very much' (ii. 193).

On 13 July, at the Registry Office in Kensington, Lawrence and Frieda were married. (Her divorce had been finalised, at long last, at the end of May.) Two days later he asked Edward Marsh – editor of *Georgian Poetry* – to lend him the pocket edition of Hardy's novels and Lascelles Abercrombie's book on Hardy. 'I am going to write a little book on Hardy's people. I think it will interest me. . .I have just finished getting together a book of short stories. Lord, how I've worked again at those stories – most of them –

---

[20] See Methuen to J. B. Pinker, 4 May and two letters on 8 May 1914, NYPL. That Methuen was eager for the book is shown by a further letter on 29 May.

[21] See *The Prussian Officer*, ed. Worthen, pp. xxvii–xxx.

forging them up' (ii. 198). The claim was justified. There is no clearer way of understanding and evaluating the development of Lawrence's art, between *Sons and Lovers* and 'The Wedding Ring', than by comparing stories like 'Odour of Chrysanthemums' and 'Daughters of the Vicar' with their earlier versions. The metaphor of the forge is a good one because it suggests the transformation, in shape and dimension, made possible by the labour, and the new energy of imagination, that had gone into the creation of the second 'Sisters' and 'The Wedding Ring' in 1914. These have almost entirely disappeared; but the essence of the development between the Lawrence of 1911–12 and the Lawrence of 1914 is clearly visible still, in the difference between the main body of 'Odour of Chrysanthemums' and the new ending, that transforms the whole mode of vision; or in the contrast between the creation of the 'Two Marriages', and the 'hinterland' that opens in 'Daughters of the Vicar' as Louisa washes Alfred's back, and later, as they kiss. Moreover these explorations, with others such as the dance in 'The White Stocking' and, (from newer stories in 1913) the restoration of Bachmann in 'The Thorn in the Flesh', and the violence springing from repressions in 'The Prussian Officer', are all directly related to scenes and themes in *The Rainbow*, of whose new vision and style they were the first published anticipation.

Lawrence was overjoyed when Marsh made him a wedding present of the books he had asked for, but still expected his own work on Hardy to be 'tiny' (ii. 200). At the beginning of August he went on a walking tour in the Lake District – and it was there he heard of the outbreak of war.

By 10 August came a severe blow: Methuen returned the typescript of 'The Wedding Ring'. 'Here is a state of affairs, –' Lawrence exclaimed to Pinker – 'what is going to become of us?' (ii. 206). In a moment, financial security had turned to real embarrassment. Nearly £100 of the £150 for the receipt of the typescript had been spent (ii. 211), the other £150 was now out of reach, and the Lawrences could not go back to Italy or its cheap living. They moved into an inexpensive cottage at Chesham in Buckinghamshire, but from now onwards money worries would be serious and pressing. It was later claimed, at the trial of *The Rainbow*, that Methuen had decided the novel 'could not be published in its then form',[22] clearly implying obscenity. This is apparently confirmed by a letter from Pinker to the Secretary of the Society of Authors, after the trial.

I gather that it was suggested that Mr. Lawrence had been unyielding on the question of alterations. This is not the case. When the MS. was delivered the publishers told me that their reader reported it as impossible for publication in its

[22] *Daily Telegraph*, Monday 15 November 1915, p. 12.

existing form. I told Mr. Lawrence of the criticism, and asked him to re-consider the MS., and Mr. Lawrence not only re-considered it but decided that he would rewrite the novel.[23]

Yet Methuen, suggesting that they had acted firmly to prevent obscenity as early as 1914, and Pinker trying to present his author as the soul of co-operation, produce a story difficult to square with Lawrence's previous and subsequent reactions to such things. His letters show not a trace of the kind of rage he had felt when Heinemann rejected *Sons and Lovers* as too improper for the libraries. Not until October is there any mention of the possibility of rewriting, and then, though there is clearly something to be done, his tone hardly suggests that there had been any serious objection, or that there could be any urgency despite his need for money. 'I don't feel quite in the humour for tackling the novel just now', he tells Pinker on 29 October. 'I suppose it will do just as well in a months time' (ii. 227–8). There is evidence, moreover, that the reaction of Methuen to the war was to suspend all new projects for six months (and therefore also the payment of royalties on them).[24] If that was what happened to 'The Wedding Ring', together with a request – perhaps conveyed more diplomatically by Pinker than expressed to him by Methuen's reader – for some 'toning down' of the 'love passages' as Kennerley had requested for America (ii. 246), Methuen's statement at the trial in 1915, and Lawrence's reactions in 1914 and later, might seem more compatible. 'I wonder what is going to happen in the book trade' is the only comment in his next note to Pinker (ii. 208), six days after the bad news from Methuen.

He was not only in financial difficulties now, but also deeply upset about the war. 'The war is just hell for me', he told Marsh on 25 August (ii. 211), 'I don't see why I should be so disturbed – but I am. I can't get away from it for a minute: live in a sort of coma, like one of those nightmares when you can't move.' But by 5 September he had thrown himself into work again. 'What a miserable world. What colossal idiocy, this war. Out of sheer rage I've begun my book about Thomas Hardy. It will be about anything but Thomas Hardy I am afraid' (ii. 212). By 5 October he was pressing his

---

[23] Pinker to G. Herbert Thring, 16 November 1915 (Carter, *TLS*).
[24] See F. Swinnerton, *The Bookman's London* (1951), p. 57: 'When the First World War began he [i.e. Methuen] assumed that books would stop selling and that it would be over in six months. He therefore invited writers such as myself to abandon authorship until the world was stable again; and he suggested to authors of renown that they should accept a fifty per cent cut in their advances.' Pinker knew in early August that 'on account of the international crisis Methuen wanted to defer payments to authors unless the money was absolutely needed'; see James Hepburn's note to a letter from Bennett to Pinker on 8 August, in his edition of *Letters of Arnold Bennett* (1966), i. 212.

friend S. S. Koteliansky ('Kot') to type it for him, and had rewritten the
first fifty pages (ii. 220). By 13 October he had done a third, 'more or less –
very much less – about Thomas Hardy' (ii. 222). On 18 November he told
the American poet and anthologist Amy Lowell that the book 'supposed to
be on Thomas Hardy' was 'in reality a sort of Confessions of my Heart',
and that he was 'just finishing' (ii. 235).

Although it was the result of a chance commission and was never
published in Lawrence's lifetime, the 'Study of Thomas Hardy'[25] was a
seminal work, which took its author by surprise. The 'little book' grew in
strange diversity. Thinking about 'Hardy's people' turned out to involve all
the concerns that were uppermost in Lawrence's mind in late 1914: not
having enough to live on; the sickness of society, and the war; the value of
work; sex and marriage; a 'Confessio Fidei' (ii. 243) – however miserable
the world – in the creative forces at work in it; and the need to understand
the working of those forces in nature, human relationships, religion and
art. Yet it is not about everything *but* Thomas Hardy. It is a very
Lawrentian self-exploration, but Hardy mapped the journey and provided
the challenge and the testing ground at each stage. Lawrence's self-
exploration ended by transforming his view of the nature and significance
of Hardy's achievement; conversely his study of Hardy helped Lawrence
find a language to articulate his own deepest beliefs, and grasp, with
greater clarity, what his fiction had been reaching towards since *Sons and
Lovers*. As soon as he finished, he turned immediately to the novel he had
thought complete, and began all over again.

He had explained to Garnett that though the first 'Sisters' had been
'flippant and often vulgar and jeering', he was primarily 'a passionately
religious man, and my novels must be written from the depth of my
religious experience' (ii. 165). Even earlier, in January 1913, he had
written his 'Foreword' to *Sons and Lovers*, which had less perhaps to do
with that novel than with a first attempt to formulate his religious
convictions, by re-casting the Christian theology of St John in terms of the
relation between man and woman. It announces that the Flesh is made
Word to dwell among us; and that Woman lies in travail to give birth to
Man, who in his hour utters his Word. 'And God the Father, the
Inscrutable, the Unknowable, we know in the Flesh, in Woman. . .In her
we go back to the Father: but like the witnesses of the Transfiguration,
blind and unconscious.' But also, as the bee moves between the hive and

[25] First published in *Phoenix*, ed. McDonald, but references in the text are to the Cambridge 'Hardy'.

the flower, man must move between the source of his renewal, and the utterance of his individuality: the glad cry: 'This is I – I am I.'[26]

Now, in 'Hardy', focussed by deepening responses to the Wessex novels, these earlier intuitions are worked out into a 'philosophy' or even 'theology' of creativity, through the marriage of opposites. Lawrence comes to see natural growth, personality, relationship, religion and art, as the outcome of creative conflict between opposed kinds of life-force, impersonal and universal. But the thought is dialectic rather than dualistic, both forces are vital to growth, and the deepest concern is with their marriage and consummation. Though separable for the sake of under-standing, they are as ultimately one as the movement at the rim of a wheel and the stillness at the centre. Lawrence is aware that all his categorising terminologies ('female' and 'male', 'God the Father' and 'God the Son', 'Law' and 'Love') are 'arbitrary, for the purpose of thought' ('Hardy' 60). Both 'male' and 'female' exist and conflict within every man and woman as well as between them; and though the sexual act is a religious mystery 'for leaping off into the unknown, as from a cliff's edge' ('Hardy' 53), sexual acts as such are not essential for laying hold of the 'beyond', and 'consummation' may take place in the spirit as well as the body.

'God the Father' is immutable, stable, all-embracing, one. Life accord-ing to this Law is a state of being in togetherness with all created things; an existence in the flesh, in sensation, linked with the whole natural universe. But equally there operates throughout evolution the opposite force of 'God the Son'. This is the impulse to movement and change, from being to knowing, from undifferentiated oneness to perception of not-self, defining the self against the other. It is differentiation into the many: into separation, distinct self-awareness, thought and utterance, ever more complete individuation. The two impulses are always in conflict, but the conflict is the ground of all growth. From every successive clash is born a new dimension of personal life, or religion, or art. But beyond the Father and the Son is the Holy Spirit; beyond sexual conflict is consummation, opening the beyond as well as giving men and women to themselves more completely; out of the dualism in the artist is created the work of art. There can however be no stasis, only a never-ending process. The whole inner history of mankind, visible in religion and art, is continual variation on the eternal dialectic. Conflict is vital; if either force becomes too dominant the consummation may be partial or crippled. Battle is the condition of growth, but the aim is always to come through, ever beyond.

This gave Lawrence a 'metaphysical' basis for his intuitive view of

[26] *Letters of D. H. Lawrence*, ed. Huxley, pp. 100–1.

human relationship, particularly marriage; not only clarifying what 'The Wedding Ring' had been trying to express, but also giving him a structural language by which to re-shape and articulate it into *The Rainbow*. Now it would be possible to write the choric prelude, the Brangwen Men and Women in their timeless world of landscape and prospect; and to shape the complex system of oppositions, which define relationships in the novel both in themselves, and by comparison and contrast. He now had, moreover, a new grasp not only of subject but also of structure. As his 'theology' re-interpreted Judaism and Christianity, so he found in the sacred history in which their theology had been embodied a hint of the shape his own 'bible' ought to have, and the point at which it should end. 'Always the threefold utterance: the declaring of the God seen approaching, the rapture of contact, the anguished joy of remembrance, when the meeting has passed into separation' ('Hardy' 61–2). He cites the story of David as an example of the first phase, Solomon of the second and Job of the third; and explains how in Solomon's case rapture turns into rupture because the man is too weak and the woman conquers, but since there had been real contact 'the living thing was conserved, kept always alive and powerful, but restrained, restricted, partial' ('Hardy' 62). So *The Rainbow* too has a threefold utterance: a beautiful but partial 'Old Testament' dominated by the Law; a world of transition in which fulfilment is fused with failure and the promised land is seen but not entered; and a new world of separation almost unto death, but retaining in extremity the memory of an abiding covenant. Thus, on rewriting, Lawrence would not only remove the Birkin material, but change a conclusion of affirmation to one of near-tragedy, while retaining an anguished joy in separation. His 'Hardy' also showed him how to begin archetypally, with a prelude showing the world of God the Father (in which he could use his sense of how Hardy's figures moved against an impersonal landscape) set against the world of God the Son. Though the three generations already existed in 'The Wedding Ring', the expansion of the first two was almost certainly an exploration, and a testing-out in human relationships, of the new 'metaphysical' insights, the third being re-shaped in comparison and contrast. Hence, even after cutting the *Women in Love* material, *The Rainbow* was still longer than 'The Wedding Ring'.[27] It is also clear why there was such a

---

[27] See above p. xxviii for the evidence of the much greater length of *The Rainbow* up to 'The Man's World'. The overall length of 'The Wedding Ring' may also be deduced, albeit only very approximately. On 1 February 1915 (*Letters*, ii. 270), DHL speaks of having written '450 pages out of 600 or so' of *The Rainbow*. On MS p. 450 Ursula and Skrebensky drive past the Hemlock Stone; and it may be assumed that, having decided to split the novel, DHL knows he will end after the final failure of the affair, and that there were 150 pages

wealth of 'theological' language; why the novel refers so continually to Biblical stories (Genesis, the Flood, the journeying Israelites, the dance of David, the fiery furnace, Lot's wife, the sons of God and the daughters of men); and why *The Rainbow* re-interprets Biblical history, theology and language in so very different a light.

Powerful symbols also awaken in 'Hardy', which the novelist's imagination could later explore with much greater complexity in terms of human relationship. The scene in Lincoln Cathedral had its beginning in a remark about 'male' and 'female' in mediæval cathedrals, in chapter VII of 'Hardy' (pp. 65–6). The axle and the wheel of chapter VI are put to sensitive use in the honeymoon of Anna and Will. The polarities of light and darkness, which Lawrence discusses in Rembrandt and Turner ('Hardy' 82–6), become a major symbolic structuring for the whole of *The Rainbow*. The column and the ellipse, in the mediæval church and in Raphael's 'Madonna degli Ansidei' (p. 72), fuse with the Biblical pillars of fire and of cloud in another symbol-system, to extend the suggestiveness of the rainbow-arch.

Finally, the study of the art of the Wessex novels, just now, must have seemed the greatest encouragement of Lawrence's own vision. Of all English novelists, here was the one who saw human life against a 'great background' and whose characters already existed in terms of being and consciousness, rather than the conduct and fixed moral scheme of what he had called 'the old stable ego' (ii. 183).

This is a constant revelation in Hardy's novels: that there exists a great background, vital and vivid, which matters more than the people who move upon it. . .This is the wonder of Hardy's novels, and gives them their beauty. The vast, unexplored morality of life itself, what we call the immorality of nature, surrounds us in its eternal incomprehensibility, and in its midst goes on the little human morality play. . . ('Hardy' 28–9)

The true moral is that man at last must learn 'to be at one, in his mind and will, with the primal impulses that rise in him' (p. 28). As he pondered

more of 'The Wedding Ring' up to that point. According to *Letters*, ii. 164, there were then another 80 pages of 'The Wedding Ring' to its end. There would also have to be a section between the failure with Skrebensky and the meeting with Birkin. Since the surviving fragment begins on p. 219 (but must come near the beginning of the last 150 pages) we get 219+150 (to the break with Skrebensky)+link+80 ('the School Inspector, and so on'); a novel of, say, 475 (more or less) pages of folio typescript, depending on the length of the linking section between the two love-affairs. Even if this were revised upwards, in *Rainbow* typescript terms, by 125 – as Charles Ross suggests in *The Composition of 'The Rainbow' and 'Women in Love'* (Charlottesville, 1979), p. 26 – or even by 150 (to 625pp.), to allow for the greater length of the 'Wedding Ring' pages, it would still be considerably shorter than the 734 pages of *The Rainbow* TS, which ended with the break with Skrebensky.

more deeply he had come to see how, in the development of Hardy's fiction, the 'great background' had become increasingly internalised in the conflict within the characters themselves, at such depth that they already showed, in human complexity, the 'allotropic' interplay of contraries that he had been struggling to grasp in his own life and writing. The increasing internalisation and self-consciousness, from *The Return of the Native*, to *Tess*, to *Jude*, is artistically recapitulated in the three generations of *The Rainbow*; and the study of Hardy's characterisation, in *Tess* and *Jude* particularly, clarified and deepened what Lawrence had been trying to say to Garnett about his new conception of character. Yet he also felt (the most liberating kind of affinity) that Hardy had not seen clearly where he was going, and had not gone far enough. Hardy had only been able, he thought, to pit the contraries against one another tragically, without exploring the possibility of the marriage of opposites. What remained to strive for was a 'supreme art' in which both sides of the dialectic would have full expression, neither over-balancing the other, and in which there would also be 'the final reconciliation, where both are equal, two-in-one, complete' ('Hardy' 128). As Lawrence turned again to 'The Wedding Ring', to make it into *The Rainbow*, that would be his aim.

The Rainbow (fourth version, November 1914–March 1915)

The last of the manuscript of the 'Hardy' was sent to Koteliansky on 5 December, but two days earlier he had already been 'working *frightfully* hard – rewriting my novel' (ii. 239); in fact he had done 'the first hundred or so pages' by the 5th when he sent them to Pinker – so must have started in late November – (ii. 240). (On p. 100 of the manuscript, hereafter MS, little Anna confronts the geese, p. 66 below.) He had also made an attempt to type a fair-copy on the typewriter recently given to him by Amy Lowell, but he soon gave up because it was taking far too long. (The effort has survived in MS, see below p. li.) On 18 December he sent Pinker another instalment (ii. 245), probably another hundred pages as he had suggested he would do. (What was then chapter IV, called 'Haste to the Wedding', begins on MS p. 199; see p. 124 and note, for Frieda's confirmation that this chapter was completed before Christmas.) By 5 January 1915 he had done three hundred pages (ii. 255), and it is clear that the novel had become quite different from 'The Wedding Ring': 'It'll be a new sort of me for you to get used to. . .I'm afraid, when Methuen gets the *Rainbow*, he'll wonder what changeling is foisted on him. For it *is* different from my other work. I am very glad with it. I am coming into my full feather at last, I think.' (MS p. 300 is concerned with Anna's response to the Cathedral, which gives point to the remark.) By 7 January when he sent this third batch to Pinker, he had finally made the crucial decision to split the novel into two volumes (ii. 256) – ensuring, as it would turn out, that *Women in Love* would become a very different book.

On 20 January he sent 'what pages of the novel I have ready' (ii. 260), because the Lawrences were about to move to the cottage on the Meynell estate near Greatham in Sussex, which their friend Viola Meynell, daughter of Wilfrid and the poet Alice, had offered rent-free. He wondered when – not whether – Methuen would want to publish, and was clearly not aware of any radical objection from them to 'The Wedding Ring'. By 1 February however (ii. 270), when he had done four hundred and fifty pages, his assurance that 'there shall be no very flagrant love-passages in it (at least, to my thinking)' tends to confirm that there must have been some request for toning down. (On MS p. 450, Ursula and Skrebensky drive past the Hemlock Stone, p. 283. It is in the early days of their courtship, and Will's episode with the girl in Nottingham, and its aftermath with Anna, did not yet exist.) At this stage Lawrence expected the novel to be about six hundred pages of manuscript, though it would turn out to be a hundred pages longer. The outburst about resurrection at the end of the previous chapter is closely related to his letter on 20 December (ii. 246–50) to Gordon Campbell – the lawyer in whose house in London they had stayed in the summer – denouncing Christianity for emphasising the Crucifixion rather than the Resurrection in the flesh. (He had been reading Mrs Henry Jenner's *Christian Symbolism*, 1910, in the Methuen series 'Little Books on Art'; ii. 250.) On 2 February he asked Campbell, who had served as a 'Sapper', for background detail about a 21-year-old-subaltern in the Royal Engineers: 'What would he be? What would he earn? What would he do? Where would he live?' (ii. 274). (Skrebensky answers Ursula's questions on p. 273.) As the rewriting went on from 'First Love', however, Lawrence's unease about Methuen became more pronounced. On 11 February he wrote of how E. M. Forster had brought to Greatham 'a ghastly rumour of the *Prussian Officer*'s being withdrawn from circulation, by order of the police' (ii. 280); and though he didn't suppose it true, he hoped 'the publishers will not think it impossible to print [*The Rainbow*] as it stands'. (By then he had almost certainly written the chapter called 'Shame' containing Ursula's lesbian relationship with Winifred Inger, which was particularly objected to by the Bow Street magistrate who subsequently ordered the destruction of the novel; see below p. l and n.) At about the same time he described to Lady Ottoline

Morrell – whom he had met in August, and who had recently brought the philosopher and mathematician Bertrand Russell to Greatham – his feelings while walking over the Downs and watching a little train far below (ii. 282), which would be transmuted into Ursula's consciousness on MS p. 667 (429–30). On 24 February he was 'very, very near the end of the novel' (ii. 293) and Viola Meynell had offered, generously again, to type it for him, though (see ii. 299) she had not yet begun. But though he enquired wistfully whether it was really too late for Spring publication, he was clearly worried now, having written the later phases of the affair between Ursula and Skrebensky, about whether Methuen would be 'ready to back up this novel of mine' and 'make some fight for it. . .and prevent the mean little fry from pulling it down' (ii. 294). On 2 March he completed the final page and wrote exultantly to Viola Meynell, 'I have finished my *Rainbow*, bended it and set it firm. Now off and away to find the pots of gold at its feet.'[28] But he also asked her, as she typed, to keep an eye open for 'repetitions and the things I can cross out' and also parts 'the publisher will decidedly object to' (ii. 299).

The revisions of *The Rainbow* (March–August 1915)

In March, April and May Lawrence revised the novel extensively, as he received batches of typescript from Viola Meynell (who did not, however, type the whole MS; see below pp. liii–liv). A host of changes, far too many to summarise, sharpen and clarify the 'opposites', and vivify and discipline the language. In one case, perhaps because of his worry about length – 'I must cross some things out' (ii. 299) – he cut a vivid passage in which Tom, busy ploughing, disturbs a peewit (see Textual apparatus for 57:32). Of greater significance, however, are the two points at which Lawrence wrote new autograph sections into the typescript (TS). The first (TS pp. 310–14) occurs in the Cathedral scene, which had been a new leap of imagination in the manuscript, but which Lawrence clearly felt, now, had come out too one-sided. He re-conceived the episode to achieve a better balance between Anna and Will, and to ensure that their partial failure to achieve the marriage of opposites is attributed as firmly to her as to him. By making Anna go through the same experience as Will before rejecting it, MS had weighted the scales in her favour; she seemed to know more than her husband. There had been a similar tendency to lay the stress at the end of 'Anna Victrix' too exclusively on the failure of Will. As Lawrence began

---

28 DHL sent her a drawing of a rainbow over a colliery, village and fields: 'I have finished my Rainbow' (reproduced in *Letters*, ii. facing p. 293).

now to correct this (and would go further still in proof), so he re-conceived their conflict in the Cathedral, in order to complicate and intensify the opposition, and make both sides seem reductive. Will's response becomes a more cogent, if still limited resolution of opposites within the inclusiveness of 'God the Father', in which, as in the natural seed, all is One. But Anna's response is transformed. She longs for even wider freedom and space; but she is now made resentful from the beginning; resisting the march to the altar, and catching at the little faces in far more anti-religious and mocking fashion. They become not merely human but wicked; and she is jeering and malicious, triumphing not merely in multiplicity but also in destructiveness. It has become a more complex conflict in which it is less possible to feel that either is in the right. Both have a half-truth, but the conflict becomes destructive because they do not marry their oppositions and go through, beyond. The second autograph insertion (TS pp. 343–55; pp. 210–22) is as remarkable a new leap of imagination at this stage as the original Cathedral scene had been in MS. There Lawrence had spoken only briefly and generally of 'some months' in which Anna:

let herself go, she gave him also his full measure, she considered nothing. Children and everything she let go, and gave way to her last desires, till she and he had gone all the devious and never-to-be-recorded ways of desire and satisfaction, to the very end, till they had had everything, and knew no more.   (MS p. 341)

Lawrence now replaced this by a new half-chapter: Will's escapade with the girl in Nottingham, and the new relation with Anna which issues in 'a sensuality violent and extreme as death', but also an 'Absolute Beauty', and a kind of liberation. He then cut a long authorial sermon at the point where Ursula looks at the cell through her microscope (see Textual apparatus at 408:40) – perhaps because its essential point had been made by his new episode.

The letters of March to May 1915 reveal a darkening sense of evil, disintegration and the savage violence of the human heart. This had first of all to do with the full realisation of what was happening in Flanders; that 'very beautiful', even 'brilliant' spring, 'upon a black undertone of the war horror' (ii. 347). But it was precipitated also by what he subsequently described as 'one of the crises in my life': the disastrous visit in March to Cambridge (which he had clearly thought of as the intellectual centre of English civilisation), only to discover what struck him as 'a form of inward corruption' in John Maynard Keynes, later reinforced by further impressions of homosexuality in Duncan Grant, and Edward Garnett's son David with Frankie Birrell. The result was nightmares of beetles and putrescence (ii. 309, 319, 320–1), and at first a kind of derangement in which 'I am afraid of the terrible things that are real, in the darkness', while in the daylight 'one is all the time walking in a pale assembly of an unreal world' (ii. 307). He became physically ill also, and reading *The Idiot* and Dostoievsky's letters (ii. 311–14), was all the more convinced that the 'disintegrating' and 'evil will' in Dostoievsky (ii. 314), disguising itself as love, was true also of the English psyche now, of himself and of his friends.

> Do not tell me there is no Devil. . .Sometimes I wish I could let go, and be really wicked – kill and murder. . .The war is no good. It is this black desire I have become conscious of. We cant so much about goodness. . .Tell Russell he does the same – let him recognise the powerful malignant will in him. This is the very worst wickedness, that we refuse to acknowledge the passionate evil that is in us. This makes us secret and rotten.   (ii. 315)

On a visit at the end of April to a Worthing swarming with soldiers, the perceptions of the marsh-malignancy of war, of murderous violence concealed by a uniform of patriotism, of the secret rottenness of insects, all came together: 'It isn't my disordered imagination. There is a wagtail sitting on the gatepost. I see how sweet and swift heaven is. But hell is slow and creeping and viscous, and insect-teeming: as is this Europe now – this England' (ii. 331). London, too, became a vision of the underworld: 'The traffic flows through the rigid grey streets like the rivers of Hell through their banks of dry, rocky ash' (ii. 339).

To look back to the middle of February, when Lawrence wrote his sermon on 'evolution' as Ursula looked into her microscope, is to see a vision that could then hold the marsh, the violent creatures and the river in a more inclusive vision, though at lower pressure. He had taken up the theme of two letters to Forster, about how life began undifferentiated (the meaning of 'Pan'), and issued in both 'demons' and 'angels'; but, as in Fra Angelico's 'Last Judgement',[29] always within a 'conception of the Whole. . .of the beginning and the end, of heaven and hell, of good and evil flowing from God through humanity as through a filter, and returning back to god' (ii. 266). So in *The Rainbow* he insisted that not only does the river of human life include the marsh and the jungle as it flows from the source to the infinite, but the soul simultaneously holds all that it has been, so may be tiger and ape, and yet be touching paradise at its tip (see Textual apparatus at 408:40). Moreover, the exploration, immediately afterwards, of the new relation of Ursula and Skrebensky after his return from Africa, had revealed a liberating potency, albeit limited, in the darkness outside

---

[29] *Letters*, ii. 265–7, 275–6. Fra Angelico's 'Last Judgement' is also discussed (and reproduced) in Mrs Jenner's *Christian Symbolism*; in 'Hardy' 69; and in *The Rainbow* 166:38 and 259:4–24.

the lighted area of human consciousness, where wild beasts prowl. Now, in revision, Lawrence both intensified the potential destructiveness already there in some of the conflicts in MS (in keeping with the letters after March); but also further explored the ways in which the darkness could set couples free. His new section reads-back the 'dark' relation of Ursula and Skrebensky (itself made more emphatic) into the new relation of Anna and Will, in a deliberately extreme, initially predatory and sexually more explicit form, developing the mere hint in MS. He strengthened the awareness in earlier chapters of Will's darkly violent potential for 'evil' – but also for a kind of life and beauty which Lawrence now felt, more than before, had to be included within the spectrum of human relation and liberation. On the other hand, as well as intensifying the polarities in the Wedding Dance in a new language of salt corrosion (see also ii. 339), he made Ursula react even more savagely against Skrebensky's dark underworld, and also against his willingness to see himself primarily as a soldier-servant of the state. Whatever view is taken of the realisation and significance of these new perspectives, they made a marked difference to the orchestration of comparison and contrast among the three generations, and to the challenge of the novel's treatment of the 'marriage' of opposites. And whereas Lawrence had begun to be worried that places in MS might be considered improper, his revision of TS had greatly increased that risk.

He began the revision when he received the first seventy-one pages (chap. I) from Viola Meynell, probably in mid-March (ii. 308). He had promised to send the TS for Lady Ottoline to read, and on 2 April he told her that, though Viola Meynell was typing slowly – actually, she had already asked for help (see below p. liii) – a 'moderately good batch' would be ready the following week (ii. 312). On 8 April he was able to send off 'one third' (ii. 314), in fact TS pp. 1–263. On the 19th he told Lady Ottoline that his agent was anxious to have the book typeset as soon as possible, and asked her to return the TS directly to Pinker (ii. 319). On 23 April he sent a second batch, which he had had to number arbitrarily from '250', because he had forgotten to note the number of the last page in the previous batch (ii. 326). The arbitrary numbering began on what is now TS p. 264. On 30 April he asked whether the last page of the arbitrary numbering in the second batch was '356' (ii. 329). In fact it was '374' (TS p. 388), and on the next page, the opening of chapter x 'The Widening Circle', begins another set of arbitrary numbering with '357'. So he had revised as far as TS p. 388 by 23 April – well past the Nottingham episode and its aftermath – which gives point to his letter to Pinker that day:

I hope you are willing to fight for this novel. It is nearly three years of hard work,[30] and I am proud of it, and it must be stood up for. I'm afraid there are parts of it Methuen wont want to publish. He must. I will take out sentences and phrases, but I won't take out paragraphs or pages. So you must tell me in detail if there are real objections to printing any parts.

You see a novel, after all this period of coming into being, has a definite organic form, just as a man has when he is grown. And we don't ask a man to cut his nose off because the public won't like it. . .

Oh God, I hope I'm not going to have a miserable time over this book, now I've at last got it pretty much to its real being.   (ii. 327)

A week later he asked Pinker whether he had received the first batch from Lady Ottoline, and promised that she would send the second batch the next day. 'That is the first half complete. The rest won't be long. We wait only for Miss Meynell.' He thanked Pinker for his 'assurances' of support (ii. 331). About 19 May he sent Lady Ottoline a third batch (ii. 342), running from TS p. 389 to at least p. 617, since it included Brinsley Street School (ii. 351), and probably to p. 631 (see Explanatory note on 391:24). Indeed her *Memoirs* record her 'discomfort' at the repetition of the word fecund 'at least twelve times on one page',[31] (actually eight on pp. 667–8) – but she may have projected back a later reading. This was the last batch sent to her, since Pinker was now pressing. On 29 May Lawrence worried about the final handing-over of the typescript to Methuen because of his fear that the 'detestable Goldbergs', the solicitors who were trying to recover the costs of Frieda's divorce from him, might be able to seize Methuen's payment. 'The MS. is being finished by Miss Meynell' (in fact by her helper, and Lawrence's new friend, Eleanor Farjeon, see below p. liii) 'this very day. I have only to revise it and let you have it' (ii. 348). On 31 May he posted the final batch to Pinker, asking him to re-number the pages and chapters and to check that nothing was missing.

I hope you will like the book: also that it is not very improper. It did not seem to me very improper, as I went through it. But then I feel very incompetent to judge on that point.

My beloved book. I am sorry to give it to you to be printed. I could weep tears in

---

[30] In fact, two years and a bit under two months. DHL is often approximate in such statements, hence the danger of seeing this one as evidence that the book might date back before March 1912. On 29 July 1915 he wrote of 'Christs in the Tirol' as having been published three years previously (*Letters*, ii. 373 n. 3), when it was two years four months – though he later corrected himself, not much more accurately, to two years. The tendency of his plea to Pinker would be to make the most of the time he had worked on the book.

[31] *Ottoline: The Early Memoirs of Lady Ottoline Morrell*, ed. Robert Gathorne-Hardy (1963), p. 283.

my heart, when I read these pages. If I had my way, I would put off the publishing
yet a while. (ii. 349)

He also asked for a dedication to Frieda's sister Else, in German, and
initially in Gothic script, though he gave in on those points – but even the
German name may have helped get *The Rainbow* into trouble when it
appeared.

By 9 July he was proof-correcting, or rather, revising extensively yet
once more in proof (ii. 362). He made so many changes in detail that
Methuen subsequently exercised their contractual option to charge for
changes exceeding printer's costs of six shillings per sheet of sixteen pages;
and deducted £9.3.9.[32] – to Lawrence's annoyance. A series of pencil
numbers in the margins of the opening chapter in TS, marking changes in
proof, is probably the result of a spot-check on what Lawrence had done,
by someone in Methuen preparing evidence in case of objection by the
author – though they might just be by a later purchaser wishing to get some
idea of the extent of the differences from the published texts. A hundred
and twenty changes are noted in that opening chapter, which is compara-
tively lightly revised, and not all were picked up.

There are no major alterations in this last revision; though Lawrence's
increasing opposition to regimentation and the war, and his new impatience with Christian democracy, in outbursts to Russell and Lady
Ottoline in July (ii. 364–8, 370–1), give a new edge to his and Ursula's
treatment of Skrebensky – and again could not have endeared the novel to
officials and patriots when it came out. Mostly (though not always) the
revisions amount to sharper focussing and improvement. However, on 13
and again on 22 July it is clear that Pinker – more imperatively now – was
asking 'for modification' (ii. 364, 369). On 26 July Lawrence sent back
'slips and pages' separately from the main series, in which he was 'now at
p. 192 of the revised proofs, the final form'.

I have cut out, as I said I would, all the *phrases* objected to. The passages and
paragraphs marked I cannot alter. There is nothing offensive in them, beyond the
very substance they contain, and that is no more offensive than that of all the rest of
the novel. The libraries won't object to the book any less, or approve of it any more,

---

[32] *Letters*, ii. 406 and n. 3; see also Methuen & Co to Pinker, 1 October 1915, NYPL. Their
claim to have warned DHL 'in June' may however be a slip for July. No such warning
could have been issued until a substantial batch of proofs had been returned by DHL. The
first mention of proof-correction is on 9 July and by 26 July he had still only reached p. 192
(ibid., ii. 370). Even if he had begun before 9 July it seems unlikely that he could have sent
back enough in June to have alerted both printer and publisher to the nature and scale of
his revision.

if these passages are cut out. And I cant cut them out, because they are living parts of an organic whole. Those who object, will object to the book altogether. These bits won't affect them particularly.   (ii. 369–70)

Presumably what Pinker sent, on Methuen's behalf, was a mixture of galleys ('slip' being the typographical term for 'a proof pulled on a long slip of paper', *OED*), in the case of passages set up in type but not yet imposed as formes, and 'pages' of proof where available – though it is just possible, if improbable, that Methuen may have sent a part of the typescript itself (see below pp. liv–lv). The letters from Pinker which might have told us not only what was sent, but the nature or even the identity of the places found objectionable, have not come to light. It is not, moreover, as simple as might be supposed, to predict what a 'respectable' publisher, with his eye on library sales in 1915, would demand should be altered. The thirteen expurgations made without Lawrence's consent in the first American edition[33] are the most likely passages that Lawrence might have refused to cut,[34] and suggest that the Nottingham episode, the relationship with Winifred Inger and the going away together of Ursula and Skrebensky were the main areas of sensitivity. The American publisher was not apparently bothered by the descriptions of the episode with the girl in Matlock, or by Anna's dancing in the nude, or by the loss of Ursula's virginity under the oak tree, or by the climax of the scene on the beach at the end. However, that might have been because of what Lawrence *had* agreed to cut or change; which is even more difficult to guess. The editorial problem posed by the knowledge that Lawrence did agree to censor himself, to some extent, is discussed below (p. lxivff.). What seem to one editor the most likely places are also indicated in the Explanatory notes.

Evidently Pinker was reasonably satisfied by what Lawrence had done, and by his justification against doing more, since Lawrence thanked him on 29 July for further assurances about Methuen and ended by hoping that 'everything is well with the novel' (ii. 372–3) – but by then his attention was turning to the re-casting of his earlier Italian sketches into the book which became *Twilight in Italy*. It is not clear exactly when he finished the last proofs of *The Rainbow*, but Methuen placed the order to print on 16 August (see below p. lvii).

---

[33] See *Letters*, iii. 652: 'Did Huebsch have your permission to cut out certain parts of *The Rainbow*? He never had mine.'
[34] See Explanatory notes on 24:21; 137:20; 219:26; 298:40; 314:1, 10; 316:4; 326:25; 421:4; 422:2; 428:32; 442:40; 444:6.

The Rainbow was published on 30 September[35] – and was very soon suppressed.

The prosecution and suppression of *The Rainbow*

Three days before publication, Methuen was 'afraid we are likely to get into trouble' and hoped Lawrence would 'try to moderate his broadmindedness' next time. The tone hardened by 18 October however, blaming 'a disastrous fiasco', since none of the big libraries or bookstalls 'would touch it', on 'the author's obstinate refusal to make the necessary alterations'.[36] But the scale of the trouble went quite beyond expectation. On 3 and 5 November the police called at Methuen with a warrant to impound all copies and unbound sheets held in stock.[37] On 11 November Inspector Draper, of Scotland Yard's Criminal Investigation Department, came again with a summons to show cause why 'the said books should not be destroyed, and to be further dealt with according to the law';[38] and on 13 November the Bow Street Magistrate, hearing the prosecution under the Obscene Publications Act of 1857, found in favour, and ordered the destruction, saying how glad he was 'to hear that the libraries refused to circulate it'. The prosecuting counsel for the Crown, Herbert Muskett, had already warned booksellers who might still be holding copies, that any who persisted in selling them 'will run the risk of prosecution'.[39]

The first warnings of a major storm had come from three hostile reviews in October, after an initially favourable one the day after publication, (see also below p. lxixff.). Robert Lynd, in the *Daily News*,[40] called the book 'a monotonous wilderness of phallicism'. James Douglas denounced it still more vehemently in the *Star*:[41] 'These people are not human beings. They

---

[35] In DHL's letter to the Society of Authors – see Carter, *TLS* and *Letters*, ii. 434 – he gives the date as 1 October, but it appears as 30 September in Methuen's ledger (now at UInd), and in their statement to Warren Roberts for his *Bibliography*.

DHL's reaction to the dust-jacket showing a sentimental painting by Frank Wright of a man and a woman embracing was 'The cover-wrapper is vile beyond words, I think Methuen is a swine to have put it on' (*Letters*, ii. 402); it is reproduced in colour in Keith Sagar, *The Life of D. H. Lawrence* (1980), facing p. 128.

[36] Methuen to Pinker, 27 September and 18 October, NYPL. The October letter draws the financial consequences: 'The result is that our sales have been up to the present 706 at 6s, 440 colonial, and the book has earned in royalties roughly £60, against an advance of £300'. Little wonder, now, that 'we shall decline to accept his next book if it at all approaches the present book in outspokenness'.

[37] The two visits are recorded in the Register of the Bow Street Clerk of the Court for 13 November 1915.

[38] Methuen & Co to the Society of Authors, Carter, *TLS*.

[39] *Daily Telegraph*, 25 November 1915, p. 12.

[40] 5 October 1915, p. 6 (Draper 91–2).   [41] 22 October 1915, p. 4 (Draper 93–5).

are creatures who are immeasurably lower than the lowest animal in the Zoo'. But, more significantly, he hinted that the book ought to be prosecuted: that when art refuses to 'conform to the ordered laws that govern human society. . .it must pay the penalty. The sanitary inspector of literature must notify it and call for its isolation. The wind of war is sweeping over our life. . .A thing like *The Rainbow* has no right to exist in the wind of war.' Clement Shorter, in the *Sphere*,[42] found more to admire, and thought the novel had been written 'from artistic impulses', but he also found that 'There is no form of viciousness, of suggestiveness, that is not reflected in these pages'. And, though he clearly had reservations about censorship by the libraries, his suggestion that, after this, no writer who was also an artist would run any risk of prosecution, might also have sounded an alarm in official ears. He too could 'find no justification whatever for the perpetration of such a book'.

Lawrence himself later believed that the prosecution was 'instigated by the National Purity League, Dr Horton and Co, nonconformity' (ii. 477) – presumably by a denunciation to the police and the Home Office, quoting the reviews – though there is no confirmation of this. There is some evidence that there may also have been a political motive for the prosecution. A Home Office minute of 1930 (when a prosecution of Martin Secker for republishing *The Rainbow* was being considered[43]) reveals that 'Although the 1915 proceedings were taken in the Commissioner's name' (i.e. the Commissioner of Police at Scotland Yard) 'they were practically initiated by the late Sir Charles Matthews', who was Director of Public Prosecutions from 1908 to 1920. As with the employment of Herbert Muskett who, according to his son, 'handled the cases of most public importance',[44] the persons involved seem too powerful for a mere case of literary obscenity. Moreover David Garnett remembered a number of visits by plain-clothes officers in August 1914, investigating denunciations by neighbours suspicious of Frieda;[45] and Ford Madox Ford claimed that his visit to Greatham in 1915, while Lawrence was in

[42] 23 October 1915, p. 104 (Draper 96–7).
[43] Public Record Office HO 45/13944, Minute 210/PB/589, Prosecutions Branch, Scotland Yard, to Sir John Anderson. Reproduced in Emile Delavenay's *D. H. Lawrence: The Man and His Work* (1972), illus. 18–19 (originally published as *D. H. Lawrence: L'homme et la genèse de son œuvre: Les années de formation 1885–1919*, 2 vols, Paris, 1969).
[44] Delavenay, *D. H. Lawrence*, p. 39; though Philip Hobsbaum states (*TLS*, 10 November 1966) that Herbert Muskett was also Secretary to the National Purity League. In a letter to Delavenay, now in Nottingham University Library, however, Muskett's son states 'I have never heard of the National Purity League and I should consider it unlikely in the extreme that he ever acted for them'.
[45] *Composite Biography*, ed. Nehls, i. 241.

Cambridge, was on behalf of 'The Minister of Information' and meant to protect Lawrence from persecution – though perhaps it was actually to make a report, as part of an intelligence-gathering operation, on an author under suspicion of being 'pro-German' (as Ford indeed calls him) as well as his wife. If this were so, Ford's later memory of the occasion, and Violet Hunt's,[46] suggest that his report would not have been favourable! There is also a note on the Home Office Memorandum prepared for the Home Secretary (to help him answer Philip Morrell's Written Question in Parliament about the prosecution) which reads: 'As to a Mrs. Weekley living at address of D. H. Lawrence see 352857', and this has been taken to confirm that there was already an 'intelligence' file dating back to 1914.[47]

However, the evidence for all this is somewhat shaky. Ford's inaccurate memory and habit of self-dramatisation make his testimony notoriously unreliable. The phrasing of the Home Office note suggests that the file on Frieda originated before her marriage to Lawrence, and therefore *before* the war, and was probably concerned initially with her immigration. Even so, it might seem also to relate to Garnett's story, yet when the number is compared with the Home Office day-books (many of whose entries concern suspected spies) it is quite wrong for 1914 or 1915, but would fit late 1917, when the Lawrences were expelled from Cornwall and were indeed under subsequent surveillance. The note is in red ink, unlike the rest of the Memorandum, and may well be of much later date. However, Lawrence had been very much occupied in the months since March 1915 in planning for 'revolution' in society and denunciation of the war, first with Bertrand Russell who lost his fellowship in Cambridge because of his pacifism, and then (after quarrelling with Russell) with John Middleton Murry and Katherine Mansfield. The final plan, announced on 5 September (ii. 385–7), was for a small magazine called *The Signature*, which would contain six essays by Lawrence (rewriting the essential philosophy of the 'Study of Thomas Hardy'); each issue being followed by a public meeting and discussion.[48] The venture was a fiasco; only a handful of people came to the meetings, and the magazine ceased after three issues on 4 and 18

[46] Ibid., i. 288 – but note Ford's vivid description of DHL who was not in fact there – and cf. Violet Hunt's account, ibid., i. 288–9.
[47] Public Record Office HO 45/13944, Minute for the Home Secretary, 22 November 1915 etc., but see above for date of red-ink note. The Minute is reproduced by Delavenay, *D. H. Lawrence*, illus. 16–17.
[48] The six essays were revised as 'The Crown' in *Reflections on the Death of a Porcupine* (Philadelphia, 1925) and are included in *Reflections on the Death of a Porcupine and Other Essays*, ed. Michael Herbert (Cambridge, 1988), pp. 253–306 and 469–79.

October and 1 November; but a number of influential people had been approached for support, and the relation of the dates with the actions of the police might seem suggestive. The German name in the dedication of *The Rainbow*, together with the evidence in the book of hostility to soldierly patriotism, and to British imperialism, in Ursula's denunciations of Skrebensky – if anyone had read carefully enough – might well have caused offence in those dark days of the war. The Home Office may have seen, in the accusations of obscenity, a good opportunity to discredit an author who was becoming, if not dangerous, at least a nuisance – though the evidence is not conclusive.

Methuen supported neither the novel nor the novelist. It becomes clear from their letter to the Society of Authors (which Lawrence had applied to join, in the hope that the Society would take up his case) how the publishers had been manoeuvred into full co-operation with the process of suppression.[49] On 3 November, Inspector Draper's first visit, 'The solicitors, in consideration of the reputation of our firm, kindly suggested that we might prefer to hand over the books rather than submit to actual search, and this we did.' The 'kindly' shows that 'the solicitors' were the Crown solicitors, and that the hinted reward for co-operation would be the preservation of Methuen's good name. As soon as the Inspector left, they telephoned Pinker, but neither then nor later had any communication with Lawrence. The Inspector's second visit, on 5 November, must have been because he had been *told*, the first time, that more sheets would be coming from the printer, since 766 sets duly arrived that day, according to Methuen's ledger, and are marked 'destroyed'. The Memorandum for the Home Secretary explains that 'The object of the Obscene Publications Acts 1857, is to enable obscene publications found on the premises which are searched to be seized and destroyed' – but clearly the sheets could not have been 'found' or 'seized' at Methuen on the 3rd, even in the notional sense that had applied to the 245 bound copies impounded then. An extra binding-order which had been placed on 1 November was also cancelled. (The letter to the Authors' Society makes no mention of this further co-operation.) On the Inspector's third visit with the summons, Methuen received the impression that this was merely 'a formal matter to obtain our formal consent on the destruction of the book' and that 'it would not be heard in a public court' – so that they did not 'obtain legal assistance or arrange to be represented' and were 'very much surprised on Saturday, the 13th, to find, on attending at the Police Court, that the case would be heard in open court'. They claimed to have asked the Inspector 'if the author

[49] See Carter, *TLS* and also Delavenay, *D. H. Lawrence*, pp. 237–8.

could have a voice in the destruction of the books, and understood him to say that the action of the Police was taken against us, and the author had no right to appear in the matter'. (This account of the law is confirmed in the Memorandum for the Home Secretary, and formed the basis of his answer to Philip Morrell, Lady Ottoline's husband, in the House of Commons.)

Pinker's letter to the Society of Authors,[50] while confirming the above account of the first visit, as given to him by Methuen's manager Mr Webster on the telephone, also shows that Methuen not only 'took no steps whatever to defend the book or to protect the author's interest', but that they had tried to discourage anyone else from doing so. A Mr Muller from Methuen had telephoned to say that they had had a call from Clive Bell, 'who was anxious to write in defence of Mr. Lawrence and his work'. Muller had referred him to Pinker 'for any information about Mr. Lawrence, but he expressed the hope that nothing would be written on the subject':

> Muller told me that he had discussed the question with one of the Directors, and they felt very strongly that the matter should be hushed up. I pointed out to him that they did not seem to have considered Mr. Lawrence's point of view, and we were going to try and get the order reversed. Mr. Muller said that they hoped I should do nothing in the matter.

Not only did Methuen never communicate with Lawrence, but Pinker also knew nothing about the proceedings in Court 'until I read of them in the newspaper'. He goes on to refute the suggestion that Lawrence 'had been unyielding on the question of alterations', in the perhaps overstated account of a co-operative author quoted (and queried) above.

In the Bow Street Court on 13 November, the Prosecutor and the Magistrate held the floor unopposed. Methuen received their reward. Muskett called them 'a publishing house of old standing and the highest repute' who had finally behaved 'with the strictest propriety' (*Telegraph*), though it was difficult to see how they had lent 'their great name' to such a work in the first place. The Magistrate, Sir John Dickinson, followed suit almost exactly, adding that their name 'on the title page of a book justified anyone in taking it into their home', which made it all the harder to understand how this one could ever have passed through their hands. Methuen took their cue and apologised – their representative suggesting (more emphatically in the *Telegraph* report than in *The Times*[51]) that they had twice acted decisively to get the author to change certain passages, both when they first received the manuscript and when they got it back; but

---

[50] See Carter, *TLS*.   [51] *The Times*, 15 November 1915, p. 3 (Draper 102–3).

that finally, having altered some, 'he refused to do anything more. No doubt the firm acted unwisely in not scrutinizing the book again more carefully, and they regretted having published it' (*Times*). Although it was quite clear that the suppression would be unopposed, both Muskett – who said he had consulted the Director of Public Prosecutions, and that 'it was considered advisable in the public interest that a statement should be made' (*Telegraph*) – and the Magistrate, went out of their way to execrate the novel, which might suggest a determination to discredit the absent author, known to be opposed to the war. (Sir John Dickinson had lost his only son at the front six weeks earlier.[52]) The two most hostile reviews were read out in Court. Muskett called *The Rainbow* 'a mass of obscenity of thought, idea, and action throughout, wrapped up in language which he supposed would be regarded in some quarters as an artistic and intellectual effort' (*Times*). Sir John, having tartly called attention to the chapter 'Shame' – to the discomfiture of Methuen's man who had said that, although he now found it 'disgraceful', two others had not been able to see anything suggestive[53] – went on to say that 'he had never read anything more disgusting than this book...It was appalling to think of the harm that such a book might have done. It was utter filth, nothing else would describe it' (*Telegraph*). Though he 'regretted' that Methuen 'did not take steps to suppress it after the criticisms had appeared in the press' (*Times*), he imposed no fine, but made the order for the destruction of the 1,011 copies and sets of sheets that had been impounded (after seven days for an appeal, though here of course there was none) and with ten guineas costs against Methuen.[54]

Lawrence first heard about the trouble on 5 November from the novelist W. L. George, who had noticed that *The Rainbow* had disappeared from the Methuen advertisement (as early, in fact, as 28 October), and telephoned them to discover why. 'I am not very much moved' Lawrence told Pinker the next day, 'am beyond that by now. I only curse them all, body and soul, root, branch and leaf, to eternal damnation' (ii. 429, 440). He wrote to Marsh the same day saying that he was 'so sick, in body and soul, that if I don't go away I shall die', and asking for financial help to emigrate to America, which the collapse of the *Signature* venture had already put in his mind (ii. 413). But W. L. George's suggestion that the

---

52 See Hobsbaum, *TLS*, 10 November 1966.

53 *Daily Telegraph*, 15 November 1915: 'It was a remarkable fact that two members of the firm read a certain chapter to which exception was taken without conceiving the suggestion it contained. Sir John Dickinson: They could not have read it very intelligently, looking at the name of the chapter – "Shame."'

54 See Clerk of the Court's Register at Bow Street, 13 November 1915.

Society of Authors might take up his case, and the response of the Secretary Herbert Thring, together with the willingness of Philip Morrell to question the Home Secretary in the Commons, decided him to stay for a little and 'fight for the book, if I can' (ii. 439). But by early December he had lost the 'spirit' to fight any more (ii. 462). The Questions in Parliament, on 18 November and 1 December, came to nothing because the Home Secretary was able to point out that, in law, only the publishers were involved, and they had pleaded guilty. The Society of Authors decided there was nothing they could do. Though there were private messages and offers of support, only one author, Arnold Bennett, spoke up belatedly in public to defend the novel (see below p. lxxiv). The plan for going to America also hung fire; but Lawrence was to do what seemed to him the next best thing, in the new year, and get as far away as possible in remote Cornwall, where, in a mood of hatred for a 'putrescent mankind' (ii. 602) and without thought of publication at first, he would take up the story of Ursula Brangwen again. It is impossible to exaggerate the effect on Lawrence himself, on his conception of his audience and therefore on the nature of his work, of the destruction of *The Rainbow* in the England of 1915.

Text

The manuscript and the typescript

The MS (November 1914–2 March 1915) of *The Rainbow* is in the possession of the Harry Ransom Humanities Research Center of the University of Texas at Austin.[55] It consists of fifteen chapters and 700 pages – nominally '707', both chapters and pages being subject to misnumbering. The final page concludes 'End of Volume I', and in different ink, 'Greatham. March 2nd 1915'. Apart from three sections of typescript, the MS is entirely in Lawrence's hand. Only at one point is there damage which might affect the reading: a tear at the foot of p. 284 (see Textual apparatus for 177:15, and Explanatory note).

MS pp. 1–7 are Lawrence's single-spaced and markedly amateur typing, the attempt which was abandoned by 5 December 1914. These seven pages replace fourteen of the original autograph manuscript, whose numbering then continues from '15'. (Since, in the close typing, a page contains a good deal more than the average two of the autograph, it is

---

[55] Roberts E331a. There is an overlapping page (548a).

possible that the prelude about the Brangwen Men and Women was added at this stage.)

MS pp. 549–604 and 608–13 are rather faint typescript, on thin 'legal'-size folio paper (343:23–390:9 and 391:38–396:4), and are all that has survived of the typescript of 'The Wedding Ring' which was prepared in duplicate, by Madge or Thomas Dunlop. They come from sections 3–5 of chapter 10 of 'The Wedding Ring', and 1–4 of chapter 11 ('Ella tries her wings', which began at what is now 387:12); and they run from Ella's first day at Brinsley Street School, to the first night in the new home in Beldover. These became chapters XII and XIII of MS, 'The Man's World' and 'The Widening Circle' – but dividing several pages earlier (see Explanatory note on 376:11). The section of autograph between the two sections of typescript has to do with the move to a new house, and probably came about because Lawrence decided to substitute a 'town' setting for a more rural outlook on the edge of the country towards Moorgreen (see Explanatory note on 390:25). At two places (MS pp. 583, 372:17 and 613, 396:2–3) the paper is frayed away or torn, but the damage probably occurred after the retyping into *The Rainbow*, since no gap appears in TS, and the readings are clear. The Dunlop typescript is revised both in pencil and in ink, and Frieda's writing occurs in many places, probably because she helped Lawrence transcribe revisions into the duplicate copy (see also Explanatory note on 365:26).

The TS (February 1915–31 May 1915) of *The Rainbow* is also in the possession of the Harry Ransom Humanities Research Center.[56] It consists of sixteen chapters, the penultimate chapter of MS having been divided into 'The Widening Circle' and 'The Bitterness of Ecstasy'; and 734 pages, with (once again) a great deal of misnumbering raising the apparent total to '747' (see also Explanatory notes on 243:1 and 309:25). The final page again concludes with an autograph note 'End of Volume I' dated from 'Greatham: April 1915' – though, as the letters show, Lawrence only received the last of the typing near the end of May and posted that to Pinker on the last day of the month. The TS was extensively revised by Lawrence with only one or perhaps two interventions by Frieda (see Explanatory note on 415:3). Significant new autograph sections were inserted into chapter VII 'The Cathedral' (TS pp. 310–14, 188:11–192:24), containing the re-conception of the Cathedral scene; and chapter VIII 'The Child' (TS pp. 345–55, 210:22–222:7), the episode in Nottingham – see above pp. xxvi, Textual apparatus and Explanatory notes.

[56] Roberts E331b.

A comparison of papers and typewriter faces suggests that the typescript was originally prepared on three different machines. (There is, however, in the typescript as we have it now, evidence of a fourth, added later, see below.)

TS pp. 1–159, 220–309 and 389–419 were prepared on the first machine, on 'Ryman's Linen Bank' paper.

TS pp. 160–219, 315–42 and 356–88 were prepared on the second machine, on 'Silver Linen' paper; and since pp. 310–14 and 343–55 are Lawrence's autograph insertions, the original batch probably ran from where it joined machine no. 1,[57] to p. 388.

TS pp. 420–508 and 559–747 were prepared on the third machine; pp. 420–99 and 595–747 on 'Silver Linen' paper of a slightly larger size, and pp. 500–8 and 559–94 on an unwatermarked paper. TS pp. 508–58 were probably also done on this machine originally, making the whole batch run from the start of chapter XI 'First Love' to the end.

The identification of the typists is, however, more problematic. Viola Meynell originally offered to do the work, but found it too much for her. Eleanor Farjeon had already begun to help before she met Lawrence in March.[58] 'It was a long manuscript, the close work strained [Viola's] eyes, and I offered to help her; and a portion of *The Rainbow* was typed on my Yost in Fellows Road. It included the stampede of horses which seemed to me epic, the work of a genius'.[59] This identifies typist and typewriter no. 3. It seems probable, then, that typewriter no. 1 belonged to Viola Meynell, who began the work but, finding it a strain, handed over the last part of MS to her friend, while she went on with the earlier part; but what remains puzzling is the subdivision of that earlier part. On the back of MS p. 495, corresponding to the last page of chapter XI 'First Love', there appears Viola Meynell's name and London address, followed by 'From Miss K. Lee, 120 Welldon Crescent, Harrow.' Perhaps, if Lawrence in his keenness to revise began to press for the typescript – he had 'only got' the first chapter by 19 March – Viola Meynell may have sought still further help from Miss Lee. But there is the difficulty that the note occurs within the continuous batch that was typed by Eleanor Farjeon; and the further

[57] Eight pages earlier in the original TS: the sub-numbering starts with '9' – hence 1–8 have gone, and been replaced by autograph. The typist of machine no. 2, in the increasing uncertainty about pagination, took to sub-numbering in the top left hand corner in order to keep track. What is now TS p. 315 (with its opening phrase deleted to make the join) is sub-numbered '9'. The division would still have come within the chapter.
[58] *Composite Biography*, ed. Nehls, i. 293, 305.
[59] Eleanor Farjeon, *Edward Thomas, The Last Four Years: Book One of the Memoirs of Eleanor Farjeon* (1958), p. 123.

difficulty that the batches done on machine no. 2 begin and end in the
middle of chapters, whereas one would expect a convenient division of
labour between two people to use the chapter divisions, as was the case
with Eleanor Farjeon's section. The most likely explanation of that would
be that both no. 1 and no. 2 were Viola Meynell, working with different
machines and supplies of paper, in London and at Greatham. If she had
already done the seventy-one pages of the first chapter before Eleanor
Farjeon's offer, this would mean a roughly equal division of the remaining
MS between the two friends. But Miss Lee then remains a puzzle.

Though the typing is not incompetent – both known typists were writers
themselves – it is also by no means professional, and interfered with the
original text quite extensively in both accidentals and substantives. Lawrence's punctuation, affecting his emphases and rhythms and showing
what he 'heard' in his head, is frequently altered. Standard English is
sometimes substituted for dialect, words are misread and on several
occasions phrases, sentences and short passages disappear. Moreover it
soon becomes clear, from the frequency with which TS errors remain
unseen and uncorrected, that as usual Lawrence, in revising, did not check
back with MS.

Pages 509–53 of TS, as we now have it, present a special problem. This
section begins just before Ursula's midnight bathe with Winifred Inger in
chapter XII, 'Shame', and ends with Ursula 'feeling she had been a fool in
her anticipations' as she is shown the large classroom of Brinsley Street
School in the next chapter. The paper is again 'Silver Linen', but size and
type-face differ from those used by the other typists. What is remarkable,
however, is that for page after page, until the last page of 'Shame', and
again later, the typescript follows the line-endings of Methuen's first
edition (E1), though in most of 'The Man's World' it ceases to do so.
When the section rejoins TS – by typing only 26 lines on p. 558 and
crossing out a passage at the top of p. 559 – it is clear that Eleanor Farjeon
had been in mid-flow in her typing of MS. The conclusion is inescapable
that pp. 509–58 in their present form were *not part of the original TS at all*,
but were done after E1 had been set up in type, and directly from it. The
reason however remains obscure. The most straightforward explanation
might be that a portion of the original TS was accidentally lost or damaged
after typesetting, so that a typist was set to work copying from E1 to make
good the loss, before a 'complete' typescript was returned to the author.
The following of line-endings may have been simply convenience – though
the possibility of faking at some later date cannot be excluded, since there
is a prima-facie resemblance to the work of typewriter no. 2.

It is also possible of course that the location of the section is no accident. 'Shame' was specifically denounced by the Bow Street Magistrate; was expurgated in several places for the first American edition (A1);[60] and was probably the chapter that Duckworth proposed to cut as a pre-condition for republishing the novel in 1920.[61] Despite what Methuen's representative said at the trial, the chapter very probably figured in the cuts that Pinker suggested at proof stage. The fact, then, that it was just *this* section of TS that went missing, might have been connected with some unsuccessful pressure for deletion (see also Explanatory note on 327:6). The 'pages' mentioned by Lawrence in his letter of 26 July (ii. 369) as accompanying the 'slips', might not have been duplicate page proofs but pages of TS, sent along with the galleys to help him to make substantial cuts; and this could have been how part of 'Shame' became detached from the rest of TS. Yet the hypothesis is not altogether convincing, since the passages considered most objectionable by the American publisher occurred *before* the midnight bathe, and the missing section is by no means confined to 'Shame'. It seems as likely to have been some kind of accident, since no other explanation will cover the loss of part of 'The Man's World' as well.

Pencilled indications of galley divisions, and of the names of the compositors A. Sayell and R. Turnham responsible for them, confirm that E1 was set from TS.

The proofs and the first edition

All proofs (July–mid-August 1915) of *The Rainbow*, with their exact identification of Lawrence's further revisions, and perhaps – since he kept the two separate (ii. 370) – of his excisions under pressure, have unfortunately disappeared. One set of revised proofs was sent on 9 September to George H. Doran,[62] who was arranging for publication in America (see below). There seems to have been another. After the court-case in November, Lawrence briefly hoped that the novel could be republished by the Parisian firm of Conard, through the influence particularly of Prince Antoine Bibesco (ii. 453, 458–9). At the end of the

---

[60] See Explanatory notes on 314:1, 10; 316:4; 326:25.

[61] *Letters*, iii. 490. DHL finally broke with Duckworth over this (*Letters*, iii. 491) and accepted Secker's offer instead, 'because you dont ask me to make alterations in the books' – an irony, since Secker was to use Huebsch's expurgated text for his edition, see below.

[62] See Pinker's annotation on DHL's letter to him of 25 January 1921 (Letter 2156 – the annotation not reproduced in *Letters*, iii. 651–2. See also note 68 below.) Doran acknowledged 'the printed sheets of THE RAINBOW' on 28 September 1915, NYPL.

lvi   *Introduction*

month he asked Koteliansky for the address of Zinaida Vengerova, and
begged him to ask her to 'let me have back the proofs of the novel, which I
sent her some time ago, so that Conard could print from them' (ii. 459).
Zinaida Athanasevna Vengerova was a translator, who rendered several
European writers into Russian, and Trotsky, later, into English. Unfortunately Lawrence's request came too late. On 4 December he wrote again
to Pinker (ii. 464) about the Conard scheme: 'I will let you have the
galley-proofs to print from – I wish I could lay hold of the revised proofs,
but I am afraid they have gone to Russia.'[63] It is not known whether
Zinaida Vengerova was merely visiting or returning to Russia. One set of
page proofs does seem to have been returned to Lawrence later. In
September 1929 he was very upset by the suspicion that manuscripts
might have disappeared from a cupboard at Frieda's ranch near Taos, New
Mexico. On 12 September he asked the Hon. Dorothy Brett to check
carefully, and to send anything she found to his agent Curtis Brown in
New York: 'When you do send the MSS. to New York, will you put in
among them also that little bundle of the page-proofs of *The Rainbow* tied
up with two old passports. That was with the MSS. in the cupboard.' By 19
September he had received from Curtis Brown's of London a list of
manuscripts in the keeping of the New York office, and had discovered
that several things were there that he had thought were at the ranch.[64]
There is no indication whether the page proofs were on that list, or
whether Brett found them at the ranch, or whether they had already
disappeared. There is the sad possibility that they might have been burnt,
along with a number of original Lawrence letters, on misunderstood
instructions from Curtis Brown of New York to their warehouse.[65]

The Methuen stock ledger which includes the entries for the first edition
(30 September 1915) of *The Rainbow* is now in the possession of the Lilly

---

[63] It seems from this letter that DHL had a complete set of galley proofs – not merely the
'slips' where self-censorship was requested – as well as the page proofs mentioned in his
letter to Pinker of 26 July 1915 (*Letters*, ii. 370). If so, these have also disappeared. Though
the Conard scheme came to nothing, hope of private publication revived in February 1916
when, through the enthusiasm of his new friend Philip Heseltine (the musician 'Peter
Warlock'), a circular for 'The Rainbow Books and Music' was printed (ii. 542). There was
some thought of acting 'in conjunction' with 'the French publisher' Paul Fernando (ii.
561, 571), who had written from Paris on 21 November 1915 to express the sympathy of 'A
large number of persons here'.
[64] Letters to Dorothy Brett, 19 and 29 September 1929.
[65] Letter from Perry H. Knowlton, President of Curtis Brown Ltd, to Warren Roberts, 11
August 1976: 'Unfortunately the old [i.e. original] D. H. Lawrence correspondence has
been lost. The storage house where we had stored all the correspondence of this

Library, University of Indiana, at Bloomington, Indiana. Sheets for 2,500 copies were ordered from the printers – Hazell, Watson and Viney – on 16 August 1915; and were received at Methuen, together with sixteen extra sets, in batches between 2 September and 5 November. Of these, 500 sets were specified as being for the Colonial edition, to be distributed abroad under a different royalty agreement. Binding orders for the English edition were placed in September (1,250 copies); and for the Colonial edition in October (300 in cloth and 200 in paper). A final binding order was placed on 1 November but subsequently cancelled, presumably after the visits of the police. 1,761 bound copies were received between 17 September and 15 November. (The extra 11 seem to have been travellers' copies.) Of the 1,250 intended for England, one was a file-copy, six went by contract to the author and 185 were confiscated by Inspector Draper on 3 and 5 November. He also confiscated 60 of the 500 Colonial copies, 245 in all. The final delivery of 766 sets of sheets was also confiscated by Inspector Draper and destroyed. It would seem, then, that 1,058 'English' copies and 439 'Colonial' copies – the last copy of the 500 only arrived on 11 November – had already been distributed for sale before the police arrived. However, during the next three months, Methuen themselves recalled and destroyed as many copies as they could: 64 in November, 10 in December, 22 in January and 88 in February,[66] of which 180 were 'English' and only 4 'Colonial', including presumably the latecomer. Eventually, therefore, a combined total of 1,195 copies and sets of sheets had been destroyed. (It is unclear whether these totals include the file-copy, the travellers' copies or the two imperfect copies which came back from the binders after 5 November.) So, up to 436 'Colonial' copies, and up to 896 'English' copies could have survived the combined operations of the police and the publishers. Lawrence was told in December that Hatchards, the bookshop, 'had sold their last copy of the *Rainbow*' (published at 6/–) 'for four guineas' (ii. 477).

The first American edition

Pinker's first agreement for the American publication of *The Rainbow* was drawn up with George H. Doran in March 1914, for 'the next three books

organisation from 1914 to 1952 misunderstood our instructions and destroyed our correspondence rather than carbon copies.'
66 Documents in the possession of Methuen & Co; see also John Worthen, 'The Reception in England of the Novels of D. H. Lawrence from *The White Peacock* to *Women in Love*', unpublished MA thesis, University of Kent at Canterbury, 1967, p. 147.

by D. H. Lawrence', i.e. after *Sons and Lovers*.[67] Doran wrote on 10 September 1915 enquiring when he might expect 'copy' of *The Rainbow*, but by 23 September he had 'heard in an indirect way that Mr. Mitchell Kennerley reviewed this book and declined to publish it'. He acknowledged receipt of 'the printed sheets' five days later, but cabled on 14 October: 'Cannot possibly publish Lawrence's Rainbow in form submitted. Am legally advised distribution would be forbidden'. The next day he explained by letter that he had had 'six separate readings of THE RAINBOW and they are all damning'. On 22 October he was having a careful study made 'of the possibility of making changes'. Lawrence commented on the 29th: 'It doesn't seem to me that it is any use altering the *Rainbow* for the Americans. Curse them, what good is it to them, altered or not. Don't you think it is best to leave it – not to publish in America at all?' (ii. 419). In fact Doran had already cabled on 27 October: 'Cannot acceptably revise rainbow Regret must positively decline'. But on the same day, having made a telephone call, he was able to cable again that another publisher would take the book over, though the 'precarious conditions' would preclude any advance on royalties. A letter on 12 November explained that the previous contract could stand, apart from that one provision, and he would remain responsible for the collection and payment of royalties.

The new publisher was Benjamin W. Huebsch, a liberal who was willing to take risks for radical authors – also publishing Joyce and Sherwood Anderson in America when nobody else would do so. Though Lawrence was at first suspicious – 'Is he somebody disreputable, or what? And why will he publish the novel if Doran wont?' (ii. 426) – he agreed on 6 November that Huebsch should go ahead, provided he was told what had just happened in London (ii. 429).

Annotation by Pinker to a letter from Lawrence dated 25 January 1921,[68] by which time Lawrence was seeking information to prove that Huebsch had broken the terms of the agreement, confirms that a set of corrected proofs was indeed sent to Doran on 9 September 1915, and '2

---

[67] Doran to Pinker, 16 March 1914, at NYPL, as are the letters from Doran referred to below.

[68] Annotation not reproduced in *Letters*, iii. 651–2; confirmed by Pinker to DHL, 1 February 1921 (attached to a Robert Mountsier letter of February 1921, Lilly Library). The two volumes were 'to obtain the interim copyright on the 30th September 1915'. This letter goes on to claim that 'Doran cabled that he could not publish "The Rainbow" in its original form and with your consent certain alterations were made'. This however accords ill with DHL's letter of 29 October 1915 quoted above (*Letters*, ii. 419), by which time Doran had already cabled that he had given up the idea of altering the book and was no longer prepared to publish. DHL was in no doubt that Huebsch never had his permission to expurgate (see *Letters*, iii. 652, to which Pinker is replying and footnote 33 above).

vols' on the 20th, three days after Methuen received the first bound copies. It was from these that Huebsch set up his type. Without any reference to Lawrence, however, he expurgated the text in thirteen places,[69] of which Lawrence only noticed five when he received a copy in December (ii. 480). There is just a possibility that Huebsch may have considered some sort of 'interpolation',[70] presumably to cover a much bigger cut, in 'Shame' perhaps, though he decided against it, and in 1955 admitted to being 'terribly sorry that I made any change'.[71]

The fullest account of the peculiar method by which (in his anxiety to prevent proceedings against the book in America) he actually published, occurs in a letter to the author Richard Aldington on 1 June 1950:[72]

I have before me the Certificate of Copyright Registration which states the date of publication as November 30, 1915, although the title page, as I stated in the Certificate, bears the date 1916. The explanation, which I think is not recorded elsewhere than in this letter, is that while the book was in process of manufacture I accepted an invitation to accompany the Ford Peace Expedition which set out on December 5 or 6, 1915. Just prior to receiving the invitation I learned of the Bow Street proceedings which resulted in the order to Methuens to withdraw the book and destroy their stock. Knowing that our smuthounds[73] would be ready to pounce on the American 'Rainbow,' and because my shop and staff were very small and included none who could face the expected proceedings, I took steps to secure the copyright and gave instructions to do no more than make such sale as to give validity to the copyright and to lock up the stock until my return, which I expected would be during January but which for reasons that I will not bore you with did not happen until March 1916. It was because of that plan that I dated the title page 1916.

Having told you so much I may as well tell you of the further procedure. Surmising that the then current Comstock was lying in wait I told my travellers (the

---

[69] See footnote 34 above.
[70] See Interviews with Huebsch conducted by Dr Louis Starr for the Oral Research Office of Columbia University in December 1954 and Spring 1955, p. 320. Referring to a suggestion in a letter by John Reed (author of *Ten Days that Shook the World*), that Huebsch had consulted him not only about excision but also some kind of interpolation, Huebsch replied: 'I don't remember any insertion such as Reed refers to – I mean, an actual rewriting. As a matter of fact, either he misunderstood something or my editor may have put in something that occurred to me in the form of a proposed interpolation, or something like that. I don't believe – I know it's impossible that I should have done something like that.' Reed's letter of disapproval was apparently dated 30 November, and it seems that Huebsch may also have consulted Carl Hovey, editor of *Metropolitan*.
[71] Huebsch, Columbia University Interviews, p. 312.   [72] Located at LC.
[73] Presumably the New York Society for the Suppression of Vice, which was to try to get *Women in Love* banned; and John Sumner, who had succeeded the late Anthony Comstock as Postal Censor.

plural makes it sound important but there surely were two!)[74] to let the book dribble out to the trade with a caution against talking too much about it, and thus the edition (I do not remember the quantity) was eventually sold out without, I think, any advertising or copies for review. Perhaps there were some reviews at that stage but if so the editors must have asked for copies; I know that I did not offer any because that would have balked my plan. The book having gone out of stock there were demands for more, of course, but I was still timid and decided to take refuge in the old trick of a limited edition, a little larger in dimensions and a little more expensively produced than the first. I have a copy dated 1920, but as I several times reprinted this 'limited' edition (at $5, which was pretty high for a novel in those days) I am not sure of the date of the first limited edition. In justice to myself let me add that I did not try to deceive anybody by the term 'limited' edition, but made it clear through the travellers that I was feeling my way, printing a lot at a time during a ticklish period. I wanted to fulfill my obligation to Lawrence by keeping the book available but I was in no position then, working almost single-handed, to defend a suit which, following on the London suppression, might have had serious consequences for me.

Much briefer and less informative explanations were given by Huebsch to Lawrence on 16 June 1916 (the letter implies that no distribution at all had yet been made), and 22 April 1919 (stating that the first printing had finally been distributed 'a few months ago').[75] It is possible that Lawrence did not know for certain until April 1919 that the book was actually current in America. The 'limited' edition was reprinted in 1921, 1922 and 1923 before a new agreement came into force with Thomas Seltzer, who had become Lawrence's American publisher, and wanted to stop the 1923 printing.[76]

The Huebsch text follows the Methuen text closely, apart from the expurgations. Some errors are corrected (sometimes mistakenly, like 'timorously' for 'temerously', 298:27, and 'beasts' for the dialect collective plural 'beast', 74:39, 76:6); and missing punctuation is supplied, particularly question marks (though Lawrence often omitted these when a sentence was mostly exclamatory). Edward D. McDonald states in his *Bibliography* that in the more expensive edition 'the text remained the same as that of the first American edition'.[77]

[74] Cf. Huebsch, Columbia University Interviews, p. 257, however: 'I just let that book trickle out. This salesman I had would go to the trade and say "Here's a book. We're not advertising it. We're not sending it out for review. It's Lawrence, though."'
[75] Huebsch letters at LC. See also *Letters*, ii. 561 n. 5, summarising letters of Doran to Pinker which suggests that distribution had not begun by 14 July 1916. Huebsch to DHL, 22 November 1921, says he had 'subscriptions for about 1000 copies' of the 'limited' edition (Charles Smith collection).
[76] Implied in DHL to Thomas Seltzer, 14 March 1923, *Letters*, iv. 409.
[77] *A Bibliography of the Writings of D. H. Lawrence* (Philadelphia, 1925), p. 39.

Subsequent editions

Seltzer published his American edition in 1924, from the Huebsch text.[78] All later editions in England and America duplicate this (with its expurgations), except for two Penguin editions: one in 1949, which reverted to E1 but also attempted to 'correct' it without reference to MS or TS, and a direct reprint of E1 in 1981.

In England, negotiations in 1920 with Duckworth broke down over the proposal to cut a chapter, almost certainly 'Shame', but Martin Secker agreed, through long negotiation, to republish *The Rainbow*, after he had published *The Lost Girl* and *Women in Love* (iii. 499).[79] By 1924 he had still not done so, and on 25 April added casually at the end of a letter 'You will not forget some time to let me have a copy of "The Rainbow", with some slight alterations to justify me in putting "new and revised edition" on the titlepage?'[80] Lawrence did no such thing;[81] but the description nevertheless appeared when Secker did finally publish, justified presumably by his having imported sheets from Seltzer containing Huebsch's expurgations. On 9 October 1925[82] he accepted Seltzer's quotation and ordered 250 copies ('folded collated and sewn', so only requiring a new title page and binding), and published what was in fact not a new edition at all, in February 1926.[83] He admitted as much to an enquirer, though disingenuously, on 9 March.[84] He seems to have followed the same sort of strategy as Huebsch. No copies were deposited in the copyright libraries – he presumably either thought it unnecessary to register a new copyright, even though he was claiming a 'revised' text; or agreed with Methuen's opinion in 1915, that after the Court had held the book 'to be indecent and obscene

---

[78] Seltzer probably bought the plates; the bill for their original manufacture by Vail Ballou Co. of Binghamton, New York, at $458.25 is mentioned in a letter of 18 April 1923, from Huebsch's lawyer Dudley F. Sichel to B. H. Stern (LC), who was acting for Seltzer and DHL.

[79] See *Women in Love*, ed. David Farmer, Lindeth Vasey and John Worthen (Cambridge, 1987), pp. xli–xliii.

[80] Secker Letter-Book, UIll.

[81] He did however once suggest in a postscript to Seltzer (whether seriously or not) 'Bring me that brown copy of *The Rainbow* if it's handy, and I'll expurgate it' (*Letters*, iv. 355) – but no such copy has come to light; Seltzer printed from Huebsch's text.

[82] Secker Letter-Book, UIll, the source also of the letters referred to below.

[83] The date is given in a letter from Secker to the *TLS*, 3 November 1966.

[84] Secker Letter-Book, UIll: 'The answer to your enquiry...is that this is the authorised American text of the book, which has circulated freely in the United States for ten years since publication. It does not purport to be a collector's item, but to give the text of the book as revised by the author for those who wish to complete their sets of his novels for ordinary reading purposes.'

... no copyright can exist'.[85] He also seems neither to have advertised nor to have sent out any copies for review; but presumably trickled out small numbers through travellers, quietly. (That there was reason to be cautious is shown by the fact that the Home Office did consider taking action in 1930,[86] though they decided against it.) Secker also protected himself financially by making Lawrence agree to be responsible for the costs of any litigation (iii. 517). He asked on 17 May 1926 whether a further order could be supplied in flat sheets, but no reply came from Seltzer, and on 20 July he ordered another 150 sets in the same format as the first. He also enquired about buying the electrotype plates, but on 28 April 1927 wrote to Lowe and Brydone for an estimate of the cost of photographic reproduction for a thin-paper edition. On 6 September 1928 he was accepting orders for the pocket-edition 'now manufacturing', and it was reprinted in 1929. By 31 July 1929 he belatedly bethought himself about royalties (on 'the small number of copies of "The Rainbow" which we imported with a view to trying out the situation') which he had overlooked 'partly from a feeling that the whole thing was *sub rosa*'. He states that 'sales between February 1926 and the current date amount to 314 copies' – but it is not clear whether that was the figure for the imported copies alone, though it probably was.

Later editions in America in the lifetime of Lawrence, still from the Huebsch text, came from the Modern Library in 1927, and A. and C. Boni in 1930. There were no more English editions in Lawrence's lifetime; the first Heinemann text appearing in 1934 and the first Penguin edition in 1949. A piracy, again of the Huebsch text, was printed in Shanghai.

The Cambridge edition

It will be obvious from the above account that no edition other than E1 has any authority, as Lawrence himself confirmed in his 'Introduction' to

[85] 9 December 1915, NYPL. This letter goes on to claim that: 'As a fact Mr Lawrence did not deliver us a copyright work at all, and there has been a complete failure of the consideration for which we paid our money. Mr Lawrence should now repay this sum' – i.e. £300.

[86] Public Record Office, HO 45/13944, Minute of March 1930 by Sir Sidney Harris calling the attention of the police to an advertisement of *The Rainbow* by Secker in the *TLS* of 6 March 1930; with reply suggesting that a few passages would still be adjudged obscene, but advising against prosecution; and Sir Sidney's concurrence, in order not to give the work further publicity. 'If only all critics would write as boldly and clearly as the author of a paragraph in the obituary in the *Telegraph* of 4 March.' (This was headed 'A Mind Diseased' and lamented 'alas! the kink in the brain developed early, and he came to write with one hand always in the slime'.)

McDonald's *Bibliography* in 1925: 'The only copy of any of my books I ever keep is my copy of Methuen's *Rainbow*. Because the American editions have all been mutilated' – like all the succeeding English ones in his lifetime, which reproduced Huebsch's text. The editorial problem is therefore confined to the transmission of the text from the last state of MS to E1, through TS and its extensive revisions (TSR), and the missing proofs whose changes (together with typesetting errors) are visible in the differences between E1 and TSR.

Lawrence's own special feeling was for 'those blue, condemned volumes';[87] but to reprint E1 is to reproduce all the mistranscriptions of the non-professional typists (including the ruining of Lawrence's punctuation which shows how he 'heard' his own voice, and wanted his prose read), as well as the errors of the compositors. It could be argued that Lawrence 'accepted' TS with all that his typists had done, where he did not change it. Yet it is clear that he not only failed to refer back to MS when revising, but did so because he read TS with a creator's and not a corrector's eye. That Lawrence was not a proof reader (making the fatal error of being interested in what was said and how) is neither an indication that he was careless about style and punctuation, nor any justification for preferring others' English to his.

Yet MS is not acceptable, as Lawrence again explicitly recognised. On 6 June 1915 he told Pinker: 'I haven't another copy of the novel, because this I sent you is so much altered from the original MS., that the latter is no good' (ii. 354). A reprint of MS would be a novel free from interference (including his own self-censorship) and containing nothing but what Lawrence himself had written, but it would not be the novel to which he gave his imprimatur. And TSR shares of course the disadvantages of both E1 and MS, and would require extensive emendation in both directions, to recapture both Lawrence's punctuation, and his proof revisions (provided the editor could be sure of distinguishing these from minor changes by the compositor, and from Lawrence's self-censorship – which is far less simple than it might seem).

What seems most important is to remain true to the nature of *The Rainbow*, as the work of a continuously revising and re-creating author; whose theory of creativity (which he began to formulate in his 'Hardy') was essentially a theory of process, of continuous and organic change, and whose individual works kept evolving out of themselves, continually refusing to be 'finished'. Even in proof Lawrence was still writing this

[87] 'Introduction' to McDonald's *Bibliography*, pp. 38–9 (reprinted in *Phoenix*, ed. McDonald, p. 234).

novel, not correcting it; and there are vital ways in which a work of Lawrence's *is* its process of becoming, which an edition should try to preserve in some fashion, however necessary it may be to choose between variants in order to produce a readable text.

This edition begins from MS and in all 'accidentals' authority resides there, except where alterations can be shown, or seem with strong probability, to be authorial; but in dubious cases the benefit of the doubt will go to MS. A few kinds of exception and standardisation are specified in the 'Note on the text'. Among these is a standardisation of paragraphing. In passages of mixed dialogue and narrative Lawrence at this time, after a speech, often began his narrative again flush with the margin, or indented less than his clear paragraph indentation. His typists and E1, however, followed the usual publishing convention by regularly using the same indentation as for a new paragraph. Since Lawrence's practice is not consistent over his career as a whole, the Cambridge edition also follows this convention. The Textual apparatus of this volume, however, differentiates between those places where the editor is confident that a genuinely new paragraph in MS was intended (noted as 'P') and others (marked with / line at the previous line ending). In substantives, MS is emended progressively through TSR to E1, but in cases where alterations in TSR have come about through typing errors, and it is unlikely that Lawrence would have made any change if he had been presented with what he had written, the MS reading is restored. (Where the change is the result of typing error, but also represents a change of imagination that might have come about in any case, TSR is preferred.) Obvious mistranscription in typesetting is of course corrected, but where (in the absence of the proofs) there is doubt whether E1 variation from TSR is owing to the author or the compositor, the E1 reading is accepted. The aim might be summarised thus: to present Lawrence, revising TS, with the accurate transcription he never received, and to follow his process of revision progressively to the end. Although this edition presents (therefore) a state of the text never seen by its author, it is closer to what he actually wrote than any other has been. The extensive Textual apparatus shows the progressive variation of the text from MS to E1.

Lawrence's self-censorship at proof stage represents a special problem. On the one hand he himself had specifically asked for advice on what might be considered objectionable, even from his typist; and had clearly agreed to make changes he regarded as relatively minor, though he refused others he considered more significant (ii. 369–70). On the other hand it is arguable that he would not have made any, had it not been for pressure from outside and the financial necessity to get the book published. If one could be certain which the changes were, there would be a case for removing them, on a similar basis to the changes which came about because of 'interference' by the typists. However, on that basis, it is necessary to balance the likelihood of objection by Methuen against other considerations that might have prompted Lawrence either to make a change himself or, having been asked to look at a passage again, to re-see and alter on other grounds than merely to meet the objection. Thus the Cambridge edition treats the different kinds of 'interference' in the same way; and where arguments are equally poised, follows the same procedure as for cases left doubtful by the loss of the proofs, giving the benefit of the doubt to E1.

Not all the cases concern the sexually 'improper'. E1 distinguishes more carefully between the Christian God and other gods or false ideas of god; capitalises pronouns more consistently where the former or Christ are meant, and also 'Bible'; and finds different forms for another two casually expletive uses of the deity. Some of this might be house-styling, or under pressure, but changes of all these kinds had begun in MS or TSR, and there is one example (see 266:7 and Explanatory note) where E1 is almost certainly Lawrence and not a house-styling typesetter. Since the pattern seems consistent with what Lawrence himself had started, and with 'a passionately religious man' seeking new prose for 'God', these changes have been retained.

Two cases involve relations between sex and religion. On the penultimate page of the novel, the MS suggestion that Ursula's future man would come 'from the loins of God' had already become in TSR 'from the Being of God', and now becomes 'out of Eternity' (457:36). Too direct a 'sonship', even in TSR, might have struck an outsider as offensive; but Lawrence's own sensitivity was already at work in TSR, and the change is almost certainly his. This may, moreover, help with the second instance, which concerns Anna's nude dancing to the Lord. Lawrence told Secker in 1920 – though on what evidence is unknown since there is none in the newspaper reports – that 'The scene to which exception was *particularly* taken was the one where Anna dances naked, when she is with child' (iii. 459). So this may well have figured in the requests for changes in proof, and E1 has certainly altered TSR in several places. Lawrence cut a first reference to David, whom Anna had 'always loved' and been 'haunted' by, in his naked dance before the Ark (see Textual apparatus for 169:34ff.). He also altered her 'lifting her hands and her body to the Lord, to the unseen Lover whose name was unutterable', to 'lifting. . .to the Unseen, to

the unseen Creator. . .to Whom she belonged'. These might well be
changes for which he had been pressed, on the grounds that the first was
improper and the second, in context, blasphemous. But the changes are
also explicable in quite different terms. Lawrence might well himself have
wanted Anna's impulse to spring, not from a youthful 'crush' or an erotic
memory of David dancing naked, but from her own inner urgency to reach
out to the Unknown and the Unseen Creator – precisely the emphasis he
then underlined at several points. The 'religious' dimension of the scene is
certainly strengthened at the expense of the erotic; but was there pressure?
And even if there was, were the changes solely owing to it, or might they
represent a significant change of imagination? There is at least much room
for argument; and since the benefit of any doubt would go to E1, the
changes are retained.

Conversely, the four occasions when Lawrence deleted 'belly' were
almost certainly urged upon him. Lady Cynthia Asquith disliked the word
even in the instances he left: 'Excellent bits of writing', her diary records of
The Rainbow, 'but still too much over-emphasis and brutality. One cannot
count how often and how gratuitously he employs the word "belly".'[88] To
an aristocratic lady it clearly sounded 'brutal', and there may be an element
of class-usage in differing connotations. For Lawrence's usage is straight-
forwardly anatomical on three of these occasions (175:4, 296:22, 316:8)
albeit in the context of nudity, and metaphorical, for a seat of bitterness, on
the fourth (335:3), the excision of which tends to confirm that the word
had been found objectionable in itself. It seems unlikely that Lawrence
would have had any reason of his own for cutting it – so the word is
restored.

There are two cases of possible self-censorship in the first generation
story. One concerns the episode with the girl at Matlock, in which
Lawrence made two quite substantial changes (see Textual apparatus for
24:18, 25). He substitutes 'he. . .was mad with desire for the girl' for
'he. . .was madly in love. . .By gad she was a tanger. . .and it *was* a
success'. He then deletes the assertions that what had happened was
because of his 'special quality of manliness' and was 'the right sort of
thing'; that Tom wanted the girl to stay with him; but that 'she wanted her
hard brutal freedom. . .her price only'. It is possible to imagine objections
here, yet these changes might have come about for quite other reasons.
The revisions from MS to TSR show that Lawrence was himself uncertain
about how he wanted to handle the episode. Moreover the first change in

[88] Lady Cynthia Asquith, *Diaries 1915–1918* (1968), p. 86. See also Kuttner's complaint,
Appendix III below.

proof hardly at all affects the explicitness of what had happened, or Tom's sexual exultation. What both changes do, however, is avoid the whole question of 'love', about which TSR is self-contradictory anyway; of any continuing relationship; and of the morality of the affair and the girl. None of these is wanted if the emphasis is to fall on a single exciting and liberating adventure, which appears to be what Lawrence finally decided. There seems at least a balance of doubt, which then goes in favour of E1. The second case occurs in the betrothal scene of Tom and Lydia (see Textual apparatus for 46:34), and is probably the most likely of all of these to have been a demand for change. A publisher's reader might well have objected to so clear an implication of erection (by contrast, say, with Henry James at the end of *Portrait of a Lady*), even though Lawrence's language has its own delicacy. Nevertheless there are other reasons, again, for Lawrence to have made the change. The new beginning of the paragraph, 'But it was too soon', might represent his own second thoughts about introducing explicit sexuality at this stage, as well as being a comment on why Lydia got up. It would then be understandable that he should emphasise, instead, the effect on Tom of the contradiction which the paragraph had already implicitly explored, between the woman lying so close upon him, and the efficient housewife ignoring him – which looks forward to Will reacting against Anna's tea-party. A change of imaginative focussing, and not merely a bowdlerisation, has occurred. Even if Mrs Grundy had put pressure upon him, which seems likely, Lawrence has shifted the emphasis from the physical to the psychological, where he might have chosen simply to cut.

Predictably, there are cases in the Nottingham episode and its aftermath. Two are concerned with the girl, 'almost swooning in the absolute of sensual knowledge'. TSR, in this case the original writing, went on (see Textual apparatus for 214:18):

Only as if mechanically she kept her knees closely shut together. And however absolutely she gave herself to his touch and discovery, she kept her knees tight shut, as if this were the reflex movement. In utter sensual delight she clenched her knees, her thighs, her loins together.

In proof, Lawrence cut all but the last sentence. Three pages earlier he had altered 'There would be pretty places in her body, that he wanted to discover. . .to know and enjoy. . .to have his fill of them' (see Textual apparatus for 211:16) to 'Her childishness whetted him keenly. She would be helpless between his hands.' Again Methuen's reader might have thought these passages too explicitly suggestive; but if so, the 'eroticism' is hardly diminished, only (again) changed in emphasis. In the earlier passage the change points to a different kind of sexuality than thoughts of places in the body; the kind that depends on a sense of power and makes some men 'whetted' by rather childish girls. In the later one, the suggestiveness is still completely there, carried by the last sentence (with a new, and mistaken, exclamation mark in E1); but the effect now, as well as economy, is to make the girl's physical movement betray excitement rather than self-preservation. These are very unconvincing as changes meant to make the fiction less 'improper', and seem likely to be Lawrence's own – revising the episode for the first time.

A much more likely case to have figured on Methuen's list is Will's new fierce sensuality with Anna where he wishes for:

a hundred men's energies, with which to enjoy her. He wished he were a cat, to lick her with a rough, grating, lascivious tongue: a tiger-cat, to lick till the blood came, so he could lap it up till it ran from the corners of his mouth: so he could tear her flesh with his mouth.

E1 cuts from 'tongue' (see Textual apparatus for 219:24); but even what was left was too much for Huebsch, who cut again from 'enjoy her'. The difficulty here is that the excessiveness of the passage is unquestionably part of its meaning, as can be confirmed from the following sentence, unchanged in all versions, and showing Lawrence perfectly well aware of Will's 'mania'. The passage is clearly related to the sermon Lawrence had cut at the point when Ursula looks through her microscope (see Textual apparatus for 408:40): 'Must I destroy myself, since I am tiger and ape?. . .Is there not room for all. . .I am all these shameful things, each in its hour. . .But none of these contradict that I am I. . .pushing on into the unknown.' But if Lawrence cut that because it was too heavy an underlining, might he not equally have cut this, for the same reason, and not wanting the emphasis on the 'shameful' and predatory to outweigh the sense of the 'undiscovered' in the same paragraph? This seems the case most open to argument; but the presence of an exactly analogous cut that is manifestly not the result of outside interference probably tips the balance. In the last sentence of the chapter, E1 cuts a final sentence which spells out the 'potent secret' which unconsciously 'darkened the mind' of little Ursula: 'It was the secret of the passion between her father and her mother. But all her limbs vibrated to it.' It seems quite likely, here again, that Lawrence himself might have thought the underlining of the *physical* effect on the child was excessive and unrealistic, in what was his first opportunity to revise this whole episode.

Finally, a cut in the Ursula story seems both certain to have been the result of outside pressure, and something that Lawrence himself had no reason to do. At 421:36, as Skrebensky comes out of the bathroom, MS originally read 'It was always a passionate adventure to go near to her. She put her arms round him, round his loins, and snuffed his warm, softened skin.' E1 changes 'passionate' to 'perfect' and cuts 'round his loins' – which seem simple bowdlerisation, and should therefore be restored.

Since these, though not all the possible candidates for Pinker's list,[89] are the likeliest, what seems most significant is that – if they were the result of outside interference – Lawrence nearly always did more than bowdlerise. This in turn makes it difficult to be certain that the new shift in emphasis should be undone, simply because he agreed to make a change. At least, readers who consider that this edition errs too far on the side of caution can now judge for themselves by consulting the Textual apparatus, and make their own restorations.

Reception

The first review of *The Rainbow* appeared in the *Standard* on 1 October 1915,[90] the day after publication, unsigned. Given all that was to happen, its understanding and open-mindedness seem quite remarkable, now. The reviewer found the book flawlessly constructed, and despite the multiplication of characters, thought that 'each has a sharply defined personality, though a certain family resemblance is preserved by them all'. Moreover, Lawrence 'seems to have excluded himself entirely from his new book'. Undeterred by a realism 'to the point of brutality' (though unlike Zola's), the review picks up both the great background and the sense of history, and also the paradox of their relation:

Assuredly *The Rainbow* is not a novel to please all. There are no draperies in it, no asterisks, no reticences, no prettiness. It reveals the latent savage in its characters, though none of the Brangwens is wholly primitive. They are strong as they rise from the soil on which for generations they have been settled, but there are influences of unrest which twist their passions this way and that. Education, the spread of a colliery town, the marriage of one of them with a Polish woman, religion, yet more education, have their necessary effect on the old stock. Something comes into them which may be called degeneracy, but is more likely a

---

[89] Some seventy-five pages were checked using the Hinmann collator on the nine copies at UT plus the editor's copy to test for possible variations; these pages included the most sensitive sections where Methuen would have been most likely to make alterations and all the pages on which printing oddities had been noted. Nothing significant was found.
[90] P. 3 (Draper 89–90).

painful and tortuous development. It is not a comfortable book. Its very foundation is an agonizing struggle between bodies and minds.

The review also notes, in the stable scene, how Lawrence can make human beings seem 'of secondary importance' against what is beyond the human. Although the language is 'not faultless', the author is 'an artist' who only needs to restrain 'too emotional descriptions'. The book may 'cause offence and be condemned, for it takes more liberties than English novelists for many years past have claimed, but, whatever its reception, it is an important piece of work'.

Then execrations mounted; but the vehemence itself – already noted in the reviews by Lynd, Douglas and Shorter – is perhaps less interesting than its causes. It is not easy now to imagine the climate of the time. Augustine Birrell, man of letters as well as politician, said on 13 November 1915 that 'He, for one, would forbid the use during the war of poetry'; and the *Observer* the same day thought that 'the war had turned the thoughts of novelists and their readers to sterner subjects. . .the war has practically killed the "problem novel" and with it the neurotic heroine'. This was no time for problematic and innovatory fiction, let alone a novel which betrayed tell-tale signs of less than whole-hearted support of soldiering for the nation. Yet if *The Rainbow* could be read for its first review so level-headedly, by a mind free from preconceptions, war-fever alone will not explain what happened. What else was responsible for the hysteria in the other responses?

In the case of Robert Lynd in the *Daily News*, the real complaint is that the characters are 'as lacking in the inhibitions of ordinary civilised life as savages. There are truthful, physiologically truthful, things in the book, but the book itself is not true. . .'; and it is this which makes him find it lacking in all the 'marks of good literature' including faith, hope, charity, honour and humour. It is basically a horror at the novel's psychological revelations, of what lies below 'the old stable ego', that makes it seem reductively 'physiological' and un-Christian. In the case of Douglas in the *Star*, behind the rodomontade, Lynd's refusal to accept that the insights could be more than bodily true has become a horrified and total rejection of them as pathological, decadent and polluting. Both he and Lynd have a picture of the human 'soul' in conflict with 'lower' nature, which is outraged by the novel – but where Lynd sees reduction, Douglas sees 'abominations' and 'putrescence', all the more dangerous because England is at war and 'public health' is vital. Lynd thought the book untrue, Douglas thinks it profoundly immoral, 'saying things that ought to be left unthought, let alone unsaid'. And Shorter in the *Sphere*, for all his pose of liberalism – 'I am not an opponent of frankness and freedom in literature' – and his recognition that 'Mr. Lawrence has written quite a good novel apart from the copious passages marked by what I can only call disease', is with Douglas. There are subjects that are obviously forms of 'viciousness' (such as lesbianism), but indeed 'the whole book is an orgie of sexiness' and it is the sexual detail itself that is 'crude' and an 'inartistic intrusion of matter' – the language is significant – 'which has no place in the development of a story and adds nothing to the subtle depicting of human beings'. Helena Maria Swanwick in the *Manchester Guardian*,[91] while she found more to like than the others, also managed to combine both approaches. Like Lynd, she sees primarily a reductiveness: there are 'innumerable fine things, and the style has individuality and poignancy' but in all the characters 'the passion of sex is so manifest as to eclipse all other passion or thought' and however 'described, embroidered, glorified, with enormous zest and skill. . .the end is tedium. . .a passion so narrowed and exaggerated would grow tiresome in one individual; when it runs through three generations. . .we cry for relief from such madness and long to turn to a world infinitely varied and bracingly sane'. The argument has become Douglas's. Some 'emotions and processes' are 'vividly and imaginatively and beautifully described', but 'Others. . .are morbid or downright insane. . .and what is disquieting about these is the suggestion that in all the various manias described (erotic, ecclesiastical, alcoholic) there is an approach to truth and insight denied to those who remain sane'; whereas these 'illusions and revelations are matter for pathological study'. She cites, as examples of the insane, 'Anna dancing to God or Ursula in her vampire mood'.

This family of reviewers are all certain that the boredom they experienced came not at all through their own psychic withdrawal, from a picture of the human being they found unbearable, but from Lawrence's manic repetition: 'a monotonous wilderness' (Lynd), 'intolerably wearisome' (Douglas), 'the horrid *ennui* caused by fixed ideas in delirium' (Swanwick). Unlike the first reviewer, they were unable to detect any element of comparison, contrast, discrimination or development. The unsigned review in the *Westminster Gazette*[92] neatly summarises the composite view:

the reader, dazed and stunned. . .wanders on into repetition after repetition, dimly conscious that this unique upheaval is taking place in Lydia or Tom or Anna or Ursula, or in an anonymous girl from Nottingham. . .The consequence is that 'The Rainbow' is a continued and violent departure from truth. . .It is not a book about marriage; it is an analytical semi-psychologic investigation of sensuality, and

[91] 28 October 1915, p. 5 (Draper 98–9).   [92] Vol. xlvi no. 6969 (October 1915), 3.

in spite of its undeniable force and of the occasional glimpses of beauty. . .it is almost impossible to read it because of the sheer weight of its numbing monotony.

Gerald Gould in the *New Statesman*[93] produces one nicely witty crack: 'I believe it has been accused of impropriety, but to me the most improper thing about it is the punctuation.' But soon there is familiar ground: the world the novel presents 'seems to consist almost entirely of fleshly people in paroxysms of emotion – largely sexual – which signify nothing. The nervous reactions are so feverish and so frequent that one ceases to take the slightest interest in them.'

Only one review, after the first, made any attempt to analyse theme and development – and that one cost Catherine Carswell her job on the *Glasgow Herald*.[94] Lawrence had befriended her, taking trouble over reading her first novel in the Summer of 1914, but the review is by no means uncritical. She begins with high praise for the book's 'emotional beauty' and 'distilled essence of profoundly passionate and individual thinking about human life'. She claims that Anna's childhood, Tom's wooing, Will Brangwen's home-life and Ursula's 'bitter baptism' as a teacher, 'must take rank with the best work done by great novelists in any age'. But Lawrence was after more than 'mere good fiction': the novel 'tells that love in our modern life, instead of being a blessed, joyous, and fruitful thing, is sterile, cruel, poisonous, and accursed'. She tries to compare the generations: finding the first marriage one 'of real passion and tenderness' (though it needed a 'beautiful spiritual movement, of sheer kindness and direct good sense' from Lydia to make it succeed); but the second marriage exposes in 'revolting detail' a bitter 'core, where the modern poison is at its disintegrating work', and in the modern 'so-called lovers' there is (familiar charge, but now made Lawrence's) 'merely an intense sexual excitement, without kindness or tenderness, without love or reverence. . .a barren, hateful thing', exposing a world 'mad and sick and sad because it knows not how to love'. It now becomes clear that although she 'longs to lavish. . .whole-hearted praise', the 'merciless, almost gloating description of the disease' is likely to be 'strongly offensive to most readers'. Moreover she likes the new style no more than Garnett had done, objecting to 'the increasingly mannered idiom' since *Sons and Lovers*, the repetition of certain words and 'a curiously vicious rhythm. . .in the more emotional passages'. Even where there was a disposition favourable to Lawrence, then, only a limited sense of the novel's exploration could come across,

[93] Vol. vi no. 133 (23 October 1915), 66–7.
[94] 4 November 1915, p. 4 (Draper 100–1).

because of the barrier of the new way of writing, which he himself had developed with such difficulty in order to subvert conventional picturings of 'the old stable ego', and to prevent people judging conventionally, according to a fixed moral scheme.

Though *The Athenæum* (on the day of the trial) found 'a strong and vivid imagination', liked the descriptions of nature and saw some psychological insight and power (if not always convincing), it also considered much of the novel 'undeniably unhealthy'. After the trial the most that liberal opinion could do was to object to the arbitrary power of the Magistrate and the police, while heartily concurring that the novel was in fact repellent.[95] More nails were hammered into its coffin by linking it with things German. G. W. de Tunzelmann, in a letter to the *Athenæum*[96] accuses Lawrence of having become 'so enamoured of his hypothesis' about sexuality 'that he has allowed himself to treat its most repulsive consequences with what evidently the court considered loving appreciation' – but 'This is but one of the many futile attempts to reconcile the facts of existence with the materialistic pseudophilosophy which has proved such a powerful instrument for the debasement of the German nation', and a source of weakness in 'our action against Germany'. And though J. C. Squire, writing as 'Solomon Eagle' in the *New Statesman*,[97] demolished some of the cant talked by Shorter and Douglas, and in Court, his own judgement would do more harm.

It is a dull and monotonous book which broods gloomily over the physical reactions of sex in a way so persistent that one wonders whether the author is under the spell of German psychologists, and so tedious that a perusal of it might send Casanova himself into a monastery, if he did not go to sleep before his revulsion against sex was complete.

He thought it a bad novel with unpalatable opinions and unhealthy tendencies. Only, this was no reason for dragging the name of an earnest young writer in the mud.

Though Lawrence received some private messages of support,[98] and

[95] *Athenæum*, no. 4594 (13 November 1915), 346; cf. *New Witness*, 18 November; *Nation*, 20 November; *Truth*, 24 November; *New Age*, 2 December.

[96] *Athenæum*, no. 4595 (20 November 1915), 369.

[97] Vol. vi (20 November 1915), 161 (Draper 104–7).

[98] See *Letters*, ii. 435 (the hope of a 'letter. . .to the papers' to be signed by Walter de la Mare, E. M. Forster, John Middleton Murry, J. D. Beresford, Hugh Walpole and Gilbert Cannan); the offer of Clive Bell to Pinker (Carter, *TLS*); *Letters*, ii. 440 ('I have had letters from a lot of people about the *Rainbow* – Oliver Lodge and others'); and ibid., ii. 447 ('John Drinkwater came in just now – he is anxious to do something'). Also Paul Fernando in Paris, see footnote 63 above. But none of these came to anything. However, in DHL's 'Introduction' to McDonald's *Bibliography*, pp. 38–9 (*Phoenix*, ed. McDonald, p. 234),

there was an abortive plan for a letter of protest to be signed by a list of writers (ii. 435), only one author defended him in public. Arnold Bennett referred to 'Mr. D. H. Lawrence's beautiful and maligned novel "The Rainbow"' in the *Daily News* on 15 December 1915. Galsworthy thought the book 'aesthetically detestable', was revolted by 'its perfervid futuristic style' and accused Lawrence of forgetting 'as no great artist does – that by dwelling on the sexual side of life so lovingly he falsifies all the values of his work', since the sexual instinct is so strong 'that any emphasis upon it drags the whole being of the reader away from seeing life steadily, truly, and whole'.[99] The assumptions about sex behind most of the reception of the novel were not often exposed quite so nakedly. Garnett showed that he had taken the point that Lawrence had made to him in 1914. He argued, in the *Dial* of 16 November 1916, in an article called 'Art and the Moralists: Mr. D. H. Lawrence's work',[100] that the moralists 'do both literature and morals a grave disservice by striving to confine aesthetic representations within too narrow a circle, and that by seeking to fetter and restrain the artist's activities they cripple art's function of deepening our consciousness and widening our recognitions' – but he does not argue a case for *The Rainbow* itself, which he continued to think 'not worthy of his remarkable talent'.[101] It is in the critic supposedly closest to Lawrence in 1915, moreover, that it becomes possible to measure the full price, in terms of incomprehension, that had to be paid for Lawrence's struggle towards a radically new imaginative art. Murry, after all, was in a unique position to understand what Lawrence was driving at. He had heard the 'Study of Thomas Hardy' expounded in Buckinghamshire, during the process of its composition;[102] and he was, as partner in the *Signature*, the only critic in England who had read all six essays of 'The Crown' – neither of which would be available to anyone else for a decade or more. Yet Murry, confronted with *The Rainbow*:

could not understand it at all. I disliked it on instinct. There was a warm, close, heavy promiscuity of flesh about it which repelled me, and I could not understand the compulsion which was upon Lawrence to write in that fashion and on

DHL mentions that, as well as Arnold Bennett, 'May Sinclair raised a kindly protest'. When McDonald tried to discover where it had been made she was unable to remember, except that it was a letter saying 'that the suppression of this book was a crime, the murder of a beautiful thing'.
[99] Letter to Pinker, Autumn 1915 (Draper 108–9).
[100] Vol. lxi, pp. 377–81 (Draper 113–20).
[101] *Manchester Guardian*, 10 December 1920, p. 5 (Draper 146).
[102] *Reminiscences of D. H. Lawrence* (1933), pp. 44–5.

those themes; neither could I understand his surprise and dismay that the critics were out for his blood. As far as mere feeling went, I felt with them. I happened to be friends with Lawrence, and Robert Lynd didn't: that was about the only difference.[103]

With such friends, what need of enemies? Yet because Murry was a genuine critic, it is not quite enough to say that. It is precisely the mark of the revolution in imagination that had taken Lawrence such a struggle to achieve, that *The Rainbow* should be so inaccessible, and remain so in England, until well after his death.[104]

In America, perhaps because the conventions of realistic fiction and character were not so entrenched, the novel gained adherents sooner, but there were no early reviews (because of the way the novel was published) and only a few later remarks to show how the novel was making its way. John Macy, reviewing *Women in Love* in 1920,[105] thought *The Rainbow* 'the stronger book' because it had more tragic power, deeper social implications and 'embraces a larger number of the manifold interests that compose the fever called living'. Louis Untermeyer in *New Republic* the previous year[106] had called *The Rainbow* 'possibly the most poetic and poignant novel of this decade'. Reviewing Seltzer's 1924 edition along with *The Boy in the Bush*, A. Donald Douglas states a preference for the earlier novels which do not try to explain emotion but are 'content to give forth the rich, tangled life of emotion and passion in color and rhythm, profound and mysterious like life'. But though *Sons and Lovers* is usually considered the favourite, 'many of us will continue to find "The Rainbow" his most certain masterpiece, a thing no one else in the world could have done. . .Most persons who shudder austerely at the "sensual scenes" of "The Rainbow" will confess (if you question them with a wise firmness) to never having read the book.'[107]

---

103 *Between Two Worlds* (1935), p. 351.
104 F. R. Leavis's early treatment – *D. H. Lawrence*, Minority Pamphlet no. 6, (?Cambridge, 1930); reprinted in *For Continuity* (Cambridge, 1933) – was still influenced by Murry. He thought *The Rainbow* 'a great deal more difficult' than *Sons and Lovers*. 'We do not doubt the urgency for the author of these shifting tensions of the inner life, this drama of the inexplicit and almost inexpressible in human intercourse, but for us the effect is one of monotony. Lawrence's fanatical concern for the "essential" often results in a strange intensity, but how limited is its range!' It was not perhaps until the three instalments of Leavis's 'The Novel as Dramatic Poem VII, *The Rainbow*' in *Scrutiny*, xviii (Winter 1951–2), 197–200, xviii (June 1952), 273–87 and xix (October 1952), 15–30, that the novel began to be seen, in England, as a major work.
105 *New York Evening Post Literary Review*, 19 March 1921, pp. 3–4 (Draper 157–8).
106 11 August 1920, pp. 314–15 (Draper 133).
107 *Public Ledger Literary Review*, 9 November 1924, pp. 3–4.

'You must not say my novel is shaky', Lawrence had written in June 1914. 'It is not perfect, because I am not expert in what I want to do. But it is the real thing, say what you like. And I shall get my reception, if not now, then before long' (ii. 183–4).

It took rather longer, and with more pain, than he had supposed.

THE RAINBOW

Note on the text

The base-text for this edition is the Manuscript (MS) which DHL completed on 2 March 1915, and from which a typescript (TS) was prepared. Emendations have been adopted from DHL's revision of the typescript in March–May; and from the revision in July and August of the unlocated proofs which were prepared from the typescript for the first English edition (E1), published by Methuen on 30 September 1915. Manuscript and typescript are in the Harry Ransom Humanities Research Center of the University of Texas at Austin.

The apparatus records all textual variants except the following silent emendations:

1. Clearly inadvertent spelling and typesetting errors have been corrected.
2. Misreadings of substantives and accidentals by typists, which were corrected back to the original before publication, are not noted.
3. Inadvertent omissions (e.g. incomplete quotation marks, the accent in hôtel and full stops omitted at the end of sentences where no other punctuation exists) have been supplied.
4. Omitted or misplaced apostrophes in possessive cases and the apostrophe in 'o'clock' have been supplied or corrected.
5. Quotation marks around the names of public houses, which DHL supplied on their first occurrence but not thereafter, have been supplied throughout. DHL's titles (e.g. St, Mr, Mrs) have been emended to his most usual form without a stop; E1 printed with the stop. The name of Brinsley Street School is silently emended from E1's 'St. Philip's' to the usual MS form 'St Philips'.
6. DHL often presented colloquial contractions without joining them up (e.g. 'does n't'), and these have been normalised ('doesn't') as they were in TS and E1.
7. E1 consistently printed 'to-day', 'to-morrow', 'to-night' whereas DHL wrote these as one unhyphenated word; his practice is followed. DHL usually wrote numbers without a hyphen as two words; TS and E1 added the hyphen, but this is not recorded.
8. DHL often followed a full stop, question mark or exclamation mark with a dash, before beginning the next sentence with a capital letter. Typists and typesetters frequently omitted the dash, which has been silently restored in this edition. E1 printed the dash with which DHL often breaks off or tails away speech as a 2-em dash (e.g. 'be——' at 27:29; this has been replaced by a 1-em dash.
9. It is often unclear whether the initial letters 'A', 'C' and 'U' in DHL's handwriting are upper or lower case. His majority use of 'angel' and 'college' has been followed silently unless MS is clearly a capital; 'Uncle', 'Aunt' and 'Cousin' are used only in direct speech, appearing otherwise as 'uncle', 'aunt' and 'cousin'; 'Church' has been used for the institution, and 'church' and 'cathedral' for the buildings, though unmistakeable capitalisation in MS is noted.

10. Some compounds, which E1 printed in a consistent form, but DHL usually in one form and sometimes in another (without nuances of meaning), are silently emended to his majority use after the first occurrence, though the minority use in MS will always be noted. E1 consistently printed 'weekday' which is here emended silently to DHL's 'week-day' except where he wrote 'week day'.

TO ELSE*

CONTENTS

Chapter I

How Tom Brangwen Married a Polish Lady

I

The Brangwens had lived for generations on the Marsh Farm, in the meadows where the Erewash twisted sluggishly through alder trees, separating Derbyshire from Nottinghamshire. Two miles away, a church-tower stood on a hill, the houses of the little country town* climbing assiduously up to it. Whenever one of the Brangwens in the fields lifted his head from his work, he saw the church-tower at Ilkeston in the empty sky. So that as he turned again to the horizontal land, he was aware of something standing above him and beyond him in the distance.

There was a look in the eyes of the Brangwens as if they were expecting something unknown, about which they were eager. They had that air of readiness for what would come to them, a kind of surety, an expectancy, the look of an inheritor.

They were fresh, blond, slow-speaking people, revealing themselves plainly, but slowly, so that one could watch the change in their eyes from laughter to anger, blue, lit-up laughter, to a hard, blue-staring anger; through all the irresolute stages of the sky when the weather is changing.

Living on rich land, on their own land, near to a growing town,* they had forgotten what it was to be in straitened circumstances. They had never become rich, because there were always children, and the patrimony was divided every time. But always, at the Marsh, there was ample.

So the Brangwens came and went without fear of necessity, working hard because of the life that was in them, not for want of the money. Neither were they thriftless. They were aware of the last halfpenny, and instinct made them not waste the peeling of their apple, for it would help to feed the cattle. But heaven and earth was* teeming around them, and how should this cease? They felt the rush of the sap in spring, they knew the wave which cannot halt, but every year throws forward the seed to begetting, and falling back,*

9

leaves the young-born on the earth. They knew the intercourse between heaven and earth, sunshine drawn into the breast and bowels, the rain sucked up in the daytime, nakedness that comes under the wind in autumn, showing the birds' nests no longer worth 5 hiding. Their life and inter-relations were such; feeling the pulse and body of the soil, that opened to their furrow for the grain, and became smooth and supple after their ploughing, and clung to their feet with a weight that pulled like desire, lying hard and unresponsive when the crops were to be shorn away. The young corn waved and 10 was silken, and the lustre slid along the limbs of the men who saw it. They took the udder of the cows, the cows yielded milk and pulse against the hands of the men, the pulse of the blood of the teats of the cows beat into the pulse of the hands of the men. They mounted their horses, and held life between the grip of their knees, they 15 harnessed their horses at the wagon, and, with hand on the bridle-rings, drew the heaving of the horses after their will.

In autumn the partridges whirred up, birds in flocks blew like spray across the fallow, rooks appeared on the grey, watery heavens, and flew cawing into the winter. Then the men sat by the fire in the 20 house where the women moved about with surety, and the limbs and the body of the men were impregnated with the day, cattle and earth and vegetation and the sky, the men sat by the fire and their brains were inert, as their blood flowed heavy with the accumulation from the living day.

25   The women were different.* On them too was the drowse of blood-intimacy, calves sucking and hens running together in droves, and young geese palpitating in the hand whilst food was pushed down their throttle. But the women looked out from the heated, blind intercourse of farm-life, to the spoken world beyond. They 30 were aware of the lips and the mind of the world speaking and giving utterance, they heard the sound in the distance, and they strained to listen.

It was enough for the men, that the earth heaved and opened its furrow to them, that the wind blew to dry the wet wheat, and set the 35 young ears of corn wheeling freshly round about; it was enough that they helped the cow in labour, or ferreted the rats from under the barn, or broke the back of a rabbit with a sharp knock of the hand. So much warmth and generating and pain and death did they know in their blood, earth and sky and beast and green plants, so much 40 exchange and interchange they had with these, that they lived full

and surcharged, their senses full fed, their faces always turned to the
heat of the blood, staring into the sun, dazed with looking towards
the source of generation, unable to turn round.

But the woman wanted another form of life than this, something
that was not blood-intimacy. Her house faced out from the farm-　5
buildings and fields, looked out to the road and the village with
church and Hall and the world beyond. She stood to see the far-off
world of cities and governments and the active scope of man, the
magic land to her, where secrets were made known and desires
fulfilled. She faced outwards to where men moved dominant and　10
creative, having turned their back on the pulsing heat of creation,
and with this behind them, were set out to discover what was beyond,
to enlarge their own scope and range and freedom; whereas the
Brangwen men faced inwards to the teeming life of creation, which
poured unresolved into their veins.　15

Looking out, as she must, from the front of her house towards the
activity of man in the world at large, whilst her husband looked out to
the back at sky and harvest and beast and land, she strained her eyes
to see what man had done in fighting outwards to knowledge,* she
strained to hear how he uttered himself in his conquest, her deepest　20
desire hung on the battle that she heard, far off, being waged on the
edge of the unknown. She also wanted to know, and to be of the
fighting host.

At home, even so near as Cossethay, was the vicar, who spoke the
other, magic language, and had the other, finer bearing, both of　25
which she could perceive, but could never attain to. The vicar moved
in worlds beyond where her own menfolk existed. Did she not know
her own menfolk: fresh, slow, full-built men, masterful enough, but
easy, native to the earth, lacking outwardness and range of motion.
Whereas the vicar, dark and dry and small beside her husband, had　30
yet a quickness and a range of being that made Brangwen, in his
large geniality, seem dull and local. She knew her husband. But in
the vicar's nature was that which passed beyond her knowledge. As
Brangwen had power over the cattle so the vicar had power over her
husband. What was it in the vicar, that raised him above the common　35
men as man is raised above the beast? She craved to know. She
craved to achieve this higher being, if not in herself, then in her
children. That which makes a man strong even if he be little and frail
in body, just as any man is little and frail beside a bull, and yet
stronger than the bull, what was it? It was not money nor power nor　40

position. What power had the vicar over Tom Brangwen—none. Yet strip them and set them on a desert island, and the vicar was the master. His soul was master of the other man's. And why—why? She decided it was a question of knowledge.

5   The curate was poor enough, and not very efficacious as a man, either, yet he took rank with those others, the superior. She watched his children being born, she saw them running as tiny things beside their mother. And already they were separate from her own children, distinct. Why were her own children marked below those others? 10 Why should the curate's children inevitably take precedence over her children, why should dominance be given them from the start? It was not money, nor even class. It was education and experience, she decided.

It was this, this education, this higher form of being, that the 15 mother wished to give to her children, so that they too could live the supreme life on earth. For her children, at least the children of her heart, had the complete nature that should take place in equality with the living, vital people in the land, not be left behind obscure among the laborers. Why must they remain obscured and stifled all their 20 lives, why should they suffer from lack of freedom to move? How should they learn the entry into the finer, more vivid circle of life?

Her imagination was fired by the squire's lady at Shelly Hall,* who came to church at Cossethay with her little children, girls in tidy capes of beaver fur, and smart little hats, herself like a winter rose, so 25 fair and delicate. So fair, so fine in mould, so luminous, what was it that Mrs Hardy felt which she, Mrs Brangwen did not feel? How was Mrs Hardy's nature different from that of the common women of Cossethay, in what was it beyond them? All the women of Cossethay talked eagerly about Mrs Hardy, of her husband, her children, her 30 guests, her dress, of her servants and her housekeeping. The lady of the Hall was the living dream of their lives, her life was the epic that inspired their lives. In her they lived imaginatively, and in gossiping of her husband who drank, of her scandalous brother, of Lord William Bentley her friend, member of Parliament for the division, 35 they had their own Odyssey* enacting itself, Penelope and Ulysses before them, and Circe and the swine and the endless web.

So the women of the village were fortunate. They saw themselves in the lady of the manor, each of them lived her own fulfilment in the life of Mrs Hardy. And the Brangwen wife at the Marsh aspired 40 beyond herself, towards the further life of the finer woman, towards

the extended being she revealed, as a traveller in his self-contained
manner reveals far-off countries present in himself. But why should
a knowledge of far-off countries make a man's life a different thing,
finer, bigger? And why is a man more than the beast and the cattle
that serve him? It is the same thing.   5

The male part of the poem was filled in by such men as the vicar and
Lord William, lean, eager men with strange movements, men who
had command of the further fields, whose lives ranged over a great
extent. Ah, it was something very desirable to know, this touch of the
wonderful men who had the power of thought and comprehension.   10
The women of the village might be much fonder of Tom Brangwen,
and more at their ease with him, yet if their lives had been robbed of
the vicar, and of Lord William, the leading shoot would have been cut
away from them, they would have been heavy and uninspired and
inclined to hate. So long as the wonder of the beyond was before   15
them, they could get along, whatever their lot. And Mrs Hardy, and
the vicar, and Lord William, these moved in the wonder of the
beyond, and were visible to the eyes of Cossethay in their motion.

II

About 1840,* a canal was constructed across the meadows of the   20
Marsh Farm, connecting the newly opened collieries of the Erewash
Valley. A high embankment travelled along the fields to carry the
canal, which passed close to the homestead, and, reaching the road,
went over in a heavy bridge.

So the Marsh was shut off from Ilkeston, and enclosed in the small   25
valley bed, which ended in a busy hill and the village spire of
Cossethay.

The Brangwens received a fair sum of money from this trespass
across their land. Then, a short time afterwards, a colliery was sunk
on the other side of the canal, and in a while the Midland Railway   30
came down the valley at the foot of the Ilkeston hill, and the invasion
was complete. The town grew rapidly, the Brangwens were kept
busy producing supplies, they became richer, they were almost
tradesmen.

Still the Marsh remained remote and original, on the old, quiet   35
side of the canal embankment, in the sunny valley where slow water
wound along in company of stiff alders, and the road went under
ash-trees past the Brangwens' garden gate.

But, looking from the garden gate down the road to the right, there, through the dark archway of the canal's square aqueduct, was a colliery spinning away in the near distance, and further, red, crude houses plastered on the valley in masses, and beyond all, the dim
5 smoking hill of the town.

The homestead was just on the safe side of civilisation, outside the gate. The house stood bare from the road, approached by a straight garden path, along which at spring the daffodils were thick in green and yellow. At the sides of the house were bushes of lilac and
10 guelder-rose and privet, entirely hiding the farm-buildings behind.

At the back a confusion of sheds spread into the home-close from out of two or three indistinct yards. The duckpond lay beyond the furthest wall, littering its white feathers on the padded earthen banks, blowing its stray, soiled feathers into the grass and the gorse
15 bushes below the canal embankment, which rose like a high rampart near at hand, so that occasionally a man's figure passed in silhouette, or a man and a towing horse traversed the sky.

At first the Brangwens were astonished by all this commotion around them. The building of a canal across their land made them
20 strangers in their own place, this raw bank of earth shutting them off disconcerted them. As they worked in the fields, from beyond the now familiar embankment came the rhythmic run of the winding engines, startling at first, but afterwards a narcotic to the brain. Then the shrill whistle of the trains re-echoed through the heart, with
25 fearsome pleasure, announcing the far-off come near and imminent.

As they drove home from town, the farmers of the land met the blackened colliers trooping from the pit-mouth. As they gathered the harvest, the west wind brought a faint, sulphurous smell of pit-refuse burning. As they pulled the turnips in November, the sharp clink-
30 clink-clink-clink-clink of empty trucks shunting on the line, vibrated in their hearts with the fact of other activity going on beyond them.

The Alfred Brangwen of this period had married a woman from Heanor, daughter of the "Black Horse." She was a slim, pretty, dark woman, quaint in her speech, whimsical,* so that the sharp things she
35 said did not hurt. She was oddly a thing to herself, rather querulous in her manner, but intrinsically separate and indifferent, so that her long lamentable complaints, when she raised her voice against her husband in particular and against everybody else after him, only made those who heard her, wonder and feel affectionately towards
40 her, even whilst they were irritated and impatient with her. She

railed long and loud about her husband, but always with a balanced, easy-flying voice and a quaint manner of speech that warmed his belly with pride and male triumph whilst he scowled with mortification at the things she said.

Consequently Brangwen himself had a humorous puckering at the eyes, a sort of fat laugh, very quiet and full, and he was spoilt like a lord of creation. He calmly did as he liked, laughed at her railing, excused himself in a teasing tone that she loved, followed his natural inclinations, and sometimes, pricked too near the quick, frightened and broke her by a deep, tense fury which seemed to fix on him and hold him for days, and which she would give anything to placate in him. They were two very separate beings, vitally connected, knowing nothing of each other, yet living in their separate ways from one root.

There were four sons and two daughters. The eldest boy ran away early to sea, and did not come back. After this the mother was more the node and centre of attraction in the home. The second boy, Alfred, whom the mother admired most, was the most reserved. He was sent to school in Ilkeston and made some progress. But in spite of his dogged, yearning effort, he could not get beyond the rudiments of anything, save of drawing. At this, in which he had some power, he worked, as if it were his hope. After much grumbling and savage rebellion against everything, after much trying and shifting about, when his father was incensed against him and his mother almost despairing, he became a draughtsman in a lace-factory in Nottingham.*

He remained heavy and somewhat uncouth, speaking with broad Derbyshire accent, adhering with all his tenacity to his work and to his town position, making good designs, and becoming fairly well-off. But at drawing, his hand swung naturally in big, bold lines, rather lax, so that it was cruel for him to pedgill* away at the lace designing, working from the tiny squares of his paper, counting and plotting and niggling. He did it stubbornly, with anguish, crushing the bowels within him, adhering to his chosen lot whatever it should cost. And he came back into life set and rigid, a rare-spoken, almost surly man.

He married the daughter of a chemist, who affected some social superiority, and he became something of a snob, in his dogged fashion, with a passion for outward refinement in the household, mad when anything clumsy or gross occurred. Later, when his three children were growing up, and he seemed a staid, almost middle-aged man, he turned after strange women, and became a silent, inscrutable follower of forbidden pleasure, neglecting his indignant bourgeois wife without a qualm.

5 Frank, the third son, refused from the first to have anything to do with learning. From the first he hung round the slaughter-house which stood away in the third yard at the back of the farm. The Brangwens had always killed their own meat, and supplied the neighbourhood. Out of this grew a regular butcher's business in connection with the farm.

10 As a child Frank had been drawn by the trickle of dark blood that ran across the pavement from the slaughter-house to the crew-yard,* by the sight of the man carrying across to the meat-shed a huge side of beef, with the kidneys showing, embedded in their heavy laps of fat.

15 He was a handsome lad with soft brown hair and regular features something like a later Roman youth. He was more easily excitable, more readily carried away than the rest, weaker in character. At eighteen he married a little factory girl, a pale, plump, quiet thing with sly eyes and a wheedling voice, who insinuated herself into him

20 and bore him a child every year and made a fool of him. When he had taken over the butchery business, already a growing callousness to it, and a sort of contempt made him neglectful of it. He drank, and was often to be found in his public-house blathering away as if he knew everything, when in reality he was a noisy fool.

25 Of the daughters, Alice, the elder, married a collier and lived for a time stormily in Ilkeston, before moving away to Yorkshire with her numerous young family. Effie, the younger, remained at home.

The last child, Tom, was considerably younger than his brothers, so had belonged rather to the company of his sisters. He was his

30 mother's favorite. She roused herself to determination, and sent him forcibly away to a Grammar School* in Derby when he was twelve years old. He did not want to go, and his father would have given way, but Mrs Brangwen had set her heart on it. Her slender, pretty, tightly covered body, with full skirts, was now the centre of resolu-

35 tion in the house, and when she had once set upon anything, which was not often, the family failed before her.

So Tom went to school, an unwilling failure from the first. He believed his mother was right in decreeing school for him, but he knew she was only right because she would not acknowledge his

40 constitution. He knew, with a child's deep, instinctive foreknowledge

of what is going to happen to him, that he would cut a sorry figure at school. But he took the infliction as inevitable, as if he were guilty of his own nature, as if his being were wrong, and his mother's conception right. If he could have been what he liked, he would have been that which his mother fondly but deludedly hoped he was. He would have been clever, and capable of becoming a gentleman. It was her aspiration for him, therefore he knew it as the true aspiration for any boy. But you can't make a silk purse out of a sow's ear, as he told his mother very early, with regard to himself; much to her mortification and chagrin.

When he got to school, he made a violent struggle against his physical inability to study. He sat gripped, making himself pale and ghastly in his effort to concentrate on the book, to take in what he had to learn. But it was no good. If he beat down his first repulsion, and got like a suicide to the stuff, he went very little further. He could not learn deliberately. His mind simply did not work.

In feeling he was developed, sensitive to the atmosphere around him, brutal perhaps, but at the same time delicate, very delicate. So he had a low opinion of himself. He knew his own limitation. He knew that his brain was a slow hopeless good-for-nothing. So he was humble.

But at the same time his feelings were more discriminating than those of most of the boys, and he was confused. He was more sensuously developed, more refined in instinct than they. For their mechanical stupidity he hated them, and suffered cruel contempt for them. But when it came to mental things, then he was at a disadvantage. He was at their mercy. He was a fool. He had not the power to controvert even the most stupid argument, so that he was forced to admit things he did not in the least believe. And having admitted them, he did not know whether he believed them or not; he rather thought he did.

But he loved anyone who could convey enlightenment to him through feeling. He sat betrayed with emotion when the teacher of literature read, in a moving fashion, Tennyson's "Ulysses" or Shelley's "Ode to the West Wind."* His lips parted, his eyes filled with a strained, almost suffering light. And the teacher read on, fired by his power over the boy. Tom Brangwen was moved by this experience beyond all calculation, he almost dreaded it, it was so deep. But when, almost secretly and shamefully, he came to take the book himself, and began the words "Oh wild west wind, thou breath

of autumn's being," the very fact of the print caused a prickly sensation of repulsion to go over his skin, the blood came to his face, his
heart filled with a bursting passion of rage and incompetence. He
threw the book down and walked over it and went out to the cricket
5   field. And he hated books as if they were his enemies. He hated
them worse than ever he hated any person.

He could not voluntarily control his attention. His mind had no
fixed habits to go by, he had nothing to get hold of, nowhere to start
from. For him there was nothing palpable, nothing known in
10 himself, that he could apply to learning. He did not know how to
begin. Therefore he was helpless when it came to deliberate understanding or deliberate learning.

He had an instinct for mathematics, but if this failed him, he was
helpless as an idiot. So that he felt that the ground was never sure
15 under his feet, he was nowhere. His final downfall was his complete
inability to attend to a question put without suggestion. If he had to
write a formal composition on the Army, he did at last learn to
repeat the few facts he knew: "You can join the army at eighteen.
You have to be over five foot eight."* But he had all the time a living
20 conviction that this was a dodge and that his commonplaces were
beneath contempt. Then he reddened furiously, felt his bowels sink
with shame, scratched out what he had written, made an agonised
effort to think of something in the real composition style, failed,
became sullen with rage and humiliation, put the pen down and
25 would have been torn to pieces rather than attempt to write another
word.

He soon got used to the Grammar School, and the Grammar
School got used to him, setting him down as a hopeless duffer at
learning, but respecting him for a generous, honest nature. Only
30 one narrow, domineering fellow, the Latin master, bullied him and
made the blue eyes mad with shame and rage. There was a horrid
scene, when the boy laid open the master's head with a slate, and
then things went on as before. The teacher got little sympathy. But
Brangwen winced and could not bear to think of the deed, not even
35 long after, when he was a grown man.

He was glad to leave school. It had not been unpleasant, he had
enjoyed the companionship of the other youths, or had thought he
enjoyed it, the time had passed very quickly, in endless activity. But
he knew all the time that he was in an ignominious position, in this
40 place of learning. He was aware of failure all the while, of incapa-

city. But he was too healthy and sanguine to be wretched, he was too much alive. Yet his soul was wretched almost to hopelessness.

He had loved one warm, clever boy who was frail in body, a consumptive type. The two had had an almost classic friendship, David and Jonathan,* wherein Brangwen was the Jonathan, the server. But he had never felt equal with his friend, because the other's mind outpaced his, and left him ashamed, far in the rear. So the two boys went at once apart on leaving school. But Brangwen always remembered his friend that had been, kept him as a sort of light, a fine experience to remember.

Tom Brangwen was glad to get back to the farm, where he was in his own again. "I've got a turnip on my shoulders, let me stick to th' fallow," he said to his exasperated mother. He had too low an opinion of himself. But he went about at his work* on the farm gladly enough, glad of the active labour and the smell of the land again, having youth and vigour and humour, and a comic wit, having the will and the power to forget his own shortcomings, finding himself violent with occasional rages, but usually on good terms with everybody and everything.

When he was seventeen, his father fell from a stack and broke his neck. Then the mother and son and daughter lived on at the farm, interrupted by occasional loud-mouthed, lamenting, jealous-spirited visitations from the butcher Frank, who had a grievance against the world, which he felt was always giving him less than his dues. Frank was particularly against the young Tom, whom he called a mardy* baby, and Tom returned the hatred violently, his face growing red and his blue eyes staring. Effie sided with Tom against Frank. But when Alfred came, from Nottingham, heavy jowled and lowering, speaking very little, but treating those at home with some contempt, Effie and the mother sided with him and put Tom into the shade. It irritated the youth that his elder brother should be made something of a hero by the women, just because he didn't live at home and was a lace-designer and almost a gentleman. But Alfred was something of a Prometheus Bound,* so the women loved him. Tom came later to understand his brother better.

As youngest son, Tom felt some importance when the care of the farm devolved on to him. He was only eighteen, but he was quite capable of doing everything his father had done. And of course, his mother remained as centre to the house.

The young man grew up very fresh and alert, with zest for every

moment of life. He worked and rode and drove to market, he went
out with companions and got tipsy occasionally and played skittles
and went to the little travelling theatres.* Once, when he was drunk
at a public-house, he went upstairs with a prostitute who seduced
5   him. He was then nineteen.

The thing was something of a shock to him. In the close intimacy
of the farm kitchen, the woman occupied the supreme position. The
men deferred to her in the house, on all household points, on all
points of morality and behaviour. The woman was the symbol for
10 that further life which comprised religion and love and morality.
The men placed in her hands their own conscience, they said to her
"Be my conscience-keeper, be the angel at the doorway* guarding
my outgoing and my incoming."* And the woman fulfilled her trust,
the men rested implicitly in her, receiving her praise or her blame
15 with pleasure or with anger, rebelling and storming, but never for a
moment really escaping in their own souls from her prerogative.
They depended on her for their stability. Without her, they would
have felt like straws in the wind, to be blown hither and thither at
random. She was the anchor and the security, she was the
20 restraining hand of God, at times highly to be execrated.

Now when Tom Brangwen, at nineteen, a youth fresh like a plant,
rooted in his mother and his sister, found that he had lain with a
prostitute woman in a common public-house, he was very much
startled. For him, there was until that time only one kind of
25 woman—his mother and sister.

But now? He did not know what to feel. There was a slight
wonder, a pang of anger, of disappointment, a first taste of ash and
of cold fear lest this was all that would happen, lest his relations with
woman were going to be no more than this nothingness; there was a
30 slight sense of shame before the prostitute, fear that she would
despise him for his inefficiency; there was a cold distaste for her,
and a fear of her; there was a moment of paralysed horror when he
felt he might have taken a disease from her; and upon all this startled
tumult of emotion, was laid the steadying hand of common sense,
35 which said it did not matter very much, so long as he had no disease.
He soon recovered balance, and really it did not matter so very
much.

But it had shocked him, and put a mistrust into his heart, and
emphasized his fear of what was within himself. He was, however, in
40 a few days going about again in his own careless, happy-go-lucky

fashion, his blue eyes just as clear and honest as ever, his face just as fresh, his appetite just as keen.

Or apparently so. He had, in fact, lost some of his buoyant confidence, and doubt hindered his outgoing.

For some time after this, he was quieter, more conscious when he 5
drank, more backward from companionship. The disillusion of his first carnal contact with woman, strengthened by his innate desire to find in a woman the embodiment of all his inarticulate, powerful religious impulses, put a bit in his mouth. He had something to lose which he was afraid of losing, which he was not sure even of 10
possessing. This first affair did not matter much: but the business of love was, at the bottom of his soul, the most serious and terrifying of all to him.

He was tormented now with sex desire, his imagination reverted always to lustful scenes. But what really prevented his returning to a 15
loose woman, over and above the natural squeamishness, was the recollection of the paucity of the last experience. It had been so nothing, so dribbling and functional, that he was ashamed to expose himself to the risk of a repetition of it.

He made a strong, instinctive fight to retain his native cheerful- 20
ness unimpaired. He had naturally a plentiful stream of life and humour, a sense of sufficiency and exuberance, giving ease. But now it tended to cause tension. A strained light came into his eyes, he had a slight knitting of the brows. His boisterous humour gave place to lowering silences, and days passed by in a sort of suspense. 25

He did not know there was any difference in him, exactly; for the most part he was filled with slow anger and resentment. But he knew he was always thinking of women, or a woman, day in, day out, and that infuriated him. He could not get free: and he was ashamed. He had one or two sweethearts, starting with them in the hope of speedy 30
development. But when he had a nice girl, he found that he was incapable of pushing the desired development. The very presence of the girl beside him made it impossible. He could not think of her like that, he could not think of her *actual* nakedness. She was a girl and he liked her, and dreaded violently even the thought of uncovering her. 35
He knew that, in these last issues of nakedness, he did not exist to her nor she to him. Again, if he had a loose girl, and things began to develop, she offended him so deeply all the time, that he never knew whether he were going to get away from her as quickly as possible, or whether he were going to take her out of inflamed necessity. Again 40

he learnt his lesson: if he took her it was a paucity which he was forced to despise. He did not despise himself nor the girl. But he despised the net result in him of the experience—he despised it deeply and bitterly.

5   Then, when he was twenty three, his mother died, and he was left at home with Effie. His mother's death was another blow out of the dark. He could not understand it, he knew it was no good his trying. One had to submit to these unforeseen blows that come unawares, and leave a bruise that remains and hurts whenever it is touched. He
10 began to be afraid of all that which was up against him. He had loved his mother.

After this, Effie and he quarrelled fiercely. They meant a very great deal to each other, but they were both under a strange, unnatural tension. He stayed out of the house as much as possible.
15 He got a special corner for himself at the "Red Lion" at Cossethay, and became a usual figure by the fire, a fresh, fair young fellow with heavy limbs and head held back, mostly silent, though alert and attentive, very hearty in his greeting of everybody he knew, shy of strangers. He teased all the women, who liked him extremely, and he
20 was very attentive to the talk of the men, very respectful.

To drink made him quickly flush very red in the face, and brought out the look of self-consciousness and unsureness, almost bewilderment, in his blue eyes. When he came home in this state of tipsy confusion his sister hated him and abused him, and he went off his
25 head, like a mad bull with rage.

He had still another turn with a light-o'love. One Whitsuntide he went a jaunt with two other young fellows, on horseback, to Matlock and thence to Bakewell.* Matlock was at that time just becoming a famous beauty-spot, visited from Manchester and from the Staf-
30 fordshire towns. In the hôtel where the young men took lunch, were two girls, and the parties struck up a friendship.

The Miss who made up to Tom Brangwen, then twenty four years old, was a handsome, reckless girl neglected for an afternoon by the man who had brought her out. She saw Brangwen, and liked him, as
35 all women did, for his warmth and his generous nature, and for the innate delicacy in him. But she saw he was one who would have to be brought to the scratch. However, she was roused and unsatisfied and made mischievous, so she dared anything. It would be an easy interlude, restoring her pride.

40   She was a handsome girl with a bosom, and dark hair, and blue

eyes, a girl full of easy laughter, flushed from the sun, inclined to
wipe her laughing face in a very natural and taking manner.

Brangwen was in a state of wonder. He treated her with his
chaffing deference, roused, but very unsure of himself, afraid to
death of being too forward, ashamed lest he might be thought   5
backward, mad with desire yet restrained by instinctive regard for
women from making any definite approach, feeling all the while that
his attitude was ridiculous, and flushing deep with confusion. She,
however, became hard and daring as he become confused, it amused
her to see him come on.   10

"When must you get back?" she asked.

"I'm not particular," he said.

There the conversation again broke down.

Brangwen's companions were ready to go on.

"Art commin' Tom," they called, "or art for stoppin'?"   15

"Ay, I'm commin'," he replied, rising reluctantly, an angry sense
of futility and disappointment spreading over him.

He met the full, almost taunting look of the girl, and he trembled
with unusedness.

"Shall you come an' have a look at my mare," he said to her, with   20
his hearty kindliness that was now shaken with trepidation.

"Oh, I should like to," she said, rising.

And she followed him, his rather sloping shoulders and his cloth
riding gaiters, out of the room. The young men got their own horses
out of the stable.   25

"Can you ride?" Brangwen asked her.

"I should like to if I could—I've never tried," she said.

"Come then, an' have a try," he said.

And he lifted her, he blushing, she laughing, into the saddle.

"I s'll slip off—it's not a lady's saddle," she cried.   30

"Hold yer tight," he said, and he led her out of the hôtel gate.

The girl sat very insecurely, clinging fast. He put a hand on her
waist, to support her. And he held her closely, he clasped her as an
embrace, he was weak with desire as he strode beside her.

The horse walked by the river.   35

"You want to sit straddle-leg," he said to her.

"I know I do," she said.

It was the time of very full skirts. She managed to get astride the
horse, quite decently, showing an intent concern for covering her
pretty leg.   40

"It's a lot better this road,"[*] she said, looking down at him.

"Ay, it is," he said, feeling the marrow melt in his bones from the look in her eyes. "I dunno why they have that side-saddle business, twistin' a woman in two."

5   "Should us leave you then—you seem to be fixed up there?" called Brangwen's companions from the road.

He went red with anger.

"Ay—don't worry," he called back.

"How long are yer stoppin'?" they asked.

10   "Not after Christmas," he said.

And the girl gave a tinkling peal of laughter.

"All right—by-bye!" called his friends.

And they cantered off, leaving him very flushed, trying to be quite normal with the girl. But presently he had gone back to the hôtel and

15   given his horse into the charge of an ostler and had gone off with the girl, into the woods, not quite knowing where he was or what he was doing. His heart thumped and he thought it the most glorious adventure, and was mad with desire for the girl.

Afterwards he glowed with pleasure. By Jove, but that was

20   something like! He stayed the afternoon with the girl, and wanted to stay the night.[*] She, however, told him this was impossible: her own man would be back by dark, and she must be with him. He, Brangwen, must not let on that there had been anything between them.

25   She gave him an intimate smile, which made him feel confused and gratified.

He could not tear himself away, though he had promised not to interfere with the girl. He stayed on at the hôtel over-night. He saw the other fellow at the evening meal; a small, middle-aged man with

30   iron-grey hair and a curious face, like a monkey's, but interesting, in its way almost beautiful. Brangwen guessed that he was a foreigner. He was in company with another, an Englishman, dry and hard. The four sat at table, two men and two women. Brangwen watched with all his eyes.

35   He saw how the foreigner treated the women with courteous contempt, as if they were pleasing animals. Brangwen's girl had put on a ladylike manner, but her voice betrayed her. She wanted to win back her man. When dessert came on, however, the little foreigner turned round from his table and calmly surveyed the room, like one

40   unoccupied. Brangwen marvelled over the cold, animal intelligence

of the face. The brown eyes were round, showing all the brown pupil, like a monkey's, and just calmly looking, perceiving the other person without referring to him at all. They rested on Brangwen. The latter marvelled at the old face turned round on him, looking at him without considering it necessary to know him at all. The eyebrows of the round, perceiving, but unconcerned eyes were rather high up, with slight wrinkles above them, just as a monkey's had. It was an old, ageless face.

The man was most amazingly a gentleman all the time, an aristocrat. Brangwen stared fascinated. The girl was pushing her crumbs about on the cloth, uneasily, flushed and angry.

As Brangwen sat motionless in the hall afterwards, too much moved and lost to know what to do, the little stranger came up to him with a beautiful smile and manner, offering a cigarette and saying:

"Will you smoke?"

Brangwen never smoked cigarettes, yet he took the one offered, fumbling painfully with thick fingers, blushing to the roots of his hair. Then he looked with his warm blue eyes at the almost sardonic, lidded eyes of the foreigner. The latter sat down beside him, and they began to talk, chiefly of horses.

Brangwen loved the other man for his exquisite graciousness, for his tact and reserve, and for his ageless, monkey-like self-surety. They talked of horses, and of Derbyshire, and of farming. The stranger warmed to the young fellow with real warmth, and Brangwen was excited. He was transported at meeting this odd, middle-aged, dry-skinned man, personally. The talk was pleasant, but that did not matter so much. It was the gracious manner, the fine contact that was all.

They talked a long while together, Brangwen flushing like a girl when the other did not understand his idiom. Then they said goodnight, and shook hands. Again the foreigner bowed and repeated his goodnight.

"Goodnight, and *bon voyage*."

Then he turned to the stairs.

Brangwen went up to his room and lay staring out at the stars of the summer night, his whole being in a whirl. What was it all? There was a life so different from what he knew it. What was there outside his knowledge, how much? What was this that he had touched? What was he in this new influence? What did everything mean? Where was life, in that which he knew or all outside him?

He fell asleep, and in the morning had ridden away before any other visitors were awake. He shrank from seeing any of them again, in the morning.

His mind was one big excitement. The girl and the foreigner: he
5 knew neither of their names. Yet they had set fire to the homestead of his nature, and he would be burned out of cover. Of the two experiences, perhaps the meeting with the foreigner was the more significant. But the girl—he had not settled about the girl.

He did not know. He had to leave it there, as it was. He could not
10 sum up his experiences.

The result of these encounters was, that he dreamed day and night, absorbedly, of a voluptuous woman and of the meeting with a small, withered foreigner of ancient breeding. No sooner was his mind free, no sooner had he left his own companions, than he began
15 to imagine an intimacy with fine-textured, subtle-mannered people such as the foreigner at Matlock, and amidst this subtle intimacy was always the satisfaction of a voluptuous woman.

He went about absorbed in the interest and the actuality of this dream. His eyes glowed, he walked with his head up, full of the
20 exquisite pleasure of aristocratic subtlety and grace, tormented with the desire for the girl.

Then gradually the glow began to fade, and the cold material of his customary life to show through. He resented it. Was he cheated in his illusion? He balked the mean enclosure of reality, stood
25 stubbornly like a bull at a gate, refusing to re-enter the well-known pound of his own life.

He drank more than usual to keep up the glow. But it faded more and more for all that. He set his teeth at the commonplace, to which he would not submit. It resolved itself starkly before him, for all that.
30 He wanted to marry, to get settled somehow, to get out of the quandary he found himself in. But how? He felt unable to move his limbs. He had seen a little creature caught in bird-lime, and the sight was a nightmare to him. He began to feel mad with the rage of impotency.
35 He wanted something to get hold of, to pull himself out. But there was nothing. Steadfastly he looked at the young women, to find a one he could marry. But not one of them did he want. And he knew that the idea of a life among such people as the foreigner was ridiculous.

Yet he dreamed of it, and stuck to his dreams, and would not have
40 the reality of Cossethay and Ilkeston. There he sat stubbornly in his

corner at the "Red Lion," smoking and musing and occasionally
lifting his beer-pot, and saying nothing, for all the world like a
gorping* farm-laborer, as he said himself.

Then a fever of restless anger came upon him. He wanted to go
away—right away. He dreamed of foreign parts. But somehow he   5
had no contact with them. And it was a very strong root which held
him to the Marsh, to his own house and land.

Then Effie got married, and he was left in the house with only
Tilly, the cross-eyed woman-servant who had been with them for
fifteen years. He felt things coming to a close. All the time, he had   10
held himself stubbornly resistant to the action of the commonplace
unreality which wanted to absorb him. But now he had to do
something.

He was by nature temperate. Being sensitive and emotional, his
nausea prevented him from drinking too much.   15

But, in futile anger, with the greatest of determination and
apparent good-humour, he began to drink in order to get drunk.
"Damn it," he said to himself, "you must have it one road or
another—you can't hitch your horse to the shadow of a gate-post—if
you've got legs you've got to rise off your backside some time or   20
other."

So he rose and went down to Ilkeston, rather awkwardly took his
place amongst a gang of young bloods, stood drinks to the company,
and discovered he could carry it off quite well. He had an idea that
everybody in the room was a man after his own heart, that everything 25
was glorious, everything was perfect. When somebody in alarm told
him his coat pocket was on fire, he could only beam from a red,
blissful face and say "Iss-all-ri-ight—iss-a'-ri-ight—it's a' right
——let it be, let it be—" and he laughed with pleasure, and was
rather indignant that the others should think it unnatural for his coat 30
pocket to burn:—it was the happiest and most natural thing in the
world—what?

He went home talking to himself and to the moon, that was very
high and small, stumbling at the flashes of moonlight from the
puddles at his feet, wondering What the Hanover!,* then laughing   35
confidently to the moon, assuring her this was first class, this was.

In the morning he woke up and thought about it, and for the first
time in his life, knew what it was to feel really acutely irritable, in a
misery of real bad temper. After bawling and snarling at Tilly, he
took himself off for very shame, to be alone. And looking at the ashen 40

fields and the putty roads, he wondered what in the name of Hell he
could do to get out of this prickly sense of disgust and physical repulsion. And he knew that this was the result of his glorious evening.

And his stomach did not want any more brandy. He went doggedly
5   across the fields with his terrier, and looked at everything with a
jaundiced eye.

The next evening found him back again in his place at the "Red
Lion," moderate and decent. There he sat and stubbornly waited for
what would happen next.

10 Did he, or did he not believe that he belonged to this world of
Cossethay and Ilkeston? There was nothing in it he wanted. Yet
could he ever get out of it? Was there anything in himself that
would carry him out of it? Or was he a dunderheaded baby, not man
enough to be like the other young fellows who drank a good deal and
15 wenched a little without any question, and were satisfied.

He went on stubbornly for a time. Then the strain became too
great for him. A hot, accumulated consciousness was always awake
in his chest, his wrists felt swelled and quivering, his mind became
full of lustful images, his eyes seemed blood-flushed. He fought with
20 himself furiously, to remain normal. He did not seek any woman. He
just went on as if he were normal. Till he must either take some
action or beat his head against the wall.

Then he went deliberately to Ilkeston, in silence, intent and
beaten. He drank to get drunk. He gulped down the brandy, and
25 more brandy, till his face became pale, his eyes burning. And still he
could not get free. He went to sleep in drunken unconsciousness,
woke up at four o'clock in the morning and continued drinking. He
would get free. Gradually the tension in him began to relax. He began
to feel happy. His riveted silence was unfastened, he began to talk
30 and babble. He was happy and at one with all the world, he was
united with all flesh in a hot blood-relationship. So, after three days
of incessant brandy-drinking, he had burned out the youth from his
blood, he had achieved this kindled state of oneness with all the
world, which is the end of youth's most passionate desire. But he had
35 achieved his satisfaction by obliterating his own individuality, that
which it depended on his manhood to preserve and develop.

So he became a bout-drinker, having at intervals these bouts of
three or four days of brandy-drinking, when he was drunk for the
whole time. He did not think about it. A deep resentment burned in
40 him. He kept aloof from any women, antagonistic.

When he was twenty eight, a thick-limbed, stiff, fair man with fresh complexion, and blue eyes staring very straight ahead, he was coming one day from Cossethay with a load of seed out of Nottingham. It was a time when he was getting ready for another bout of drinking, so he stared fixedly before him, watchful yet absorbed, seeing everything and aware of nothing, coiled in himself. It was early in the year.

He walked steadily beside the horse, the load clanked behind as the hill descended steeper. The road curved downhill before him, under banks and hedges, seen only for a few yards ahead.

Slowly turning the curve at the steepest part of the slope, his horse britching* between the shafts, he saw a woman approaching. But he was thinking for the moment of the horse.

Then he turned to look at her. She was dressed in black, was apparently rather small and slight, beneath her long black cloak, and she wore a black bonnet. She walked hastily, as if unseeing, her head rather forward. It was her curious, absorbed, flitting motion, as if she were passing unseen by everybody, that first arrested him.

She had heard the cart, and looked up. Her face was pale and clear, she had thick dark eyebrows and a wide mouth, curiously held. He saw her face clearly, as if by a light in the air. He saw her face so distinctly, that he ceased to coil on himself, and was suspended.

"That's her," he said involuntarily. As the cart passed by, splashing through the thin mud, she stood back against the bank. Then, as he walked still beside his britching horse, his eyes met hers. He looked quickly away, pressing back his head, a pain of joy running through him. He could not bear to think of anything.

He turned round at the last moment. He saw her bonnet, her shape in the black cloak, the movement as she walked. Then she was gone round the bend.

She had passed by. He felt as if he were walking again in a far world, not Cossethay, a far world, the fragile reality. He went on, quiet, suspended, rarified. He could not bear to think or to speak, nor make any sound or sign, nor change his fixed motion. He could scarcely bear to think of her face. He moved within the knowledge of her, in the world that was beyond reality.

The feeling that they had exchanged recognition possessed him like a madness, like a torment. How could he be sure, what confirmation had he? The doubt was like a sense of infinite space, a

nothingness, annihilating. He kept within his breast the will to
surety. They had exchanged recognition.

   He walked about in this state for the next few days. And then again
like a mist it began to break to let through the common, barren
5 world. He was very gentle with man and beast, but he dreaded the
starkness of disillusion cropping through again.

   As he was standing with his back to the fire after dinner a few days
later, he saw the woman passing. He wanted to know that she knew
him, that she was aware. He wanted it said that there was something
10 between them. So he stood anxiously watching, looking at her as she
went down the road. He called to Tilly.

   "Who might that be?" he asked.

   Tilly, the cross-eyed woman of forty, who adored him, ran gladly
to the window to look. She was glad when he asked her for anything.
15 She craned her head over the short curtain, the little tight knob of
her black hair sticking out pathetically as she bobbed about.

   "Oh why—" she lifted her head and peered with her twisted, keen
brown eyes—"why, you know who it is—it's her from th' vicarage—
you know—"

20   "*How* do I know, you hen-bird," he shouted.

   Tilly blushed and drew her neck in and looked at him with her
squinting, sharp, almost reproachful look.

   "Why you do—it's the new housekeeper."

   "Ay—an' what by that?"

25   "Well, an' *what* by that?" rejoined the indignant Tilly.

   "She's a woman, isn't she, housekeeper or no housekeeper? She's
got more to her than that! Who is she—she's got a name?"

   "Well, if she has, *I* don't know," retorted Tilly, not to be badgered
by this lad who had grown up into a man.

30   "What's her name?" he asked, more gently.

   "I'm sure I couldn't tell you," replied Tilly, on her dignity.

   "An' is that all as you've gathered, as she's housekeeping at the
vicarage?"

   "I've 'eered mention of 'er name, but I couldn't remember it for
35 my life."

   "Why yer riddle-skulled woman o' nonsense, what have you got a
head for?"

   "For what other folks 'as got theirs for," retorted Tilly, who loved
nothing more than these tilts when he would call her names.

There was a lull.

"I don't believe as anybody could keep it in their head," the woman-servant continued, tentatively.

"What?" he asked.

"Why, 'er name." 5

"How's that?"

"She's fra some foreign parts or other."

"Who told you that?"

"That's all I do know, as she is."

"An' wheer do you reckon she's from, then?" 10

"I don't know. They do say as she hails fra th' Pole. *I* don't know," Tilly hastened to add, knowing he would attack her.

"Fra th' Pole, why do *you* hail fra th' Pole? Who's set up that menagerie confabulation?"*

"That's what they say—*I* don't know—" 15

"Who says?"

"Mrs Bentley—says as she's fra th' Pole—else she *is* a Pole, or summat."*

Tilly was only afraid she was landing herself deeper now.

"Who says she's a Pole?" 20

"They all say so."

"Then what's brought her to these parts?"

"I couldn't tell you. She's got a little girl with her."

"Got a little girl with her?"

"Of three or four, with a head like a fuzz-ball."* 25

"Black?"

"White—fair as can be, an' all of a fuzz."

"Is there a father, then?"

"Not to my knowledge. I don't know."

"What brought her here?" 30

"I couldn't say, without th' vicar axed* her."

"Is the child her child?"

"I s'd think so—they say so."

"Who told you about her?"

"Why Lizzie—a-Monday—we seed her goin' past." 35

"You'd have to be rattling your tongues if anything went past."

Brangwen stood musing. That evening he went up to Cossethay to the "Red Lion," half with the intention of hearing more.

She was the widow of a Polish doctor, he gathered. Her husband had died, a refugee, in London. She spoke a bit foreign like, but you could easily make out what she said. She had one little girl, named Anna. Lensky was the woman's name, Mrs Lensky.

Brangwen felt that here was the unreality established at last. He
5 felt also a curious certainty about her, as if she were destined to him. It was to him a profound satisfaction that she was a foreigner.

A swift change had taken place on the earth for him, as if a new creation were fulfilled, in which he had real existence. Things had all been stark, unreal, barren, mere nullities before. Now they were
10 actualities that he could handle.

He dared scarcely think of the woman. He was afraid. Only all the time he was aware of her presence not far off, he lived in her. But he dared not know her, even acquaint himself with her by thinking of her.

15 One day he met her walking along the road with her little girl. It was a child with a face like a bud of apple-blossom, and glistening fair hair like thistle-down sticking out in straight, wild, flamy pieces, and very dark eyes. The child clung jealously to her mother's side when he looked at her, staring with resentful black eyes. But the
20 mother glanced at him again, almost vacantly. And the very vacancy of her look inflamed him. She had wide grey-brown eyes with very dark, fathomless pupils. He felt the fine flame running under his skin, as if all his veins had caught fire on the surface. And he went on walking without knowledge.

25 It was coming, he knew, his fate. The world was submitting to its transformation. He made no move: it would come, what would come.

When his sister Effie came to the Marsh for a week, he went with her for once to church. In the tiny place, with its mere dozen pews,
30 he sat not far from the stranger. There was a fineness about her, a poignancy about the way she sat and held her head lifted. She was strange, from far off, yet so intimate. She was from far away, a presence, so close to his soul. She was not really there, sitting in Cossethay church beside her little girl. She was not living the
35 apparent life of her days. She belonged to somewhere else. He felt it poignantly, as something real and natural. But a pang of fear for his own concrete life, that was only Cossethay, hurt him, and gave him misgiving.

Her thick dark brows almost met above her irregular nose, she
40 had a wide, rather thick mouth. But her face was lifted to another

world of life: not to heaven or death: but to some place where she still lived, in spite of her body's absence.

The child beside her watched everything with wide, black eyes. She had an odd little defiant look, her little red mouth was pinched shut. She seemed to be jealously guarding something, to be always 5 on the alert for defense. She met Brangwen's near, vacant, intimate gaze, and a palpitating hostility, almost like a flame of pain, came into the wide, over-conscious dark eyes.

The old clergyman droned on, Cossethay sat unmoved as usual. And there was the foreign woman with a foreign land vivid* about 10 her, inviolate, and the strange child, also foreign, jealously guarding something.

When the service was over, he walked in the daze of another existence out of the church. As he went down the church-path with his sister, behind the woman and child, the little girl suddenly broke 15 from her mother's hand, and slipped back with quick, almost invisible movement, and was picking at something almost under Brangwen's feet. Her tiny fingers were fine and quick, but they missed the red button.

"Have you found something?" said Brangwen to her. 20

And he also stooped for the button. But she had got it, and she stood back with it pressed against her little coat, her black eyes flaring at him, as if to forbid him to notice her. Then, having silenced him, she turned with a swift

"Mother—," and was gone down the path. 25

The mother had stood watching impassive, looking not at the child, but at Brangwen. He became aware of the woman looking at him, standing there isolated yet for him dominant in her foreign existence.

He did not know what to do, and turned to his sister. But the wide 30 grey eyes, almost vacant yet so moving, held him beyond himself.

"Mother, I may have it, mayn't I?" came the child's proud, silvery tones. "Mother"—she seemed always to be calling her mother to remember her—"Mother—" and she had nothing to continue, now her mother had replied "Yes my child." But, with ready invention, 35 the child stumbled and ran on "What are those people's names?"

Brangwen heard the abstract:

"I don't know dear."

He went on down the road as if he were not living inside himself, but somewhere outside. 40

"Who *was* that person?" his sister Effie asked.

"I couldn't tell you," he answered unknowing.

"She's *somebody* very funny," said Effie, almost in condemnation. "That child's like one bewitched."

5   "Bewitched—how bewitched?" he repeated.

"You can see for yourself. The mother's plain, I must say—but the child is like a changeling. She'd be about thirty five."

But he took no notice. His sister talked on.

"There's your woman for you," she continued. "You'd better
10 marry *her*." But still he took no notice. Things were as they were.

Another day, at tea-time, as he sat alone at table, there came a knock at the front door. It startled him like a portent. No-one ever knocked at the front door. He rose and began slotting back the bolts, turning the big key. When he had opened the door, the strange
15 woman stood on the threshold.

"Can you give me a pound of butter?" she asked, in the curious detached way of one speaking a foreign language.

He tried to attend to her question. She was looking at him questioningly. But underneath the question, what was there, in her
20 very standing motionless, which affected him?

He stepped aside and she at once entered the house, as if the door had been opened to admit her. That startled him. It was the custom for everybody to wait on the doorstep till asked inside. He went into the kitchen and she followed.

25 His tea-things were spread on the scrubbed deal table, a big fire was burning, a dog rose from the hearth and went to her. She stood motionless just inside the kitchen.

"Tilly," he called loudly, "have we got any butter?"

The stranger stood there like a silence in her black cloak.

30 "Eh?" came the shrill cry from the distance.

He shouted his question again.

"We've got what's on t' table," answered Tilly's shrill voice out of the dairy.

Brangwen looked at the table. There was a large pat of butter on a
35 plate, almost a pound. It was round, and stamped with acorns and oak-leaves.

"Can't you come when you're wanted?" he shouted. ·

"Why what d'you want?" Tilly protested, as she came peeking inquisitively through the other door.

She saw the strange woman, stared at her with cross eyes, but said nothing.

"*Haven't* we any butter?" asked Brangwen again, impatiently, as if he could command some by his question.

"I tell you there's what's on t' table," said Tilly, impatient that she   5
was unable to create any to his demand. "We haven't a morsel besides."

There was a moment's silence.

Then the stranger spoke, in her curiously distinct, detached manner of one who must think her speech first.   10

"Oh, then thank you very much. I am sorry that I have come to trouble you."

She could not understand the entire lack of manners, was slightly puzzled. Any politeness would have made the situation quite impersonal. But here it was a case of wills in confusion. Brangwen   15
flushed at her polite speech. Still he did not let her go.

"Get summat an' wrap *that* up for her," he said to Tilly, looking at the butter on the table.

And taking a clean knife, he cut off that side of the butter where it was touched.   20

His speech, the "for her," penetrated slowly into the foreign woman, and angered Tilly.

"Vicar has his butter fra Brown's by rights," said the insuppressible servant-woman. "We s'll be churnin' tomorrow mornin' first thing."   25

"Yes"—the long-drawn foreign yes—"Yes," said the Polish woman, "I went to Mrs Brown's. She hasn't any more."

Tilly bridled her head, bursting to say that, according to the etiquette of people who bought butter, it was no sort of manners whatever coming to a place as cool as you like and knocking at the   30
front door asking for a pound as a stop-gap while your other people were short. If you go to Brown's you go to Brown's, an' my butter isn't just to make shift when Brown's has got none.

Brangwen understood perfectly this unspoken speech of Tilly's. The Polish lady did not. And as she wanted butter for the vicar, and   35
as Tilly was churning in the morning, she waited.

"Sluther up* now," said Brangwen loudly after this silence had resolved itself out; and Tilly disappeared through the inner door.

"I am afraid that I should not come, so," said the stranger, looking at him inquiringly, as if referring to him for what it was usual to do.

He felt confused.

"How's that?" he said, trying to be genial and being only
5   protective.

"Do you—?" she began deliberately. But she was not sure of her ground, and the conversation came to an end. Her eyes looked at him all the while, because she could not speak the language.

They stood facing each other. The dog walked away from her to
10 him. He bent down to it.

"And how's your little girl?" he asked.

"Yes, thank you, she is very well," was the reply, a phrase of polite speech in a foreign language, merely.

"Sit you down," he said.

15 And she sat in a chair, her slim arms, coming through the slits of her cloak, resting on her lap.

"You're not used to these parts," he said, still standing on the hearthrug with his back to the fire, coatless, looking with curious directness at the woman. Her self-possession pleased him and
20 inspired him, set him curiously free. It seemed to him almost brutal to feel so master of himself and of the situation.

Her eyes rested on him for a moment, questioning, as she thought of the meaning of his speech.

"No," she said, understanding. "No—it is strange."

25 "You find it middlin' rough?" he said.

"—a— —" Her eyes waited on him, so that he should say it again.

"Our ways are rough to you," he repeated.

"Yes—yes, I understand. Yes, it is different, it is strange. But I was in Yorkshire—"

30 "Oh well then," he said, "it's no worse here than what they are up there."

She did not quite understand. His protective manner, and his sureness, and his intimacy, puzzled her. What did he mean? If he was her equal, why did he behave so without formality?

35 "No—" she said, vaguely, her eyes resting on him.

She saw him fresh and naïve, uncouth, almost entirely beyond relationship with her. Yet he was good-looking, with his fair hair and blue eyes full of energy, and with his healthy body that seemed to take equality with her. She watched him steadily. He was difficult for
40 her to understand, warm, uncouth, and confident as he was, sure on

his feet as if he did not know what it was to be unsure. What then was
it that gave him this curious stability?

She did not know. She wondered. She looked round the room he
lived in. It had a close intimacy that fascinated and almost frightened
her. The furniture was old and familiar as old people, the whole   5
place seemed so kin to him, as if it partook of his being, that she was
uneasy.

"It is already a long time that you have lived in this house—yes?"
she asked.

"I've always lived here," he said.   10

"Yes—but your people—your family?"

"We've been here above *two* hundred years,"* he said.

Her eyes were on him all the time, wide-open and trying to grasp
him. He felt that he was there for her.

"It is your own place, the house, the farm—?"   15

"Yes," he said.

He looked down at her and met her look. It disturbed her. She did
not know him. He was a foreigner, they had nothing to do with each
other. Yet his look disturbed her to knowledge of him. He was so
strangely confident and direct.   20

"You live quite alone?"

"Yes—if you call it alone."

She did not understand. It seemed unusual to her. What was the
meaning of it?

And whenever her eyes, after watching him for some time,   25
inevitably met his, she was aware of a heat beating up over her
consciousness. She sat motionless and in conflict. Who was this
strange man who was at once so near to her? What was happening to
her? Something in his young, warm-twinkling eyes seemed to
assume a right to her, to speak to her, to extend her his protection. 30
But how? Why did he speak to her! Why were his eyes so certain, so
full of light and confident, waiting for no permission nor signal.

Tilly returned with a large leaf* and found the two silent. At once
he felt it incumbent on him to speak, now the serving-woman had
come back.   35

"How old is your little girl?" he asked.

"Four years,"* she replied.

"Her father hasn't been dead long, then?" he asked.

"She was one year when he died."

"Three years?"   40

"Yes, three years that he is dead—yes."

Curiously quiet she was, almost abstracted, answering these questions. She looked at him again, with some maidenhood opening in her eyes. He felt he could not move, neither towards her nor away
5 from her. Something about her presence hurt him, till he was almost rigid before her. He saw the girl's wondering look rise in her eyes.

Tilly handed her the butter, and she rose.

"Thank you very much," she said. "How much is it?"

"We'll make th' vicar a present of it," he said. "It'll do for me goin'
10 to church."

"It 'ud look better of you if you went to church and took th' money for your butter," said Tilly, persistent in her claim to him.

"You'd have to put in, shouldn't you?" he said.

"How much, please?" said the Polish woman to Tilly.
15 Brangwen stood by and let be.

"Then, thank you very much," she said.

"Bring your little girl down sometime to look at th' fowls and horses," he said; "—if she'd like it."

"Yes, she would like it," said the stranger.
20 And she went. Brangwen stood dimmed by her departure. He could not notice Tilly, who was looking at him uneasily, wanting to be reassured. He could not think of anything. He felt that he had made some invisible connection with the strange woman.

A daze had come over his mind, he had another centre of
25 consciousness. In his breast, or in his bowels, somewhere in his body, there had started another activity. It was as if a strong light were burning there, and he was blind within it, unable to know anything, except that this transfiguration burned between him and her, connecting them, like a secret power.
30 Since she had come to the house he went about in a daze, scarcely seeing even the things he handled, drifting, quiescent, in a state of metamorphosis. He submitted to that which was happening to him, letting go of his will, suffering the loss of himself, dormant always on the brink of ecstasy, like a creature evolving to a new birth.
35 She came twice with her child to the farm, but there was this lull between them, an intense calm and passivity like a torpor upon them, so that* no active change took place. He was almost unaware of the child, yet by his native good-humour he gained her confidence, even her affection, setting her on the horse to ride, giving her corn
40 for the fowls.

Once he drove the mother and child from Ilkeston, picking them up on the road. The child huddled close to him as if for love, the mother sat very still. There was a vagueness, like a soft mist over all of them, and a silence as if their wills were suspended. Only he saw her hands, ungloved, folded in her lap, and he noticed the wedding-ring* on her finger. It excluded him: it was a closed circle. It bound her life, the wedding-ring, it stood for her life in which he could have no part. Nevertheless, beyond all this, there was herself and himself which should meet.

As he helped her down from the trap, almost lifting her, he felt he had some right to take her thus between his hands. She belonged as yet to that other, to that which was behind. But he must care for her also. She was too living to be neglected.

Sometimes her vagueness, in which he was lost, made him angry, made him rage. But he held himself still as yet. She had no response, no being towards him. It puzzled and enraged him, but he submitted for a long time. Then, from the accumulated troubling of her ignoring him, gradually a fury broke out, destructive, and he wanted to go away, to escape her.

It happened she came down to the Marsh with the child whilst he was in this state. Then he stood over against her, strong and heavy in his revolt, and though he said nothing, still she felt his anger and heavy impatience grip hold of her, she was shaken again as out of a torpor. Again her heart stirred with a quick, out-running impulse, she looked at him, at the stranger who was not a gentleman yet who insisted on coming into her life, and the pain of a new birth in herself strung all her veins to a new form. She would have to begin again, to find a new being, a new form, to respond to that blind, insistent figure standing over against her.

A shiver, a sickness of new birth passed over her, the flame leaped up him, under his skin. She wanted it, this new life from him, with him, yet she must defend herself against it, for it was a destruction.

As he worked alone on the land, or sat up with his ewes at lambing time, the facts and material of his daily life fell away, leaving the kernel of his purpose clean. And then it came upon him that he would marry her and she would be his life.

Gradually, even without seeing her, he came to know her. He would have liked to think of her as of something given into his protection, like a child without parents. But it was forbidden him. He had to come down from this pleasant view of the case. She might refuse him. And besides, he was afraid of her.

But during the long February nights with the ewes in labour, looking out from the shelter into the flashing stars, he knew he did
5   not belong to himself. He must admit that he was only fragmentary, something incomplete and subject. There were the stars in the dark heaven travelling, the whole host passing by on some eternal voyage. So he sat small and submissive to the greater ordering.

Unless she would come to him, he must remain as a nothingness.
10 It was a hard experience. But, after her repeated obliviousness to him, after he had seen so often that he did not exist for her, after he had raged and tried to escape, and said he was good enough by himself, he was a man, and could stand alone, he must, in the starry multiplicity of the night humble himself, and admit and know that
15 without her he was nothing.

He was nothing. But with her, he would be real. If she were now walking across the frosty grass near the sheep-shelter, through the fretful bleating of the ewes and lambs, she would bring him completeness and perfection. And if it should be so, that she should
20 come to him! It should be so—it was ordained so.

He was a long time resolving definitely to ask her to marry him. And he knew, if he asked her, she must really acquiesce. She must, it could not be otherwise.

He had learned a little of her. She was poor, quite alone, and had
25 had a hard time in London, both before and after her husband died. But in Poland she was a lady well born, a landowner's daughter.

All these things were only words to him, the fact of her superior birth, the fact that her husband had been a brilliant doctor, the fact that he himself was her inferior in almost every way of distinction.
30 There was an inner reality, a logic of the soul, which connected her with him.

One evening in March, when the wind was roaring outside, came the moment to ask her. He had sat with his hands before him leaning to the fire. And as he watched the fire, he knew almost without
35 thinking that he was going this evening.

"Have you got a clean shirt?" he asked Tilly.

"You know you've got clean shirts," she said.

"Ay,—bring me a white one."

Tilly brought down one of the linen shirts he had inherited from
40 his father, putting it before him to air at the fire. She loved him with a

dumb, aching love as he sat leaning with his arms on his knees, still
and absorbed, unaware of her. Lately, a quivering inclination to cry
had come over her, when she did anything for him in his presence.
Now her hands trembled as she spread the shirt. He was never
shouting and teasing now. The deep stillness there was in the house 5
made her tremble.

He went to wash himself. Queer little breaks of consciousness
seemed to rise and burst like bubbles out of the depths of his
stillness.

"It's got to be done," he said as he stooped to take the shirt out of 10
the fender, "it's got to be done, so why balk it?" And as he combed
his hair before the mirror on the wall, he retorted to himself,
superficially: "The woman's not speechless dumb. She's not clutterin'* at the nipple. She's got the right to please herself, and
displease whosoever she likes." 15

This streak of commonsense carried him a little further.

"Did you want anythink?" asked Tilly, suddenly appearing,
having heard him speak. She stood watching him comb his fair
beard. His eyes were calm and uninterrupted.

"Ay," he said, "where have you put the scissors." 20

She brought them to him, and stood watching as, chin forward, he
trimmed his beard.

"Don't go an' crop yourself as if you was at a shearin' contest," she
said, anxiously. He blew the fine-curled hair quickly off his lips.

He put on all clean clothes, folded his stock carefully, and donned 25
his best coat. Then, being ready, as grey twilight was falling, he went
across to the orchard to gather the daffodils. The wind was roaring in
the apple-trees, the yellow flowers swayed violently up and down, he
heard even the fine whisper of their spears as he stooped to break the
flattened, brittle stems of the flowers. 30

"What's to-do?" shouted a friend who met him as he left the
garden gate.

"Bit of courtin', like," said Brangwen.

And Tilly, in a great state of trepidation and excitement, let the
wind whisk her over the field to the big gate, whence she could watch 35
him go.

He went up the hill and on towards the vicarage, the wind roaring
through the hedges, whilst he tried to shelter his bunch of daffodils
by his side. He did not think of anything, only knew that the wind was
blowing. 40

Night was falling, the bare trees drummed and whistled. The vicar, he knew, would be in his study, the Polish woman in the kitchen, a comfortable room, with her child. In the darkest of twilight, he went through the gate and down the path where a few
5　daffodils stooped in the wind, and shattered crocuses made a pale, colourless ravel.

There was a light streaming on to the bushes at the back from the kitchen window. He began to hesitate. How could he do this? Looking through the window, he saw her seated in the rocking chair
10　with the child, already in its nightdress, sitting on her knee. The fair head with its wild, fierce hair was drooping towards the fire-warmth, which reflected on the bright cheeks and clear skin of the child, who seemed to be musing, almost like a grown-up person. The mother's face was dark and still, and he saw, with a pang, that she was away
15　back in the life that had been. The child's hair gleamed like spun glass, her face was illuminated till it seemed like wax lit up from the inside. The wind boomed strongly. Mother and child sat motionless, silent, the child staring with vacant dark eyes into the fire, the mother looking into space. The little girl was almost asleep. It was her will
20　which kept her eyes so wide.

Suddenly she looked round, troubled, as the wind shook the house, and Brangwen saw the small lips move. The mother began to rock, he heard the slight crunch of the rockers of the chair. Then he heard the low, monotonous murmur of a song in a foreign language.
25　Then a great burst of wind, the mother seemed to have drifted away, the child's eyes were black and dilated. Brangwen looked up at the clouds which packed in great, alarming haste across the dark sky.

Then there came the child's high, complaining, yet imperative voice:
30　"Don't sing that stuff, mother, I don't want to hear it."

The singing died away.

"You will go to bed," said the mother.

He saw the clinging protest of the child, the unmoved far-awayness of the mother, the clinging, grasping effort of the child.
35　Then suddenly the clear childish challenge:

"I want you to tell me a story."

The wind blew, the story began, the child nestled against the mother, Brangwen waited outside, suspended, looking at the wild waving of the trees in the wind and the gathering darkness. He had
40　his fate to follow, he lingered here at the threshold.

The child crouched distinct and motionless, curled in against her mother, the eyes dark and unblinking among the keen fleece* of hair, like a curled up animal asleep but for the eyes. The mother sat as if in shadow, the story went on as if by itself. Brangwen stood outside seeing the night fall. He did not notice the passage of time. 5
The hand that held the daffodils was fixed and cold.

The story came to an end, the mother rose at last, with the child clinging round her neck. She must be strong, to carry so large a child so easily. The little Anna clung round her mother's neck. The fair, strange face of the child looked over the shoulder of the 10
mother, all asleep but the eyes, and these, wide and dark, kept up the resistance and the fight with something unseen.

When they were gone, Brangwen stirred for the first time from the place where he stood, and looked round at the night. He wished it were really as beautiful and familiar as it seemed in these few 15
moments of release. Along with the child, he felt a curious strain on him, a suffering, like a fate.

The mother came down again, and began folding the child's clothes. He knocked. She opened wondering, a little bit at bay, like a foreigner, uneasy. 20

"Good-evening," he said. "I'll just come in a minute."

A change went quickly over her face; she was unprepared. She looked down at him as he stood in the light from the window, holding the daffodils, the darkness behind. In his black clothes she again did not know him, she was almost afraid. 25

But he was already stepping on to the threshold, and closing the door behind him. She turned into the kitchen, startled out of herself by this invasion from the night. He took off his hat, and came towards her. Then he stood in the light, in his black clothes and his black stock, hat in one hand and yellow flowers in the other. 30
She stood away, at his mercy, snatched out of herself. She did not know him, only she knew he was a man come for her. She could only see the dark-clad man's figure standing there upon her, and the gripped fist of flowers. She could not see the face and the living eyes. 35

He was watching her, without knowing her, only aware underneath of her presence.

"I come to have a word with you," he said, striding forward to the table, laying down his hat and the flowers, which tumbled apart and lay in a loose heap. She had flinched from his advance. She 40 had no will, no being. The wind boomed in the chimney, and he waited. He had disembarrassed his hands. Now he shut his fists.

He was aware of her standing there unknown, dread, yet related to him.

5 "I came up," he said, speaking curiously matter-of-fact and level, "to ask if you'd marry me. You are free, aren't you?"

There was a long silence, whilst his blue eyes, strangely impersonal, looked into her eyes to seek an answer to the truth. He was looking for the truth out of her. And she, as if hypnotised, must
10 answer at length:

"Yes. I am free to marry."

The expression of his eyes changed, became less impersonal, as if he were looking almost at her, for the truth of her.* Steady and intent and eternal they were, as if they would never change. They seemed
15 to fix and to resolve her. She quivered, feeling herself created, will-less, lapsing into him, into a common will with him.

"You want me?" she said.

A pallor came over his face.

"Yes," he said.
20 Still there was suspense and silence.

"No," she said, not of herself. "No, I don't know."

He felt the tension breaking up in him, his fists slackened, he was unable to move. He stood looking at her, helpless in his vague collapse. For the moment she had become unreal to him. Then he
25 saw her come to him, curiously direct and as if without movement, in a sudden flow. She put her hand to his coat.

"Yes I want to," she said, impersonally, looking at him with wide, candid, newly-opened eyes, opened now with supreme truth. He went very white as he stood, and did not move, only his eyes were
30 held by hers, and he suffered. She seemed to see him with her newly-opened, wide eyes, almost of a child, and with a strange movement, that was agony to him, she reached slowly forward her dark face and her breast to him, with a slow insinuation of a kiss that made something break in his brain, and it was darkness over him for
35 a few moments.

He had her in his arms, and, obliterated, was kissing her. And it was sheer, blenched agony to him, to break away from himself. She was there so small and light and accepting in his arms, like a child, and yet with such an insinuation of embrace, of infinite embrace, that
40 he could not bear it, he could not stand.

He turned and looked for a chair, and keeping her still in his arms, sat down with her close to him, to his breast. Then, for a few seconds, he went utterly to sleep, asleep and sealed in the darkest sleep, utter, extreme oblivion.

From which he came to gradually, always holding her warm and   5 close upon him, and she as utterly silent as he, involved in the same oblivion, the fecund darkness.

He returned gradually, but newly created, as after a gestation, a new birth, in the womb of darkness. Aërial and light everything was, new as a morning, fresh and newly begun. Like a dawn the newness   10 and the bliss filled in. And she sat utterly still with him, as if in the same.

Then she looked up at him, the wide, young eyes blazing with light. And he bent down and kissed her on the lips. And the dawn blazed in them, their new life came to pass, it was beyond all   15 conceiving good, it was so good, that it was almost like a passing-away, a trespass.* He drew her suddenly close to him.

For soon the light began to fade in her, gradually, and as she was in his arms, her head sank, she leaned it against him, and lay still, with sunk head, a little tired, effaced because she was tired. And in   20 her tiredness was a certain negation of him.

"There is the child," she said, out of the long silence.

He did not understand. It was a long time since he had heard a voice. Now also he heard the wind roaring, as if it had just begun again.   25

"Yes," he said, not understanding. There was a slight contraction of pain at his heart, a slight tension on his brows. Something he wanted to grasp and could not.

"You will love her?" she said.

The quick contraction, like pain, went over him again.   30

"I love her now," he said.

She lay still against him, taking his physical warmth without heed. It was great confirmation for him to feel her there, absorbing the warmth from him, giving him back her weight and her strange confidence. But where was she, that she seemed so absent? His mind   35 was open with wonder. He did not know her.

"But I am much older than you," she said.

"How old?" he asked.

"I am thirty four," she said.

"I am twenty eight,"* he said.   40

"Six years."

She was oddly concerned, even as if it pleased her a little. He sat
and listened and wondered. It was rather splendid, to be so ignored
by her, whilst she lay against him, and he lifted her with his
5   breathing, and felt her weight upon his living, so he had a completeness and an inviolable power. He did not interfere with her. He
did not even know her. It was so strange that she lay there with her
weight abandoned upon him. He was silent with delight. He felt
strong, physically, carrying her on his breathing. The strange,
10   inviolable completeness of the two of them made him feel as sure and
as stable as God. Amused, he wondered what the vicar would say if
he knew.

"You needn't stop here much longer, housekeeping," he said.

"I like it also, here," she said. "When one has been in many
15   places, it is very nice here."

He was silent again at this. So close on him she lay, and yet she
answered him from so far away. But he did not mind.

"What was your own home like, when you were little?" he asked.

"My father was a landowner," she replied. "It was near a river."

20   This did not convey much to him. All was as vague as before. But
he did not care, whilst she was so close.

"I am a landowner—a little one," he said.

"Yes," she said.

He had not dared to move. He sat there with his arms round her,
25   her lying motionless on his breathing, and for a long time he did not
stir. Then softly, timidly, his hand settled on the roundness of her
arm, on the unknown. She seemed to lie a little closer. A hot flame
licked up from his belly to his chest.

But it was too soon. She rose, and went across the room to a
30   drawer, taking out a little tray-cloth. There was something quiet and
professional about her. She had been a nurse beside her husband,
both in Warsaw and in the rebellion afterwards. She proceeded to set
a tray. It was as if she ignored Brangwen. He sat up, unable to bear a
contradiction in her.* She moved about inscrutably.

35   Then, as he sat there, all unused and wondering, she came near to
him, looking at him with wide, grey eyes that almost smiled with a
low light. But her ugly-beautiful mouth was still unmoved and sad.
He was afraid.

His eyes, strained and roused with unusedness, quailed a little
40   before her, he felt himself quailing and yet he rose, as if obedient,

and as if obedient to her, he bent and kissed her heavy, sad, wide
mouth, that was kissed, and did not alter. Fear was too strong in him.
Again he had not got her.

She turned away. The vicarage kitchen was untidy, and yet to him
beautiful with the untidiness of her and her child. Such a wonderful   5
remoteness there was about her, and then something in touch with
him, that made his heart knock in his chest. He stood there and
waited, suspended.

Again she came to him, as he stood in his black clothes, with blue
eyes very bright and puzzled for her, his face tensely alive, his hair   10
dishevelled. She came close up to him, to his intent, black-clothed
body, and laid her hand on his arm. He remained unmoved. Her
eyes, with a blackness of memory struggling with passion, primitive
and electric away at the back of them, rejected him and absorbed him
at once. But he remained himself. He breathed with difficulty, and   15
sweat came out at the roots of his hair, on his forehead.

"Do you want to marry me?" she asked slowly, always uncertain.

He was afraid lest he could not speak. He drew breath hard,
saying:

"I do."   20

Then again, what was agony to him, with one hand lightly resting
on his arm, she leaned forward a little, and with a strange, primeval
suggestion of embrace, held him her mouth. It was ugly-beautiful,
and he could not bear it. He put his mouth on hers, and slowly,
slowly the response came, gathering force and passion, till it seemed   25
to him she was thundering at him till he could bear no more. He
drew away, white, unbreathing. Only, in his blue eyes, was something of himself concentrated. And in her eyes was a little smile upon
a black void.

She was drifting away from him again. And he wanted to go away.   30
It was intolerable. He could bear no more. He must go. Yet he was
irresolute. But she turned away from him.

With a little pang of anguish, of denial, it was decided.

"I'll come an' speak to the vicar tomorrow," he said, taking his hat.

She looked at him, her eyes expressionless and full of darkness.   35
He could see no answer.

"That'll do, won't it?" he said.

"Yes," she answered, mere echo without body or meaning.

"Goodnight," he said.

"Goodnight."   40

He left her standing there, expressionless and void as she was. Then she went on laying the tray for the vicar. Needing the table, she put the daffodils aside on the dresser without noticing them. Only their coolness, touching her hand, remained echoing there a long
5   while.

They were such strangers, they must forever be such strangers, that his passion was a clanging torment to him. Such intimacy of embrace, and such utter foreignness of contact! It was unbearable. He could not bear to be near her, and know the utter foreignness
10 between them, know how entirely they were strangers to each other. He went out into the wind. Big holes were blown into the sky, the moonlight blew about. Sometimes a high moon, liquid-brilliant, scudded across a hollow space and took cover under electric, brown-iridescent cloud-edges. Then there was a blot of cloud, and
15 shadow. Then somewhere in the night a radiance again, like a vapour. And all the sky was teeming and tearing along, a vast disorder of flying shapes and darknesses and ragged fumes of light and a great brown circling halo, then the terror of a moon running liquid-brilliant into the open for a moment, hurting the eyes before
20 she plunged under cover of cloud again.

Chapter II

They Live at the Marsh

She was the daughter of a Polish landowner* who, deeply in debt to the Jews, had married a German wife with money, and who had died just before the rebellion. Quite young, she had married Paul Lensky, an intellectual who had studied at Berlin, and had returned to Warsaw a patriot.* Her mother had married a German merchant and gone away.

Lydia Lensky, married to the young doctor, became with him a patriot and an émancipée. They were poor, but they were very conceited. She learned nursing as a mark of her emancipation. They represented in Poland the new movement just begun in Russia. But they were very patriotic: and, at the same time, very "European."*

They had two children. Then came the great rebellion.* Lensky, very ardent and full of words, went about inciting his countrymen. Little Poles flamed down the streets of Warsaw, on the way to shoot every Muscovite. So they crossed into the south of Russia, and it was common for six little insurgents to ride into a Jewish village, brandishing swords and words, emphasising the fact that they were going to shoot every living Muscovite.*

Lensky was something of a fire-eater also. Lydia, tempered by her German blood, coming of a different family, was obliterated, carried along in her husband's emphasis of declaration, and his whirl of patriotism. He was indeed a brave man, but no bravery could quite have equalled the vividness of his talk. He worked very hard, till nothing lived in him but his eyes. And Lydia, as if drugged, followed him like a shadow, serving, echoing. Sometimes she had her two children, sometimes they were left behind.

She returned once to find them both dead of diphtheria. Her husband wept aloud, unaware of everybody. But the war went on, and soon he was back at his work. A darkness had come over Lydia's mind. She walked always in a shadow, silenced, with a strange, deep terror having hold of her, her desire was to seek satisfaction in dread, to enter a nunnery, to satisfy the instincts of dread in her through service of a dark religion. But she could not.

49

Then came the flight to London. Lensky, the little, thin man, had got all his life locked into a resistance and could not relax again. He lived in a sort of insane irritability, touchy, haughty to the last degree, fractious, so that as assistant doctor in one of the hospitals he soon
5 became impossible. They were almost beggars. But he kept still his great ideas of himself, he seemed to live in a complete hallucination, where he himself figured vivid and lordly. He guarded his wife jealously against the ignominy of her position, rushed round her like a brandished weapon,* an amazing sight to the English eye, had her
10 in his power, as if he hypnotised her. She was passive, dark, always in shadow.

He was wasting away. Already when the child was born he seemed nothing but skin and bone and fixed idea. She watched him dying, nursed him, nursed the baby, but really took no notice of anything. A
15 darkness was on her, like remorse, or like a remembering of the dark, savage, mystic ride of dread, of death,* of the shadow of revenge. When her husband died, she was relieved. He would no longer dart about her.

England fitted her mood, its aloofness and foreignness. She had
20 known a little of the language before coming, and a sort of parrot-mind made her pick it up fairly easily. But she knew nothing of the English, nor of English life. Indeed, these did not exist for her. She was like one walking in the Underworld, where the shades throng intelligibly but have no connection with one. She felt the
25 English people as a potent, cold, slightly hostile host amongst whom she walked isolated.

The English people themselves were most deferential to her, the Church saw that she did not want. She walked without passion, like a shade, tormented into moments of love by the child. Her dying
30 husband with his tortured eyes and the skin drawn tight over his face, he was as a vision to her, not a reality. In a vision he was buried and put away. Then the vision ceased, she was untroubled, time went on grey, uncoloured, like a long journey where she sat unconscious as the landscape unrolled beside her. When she rocked her baby at
35 evening, maybe she fell into a Polish slumber song, or she talked sometimes to herself in Polish. Otherwise she did not think of Poland, nor of that life to which she had belonged. It was a great blot looming blank in its darkness. In the superficial activity of her life, she was all English. She even thought in English. But her long blanks
40 and darknesses of abstraction were Polish.

So she lived for some time. Then, with slight uneasiness, she used half to awake to the streets of London. She realised that there was something around her, very foreign, she realised she was in a strange place. And then, she was sent away into the country. There came into her mind now the memory of her home where she had been a child, the big house among the land, the peasants of the village.

She was sent to Yorkshire, to nurse an old rector in his rectory by the sea. This was the first shake of the kaleidoscope that brought in front of her eyes something she must see. It hurt her brain, the open country and the moors. It hurt her and hurt her. Yet it forced itself upon her as something living, it roused some potency of her childhood in her, it had some relation to her.

There was green and silver and blue in the air about her now. And there was a strange insistence of light from the sea, to which she must attend. Primroses glimmered around, many of them, and she stooped to the disturbing influence near her feet, she even picked one or two flowers, faintly remembering in the new colour of life, what had been. All the day long, as she sat at the upper window, the light came off the sea, constantly, constantly, without refusal, till it seemed to bear her away, and the noise of the sea created a drowsiness in her, a relaxation like sleep. Her automatic consciousness gave way a little, she stumbled sometimes, she had a poignant, momentary vision of her living child, that hurt her unspeakably. Her soul roused to attention.

Very strange was the constant glitter of the sea unsheathed in heaven, very warm and sweet the graveyard, in a nook of the hill catching the sunshine and holding it as one holds a bee between the palms of the hands, when it is benumbed. Grey grass and lichens and a little church, and snowdrops among coarse grass, and a cupful of incredibly warm sunshine.

She was troubled in spirit. Hearing the rushing of the beck away down under the trees, she was startled, and wondered what it was. Walking down, she found the bluebells around her glowing like a presence, among the trees.

Summer came, the moors were tangled with harebells like water in the ruts of the roads, the heather came rosy under the skies, setting the whole world awake. And she was uneasy. She went past the gorse bushes shrinking from their presence, she stepped into the heather as into a quickening bath that almost hurt. Her fingers

moved over the clasped fingers of the child, she heard the anxious
voice of the baby, as it tried to make her talk, distraught.

And she shrank away again, back into her darkness, and for a long
while remained blotted safely away from living. But autumn came
5   with the faint red glimmer of robins singing, winter darkened the
moors, and almost savagely she turned again to life, demanding her
life back again, demanding that it should be as it had been when she
was a girl, on the land at home, under the sky. Snow lay in great
expanses, the telegraph posts strode over the white earth, away
10 under the gloom of the sky. And savagely her desire rose in her
again, demanding that this was Poland, her youth, that all was her
own again.

But there were no sledges nor bells, she did not see the peasants
coming out like new people, in their sheepskins and their fresh,
15 ruddy, bright faces, that seemed to become new and vivid when the
snow lit up the ground. It did not come to her, the life of her youth, it
did not come back. There was a little agony of struggle, then a
relapse into the darkness of the convent, where Satan and the devils
raged round the walls, and Christ was white on the cross of victory.
20 She watched from the sick-room the snow whirl past, like flocks of
shadows in haste, flying on some final mission out to a leaden,
inalterable sea, beyond the final whiteness of the curving shore, and
the snow-speckled blackness of the rocks half-submerged. But near
at hand on the trees the snow was soft in bloom. Only the voice of the
25 dying vicar spoke grey and querulous from behind.

By the time the snowdrops were out, however, he was dead. He
was dead. But with curious equanimity the returning woman
watched the snowdrops on the edge of the grass below, blown white
in the wind, but not to be blown away. She watched them fluttering
30 and bobbing, the white, shut flowers, anchored by a thread to the
grey-green grass, yet never blown away, not drifting with the wind.

As she rose in the morning, the dawn was beating up white, gusts
of light blown like a thin snowstorm from the east, blown stronger
and fiercer, till the rose appeared, and the gold, and the sea lit up
35 below. She was impassive and indifferent. Yet she was outside the
enclosure of darkness.

There passed a space of shadow again, the familiarity of dread-
worship, during which she was moved oblivious to Cossethay.
There, at first, there was nothing—just grey nothing. But then one
40 morning there was a light from the yellow jasmine caught her, and

after that, morning and evening, the persistent ringing of thrushes from the shrubbery, till her heart, beaten upon, was forced to lift up its voice in rivalry and answer. Little tunes came into her mind. She was full of trouble almost like anguish. Resistant, she knew she was beaten, and from fear of darkness turned to fear of light. She would have hidden herself indoors, if she could. Above all, she craved for the peace and heavy oblivion of her old state. She could not bear to come to, to realise. The first pangs of this new parturition were so acute, she knew she could not bear it. She would rather remain out of life, than be torn, mutilated into this birth, which she could not survive. She had not the strength to come to life now, in England, so foreign, skies so hostile. She knew she would die like an early, colourless, scentless flower that the end of the winter puts forth mercilessly. And she wanted to harbour her modicum of twinkling life.

But a sunshiny day came full of the scent of a mezereon tree,* when bees were tumbling into the yellow crocuses, and she forgot, she felt like somebody else, not herself, a new person, quite glad. But she knew it was fragile, and she dreaded it. The vicar put pea-flour* into the crocuses, for his bees to roll in, and she laughed. Then night came, with brilliant stars that she knew of old, from her girlhood. And they flashed so bright, she knew they were victors.

She could neither wake nor sleep. As if crushed between the past and the future, like a flower that comes above-ground to find a great stone lying above it, she was helpless.

The bewilderment and helplessness continued, she felt surrounded by great moving masses that must crush her. And there was no escape. Save in the old obliviousness, the cold darkness she strove to retain. But the vicar showed her eggs in the thrush's nest near the back door. She saw herself the mother-thrush upon the nest, and the way her wings were spread, so eager down upon her secret. The tense, eager, nesting wings moved her beyond endurance. She thought of them in the morning, when she heard the thrush whistling as he got up, and she thought "Why didn't I die out there, why am I brought here?"

She was aware of people who passed around her, not as persons, but as looming presences. It was very difficult for her to adjust herself. In Poland, the peasantry, the people, had been cattle to her, they had been her cattle that she owned and used. What were these people? Now she was coming awake, she was lost.

But she had felt Brangwen go by almost as if he had brushed her. She had tingled in body as she had gone on up the road. After she had been with him in the Marsh kitchen, the voice of her body had risen strong and insistent. Soon, she wanted him. He was the man who had come nearest to her for her awakening.

Always, however, between-whiles she lapsed into the old unconsciousness, indifference, and there was a will in her, to save herself from living any more. But she would wake in the morning one day and feel her blood running, feel herself lying open like a flower unsheathed in the sun, insistent and potent with demand.

She got to know him better, and her instinct fixed on him—just on him. Her impulse was strong against him, because he was not of her own sort. But one blind instinct led her, to take him, to have him, and then to relinquish herself to him. It would be safety. She felt the rooted safety of him, and the life in him. Also he was young and very fresh. The blue, steady livingness of his eyes she enjoyed like morning. He was very young.

Then she lapsed again to stupor and indifference. This, however, was bound to pass. The warmth flowed through her, she felt herself opening, unfolding, asking, as a flower opens in full request under the sun, as the beaks of tiny birds open flat to receive, to receive. And unfolded she turned to him, straight to him. And he came, slowly, afraid, held back by uncouth fear, and driven by a desire bigger than himself.

When she opened and turned to him, then all that had been and all that was, was gone from her, she was as new as a flower that unsheathes itself and stands always ready, waiting, receptive. He could not understand this. He forced himself, through lack of understanding, to an adherence to the line of honorable courtship and sanctioned, licensed marriage. Thereafter, after he had gone to the vicarage and asked for her, she remained for some days held in this one spell, open, receptive to him, before him. He was roused to chaos. He spoke to the vicar and gave in the banns. Then he stood to wait.

She remained attentive and instinctively expectant before him, unfolded, ready to receive him. He could not act, because of self-fear and because of his conception of honor towards her. So he remained in a state of chaos.

And after a few days, gradually she closed again, away from him, was sheathed over, impervious to him, oblivious. Then a black, bottomless despair became real to him, he knew what he had lost. He felt he had lost it for good, he knew what it was to have been in communication with her, and to be cast off again. In misery, his heart like a heavy stone, he went about unliving.

Till gradually he became desperate, lost his understanding, was plunged in a revolt that knew no bounds. Inarticulate, he moved with her at the Marsh in violent, gloomy, wordless passion, almost in hatred of her. Till gradually, she became aware of him, aware of herself with regard to him, her blood stirred to life, she began to open towards him, to flow towards him again. He waited, till the spell was between them again, till they were together within one rushing, hastening flame. And then again he was bewildered, he was tied up as with cords, and could not move to her. So she came to him, and unfastened the breast of his waistcoat and his shirt, and put her hand on him, needing to know him. For it was cruel to her, to be open and offered to him, yet not to know what he was, not even that he was there. She gave herself to the hour, but he could not, and he bungled in taking her.

So that he lived in suspense, as if only half his faculties worked, until the wedding. She did not understand. But the vagueness came over her again, and the days lapsed by. He could not get definitely into touch with her. For the time being, she let him go again.

He suffered very much from the thought of actual marriage, the intimacy and nakedness of marriage. He knew her so little. They were so foreign to each other, they were such strangers. And they could not talk to each other. When she talked, of Poland or of what had been, it was all so foreign, she scarcely communicated anything to him. And when he looked at her, an over-much reverence and fear of the unknown changed the nature of his desire into a sort of worship, holding her aloof from his physical desire, self-thwarting.

She did not know this, she did not understand. They had looked at each other, and had accepted each other. It was so, then there was nothing to balk at, it was complete between them.

At the wedding, his face was stiff and expressionless. He wanted to drink, to get rid of his forethought and afterthought, to set the moment free. But he could not. The suspense only tightened at his heart. The jesting and joviality and jolly, broad insinuation of the guests only coiled him more. He could not hear. That which was impending obsessed him, he could not get free.

She sat quiet, with a strange, still smile. She was not afraid.

Having accepted him, she wanted to take him, she belonged altogether to the hour, now. No future, no past, only this, her hour. She
did not even notice him, as she sat beside him at the head of the
table. He was very near, their coming together was close at hand.
5 What more!

As the time came for all the guests to go, her dark face was softly
lighted, the bend of her head was proud, her grey eyes clear and
dilated, so that the men could not look at her, and the women were
elated by her, they served her. Very wonderful she was, as she bade
10 farewell, her ugly wide mouth smiling with pride and recognition,
her voice speaking softly and richly in the foreign accent, her dilated
eyes ignoring one and all the departing guests. Her manner was
gracious and fascinating, but she ignored the being of him or her to
whom she gave her hand.

15 And Brangwen stood beside her, giving his hearty handshake to
his friends, receiving their regard gratefully, glad of their attention.
His heart was tormented within him, he did not try to smile. The
time of his trial and his admittance, his Gethsemane and his
Triumphal Entry* in one, had come now.

20 Behind her, there was so much unknown to him. When he
approached her, he came to such a terrible painful unknown. How
could he embrace it and fathom it? How could he close his arms
round all this darkness and hold it to his breast and give himself to
it? What might not happen to him? If he stretched and strained for
25 ever he would never be able to grasp it all. And to yield himself
naked out of his own hands into an unknown power! How could a
man be strong enough to take her, put his arms round her and
have her, and be sure he could conquer this awful unknown next
his heart? What was it then that she was, to which he must also
30 deliver himself up, and which at the same time he must embrace,
contain?

He was to be her husband. It was established so. And he wanted it
more than he wanted life, or anything. She stood beside him in her
silk dress, looking at him, strangely, so that a certain terror, horror
35 took possession of him, because she was strange and impending and
he had no choice. He could not bear to meet her look from under her
strange, thick brows.

"Is it late?" she said.

He looked at his watch.

40 "No—half past eleven," he said. And he made an excuse to go

into the kitchen, leaving her standing in the room among the disorder and the drinking-glasses.

Tilly was seated beside the fire in the kitchen, her head in her hands. She started up when he entered.

"Why haven't you gone to bed?" he said.

"I thought I'd better stop an' lock up an' do," she said.

Her agitation quieted him. He gave her some little order, then returned, steadied now, almost ashamed, to his wife. She stood a moment watching him, as he moved with averted face. Then she said:

"You will be good to me, won't you?"

She was small and girlish and terrible, with a queer, wide look in her eyes. His heart leaped in him, in anguish of love and desire, he went blindly to her and took her in his arms.

"I want to," he said, as he drew her closer and closer in. She was soothed by the stress of his embrace, and remained quite still, relaxed against him, mingling in to him. And he let himself go from past and future, was reduced to the moment with her. In which he took her and was with her and there was nothing beyond, they were together in an elemental embrace beyond their superficial foreign- ness. But in the morning he was uneasy again. She was still foreign and unknown to him. Only, within the fear was pride, belief in himself as mate for her. And she, everything forgotten in her new hour of coming to life, radiated vigour and joy, so that he quivered to touch her.

It made a great difference to him, marriage. Things became so remote and of so little significance, as he knew the powerful source of his life, his eyes opened on a new universe, and he wondered in thinking of his triviality before. A new, calm relationship showed to him in the things he saw, in the cattle he used, the young wheat as it eddied in a wind.

And* each time he returned home, he went steadily, expectantly, like a man who goes to a profound, unknown satisfaction. At dinner-time, he appeared in the doorway, hanging back a moment from entering, to see if she was there. He saw her setting the plates on the white-scrubbed table. Her arms were slim, she had a slim body and full skirts, she had a dark, shapely head with close-banded hair. Somehow, it was her head, so shapely and poignant, that revealed her his woman to him. As she moved about clothed closely, full-skirted and wearing her little silk apron, her dark hair smoothly

parted, her head revealed itself to him in all its subtle, intrinsic
beauty, and he knew she was his woman, he knew her essence, that it
was his to possess. And he seemed to live thus in contact with her, in
contact with the unknown, the unaccountable and incalculable.

5   They did not take much notice of each other, consciously.

"I'm betimes," he said.

"Yes," she answered.

He turned to the dogs, or to the child if she were there. The little
Anna played about the farm, flitting constantly in to call something to
10   her mother, to fling her arms round her mother's skirts, to be
noticed, perhaps caressed, then, forgetting, to slip out again.

Then Brangwen, talking to the child, or to the dog between his
knees, would be aware of his wife, as, in her tight, dark bodice and
her lace fichu, she was reaching up to the corner cupboard. He
15   realised with a sharp pang that she belonged to him, and he to her.
He realised that he lived by her. Did he own her? Was she here for
ever? Or might she go away? She was not really his, it was not a real
marriage, this marriage between them. She might go away. He did
not feel like a master, husband, father of her children. She belonged
20   elsewhere. Any moment, she might be gone. And he was ever drawn
to her, drawn after her, with ever-raging, ever-unsatisfied desire. He
must always turn home, wherever his steps were taking him, always
to her, and he could never quite reach her, he could never quite be
satisfied, never be at peace, because she might go away.

25   At evening, he was glad. Then, when he had finished in the yard,
and come in and washed himself, when the child was put to bed, he
could sit on the other side of the fire with his beer on the hob and his
long white pipe in his fingers, conscious of her there opposite him, as
she worked at her embroidery, or as she talked to him, and he was
30   safe with her now, till morning. She was curiously self-sufficient,
and did not say very much. Occasionally she lifted her head, her grey
eyes shining with a strange light, that had nothing to do with him or
with this place, and would tell him about herself. She seemed to be
back again in the past, chiefly in her childhood or her girlhood, with
35   her father. She very rarely talked of her first husband. But sometimes, all shining-eyed, she was back at her own home, telling him
about the riotous times, the trip to Paris with her father, tales of the
mad acts of the peasants when a burst of religious, self-hurting
fervour had passed over the country.

40   She would lift her head and say:

"When they brought the railway across the country, they made afterwards smaller railways, of shorter width, to come down to our town—a hundred miles. When I was a girl, Gisla, my German gouvernante, was very shocked and she would not tell me. But I heard the servants talking. I remember, it was Pierre, the coachman. 5 And my father, and some of his friends, landowners, they had taken a wagon, a whole railway wagon—that you travel in—"

"A railway-carriage," said Brangwen.

She laughed to herself.

"I know it was a great scandal: yes—a whole wagon, and they had 10 girls, you know, *filles,** naked, all the wagon full, and so they came down to our village. They came through villages of the Jews, and it was a great scandal. Can you imagine? All the countryside! And my mother, she did not like it. Gisla said to me, 'Madame, she must not know that you have heard such things'— — — 15

"My mother, she used to cry, and she wished to beat my father, plainly beat* him. He would say, when she cried because he sold the forest, the wood, to jingle money in his pocket, and go to Warsaw or Paris or Kiev, when she said, he must take back his word, he must not sell the forest, he would stand and say 'I know, I know, I have 20 heard it all, I have heard it all before. Tell me some new thing. I know, I know, I know— —' Oh, but can you understand, I loved him when he stood there under the door, saying only 'I know, I know, I know it all already.' She could not change him, no, not if she killed herself for it. And she could change everybody else, but him, she 25 could not change him— —"

Brangwen could not understand. He had pictures of a cattle-truck full of naked girls riding from nowhere to nowhere, of Lydia laughing because her father made great debts and said "I know, I know"; of Jews running down the street shouting in Yiddish "Don't 30 do it, don't do it," and being cut down by demented peasants—she called them "cattle"—whilst she looked on interested and even amused; of tutors and governesses and Paris and a convent—. It was too much for him. And there she sat, telling the tales to the open space, not to him, arrogating a curious superiority to him, a distance 35 between them, something strange and foreign and outside his life, talking, rattling, without rhyme or reason, laughing when he was shocked or astounded, condemning nothing, confounding his mind and making the whole world a chaos, without order or stability of any kind. Then, when they went to bed, he knew that he had nothing to 40

do with her. She was back in her childhood, he was a peasant, a serf, a servant, a lover, a paramour, a shadow, a nothing. He lay still in amazement, staring at the room he knew so well, and wondering whether it was really there, the window, the chest of drawers, or
5 whether it was merely a figment in the atmosphere. And gradually he grew into a raging fury against her. But because he was so much amazed, and there was as yet such a distance between them, and she was such an amazing thing to him, with all wonder opening out behind her, he made no retaliation on her. Only he lay still and
10 wide-eyed with rage, inarticulate, not understanding, but solid with hostility.

And he remained wrathful and distinct from her, unchanged outwardly to her, but underneath a solid power of antagonism to her. Of which she became gradually aware. And it irritated her to be
15 made aware of him as a separate power. She lapsed into a sort of sombre exclusion, a curious communion with mysterious powers, a sort of mystic, dark state which drove him and the child nearly mad. He walked about for days stiffened with resistance to her, stiff with a will to destroy her as she was. Then suddenly, out of nowhere, there
20 was connection between them again. It came on him as he was working in the fields. The tension, the bond, burst, and the passionate flood broke forward into a tremendous, magnificent rush, so that he felt he could snap off the trees as he passed, and create the world afresh.

25 And when he arrived home, there was no sign between them. He waited and waited till she came. And as he waited, his limbs seemed strong and splendid to him, his hands seemed like passionate servants to him, goodly, he felt a stupendous power in himself, of life, and of urgent, strong blood.

30 She was sure to come at last, and touch him. Then he burst into flame for her, and lost himself.* They looked at each other, a deep laugh at the bottom of their eyes, and he went to take of her again, wholesale, mad to revel in the inexhaustible wealth of her, to bury himself in the depths of her in an inexhaustible exploration, she all
35 the while revelling in that he revelled in her, tossed all her secrets aside and plunged to that which was secret to her as well, whilst she quivered with fear and the last anguish of delight.

What did it matter who they were, whether they knew each other or not?

40 The hour passed away again, there was severance between them,

and rage and misery and bereavement for her, and deposition and toiling at the mill with slaves* for him. But no matter. They had had their hour, and should it chime again, they were ready for it, ready to renew the game at the point where it was left off, on the edge of the outer darkness,* when the secrets within the woman are game for the man, hunted doggedly, when the secrets of the woman are the man's adventure, and they both give themselves to the adventure.

She was with child, and there was again the silence and distance between them. She did not want him nor his secrets nor his game, he was deposed, he was cast out. He seethed with fury at the small, ugly-mouthed woman who had nothing to do with him. Sometimes his anger broke on her, but she did not cry. She turned on him like a tiger, and there was battle.

He had to learn to contain himself again, and he hated it. He hated her that she was not there for him. And he took himself off, anywhere.

But an instinct of gratitude and a knowledge that she would receive him back again, that later on she would be there for him again, prevented his straying very far. He cautiously did not go too far. He knew she might lapse into ignorance of him, lapse away from him, farther, farther, farther, till she was lost to him. He had sense enough, premonition enough in himself, to be aware of this and to measure himself accordingly. For he did not want to lose her: he did not want her to lapse away.

Cold, he called her, selfish, only caring about herself, a foreigner with a bad nature, caring really about nothing, having no proper feelings at the bottom of her, and no proper niceness. He raged, and piled up accusations that had some measure of truth in them all. But a certain grace in him forbade him from going too far. He knew, and he quivered with rage and hatred, that she was all these vile things, that she was everything vile and detestable. But he had grace at the bottom of him, which told him, that above all things, he did not want to lose her, he was not going to lose her.

So he kept some consideration for her, he preserved some relationship. He went out more often, to the "Red Lion" again, to escape the madness of sitting next to her when she did not belong to him, when she was as absent as any woman in indifference could be. He could not stay at home. So he went to the "Red Lion." And sometimes he got drunk. But he preserved his measure, some things between them he never forfeited.

A tormented look came into his eyes, as if something were always dogging him. He glanced sharp and quick, he could not bear to sit still doing nothing. He had to go out, to find company, to give himself away there. For he had no other outlet, he could not work to give
5 himself out, he had not the knowledge.

As the months of her pregnancy went on, she left him more and more alone, she was more and more unaware of him, his existence was annulled. And he felt bound down, bound, unable to stir, beginning to go mad, ready to rave. For she was quiet and polite, as if
10 he did not exist, as one is quiet and polite to a servant.

Nevertheless she was great with his child, it was his turn to submit. She sat opposite him, sewing, her foreign face inscrutable and indifferent. He felt he wanted to break her into acknowledgment of him, into awareness of him. It was insufferable that she had so
15 obliterated him. He would smash her into regarding him. He had a raging agony of desire to do so.

But something bigger in him withheld him, kept him motionless. So he went out of the house for relief. Or he turned to the little girl for her sympathy and her love, he appealed with all his power to the
20 small Anna. So soon they were like lovers, father and child.

For he was afraid of his wife. As she sat there with bent head, silent, working or reading, but so unutterably silent that his heart seemed under the millstone of it, she became herself like the upper millstone* lying on him, crushing him, as sometimes a heavy sky lies
25 on the earth.

Yet he knew he could not tear her away from the heavy obscurity into which she was merged. He must not try to tear her into recognition of himself, and agreement with himself. It were disastrous, impious. So, let him rage as he might, he must withhold
30 himself. But his wrists trembled and seemed mad, and seemed as if they would burst.

When, in November, the leaves came beating against the window shutters, with a lashing sound, he started, and his eyes flickered with flame. The dog looked up at him, he sunk his head to the fire. But his
35 wife was startled. He was aware of her listening.

"They blow up with a rattle," he said.

"What?" she asked.

"The leaves."

She sank away again. The strange leaves beating in the wind on
40 the wood had come nearer than she. The tension in the room was

overpowering, it was difficult for him to move his head. He sat with every nerve, every vein, every fibre of muscle in his body stretched on a tension. He felt like a broken arch thrust sickeningly out from support. For her response was gone, he thrust at nothing. And he remained himself, he saved himself from crashing down into nothingness, from being squandered into fragments, by sheer tension, sheer backward resistance. 5

During the last months of her pregnancy, he went about in a surcharged, imminent state that did not exhaust itself. She was also depressed, and sometimes she cried. It needed so much life to begin afresh, after she had lost so lavishly. Sometimes she cried. Then he stood stiff, feeling his heart would burst. For she did not want him, she did not want even to be made aware of him. By the very puckering of her face he knew that he must stand back, leave her intact, alone. For it was the old grief come back in her, the old loss, the pain of the old life, the dead husband, the dead children. This was sacred to her, and he must not violate her with his comfort. For what she wanted she would come to him. He stood aloof with turgid heart. 10 15

He had to see her tears come, fall over her scarcely moving face, that only puckered sometimes, down on to her breast, that was so still, scarcely moving. And there was no noise, save now and again, when, with a strange, somnambule movement, she took her handkerchief and wiped her face and blew her nose, and went on with the noiseless weeping. He knew that any offer of comfort from himself would be worse than useless, hateful to her, jangling her. She must cry. But it drove him insane. His heart was scalded, his brain hurt in his head, he went away, out of the house. 20 25

His great and chiefest source of solace was the child. She had been at first aloof from him, reserved. However friendly she might seem one day, the next she would have lapsed to her original disregard of him, cold, detached, at her distance. 30

The first morning after his marriage he had discovered it would not be so easy with the child. At the break of dawn he had started awake hearing a small voice outside the door saying plaintively: 35
"Mother!"

He rose and opened the door. She stood on the threshold in her nightdress, as she had climbed out of bed, black eyes staring round and hostile, her fair hair sticking out in a wild fleece. The man and child confronted each other. 40

"I want my mother," she said, jealously accenting the "my."

"Come on then," he said gently.

"Where's my mother?"

"She's here—come on."

5   The child's eyes, staring at the man with ruffled hair and beard, did not change. The mother's voice called softly. The little bare feet entered the room with trepidation.

"Mother!"

"Come, my dear."

10   The small bare feet approached swiftly.

"I wondered where you were," came the plaintive voice.

The mother stretched out her arms. The child stood beside the high bed. Brangwen lightly lifted the tiny girl, with an "up-a-daisy," then took his own place in the bed again.

15   "Mother!" cried the child sharply, as in anguish.

"What, my pet?"

Anna wriggled close into her mother's arms, clinging tight, hiding from the fact of the man. Brangwen lay still, and waited. There was a long stillness.

20   Then suddenly, Anna looked round, as if she thought he would be gone. She saw the face of the man lying upturned to the ceiling. Her black eyes stared antagonistic from her exquisite face, her arms clung tightly to her mother, afraid. He did not move for some time, not knowing what to say. His face was smooth and soft-skinned with

25   love, his eyes full of soft light. He looked at her, scarcely moving his head, his eyes smiling.

"Have you just wakened up?" he said.

"Go away," she retorted, with a little darting forward of the head, something like a viper.

30   "Nay," he answered, "*I'm* not going. You can go."

"Go away," came the sharp little command.

"There's room for you," he said.

"You can't send your father from his own bed, my little bird," said her mother, pleasantly.

35   The child glowered at him, miserable in her impotence.

"There's room for you as well," he said. "It's a big bed, enough."

She glowered without answering, then turned and clung to her mother. She would not allow it.

During the day, she asked her mother several times:

40   "When are we going home, mother?"

"We are at home, darling, we live here now. This is our house, we live here with your father."

The child was forced to accept it. But she remained against the man. As night came on, she asked:

"Where are you going to sleep, mother?"

"I sleep with the father now."

And when Brangwen came in, the child asked fiercely:

"*Why* do you sleep with *my* mother? My mother sleeps with me," her voice quivering.

"You come as well, an' sleep with both of us," he coaxed.

"Mother!" she cried, turning, appealing against him.

"But I must have a husband, darling. All women must have a husband."

"And you like to have a father with your mother, don't you?" said Brangwen.

Anna glowered at him. She seemed to cogitate.

"No," she cried fiercely at length, "no, I don't *want*."

And slowly her face puckered, she sobbed bitterly. He stood and watched her, sorry. But there could be no altering it.

Which, when she knew, she became quiet. He was easy with her, talking to her, taking her to see the live creatures, bringing her the first chickens in his cap, taking her to gather the eggs, letting her throw crusts to the horse. She would easily accompany him, and take all he had to give, but she remained neutral still.

She was curiously, incomprehensibly jealous of her mother, always anxiously concerned about her. If Brangwen drove with his wife to Nottingham, Anna ran about happily enough, or unconcerned, for a long time. Then, as afternoon came on, there was only one cry—"I want my mother, I want my mother—" and a bitter, pathetic sobbing that soon had the soft-hearted Tilly sobbing too. The child's anguish was that her mother was gone, gone.

Yet as a rule, Anna seemed cold, resenting her mother, critical of her. It was:

"I don't like you to do that, mother," or, "I don't like you to say that." She was a sore problem to Brangwen and to all the people at the Marsh. As a rule, however, she was active, lightly flitting about the farmyard, only appearing now and again to assure herself of her mother. Happy she never seemed, but quick, sharp, absorbed, full of imagination and changeability. Tilly said she was bewitched. But it did not matter so long as she did not cry. There was something

heartrending about Anna's crying, her childish anguish seemed so
utter and so timeless, as if it were a thing of all the ages.

She made playmates of the creatures of the farmyard, talking to
them, telling them the stories she had from her mother, counselling
5   them and correcting them.

Brangwen found her at the gate leading to the paddock and to the
duckpond. She was peering through the bars and shouting to the
stately white geese, that stood in a curving line:

"You're *not* to call at people when they want to come. You must
10 not do it."

The heavy, balanced birds looked at the fierce little face and the
fleece of keen hair thrust between the bars, and they raised their
heads and swayed off, producing the long, can-canking, protesting
noise of geese, rocking their ship-like, beautiful white bodies in a
15 line beyond the gate.

"You're naughty, you're naughty," cried Anna, tears of dismay
and vexation in her eyes. And she stamped her slipper.*

"Why, what are they doing?" said Brangwen.

"They won't let me come in," she said, turning her flushed little
20 face to him.

"Yi, they will. You can go in if you want to," and he pushed open
the gate for her.

She stood irresolute, looking at the group of bluey-white geese
standing monumental under the grey, cold day.

25 "Go on," he said.

She marched valiantly a few steps in. Her little body started
convulsively at the sudden, derisive Can-cank-ank of the geese. A
blankness spread over her. The geese trailed away with uplifted
heads under the low grey sky.

30 "They don't know you," said Brangwen. "You should tell 'em
what your name is."

"They're *naughty* to shout at me," she flashed.

"They think you don't live here," he said.

Later he found her at the gate calling shrilly and imperiously:

35 "My name is Anna, Anna Lensky, and I live here, because Mr
Brangwen's my father now. He *is*—yes he *is*. And I live here."

This pleased Brangwen very much. And gradually, without
knowing it herself, she clung to him, in her lost, childish, desolate
moments, when it was good to creep up to something big and warm,
40 and bury her little self in his big, unlimited being. Instinctively he

was careful of her, careful to recognise her and to give himself to her disposal.

She was difficult of her affections. For Tilly, she had a childish, essential contempt, almost dislike, because the poor woman was such a servant. The child would not let the serving-woman attend to her, do intimate things for her, not for a long time. She treated her as one of an inferior race. Brangwen did not like it.

"Why aren't you fond of Tilly?" he asked.

"Because—because—because she looks at me with her eyes bent."

Then gradually she accepted Tilly as belonging to the household, never as a person.

For the first weeks, the black eyes of the child were forever on the watch. Brangwen, good-humoured but impatient, spoiled by Tilly, was an easy blusterer. If for a few minutes he upset the household with his noisy impatience, he found at the end the child glowering at him with intense black eyes, and she was sure to dart forward her little head, like a serpent, with her biting:

"Go away."

"I'm *not* going away," he shouted, irritated at last. "Go yourself—hustle—stir thysen*—hop." And he pointed to the door.

The child backed away from him, pale with fear. Then she gathered her courage, seeing him become patient.

"We don't live with *you*," she said, thrusting forward her little head at him: "You—you're—you're a bomakle."*

"A what?" he shouted.

Her voice wavered—but it came—

"A bomakle."

"Ay, an' you're a comakle."

She meditated. Then she hissed forward her head.

"I'm not."

"Not what?"

"A comakle."

"No more am I a bomakle."

He was really cross.

Other times she would say:

"My mother *doesn't* live here."

"Oh ay?"

"I want her to go away."

"Then want's your portion," he replied, laconically.

So they drew nearer together. He would take her with him when he went out in the trap. The horse ready at the gate, he came noisily into the house, which seemed quiet and peaceful till he appeared to set everything awake.

5   "Now then, Topsy,* pop into thy bonnet."

The child drew herself up, resenting the indignity of the address.

"I can't fasten my bonnet myself," she said haughtily.

"Not man enough yet," he said, tying the ribbons under her chin with clumsy fingers.

10   She held up her face to him. Her little, bright-red lips moved as he fumbled under her chin.

"You talk—nonsents," she said, re-echoing one of his phrases.

"*That* face shouts for th' pump," he said, and taking out a big red handkerchief, that smelled of strong tobacco, began wiping round

15   her mouth.

"Is Kitty waiting for me?" she asked.

"Ay," he said. "Let's finish wiping your face—it'll pass wi' a cat-lick."

She submitted prettily. Then, when he let her go, she began to

20   skip, with a curious flicking up of one leg behind her.

"Now my young buck-rabbit," he said. "Slippy!"*

She came and was shaken into her coat, and the two set off. She sat very close beside him in the gig, tucked tightly, feeling his big body sway against her, very splendid. She loved the rocking of the gig,

25   when his big, live body swayed upon her, against her. She laughed, a poignant little shrill, and her black eyes glowed.

She was curiously hard, and then passionately tender-hearted. Her mother was ill, the child stole about on tip-toe in the bedroom for hours, being nurse, and doing the thing thoughtfully and

30   diligently. Another day, her mother was unhappy, Anna would stand with legs apart, glowering, balancing on the sides of her slippers. She laughed when the goslings wriggled in Tilly's hand, as the pellets of food were rammed down their throats with a skewer, she laughed nervously. She was hard and imperious with the animals, squander-

35   ing no love, running about amongst them like a cruel mistress.

Summer came, and hay-harvest, Anna was a brown elvish mite dancing about. Tilly always marvelled over her, more than she loved her.

But always in the child was some anxious connection with the

40   mother. So long as Mrs Brangwen was all right, the little girl played

about and took very little notice of her. But corn-harvest went by, the autumn drew on, and the mother, the later months of her pregnancy beginning, was strange and detached, Brangwen began to knit his brows, the old, unhealthy uneasiness, the unskinned susceptibility came on the child again. If she went to the fields with her father, 5 then, instead of playing about carelessly, it was:

"I want to go home."

"Home, why tha's nobbut* this minute come."

"I want to go home."

"What for? What ails thee?" 10

"I want my mother."

"Thy mother! Thy mother none wants thee."

"I want to go home."

There would be tears in a moment.

"Can ter* find t'road, then?" 15

And he watched her scudding, silent and intent along the hedge-bottom, at a steady, anxious pace, till she turned and was gone through the gateway. Then he saw her two fields off, still pressing forward, small and urgent. His face was clouded as he turned to plough up the stubble. 20

The year drew on, in the hedges the berries shone red and twinkling above bare twigs, robins were seen, great droves of birds dashed like spray from the fallow, rooks appeared, black and flapping down to earth, the ground was cold as he pulled the turnips, the roads were churned deep in mud. Then the turnips were pitted* and 25 work was slack.

Inside the house it was dark, and quiet. The child flitted uneasily round, and now and again came her plaintive, startled cry:

"Mother!"

Mrs Brangwen was heavy and unresponsive, tired, lapsed back. 30 Brangwen went on working out of doors.

At evening, when he came in to milk, the child would run behind him. Then, in the cosy cowsheds, with the doors shut and the air looking warm by the light of the hanging lantern, above the branching horns of the cows, she would stand watching his hands 35 squeezing rhythmically the teats of the placid beast, watch the froth and the leaping squirt of milk, watch his hand sometimes rubbing slowly, understandingly, upon a hanging udder. So they kept each other company, but at a distance, rarely speaking.

The darkest days of the year came on, the child was fretful, 40

sighing as if some oppression were on her, running hither and
thither without relief. And Brangwen went about at his work, heavy,
his heart heavy as the sodden earth.

5 The winter nights fell early, the lamp was lighted before tea-time,
the shutters were closed, they were all shut into the room with the
tension and stress. Mrs Brangwen went early to bed, Anna playing
on the floor beside her. Brangwen sat in the emptiness of the
downstairs room, smoking, scarcely conscious even of his own
misery. And very often he went out to escape it.

10 Christmas passed, the wet, drenched, cold days of January
recurred monotonously, with now and then a brilliance of blue
flashing in, when Brangwen went out into a morning like crystal,
when every sound rang again, and the birds were many and sudden
and brusque in the hedges. Then an elation came over him in spite of
15 everything, whether his wife were strange or sad, or whether he
craved for her to be with him, it did not matter, the air rang with clear
noises, the sky was like crystal, like a bell, and the earth was hard.
Then he worked and was happy, his eyes shining, his cheeks flushed.
And the zest of life was strong in him.

20 The birds pecked busily round him, the horses were fresh and
ready, the bare branches of the trees flung themselves up like a man
yawning, taut with energy, the twigs radiated off into the clear light.
He was alive and full of zest for it all. And if his wife were heavy,
separated from him, extinguished, then let her be, let him remain
25 himself. Things would be as they would be. Meanwhile he heard the
ringing crow of a cockerel in the distance, he saw the pale shell of the
moon effaced on a blue sky.

So he shouted to the horses, and was happy. If, driving into
Ilkeston, a fresh young woman were going in to do her shopping, he
30 hailed her, and reined in his horse, and picked her up. Then he was
glad to have her near him, his eyes shone, his voice, laughing, teasing
in a warm fashion, made the poise of her head more beautiful, her
blood ran quicker. They were both stimulated, the morning was fine.

What did it matter that, at the bottom of his heart, was care and
35 pain? It was at the bottom, let it stop at the bottom. His wife, her
suffering, her coming pain—well, it must be so. She suffered, but he
was out of doors, full in life, and it would be ridiculous, indecent, to
pull a long face and to insist on being miserable. He was happy, this
morning, driving to town, with the hoofs of the horse spanking the
40 hard earth. Well, he was happy, if half the world were weeping at the

funeral of the other half. And it was a jolly girl sitting beside him. And Woman was immortal, whatever happened, whoever turned towards death. Let the misery come when it could not be resisted.

The evening arrived later very beautiful, with a rosy flush hovering above the sunset, and passing away into violet and lavender with turquoise green north and south in the sky, and in the east, a great, yellow moon hanging heavy and radiant. It was magnificent to walk between the sunset and the moon, on a road where little holly trees thrust black into the rose and lavender, and starlings flickered in droves across the light. But what was the end of the journey.

The pain came right enough, later on, when his heart and his feet were heavy, his brain dead, his life stopped.

One afternoon, the pains began, Mrs Brangwen was put to bed, the midwife came. Night fell, the shutters were closed, Brangwen came in to tea, to the loaf and the pewter tea-pot, the child, silent and quivering, playing with glass beads, the house, empty, it seemed, or exposed to the winter night, as if it had no walls.

Sometimes there sounded, long and remote in the house, vibrating through everything, the moaning cry of a woman in labour. Brangwen, sitting downstairs, was divided. His lower, deeper self was with her, bound to her, suffering. But the big shell of his body remembered the sound of owls that used to fly round the farmstead when he was a boy. He was back in his youth, a boy, haunted by the sound of the owls, waking up his brother to speak to him. And his mind drifted away to the birds, their solemn, dignified faces, their flight so soft and broad-winged. And then to the birds his brother had shot, fluffy, dust-coloured, dead heaps of softness with faces absurdly asleep. It was a queer thing, a dead owl.

He lifted his cup to his lips, he watched the child with the beads. But his mind was occupied with owls, and the atmosphere of his boyhood, with his brothers and sisters. Elsewhere, fundamental, he was with his wife in labour, the child was being brought forth out of their one flesh.* He and she, one flesh, out of which life must be put forth. The rent was not in his body, but it was of his body. On her the blows fell, but the quiver ran through to him, to his last fibre. She must be torn asunder for life to come forth, yet still they were one flesh, and still, from further back, the life came out of him to her, and still he was the unbroken that has the broken rock* in its arms, their flesh was one rock from which the life gushed, out of her who was smitten and rent, from him who quivered and yielded.

He went upstairs to her. As he came to the bedside she spoke to him in Polish.

"Is it very bad?" he asked.

5　She looked at him, and oh, the weariness to her, of the effort to understand another language, the weariness of hearing him, attending to him, making out who he was, as he stood there fair-bearded and alien, looking at her. She knew something of him, of his eyes. But she could not grasp him. She closed her eyes.

He turned away, white to the gills.

10　"It's not so very bad," said the midwife.

He knew he was a strain on his wife. He went downstairs.

The child glanced up at him, frightened.

"I want my mother," she quavered.

"Ay, but she's badly," he said mildly, unheeding.

15　She looked at him with lost, frightened eyes.

"Has she got a headache?"

"No—she's going to have a baby."

The child looked round. He was unaware of her. She was alone again in terror.

20　"I want my mother," came the cry of panic.

"Let Tilly undress you," he said. "You're tired."

There was another silence. Again came the cry of labour.

"I want my mother," rang automatically from the wincing, panic-stricken child, that felt cut off and lost in a horror of desola-

25　tion.

Tilly came forward, her heart wrung.

"Come an' let me undress her then, pet-lamb," she crooned. "You s'll have your mother in th' mornin', don't you fret, my duckie; never mind, angel."

30　But Anna stood upon the sofa, her back to the wall.

"I want my mother," she cried, her little face quivering, and the great tears of childish, utter anguish falling.

"She's poorly, my lamb, she's poorly tonight, but she'll be better by mornin'. Oh don't cry, don't cry, love, she doesn't want you to cry,

35　precious little heart, no, she doesn't."

Tilly took gently hold of the child's skirts. Anna snatched back her dress, and cried, in a little hysteria:

"No, you're not to undress me.—I want my mother—", and her child's face was running with grief and tears, her body shaken.

40　"Oh, but let Tilly undress you. Let Tilly undress you, who loves you, don't be wilful tonight. Mother's poorly, she doesn't want you to cry."

The child sobbed distractedly, she could not hear.

"I want my mother," she wept.

"When you're undressed you s'll go up to see your mother—when you're undressed, pet, when you've let Tilly undress you, when you're a little jewel in your nightie, love. Oh don't you cry, don't you—"

Brangwen sat stiff in his chair. He felt his brain going tighter. He crossed over the room, aware only of the maddening sobbing.

"Don't make a noise," he said.

And a new fear shook the child from the sound of his voice. She cried mechanically, her eyes looking watchful through her tears, in terror, alert to what might happen.

"I want—my—mother," quavered the sobbing, blind voice.

A shiver of irritation went over the man's limbs. It was the utter, persistent unreason, the maddening blindness of the voice and the crying.

"You must come and be undressed," he said, in a quiet voice that was thin with anger.

And he reached his hand and grasped her. He felt her body catch in a convulsive sob. But he too was blind, and intent, irritated into mechanical action. He began to unfasten her little apron. She would have shrunk from him, but could not. So her small body remained in his grasp, while he fumbled at the little buttons and tapes, unthinking, intent, unaware of anything but the irritation of her. Her body was held taut and resistant, he pushed off the little dress and the petticoats, revealing the white arms. She kept stiff, overpowered, violated, he went on with his task. And all the while, she sobbed, choking:

"I want my mother."

He was unheedingly silent, his face stiff. The child was now incapable of understanding, she had become a little, mechanical thing of fixed will. She wept, her body convulsed, her voice repeating the same cry.

"Eh dear o' me!" cried Tilly, becoming distracted herself.

Brangwen, slow, clumsy, blind, intent, got off all the little garments, and stood the child naked in its shift upon the sofa.

"Wheer's her nightie?" he asked.

Tilly brought it, and he put it on her. Anna did not move her limbs to his desire. He had to push them into place. She stood, with fixed, blind will, resistant, a small, convulsed, unchangeable thing weeping ever and repeating the same phrase. He lifted one foot after the other, pulled off slippers and socks. She was ready.

5   "Do you want a drink?" he asked.

She did not change. Unheeding, uncaring, she stood on the sofa, standing back, alone, her hands shut and half lifted, her face, all tears, raised and blind. And through the sobbing and choking came the broken:

10   "I—want—my—mother."

"Do you want a drink?" he said again.

There was no answer. He lifted the stiff, denying body between his hands. Its stiff blindness made a flash of rage go through him. He would like to break it.

15   He set the child on his knee, and sat again in his chair beside the fire, the wet, sobbing, inarticulate noise going on near his ear, the child sitting stiff, not yielding to him or anything, not aware.

A new degree of anger came over him. What did it all matter? What did it matter if the mother talked Polish and cried in labour, if

20   this child were stiff with resistance, and crying? Why take it to heart? Let the mother cry in labour, let the child cry in resistance, since they would do so. Why should he fight against it, why resist? Let it be, if it were so. Let them be as they were, if they insisted.

And in a daze he sat, offering no fight. The child cried on, the

25   minutes ticked away, a sort of torpor was on him.

It was some little time before he came to, and turned to attend to the child. He was shocked by her little, wet, blinded face. A bit dazed, he pushed back the wet hair. Like a living statue of grief, her blind face cried on.

30   "Nay," he said, "not as bad as that. It's not as bad as that, Anna, my child. Come, what are you crying for so much? Come, stop now, it'll make you sick. I wipe you dry, don't wet your face any more. Don't cry any more wet tears, don't, it's better not to. Don't cry—it's not so bad as all that. Hush now, hush—let it be enough."

35   His voice was queer and distant and calm. He looked at the child. She was beside herself now. He wanted her to stop, he wanted it all to stop, to become natural.

"Come," he said, rising to turn away, "We'll go an' supper-up the beast."*

He took a big shawl, folded her round, and went out into the kitchen for the lantern.

"You're never taking the child out, of a night like this," said Tilly.

"Ay, it'll quieten her," he answered.

It was raining. The child was suddenly still, shocked, finding the rain on its face, the darkness.

"We'll just give the cows their something-to-eat, afore they go to bed," Brangwen was saying to her, holding her close and sure.

There was a trickling of water into the butt, a burst of rain-drops sputtering on to her shawl, and the light of the lantern swinging, flashing on a wet pavement and the base of a wet wall. Otherwise it was black darkness: one breathed darkness.

He opened the doors, upper and lower, and they entered into the high, dry barn, that smelled warm even if it were not warm. He hung the lantern on the nail, and shut the door. They were in another world now. The light shed softly on the timbered barn, on the white-washed walls, and the great heap of hay; instruments cast their shadows largely, a ladder rose to the dark arch of a loft. Outside there was the driving rain, inside, the softly-illuminated stillness and calmness of the barn.

Holding the child on one arm, he set about preparing the food for the cows, filling a pan with chopped hay and brewer's grains* and a little meal. The child, all wonder, watched what he did. A new being was created in her for the new conditions. Sometimes, a little spasm, eddying from the bygone storm of sobbing, shook her small body. Her eyes were wide and wondering, pathetic. She was silent, quite still.

In a sort of dream, his heart sunk to the bottom, leaving the surface of him still, quite still, he rose with the panful of food, carefully balancing the child on one arm, the pan in the other hand. The silky fringe of the shawl swayed softly, grains and hay trickled to the floor; he went along a dimly-lit passage behind the mangers, where the horns of the cows pricked out of the obscurity. The child shrank, he balanced stiffly, rested the pan on the manger wall, and tipped out the food, half to this cow, half to the next. There was a noise of chains running, as the cows lifted or dropped their heads sharply; then a contented, soothing sound, a long snuffing as the beast ate in silence.

The journey had to be performed several times. There was the

rhythmic sound of the shovel in the barn, then the man returned, walking stiffly between the two weights, the face of the child peering out from the shawl. Then the next time, as he stooped, she freed her arm and put it round his neck, clinging soft and warm, making all
5　easier.

The beast fed, he dropped the pan and sat down on a box, to arrange the child.

"Will the cows go to sleep now?" she said, catching her breath as she spoke.
10　"Yes."

"Will they eat all their stuff up first?"

"Yes. Hark at them."

And the two sat still, listening to the snuffing and breathing of cows feeding in the sheds communicating with this small barn. The
15　lantern shed a soft, steady light from one wall. All outside was still in the rain. He looked down at the silky folds of the paisley shawl.* It reminded him of his mother. She used to go to church in it. He was back again in the old irresponsibility and security, a boy at home.

The two sat very quiet. His mind, in a sort of trance, seemed to
20　become more and more vague. He held the child close to him. A quivering little shudder, re-echoing from her sobbing, went down her limbs. He held her closer. Gradually she relaxed, the eyelids began to sink over her dark, watchful eyes. As she sank to sleep, his mind became blank.
25　When he came to, as if from sleep, he seemed to be sitting in a timeless stillness. What was he listening for? He seemed to be listening for some sound a long way off, from beyond life. He remembered his wife. He must go back to her. The child was asleep, the eyelids not quite shut, showing a slight film of black pupil
30　between. Why did she not shut her eyes? Her mouth was also a little open.

He rose quietly and went back to the house.

"Is she asleep?" whispered Tilly.

He nodded. The servant-woman came to look at the child who
35　slept in the shawl, with cheeks flushed hot and red, and a whiteness, a wanness round the eyes.

"God-a-mercy!" whispered Tilly, shaking her head.

He pushed off his boots and went upstairs with the child. He became aware of the anxiety grasped tight at his heart, because of his
40　wife. But he remained still. The house was silent save for the wind

outside, and the noisy trickling and splattering of water in the water-butts. There was a slit of light under his wife's door.

He put the child into bed wrapped as she was in the shawl, for the sheets would be cold. Then he was afraid that she might not be able to move her arms, so he loosened her. The black eyes opened, rested on him vacantly, sank shut again. He covered her up. The last little quiver from the sobbing shook her breathing.

This was his room, the room he had had before he married. It was familiar. He remembered what it was to be a young man, untouched.

He remained suspended. The child slept, pushing her small fists from the shawl. He could tell the woman her child was asleep. But he must go to the other landing. He started. There was the sound of the owls—the moaning of the woman. What an uncanny sound! It was not human—at least to a man.

He went down to her room, entering softly. She was lying still, with eyes shut, pale, tired. His heart leapt, fearing she was dead. Yet he knew perfectly well she was not. He saw the way her hair went loose over her temples, her mouth was shut with suffering in a sort of grin. She was beautiful to him—but it was not human. He had a dread of her as she lay there. What had she to do with him?* She was other than himself.

Something made him go and touch her fingers that were still grasped on the sheet. Her brown-grey eyes opened and looked at him. She did not know him as himself. But she knew him as the man. She looked at him as a woman in childbirth looks at the man who begot the child in her; an impersonal look, in the extreme hour, female to male. Her eyes closed again. A great, scalding peace went over him, burning his heart and his entrails, passing off into the infinite.

When her pains began afresh, tearing her, he turned aside, and could not look. But his heart in torture was at peace, his bowels were glad. He went downstairs, and to the door, outside, lifted his face to the rain, and felt the darkness striking unseen and steadily upon him.

The swift, unseen threshing of the night upon him silenced him and he was overcome. He turned away indoors, humbly. There was the infinite world, eternal, unchanging, as well as the world of life.

Chapter III

Childhood of Anna Lensky

Tom Brangwen never loved his own son as he loved his step-child Anna. When they told him it was a boy, he had a thrill of pleasure. He liked the confirmation of fatherhood. It gave him satisfaction to know he had a son. But he felt not very much outgoing to the baby itself. He was its father, that was enough.

He was glad that his wife was mother of his child. She was serene, a little bit shadowy, as if she were transplanted. In the birth of the child she seemed to lose connection with her former self. She became now really English, really Mrs Brangwen. Her vitality, however, seemed lowered.

She was still, to Brangwen, immeasurably beautiful. She was still passionate, with a flame of being. But the flame was not robust and present. Her eyes shone, her face glowed for him, but like some flower opened in the shade, that could not bear the full light. She loved the baby. But even this, with a sort of dimness, a faint absence about her, a shadowiness even in her mother-love. When Brangwen saw her nursing his child, happy, absorbed in it, a pain went over him like a thin flame. For he perceived how he must subdue himself in his approach to her. And he wanted again the robust, mortal exchange of love and passion such as he had had at first with her, at one time and another, when they were matched at their highest intensity. This was the one experience for him now. And he wanted it, always, with remorseless craving.

She came to him again, with the same lifting her mouth as had driven him almost mad with trammelled passion at first. She came to him again, and, his heart delirious in delight and readiness, he took her. And it was almost as before.

Perhaps it was quite as before. At any rate, it made him know perfection, it established in him a constant, eternal knowledge.

But it died down before he wanted it to die down. She was finished, she could take no more. And he was not exhausted, he wanted to go on. But it could not be.

So he had to begin the bitter lesson, to abate himself, to take less

78

than he wanted. For she was Woman to him, all other women were
her shadows. For she had satisfied him. And he wanted it to go on.
And it could not. However he raged, and, filled with suppression that
became hot and bitter, hated her in his soul that she did not want
him, however he had mad outbursts, and drank and made ugly
scenes, still he knew, he was only kicking against the pricks.* It was
not, he had to learn, that she *would* not want him enough, as much as
he demanded that she should want him. It was, that she could not.
She could only want him in her own way, and to her own measure.
And she had spent much life before he found her as she was, the
woman who could take him and give him fulfilment. She had taken
him and given him fulfilment. She still would do so, in her own times
and ways. But he must control himself, measure himself to her.

He wanted to give her all his love, all his passion, all his essential
energy. But it could not be. He must find other things than her, other
centres of living. She sat close and impregnable with the child. And
he was jealous of the child.

But he loved her, and time came to give some sort of course to his
troublesome current of life, so that it did not foam and flood and
make misery. He formed another centre of love in her child, Anna.
Gradually a part of his stream of life was diverted to the child,
relieving the main flood to his wife. Also he sought the company of
men, he drank heavily now and again.

The child ceased to have so much anxiety for her mother after the
baby came. Seeing the mother with the baby boy, delighted and
serene and secure, Anna was at first puzzled, then gradually she
became indignant, and at last her little life settled on its own swivel,
she was no more strained and distorted to support her mother. She
became more childish, not so abnormal, not charged with cares she
could not understand. The charge of the mother, the satisfying of the
mother, had devolved elsewhere than on her. Gradually the child
was freed, she became an independent, forgetful little soul, loving
from her own centre.

Of her own choice, she then loved Brangwen most, or most
obviously. For these two made a little life together, they had a joint
activity. It amused him, at evening, to teach her to count, or to say her
letters. He remembered for her all the little nursery rhymes and
childish songs that lay forgotten at the bottom of his brain.

At first she thought them rubbish. But he laughed, and she
laughed. They became to her a huge joke. Old King Cole she

thought was Brangwen, Mother Hubbard was Tilly, her mother was the old woman who lived in a shoe. It was a huge, it was a frantic delight to the child, this nonsense, after her years with her mother, after the poignant folk-tales she had had from her mother, which
5   always troubled and mystified her soul.

She shared a sort of recklessness with her father, a complete, chosen carelessness that had the laugh of ridicule in it. He loved to make her voice go high and shouting and defiant with laughter. The baby was dark-skinned and dark-haired, like the mother, and had
10   hazel eyes. Brangwen called him the black-bird.

"Hallo," Brangwen would cry, starting as he heard the wail of the child announcing it wanted to be taken out of the cradle, "there's the black-bird tuning-up."

"The black-bird's singing," Anna would shout with delight, "the
15   black-bird's singing."

"When the pie was opened," Brangwen shouted in his bawling bass voice, going over to the cradle, "the bird began to sing."

"Wasn't it a dainty dish to set before a king?"* cried Anna, her eyes flashing with joy as she uttered the cryptic words, looking at
20   Brangwen for confirmation. He sat down with the baby, saying loudly:

"Sing up, my lad, sing up."

And the baby cried loudly, and Anna shouted lustily, dancing in wild bliss:

25   "'Sing a song of sixpence
                            Pocketful of posies,
                            Ascha! Ascha!'—"

Then she stopped suddenly in silence and looked at Brangwen again, her eyes flashing, as she shouted loudly and delightedly:
30   "I've got it wrong, I've got it wrong."

"Oh my sirs!" said Tilly entering, "What a racket!"

Brangwen hushed the child and Anna flipped and danced on. She loved her wild bursts of rowdiness with her father. Tilly hated it, Mrs Brangwen did not mind.
35   Anna did not care much for other children. She domineered them, she treated them as if they were extremely young and incapable, to her they were little people, they were not her equals. So she was mostly alone, flying round the farm, entertaining the farmhands and Tilly and the servant-girl, whirling on and never ceasing.

She loved driving with Brangwen in the trap. Then, sitting high up and bowling along, her passion for eminence and dominance was satisfied. She was like a little savage in her arrogance. She thought her father important, she was installed beside him on high. And they spanked along, beside the high, flourishing hedge-tops, surveying 5 the activity of the countryside. When people shouted a greeting to them from the road below, and Brangwen shouted jovially back, her little voice was soon heard shrilling along with his, followed by her chuckling laugh, when she looked up at her father with bright eyes, and they laughed at each other. And soon it was the custom for the 10 passer-by to sing out: "How are ter, Tom? Well, my lady!" or else "Mornin' Tom, mornin' my Lass!" or else "You're off together then?" or else "You're lookin' rarely,* you two."

Anna would respond, with her father: "How are you, John! *Good* mornin', William! Ay, makin' for Derby," shrilling as loudly as she 15 could. Though often, in response to "You're off out a bit then," she would reply, "Yes, we are," to the great joy* of all. She did not like the people who saluted him and did not salute her.

She went into the public-house with him, if he had to call, and often sat beside him in the bar-parlour as he drank his beer or 20 brandy. The landladies paid court to her, in the obsequious way landladies have.

"Well, little lady, an' what's your name?"

"Anna Brangwin," came the immediate, haughty answer.

"Indeed it is! An' do you like driving in a trap with your 25 father?"

"Yes," said Anna, shy, but bored by these inanities.

She had a touch-me-not way of blighting the inane inquiries of grown-up people.

"My word, she's a fawce* little thing," the landlady would say to 30 Brangwen.

"Ay," he answered, not encouraging comment on the child.

Then there followed the present of a biscuit, or of cake, which Anna accepted as her dues.

"What does she say, that I'm a fawce little thing?" the small girl 35 asked afterwards.

"She means you're a sharp-shins."*

Anna hesitated. She did not understand. Then she laughed at some absurdity she found.

Soon he took her every week to market with him. 40

"I can come, can't I?' she asked every Saturday, or Thursday morning, when he made himself look fine in his dress of a gentleman-farmer. And his face clouded at having to refuse her.

So at last, he overcame his own shyness, and tucked her beside
5 him. They drove in to Nottingham and put up at the "Black Swan."*
So far all right. Then he wanted to leave her at the inn. But he saw her face, and knew it was impossible. So he mustered his courage, and set off with her, holding her hand, to the cattle-market.

She stared in bewilderment, flitting silent at his side. But in the
10 cattle-market she shrank from the press of men, all men, all in heavy, filthy boots, and leathern leggings. And the road underfoot was all nasty with cow-muck. And it frightened her to see the cattle in the square pens, so many horns, and so little enclosure, and such a madness of men and a yelling of drovers. Also she felt her father was
15 embarrassed by her, and ill-at-ease.

He bought her a cake at the refreshment booth, and set her on a seat. A man hailed him.

"*Good* morning, Tom. That thine, then?"—and the bearded farmer jerked his head at Anna.
20 "Ay," said Brangwen, deprecating.

"I didna know tha'd one that old."

"No, it's my Missis's."

"Oh, that's it!" And the man looked at Anna as if she were some odd little cattle. She glowered with black eyes.
25 Brangwen left her there, in charge of the bar-man, whilst he went to see about the selling of some young stirks.* Farmers, butchers, drovers, dirty, uncouth men from whom she shrank instinctively stared down at her as she sat on her seat, then went to get their drink, talking in unabated tones. All was big and violent about her.
30 "Whose child met* that be?" they asked of the barman.

"It belongs to Tom Brangwen."

The child sat on in neglect, watching the door for her father. He never came; many, many men came, but not he, and she sat like a shadow. She knew one did not cry in such a place. And every man
35 looked at her inquisitively, she shut herself away from them. A deep, gathering coldness of isolation took hold on her. He was never coming back. She sat on, frozen, unmoving.

When she had become blank and timeless, he came, and she slipped off her seat to him, like one come back from the dead. He
40 had sold his beast as quickly as he could. But all the business was not

finished. He took her again through the hurtling welter of the cattle-market.

Then at last they turned and went out through the gate. He was always hailing one man or another, always stopping to gossip about land and cattle and horses and other things she did not understand, standing in the filth and the smell, among the legs and great boots of men. And always she heard the question:

"What lass is that, then? I didn't know tha'd one o' that age."

"It belongs to my Missis."

Anna was very conscious of her derivation from her mother, in the end, and of her alienation.

But at last they were away, and Brangwen went with her into a little, dark, ancient eating-house in the Bridlesmith-Gate. They had cow's-tail soup, and meat and cabbage and potatoes. Other men, other people came into the dark, vaulted place, to eat. Anna was wide-eyed and silent with wonder.

Then they went into the big market, into the corn exchange, then to shops. He bought her a little book off a stall. He loved buying things, odd things that he thought would be useful. Then they went to the "Black Swan," and she drank milk and he brandy, and they harnessed the horse and drove off, up the Derby Road.

She was tired out with wonder and marvelling. But the next day, when she thought of it, she skipped, flipping her leg in the odd dance she did, and talked the whole time of what had happened to her, of what she had seen. It lasted her all the week. And the next Saturday she was eager to go again.

She became a familiar figure in the cattle-market, sitting waiting in the little booth. But she liked best to go to Derby. There her father had more friends. And she liked the familiarity of the smaller town, the nearness of the river, the strangeness that did not frighten her, it was so much smaller. She liked the covered-in market, and the old women. She liked the "George Inn,"* where her father put up. The landlord was Brangwen's old friend, and Anna was made much of. She sat many a day in the cosy parlour talking to Mr Wigginton, a fat man with red hair, the landlord. And when the farmers all gathered at twelve o'clock, for dinner, she was a little heroine.

At first she would only glower or hiss at these strange men with their uncouth accent. But they were good-humoured. She was a little oddity, with her fierce fair hair like spun glass sticking out in a

flamy halo round her apple-blossom face* and her black eyes, and
the men liked an oddity. She kindled their attention.

She was very angry because Marriott, a gentleman-farmer from
Ambergate, called her the little pole-cat.

5 "Why you're a pole-cat," he said to her.

"I'm not," she flashed.

"You are. That's just how a pole-cat goes."

She thought about it.

"Well you're—you're—" she began.

10 "I'm what?"

She looked him up and down.

"You're a bow-leg man."

Which he was. There was a roar of laughter. They loved her that
she was indomitable.

15 "Ah," said Marriott. "Only a pole-cat says that."

"Well I *am* a pole-cat," she flamed.

There was another roar of laughter from the men.

They loved to tease her.

"Well ma little maid," Braithwaite would say to her, "an' how's th'
20 lamb's wool?"

He gave a tug at a glistening, pale piece of her hair.

"It's not lamb's wool," said Anna, indignantly putting back her
offended lock.

"Why, what'st ca' it then?"

25 "It's hair."*

"Hair! Wheriver dun they rear that sort?"

"Wheriver dun they?" she asked, in dialect, her curiosity overcoming her.

Instead of answering he shouted with joy. It was the triumph, to
30 make her speak dialect.

She had one enemy, the man they called Nut-Nat, or Nat-Nut, a
crétin, with inturned feet, who came flap-lapping along, shoulder
jerking up at every step. This poor creature sold nuts in the
public-houses where he was known. He had no roof to his mouth,
35 and the men used to mock his speech.

The first time he came into the "George" when Anna was there,
she asked, after he had gone, her eyes very round:

"Why does he do that when he walks?"

"'E canna 'elp 'isself, Duckie, it's tha' make o' th' fellow."

She thought about it, then she laughed nervously. And then she bethought herself, her cheeks flushed, and she cried:

"He's a *horrid* man."

"Nay, he's non horrid; he canna help it if he wor struck that road."

But when poor Nat came wambling* in again, she slid away. And 5 she would not eat his nuts, if the men bought them for her. And when the farmers gambled at dominoes for them, she was angry.

"They are dirty-man's nuts," she cried.

So a revulsion started against Nat, who had not long after to go to the workhouse. 10

There grew in Brangwen's heart now a secret desire to make her a lady. His brother Alfred, in Nottingham, had caused a great scandal by becoming the lover of an educated woman, a lady, widow of a doctor. Very often, Alfred Brangwen went down as a friend to her cottage, which was in Derbyshire, leaving his wife and family for a 15 day or two, then returning to them. And no-one dared gainsay him, for he was a strong-willed, direct man, and he said he was a friend of this widow.

One day Brangwen met his brother on the station.

"Where are *you* going to, then?" asked the younger brother. 20

"I'm going down to Wirksworth."

"You've got friends down there, I'm told."

"Yes."

"I s'll have to be lookin' in when I'm down that road."

"You please yourself." 25

Tom Brangwen was so curious about the woman, that the next time he was in Wirksworth he asked for her house.

He found a beautiful cottage on the steep side of a hill, looking clean over the town, that lay in the bottom of the basin, and away at the old quarries on the opposite side of the space. Mrs Forbes was in 30 the garden. She was a tall woman with white hair. She came up the path taking off her thick gloves, laying down her shears. It was autumn. She wore a wide-brimmed hat.

Brangwen blushed to the roots of his hair, and did not know what to say. 35

"I thought I might look in," he said, "knowing you were friends of my brother's. I had to come to Wirksworth."

She saw at once he was a Brangwen.

"Will you come in," she said. "My father is lying down."

She took him into a drawing room, full of books, with a piano and a violin-stand. And they talked, she simply and easily. She was full of dignity. The room was of a kind Brangwen had never known; the atmosphere seemed open and spacious, like a mountain-top to
5 him.

"Does my brother like reading?" he asked.

"Some things. He has been reading Herbert Spencer—and we read Browning* sometimes."

Brangwen was full of admiration, deep, thrilling, almost rever-
10 ential admiration. He looked at her with lit-up eyes when she said "we read." At last he burst out, looking round the room:

"I didn't know our Alfred was this way inclined."

"He is quite an unusual man."

He looked at her in amazement. She evidently had a new idea of
15 his brother: she evidently appreciated him. He looked again at the woman. She was about forty, straight, rather hard, a curious, separate creature. Himself, he was not in love with her. There was something chilling about her. But he was filled with boundless admiration.

20 At tea-time, he was introduced to her father, an invalid who had to be helped about, but who was ruddy and well-favoured, with snowy hair and watery blue eyes, and a courtly, naïve manner that again was new and strange to Brangwen, so suave, so merry, so innocent.

His brother was this woman's lover! It was too amazing. Brangwen
25 went home despising himself for his own poor way of life. He was a clod-hopper and a boor, dull, stuck in the mud. More than ever he wanted to clamber out, to this visionary polite world.

He was well-off. He was as well-off as Alfred, who could not have above six hundred a year, all told. He himself made about four
30 hundred, and could make more. His investments got better every day. Why did he not do something? His wife was a lady also.

But when he got to the Marsh, he realised how fixed everything was, how the other form of life was beyond him, and he regretted, for the first time, that he had succeeded to the farm. He felt a prisoner,
35 sitting safe and easy and unadventurous. He might, with risk, have done more with himself. He could neither read Browning nor Herbert Spencer, nor have access to such a room as Mrs Forbes'. All that form of life was outside him.

But then, he said he did not want it. The excitement of the visit
40 began to pass off. The next day he was himself, and if he thought of

the other woman, there was something about her and her place that he did not like, something cold, something alien, as if she were not a woman, but an inhuman being who used up human life for cold, unliving purposes.

The evening came on, he played with Anna, and then sat alone 5 with his own wife. She was sewing. He sat very still, smoking, perturbed. He was aware of his wife's quiet figure and quiet, dark head bent over her needle. It was too quiet for him. It was too peaceful. He wanted to smash the walls down, and let the night in, so that his wife should not be so secure and quiet, sitting there. He 10 wished the air were not so close and narrow. His wife was obliterated from him, she was in her own world, quiet, secure, unnoticed, unnoticing. He was shut down by her.

He rose to go out. He could not sit still any longer. He must get out of this oppressive, shut-down, woman-haunt. 15

His wife lifted her head and looked at him.

"Are you going out?" she asked.

He looked down and met her eyes. They were darker than darkness, and gave deeper space. He felt himself retreating before her, defensive, whilst her eyes followed and tracked him down. 20

"I was just going up to Cossethay," he said.

She remained watching him.

"Why do you go?" she said.

His heart beat fast, and he sat down, slowly.

"No reason particular," he said, beginning to fill his pipe again, 25 mechanically.

"Why do you go away so often?" she said.

"But you don't want me," he replied.

She was silent for a while.

"You do not want to be with me any more," she said. 30

It startled him. How did she know this truth? He thought it was his secret.

"Yi," he said.

"You want to find something else," she said.

He did not answer. Did he?, he asked himself. 35

"You should not want so much attention," she said. "You are not a baby."

"I'm not grumbling," he said. Yet he knew he was.

"You think you have not enough," she said.

"How enough?" 40

"You think you have not enough in me. But how do you know me? What do you do to make me love you?"

He was flabbergasted.

"I never said I hadn't enough in you," he replied. "I didn't know
5 you wanted making to love me. What do you want?"

"You don't make it good between us any more, you are not interested. You do not make me want you."

"And you don't make me want *you*—do you now?"

There was a silence. They were such strangers.
10 "Would you like to have another woman?" she asked.

His eyes grew round, he did not know where he was. How could she, his own wife, say such a thing? But she sat there small and foreign and separate. It dawned upon him she did not consider herself his wife, except in so far as they agreed. She did not feel she
15 had married him. At any rate, she was willing to allow he might want another woman. A gap, a space opened before him.

"No," he said, slowly. "What other woman should I want?"

"Like your brother," she said.

He was silent for some time, ashamed also.
20 "What of her?" he said "I didn't like the woman."

"Yes, you liked her," she answered persistently.

He stared in wonder at his wife as she told him his own heart so callously. And he was indignant. What right had she to sit there telling him these things. She was his wife, what right had she to
25 speak to him like this, as if she were a stranger.

"I didn't," he said. "I want no woman."

"Yes, you would like to be like Alfred."

His silence was one of angry frustration. He was astonished. He had told her of his visit to Wirksworth, but briefly, without interest,
30 he thought.

As she sat with her strange dark face turned towards him, her eyes watched him, inscrutable, casting him up. He began to oppose her. She was again the active unknown facing him. Must he admit her? He resisted involuntarily.
35 "Why should you want to find a woman who is more to you than me?" she said.

The turbulence raged in his breast.

"I don't," he said.

"Why do you?" she repeated. "Why do you want to deny me?"
40 Suddenly, in a flash, he saw she might be lonely, isolated, unsure.

She had seemed to him the utterly certain, satisfied, absolute, excluding him. Could she need anything?

"Why aren't you satisfied with me?—I'm not satisfied with you. Paul used to come to me and take me like a man does. You only leave me alone, or come to me like your cattle, quickly, to forget me again—so that you can forget me again."

"What am I to remember about you?" said Brangwen.

"I want you to know there is somebody there besides yourself."

"Well don't I know it?"

"You come to me as if it was for nothing, as if I was nothing there. When Paul came to me, I *was* something to him—a woman, I was. To you I am nothing—it is like cattle—or nothing—"

"You make me feel as if *I* was nothing," he said.

They were silent. She sat watching him. He could not move, his soul was seething and chaotic. She turned to her sewing again. But the sight of her bent before him held him and would not let him be. She was a strange, hostile, dominant thing. Yet not quite hostile. As he sat he felt his limbs were strong and hard, he sat in strength.

She was silent for a long time, stitching. He was aware, poignantly, of the round shape of her head, very intimate, compelling. She lifted her head and sighed. The blood burned in him, her voice ran to him like fire.

"Come here," she said, unsure.

For some moments he did not move. Then he rose slowly and went across the hearth. It required an almost deathly effort of volition, or of acquiescence. He stood before her and looked down at her. Her face was shining again, her eyes were shining again like terrible laughter. It was to him terrible, how she could be transfigured. He could not look at her, it burnt his heart.

"My love!" she said.

And she put her arms round him as he stood before her, round his thighs, pressing him against her breast. And her hands on him seemed to reveal to him the mould of his own nakedness, he was passionately lovely to himself. He could not bear to look at her.

"My dear!" she said. He knew she spoke a foreign language. The fear was like bliss in his heart. He looked down. Her face was shining, her eyes were full of light, she was awful. He suffered from the compulsion to her. She was the awful unknown. He bent down to her, suffering, unable to let go, unable to let himself go, yet drawn, driven. She was now the transfigured, she was wonderful, beyond

him. He wanted to go. But he could not as yet kiss her. He was himself, apart. Easiest he could kiss her feet. But he was ashamed for the actual deed, which were like an affront. She waited for him to meet her, not to bow before her, and serve her. She wanted his active
5   participation, not his submission.

She put her fingers on him. And it was torture to him, that he must give himself to her actively, participate in her, that he must meet and embrace and know her, who was other than himself. There was that in him which shrank from yielding to her, resisted the relaxing
10 towards her, opposed the mingling with her, even whilst he most desired it. He was afraid, he wanted to save himself.

There were a few moments of stillness. Then gradually, the tension, the withholding relaxed in him, and he began to flow towards her. She was beyond him, the unattainable. But he let go his
15 hold on himself, he relinquished himself, and knew the subterranean force of his desire to come to her, to be with her, to mingle with her, losing himself to find her, to find himself in her. He began to approach her, to draw near.

His blood beat up in waves of desire. He wanted to come to her, to
20 meet her. She was there, if he could reach her. The reality of her who was just beyond him absorbed him. Blind and destroyed, he pressed forward, nearer, nearer, to receive the consummation of himself, be received within the darkness which should swallow him and yield him up to himself. If he could come really within the
25 blazing kernel of darkness, if really he could be destroyed, burnt away till he lit with her in one consummation, that were supreme, supreme.

Their coming together now, after two years of married life, was much more wonderful to them than it had been before. It was the
30 entry into another circle of existence, it was the baptism to another life, it was the complete confirmation.* Their feet trod strange ground of knowledge, their footsteps were lit-up with discovery. Wherever they walked, it was well, the world re-echoed round them in discovery. They went gladly and forgetful. Everything was lost,
35 and everything was found.* The new world was discovered, it remained only to be explored.

They had passed through the doorway into the further space, where movement was so big, that it contained bonds and constraints and labours, and still was complete liberty.* She was the doorway to
40 him, he to her. At last they had thrown open the doors, each to the

other, and had stood in the doorways facing each other, whilst the light flooded out from behind on to each of their faces, it was the transfiguration, the glorification, the admission.*

And always the light of the transfiguration burned on in their hearts. He went his way, as before, she went her way, to the rest of the world, there seemed no change. But to the two of them, there was the perpetual wonder of the transfiguration.

He did not know her any better, any more precisely, now that he knew her altogether. Poland, her husband, the war—he understood no more of this in her. He did not understand her foreign nature, half German, half Polish, nor her foreign speech. But he knew her, he knew her meaning, without understanding. What she said, what she spoke, this was a blind gesture on her part. In herself she walked strong and clear, he knew her, he saluted her, was with her. What was memory after all, but the recording of a number of possibilities which had never been fulfilled? What was Paul Lensky to her, but an unfulfilled possibility of which he, Brangwen, was the reality and the fulfilment. What did it matter, that Anna Lensky was born of Lydia and Paul? God was her father and her mother, He had passed through the married pair without fully making Himself known to them.

Now He was declared to Brangwen and to Lydia Brangwen, as they stood together. When at last they had joined hands, the house was finished, and the Lord took up His abode.* And they were glad.

The days went on as before, Brangwen went out to his work, his wife nursed her child and attended in some measure to the farm. They did not think of each other—why should they? Only when she touched him, he knew her instantly, that she was with him, near him, that she was the gateway and the way out, that she was beyond, and that he was travelling in her through the beyond. Whither?—What does it matter? He responded always. When she called, he answered, when he asked, her response came at once, or at length.

Anna's soul was put at peace between them. She looked from one to the other, and she saw them established to her safety, and she was free. She played between the pillar of fire and the pillar of cloud* in confidence, having the assurance on her right hand and the assurance on her left. She was no more called upon to uphold with her childish might the broken end of the arch. Her father and her mother now met to the span of the heavens, and she, the child, was free to play in the space beneath, between.

Chapter IV

Girlhood of Anna Brangwen

When Anna was nine years old, Brangwen sent her to the dame's school* in Cossethay. There she went, flipping and dancing in her
5 inconsequential fashion, doing very much as she liked, disconcerting old Miss Coates by her indifference to respectability and by her lack of reverence. Anna only laughed at Miss Coates, liked her, and patronised her in superb, childish fashion.

The girl was at once shy and wild. She had a curious contempt for
10 ordinary people, a benevolent superiority. She was very shy, and tortured with misery when people did not like her. On the other hand, she cared very little for anybody save her mother, whom she still rather resentfully worshipped, and her father, whom she loved and patronised, but upon whom she depended. These two, her
15 mother and father, held her still in fee.* But she was free of other people, towards whom, on the whole, she took the benevolent attitude. She deeply hated ugliness or intrusion or arrogance, however. As a child, she was as proud and shadowy as a tiger, and as aloof. She could confer favours, but, save from her mother and father, she
20 could receive none. She hated people who came too near to her. Like a wild thing, she wanted her distance. She mistrusted intimacy.

In Cossethay and Ilkeston she was always an alien. She had plenty of acquaintances, but no friends. Very few people whom she met were significant to her. They seemed parts of a herd, undis-
25 tinguished. She did not take people very seriously.

She had two brothers, Tom, dark-haired, small, volatile, whom she was intimately related to but whom she never mingled with, and Fred, fair and responsive, whom she adored but did not consider as a real, separate being. She was too much the centre of her own
30 universe, too little aware of anything outside.

The first *person* she met, who affected her as a real living person, whom she regarded as having definite existence, was Baron Skrebensky,* her mother's friend. He also was a Polish exile, who had taken orders, and had received from Mr Gladstone* a small
35 country living in Yorkshire.

When Anna was about ten years old, she went with her mother to
spend a few days with the Baron Skrebensky. He was very unhappy
in his red-brick vicarage. He was vicar of a country church, a living
worth a little over two hundred pounds a year, but he had a large
parish containing several collieries, with a new, raw, heathen   5
population. He went to the north of England expecting homage from
the common people, for he was an aristocrat. He was roughly, even
cruelly received. But he never understood it. He remained a fiery
aristocrat. Only he had to learn to avoid his parishioners.

Anna was very much impressed by him. He was a smallish man   10
with a rugged, rather crumpled face and blue eyes set very deep and
glowing. His wife was a tall thin woman, of noble Polish family, mad
with pride. He still spoke broken English, for he had kept very close
to his wife, both of them forlorn in this strange, inhospitable country,
and they always spoke in Polish together. He was disappointed with   15
Mrs Brangwen's soft, natural English, very disappointed that her
child spoke no Polish.

Anna loved to watch him. She liked the big, new, rambling
vicarage, desolate and stark on its hill. It was so exposed, so bleak and
bold after the Marsh. The Baron talked endlessly in Polish to Mrs   20
Brangwen; he made furious gestures with his hands, his blue eyes
were full of fire. And to Anna, there was a significance about his
sharp, flinging movements. Something in her responded, to his
extravagance and his exuberant manner. She thought him a very
wonderful person. She was shy of him, she liked him to talk to her.   25
She felt a sense of freedom near him.

She never could tell how she knew it, but she did know that he was
a knight of Malta.* She could never remember whether she had seen
his star, or cross, or his order or not, but it flashed in her mind, like a
symbol. He at any rate represented to the child the real world, where   30
kings and lords and princes moved and fulfilled their shining lives,
whilst queens and ladies and princesses upheld the noble order.

She had recognised the Baron Skrebensky as a real person, he had
had some regard for her. But when she did not see him any more, he
faded and became a memory. But as a memory he was always alive to   35
her.

Anna became a tall, awkward girl. Her eyes were still very dark
and quick, but they had grown careless, they had lost their watchful,
hostile look. Her fierce, spun hair turned brown, it grew heavier and
was tied back. She was sent to a young ladies' school in Nottingham.*   40

And at this period she was absorbed in becoming a young lady.
She was intelligent enough, but not interested in learning. At first,
she thought all the girls at school very ladylike and wonderful, and
she wanted to be like them. She came to a speedy disillusion: they
5 galled and maddened her, they were petty and mean. After the loose,
generous atmosphere of her home, where little things did not count,
she was always uneasy in the world, that would snap and bite at every
trifle.

A quick change came over her. She mistrusted herself, she
10 mistrusted the outer world. She did not want to go on, she did not
want to go out into it, she wanted to go no further.

"What do *I* care about that lot of girls?" she would say to her
father, contemptuously, "they are nobody."

The trouble was that the girls could not accept Anna at her
15 measure. They would have her according to themselves or not at all.
So she was confused, seduced, she became as they were for a time,
and then, in revulsion, she hated them furiously.

"Why don't you ask some of your girls here?" her father would
say.

20 "They're not coming here," she cried.

"And why not."

"They're bagatelle,"* she said, using one of her mother's rare
phrases.

"Bagatelles or billiards, it makes no matter, they're nice young
25 lasses enough."

But Anna was not to be won over. She had a curious shrinking
from commonplace people, and particularly from the young lady of
her day. She would not go into company because of the ill-at-ease
feeling other people brought upon her. And she never could decide
30 whether it were her fault or theirs. She half respected these other
people, and continuous disillusion maddened her. She wanted to
respect them. Still she thought the people she did not *know* were
wonderful. Those she knew seemed always to be limiting her, tying
her up in little falsities that irritated her beyond bearing. She would
35 rather stay at home, and avoid the rest of the world, leave it illusory.

For at the Marsh life had indeed a certain freedom and largeness.
There was no fret about money, no mean little precedence, nor care
for what other people thought, because neither Mrs Brangwen nor
Brangwen could be sensible of any judgment passed on them from
40 outside. Their lives were too separate.

So Anna was only easy at home, where the common sense and the supreme relation between her parents produced a freer standard of being than she could find outside. Where, outside the Marsh, could she find the tolerant dignity she had been brought up in? Her parents stood undiminished and unaware of criticism. The people she met 5 outside seemed to begrudge her her very existence. They seemed to want to belittle her also. She was exceedingly reluctant to go amongst them. She depended upon her mother and her father. And yet she wanted to go out.

At school, or in the world, she was usually at fault, she felt usually 10 that she ought to be slinking in disgrace. She was never quite sure, in herself, whether she were wrong, or whether the others were wrong. She had not done her lessons: well, she did not see any reason why she *should* do her lessons, if she did not want to. Was there some occult reason why she should? Were these people, school- 15 mistresses, representatives of some mystic Right, some Higher Good? They seemed to think so themselves. But she could not for her life see why a woman should bully and insult her because she did not know thirty lines of "As You Like It."* After all, *what* did it matter if she knew them or not? Nothing could persuade her that it 20 was of the slightest importance. Because she despised inwardly the coarsely working nature of the mistress. Therefore she was always at outs with authority. From constant telling, she came almost to believe in her own badness, her own intrinsic inferiority. She felt that she ought to be always in a state of slinking disgrace, if she fulfilled 25 what was expected of her. But she rebelled. She never really believed in her own badness. At the bottom of her heart she despised the other people, who carped and were loud over trifles. She despised them, and wanted revenge on them. She hated them whilst they had power over her. 30

Still she kept an ideal: a free, proud lady absolved from the petty ties, existing beyond petty considerations. She would see such ladies in pictures: Alexandra,* Princess of Wales, was one of her models. This lady was proud and royal, and stepped indifferently over all small, mean desires: so thought Anna, in her heart. And the girl did 35 up her hair high under a little slanting hat, her skirts were fashionably bunched up, she wore an elegant, skin-fitting coat.

Her father was delighted. Anna was very proud in her bearing, too naturally indifferent to smaller bonds to satisfy Ilkeston, which would have liked to put her down. But Brangwen was having no such 40 thing. If she chose to be royal, royal she should be. He stood like a rock between her and the world.

After the fashion of his family, he grew stout and handsome. His blue eyes were full of light, twinkling and sensitive, his manner was deliberate, but hearty, warm. His capacity for living his own life without attention from his neighbours made them respect him. They would run to do anything for him. He did not consider them, but was open-handed towards them, so they made profit of their willingness. He liked people, so long as they remained in the background.

Mrs Brangwen went on in her own way, following her own devices. She had her husband, her two sons, and Anna. These staked out and marked her horizon. The other people were outsiders. Inside her own world, her life passed along like a dream for her, it lapsed, and she lived within its lapse, active and always pleased, intent. She scarcely noticed the outer things at all. What was outside was outside, non-existent. She did not mind if the boys fought, so long as it was out of her presence. But if they fought when she was by, she was angry, and they were afraid of her. She did not care if they broke a window of a railway carriage or sold their watches to have a revel at the Goose Fair.* Brangwen was perhaps angry over these things. To the mother they were insignificant.

It was odd little things that offended her. She was furious if the boys hung round the slaughter-house, she was displeased when the school reports were bad. It did not matter how many sins her boys were accused of, so long as they were not stupid, or inferior. If they seemed to brook insult, she hated them. And it was only a certain *gaucherie*, a gawkiness on Anna's part that irritated her against the girl. Certain forms of clumsiness, grossness, made the mother's eyes glow with curious rage. Otherwise she was pleased, indifferent.

Pursuing her splendid-lady ideal, Anna became a lofty demoiselle of sixteen, plagued by family shortcomings. She was very sensitive to her father. She knew if he had been drinking, were he ever so little affected, and she could not bear it. He flushed when he drank, the veins stood out on his temples, there was a twinkling, cavalier boisterousness in his eyes, his manner was jovially overbearing and mocking. And it angered her. When she heard his loud, roaring, boisterous mockery, an anger of resentment filled her. She was quick to forestall him, the moment he came in.

"You look a sight, you do, red in the face," she cried.

"I might look worse if I was green," he answered.

"Boozing in Ilkeston."

"And what's wrong wi' Il'son?"

She flounced away. He watched her with amused, twinkling eyes, yet in spite of himself sad that she flouted him.

They were a curious family, a law to themselves, separate from the 5 world, isolated, a small republic set in invisible bounds. The mother was quite indifferent to Ilkeston and Cossethay, to any claims made on her from outside, she was very shy of any outsider, exceedingly courteous, winning even. But the moment a visitor had gone, she laughed and dismissed him, he did not exist. It had been all a game to 10 her. She was still a foreigner, unsure of her ground. But alone with her own children and husband at the Marsh, she was mistress of a little native land that lacked nothing.

She had some beliefs somewhere, never defined. She had been brought up a Roman Catholic. She had gone to the Church of 15 England for protection. The outward form was a matter of indifference to her. Yet she had some fundamental religion. It was as if she worshipped God as a Mystery, never seeking in the least to define what He was.

And inside her, the subtle sense of the Great Absolute wherein 20 she had her being was very strong. The English dogma never reached her: the language was too foreign. Through it all she felt the great Separator* who held life in His hands, gleaming, imminent, terrible, the Great Mystery, immediate beyond all telling.

She shone and gleamed to the Mystery, Whom she knew through 25 all her senses, she glanced with strange, mystic superstitions that never found expression in the English language, never mounted to thought in English. But so she lived, within a potent, sensuous belief that included her family and contained her destiny.

To this she had reduced her husband. He existed with her entirely 30 indifferent to the general values of the world. Her very ways, the very mark of her eyebrows were symbols and indication to him. There, on the farm with her, he lived through a mystery of life and death and creation, strange, profound ecstasies and incommunicable satisfactions, of which the rest of the world knew nothing; which made the 35 pair of them apart and respected in the English village, for they were also well-to-do.

But Anna was only half safe within her mother's unthinking knowledge. She had a mother-of-pearl rosary that had been her own father's. What it meant to her she could never say. But the string of 40

moonlight and silver, when she had it between her fingers, filled her
with strange passion. She learned at school a little Latin, she learned
an Ave Maria and a Pater Noster,* she learned how to say her rosary.
But that was no good. "Ave Maria, gratia plena, Dominus tecum,
5 benedicta tu in mulieribus et benedictus fructus ventris tui Jesus.
Ave Maria, Sancta Maria, ora pro nobis peccatoribus, nunc et in
hora mortis nostrae, Amen."

It was not right, somehow. What these words meant when
translated was not the same as the pale rosary meant. There was a
10 discrepancy, a falsehood. It irritated her to say "Dominus tecum," or
"benedicta tu in mulieribus." She loved the mystic words "Ave
Maria, Sancta Maria": she was moved by "benedictus fructus ventris
tui Jesus," and by "nunc et in hora mortis nostrae." But none of it
was quite real. It was not satisfactory, somehow.

15 She avoided her rosary, because, moving her with curious passion
as it did, it *meant* only these not very significant things. She put it
away. It was her instinct to put all these things away. It was her
instinct to avoid thinking, to avoid it, to save herself.

She was seventeen, touchy, full of spirits, and very moody: quick
20 to flush, and always uneasy, uncertain. For some reason or other, she
turned more to her father, she felt almost flashes of hatred for her
mother. Her mother's dark muzzle and curiously insidious ways, her
mother's utter surety and confidence, her strange satisfaction, even
triumph, her mother's way of laughing at things, and her mother's
25 silent overriding of vexatious propositions, most of all her mother's
triumphant power maddened the girl.

She became sudden and incalculable. Often she stood at the
window, looking out, as if she wanted to go. Sometimes she went, she
mixed with people. But always she came home in anger, as if she
30 were diminished, belittled, almost degraded.

There was over the house a kind of dark silence and intensity, in
which passion worked its inevitable conclusions. There was in the
house a sort of richness, a deep, inarticulate interchange which
made other places seem thin and unsatisfying. Brangwen could sit
35 silent, smoking in his chair, the mother could move about in her
quiet, insidious way, and the sense of the two presences was powerful, sustaining. The whole intercourse was wordless, intense and
close.

But Anna was uneasy. She wanted to get away. Yet wherever she
40 went, there came upon her that feeling of thinness, as if she were
made smaller, belittled. She hastened home.

There she raged and interrupted the strong, settled interchange. Sometimes her mother turned on her with a fierce, destructive anger, in which was no pity nor consideration. And Anna shrank, afraid. She went to her father.

He would still listen to the spoken word, which fell sterile on the unheeding mother. Sometimes Anna talked to her father. She tried to discuss people, she wanted to know what was meant. But her father became uneasy. He did not want to have things dragged into consciousness. Only out of consideration for her he listened. And there was a kind of bristling rousedness in the room. The cat got up and stretched* itself, went uneasily to the door. Mrs Brangwen was silent, she seemed ominous. Anna could not go on with her fault-finding, her criticism, her expression of dissatisfactions. She felt even her father against her. He had a strong, dark bond with her mother, a potent intimacy that existed inarticulate and wild, following its own course, and savage if interrupted, uncovered.

Nevertheless Brangwen was uneasy about the girl, the whole house continued to be disturbed. She had a pathetic, baffled appeal. She was hostile to her parents, even whilst she lived entirely within them, within their spell.

Many ways she tried, of escape. She became an assiduous church-goer. But the *language* meant nothing to her: it seemed false. She hated to hear things expressed, put into words. Whilst the religious feelings were inside her, they were passionately moving. In the mouth of the clergyman, they were false, indecent. She tried to read. But again the tedium and the sense of the falsity of the spoken word put her off. She went to stay with girl friends. At first she thought it splendid. But then the inner boredom came on, it seemed to her all nothingness. And she felt always belittled, as if never, never could she stretch her length and stride her stride.

Her mind reverted often to the torture cell of a certain Bishop of France,* in which the victim could neither stand nor lie stretched out, never. Not that she thought of herself in any connection with this. But often there came into her mind the wonder, how the cell was built, and she could feel the horror of the crampedness, as something very real.

She was, however, only eighteen when a letter came from Mrs Alfred Brangwen, in Nottingham, saying that her son William was coming to Ilkeston to take a place as junior draughtsman, scarcely more than apprentice, in a lace-factory. He was twenty years old, and would the Marsh Brangwens be friendly with him.

Tom Brangwen at once wrote offering the young man a home at
the Marsh. This was not accepted, but the Nottingham Brangwens
expressed gratitude.

There had never been much love lost between the Nottingham
5 Brangwens and the Marsh. Indeed, Mrs Alfred, having inherited
three thousand pounds, and having occasion to be dissatisfied with
her husband, held aloof from all the Brangwens whatsoever. She
affected, however, some esteem of Mrs Tom, as she called the Polish
woman, saying that at any rate she was a lady.

10 Anna Brangwen was faintly excited at the news of her cousin
Will's coming to Ilkeston. She knew plenty of young men, but they
had never become real to her. She had seen in this young gallant a
nose she liked, in that a pleasant moustache, in the other a nice way
of wearing clothes, in one a ridiculous fringe of hair, in another a
15 comical way of talking. They were objects of amusement and faint
wonder to her, rather than real beings, the young men.

The only man she knew was her father; and, as he was something
large, looming, a kind of Godhead, he embraced all manhood for
her, and other men were just incidental.

20 She remembered her cousin Will. He had town clothes and was
thin, with a very curious head, black as jet, with hair like sleek, thin
fur. It was a curious head: it reminded her she knew not of what: of
some animal, some mysterious animal that lived in the darkness
under the leaves and never came out, but which lived vividly, swift
25 and intense. She always thought of him with that black, keen, blind
head. And she considered him odd.

He appeared at the Marsh one Sunday morning: a rather long,
thin youth with a bright face and a curious self-possession among his
shyness, a native unawareness of what other people might be, since
30 he was himself.

When Anna came downstairs in her Sunday clothes, ready for
church, he rose and greeted her conventionally, shaking hands. His
manners were better than hers. She flushed. She noticed that he now
had a black fledge on his upper lip, a black, finely-shapen line
35 marking his wide mouth. It rather repelled her. It reminded her of
the thin, fine fur of his hair. She was aware of something strange in
him.

His voice had rather high upper notes, and very resonant middle
notes. It was queer. She wondered why he did it. But he sat very
40 naturally in the Marsh living-room. He had some uncouthness,

some natural self-possession of the Brangwens, that made him at home there.

Anna was rather troubled by the intimate,* affectionate way her father had towards this young man. He seemed gentle towards him, he put himself aside in order to fill out the young man. This irritated 5 Anna.

"Father," she said abruptly, "give me some collection."

"What collection?" asked Brangwen.

"Don't be ridiculous," she cried, flushing.

"Nay," he said, "what collection's this?" 10

"You know it's the first Sunday of the month."

Anna stood confused. Why was he doing this, why was he making her conspicuous before this stranger!

"I want some collection," she re-asserted.

"So tha says," he replied indifferently, looking at her then turning 15 again to his nephew.

She went forward, and thrust her hand into his breeches pocket. He smoked stolidly, making no resistance, talking to his nephew. Her hand groped about in his pocket, and then drew out his leathern purse. Her colour was bright in her clear cheeks, her eyes 20 shone. Brangwen's eyes were twinkling. The nephew sat sheepishly. Anna, in her finery, sat down and slid all the money into her lap. There was silver and gold. The youth could not help watching her. She was bent over the heap of money, fingering the different coins. 25

"I've a good mind to take half a sovereign," she said, and she looked up with glowing dark eyes. She met the light-brown eyes of her cousin, close and intent upon her. She was startled. She laughed quickly, and turned to her father.

"I've a good mind to take half a sovereign, our Dad," she said. 30

"Yes, nimble fingers," said her father. "You take what's your own."

"Are you coming, our Anna?" asked her brother from the door.

She suddenly chilled to normal, forgetting both her father and her cousin. 35

"Yes, I'm ready," she said, taking sixpence from the heap of money and sliding the rest back into the purse, which she laid on the table.

"Give it here," said her father.

Hastily she thrust the purse into his pocket and was going out. 40

"You'd better go wi' 'em, lad, hadn't you?" said the father to the nephew.

Will Brangwen rose uncertainly. He had golden-brown, quick, steady eyes, like a bird's, like a hawk's, which cannot look afraid.

5 "Your Cousin Will 'll come with you," said the father.

Anna glanced at the strange youth again. She felt him waiting there for her to notice him. He was hovering on the edge of her consciousness, ready to come in. She did not want to look at him: she was antagonistic to him.

10 She waited without speaking. Her cousin took his hat and joined her. It was summer outside. Her brother Fred was plucking a sprig of flowering currant to put in his coat, from the bush at the angle of the house. She took no notice. Her cousin followed just behind her.

They were on the high-road. She was aware of a strangeness in

15 her being. It made her uncertain. She caught sight of the flowering currant in her brother's buttonhole.

"Oh, our Fred," she cried. "Don't wear that stuff to go to church."

Fred looked down protectively at the pink adornment on his

20 breast.

"Why, I like it," he said.

"Then you're the only one who does, I'm sure," she said. And she turned to her cousin.

"Do *you* like the smell of it?" she asked.

25 He was there beside her, tall and uncouth and yet self-possessed. It excited her.

"I can't say whether I do or not," he replied.

"Give it here, Fred, don't have it smelling in church," she said to the little boy, her page.

30 Her fair, small brother handed her the flower dutifully. She sniffed it and gave it without a word to her cousin, for his judgment. He smelled the dangling flower curiously.

"It's a funny smell," he said.

And suddenly she laughed, and a quick light came on all their

35 faces, there was a blithe trip in the small boy's walk.

The bells were ringing, they were going up the summery hill in their Sunday clothes. Anna was very fine in a silk frock of brown and white stripes, tight along the arms and the body, bunched up very elegantly behind the skirt. There was something of the cavalier about

40 Will Brangwen, and he was well dressed.

He walked along with the sprig of currant-blossom dangling between his fingers, and none of them spoke. The sun shone brightly on little showers of buttercup down the bank, in the fields the fool's-parsley was foamy, held very high and proud above a number of flowers that flitted in the greenish twilight of the mowing-grass below.

They reached the church. Fred led the way to the pew, followed by the cousin, then Anna. She felt very conspicuous and important. Somehow, this young man gave her away to the other people. He stood aside and let her pass to her place, then sat next to her. It was a curious sensation, to sit next to him.

The colour came streaming from the painted window above her. It lit on the dark wood of the pew, on the stone, worn aisle, on the pillar behind her cousin, and on her cousin's hands, as they lay on his knees. She sat amid illumination, illumination and luminous shadow all around her, her soul very bright. She sat, without knowing it, conscious of the hands and motionless knees of her cousin. Something strange had entered into her world, something entirely strange and unlike what she knew.

She was curiously elated. She sat in a glowing world of unreality, very delightful. A brooding light, like laughter, was in her eyes. She was aware of a strange influence entering in to her, which she enjoyed. It was a dark, enrichening influence she had not known before. She did not think of her cousin. But she was startled when his hands moved.

She *wished* he would not say the responses so plainly. It diverted her from her vague enjoyment. Why would he obtrude, and draw notice to himself? It was bad taste. But she went on all right till the hymn came. He stood up beside her to sing, and that pleased her. Then suddenly, at the very first word, his voice came strong and over-riding, filling the church. He was singing the tenor. Her soul opened in amazement. His voice filled the church! It rang out like a trumpet, and rang out again. She started to giggle over her hymn-book. But he went on, perfectly steady. Up and down rang his voice, going its own way. She was helplessly shocked into laughter. Between moments of dead silence in herself she shook with laughter. On came the laughter, seized her and shook her till the tears were into her eyes. She was amazed, and rather enjoyed it. And still the hymn rolled on, and still she laughed. She bent over her hymn-book crimson with confusion, but still her sides shook with laughter. She

pretended to cough, she pretended to have a crumb in her throat.
Fred was gazing up at her with clear blue eyes. She was recovering
herself. And then a slur in the strong, blind voice at her side brought
it all on again, in a gust of mad laughter.

5   She bent down to prayer in cold reproof of herself. And yet, as she
knelt, little eddies of giggling went over her. The very sight of his
knees on the praying cushion sent the little shock of laughter over
her.

She gathered herself together and sat with prim, pure face, white
10   and pink and cold as a christmas rose, her hands in her silk gloves
folded on her lap, her dark eyes all vague, abstracted in a sort of
dream, oblivious of everything.

The sermon rolled on vaguely, in a tide of pregnant peace. Her
cousin took out his pocket handkerchief. He seemed to be drifted
15   absorbed into the sermon. He put his handkerchief to his face. Then
something dropped on to his knee. There lay the bit of flowering
currant! He was looking down at it in real astonishment. A wild snirt*
of laughter came from Anna. Everybody heard: it was torture. He
had shut the crumpled flower in his hand and was looking up again
20   with the same absorbed attention to the sermon. Another snirt of
laughter from Anna. Fred nudged her remindingly. Her cousin sat
motionless. Somehow she was aware that his face was red. She could
feel him. His hand, closed over the flower, remained quite still,
pretending to be normal. Another wild struggle in Anna's breast, and
25   the snirt of laughter. She bent forward shaking with laughter. It was
now no joke. Fred was nudge-nudging at her. She nudged him back
fiercely. Then another vicious spasm of laughter seized her. She
tried to ward it off in a little cough. The cough ended in a suppressed
whoop. The whole church heard it. She wanted to die. And the
30   closed hand crept away to the pocket. Whilst she sat in taut suspense,
the laughter rushed back at her, knowing he was fumbling in his
pocket to shove the flower away.

In the end, she felt weak, exhausted, and thoroughly depressed. A
blankness of wincing depression came over her. She hated the
35   presence of the other people. Her face became quite haughty. She
was unaware of her cousin any more.

When the collection arrived, with the last hymn, her cousin was
again singing resoundingly. And still it amused her. In spite of the
shameful exhibition she had made of herself, it amused her still. She
40   listened to it in a spell of amusement. And the bag was thrust in front

of her, and her sixpence was mingled in the folds of her glove. In her haste to get it out, it flipped away and went tinkling in the next pew. She stood and giggled. She could not help it: she laughed outright, a figure of shame.

"What were you laughing about, our Anna?" asked Fred, the 5 moment they were out of the church.

"Oh, I couldn't help it," she said, in her careless, half mocking fashion. "I don't know *why* Cousin Will's singing set me off."

"What was there in my singing to make you laugh?" he asked.

"It was so loud," she said.   10

They did not look at each other, but they both laughed again, both reddening.

"What were you snorting o'laughing for, our Anna?" asked Tom, the elder brother, at the dinner table, his hazel eyes bright with joy. "Everybody stopped to look at you." Tom was in the choir.   15

She was aware of Will's eyes shining steadily upon her, waiting for her to speak.

"It was Cousin Will's singing," she said.

At which her cousin burst into a suppressed, chuckling laugh, suddenly showing all his small, regular, rather sharp teeth, and just 20 as quickly closing his mouth again.

"Has he got such a remarkable voice on him then?" asked Brangwen.

"No, it's not that," said Anna. "Only it tickled me—I couldn't tell you why."   25

And again a ripple of laughter went down the table. Will Brangwen thrust forward his dark face, his eyes dancing, and said:

"I'm in the choir of St Nicholas'."

"Oh, you go to church then?" said Brangwen.

"Mother does—father doesn't," replied the youth.   30

It was the little things, his movement, the funny tones of his voice, that showed up big to Anna. The matter-of-fact things he said were absurd in contrast. The things her father said seemed meaningless and neutral.

During the afternoon they sat in the parlour, that smelled of 35 geranium, and they ate cherries, and talked. Will Brangwen was called on to give himself forth. And soon he was drawn out.

He was interested in churches, in church architecture. The influence of Ruskin had stimulated him to a pleasure in the mediæval forms.* His talk was fragmentary, he was only half articulate. But 40

listening to him, as he spoke of church after church, of nave and chancel and transept, of rood-screen and font, of hatchet-carving and moulding and tracery, speaking always with close passion of particular things, particular places, there gathered in her heart a
5   pregnant hush of churches, a mystery, a ponderous significance of bowed stone, a dim coloured light through which something took place obscurely, passing into darkness: a high, delighted framework of the mystic screen, and beyond, in the furthest beyond, the altar. It was a very real experience. She was carried away. And the land
10   seemed to be covered with a vast, mystic church, reserved in gloom, thrilled with an unknown Presence.

Almost it hurt her, to look out of the window and see the lilacs towering in the vivid sunshine. Or was this the jewelled glass?

He talked of Gothic and Renaissance and Perpendicular, and
15   Early English and Norman. The words thrilled her.

"Have you been to Southwell?" he said. "I was there at twelve o'clock, at midday, eating my lunch in the churchyard. And the bells played a hymn.*

"Ay, it's a fine Minster, Southwell, heavy. It's got heavy, round
20   arches, rather low, on thick pillars. It's grand, the way those arches travel forward.

"There's a sedilia* as well—pretty. But I like the main body of the church—and that north porch—"

He was very much excited and filled with himself that afternoon. A
25   flame kindled round him, making his experience passionate and glowing, burningly real.

His uncle listened with twinkling eyes, half moved. His aunt bent forward her dark face, half moved, but held by other knowledge. Anna went with him.
30   He returned to his lodgings at night treading quick, his eyes glittering and his face shining darkly as if he came from some passionate, vital tryst.

The glow remained in him, the fire burned, his heart was fierce like a sun. He enjoyed his unknown life and his own self. And he was
35   ready to go back to the Marsh.

Without knowing it, Anna was wanting him to come. In him she had escaped. In him the bounds of her experience were transgressed: he was a hole in the wall, beyond which the sunshine blazed on an outside world.
40   He came. Sometimes, not often, but sometimes, talking again,

there recurred the strange, remote reality which carried everything before it. Sometimes he talked of his father, whom he hated with a hatred that was burningly close to love, of his mother, whom he loved with a love that was keenly close to hatred, or to revolt. His sentences were clumsy, he was only half articulate. But he had the wonderful 5 voice, that could ring its vibration through the girl's soul, transport her into his feeling. Sometimes his voice was hot and declamatory, sometimes it had a strange, twanging, almost cat-like sound, sometimes it hesitated, puzzled, sometimes there was the break of a little laugh. Anna was taken by him. She loved the running flame that 10 coursed through her as she listened to him. And his mother and his father became to her two separate people in her life.

For some weeks the youth came frequently, and was received gladly by them all. He sat amongst them, his dark face glowing, an eagerness and a touch of derisiveness on his wide mouth, something 15 grinning and twisted, his eyes always shining like a bird's, utterly without depth. There was no getting hold of the fellow, Brangwen irritably thought. He was like a grinning young tom-cat, that came when he thought he would, and without cognisance of the other person. 20

At first the youth had looked towards Tom Brangwen when he talked; and then he looked towards his aunt, for her appreciation, valuing it more than his uncle's; and then he turned to Anna, because from her he got what he wanted, which was not in the older people.

So that the two young people, from being always attendant on the 25 elder, began to draw apart and establish a separate kingdom. Sometimes Tom Brangwen was irritated. His nephew irritated him. The lad seemed to him too special, self-contained. His nature was fierce enough, but too much abstracted, like a separate thing, like a cat's nature. A cat could lie perfectly peacefully, on the hearthrug 30 whilst its master or mistress writhed in agony a yard away. It had nothing to do with other people's affairs. What did the lad really care about anything, save his own instinctive affairs.

Brangwen was irritated. Nevertheless he liked and respected his nephew. Mrs Brangwen was irritated by Anna, who was suddenly 35 changed, under the influence of the youth. The mother liked the boy: he was not quite an outsider. But she did not like her daughter to be so much under the spell.

So that gradually the two young people drew apart, escaped from the elders, to create a new thing by themselves. He worked in the 40

garden to propitiate his uncle. He talked churches to propitiate his aunt. He followed Anna like a shadow: like a long, persistent, unswerving black shadow he went after the girl. It irritated Brangwen exceedingly. It exasperated him beyond bearing, to see
5 the lit-up grin, the cat-grin as he called it, on his nephew's face.

And Anna had a new reserve, a new independence. Suddenly she began to act independently of her parents, to live beyond them. Her mother had flashes of anger.

But the courtship went on. Anna would find occasion to go
10 shopping in Ilkeston at evening. She always returned with her cousin, he walking with his head over her shoulder, a little bit behind her, like the Devil looking over Lincoln,* as Brangwen noted angrily and yet with satisfaction.

To his own wonder, Will Brangwen found himself in an electric
15 state of passion. To his wonder, he had stopped her at the gate as they came home from Ilkeston one night, and had kissed her, blocking her way and kissing her whilst he felt as if some blow were struck at him in the dark. And when they went indoors, he was acutely angry that her parents looked up scrutinisingly at him and
20 her. What right had they there: why should they look up! Let them remove themselves, or look elsewhere.

And the youth went home with the stars in heaven whirling fiercely about the blackness of his head, and his heart fierce, insistent, but fierce as if he felt something balking him. He wanted to
25 smash through something.

A spell was cast over her. And how uneasy her parents were, as she went about the house unnoticing, not noticing them, moving in a spell as if she were invisible to them. She *was* invisible to them. It made them angry. Yet they had to submit. She went about absorbed,
30 obscured for a while.

Over him too the darkness of obscurity settled. He seemed to be hidden in a tense, electric darkness, in which his soul, his life was intensely active, but without his aid or attention. His mind was obscured. He worked swiftly and mechanically, and he produced
35 some beautiful things.

His favorite work was wood-carving.* The first thing he made for her was a butter stamper. In it he carved a mythological bird, a phœnix,* something like an eagle, rising on symmetrical wings, from a circle of very beautiful flickering flames that rose upwards from the
40 rim of the cup.

Anna thought nothing of the gift on the evening when he gave it to her. In the morning, however, when the butter was made, she fetched his seal in place of the old wooden stamper of oak-leaves and acorns. She was curiously excited to see how it would turn out. Strange, the uncouth bird moulded there, in the cup-like hollow, with curious, thick waverings running inwards from a smooth rim. She pressed another mould. Strange, to lift the stamp and see that eagle-beaked bird raising its breast to her. She loved creating it over and over again. And every time she looked, it seemed a new thing come to life. Every piece of butter became this strange, vital emblem.

She showed it to her mother and father.

"That is beautiful," said her mother, a little light coming on to her face.

"Beautiful!" exclaimed the father, puzzled, fretted. "Why what sort of a bird does he call it?"

And this was the question put by the customers during the next weeks.

"What sort of a bird do you call *that*, as you've got on th' butter?"

When he came in the evening, she took him into the dairy to show him.

"Do you like it?" he asked, in his loud, vibrating voice that always sounded strange, re-echoing in the dark places of her being.

They very rarely touched each other. They liked to be alone together, near to each other, but there was still a distance between them.

In the cool dairy the candle-light lit on the large, white surfaces of the cream pans. He turned his head sharply. It was so cool and remote in there, so remote. His mouth was open in a little, strained laugh. She stood with her head bent, turned aside. He wanted to go near to her. He had kissed her once. Again his eye rested on the round blocks of butter, where the emblematic bird lifted its breast from the shadow cast by the candle flame. What was restraining him? Her breast was near him; his head lifted like an eagle's. She did not move. Suddenly, with an incredibly quick, delicate movement, he put his arms round her and drew her to him. It was quick, cleanly done, like a bird that swoops and sinks close, closer.

He was kissing her throat. She turned and looked at him. Her eyes were dark and flowing with fire. His eyes were hard and bright with a fierce purpose and gladness, like a hawk's. She felt him flying into the dark space of her flames, like a brand, like a gleaming hawk.

They had looked at each other, and seen each other strange, yet near, very near, like a hawk stooping, swooping, dropping into a flame of darkness. So she took the candle and they went back to the kitchen.

5   They went on in this way for some time, always coming together, but rarely touching, very seldom did they kiss. And then, often, it was merely a touch of the lips, a sign. But her eyes began to waken with a constant fire, she paused often in the midst of her transit, as if to recollect something, or to discover something.

10   And his face became sombre, intent, he did not readily hear what was said to him.

One evening in August he came when it was raining. He came in with his jacket collar turned up, his jacket buttoned close, his face wet. And he looked so slim and definite, coming out of the chill rain,
15   she was suddenly blinded with love for him. Yet he sat and talked with her father and mother, meaninglessly, whilst her blood seethed to anguish in her. She wanted to touch him now, only to touch him.

There was the queer, abstract look on her silvery radiant face that maddened her father, her dark eyes were hidden. But she raised
20   them to the youth. And they were dark with a flare that made him quail for a moment.

She went into the second kitchen and took a lantern. Her father watched her as she returned.

"Come with me, Will," she said to her cousin. "I want to see if I
25   put the brick over where that rat comes in."

"You've no need to do that," retorted her father.

She took no notice. The youth was between the two wills. The colour mounted into the father's face, his blue eyes stared. The girl stood near the door, her head held slightly back, like an indication
30   that the youth must come. He rose, in his silent, intent way, and was gone with her. The blood swelled in Brangwen's forehead veins.

It was raining. The light of the lantern flashed on the cobbled path and the bottom of the wall. She came to a small ladder, and climbed up. He reached her the lantern, and followed. Up there in the
35   fowl-loft, the birds sat in fat bunches on the perches, the red combs shining like fire. Bright, sharp eyes opened. There was a sharp crawk of expostulation as one of the hens shifted over. The cock sat watching, his yellow neck-feathers bright as glass. Anna went across the dirty floor. Brangwen crouched in the loft, watching. The light
40   was soft under the red, naked tiles. The girl crouched in a corner.

There was another explosive bustle of a hen springing from her perch.

Anna came back, stooping under the perches. He was waiting for her near the door. Suddenly she had her arms round him, was clinging close to him, cleaving her body against his, and crying, in a 5 whispering, whimpering sound:

"Will, I love you, I love you, Will, I love you."

It sounded as if it were tearing her.

He was not even very much surprised. He held her in his arms, and his bones melted. He leaned back against the wall. The door of 10 the loft was open. Outside, the rain slanted by in fine, steely, mysterious haste, emerging out of the gulf of darkness. He held her in his arms, and he and she together seemed to be swinging in big, swooping oscillations, the two of them clasped together up in the darkness. Outside the open door of the loft in which they stood, 15 beyond them and below them, was darkness, with a travelling veil of rain.

"I love you, Will, I love you," she moaned, "I love you, Will."

He held her as though they were one, and was silent.

In the house, Tom Brangwen waited a while. Then he got up and 20 went out. He went down the yard. He saw the curious misty shaft coming from the loft door. He scarcely knew it was the light in the rain. He went on till the illumination fell on him dimly. Then looking up, through the blur* he saw the youth and the girl together, the youth with his back against the wall, his head sunk over the head of 25 the girl. The elder man saw them blurred through the rain, but lit up. They thought themselves so buried in the night. He even saw the lighted dryness of the loft behind, and shadows and bunches of roosting fowl, up in the night, strange shadows cast from the lantern on the floor. 30

And a black gloom of anger, and a tenderness of self-effacement, fought in his heart. She did not understand what she was doing. She betrayed herself. She was a child, a mere child. She did not know how much of herself she was squandering. And he was blackly and furiously miserable. Was he then an old man, that he should be 35 giving her away in marriage? Was he old? He was not old. He was younger than that young thoughtless fellow in whose arms she lay. Who knew her—he or that blind-headed youth? To whom did she belong, if not to himself?

He thought again of the child he had carried out at night into the 40

barn, whilst his wife was in labour with the young Tom. He remembered the soft, warm weight of the little girl on his arm, round his neck. Now she would say he was finished. She was going away, to deny him, to leave an unendurable emptiness in him, a void that he
5 could not bear. Almost he hated her. How dared she say he was old. He walked on in the rain, sweating with pain, with the horror of being old, with the agony of having to relinquish what was life to him.

Will Brangwen went home without having seen his uncle. He held his hot face to the rain, and walked on in a trance. "I love you, Will, I
10 love you." The words repeated themselves endlessly. The veils had ripped* and issued him naked into endless space, and he shuddered. The walls had thrust him out, and given him a vast space to walk in. Whither, through this darkness of infinite space, was he walking blindly? Where, at the end of all the darkness, was God the Almighty
15 still darkly seated, thrusting him on? "I love you, Will, I love you." He trembled with fear as the words beat in his heart again. And he dared not think of her face, of her eyes which shone, and of her strange, transfigured face. The hand of the Hidden Almighty, burning bright, had thrust out of the darkness and gripped him. He
20 went on subject, and in fear, his heart gripped and burning from the touch.

The days went by, they ran on dark-padded feet in silence. He went to see Anna, but again there had come a reserve between them. Tom Brangwen was gloomy, his blue eyes sombre. Anna was strange
25 and delivered up. Her face in its delicate colouring was mute, touched dumb and poignant. The mother bowed her head and moved in her own dark world, that was pregnant again with fulfilment.

Will Brangwen worked at his wood-carving. It was a passion, a
30 passion for him to have the chisel under his grip. Verily the passion of his heart lifted the fine bite of steel. He was carving, as he had always wanted, the Creation of Eve.* It was a panel in low relief, for a church. Adam lay asleep as if suffering, and God, a dim, large figure, stooped towards him, stretching forward His unveiled hand; an Eve,
35 a small, vivid, naked female shape, was issuing like a flame towards the hand of God, from the torn side of Adam.

Now, Will Brangwen was working at the Eve. She was thin, a keen, unripe thing. With trembling passion, fine as a breath of air, he sent the chisel over her belly, her hard, unripe, small belly. She was a stiff
40 little figure, with sharp lines, in the throes and torture and ecstasy of

her creation. But he trembled as he touched her. He had not finished
any of his figures. There was a bird on a bough overhead, lifting its
wings for flight, and a serpent wreathing up to it. It was not finished
yet. He trembled with passion, at last able to create the new, sharp
body of his Eve.   5

At the sides, at the far sides, at either end, were two angels
covering their faces with their wings.* They were like trees. As he
went to the Marsh, in the twilight, he felt that the angels with covered
faces were standing back as he went by. The darkness was of their
shadows and the covering of their faces. When he went through the   10
canal bridge, the evening glowed in its last deep colours, the sky was
dark blue, the stars glittered from afar, very remote and approaching
above the darkening cluster of the farm, above the puther* of crystal
along the edge of the heavens.

She waited for him like the glow of light, and as if his face were   15
covered. And he dared not lift his face to look at her.

Corn-harvest came on. One evening they walked out through the
farm-buildings at nightfall. A large gold moon hung heavily to the
grey horizon, trees hovered tall, standing back in the dusk, waiting.
Anna and the young man went on noiselessly by the hedge, along   20
where the farm-carts had made dark ruts in the grass. They came
through a gate into a wide open field where still much light seemed to
spread against their faces. In the under-shadow the sheaves lay on
the ground where the reapers had left them, many sheaves like
bodies prostrate in shadowy bulk; others were riding hazily in   25
shocks, like ships in the haze of moonlight and of dusk, further off.

They did not want to turn back, yet whither they were to go,
towards the moon? For they were separate, single.

"We will put up some sheaves," said Anna.

So they could remain there in the broad, open place.   30

They went across the stubble to where the long rows of upreared
shocks ended. Curiously populous that part of the field looked,
where the shocks rode erect; the rest was open and prostrate.

The air was all hoary silver. She looked around her. Trees stood
vaguely at their distance, as if waiting, like heralds, for the signal to 35
approach. In this space of vague crystal her heart seemed like a bell
ringing. She was afraid lest the sound should be heard.

"You take this row," she said to the youth, and passing on, she
stooped in the next row of lying sheaves, grasping her hands in the
tresses of the oats, lifting the heavy corn in either hand, carrying it, as 40

it hung heavily against her, to the cleared space, where she set the
two sheaves sharply down, bringing them together with a faint, keen
clash. Her two bulks stood leaning together. He was coming, walking
shadowily with the gossamer dusk, carrying his two sheaves. She
5   waited near by. He set his sheaves with a keen, faint clash, next to her
sheaves. They rode unsteadily. He tangled the tresses of corn. It
hissed like a fountain. He looked up and laughed.

Then she turned away towards the moon, which seemed glowingly
to uncover her bosom every time she faced it. He went to the vague
10 emptiness of the field opposite, dutifully.

They stooped, grasped the wet, soft hair of the corn, lifted the
heavy bundles, and returned. She was always first. She set down her
sheaves, making a pent-house with those others. He was coming
shadowy across the stubble, carrying his bundles. She turned away,
15 hearing only the sharp hiss of his mingling corn. She walked between
the moon and his shadowy figure.

She took her new two sheaves and walked towards him, as he rose
from stooping over the earth. He was coming out of the near
distance. She set down her sheaves to make a new stook. They were
20 unsure. Her hands fluttered. Yet she broke away, and turned to the
moon, which laid bare her bosom, so she felt as if her bosom were
heaving and panting with moonlight.—And he had to put up her two
sheaves, which had fallen down. He worked in silence. The rhythm
of the work carried him away again, as she was coming near.

25 They worked together, coming and going, in a rhythm, which
carried their feet and their bodies in tune. She stooped, she lifted the
burden of sheaves, she turned her face to the dimness where he was,
and went with her burden over the stubble. She hesitated, set down
her sheaves, there was a swish and hiss of mingling oats, he was
30 drawing near, and she must turn, again. And there was the flaring
moon laying bare her bosom again, making her drift and ebb like a
wave.

He worked steadily, engrossed, threading backwards and forwards like a shuttle across the strip of cleared stubble, weaving the
35 long line of riding shocks, nearer and nearer to the shadowy trees,
threading his sheaves with hers.

And always she was gone before he came. As he came, she drew
away, as he drew away, she came. Were they never to meet?
Gradually a low, deep-sounding will in him vibrated to her, tried to
40 set her in accord, tried to bring her gradually to him, to a meeting, till

they should be together, till they should meet as the sheaves that
swished together.

And the work went on. The moon grew brighter, clearer, the corn
glistened. He bent over the prostrate bundles, there was a hiss as the
sheaves left the ground, a trailing of heavy bodies against him, a 5
dazzle of moonlight on his eyes. And then he was setting the corn
together at the stook. And she was coming near.

He waited for her, he fumbled at the stook. She came. But she
stood back till he drew away. He saw her in shadow, a dark column,
and spoke to her, and she answered. She saw the moonlight flash 10
question on his face. But there was a space between them, and he
went away, the work carried them, rhythmic.

Why was there always a space between them, why were they apart?
Why, as she came up from under the moon, would she halt and stand
off from him? Why was he held away from her? His will drummed 15
persistently, darkly, it drowned everything else.

Into the rhythm of his work there came a pulse and a steadied
purpose. He stooped, he lifted the weight, he heaved it towards her,
setting it as in her, under the moonlit space. And he went back for
more. Ever with increasing closeness he lifted the sheaves and swung 20
striding to the centre with them, ever he drove her more nearly to the
meeting, ever he did his share, and drew towards her, overtaking her.
There was only the moving to and fro in the moonlight, engrossed,
the swinging in the silence, that was marked only by the splash of
sheaves, and silence, and a splash of sheaves. And ever the splash of 25
his sheaves broke swifter, beating up to hers, and ever the splash of
her sheaves recurred monotonously, unchanging, and ever the
splash of his sheaves beat nearer.

Till at last, they met at the shock, facing each other, sheaves in
hand. And he was silvery with moonlight, with a moonlit, shadowy 30
face that frightened her. She waited for him.

"Put yours down," she said.

"No, it's your turn."

His voice was twanging and insistent.

She set her sheaves against the shock. He saw her hands glisten 35
among the spray of grain. And he dropped his sheaves and he
trembled as he took her in his arms. He had overtaken her, and it was
his privilege, to kiss her. She was sweet and fresh with the night air,
and sweet with the scent of grain. And the whole rhythm of him beat
into his kisses, and still he pursued her, in his kisses, and still she was 40

not quite overcome. He wondered over the moonlight on her nose! All the moonlight upon her, all the darkness within her! All the night in his arms, darkness and shine, he possessed of it all! All the night for him now, to unfold, to venture within, all the mystery to be

5   entered, all the discovery to be made.

Trembling with keen triumph, his heart was white as a star as he drove his kisses nearer.

"My love!" she called, in a low voice, from afar.

The low sound seemed to call to him from far off, under the

10   moon, to him who was unaware. He stopped, quivered, and listened.

"My love," came again the low, plaintive call, like a bird unseen in the night.

He was afraid. His heart quivered and broke. He was stopped.

"Anna," he said, as if he answered her from a distance, unsure.

15   "My love."

And he drew near, and she drew near.

"Anna," he said, in wonder and birthpain of love.

"My love," she said, her voice growing rapturous.

And they kissed on the mouth, in rapture and surprise, long, real

20   kisses. The kiss lasted, there among the moonlight. He kissed her again, and she kissed him. And again they were kissing together. Till something happened in him, he was strange. He wanted her. He wanted her exceedingly. She was something new. They stood there folded, suspended in the night. And his whole being quivered

25   with surprise, as from a blow. He wanted her, and he wanted to tell her so. But the shock was too great to him. He had never realised before. He trembled with initiation and unusedness, he did not know what to do. He held her more gently, gently, much more gently. The conflict was gone by. And he was glad, and breathless,

30   and almost in tears. But he knew he wanted her. Something fixed in him for ever. He was hers. And he was very glad, and afraid. He did not know what to do, as they stood there in the open, moonlit fields. He looked through her hair at the moon, which seemed to swim liquid-bright.

35   She sighed, and seemed to wake up. Then she kissed him again. Then she loosened herself away from him and took his hand. It hurt him when she drew away from his breast. It hurt him with a chagrin. Why did she draw away from him? But she held his hand.

"I want to go home," she said, looking at him in a way he could not

40   understand.

He held close to her hand. He was dazed and he could not move, he did not know how to move. She drew him away.

He walked helplessly beside her, holding her hand. She went with bent head. Suddenly he said, as the simple solution stated itself to him:

"We'll get married, Anna."

She was silent.

"We'll get married, Anna, shall we?"

She stopped in the field again and kissed him, clinging to him passionately, in a way he could not understand. He could not understand. But he left it all now, to marriage. That was the solution now, fixed ahead. He wanted her, he wanted to be married to her, he wanted to have her altogether, as his own for ever. And he waited, intent, for the accomplishment. But there was all the while a slight tension of irritation.*

He spoke to his uncle and aunt that night.

"Uncle," he said, "Anna and me think of getting married."

"Oh ay!" said Brangwen.

"But how, you have no money," said the mother.

The youth went pale. He hated these words. But he was like a gleaming, bright pebble, something bright and inalterable. He did not think. He sat there in his hard brightness, and did not speak.

"Have you mentioned it to your own mother?" asked Brangwen.

"No—I s'll tell her on Saturday."

"You'll go and see her?"

"Yes."

There was a long pause.

"And what are you going to marry on—your pound a week?"

Again the youth went pale, as if the spirit were being injured in him.

"I don't know," he said, looking at his uncle with his bright, inhuman eyes, like a hawk's.

Brangwen stirred in hatred.

"It needs knowing," he said.

"I shall have money later on," said the nephew. "I will raise some now, and pay it back then."

"Oh ay!—And why this desperate hurry? She's a child of eighteen, and you're a boy of twenty. You're neither of you of age to do as you like yet."

Will Brangwen ducked his head and looked at his uncle with swift, bright, mistrustful eyes, like a caged hawk.

"What does it matter how old she is, and how old I am," he said. "What's the difference between me now and when I'm thirty?"

5   "A big difference, let us hope."

"But you have no experience—you have no experience, and no money. Why do you want to marry, without experience or money?" asked the aunt.

"What experience do I want, Aunt?" asked the boy.

10   And if Brangwen's heart had not been hard and intact with anger, like a precious stone, he would have agreed.

Will Brangwen went home strange and untouched. He felt he could not alter from what he was fixed upon, his will was set. To alter it he must be destroyed. And he would not be destroyed. He had no

15   money. But he would get some from somewhere, it did not matter. He lay awake for many hours, hard and clear and unthinking, his soul crystallising more inalterably. Then he went fast asleep.

It was as if his soul had turned into a hard crystal. He might tremble and quiver and suffer, *it* did not alter.

20   The next morning Tom Brangwen, inhuman with anger, spoke to Anna.

"What's this about wanting to get married?" he said.

She stood, paling a little, her dark eyes springing to the hostile, startled look of a savage thing that will defend itself, but trembles

25   with sensitiveness.

"I do," she said, out of her unconsciousness.

His anger rose, and he would have liked to break her.

"You do—you do—and what for?" he sneered with contempt.

The old, childish agony, the blindness that could recognise

30   nobody, the palpitating antagonism as of a raw, helpless, undefended thing came back on her.

"I do because I do," she cried, in the shrill, hysterical way of her childhood. "*You* are not my father—my father is dead—*you* are not my father."

35   She was still a stranger. She did not recognise him. The cold blade cut down, deep into Brangwen's soul. It cut him off from her.

"And what if I'm not?" he said.

But he could not bear it. It had been so passionately dear to him, her "Father—Daddie."

40   He went about for some days as if stunned. His wife was bemused.

She did not understand. She only thought the marriage was impeded for want of money and position.

There was a horrible silence in the house. Anna kept out of sight as much as possible. She could be for hours alone.

Will Brangwen came back, after stupid scenes at Nottingham. He too was pale and blank, but unchanging. His uncle hated him. He hated this youth, who was so inhuman and obstinate. Nevertheless, it was to Will Brangwen that the uncle, one evening, handed over the shares which he had had transferred to Anna Lensky. They were for two thousand five hundred pounds. Will Brangwen looked at his uncle. It was a great deal of the Marsh capital here given away. The youth, however, was only colder and more fixed. He was abstract, purely a fixed will. He gave the shares to Anna.

After which she cried for a whole day, sobbing her eyes out. And at night, when she had heard her mother go to bed, she slipped down and hung in the doorway. Her father sat in his heavy silence, like a monument. He turned his head slowly.

"Daddy," she cried from the doorway, and she ran to him sobbing as if her heart would break. "Daddy—daddy—daddy—"

She crouched on the hearthrug with her arms round him and her face against him. His body was so big and comfortable. But something hurt her heart intolerably. She sobbed almost with hysteria.

He was silent, with his hand on her shoulder. His heart was bleak. He was not her father. That beloved image she had broken. Who was he then? A man put apart with those whose life has no more developments. He was isolated from her. There was a generation between them, he was old, he had died out from hot life. A great deal of ash was in his fire, cold ash. He felt the inevitable coldness, and in bitterness forgot the fire. He sat in his coldness of age and isolation. He had his own wife. And he blamed himself, he sneered at himself, for this clinging to the young, wanting the young to belong to him.

The child who clung to him wanted her child-husband, as was natural. And from him, Brangwen, she wanted help, so that her life might be properly fitted out. But love she did not want. Why should there be love between them, between the stout, middle-aged man and this child. How could there be anything between them, but mere human willingness to help each other? He was her guardian, no more. His heart was like ice, his face cold and expressionless. She could not move him any more than a statue.

She crept to bed, and cried. But she was going to be married to
Will Brangwen, and then she need not bother any more. Brangwen
went to bed with a hard, cold heart, and cursed himself. He looked at
his wife. She was still his wife. Her dark hair was threaded with grey,
5   her face was beautiful in its gathering age. She was just fifty. How
poignantly he saw her! And he wanted to cut out some of his own
heart, which was incontinent, and demanded still to share the rapid
life of youth. How he hated himself.

His wife was so poignant and timely. She was still young and
10 naïve, with some girl's freshness. But she did not want any more the
fight, the battle, the control, as he, in his incontinence, still did. She
was so natural, and he was ugly, unnatural, in his inability to yield
place. How hideous, this greedy middle-age, which must stand in the
way of life, like a large demon.

15 What was missing in his life, that, in his ravening soul, he was not
satisfied? He had had that friend at school, his mother, his wife, and
Anna. What had he done? He had failed with his friend, he had been
a poor son; but he had known satisfaction with his wife, let it be
enough; he loathed himself for the state he was in over Anna. Yet he
20 was *not* satisfied. It was agony to know it.

Was his life nothing? Had he nothing to show, no work? He did
not count his work, anybody could have done it. What had he known,
but the long, marital embrace with his wife? Curious, that this was
what his life amounted to! At any rate, it was something, it was
25 eternal. He would say so to anybody, and be proud of it. He lay with
his wife in his arms, and she was still his fulfilment, just the same as
ever. And that was the be-all and the end-all.* Yes, and he was proud
of it.

But the bitterness, underneath, that there still remained an
30 unsatisfied Tom Brangwen, who suffered agony because a girl cared
nothing for him. He loved his sons—he had them also. But it was the
further, the creative life* with the girl, he wanted as well. Oh, and he
was ashamed. He trampled himself, to extinguish himself.

What weariness! There was no peace, however old one grew! One
35 was never right, never decent, never master of oneself. It was as if his
hope had been in the girl.

Anna quickly lapsed again into her love for the youth. Will
Brangwen had fixed his marriage for the Saturday before Christmas.
And he waited for her, in his bright, unquestioning fashion, until
40 then. He wanted her, she was his, he suspended his being till the day

should come. The wedding day, December the twenty third, had come into being for him as an absolute thing. He lived in it.

He did not count the days. But like a man who journeys in a ship, he was suspended till the coming to port.

He worked at his carving, he worked in his office, he came to see her: all was but a form of waiting, without thought or question.

She was much more alive. She wanted to enjoy courtship. He seemed to come and go like the wind, without asking why or whither. But she wanted to enjoy his presence. For her, he was the kernel of life, to touch him alone was bliss. But for him, she was the essence of life: she existed as much when he was at his carving in his lodging in Ilkeston, as when she sat looking at him in the Marsh kitchen. In himself, he knew her. But his outward faculties seemed suspended. He did not see her with his eyes, nor hear her with his voice.

And yet he trembled,* sometimes into a kind of swoon, holding her in his arms. They would stand sometimes folded together in the barn, in silence. Then to her, as she felt his young, tense figure with her hands, the bliss was intolerable, intolerable the sense that she possessed him. For his body was so keen and wonderful, it was the only reality in her world. In her world, there was this one tense, vivid body of a man, and then many other shadowy men, all unreal. In him she touched the centre of reality. And they were together, he and she, at the heart of the secret. How she clutched him to her, his body the central body of all life. Out of the rock of his form the very fountain of life flowed.

But to him, she was a flame that consumed him. The flame flowed up his limbs, flowed through him, till he was consumed, till he existed only as an unconscious, dark transit of flame, deriving from her.

Sometimes, in the darkness, a cow coughed. There was, in the darkness, a slow sound of cud chewing. And it all seemed to flow round them and upon them as the hot blood flows through the womb, laving the unborn young.

Sometimes, when it was cold, they stood to be lovers in the stables, where the air was warm and sharp with ammonia. And during these dark vigils, he learned to know her, her body against his, they drew nearer and nearer together, the kisses came more subtly close and fitting. So when in the thick darkness, a horse suddenly scrambled to its feet, with a dull, thunderous sound, they listened as one person listening, they knew as one person, they were conscious of the horse.

Tom Brangwen had taken them a cottage at Cossethay, on a twenty one years lease. Will Brangwen's eyes lit up as he saw it. It was the cottage next the church,* with dark yew-trees, very black old trees, along the side of the house and the grassy front garden; a red,
5   squarish cottage with a low slate roof, and low windows. It had a long dairy-scullery, a big flagged kitchen, and a low parlour, that went up one step from the kitchen. There were whitewashed beams across the ceilings, and odd corners with cupboards. Looking out through the windows, there was the grassy garden, the procession of black
10 yew-trees down one side, and along the other sides, a red wall with ivy separating the place from the high-road and the churchyard. The old, little church, with its small spire on a square tower, seemed to be looking back at the cottage windows.

"There'll be no need to have a clock," said Will Brangwen,
15 peeping out at the white clock-face on the tower, his neighbour.

At the back of the house was a garden adjoining the paddock, a cowshed with standing for two cows, pig-cotes and fowl-houses. Will Brangwen was very happy. Anna was glad to think of being mistress of her own place.
20 Tom Brangwen was now the fairy god-father. He was never happy unless he was buying something. Will Brangwen, with his interest in all wood-work, was getting the furniture. He was left to buy tables and round-staved chairs and dressers, quite ordinary stuff, but such as was identified with his cottage.
25 Tom Brangwen, with more particular thought, spied out what he called handy little things for her. He appeared with a set of new-fangled cooking-pans, with a special sort of hanging lamp, though the rooms were so low, with canny little machines for grinding meat or mashing potatoes or whisking eggs.
30 Anna took a sharp interest in what he bought, though she was not always pleased. Some of the little contrivances, which he thought so canny, left her doubtful. Nevertheless she was always expectant, on market days there was always a long thrill of anticipation. He arrived with the first darkness, the copper lamps of his cart glowing. And she
35 ran to the gate, as he, a dark, burly figure up in the cart, was bending over his parcels.

"It's cupboard love as brings you out so sharp," he said, his voice resounding in the cold darkness. Nevertheless he was excited. And she, taking one of the cart lamps, poked and peered among the jumble of things he had brought, pushing aside the oil or implements he had got for himself.

She dragged out a pair of small, strong bellows, registered them in her mind, and then pulled uncertainly at something else. It had a long handle, and a piece of brown paper round the middle of it, like a waistcoat.

"What's this?" she said, poking.

He stopped to look at her. She went to the lamp-light by the horse, and stood there bent over the new thing, while her hair was like bronze, her apron white and cheerful. Her fingers plucked busily at the paper. She dragged forth a little wringer, with clean indiarubber rollers. She examined it critically, not knowing quite how it worked.

She looked up at him. He stood a shadowy presence beyond the light.

"How does it go?" she asked.

"Why, it's for pulpin' turnips," he replied.

She looked at him. His voice disturbed her.

"Don't be silly. It's a little mangle," she said. "How do you stand it though?"

"You screw it on th' side o' your wash-tub."

He came and held it out to her.

"Oh yes!" she cried, with one of her little skipping movements, which still came when she was suddenly glad.

And without another thought she ran off into the house, leaving him to untackle the horse. And when he came in to the scullery, he found her there, with the little wringer fixed on the dolly-tub,* turning blissfully at the handle, and Tilly beside her, exclaiming:

"My word, that's a natty little thing! That'll save you luggin' your inside out. That's the latest contraption, that is."

And Anna turned away at the handle, with great gusto of possession. Then she let Tilly have a turn.

"It fair runs by itself," said Tilly, turning on and on. "Your clothes'll nip out onto th' line."

Chapter V

Wedding at the Marsh

It was a beautiful sunny day for the wedding,* a muddy earth but a bright sky. They had three cabs and two big closed-in vehicles.*
5 Everybody crowded in the parlour in excitement. Anna was still upstairs. Her father kept taking a nip of brandy. He was handsome in his black coat and grey trousers. His voice was hearty but troubled. His wife came down in dark grey silk with lace, and a touch of peacock blue in her bonnet. Her little body was very sure
10 and definite. Brangwen was thankful she was there, to sustain him among all these people.

The carriages! The Nottingham Mrs Brangwen, in silk brocade, stands in the doorway saying who must go with whom. There is a great bustle. The front door is opened, and the wedding guests are
15 walking down the garden path, whilst those still waiting peer through the window, and the little crowd at the gate gorps and stretches. How funny such dressed-up people look in the winter sunshine!

They are gone—another lot! There begins to be more room. Anna comes down, blushing and very shy, to be viewed in her white silk
20 and her veil. Her mother-in-law surveys her objectively, twitches the white train, arranges the folds of the veil, and asserts herself.

Loud exclamations from the window that the bridegroom's carriage has just passed.

"Where's your hat, father, and your gloves?" cries the bride,
25 stamping her white slipper, her eyes flashing through her veil. He hunts round—his hair is ruffled. Everybody has gone but the bride and her father. He is ready—his face very red and daunted. Tilly dithers in the little porch, waiting to open the door. A waiting woman walks round Anna, who asks:
30 "Am I all right?"

She is ready. She bridles herself and looks queenly. She waves her hand sharply to her father:

"Come here!"

He goes. She puts her hand very lightly on his arm, and holding
35 her bouquet like a shower, stepping oh very graciously, just a little

124

impatient with her father for being so red in the face, she sweeps
slowly past the fluttering Tilly, and down the path. There are hoarse
shouts at the gate, and all her floating, foamy whiteness passes slowly
into the cab.

Her father notices her slim ankle and foot as she steps up: a child's   5
foot. His heart is hard with tenderness. But she is in ecstasies with
herself for making such a lovely spectacle. All the way she sat
flamboyant with bliss because it was all so lovely. She looked down
solicitously at her bouquet: white roses and lilies of the valley and
tuberoses and maiden-hair fern—very rich and cascade-like.   10

Her father sat bewildered with all this strangeness, his heart was
so full it felt hard, and he couldn't think of anything.

The church was decorated for Christmas, dark with evergreens,
cold and snowy with white flowers. He went vaguely down to the
altar. How long was it since he had gone to be married himself? He   15
was not sure whether he was going to be married now, or what he had
come for. He had a troubled notion that he had to do something or
other. He saw his wife's bonnet, and wondered why *she* wasn't there
with him.

They stood before the altar. He was staring up at the east window,   20
that glowed intensely, a sort of blue purple: it was deep blue glowing,
and some crimson, and little yellow flowers, held fast in veins of
shadow, in a heavy web of darkness. How it burned alive in radiance
among its black web.

"Who giveth this woman to be married to this man?"   25

He felt somebody touch him. He started. The words still re-
echoed in his memory, but were drawing off.

"Me," he said hastily.

Anna bent her head and smiled in her veil. How absurd he
was!   30

Brangwen was staring away at the burning blue window at the
back of the altar, and wondering vaguely, with pain, if he ever *should*
get old, if he ever should feel arrived and established. He was here at
Anna's wedding. Well, what right had he to feel responsible, like a
father? He was still as unsure and unfixed as when he had married   35
himself. His wife and he! With a pang of anguish he realised what
uncertainties they both were. He was a man of forty five. Forty five!
In five more years, fifty. Then, sixty—then seventy—then it was
finished. My God—and one still was so unestablished!

How did one grow old—how could one become confident? He   40

wished he felt older. Why, what difference was there, as far as he felt matured or completed, between him now and him at his own wedding? He might be getting married over again—he and his wife. He felt himself tiny, a little, upright figure on a plain circled round
5 with the immense, roaring sky: he and his wife, two little, upright figures walking across this plain, whilst the heavens shimmered and roared about them. When did one come to an end? In which direction was it finished? There was no end, no finish, only this roaring vast space. Did one never get old, never die? That was the
10 clue. He exulted strangely, with torture. He would go on with his wife, he and she like two children camping in the plains. What was sure but the endless sky? But that was so sure, so boundless.

Still the royal blue colour burned and blazed and sported itself in the web of darkness before him, unwearyingly rich and splendid.
15 How rich and splendid his own life was, red and burning and blazing and sporting itself in the dark meshes of his body: and his wife, how she glowed and burned dark within her meshes! Always it was so unfinished and unformed!

There was a loud noise of the organ. The whole party was
20 trooping to the vestry. There was a blotted, scrawled book—and that young girl putting back her veil in her vanity, and laying her hand with the wedding-ring self-consciously conspicuous, and signing her name proudly because of the vain spectacle she made.

"Anna Theresa Lensky."
25   "Anna Theresa Lensky"—what a vain, independent minx she was! The bridegroom, slender in his black swallow-tail and grey trousers, solemn as a young solemn cat, was writing seriously:

"William Brangwen."

That looked more like it.
30   "Come and sign father," cried the imperious young hussy.

"'Thomas Brangwen'—clumsy-fist," he said to himself as he signed.

Then his brother, a big, sallow fellow with black side-whiskers wrote:
35   "Alfred Brangwen."

"How many more Brangwens?" said Tom Brangwen, ashamed of the too-frequent recurrence of his family name.

When they were out again in the sunshine, and he saw the frost hoary and blue among the long grass under the tombstones, the
40 holly-berries overhead twinkling scarlet as the bells rang, the yew-

trees hanging their black, motionless, ragged boughs, everything seemed like a vision.

The marriage party went across the graveyard to the wall, mounted it by the little steps, and descended. Oh a vain white peacock of a bride perching herself on the top of the wall and giving her hand to the bridegroom on the other side, to be helped down! The vanity of her white, slim, daintily-stepping feet, and her arched neck. And the regal impudence with which she seemed to dismiss them all, the others, parents and wedding guests, as she went with her young husband.

In the cottage big fires were burning, there were dozens of glasses on the table, and holly and mistletoe hanging up. The wedding party crowded in, and Tom Brangwen, becoming roisterous, poured out drinks. Everybody must drink. The bells were ringing away against the windows.

"Lift your glasses up," shouted Tom Brangwen from the parlour, "lift your glasses up, an' drink to the hearth an' home—hearth an' home, an' may they enjoy it."

"Night an' day, an' may they enjoy it," shouted Frank Brangwen, in addition.

"Hammer an' tongs, and may they enjoy it," shouted Alfred Brangwen, the saturnine.

"Fill your glasses up, an' let's have it all over again," shouted Tom Brangwen.

"Hearth and home, an' may ye enjoy it."

There was a ragged shout of the company in response.

"Bed an' blessin', an' may ye enjoy it," shouted Frank Brangwen.

There was a swelling chorus in answer.

"Comin' and goin', an' may ye enjoy it," shouted the saturnine Alfred Brangwen, and the men roared by now boldly, and the women said "Just hark, now!"

There was a touch of scandal in the air.

Then the party rolled off in the carriages, full speed back to the Marsh, to a large meal of the high-tea order, which lasted for an hour and a half. The bride and bridegroom sat at the head of the table, very prim and shining both of them, wordless, whilst the company raged down the table.

The Brangwen men had brandy in their tea, and were becoming unmanageable. The saturnine Alfred had glittering, unseeing eyes, and a strange, fierce way of laughing that showed his teeth. His wife glowered at him and jerked her head at him like a snake. He was oblivious. Frank Brangwen, the butcher, flushed and florid and handsome, roared echoes to his two brothers. Tom Brangwen, in his solid fashion, was letting himself go at last.

5 These three brothers dominated the whole company. Tom Brangwen wanted to make a speech. For the first time in his life, he must spread himself wordily.

"Marriage," he began, his eyes twinkling and yet quite profound, for he was deeply serious and hugely amused at the same time; 10 "Marriage," he said, speaking in the slow, full-mouthed way of the Brangwens, "is what we're made for—"

"Let him talk," said Alfred Brangwen, slowly and inscrutably, "let him talk." Mrs Alfred darted indignant eyes at her husband.

"A man," continued Tom Brangwen, "enjoys being a man: for 15 what purpose was he made a man, if not to enjoy it?"

"That's a true word," said Frank, floridly.

"And likewise," continued Tom Brangwen, "a woman enjoys being a woman: at least we surmise she does—"

"Oh, don't you bother—" called a farmer's wife.

20 "You may back your life they'd be summisin'," said Frank's wife.

"Now," continued Tom Brangwen, "for a man to be a man, it takes a woman—"

"It does that," said a woman grimly.

"And for a woman to be a woman, it takes a *man*—" continued 25 Tom Brangwen.

"All speak up, men," chimed in a feminine voice.

"Therefore we have marriage," continued Tom Brangwen.

"Hold, hold," said Alfred Brangwen. "Don't run us off our legs."

And in dead silence the glasses were filled. The bride and 30 bridegroom, two children, sat with intent, shining faces at the head of the table, abstracted.

"There's no marriage in heaven,"* went on Tom Brangwen; "but on earth there *is* marriage."

"That's the difference between 'em," said Alfred Brangwen, 35 mocking.

"Alfred," said Tom Brangwen, "keep your remarks till afterwards, and then we'll thank you for them.—There's very little else, on earth, but marriage. You can talk about making money, or saving souls. You can save your soul seven times over, and you may have a 40 mint of money, but your soul goes gnawin', gnawin', gnawin', and it

says there's something it must have. In heaven there is no marriage.
But on earth there *is* marriage, else heaven drops out, and there's no
bottom to it."

"Just hark you now," said Frank's wife.

"Go on, Thomas," said Alfred sardonically.

"*If* we've got to be angels," went on Tom Brangwen, haranguing
the company at large, "and if there is no such thing as a man nor a
woman amongst them, then it seems to me as a married couple
makes *one* angel."

"It's the brandy," said Alfred Brangwen wearily.

"For," said Tom Brangwen, and the company was listening to the
conundrum, "an angel can't be *less* than a human being. And if it was
only the soul of a man *minus* the man, then it would be *less* than a
human being—"

"Decidedly," said Alfred.

And a laugh went round the table. But Tom Brangwen was inspired.

"An angel's *got* to be more than a human being," he continued.
"So I say, an angel is the soul of man and woman in one: they rise
united at the Judgment Day, as one angel—"

"Praising the Lord," said Frank.

"Praising the Lord," repeated Tom.

"And what about the women left over?" asked Alfred, jeering. The
company was getting uneasy.*

"That I can't tell. How do I know as there *is* anybody left over at
the Judgment Day? Let that be. What I say is, that when a man's soul
and a woman's soul unites together—that makes one angel."*

"I dunno about souls. I know as one plus one makes three,
sometimes," said Frank. But he had the laugh to himself.

"Bodies and souls, it's the same," said Tom.

"And what about your Missis, who was married afore you knew
her?" asked Alfred, set on edge by this discourse.

"That I can't tell you. If I am to become an angel, it'll be my
married soul, and not my single soul. It'll not be the soul of me when
I was a lad: for I hadn't a soul as would *make* an angel then."

"I can always remember," said Frank's wife, "when our Harold
was bad, he did nothink but see an angel at th' back o' th' lookin'
glass. 'Look mother,' 'e said, 'at that angel.' 'Theer isn't no angel, my
duck,' I said, but he wouldn't have it. I took th' lookin' glass off'n th'
dressin' table, but it made no difference. He kep' on sayin' it was

there. My word, it did give me a turn. I thought for sure as I'd lost him."

"I can remember," said another man, Tom's sister's husband, "my mother gave me a good hidin' once, for sayin' I'd got an angel up
5 my nose. She seed me pokin', an' she said: 'What are you pokin' at your nose for—give over.' 'There's an angel up it,' I said, an' she fetched me such a wipe. But there was. We used to call them thistle things 'angels,' as wafts about. An' I'd pushed one o' these up my nose, for some reason or other."

10 "It's wonderful what children will get up their noses," said Frank's wife. "I c'n remember our Hemmie, she shoved one o' them bluebell things out o' th' middle of a bluebell, what they call 'candles,' up her nose, and oh we had some work! I'd seen her stickin' 'em on the end of her nose, like, but I never thought she'd be
15 so soft as to shove it right up. She was a gel of eight or more. Oh my word, we got a crochet-hook an' I don't know what— — —"

Tom Brangwen's mood of inspiration began to pass away. He forgot all about it, and was soon roaring and shouting with the rest. Outside the wake* came, singing the carols. They were invited into
20 the bursting house. They had two fiddles and a piccolo. There in the parlour they played carols, and the whole company sang them at the top of its voice. Only the bride and bridegroom sat with shining eyes and strange, bright faces, and scarcely sang, or only with just moving lips.

25 The wake departed, and the guysers* came. There was loud applause, and shouting and excitement as the old mystery play of St George, in which every man present had acted as a boy, proceeded, with banging and thumping of club and dripping pan.*

"By Jove, I got a crack once, when I was playin' Beelzebub," said
30 Tom Brangwen, his eyes full of water with laughing. "It knocked all th' sense out of me as you'd crack an egg. But I tell you, when I come to, I played Old Johnny Roger with St George, I did that."

He was shaking with laughter. Another knock came at the door. There was a hush.

35 "It's th' cab," said somebody from the door.

"Walk in," shouted Tom Brangwen, and a red-faced, grinning man entered.

"Now you two, get yourselves ready an' off to blanket fair," shouted Tom Brangwen. "Strike a daisy,* but if you're not off like a
40 blink o' lightnin', you shanna go, you s'll sleep separate."

Anna rose silently and went to change her dress. Will Brangwen would have gone out, but Tilly came with his hat and coat. The youth was helped on.

"Well, here's luck, my boy," shouted his father.

"When th' fat's in th' fire, let it frizzle," admonished his uncle 5
Frank.

"Fair and *softly* does it, fair an' *softly* does it," cried his aunt,
Frank's wife, contrary.

"You don't want to fall over yourself," said his uncle by marriage.
"You're not a bull at a gate." 10

"Let a man have his own road," said Tom Brangwen testily.
"Don't be so free of your advice—it's his wedding this time, not
yours."

" 'E won't want many sign-posts," said his father. "There's some
roads a man has to be led, an' there's some roads a boz-eyed* man 15
can only follow wi' one eye shut. But this road can't be lost by a blind
man nor a boz-eyed man nor a cripple—And he's neither, thank
God."

"Don't you be so sure o' your walkin' powers," cried Frank's wife.
"There's many a man gets no further than half way, nor can't to save 20
his life, let him live for ever."

"Why how do you know?" said Alfred.

"It's plain enough in th' looks o' some," retorted Lizzie, his
sister-in-law.

The youth stood with a faint, half-hearing smile on his face. He 25
was tense and abstracted. These things, or anything, scarcely
touched him.

Anna came down, in her day dress, very elusive. She kissed
everybody, men and women, Will Brangwen shook hands with
everybody, kissed his mother, who began to cry, and the whole party 30
went surging out to the cab.

The young couple were shut up, last injunctions shouted at them.

"Drive on," shouted Tom Brangwen.

The cab rolled off. They saw the lights diminish under the
ash-trees. Then the whole party, quietened, went indoors. 35

"They'll have three good fires burning," said Tom Brangwen,
looking at his watch. "I told Emma to make 'em up at nine, an' then
leave the door on th' latch. It's only half past. They'll have three fires
burning, an' lamps lighted, an' Emma will ha' warmed th' bed wi' th'
warmin' pan. So I s'd think they'll be all right." 40

The party was much quieter. They talked of the young couple.

"She said she didn't want a servant in,"* said Tom Brangwen. "The house isn't big enough, she'd always have the creature under her nose. Emma'll do what is wanted of her, an' they'll be to themselves."

"It's best," said Lizzie, "you're more free."

The party talked on slowly. Brangwen looked at his watch.

"Let's go an' give 'em a carol," he said. "We s'll find th' fiddles at the 'Cock an' Robin.'"

"Ay, come on," said Frank.

Alfred rose in silence. The brother-in-law and one of Will's brothers rose also.

The five men went out. The night was flashing with stars. Sirius blazed like a signal at the side of the hill, Orion, stately and magnificent, was sloping along.

Tom walked with his brother Alfred. The men's heels rang on the ground.

"It's a fine night," said Tom.

"Ay," said Alfred.

"Nice to get out."

"Ay."

The brothers walked close together, the bond of blood strong between them. Tom always felt very much the junior to Alfred.

"It's a long while since *you* left home," he said.

"Ay," said Alfred. "I thought I was getting a bit oldish—but I'm not. It's the things you've got as gets worn out, it's not you yourself."

"Why, what's worn out?"

"Most folks as I've anything to do with—as has anything to do with me. They all break down. You've got to go on by yourself, if it's only to perdition. There's nobody going alongside even there."

Tom Brangwen meditated this.

"Maybe you was never broken in," he said.

"No, I never was," said Alfred proudly.

And Tom felt his elder brother despised him a little. He winced under it.

"Everybody's got a way of their own," he said, stubbornly. "It's only a dog as hasn't. An' them as can't take what they give an' give what they take, they must go by themselves, or get a dog as'll follow 'em."

"They can do without the dog," said his brother.

And again Tom Brangwen was humble, thinking his brother was bigger than himself. But if he was, he was. And if it were finer to go alone, it was: he did not want to, for all that.

They went over the field, where a thin, keen wind blew round the ball of the hill; in the starlight. They came to the stile, and to the side 5 of Anna's house. The lights were out, only on the blinds of the rooms downstairs, and of a bedroom upstairs, firelight flickered.

"We'd better leave 'em alone," said Alfred Brangwen.

"Nay nay," said Tom. "We'll carol 'em, for th' last time."

And in a quarter of an hour's time, eleven silent, rather tipsy men 10 scrambled over the wall, and into the garden by the yew-trees, outside the windows where faint firelight glowed on the blinds. There came a shrill sound, two violins and a piccolo shrilling on the frosty air.

"In the fields with their flocks abiding."* A commotion of men's 15 voices broke out singing in ragged unison.

Anna Brangwen had started up, listening, when the music began. She was afraid.

"It's the wake," he whispered.

She remained tense, her heart beating heavily, possessed with 20 strange, strong fear. Then there came the burst of men's singing, rather uneven. She strained still, listening.

"It's Dad," she said, in a low voice.

They were silent, listening.

"And my father," he said. 25

She listened still. But she was sure. She sank down again into bed, into his arms. He held her very close, kissing her. The hymn rambled on outside, all the men singing their best, having forgotten everything else under the spell of the fiddles and the tune. The firelight glowed against the darkness in the room. Anna could hear 30 her father singing with gusto.

"Aren't they silly?" she whispered.

And they crept closer, closer together, hearts beating to one another. And even as the hymn rolled on, they ceased to hear it.

Chapter VI

Anna Victrix*

Will Brangwen had some weeks of holiday after his marriage, so the two took their honeymoon in full hands, alone in their cottage together.

And to him, as the days went by, it was as if the heavens had fallen, and he were sitting with her among the ruins, in a new world, everybody else buried, themselves two blissful survivors, with everything to squander as they would. At first, he could not get rid of a culpable sense of licence on his part. Wasn't there some duty outside, calling him and he did not come?

It was all very well at night, when the doors were locked and the darkness drawn round the two of them. Then they *were* the only inhabitants of the visible earth, the rest were under the flood.* And being alone in the world, they were a law unto themselves, they could enjoy and squander and waste like conscienceless gods.

But in the morning, as the carts clanked by, and children shouted down the lane: as the hucksters came calling their wares, and the church clock struck eleven, and he and she had not got up yet, even to breakfast: he could not help feeling guilty, as if he were committing a breach of the law—ashamed that he was not up and doing.

"Doing what?" she asked. "What is there to do? You will only lounge about."

Still, even lounging about was respectable. One was at least in connection with the world, then. Whereas now, lying so still and peacefully while the daylight came obscurely through the drawn blind, one was severed from the world, one shut oneself off in tacit denial of the world. And he was troubled.

But it was so sweet and satisfying lying there talking desultorily with her. It was sweeter than sunshine, and not so evanescent. It was even irritating the way the church clock kept on chiming: there seemed no space between the hours, just a moment, golden and still, whilst she traced his features with her finger-tips, utterly careless and happy, and he loved her to do it.

But he was strange and unused. So suddenly, everything that had been before was shed away and gone. One day, he was a bachelor, living with the world. The next day, he was with her, as remote from the world as if the two of them were buried like a seed in darkness. Suddenly, like a chestnut falling out of a burr, he was shed naked and glistening on to a soft, fecund earth, leaving behind him the hard 5 rind of worldly knowledge and experience. There it lay, cast off, the worldly experience. He heard it in the hucksters' cries, the noise of carts, the calling of children. And it was like the hard shed rind, discarded. Inside, in the softness and stillness of the room, was the naked kernel, that palpitated in silent activity, absorbed in reality. 10

Inside the room was a great steadiness, a core of living eternity. Only far outside, at the rim, went on the noise and the distraction. Here at the centre the great wheel* was motionless, centred upon itself. Here was a poised, unflawed stillness that was beyond time, because it remained the same, inexhaustible, unchanging, unex- 15 hausted.

As they lay close together, complete and beyond the touch of time or change, it was as if they were at the very centre of all the slow wheeling of space and the rapid agitation of life, deep, deep inside them all, at the centre where there is utter radiance, and eternal 20 being, and the silence absorbed in praise: the steady core of all movements, the unawakened sleep of all wakefulness. They found themselves there, and they lay still, in each other's arms; for their moment they were at the heart of eternity, whilst time roared far off, forever far off, towards the rim. 25

Then gradually they were passed away from the supreme centre, down the circles of praise and joy and gladness, further and further out, towards the noise and the friction. But their hearts had burned and were tempered by the inner reality, they were unalterably glad.

Gradually they began to wake up, the noises outside became more 30 real. They understood and answered the call outside. They counted the strokes of the bell. And when they counted midday, they understood that it was midday, in the world, and for themselves also.

It dawned upon her that she was hungry. She had been getting hungrier for a lifetime. But even yet it was not sufficiently real to 35 rouse her. A long way off she could hear the words "I am dying of hunger." Yet she lay still, separate, at peace, and the words were unuttered. There was still another lapse.

And then, quite calmly, even a little surprised, she was in the present, and was saying: 40

"I am dying with hunger."

"So am I," he said calmly, as if it were of not the slightest significance. And they relapsed into the warm, golden stillness. And the minutes flowed unheeded past the window outside.

5   Then suddenly she stirred against him.

"My dear, I am dying of hunger," she said.

It was a slight pain to him to be brought to.

"We'll get up," he said, unmoving.

And she sank her head on to him again, and they lay still, lapsing.
10   Half consciously, he heard the clock chime the hour. She did not hear.

"Do get up," she murmured at length, "and give me something to eat."

"Yes," he said, and he put his arms round her, and she lay with
15   her face on him. They were faintly astonished that they did not move. The minutes rustled louder at the window.

"Let me go then," he said.

She lifted her head from him, relinquishingly. With a little breaking away, he moved out of bed, and was taking his clothes. She
20   stretched out her hand to him.

"You are so nice," she said, and he went back for a moment or two.

Then actually he did slip into some clothes, and, looking round quickly at her, was gone out of the room. She lay translated again
25   into a pale, clearer peace. As if she were a spirit, she listened to the noise of him downstairs, as if she were no longer of the material world.

It was half past one. He looked at the silent kitchen, untouched from last night, dim with the drawn blind. And he hastened to draw
30   up the blind, so people should know they were not in bed any later. Well, it was his own house, it did not matter. Hastily he put wood in the grate and made a fire. He exulted in himself, like an adventurer on an undiscovered island. The fire blazed up, he put on the kettle. How happy he felt! How still and secluded the house was! There
35   were only he and she in the world.

But when he unbolted the door, and, half dressed, looked out, he felt furtive and guilty. The world *was* there, after all. And he had felt so secure, as though this house were the Ark in the flood,* and all the rest was drowned. The world was there: and it was afternoon. The
40   morning had vanished and gone by, the day was growing old. Where

was the bright, fresh morning? He was accused. Was the morning gone, and he had lain with blinds drawn, let it pass by unnoticed?

He looked again round the chill, grey afternoon. And he himself so soft and warm and glowing! There were two sprigs of yellow jasmine in the saucer that covered the milk-jug. He wondered who had been and left the sign. Taking the jug, he hastily shut the door. Let the day and the daylight drop out, let it go by unseen. He did not care. What did one day more or less matter to him. It could fall into oblivion unspent, if it liked, this one course of daylight.

"Somebody has been and found the door locked," he said when he went upstairs with the tray. He gave her the two sprigs of jasmine. She laughed as she sat up in bed, childishly threading the flowers in the breast of her nightdress. Her brown hair stuck out like a nimbus, all fierce, round her softly glowing face. Her dark eyes watched the tray eagerly.

"How good!" she cried, sniffing the cold air. "I'm glad you did a lot." And she held out her hands eagerly for her plate.—"Come back to bed, quick—it's cold." She rubbed her hands together sharply.

He put off what little clothing he had on, and* sat beside her in the bed.

"You look like a lion, with your mane sticking out, and your nose pushed over your food," he said.

She tinkled with laughter, and gladly ate her breakfast.

The morning was sunk away unseen, the afternoon was steadily going too, and he was letting it go. One bright transit of daylight gone by unacknowledged! There was something unmanly, recusant in it. He could not quite reconcile himself to the fact. He felt he ought to get up, go out quickly into the daylight, and work or spend himself energetically in the open air of the afternoon, retrieving what was left to him of the day.

But he did not go. Well, one might as well be hung for a sheep as for a lamb. If he had lost this day of his life, he had lost it. He gave it up. He was not going to count his losses. *She* didn't care. *She* didn't care in the least. Then why should he? Should he be behind her in recklessness and independence? She was superb in her indifference. He wanted to be like her.

She took her responsibilities lightly. When she spilled her tea on the pillow, she rubbed it carelessly with a handkerchief, and turned over the pillow. He would have felt guilty. She did not. And it pleased him. It pleased him very much to see how these things did not matter to her.

When the meal was over, she wiped her mouth on her handkerchief quickly, satisfied and happy, and settled down on the pillows
5   again, with her fingers in his close, strange, fur-like hair.

The evening began to fall, the light was half alive, livid. He hid his face against her.

"I don't like the twilight," he said.

"I love it," she answered.

10   He hid his face against her, who was warm and like sunlight. She seemed to have sunlight inside her. Her heart beating seemed like sunlight upon him. In her was a more real day than the day could give: so warm and steady and restoring. He hid his face against her whilst the twilight fell, whilst she lay staring out with her unseeing
15   dark eyes, as if she wandered forth untrammelled in the vagueness. The vagueness gave her scope and set her free.

To him, turned towards her heart-pulse, all was very still and very warm and very close, like noon-tide. He was glad to know this warm, full noon. It ripened him and took away his responsibility, some of
20   his conscience.

They got up when it was quite dark. She hastily twisted her hair into a knot, and was dressed in a twinkling. Then they went downstairs, drew to the fire, and sat in silence, saying a few words now and then.

25   Her father was coming. She bundled the dishes away, flew round and tidied the room, assumed another character, and again seated herself. He sat thinking of his carving of Eve. He loved to go over his carving in his mind, dwelling on every stroke, every line. How he loved it now! When he went back to his Creation-
30   panel again, he would finish his Eve, tender and sparkling. It did not satisfy him yet. The Lord should labour over her in a silent passion of Creation, and Adam should be tense as if in a dream of immortality, and Eve should take form glimmeringly, shadowily, as if the Lord must wrestle with His own soul for her, yet she was a
35   radiance.

"What are you thinking about?" she asked.

He found it difficult to say. His soul became shy when he tried to communicate it.

"I was thinking my Eve was too hard and lively."

40   "Why?"

"I don't know. She should be more—," he made a gesture of infinite tenderness.

There was a stillness with a little joy. He could not tell her any more. Why could he not tell her any more? She felt a pang of disconsolate sadness. But it was nothing. She went to him. 5

Her father came, and found them both very glowing, like an open flower. He loved to sit with them. Where there was a perfume of love, anyone who came must breathe it. They were both very quick and alive, lit up from the other-world, so that it was quite an experience for them, that anyone else could exist. 10

But still it troubled Will Brangwen a little, in his orderly, conventional mind, that the established rule of things had gone so utterly. One ought to get up in the morning and wash oneself and be a decent social being. Instead, the two of them stayed in bed till nightfall, then got up; she never washed her face, but sat there 15 talking to her father as bright and shameless as a daisy opened out of the dew. Or she got up at ten o'clock, and quite blithely went to bed again at three, or at half past four, stripping him naked in the daylight, and all so gladly and perfectly, oblivious quite of his qualms. He let her do as she liked with him, and shone with strange 20 pleasure. She was to dispose of him as she would. He was translated with gladness to be in her hands. And down went his qualms, his maxims, his rules, his smaller beliefs, she scattered them like an expert skittle-player. He was very much astonished and delighted to see them scatter. 25

He stood and gazed and grinned with wonder whilst his Tablets of Stone* went bounding and bumping and splintering down the hill, dislodged for ever. Indeed, it was true as they said, that a man wasn't born before he was married. What a change indeed!

He surveyed the rind of the world: houses, factories, trams, the 30 discarded rind; people scurrying about, work going on, all on the discarded surface. An earthquake had burst it all from inside. It was as if the surface of the world had been broken away entire: Ilkeston, streets, church, people, work, rule-of-the-day, all intact; and yet peeled away into unreality, leaving here exposed the inside, the 35 reality: one's own being, strange feelings and passions and yearnings and beliefs and aspirations, suddenly become present, revealed, the permanent bedrock, knitted one rock with the woman one loved. It was confounding. Things are not what they seem! When he was a child, he had thought a woman was a woman merely by virtue of her 40 skirts and petticoats. And now, lo, the whole world could be divested of its garment, the garment could lie there shed away intact, and one could stand in a new world, a new earth, naked in a new, naked universe. It was too astounding and miraculous.

This then was marriage! The old things didn't matter any more. One got up at four o'clock, and had broth at tea-time and made toffee in the middle of the night. One didn't put on one's clothes or one did put on one's clothes. He still was not quite sure it was not criminal. But it was a discovery to find one might be so supremely absolved. All that mattered was that he should love her and she should love him and they should live kindled to one another, like the Lord in two burning bushes that were not consumed.* And so they lived for the time.

She was less hampered than he, so she came more quickly to her fulness, and was sooner ready to enjoy again a return to the outside world. She was going to give a tea-party. His heart sank. He wanted to go on, to go on as they were. He wanted to have done with the outside world, to declare it finished for ever. He was anxious with a deep desire and anxiety that she should stay with him where they were in the timeless universe of free, perfect limbs and immortal breast, affirming that the old, outward order was finished. The new order was begun to last for ever, the living life, palpitating from the gleaming core, to action, without crust or cover or outward lie. But no, he could not keep her. She wanted the dead world again—she wanted to walk on the outside once more. She was going to give a tea-party. It made him frightened and furious and miserable. He was afraid all would be lost that he had so newly come unto: like the youth in the fairy tale, who was king for one day in the year, and for the rest a beaten herd:* like Cinderella also, at the feast. He was sullen. But she blithely began to make preparations for her tea-party. His fear was too strong, he was troubled, he hated her shallow anticipation and joy. Was she not forfeiting the reality, the one reality, for all that was shallow and worthless? Wasn't she carelessly taking off her crown to be an artificial figure having other artificial women to tea: when she might have been perfect with him, and kept him perfect, in the land of intimate connection? Now he must be deposed, his joy must be destroyed, he must put on the vulgar, shallow death of an outward existence.

He ground his soul in uneasiness and fear. But she rose to a real outburst of housework, turning him away as she shoved the furniture

aside to her broom. He stood hanging miserably near. He wanted
her back. Dread and desire for her to stay with him and shame at his
own dependence on her drove him to anger. He began to lose his
head. The wonder was going to pass away again. All the love, the
magnificent new order was going to be lost, she would forfeit it all for 5
the outside things. She would admit the outside world again, she
would throw away the living fruit for the ostensible rind. He began to
hate this in her. Driven by fear of her departure into a state of
helplessness, almost of imbecility, he wandered about the house.

And she, with her skirts kilted up, flew round at her work, 10
absorbed.

"Shake the rug then, if you must hang round," she said.

And fretting with resentment, he went to shake the rug. She was
blithely unconscious of him. He came back, hanging near to her.

"Can't you do anything?" she said, as if to a child, impatiently. 15
"Can't you do your wood-work?"

"Where shall I do it?" he asked, harsh with pain.

"Anywhere."

How furious that made him.

"Or go for a walk," she continued. "Go down to the Marsh. Don't 20
hang about as if you were only half there."

He winced and hated it. He went away to read. Never had his soul
felt so flayed and uncreated.*

And soon he must come down again to her. His hovering near her,
wanting her to be with him, the futility of him, the way his hands 25
hung, irritated her beyond bearing. She turned on him blindly and
destructively, he became a mad creature, black and electric with
fury. The dark storms rose in him, his eyes glowed black and evil, he
was fiendish in his thwarted soul.

There followed two black and ghastly days, when she was set in 30
anguish against him, and he felt as if he were in a black, violent
underworld, and his wrists quivered murderously. And she resisted
him. He seemed a dark, almost evil thing pursuing her, hanging on to
her, burdening her. She would give anything to have him removed.

"You need some work to do," she said. "You ought to be at work. 35
Can't you *do* something?"

His soul only grew the blacker. His condition now became
complete, the darkness of his soul was thorough. Everything had
gone: he remained complete in his own tense, black will. He was now
unaware of her. She did not exist. His dark, passionate soul had 40

recoiled upon itself, and now, clinched and coiled round a centre of hatred, existed in its own power. There was a curiously ugly pallor, an expressionlessness in his face. She shuddered from him. She was afraid of him. His will seemed grappled upon her.

5   She retreated before him. She went down to the Marsh, she entered again the immunity of her parents' love for her. He remained at Yew Cottage, black and clinched, his mind dead. He was unable to work at his wood-carving. He went on working monotonously at the garden, blindly, like a mole.

10   As she came home, up the hill, looking away at the town dim and blue on the hill, her heart relaxed and became yearning. She did not want to fight him any more. She wanted love—oh, love. Her feet began to hurry. She wanted to get back to him. Her heart became tight with yearning for him.

15   He had been making the garden in order, cutting the edges of the turf, laying the path with stones. He was a good, capable workman.

"How nice you've made it," she said, approaching tentatively down the path.

But he did not heed, he did not hear. His brain was solid and dead.

20   "Haven't you made it nice?" she repeated, rather plaintively.

He looked up at her, with that fixed, expressionless face and unseeing eyes which shocked her, made her go dazed and blind. Then he turned away. She saw his slender, stooping figure groping. A revulsion came over her. She went indoors.

25   As she took off her hat in the bedroom, she found herself weeping bitterly, with some of the old, anguished, childish desolation. She sat still and cried on. She did not want him to know. She was afraid of his hard, evil movements, the head dropped a little, rigidly, in a crouching, cruel way. She was afraid of him. He seemed to lacerate

30   her sensitive femaleness. He seemed to hurt her womb, to take pleasure in torturing her.

He came in to the house. The sound of his footsteps in his heavy boots filled her with horror: a hard, cruel, malignant sound. She was afraid he would come upstairs. But he did not. She waited appre-

35   hensively. He went out.

Where she was most vulnerable, he hurt her. Oh, where she was delivered over to him, in her very soft femaleness, he seemed to lacerate her and desecrate her. She pressed her hands over her womb in anguish, whilst the tears ran down her face. And why, and

40   why? Why was he like this?

Suddenly she dried her tears. She must get the tea ready. She went downstairs and set the table. When the meal was ready, she called to him.

"I've mashed the tea, Will, are you coming?"

She herself could hear the sound of tears in her own voice, and she began to cry again. He did not answer, but went on with his work. She waited a few minutes, in anguish. Fear came over her, she was panic-stricken with terror, like a child; and she could not go home again to her father; she was held by the power in this man who had taken her.

She turned indoors so that he should not see her tears. She sat down to table. Presently he came in to the scullery. His movements jarred on her, as she heard them. How horrible was the way he pumped, exacerbating, so cruel! How she hated to hear him! How he hated her! How his hatred was like blows upon her! The tears were coming again.

He came in, his face wooden and lifeless, fixed, persistent. He sat down to tea, his head dropped over his cup, uglily. His hands were red from the cold water, and there were rims of earth in his nails. He went on with his tea.

It was negative insensitiveness to her that she could not bear, something clayey and ugly. His intelligence was self-absorbed. How unnatural it was to sit with a self-absorbed creature, like something negative ensconced opposite one. Nothing could touch him—he could only absorb things into his own self.

The tears were running down her face. Something startled him, and he was looking up at her with his hateful, hard, bright eyes, hard and unchanging as a bird of prey.

"What are you crying for?" came the grating voice.

She winced through her womb. She could not stop crying.

"What are you crying for?" came the question again, in just the same tone. And still there was silence, with only the sniff of her tears.

His eyes glittered evilly, and as if with malignant desire. She shrank and became blind. She was like a bird being beaten down. A sort of swoon of helplessness came over her. She was of another order than he, she had no defence against him. Against such an influence, she was only vulnerable, she was given up.

He rose and went out of the house, possessed by the evil spirit. It tortured him and wracked him, and fought in him. And whilst he

worked, in the deepening twilight, it left him. Suddenly he saw that
she was hurt. He had only seen her triumphant before. Suddenly his
heart was torn with compassion for her. He became alive again, in an
anguish of compassion. He could not bear to think of her tears—he
5 could not bear it. He wanted to go to her and pour out his heart's
blood to her. He wanted to give everything to her, all his blood, his
life, to the last dregs, pour everything away to her. He yearned with
passionate desire to offer himself to her, utterly.

The evening star came, and the night. She had not lighted the
10 lamp. His heart burned with pain and with grief. He trembled to go
to her.

And at last he went, hesitating, burdened with a great offering.
The hardness had gone out of him, his body was sensitive, slightly
trembling. His hand was curiously sensitive, shrinking, as he shut
15 the door. He fixed the latch almost tenderly.

In the kitchen was only the fireglow, he could not see her. He
quivered with dread lest she had gone—he knew not where. In
shrinking dread, he went through to the parlour, to the foot of the
stairs.

20 "Anna," he called.

There was no answer. He went up the stairs, in dread of the empty
house—the horrible emptiness that made his heart ring with
insanity. He opened the bedroom door, and his heart flashed with
certainty that she had gone, that he was alone.

25 But he saw her on the bed, lying very still and scarcely noticeable,
with her back to him. He went and put his hand on her shoulder,
very gently, hesitating, in a great fear and self-offering. She did not
move. He waited. The hand that touched her shoulder hurt him, as if
she were sending it away. He stood dim with pain.

30 "Anna," he said.

But still she was motionless, like a curled up, oblivious creature.
His heart beat with strange throes of pain. Then, by a motion under
his hand, he knew she was crying, holding herself hard so that her
tears should not be known. He waited. The tension continued—
35 perhaps she was not crying—then suddenly relaxed with a sharp
catch of a sob. His heart flamed with love and suffering for her.
Kneeling carefully on the bed, so that his earthy boots should not
touch it, he took her in his arms to comfort her. The sobs gathered in
her, she was sobbing bitterly. But not to him. She was still away from
40 him.

He held her against his breast, whilst she sobbed, withheld from him, and all his body vibrated against her.

"Don't cry—don't cry," he said, with an odd simplicity. His heart was calm and numb with a sort of innocence of love, now.

She still sobbed, ignoring him, ignoring that he held her. His lips were dry.

"Don't cry, my love," he said, in the same abstract way. In his breast his heart burned like a torch, with suffering. He could not bear the desolateness of her crying. He would have soothed her with his blood. He heard the church clock chime, as if it touched him, and he waited in suspense for it to have gone by. It was quiet again.

"My love," he said to her, bending to touch her wet face with his mouth. He was afraid to touch her. How wet her face was! His body trembled as he held her. He loved her till he felt his heart and all his veins would burst and flood her with his hot, healing blood. He knew his blood would heal and restore her.

She was becoming quieter. He thanked the God of mercy that at last she was becoming quieter. His head felt so strange and blazed. Still he held her close, with trembling arms. His blood seemed very strong, enveloping her.

And at last she began to draw near him, she nestled to him. His limbs, his body, took fire and beat up in flames. She clung to him, she cleaved to his body. The flames swept him, he held her in sinews of fire. If she would kiss him! He bent his mouth down. And her mouth, soft and moist, received him. He felt his veins would burst with anguish of thankfulness, his heart was mad with gratefulness, he could pour himself out upon her for ever.

When they came to themselves, the night was very dark. Two hours had gone by. They lay still and warm and weak, like the new-born, together. And there was a silence almost of the unborn. Only his heart was weeping happily, after the pain. He did not understand, he had yielded, given way. There *was* no understanding. There could be only acquiescence and submission, and tremulous wonder of consummation.

The next morning, when they woke up, it had snowed. He wondered what was the strange pallor in the air, and the unusual tang. Snow was on the grass and the window-sill, it weighed down the black, ragged branches of the yews, and smoothed the graves in the churchyard.

Soon, it began to snow again, and they were shut in. He was glad, for then they were immune in a shadowy silence, there was no world, no time.

The snow lasted for some days. On the Sunday they went to church. They made a line of foot-prints across the garden, he left a
5 flat snow-print of his hand on the wall as he vaulted over, they traced the snow across the churchyard. For three days they had been immune in a perfect love.

There were very few people in church, and she was glad. She did not care much for church. She had never questioned any beliefs, and
10 she was, from habit and custom, a regular attendant at morning service. But she had ceased to come with any anticipation. Today, however, in the strangeness of snow, after such consummation of love, she felt expectant again, and delighted. She was still in the eternal world.

15 She used, after she went to the High School and wanted to be a lady, wanted to fulfil some mysterious ideal, always to listen to the sermon and to try to gather suggestions. That was all very well for a while. The vicar told her to be good in this way and in that. She went away feeling it was her highest aim to fulfil these injunctions.

20 But quickly this palled. After a short time, she was not very much interested in being good. Her soul was in quest of something, which was not just being good, and doing one's best. No, she wanted something else: something that was not her ready-made duty. Everything seemed to be merely a matter of social duty, and never of
25 her *self*. They talked about her soul, but somehow never managed to rouse or to implicate her soul. As yet her soul was not brought in at all.

So that whilst she had an affection for Mr Loverseed, the vicar, and a protective sort of feeling for Cossethay church, wanting always
30 to help it and defend it, it counted very small in her life.

Not but that she was conscious of some unsatisfaction. When her husband was roused by the thought of the churches, then she became hostile to the ostensible Church, she hated it for not fulfilling anything in her. The Church told her to be good: very well,
35 she had no idea of contradicting what it said. The Church talked about her soul, and about the welfare of mankind, as if the saving of her soul lay in her performing certain acts conducive to the welfare of mankind. Very good, she heard it all and was sure it was true. The salvation of her soul lay in her contributing to the welfare of
40 mankind. Well and good—it was so, then.

Nevertheless, as she sat in church her face had a pathos and poignancy. Was this what she had come to hear: how, by doing this thing and by not doing that, she could save her soul? She did not contradict it. But the pathos of her face gave the lie. There was something else she wanted to hear, it was something else she asked 5 for from the Church.

But who was *she* to affirm it? And what was *she* doing with unsatisfied desires? She was ashamed. She ignored them and left them out of count as much as possible, her underneath yearnings. They angered her. She wanted to be like other people, decently 10 satisfied.

He angered her more than ever. Church had an irresistible attraction for him. And he paid no more attention to that part of the service which was Church to her, than if he had been an angel or a fabulous beast sitting there. He simply paid no heed to the sermon or 15 to the meaning of the service. There was something thick, dark, dense, powerful about him that irritated her too deeply for her to speak of it. The Church teaching in itself meant nothing to him. "And forgive us our trespasses as we forgive them that trespass against us—"* it simply did not touch him. It might have been mere 20 sounds, and it would have acted upon him in the same way. He did not want things to be intelligible. And he did not care about his trespasses, neither about the trespasses of his neighbour, when he was in church. Leave that care for week-days. When he was in church, he took no more notice of his daily life. It was week-day 25 stuff. As for the welfare of mankind,—he merely did not realise that there was any such thing: except on week-days, when he was good natured enough. In church, he wanted a dark, nameless emotion, the emotion of all the great mysteries of passion.

He was not interested in the *thought* of himself or of her: oh, and 30 how that irritated her! He ignored the sermon, he ignored the greatness of mankind, he did not admit the immediate importance of mankind. He did not care about himself as a human being. He did not attach any vital importance to his life in the drafting office, or his life among men. That was just merely the margin to the text. The 35 verity was his connection with Anna and his connection with the Church, his real being lay in his dark emotional experience of the Infinite, of the Absolute. And the great, mysterious, illuminated capitals to the text, were his feelings with the Church.

It exasperated her beyond measure. She could not get out of the 40

Church the satisfaction he got. The thought of her soul was intimately mixed up with the thought of her own self. Indeed, her soul and her own self were one and the same in her. Whereas he seemed simply to ignore the fact of his own self, almost to refute it.
5 He had a soul—a dark, inhuman thing caring nothing for humanity. So she conceived it. And in the gloom and the mystery of the Church his soul lived and ran free, like some strange, underground thing, abstract.

He was very strange to her, and, in this Church spirit, in
10 conceiving himself as a soul, he seemed to escape and run free of her. In a way, she envied it him, this dark freedom and jubilation of the soul, some strange entity in him. It fascinated her. Again she hated it. And again, she despised him, wanted to destroy it in him.

This snowy morning, he sat with a dark-bright face beside her, not
15 aware of her, and somehow, she felt he was conveying to strange, secret places the love that sprang in him for her. He sat with a dark-rapt, half-delighted face, looking at a little stained window. She saw the ruby-coloured glass, with the shadow heaped along the bottom from the snow outside, and the familiar yellow figure of the
20 lamb holding the banner,* a little darkened now, but in the murky interior, strangely luminous, pregnant.

She had always liked this little red and yellow window. The lamb, looking very silly and self-conscious, was holding up a fore-paw, in the cleft of which was dangerously perched a little flag with a red
25 cross. Very pale yellow, the lamb, with greenish shadows. Since she was a child she had liked this creature, with the same feeling she felt for the little woolly lambs on green legs that the children carried home from the fair every year. She had always liked those toys, and she had the same amused, childish liking for this church lamb. Yet
30 she had always been uneasy about it. She was never sure that this Lamb with a flag did not want to be more than it appeared. So she half mistrusted it, there was a mixture of dislike in her attitude to it.

Now, by a curious gathering, knitting of his eyes, the faintest tension of ecstasy on his face, he gave her the uncomfortable feeling
35 that he was in correspondence with the creature, the lamb in the window. A cold wonder came over her—her soul was perplexed. There he sat, motionless, timeless, with the faint bright tension on his face. What was he doing? What connection was there between him and the lamb in the glass?
40 Suddenly it gleamed to her dominant, this lamb with the flag.

Suddenly she had a powerful mystic experience, the power of the tradition seized on her, she was transported to another world. And she hated it, resisted it.

Instantly, it was only a silly lamb in the glass again. And dark, violent hatred of her husband swept up in her. What was he doing, 5 sitting there gleaming, carried away, soulful?

She shifted sharply, she knocked him as she pretended to pick up her glove, she groped among his feet.

He came to, rather bewildered, exposed. Anybody but her would have pitied him. She wanted to rend him. He did not know what was 10 amiss, what he had been doing.

As they sat at dinner, in their cottage, he was dazed by the chill of antagonism from her. She did not know why she was so angry. But she was incensed.

"Why do you never listen to the sermon?" she asked, seething with 15 hostility and violation.

"I do," he said.

"You don't—you don't hear a single word."

He retired into himself, to enjoy his own sensation. There was something subterranean about him, as if he had an underworld 20 refuge. The young girl hated to be in the house with him when he was like this.

After dinner, he retired into the parlour, continuing in the same state of abstraction, which was a burden intolerable to her. Then he went to the book-shelf and took down books to look at, that she had 25 scarcely glanced over.

He sat absorbed over a book on the illuminations in old missals, and then over a book on paintings in churches; Italian, English, French and German. He had, when he was sixteen, discovered a Roman Catholic bookshop where he could find such things. 30

He turned the leaves in absorption, absorbed in looking, not thinking. He was like a man whose eyes were in his chest, she said of him later.

She came to look at the things with him. Half they fascinated her. She was puzzled, interested, and antagonistic. 35

It was when she came to pictures of the Pietà* that she burst out.

"I do think they're loathsome," she cried.

"What?" he said, surprised, abstracted.

"Those bodies with slits in them, posing to be worshipped."

"You see, it means the Sacraments, the Bread," he said, slowly. 40

"Does it!" she cried. "Then it's worse. *I* don't want to see your chest slit, nor to eat your dead body, even if you offer it me. Can't you see it's horrible?"

"It isn't me, it's Christ."

5   "What if it is, it's you! And it's horrible, you wallowing in your own dead body, and thinking of eating it in the Sacrament."

"You've to take it for what it means."

"It means your human body put up to be slit and killed and then worshipped—what else?"

10 They lapsed into silence. His soul grew angry and aloof.

"And I think that Lamb in Church," she said, "is the biggest joke in the parish—"

She burst into a 'Pouf' of ridiculing laughter.

"It might be, to those that see nothing in it," he said. "You know

15 it's the symbol of Christ, of His innocence and sacrifice."

"Whatever it means, it's a *lamb*," she said. "And I like lambs too much to treat them as if they had to mean something. As for the Christmas-tree flag—no—"

And again she poufed with mockery.

20 "It's because you don't know anything," he said violently, harshly. "Laugh at what you know, not at what you don't know."

"What don't I know?"

"What things mean."

"And what does it mean?"

25 He was reluctant to answer her. He found it difficult.

"*What* does it mean?" she insisted.

"It means the triumph of the Resurrection."

She hesitated, baffled. A fear came upon her. What were these things? Something dark and powerful seemed to extend before her.

30 Was it wonderful after all?

But no—she refused it.

"Whatever it may pretend to mean, what it *is* is a silly absurd toy-lamb with a Christmas-tree flag ledged on its paw—and if it wants to mean anything else, it must look different from that."

35 He was in a state of violent irritation against her. Partly he was ashamed of his love for these things; he hid his passion for them. He was ashamed of the ecstasy into which he could throw himself with these symbols. And for a few moments he hated the Lamb and the mystic pictures of the Eucharist, with a violent, ashy hatred. His fire

40 was put out, she had thrown cold water on it. The whole thing was

distasteful to him, his mouth was full of ashes. He went out cold with corpse-like anger, leaving her alone. He hated her. He walked through the white snow, under a sky of lead.

And she wept again, in bitter recurrence of the previous gloom. But her heart was easy—oh, much more easy.

She was quite willing to make it up with him when he came home again. He was black and surly, but abated. She had broken a little of something in him. And at length he was glad to forfeit from his soul all his symbols, to have her making love to him. He loved it when she put her head on his knee, and he had not asked her to or wanted her to, he loved her when she put her arms round him and made bold love to him, and he did not make love to her. He felt a strong blood in his limbs again.

And she loved the intent, far look of his eyes when they rested on her: intent, yet far, not near, not with her. And she wanted to bring them near. She wanted his eyes to come to hers, to know her. And they would not. They remained intent, and far, and proud, like a hawk's, naïve and inhuman as a hawk's. So she loved him and caressed him and roused him like a hawk, till he was keen and instant, but without tenderness. He came to her fierce and hard, like a hawk striking and taking her. He was no mystic any more, she was his aim and object, his prey. And she was carried off, and he was satisfied, or satiated at last.

Then immediately she began to retaliate on him. She too was a hawk. If she imitated the pathetic plover running plaintive to him, that was part of the game. When he, satisfied, moved with a proud, insolent slouch of the body and a half-contemptuous drop of the head, unaware of her, ignoring her very existence after taking his fill of her and getting his satisfaction of her, her soul roused, its pinions became like steel, and she struck at him. When he sat on his perch glancing sharply round with solitary pride, pride eminent and fierce, she dashed at him and threw him from his station savagely, she goaded him from his keen dignity of a male, she harassed him from his unperturbed pride, till he was mad with rage, his light brown eyes burned with fury, they saw her now, like flames of anger they flared at her and recognised her as the enemy.

Very good, she was the enemy, very good. As he prowled round her, she watched him. As he struck at her, she struck back.

He was angry because she had carelessly pushed away his tools so that they got rusty.

"Don't leave them littering in my way, then," she said.

"I shall leave them where I like," he cried.

"Then I shall throw them where I like."

They glowered at each other, he with rage in his hands, she with
5   her soul fierce with victory. They were very well matched. They
would fight it out.

She turned to her sewing. Immediately the tea-things were
cleared away, she fetched out the stuff, and his soul rose in rage. He
hated beyond measure to hear the shriek of calico as she tore the web
10 sharply, as if with pleasure. And the run of the sewing-machine
gathered a frenzy in him at last.

"Aren't you going to stop that row." he shouted. "Can't you do it
in the daytime?"

She looked up sharply, hostile from her work.

15 "No, I can't do it in the daytime, I have other things to do. Besides,
I like sewing, and you're not going to stop me doing it."

Whereupon she turned back to her arranging, fixing, stitching, his
nerves jumped with anger as the sewing-machine started and
stuttered and buzzed.

20 But she was enjoying herself, she was triumphant and happy as the
darting needle danced ecstatically down a hem, drawing the stuff
along under its vivid stabbing, irresistibly. She made the machine
hum. She stopped it imperiously, her fingers were deft and swift and
mistress.

25 If he sat behind her stiff with impotent rage—it only made a
trembling vividness come into her energy. On she worked. At last he
went to bed in a rage, and lay stiff, away from her. And she turned
her back on him. And in the morning they did not speak, except in
mere cold civilities.

30 And when he came home at night, his heart relenting and growing
hot for love of her, when he was just ready to feel he had been wrong,
and when he was expecting her to feel the same, there she sat at the
sewing-machine, the whole house was covered with clipped calico,
the kettle was not even on the fire.

35 She started up, affecting concern.

"Is it so late?" she cried.

But his face had gone stiff with rage. He walked through to the
parlour, then he walked back and out of the house again. Her heart
sank. Very swiftly she began to make his tea.

40 He went black-hearted down the road to Ilkeston. When he was in

this state he never thought. A bolt shot across the doors of his mind and shut him in, a prisoner. He went back to Ilkeston, and drank a glass of beer. What was he going to do? He did not want to see anybody.

He would go to Nottingham, to his own town. He went to the 5 station and took a train. When he got to Nottingham, still he had nowhere to go. However, it was more agreeable to walk familiar streets. He paced them with a mad restlessness, as if he were running amok. Then he turned to a bookshop and found a book on Bamberg Cathedral.* Here was a discovery! here was something for him! He 10 went into a quiet restaurant to look at his treasure. He lit up with thrills of bliss as he turned from picture to picture. He had found something at last, in these carvings. His soul had great satisfaction. Had he not come out to seek, and had he not found! He was in a passion of fulfilment. These were the finest carvings, statues, he had 15 ever seen. The book lay in his hands like a doorway. The world around was only an inclosure, a room. But he was going away. He lingered over the lovely statues of women. A marvellous, finely wrought universe crystallised out around him as he looked again, at the crowns, the twining hair, the woman-faces. 20

He liked all the better the unintelligible text of the German. He preferred things he could not understand with the mind. He loved the undiscovered and the undiscoverable. He pored over the pictures intensely. And these were wooden statues! "Holz"—he believed that meant wood. Wooden statues so shapen to his soul! He 25 was a million times gladdened. How undiscovered the world was, how it revealed itself to his soul! What a fine, exciting thing his life was, at his hand! Did not Bamberg Cathedral make the world his own? He celebrated his triumphant strength and life and verity, and embraced the vast riches he was inheriting. 30

But it was about time to go home. He had better catch a train. All the time there was a steady bruise at the bottom of his soul, but so steady as to be forgettable. He caught a train for Ilkeston.

It was ten o'clock as he was mounting the hill to Cossethay, carrying his limp book on Bamberg Cathedral. He had not yet 35 thought of Anna, not definitely. The dark finger pressing a bruise controlled him thoughtlessly.

Anna had started guiltily when he left the house. She had hastened preparing the tea, hoping he would come back. She had made some toast, and got all ready. Then he didn't come. She cried 40

with vexation and disappointment. Why had he gone? Why couldn't
he come back now? Why was it such a battle between them? She
loved him—she did love him—why couldn't he be kinder to her,
nicer to her?

5   She waited in distress—then her mood grew harder. He passed
out of her thoughts. She had considered, indignantly, what right he
had to interfere with her sewing? She had indignantly refused his
right to interfere with her at all. She was not to be interfered with.
Was she not herself, and he the outsider?

10   Yet a quiver of fear went through her. If he should leave her? That
would destroy her. She never quite knew what he would do next. She
disliked him that he was so unsure, so unfixed. What if he did leave
her? She sat conjuring fears and sufferings, till she wept with very
self-pity. She did not know what she would do if he left her, or if he

15 turned against her. The thought of it chilled her, made her desolate
and hard. And against him, the stranger, the outside being* who
wanted to arrogate authority, she remained steadily fortified. Was
she not herself? How could one who was not of her own kind
presume with authority? She knew she was immutable, unchange-

20 able, she was not afraid for her own being. She was only afraid of all
that was not herself. It pressed round her, it came to her and took
part in her, in form of her man, this vast, resounding, alien world
which was not herself. And he had so many weapons, he might strike
from so many sides.

25   When he came in at the door, his heart was blazed with pity and
tenderness, she looked so lost and forlorn and young. She glanced
up, afraid. And she was surprised to see him, shining-faced, clear
and beautiful in his movements, as if he were clarified. And a startled
pang of fear, and shame of herself went through her.

30   They waited for each other to speak.

"Do you want to eat anything?" she said.

"I'll get it myself," he answered, not wanting her to serve him.

But she brought out food. And it pleased him she did it for him.
He was again a bright lord.

35   "I went to Nottingham," he said mildly.

"To your mother?" she asked, in a flash of contempt.

"No—I didn't go home."

"Who did you go to see?"

"I went to see nobody."

40   "Then why did you go to Nottingham?"

"I went because I wanted to go."

He was getting angry that she again rebuffed him when he was so clear and shining.

"And who did you see?"

"I saw nobody." 5

"Nobody?"

"No—who should I see?"

"You saw nobody you knew?"

"No, I didn't," he replied irritably.

She believed him, and her mood became cold. 10

"I bought a book," he said, handing her the propitiatory volume.

She idly looked at the pictures. Beautiful, the pure women with their clear-dropping gowns. Her heart became colder. What did they mean to *him*.

He sat and waited for her. She bent over the book. 15

"Aren't they nice?" he said, his voice roused and glad.

Her blood flushed, but she did not lift her head.

"Yes," she said. In spite of herself, she was compelled by him. He was strange, attractive, exerting some power over her.

He came over to her, and touched her delicately. Her heart beat 20 with wild passion, wild raging passion. But she resisted as yet. It was always the unknown, always the unknown, and she clung fiercely to her known self. But the rising flood carried her away.

They loved each other to transport again, passionately and fully.

"Isn't it more wonderful than ever?" she asked him, radiant like a 25 newly-opened flower, with tears like dew.

He held her closer. He was strange and abstracted.

"It is always more wonderful," she asseverated, in a glad, child's voice, remembering her fear, and not quite cleared of it yet.

So it went on continually, the recurrence of love and conflict 30 between them. One day it seemed as if everything was shattered, all life spoiled, ruined, desolated and laid waste. The next day it was all marvellous again, just marvellous. One day she thought she would go mad from his very presence, the sound of his drinking was detestable to her. The next day she loved and rejoiced in the way he crossed the 35 floor,* he was sun, moon and stars in one.

She fretted, however, at last, over the lack of stability. When the perfect hours came back, her heart did not forget that they would pass away again. She was uneasy. The surety, the surety, the inner surety, the confidence in the abidingness of love: that was what she 40

wanted. And that she did not get. She knew also that he had not got
it.

Nevertheless it was a marvellous world, she was for the most part
lost in the marvellousness of it. Even her great woes were marvellous
5 to her.

She could be very happy. And she wanted to be happy. She
resented it when he made her unhappy. Then she could kill him, cast
him out. Many days, she waited for the hour when he would be gone
to work. Then the flow of her life, which he seemed to dam up, was
10 let loose, and she was free. She was free, she was full of delight.
Everything delighted her. She took up the rug and went to shake it in
the garden. Patches of snow were on the fields, the air was light. She
heard the ducks shouting on the pond, she saw them charge and sail
across the water as if they were setting off on an invasion of the
15 world. She watched the rough horses, one of which was clipped
smooth on the belly, so that he wore a jacket and long stockings of
brown fur, stand kissing each other in the wintry morning by the
churchyard wall. Everything delighted her, now he was gone, the
insulator, the obstruction removed, the world all hers, in connection
20 with her.

She was joyfully active. Nothing pleased her more than to hang
out the washing in a high wind that came full-butt* over the round of
the hill, tearing the wet garments out of her hands, making flap-
flap-flap of the waving stuff. She laughed and struggled and grew
25 angry. But she loved her solitary days.

Then he came home at night, and she knitted her brows because
of some endless contest between them. As he stood in the doorway,
her heart changed. It steeled itself. The laughter and zest of the day
disappeared from her. She was stiffened.

30 They fought an unknown battle, unconsciously. Still they were in
love with each other, the passion was there. But the passion was
consumed in a battle. And the deep, fierce, unnamed battle went on.
Everything glowed intensely about them, the world had put off its
clothes and was awful, with new, primal nakedness.

35 Sunday came, when the strange spell was cast over her by him.
Half she loved it. She was becoming more like him. All the
week-days, there was a glint of sky and fields, the little church
seemed to babble away to the cottages the morning through. But on
Sundays, when he stayed at home, a deeply-coloured, tense gloom
40 seemed to gather on the face of the earth, the church seemed to fill

itself with shadow, to become big, a universe to her, there was a burning of blue and ruby, a sound of worship about her. And when the doors were opened, and she came out into the world, it was a world new-created, she stepped into the resurrection of the world, her heart beating to the memory of the darkness and the Passion.* 5

If, as very often, they went to the Marsh for tea on Sundays, then she regained another, lighter world, that had never known the gloom and the stained glass and the ecstasy of chanting. Her husband was obliterated, she was with her father again, who was so fresh and free and all daylight. Her husband, with his intensity and his darkness, 10 was obliterated. She left him, she forgot him, she accepted her father.

Yet, as she went home again with the young man, she put her hand on his arm tentatively, a little bit ashamed, her hand pleaded that he would not hold it against her, her recusancy. But he was obscured. 15 He seemed to become blind, as if he were not there with her.

Then she was afraid. She wanted him. When he was oblivious of her, she almost went mad with fear. For she had become so vulnerable, so exposed. She was in touch so intimately. All things about her had become intimate, she had known them near and 20 lovely, like presences hovering upon her. What if they should all go hard and separate again, standing back from her terrible and distinct, and she, having known them, should be at their mercy.

This frightened her. Always, her husband was to her the unknown to which she was delivered up. She was a flower that has been 25 tempted forth into blossom, and has no retreat. He had her nakedness in his power. And who was he, what was he? A blind thing, a dark force, without knowledge. She wanted to preserve herself.

Then she gathered him to herself again and was satisfied for a moment. But as time went on, she began to realise more and more 30 that he did not alter, that he was something dark, alien to herself. She had thought him just the bright reflex of herself. As the weeks and months went by she realised that he was a dark opposite to her, that they were opposites, not complements.*

He did not alter, he remained separately himself, and he seemed to 35 expect her to be part of himself, the extension of his will. She felt him trying to gain power over her, without knowing her. What did he want? Was he going to bully her?

What did she want herself? She answered herself, that she wanted to be happy, to be natural, like the sunlight and the busy daytime. 40

And, at the bottom of her soul, she felt he wanted her to be dark, unnatural. Sometimes, when he seemed like the darkness covering and smothering her, she revolted almost in horror, and struck at him. She struck at him, and made him bleed, and he became wicked.

5 Because she dreaded him and held him in horror, he became wicked, he wanted to destroy. And then the fight between them was cruel.

She began to tremble. He wanted to impose himself on her. And he began to shudder. She wanted to desert him, to leave him a prey to the open, with the unclean dogs of the darkness setting on to

10 devour him. He must beat her, and make her stay with him. Whereas she fought to keep herself free of him.

They went their ways now shadowed and stained with blood, feeling the world far off, unable to give help. Till she began to get tired. After a certain point, she became impassive, detached utterly

15 from him. He was always ready to burst out murderously against her. Her soul got up and left him, she went her way. Nevertheless in her apparent blitheness, that made his soul black with opposition, she trembled as if she bled.

And ever and again, the pure love came in sunbeams between

20 them, when she was like a flower in the sun to him, so beautiful, so shining, so intensely dear that he could scarcely bear it. Then as if his soul had six wings of bliss* he stood absorbed in praise, feeling the radiance from the Almighty beat through him like a pulse, as he stood in the upright flame of praise, transmitting the pulse of

25 Creation.

And ever and again he appeared to her as the dread flame of power. Sometimes, when he stood in the doorway, his face lit up, he seemed like an Annunciation* to her, her heart beat fast. And she watched him, suspended. He had a dark, burning being that she dreaded and

30 resisted. She was subject to him as to the Angel of the Presence.* She waited upon him and heard his will, and she trembled in his service.

Then all this passed away. Then he loved her for her childishness and for her strangeness to him, for the wonder of her soul which was different from his soul, and which made him genuine when he would

35 be false. And she loved him for the way he sat loosely in a chair, or for the way he came through a door with his face open and eager. She loved his ringing, eager voice, and the touch of the unknown about him, his absolute simplicity.

Yet neither of them was quite satisfied. He felt, somewhere, that

40 she did not respect him. She only respected him as far as he was

related to herself. For what he was, beyond her, she had no care. She did not care for what he represented in himself. It is true, he did not know himself what he represented. But whatever it was, she did not really honor it. She did no service to his work as a lace-designer, nor to himself as bread-winner. Because he went down to the office and worked every day—that entitled him to no respect or regard from her, he knew. Rather she despised him for it. And he almost loved her for this, though at first it maddened him like an insult.

What was much deeper, she soon came to combat his deepest feelings. What he thought about life and about society and mankind did not matter very much to her: he was right enough to be insignificant. This was again galling to him. She would judge beyond him on these things. But at length he came to accept her judgments, discovering them as if they were his own. It was not here the deep trouble lay. The deep root of his enmity lay in the fact that she jeered at his soul. He was inarticulate and stupid in thought. But to some things he clung passionately. He loved the Church. If she tried to get out of him, what he *believed*, then they were both soon in a white rage.

Did he believe the water turned to wine at Cana?* She would drive him to the thing as a historical fact: so much rain-water—look at it—can it become grape-juice, wine? For an instant, he saw with the clear eyes of the mind and said no, his clear mind, answering her for a moment, rejected the idea. And immediately his whole soul was crying in a mad, inchoate hatred against this violation of himself. It *was* true for him. His mind was extinguished again at once, his blood was up. In his blood and bones, he wanted the scene, the wedding, the water brought forward from the firkins as red wine: and Christ saying to His mother:

"Woman, what have I to do with thee?—mine hour is not yet come."

And then:

"His mother saith unto the servants, 'Whatsoever he saith unto you, do it.'"

Brangwen loved it, with his bones and blood he loved it, he could not let it go. Yet she forced him to let it go. She hated his blind attachments.

Water, natural water, could it suddenly and unnaturally turn into wine, depart from its being and at hap-hazard take on another being? Ah no, he knew it was wrong.

She became again the palpitating, hostile child, hateful, putting

things to destruction. He became mute and dead. His own being
gave him the lie. He knew it was so: wine was wine, water was water,
for ever: the water had not become wine. The miracle was not a real
fact. She seemed to be destroying him. He went out, dark* and
5   destroyed, his soul running its blood. And he tasted of death.*
Because his life was formed in these unquestioned concepts.

She, desolate again as she had been when she was a child, went
away and sobbed. She did not care, she did not care whether the
water had turned to wine or not. Let him believe it if he wanted to.
10 But she knew she had won. And an ashy desolation came over her.

They were ashenly miserable for some time. Then the life began
to come back. He was nothing if not dogged. He thought again of the
chapter of St John. There was a great biting pang. "But thou hast
kept the good wine until now." "The best wine!" The young man's
15 heart responded in a craving, in a triumph, although the knowledge
that it was not true in fact bit at him like a weasel in his heart. Which
was stronger, the pain of the denial or the desire for affirmation? He
was stubborn in spirit, and abode by his desire. But he would not any
more affirm the miracles as true.

20 Very well, it was not true, the water had not turned into wine. The
water had not turned into wine. But for all that he would live in his
soul as if the water *had* turned into wine. For truth of fact, it had not.
But for his soul, it had.

"Whether it turned into wine or whether it didn't," he said, "it
25 doesn't bother me. I take it for what it is."

"And *what* is it?" she asked, quickly, hopefully.

"It's the Bible," he said.

That answer enraged her, and she despised him. She did not
actively question the Bible herself. But he drove her to contempt.
30 And yet he did not care about the Bible, the written letter.
Although he could not satisfy her, yet she knew of herself that he had
something real. He was not a dogmatist. He did not believe in *fact*
that the water turned into wine. He did not want to make a fact out of
it. Indeed, his attitude was without criticism. It was purely individual.
35 He took that which was of value to him from the Written Word, he
added to his spirit. His mind he let sleep.

And she was bitter against him, that he let his mind sleep. That
which was human, belonged to mankind, he would not exert. He
cared only for himself. He was no Christian. Above all, Christ had
40 asserted the brotherhood of man.*

She, almost against herself, clung to the worship of the human knowledge. Man must die in the body, but in his knowledge he was immortal. Such, somewhere, was her belief, quite obscure and unformulated. She believed in the omnipotence of the human mind.

He, on the other hand, blind as a subterranean thing, just ignored   5
the human mind and ran after his own dark-souled desires, following his own tunnelling nose. She felt often she must suffocate. And she fought him off.

Then he, knowing he was blind, fought madly back again, frantic in sensual fear. He did foolish things. He asserted himself on his   10
rights, he arrogated the old position of master of the house.

"You've a right* to do as I want," he cried.

"Fool!" she answered. "Fool!"

"I'll let you know who's master," he cried.

"Fool!" she answered. "Fool! I've known my own father, who   15
could put a dozen of you in his pipe and push them down with his finger-end. Don't I know what a fool you are."

He knew himself what a fool he was, and was flayed by the knowledge. Yet he went on trying to steer the ship of their dual life. He asserted his position as the captain of the ship.* And captain and   20
ship bored her. He wanted to loom important as master of one of the innumerable domestic craft that make up the great fleet of society. It seemed to her a ridiculous armada of tubs jostling in futility. She felt no belief in it. She jeered at him as master of the house, master of their dual life. And he was black with shame and rage. He knew, with   25
shame, how her father had been a man without arrogating any authority.

He had gone on the wrong tack, and he felt it hard to give up the expedition. There was great surging and shame. Then he yielded. He had given up the master-of-the-house idea.   30

There was something he wanted, nevertheless, some form of mastery. Ever and anon, after his collapses into the petty and the shameful, he rose up again, and, stubborn in spirit, strong in his power to start afresh, set out once more in his male pride of being to fulfil the hidden passion of his spirit.   35

It began well, but it ended always in war between them, till they were both driven almost to madness. He said, she did not respect him. She laughed in hollow scorn of this. For her it was enough that she loved him.

"Respect what?" she asked.   40

But he always answered the wrong thing. And though she cudgelled her brains, she could not come at it.

"Why don't you go on with your wood-carving?" she said. "Why don't you finish your Adam and Eve?"

5   But she did not care for the Adam and Eve, and he never put another stroke to it. She jeered at the Eve, saying:

"She is like a little marionette. Why is she so small? You've made Adam as big as God, and Eve like a doll.

"It is impudence to say that Woman was made out of Man's
10 body,"* she continued, "when every man is born of woman. What impudence men have, what arrogance!"

In a rage one day, after trying to work on the board, and failing, so that his belly was a flame of nausea, he chopped up the whole panel and put it on the fire. She did not know. He went about for some days
15 very quiet and subdued after it.

"Where is the Adam and Eve board?" she asked him.

"Burnt."

She looked at him.

"But your carving."
20 "I burned it."

"When?"

She did not believe him.

"On Friday night."

"When I was at the Marsh?"
25 "Yes."

She said no more.

Then, when he had gone to work, she wept for a whole day, and was much chastened in spirit. So that a new, fragile flame of love came out of the ashes of this last pain.
30 Directly, it occurred to her that she was with child. There was a great trembling of wonder and anticipation through her soul. She wanted a child. Not that she loved babies so much, though she was touched by all young things. But she wanted to bear children. And a certain hunger in her heart wanted to unite her husband with herself,
35 in a child.

She wanted a son. She felt, a son would be everything. She wanted to tell her husband. But it was such a trembling, intimate thing to tell him, and he was at this time hard and unresponsive. So that she went away and wept. It was such a waste of a beautiful opportunity, such a
40 frost that nipped in the bud one of the beautiful moments of her life.

She went about heavy and tremulous with her secret, wanting to touch him, oh, most delicately, and see his face, dark and sensitive, attend to her news. She waited and waited for him to become gentle and still towards her. But he was always harsh and he bullied her.

So that the buds shrivelled from her confidence, she was chilled. 5 She went down to the Marsh.

"Well," said her father, looking at her and seeing her at the first glance; "what's amiss wi' you now?"

The tears came at the touch of his careful love.

"Nothing," she said. 10

"Can't you hit it off, you two?" he said.

"He's so obstinate," she quivered; but her soul was obdurate itself.

"Ay, an' I know another who's all that," said her father.

She was silent. 15

"You don't want to make yourselves miserable," said her father: "all about nowt."

"*He* isn't miserable," she said.

"I'll back my life, if you can do nowt else, you can make him as miserable as a dog. You'd be a dab hand at that, my lass." 20

"*I* do nothing to make him miserable," she retorted.

"Oh no—oh no! A packet o' butterscotch, you are."

She laughed a little.

"You mustn't think I *want* to be miserable," she cried. "I don't."

"We quite readily believe it," retorted Brangwen. "Neither do you 25 intend him to be hopping for joy like a fish in a pond."

This made her think. She was rather surprised to find that she did *not* intend her husband to be hopping for joy like a fish in a pond.

Her mother came, and they all sat down to tea, talking casually.

"Remember, child," said her mother, "that everything is not 30 waiting for *your* hand just to take or leave. You mustn't expect it. Between two people, the love itself is the important thing, and that is neither you nor him. It is a third thing you must create. You mustn't expect it to be just your way."

"Ha—nor do I. If I did, I should soon find my mistake out. If *I* put 35 my hand out to take anything, my hand is very soon bitten, I can tell you."

"Then you must mind where you put your hand," said her father.

Anna was rather indignant that they took the tragedy of her young married life with such equanimity. 40

"You love the man right enough," said her father, wrinkling his forehead in distress. "That's all as counts."

"I *do* love him, more shame to him," she cried. "I want to tell him—I've been waiting for four days now to tell him—" her face
5 began to quiver, the tears came. Her parents watched her in silence. She did not go on.

"Tell him what?" said her father.

"That we're going to have an infant," she sobbed, "and he's never, never let me, not once, every time I've come to him, he's been
10 horrid to me, and I wanted to tell him, I did. And he won't let me—he's cruel to me."

She sobbed as if her heart would break. Her mother went and comforted her, put her arms round her, and held her close. Her father sat with a queer, wrinkled brow, and was rather paler than
15 usual. His heart went tense with hatred of his son-in-law.

So that, when the tale was sobbed out, and comfort administered, and tea sipped, and something like calm restored to the little circle, the thought of Will Brangwen's entry was not pleasantly entertained.

Tilly was set to watch out for him as he passed by on his way home.
20 The little party at table heard the woman-servant's shrill call:

"You've got to come in, Will. Anna's here."

After a few moments, the youth entered.

"Are you stopping?" he asked in his hard, harsh voice.

He seemed like a blade of destruction standing there. She
25 quivered to tears.

"Sit you down," said Tom Brangwen, "an' take a bit off your length."

Will Brangwen sat down. He felt something strange in the atmosphere. He was dark browed, but his eyes had the keen, intent,
30 sharp look, as if he could only see in the distance; which was a beauty in him, and which made Anna so angry.

"Why does he always deny me?" she said to herself. "Why is it nothing to him, what I am?"

And Tom Brangwen, blue-eyed and warm, sat in opposition to the
35 youth.

"How long are you stopping?" the young husband asked his wife.

"Not very long," she said.

"Get your tea, lad," said Tom Brangwen. "Are you itchin' to be off the moment you enter?"
40 They talked of trivial things. Through the open door the level rays

of sunset poured in, shining on the floor. A grey hen appeared stepping swiftly in the doorway, pecking, and the light through her comb and her wattles made an oriflamme tossed here and there, as she went, her grey body was like a ghost.

Anna, watching, threw scraps of bread, and she felt the child flame within her. She seemed to remember again forgotten, burning, far-off things.

"Where was I born, mother?" she asked.

"In London."

"And was my father—" she spoke of him as if he were merely a strange name: she could never connect herself with him—"was he dark?"

"He had dark-brown hair and dark eyes and a fresh colouring. He went bald, rather bald, when he was quite young," replied the mother, also as if telling a tale which was just old imagination.

"Was he good-looking?"

"Yes—he was very good-looking—rather small. I have never seen an Englishman who looked like him."

"Why?"

"He was—" the mother made a quick, running movement with her hands—"his figure was alive and changing—it was never fixed. He was not in the least steady—like a running stream."

It flashed over the youth—Anna too was like a running stream. Instantly he was in love with her again.

Tom Brangwen was frightened. His heart always filled with fear, fear of the unknown, when he heard his women speak of their bygone men as of strangers they had known in passing and had taken leave of again.

In the room, there came a silence and a singleness over all their hearts. They were separate people with separate destinies. Why should they seek each to lay violent hands of claim on the other?

The young people went home as a sharp little moon was setting in a dusk of spring. Tufts of trees hovered in the upper air, the little church pricked up shadowily at the top of the hill, the earth was a dark blue shadow.

She put her hand lightly on his arm, out of her far distance. And out of the distance, he felt her touch him. They walked on, hand in hand, along opposite horizons,* touching across the dusk. There was a sound of thrushes calling in the dark-blue twilight.

"I think we are going to have an infant, Bill," she said, from far off.

He trembled, and his fingers tightened on hers.

"Why?" he asked, his heart beating. "You don't know?"

"I do," she said.

5 They continued without saying any more, walking along opposite horizons, hand in hand across the intervening space, two separate people. And he trembled as if a wind blew on to him in strong gusts, out of the unseen. He was afraid. He was afraid to know he was alone. For she seemed fulfilled and separate and sufficient in her half of the world. He could not bear to know that he was cut off. Why
10 could he not be always one with her? It was he who had given her the child. Why could she not be with him, one with him? Why must he be set in this separateness, why could she not be with him, close, close, as one with him? She must be one with him.

He held her fingers tightly in his own. She did not know what he
15 was thinking. The blaze of light on her heart was too beautiful and dazzling, from the conception in her womb. She walked glorified, and the sound of the thrushes, of the trains in the valley, of the far-off faint noises of the town, were her "Magnificat."*

But he was struggling in silence. It seemed as though there were
20 before him a solid wall of darkness that impeded him and suffocated him and made him mad. He wanted her to come to him, to complete him, to stand before him so that his eyes did not, should not meet the naked darkness. Nothing mattered to him but that she should come and complete him. For he was ridden by the awful sense of his own
25 limitation. It was as if he ended uncompleted, as yet uncreated on the darkness, and he wanted her to come and liberate him into the whole.

But she was complete in herself, and he was ashamed of his need, his helpless need of her. His need, and his shame of need, weighed
30 on him like a madness. Yet still he was quiet and gentle, in reverence of her conception, and because she was with child by him.

And she was happy in showers of sunshine. She loved her husband, as a presence, as a grateful condition. But for the moment her need was fulfilled, and now she wanted only to hold her husband
35 by the hand in sheer happiness, without taking thought, only being glad.

He had various folios of reproductions, and among them a cheap print from Fra Angelico's "Entry of the Blessed into Paradise."* This filled Anna with bliss. The beautiful, innocent way in which the
40 Blessed held each other by the hand as they moved towards the

radiance, the real, real, angelic melody, made her weep with happiness. The floweriness, the beams of light, the linking of hands, was almost too much for her, too innocent.

Day after day came shining through the door of Paradise, day after day she entered into the brightness. The child in her shone till she herself was a beam of sunshine; and how lovely was the sunshine that loitered and wandered out of doors, where the catkins on the big hazel bushes at the end of the garden hung in their shaken, floating aureole, where little fumes like fire burst out from the black yew-trees as a bird settled clinging to the branches. One day bluebells were along the hedge-bottoms, then cowslips twinkled like manna, golden and evanescent on the meadows. She was full of a rich drowsiness and loveliness. How happy she was, how gorgeous it was to live: to have known herself, her husband, the passion of love and begetting; and to know that all this lived and waited and burned on around her, a terrible purifying fire, through which she had passed for once to come to this peace of golden radiance, when she was with child, and innocent, and in love with her husband and with all the many angels hand in hand. She lifted her throat to the breeze that came across the fields, and she felt it handling her like sisters fondling her, she drank it in perfume of cowslips and of apple-blossoms.

And in all the happiness a black shadow, shy, wild, a beast of prey, roamed and vanished from sight, and like strands of gossamer blown across her eyes, there was a dread for her.

She was afraid when he came home at night. As yet, her fear never spoke, the shadow never rushed upon her. He was gentle, humble, he kept himself withheld. His hands were delicate upon her, and she loved them. But there ran through her the thrill, crisp as pain, for she felt the darkness and other-world still in his soft, sheathed hands.

But the summer drifted in with the silence of a miracle, she was almost always alone. All the while, went on the long, lovely drowsi-ness, the maidenblush roses in the garden were all shed, washed away in a pouring rain, summer drifted into autumn, and the long, vague, golden day began to close. Crimson clouds fumed about the west, and as night came on, all the sky was fuming and steaming, and the moon, far above the swiftness of vapours, was white, bleared, the night was uneasy. Suddenly the moon would appear at a clear window in the sky, looking down from far above, like a captive. And

Anna did not sleep. There was a strange, dark tension about her husband.

She became aware that he was trying to force his will upon her,* there was something he wanted, as he lay there dark and tense. And 5 her soul sighed in weariness.

Everything was so vague and lovely, and he wanted to wake her up to the hard, hostile reality. She drew back in resistance. Still he said nothing. But she felt his power persisting on her, till she became aware of the strain, she cried out against the exhaustion. He was 10 forcing her, he was forcing her. And she wanted so much the joy and the vagueness and the innocence of her pregnancy. She did not want his bitter-corrosive love, she did not want it poured into her, to burn her. Why must she have it? Why, oh why was he not content, contained?

15 She sat many hours by the window, in those days when he drove her most with the black constraint of his will, and she watched the rain falling on the yew-trees. She was not sad, only wistful, blanched. The child under her heart was a perpetual warmth. And she was sure. The pressure was only upon her from the outside, her soul had 20 no stripes.

Yet in her heart itself was always this same strain, tense, anxious. She was not safe, she was always exposed, she was always attacked. There was a yearning in her for a fulness of peace and blessedness. What a heavy yearning it was—so heavy.

25 She knew, vaguely, that all the time he was not satisfied, all the time he was trying to force something from her. Ah, how she wished she could succeed with him, in her own way! He was there, so inevitable. She lived in him also. And how she wanted to be at peace with him, at peace. She loved him. She would give him love, pure 30 love. With a strange, rapt look on her face, she awaited his homecoming that night.

Then, when he came, she rose with her hands full of love, as of flowers, radiant, innocent. A dark spasm crossed his face. As she watched, her face shining and flower-like with innocent love, his face 35 grew dark and tense, the cruelty gathered in his brows, his eyes turned aside, she saw the whites of his eyes as he looked aside from her. She waited, touching him with her hands. But from his body through her hands came the bitter-corrosive shock of his passion upon her, destroying her in blossom. She shrank. She rose from her knees and went away from him, to preserve herself. And it was great pain to her.

To him also it was agony. He saw the glistening, flower-like love in her face, and his heart was black because he did not want it. Not this—not this. He did not want flowery innocence. He was un- 5 satisfied. The rage and storm of unsatisfaction tormented him ceaselessly. Why had she not satisfied him? He had satisfied her. She was satisfied, at peace, innocent round the doors of her own paradise.

And he was unsatisfied, unfulfilled, he raged in torment, wanting, 10 wanting. It was for her to satisfy him: then let her do it. Let her not come with flowery handfuls of innocent love. He would throw these aside and trample the flowers to nothing. He would destroy her flowery, innocent bliss. Was he not entitled to satisfaction from her, and was not his heart all raging desire, his soul a black torment of 15 unfulfilment. Let it be fulfilled in him, then, as it was fulfilled in her. He had given her her fulfilment. Let her rise up and do her part.

He was cruel to her. But all the time he was ashamed. And being ashamed, he was more cruel. For he was ashamed that he could not come to fulfilment without her. And he could not. And she would not 20 heed him. He was shackled and in darkness of torment.

She beseeched him to work again, to do his wood-carving. But his soul was too black. He had destroyed his panel of Adam and Eve. He could not begin again, least of all now, whilst he was in this condition. 25

For her there was no final release, since he could not be liberated from himself. Strange and amorphous, she must go yearning on through the trouble, like a warm, glowing cloud blown in the middle of a storm. She felt so rich, in her warm vagueness, that her soul cried out on him, because he harried her and wanted to 30 destroy her.

She had her moments of exaltation still, re-births of old exaltations. As she sat by her bedroom window, watching the steady rain, her spirit was somewhere far off.

She sat in pride and curious pleasure. Where there was no-one to 35 exult with, and the unsatisfied soul must dance and play, then one danced before the Unknown.

Suddenly she realised that this was what she wanted to do. Big with child as she was, she danced there in the bedroom by herself, lifting her hands and her body to the Unseen, to the unseen Creator who had chosen her, to Whom she belonged.

She would not have had anyone know. She danced in secret, and her soul rose in bliss. She danced in secret before the Creator, she
5 took off her clothes and danced in the pride of her bigness.

It surprised her, when it was over. She was shrinking and afraid. To what was she now exposed? She half wanted to tell her husband. Yet she shrank from him.

All the time she ran on by herself. She liked the story of David,
10 who danced before the Lord, and uncovered himself exultingly. Why should he uncover himself to Michal,* a common woman? He uncovered himself to the Lord.

"Thou comest to me with a sword and a spear and a shield, but I come to thee in the name of the Lord:—for the battle is the Lord's,
15 and he will give you into our hands."*

Her heart rang to the words. She walked in her pride. And her battle was her own Lord's, her husband was delivered over.

In these days she was oblivious of him. Who was he, to come against her? No, he was not even the Philistine, the Giant. He was
20 like Saul proclaiming his own kingship.* She laughed in her heart. Who was he, proclaiming his kingship? She laughed in her heart with pride.

And she had to dance in exultation beyond him. Because he was in the house, she had to dance before her Creator in exemption from
25 the man. On a Saturday afternoon, when she had a fire in her bedroom, again she took off her things and danced, lifting her knees and her hands in a slow, rhythmic exulting. He was in the house, so her pride was fiercer. She would dance his nullification, she would dance to her unseen Lord. She was exalted over him, before* the
30 Lord.

She heard him coming up the stairs, and she flinched. She stood with the firelight on her ankles and feet, naked in the shadowy, late afternoon, fastening up her hair. He was startled. He stood in the doorway, his brows black and lowering.
35   "What are you doing?" he said, gratingly. "You'll catch a cold."

And she lifted her hands and danced again, to annul him, the light glanced on her knees as she made her slow, fine movements down the far side of the room, across the firelight. He stood away near the door in blackness of shadow, watching, transfixed. And with slow,
40 heavy movements, she swayed backwards and forwards, like a full ear

of corn, pale in the dusky afternoon, threading before the firelight, dancing his non-existence, dancing herself to the Lord, to exultation.

He watched, and his soul burned in him. He turned aside, he could not look, it hurt his eyes. Her fine limbs lifted and lifted, her hair was sticking out all fierce, and her belly, big, strange, terrifying, uplifted to the Lord. Her face was rapt and beautiful, she danced exulting before her Lord, and knew no man.

It hurt him as he watched as if he were at the stake. He felt he was being burned alive. The strangeness, the power of her in her dancing consumed him, he was burned, he could not grasp, he could not understand. He waited obliterated. Then his eyes became blind to her, he saw her no more. And through the unseeing veil between them he called to her, in his jarring voice:

"What are you doing that for?"

"Go away," she said. "Let me dance by myself."

"That isn't dancing," he said harshly. "What do you want to do that for?"

"I don't do it for you," she said, "you go away."

Her strange, lifted belly, big with his child! Had he no right to be there? He felt his presence a violation. Yet he had his right to be there. He went and sat on the bed.

She stopped dancing, and confronted him, again lifting her slim arms and twisting at her hair. Her nakedness hurt her, opposed to him.

"I can do as I like in my bedroom," she cried. "Why do you interfere with me?"

And she slipped on a dressing-gown and crouched before the fire. He was more at ease now she was covered up. The vision of her tormented him all the days of his life, as she had been then, a strange, exalted thing having no relation to himself.

After this day, the door seemed to shut on his mind. His brow shut and became impervious. His eyes ceased to see, his hands were suspended. Within himself his will was coiled like a beast, hidden under the darkness, but always potent, working.

At first she went on blithely enough with him shut down beside her. But then his spell began to take hold of her. The dark, seething potency of him, the power of a creature that lies hidden and exerts its will to the destruction of the free-running creature, as the tiger lying in the darkness of the leaves steadily enforces the fall and the death

of the light creatures that drink by the waterside in the morning, gradually began to take effect on her. Though he lay there in his darkness and did not move, yet she knew he lay waiting for her. She felt his will fastening on her and pulling her down, even whilst he was
5   silent and obscure.

She found that, in all her outgoings and her incomings, he prevented her.* Gradually she realised that she was being borne down by him, borne down by the clinging, heavy weight of him, that he was pulling her down as a leopard clings to a wild cow and
10   exhausts her and pulls her down.

Gradually she realised that her life, her freedom, was sinking under the silent grip of his physical will. He wanted her in his power. He wanted to devour her at leisure, to have her. At length she realised that her sleep was a long ache and a weariness and
15   exhaustion, because of his will fastened upon her, as he lay there beside her, during the night.

She realised it all, and there came a momentous pause, a pause in her swift running, a moment's suspension in her life, when she was lost.

20   Then she turned fiercely on him, and fought him. He was not to do this to her, it was monstrous. What horrible hold did he want to have over her body? Why did he want to drag her down, and kill her spirit? Why did he want to deny her spirit? Why did he deny her spirituality, hold her for a body only? And was he to claim her
25   carcase?

Some vast, hideous darkness he seemed to represent to her.

"What do you do to me?" she cried. "What beastly thing do you do to me? You put a horrible pressure on my head, you don't let me sleep, you don't let me *live*. Every moment of your life you are doing
30   something to me, something horrible, that destroys me. There is something horrible in you, something dark and beastly in your will. What do you want of me? What do you want to do to me?"

All the blood in his body went black and powerful and corrosive as he heard her. Black and blind with hatred of her he was. He was in a
35   very black hell, and could not escape.

He hated her for what she said. Did he not give her everything, was she not everything to him? And the shame was a bitter fire in him, that she was everything to him, that he had nothing but her. And then that she should taunt him with it, that he could not escape!
40   The fire went black in his veins. For try as he might, he could not

escape. She was everything to him, she was his life and his
derivation. He depended on her. If she were taken away, he would
collapse as a house from which the central pillar is removed.

And she hated him, because he depended on her so utterly. He
was horrible to her. She wanted to thrust him off, to set him apart. It 5
was horrible that he should cleave to her, so close, so close, like a
leopard that had leapt on her, and fastened.

He went on from day to day in a blackness of rage and shame and
frustration. How he tortured himself, to be able to get away from her.
But he could not. She was as the rock on which he stood, with deep, 10
heaving water all round, and he unable to swim. He *must* take his
stand on her, he must depend on her.

What had he in life, save her? Nothing. The rest was a great,
heaving flood. The terror of the night of heaving, overwhelming
flood, which was his vision of life without her, was too much for him. 15
He clung to her fiercely and abjectly.

And she beat him off, she beat him off. Where could he turn, like a
swimmer in a dark sea beaten off from his hold, whither could he
turn? He wanted to leave her, he wanted to be able to leave her. For
his soul's sake, for his manhood's sake, he must be able to leave her. 20

But for what? She was the ark, and the rest of the world was flood.*
The only tangible, secure thing was the woman. He could leave her
only for another woman. And where was the other woman, and who
was the other woman? Besides, he would be just in the same state.
Another woman would be woman, the case would be the same. 25

Why was she the all, the everything, why must he live only through
her, why must he sink if he were detached from her? Why must he
cleave to her in a frenzy as for his very life?

The only other way to leave her was to die. The only straight way
to leave her was to die. His dark, raging soul knew that. But he had 30
no desire for death.

Why could he not leave her? Why could he not throw himself
into the hidden water to live or die, as might be? He could not, he
could not. But supposing he went away, right away, and found
work, and had a lodging again. He could be again as he had been 35
before.

But he knew he could not. A woman, he must have a woman. And
having a woman, he must be free of her. It would be the same
position. For he could not be free of her.

For how can a man stand, unless he have something sure under 40 his feet. Can a man tread the unstable water all his life, and call that standing? Better give in and drown at once.

And upon what could he stand, save upon a woman? Was he then like the old man of the seas,* impotent to move save upon the back of
5　another life? Was he impotent, or a cripple, or a defective, or a fragment?

It was black, mad, shameful torture, the frenzy of fear, the frenzy of desire, and the horrible, grasping back-wash of shame.

What was he afraid of? Why did life, without Anna, seem to him
10　just a horrible welter, everything jostling in a meaningless, dark, fathomless flood? Why, if Anna left him even for a week, did he seem to be clinging like a madman to the edge of reality, and slipping surely, surely into the flood of unreality that would drown him. This horrible slipping into unreality drove him mad, his soul screamed
15　with fear and agony.

Yet she was pushing him off from her, pushing him away, breaking his fingers from their hold on her, persistently, ruthlessly. He wanted her to have pity. And sometimes for a moment she had pity. But she always began again, thrusting him off, into the deep water,
20　into the frenzy and agony of uncertainty.

She became like a fury* to him, without any sense of him. Her eyes were bright with a cold, unmoving hatred. Then his heart seemed to die in its last fear. She might push him off into the deeps.

She would not sleep with him any more. She said he destroyed her
25　sleep. Up started all his frenzy and madness of fear and suffering. She drove him away. Like a cowed, lurking devil he was driven off, his mind working cunningly against her, devising evil for her. But she drove him off. In his moments of intensest suffering, she seemed to him inconceivable, a monster, the principle of cruelty.

30　However her pity might give way for moments, she was hard and cold as a jewel. He must be put off from her, she must sleep alone. She made him a bed in the small room.

And he lay there whipped, his soul whipped almost to death, yet unchanged. He lay in agony of suffering, thrown back into unreality,
35　like a man thrown overboard into a sea, to swim till he sinks, because there is no hold, only a wide, weltering sea.

He did not sleep, save for the white sleep when a thin veil is drawn over the mind. It was not sleep. He was awake, and he was not awake. He could not be alone. He needed to be able to put his arms round
40　her. He could not bear the empty space against his breast and belly,

where she used to be. He could not bear it. He felt as if he were suspended in space, held there by the grip of his will. If he relaxed his will he would fall, fall through endless space, into the bottomless pit, always falling, will-less, helpless, non-existent, just dropping to extinction, falling till the fire of friction had burned out, like a falling star, then nothing, nothing, complete nothing.

He rose in the morning grey and unreal. And she seemed fond of him again, she seemed to make up to him a little.

"I slept well," she said, with her slightly false brightness. "Did you?"

"All right," he answered.

He would never tell her.

For three or four nights he lay alone through the white sleep, his will unchanged, unchanged, still tense, fixed in its grip. Then, as if she were revived and free to be fond of him again, deluded by his silence and seeming acquiescence, moved also by pity, she took him back again.

Each night, in spite of all the shame, he had waited with agony for bed-time, to see if she would shut him out. And each night, as, in her false brightness, she said Goodnight, he felt he must kill her or himself. But she asked for her kiss, so pathetically, so prettily. So he kissed her, whilst his heart was ice.

And sometimes he went out. Once he sat for a long time in the church porch, before going in to bed. It was dark with a wind blowing. He sat in the church porch and felt some shelter, some security. But it grew cold, and he must go in to bed.

Then came the night when she said, putting her arms round him and kissing him fondly:

"Stay with me tonight, will you?"

And he had stayed without demur. But his will had not altered. He would have her fixed to him.

So that soon she told him again she must be alone.

"I don't *want* to send you away. I *want* to sleep with you. But I can't sleep, you don't let me sleep."

His blood turned black in his veins.

"What do you mean by such a thing? It's an arrant lie. *I* don't let you sleep—!"

"But you don't. I sleep so well when I'm alone. And I can't sleep when you're there. You do something to me, you put a pressure on my head. And I *must* sleep now, now the child is coming."

"It's something in yourself," he replied, "something wrong in you."

Horrible in the extreme were these nocturnal combats, when all the world was asleep, and they two were alone, alone in the world, and repelling each other. It was hardly to be borne.

He went and lay down alone. And at length, after a grey and livid and ghastly period, he relaxed, something gave way in him. He let go, he did not care what became of him. Strange and dim he became to himself, to her, to everybody. A vagueness had come over everything, like a drowning. And it was an infinite relief to drown, a relief, a great, great relief.

He would insist no more, he would force her no more. He would force himself upon her no more. He would let go, relax, lapse, and what would be, should be.

Yet he wanted her still, he always, always wanted her. In his soul, he was desolate as a child, he was so helpless. Like a child on its mother, he depended on her for his living. He knew it, and he knew he could hardly help it.

Yet he must be able to be alone. He must be able to lie down alongside the empty space, and let be. He must be able to leave himself to the flood, to sink or live as might be. For he recognised at length his own limitation, and the limitation of his power. He had to give in.

There was a stillness, a wanness between them. Half at least of the battle was over. Sometimes she wept as she went about, her heart was very heavy. But the child was always warm in her womb.

They were friends again, new, subdued friends. But there was a wanness between them. They slept together once more, very quietly, and distinct, not one together as before. And she was intimate with him as at first. But he was very quiet, and not intimate. He was glad in his soul, but for the time being he was not alive.

He could sleep with her, and let her be. He could be alone now. He had just learned what it was to be able to be alone. It was right and peaceful. She had given him a new, deeper freedom. The world might be a welter of uncertainty, but he was himself now. He had come into his own existence. He was born for a second time,* born at last unto himself, out of the vast body of humanity. Now at last he had a separate identity, he existed alone, even if he were not quite alone. Before, he had only existed in so far as he had relations with another being. Now he had an absolute self, as well as a relative self.

But it was a very dumb, weak, helpless self, a crawling nursling. He went about very quiet and in a way, submissive. He had an unalterable self at last, free, separate, independent.

She was relieved, she was free of him. She had given him to himself. She wept sometimes with tiredness and helplessness. But he was a husband. And she seemed, in the child that was coming, to forget. It seemed to make her warm and drowsy. She lapsed into a long muse, indistinct, warm, vague, unwilling to be taken out of her vagueness. And she rested on him also.

Sometimes she came to him with a strange light in her eyes, poignant, pathetic, as if she were asking for something. He looked, and he could not understand. She was so beautiful, so visionary, the rays seemed to go out of his breast to her, like a shining. He was there for her, all for her. And she would hold his breast, and kiss it, and kiss it, kneeling beside him [almost dev]otionally,* she who was waiting for the hour of her delivery. And he would lie looking down at his breast, till it seemed that his breast was not himself, that he had left it lying there. Yet it was himself also, and beautiful and bright with her kisses. He was glad with a strange, radiant pain. Whilst she kneeled beside him, and kissed his breast with a slow, rapt, half devotional movement.

He knew she wanted something, his heart yearned to give it her. His heart yearned over her. And as she lifted her face, that was radiant and rosy as a little cloud, his heart still yearned over her, and, now from the distance, adored her. She had a flower-like presence which he adored as he stood far off, a stranger.

The weeks passed on, the time drew near, they were very gentle, and delicately happy. The insistent, passionate, dark soul, the powerful unsatisfaction in him seemed stilled and tamed, the lion lay down with the lamb* in him.

She loved him very much indeed, and he waited near her. She was a precious, remote thing to him at this time, as she waited for her child. Her soul was glad with an ecstasy because of the coming infant. She wanted a boy: oh very much she wanted a boy.

But she seemed so young and so frail. She was indeed only a girl. As she stood by the fire washing herself—she was proud to wash herself at this time—and he looked at her, his heart was full of extreme tenderness for her. Such fine, fine limbs, her slim, round arms like chasing lights, and her legs so simple and childish, yet so very proud. Oh, she stood on proud legs, with a lovely reckless balance of her full belly, and the adorable little roundnesses, and the breasts becoming important. Above it all, her face was like a rosy cloud shining.

How proud she was, what a lovely proud thing her young body!
And she loved him to put his hand on her ripe fulness, so that he should thrill also with the stir and the quickening there. He was afraid and silent, but she flung her arms round his neck with proud, impudent joy.

The pains came on, and OO—how she cried! She would have him stay with her. And after her long cries she would look at him, with tears in her eyes and a sobbing laugh on her face, saying:

"I don't mind it really."

It was bad enough. But to her it was never deathly. Even the fierce, tearing pain was exhilarating. She screamed and suffered, but was all the time curiously alive and vital. She felt so powerfully alive and in the hands of such a masterly force of life, that her bottommost feeling was one of exhilaration. She knew she was winning, winning, she was always winning, with each onset of pain she was nearer to victory.

Probably he suffered more than she did. He was not shocked or horrified. But he was screwed very tight in the vise of suffering.

It was a girl. The second of silence on her face when they said so showed him she was disappointed. And a great, blazing passion of resentment and protest sprang up in his heart. In that moment he claimed the child.

But when the milk came, and the infant sucked her breast, she seemed to be leaping with extravagant bliss.

"It sucks me, it sucks me, it likes me—oh, it loves it!" she cried, holding the child to her breast with her two hands covering it, passionately.

And in a few moments, as she became used to her bliss, she looked at the youth with glowing, unseeing eyes, and said:

"Anna Victrix."

He went away, trembling, and slept. To her, her pains were the wound-smart of a victor, she was the prouder.

When she was well again she was very happy. She called the baby Ursula. Both Anna and her husband felt they must have a name that gave them private satisfaction. The baby was tawny skinned, it had a curious downy skin, and wisps of bronze hair, and the yellow grey eyes that wavered, and then became golden-brown like the father's. So they called her Ursula because of the picture of the saint.*

It was a rather delicate baby at first, but soon it became stronger, and was restless as a young eel. Anna was worn out with the day-long wrestling with its young vigour.

As a little animal, she loved and adored it and was happy. She loved her husband, she kissed his eyes and nose and mouth, and made much of him, she said his limbs were beautiful, she was fascinated by the physical form of him.

And she was indeed Anna Victrix. He could not combat her any more. He was out in the wilderness, alone with her. Having occasion to go to London, he marvelled, as he returned, thinking of naked, lurking savages on an island, how these had built up and created the great mass of Oxford Street or Piccadilly. How had helpless savages, running with their spears on the river-side, after fish, how had they come to rear up this great London, the ponderous, massive, ugly superstructure of a world of man upon a world of nature? It frightened and awed him. Man was terrible, awful in his works. The works of man were more terrible than man himself, almost monstrous.

And yet, for his own part, for his private being, Brangwen felt that the whole of the man's world was exterior and extraneous to his own real life with Anna. Sweep away the whole monstrous superstructure of the world of today, cities and industries and civilisation, leave only the bare earth with plants growing and waters running, and he would not mind, so long as he were whole, had Anna and the child and the new, strange certainty in his soul. Then, if he were naked, he would find clothing somewhere, he would make a shelter and bring food to his wife.

And what more? What more would be necessary? The great mass of activity in which mankind was engaged meant nothing to him. By nature, he had no part in it. What did he live for, then? For Anna only, and for the sake of living? What did he want on this earth? Anna only, and his children, and his life with his children and her? Was there no more?

He was attended by a sense of something more, something further, which gave him absolute being. It was as if now he existed in Eternity, let Time be what it might. What was there outside? The fabricated world, that he did not believe in? What should he bring to her, from outside? Nothing? Was it enough, as it was? He was

troubled in his acquiescence. She was not with him. Yet he scarcely
believed in himself, apart from her, though the whole Infinite was
with him. Let the whole world slide down and over the edge of
oblivion, he would stand alone. But he was unsure of her. And he
5   existed also in her. So he was unsure.

He hovered near to her, never quite able to forget the vague,
haunting uncertainty, that seemed to challenge him, and which he
would not hear. A pang of dread, almost guilt, as of insufficiency,
would go over him as he heard her talking to the baby. She stood
10 before the window, with the month-old child in her arms, talking in a
musical, young singsong that he had not heard before, and which
rang on his heart like a claim from the distance, or the voice of
another world sounding its claim on him. He stood near, listening,
and his heart surged, surged to rise and submit. Then it shrank back,
15 and stayed aloof. He could not move, a denial was upon him, as if he
could not deny himself. He must, he must be himself.

"Look at the silly blue-caps, my beauty," she crooned, holding up
the infant to the window, where shone the white garden, and the
blue-tits scuffling in the snow: "look at the silly blue-caps, my
20 darling, having a fight in the snow! Look at them, my bird;—beating
the snow about with their wings, and shaking their heads. Oh, aren't
they wicked things, wicked things! Look at their yellow feathers on
the snow there! They'll miss them, won't they, when they're cold
later on.

25   "Must we tell them to stop, must we say 'stop it' to them, my bird?
But they are naughty, naughty! Look at them!"

Suddenly her voice broke loud and fierce, she rapped the pane
sharply:

"Stop it," she cried, "stop it, you little nuisances. Stop it!"
30 She called louder, and rapped the pane more sharply. Her voice
was fierce and imperative.

"Have more sense," she cried.

"There, now they've gone. Where have they gone, the silly things?
What will they say to each other? What will they say, my lambkin?
35 They'll forget, won't they, they'll forget all about it, out of their silly
little heads, and their blue caps."

After a moment, she turned her bright face to her husband.

"They were *really* fighting, they were really fierce with each
other!" she said, her voice keen with excitement and wonder, as if she
40 belonged to the birds' world, were identified with the race of birds.

"Ay, they'll fight, will blue-caps," he said, glad when she turned to

him with her glow from elsewhere. He came and stood beside her
and looked out at the marks on the snow where the birds had
scuffled, and at the yew-trees' burdened, white and black branches.
What was the appeal it made to him, what was the question of her
bright face, what was the challenge he was called to answer? He did   5
not know. But as he stood there he felt some responsibility which
made him glad, but uneasy, as if he must put out his own light. And
he could not move as yet.

Anna loved the child very much, oh very much. Yet still she was
not quite fulfilled. She had a slight expectant feeling, as of a door half   10
opened. Here she was, safe and still in Cossethay. But she felt as if
she were not in Cossethay at all. She was straining her eyes to
something beyond. And from her Pisgah mount,* which she had
attained, what could she see? A faint, gleaming horizon, a long way
off, and a rainbow like an archway, a shadow-door with faintly   15
coloured coping above it.* Must she be moving thither?

Something she had not, something she did not grasp, could not
arrive at. There was something beyond her. But why must she start
on the journey? She stood so safely on this Pisgah mountain.

In the winter, when she rose with the sunrise, and out of the back   20
windows saw the east flaming yellow and orange above the green,
glowing grass, while the great pear-tree in between stood dark and
magnificent as an idol, and under the dark pear-tree, the little sheet
of water spread smooth in burnished, yellow light, she said, "It is
here." And when, at evening, the sunset came in a red glare through   25
the big opening in the clouds, she said again, "It is beyond."

Dawn and sunset were* the feet of the rainbow that spanned the
day, and she saw the hope, the promise. Why should she travel any
further?

Yet she always asked the question. As the sun went down in his   30
fiery winter haste, she faced the blazing close of the affair, in which
she had not played her fullest part, and she made her demand still:
"What are you doing, making this big shining commotion? What is it
that you keep so busy about, that you will not let us alone?"

She did not turn to her husband, for him to lead her. He was apart   35
from her, with her, according to her different conceptions of him.
The child she might hold up, she might toss the child forward into
the furnace, the child might walk there, amid the burning coals and
the incandescent roar of heat, as the three witnesses walked with the
angel in the fire.*   40

Soon, she felt sure of her husband. She knew his dark face and the extent of its passion. She knew his slim, vigorous body, she said it was hers. Then there was no denying her. She was a rich woman enjoying her riches.

5   And soon again she was with child. Which made her satisfied and took away her discontent. She forgot that she had watched the sun climb up and pass his way, a magnificent traveller surging forward. She forgot that the moon had looked through a window of the high, dark night, and nodded like a magic recognition, signalled to her to
10 follow. Sun and moon travelled on, and left her, passed her by, a rich woman enjoying her riches. She should go also. But she could not go, when they called, because she must stay at home now. With satisfaction she relinquished the adventure to the unknown. She was bearing her children.

15   There was another child coming, and Anna lapsed into vague content. If she were not the wayfarer to the unknown, if she were arrived now, settled in her builded house,* a rich woman, still her doors opened under the arch of the rainbow, her threshold reflected the passing of the sun and moon, the great travellers, her house was
20 full of the echo of journeying.

She was a door and a threshold, she herself. Through her another soul was coming, to stand upon her as upon the threshold, looking out, shading its eyes for the direction to take.

Chapter VII

The Cathedral

During the first year of her marriage, before Ursula was born, Anna Brangwen and her husband went to visit her mother's friend, the Baron Skrebensky. The latter had kept a slight connection with Anna's mother, and had always preserved some officious interest in the young girl, because she was a pure Pole.

When Baron Skrebensky was about forty years old, his wife died, and left him raving disconsolate. Lydia had visited him then, taking Anna with her. It was when the girl was fourteen years old.* Since then she had not seen him. She remembered him as a small, sharp clergyman who cried and talked and terrified her, whilst her mother was most strangely consoling, in a foreign language.

The little Baron never quite approved of Anna, because she spoke no Polish. Still, he considered himself in some way her guardian, on Lensky's behalf, and he presented her with some old, heavy, Russian jewellery, the least valuable of his wife's relics. Then he lapsed out of the Brangwen life again, though he lived only about thirty miles away.

Three years later came the startling news that he had married a young English girl of good family. Everybody marvelled. Then came a copy of "The History of the Parish of Briswell—by Rudolph, Baron Skrebensky, Vicar of Briswell."* It was a curious book, incoherent, full of interesting exhumations. It was dedicated: "To my wife, Millicent Maud Pearse, in whom I embrace the generous spirit of England."

"If he embraces no more than the spirit of England," said Tom Brangwen, "it's a bad look-out for him."

But paying a formal visit with his wife, he found the new Baroness a little, creamy-skinned, insidious thing with red-brown hair and a mouth that one must always watch, because it curved back continually in an incomprehensible, strange laugh that exposed her rather prominent teeth. She was not beautiful, yet Tom Brangwen was immediately under her spell. She seemed to snuggle like a kitten within his warmth, whilst she was at the same time elusive and ironical, suggesting the fine steel of her claws.

The Baron was almost dotingly courteous and attentive to her.
She, almost mockingly, yet quite happy, let him dote. Curious little
thing she was, she had the soft, creamy, elusive beauty of a ferret.
Tom Brangwen was quite at a loss, at her mercy, and she laughed, a
5 little breathlessly, as if tempted to cruelty. She did put fine torments
on the elderly Baron.

When some months later she bore a son, the Baron Skrebensky
was loud with delight.

Gradually she gathered a circle of acquaintants in the country.
10 For she was of good family, half Venetian, educated in Dresden.
The little foreign vicar attained to a social status which almost
satisfied his maddened pride.

Therefore the Brangwens were surprised when the invitation
came for Anna and her young husband to pay a visit to Briswell
15 vicarage. For the Skrebenskys were now moderately well off,
Millicent Skrebensky having some fortune of her own.

Anna took her best clothes, recovered her best high-school
manner, and arrived with her husband. Will Brangwen, ruddy,
bright, with long limbs and a small head, like some uncouth bird, was
20 not changed in the least. The little Baroness was smiling, showing
her teeth. She had a real charm, a kind of joyous coldness, laughing,
delighted, like some weasel. Anna at once respected her, and was on
her guard before her, instinctively attracted by the strange, child-like
surety of the Baroness, yet mistrusting it, fascinated. The little Baron
25 was now quite white-haired, very brittle. He was wizened and
wrinkled, yet fiery, unsubdued. Anna looked at his lean body, at his
small, fine, lean legs and lean hands as he sat talking, and she
flushed. She recognised the quality of the male in him, his lean,
concentrated age, his informed fire, his faculty for sharp, deliberate
30 response. He was so detached, so purely objective. A woman was
thoroughly outside him. There was no confusion. So he could give
that fine, deliberate response.

He was something separate and interesting; his hard, intrinsic
being, whittled down by age to an essentiality and a directness almost
35 death-like, cruel, was yet so unswervingly sure in its action, so
distinct in its surety, that she was attracted to him. She watched his
cool, hard, separate fire, fascinated by it. Would she rather have it
than her husband's diffuse heat, than his blind, hot youth?

She seemed to be breathing high, sharp air, as if she had just come
40 out of a hot room. These strange Skrebenskys made her aware of

another, freer element, in which each person was detached and isolated. Was not this her natural element? Was not the close Brangwen life stifling to her?

Meanwhile the little Baroness, with always a subtle light stirring in her full, lustrous, hazel eyes, was playing with Will Brangwen. He was not quick enough to see all her movements. Yet he watched her steadily, with unchanging, lit-up eyes. She was a strange creature to him. But she had no power over him. She flushed, and was irritated. Yet she glanced again and again at his dark, living face, curiously, as if she despised him. She despised his uncritical, unironical nature, it had nothing for her. Yet it angered her as if she were jealous. He watched her with deferential interest as he would watch a stoat playing. But he himself was not implicated. He was different in kind. She was all lambent, biting flames, he was a red fire glowing steadily. She could get nothing out of him. So she made him flush darkly by assuming a biting, subtle class-superiority. He flushed, but still he did not object. He was too different.

Her little boy came in with the nurse. He was a quick, slight child, with fine perceptiveness, and a cool transitoriness in his interest. At once he treated Will Brangwen as an outsider. He stayed by Anna for a moment, acknowledged her, then was gone again, quick, observant, restless, with a glance of interest at everything.

The father adored him, and spoke to him in Polish. It was queer, the stiff, aristocratic manner of the father with the child, the distance in their relationship, the classic fatherhood on the one hand, the filial subordination on the other. They played together, in their different degrees very separate, two different beings, differing as it were in rank rather than in relationship. And the Baroness smiled, smiled, smiled, always smiled, showing her rather protruding teeth, having always a mysterious attraction and charm.

Anna realised how different her own lot might have been, how different her own being. Her soul stirred, she became as another person. Her intimacy with her husband passed away, the curious enveloping Brangwen intimacy, so warm, so close, so stifling, when one seemed always to be in contact with the other person, like a blood-relation, was annulled. She denied it, this close relationship with her young husband. He and she were not one. His heat was not always to suffuse her, suffuse her, through her mind and her individuality, till she was of one heat with him, till she had not her own self apart. She wanted her own life. He seemed to lap her and suffuse her with his being, his hot life, till she did not know whether she were herself, or whether she were another creature, united with him in a world of close blood-intimacy that closed over her and excluded her from all the cool outside.

5   She wanted her own, old, sharp self, detached, detached, active but not absorbed, active for her own part, taking and giving, but never absorbed. Whereas he wanted this strange absorption with her, which still she resisted. But she was partly helpless against it. She had lived so long in Tom Brangwen's love, beforehand.

10   From the Skrebenskys' they went to Will Brangwen's beloved Lincoln Cathedral, because it was not far off. He had promised her, that one by one, they should visit all the cathedrals of England. They began with Lincoln, which he knew well.

    He began to get excited as the time drew near to set off. What was

15 it that changed him so much? She was almost angry, coming as she did from the Skrebenskys. But now he ran on alone. His very breast seemed to open its doors to watch for the great church brooding over the town. His soul ran ahead.

    When he saw the cathedral in the distance, dark blue lifted

20 watchful in the sky, his heart leapt. It was the sign in heaven, it was the Spirit hovering like a dove, like an eagle over the earth. He turned his glowing, ecstatic face to her, his mouth opened with a strange, ecstatic grin.

    "There she is," he said.

25   The "she" irritated her. Why "she"? It was "it." What was the cathedral, a big building, a thing of the past, obsolete, to excite him to such a pitch? She began to stir herself to readiness.

    They pressed up the steep hill, he eager as a pilgrim arriving at the shrine. As they came near the precincts, with castle on one side and

30 cathedral on the other, his veins seemed to break into fiery blossom, he was transported.

    They had passed through the gate, and the great west front was before them, with all its breadth and ornament.

    "It is a false front," he said, looking at the golden stone and the

35 twin towers, and loving them just the same. In a little ecstasy he found himself in the porch, on the brink of the unrevealed. He looked up to the lovely unfolding of the stone. He was to pass within to the perfect womb.

    Then he pushed open the door, and the great, pillared gloom was

40 before him, in which his soul shuddered and rose from her nest. His

soul leapt, soared up into the great church. His body stood still, absorbed by the height. His soul leapt up into the gloom, into possession, it reeled, it swooned with a great escape, it quivered in the womb, in the hush and the gloom of fecundity, like seed of procreation in ecstasy.   5

She too was overcome with wonder and awe. She followed him in his progress. Here, the twilight was the very essence of life, the coloured darkness was the embryo of all light, and the day. Here, the very first dawn was breaking, the very last sunset sinking, and the immemorial darkness, whereof life's day would blossom and fall   10 away again, re-echoed peace and profound, immemorial silence.

Away from time, always outside of time!* Between east and west, between dawn and sunset, the church lay like a seed in silence, dark before germination, silenced after death. Containing birth and death, potential with all the noise and transitation* of life, the   15 cathedral remained hushed, a great, involved seed whereof the flower would be radiant life inconceivable, but whose beginning and whose end were the circle of silence. Spanned round with the rainbow, the jewelled gloom folded music upon silence, light upon darkness, fecundity upon death, as a seed folds leaf upon leaf and   20 silence upon the root and the flower, hushing up the secret of all between its parts, the death out of which it fell, the life into which it has dropped, the immortality it involves, and the death it will embrace again.

Here in the church, "before" and "after" were folded together, all   25 was contained in oneness.* Brangwen came to his consummation. Out of the doors of the womb he had come, putting aside the wings of the womb and proceeding into the light. Through daylight and day-after-day he had come, knowledge after knowledge and experience after experience, remembering the darkness of the womb,   30 having prescience of the darkness after death. Then betweenwhiles he had pushed open the doors of the cathedral, and entered the twilight of both darknesses, the hush of the two-fold silence, where dawn was sunset, and the beginning and the end were one.

Here the stone leapt up from the plain of earth, leapt up in a   35 manifold, clustered desire each time, up, away from the horizontal earth, through twilight and dusk and the whole range of desire, through the swerving, the declination, ah, to the ecstasy, the touch, to the meeting and the consummation, the meeting, the clasp, the close embrace, the neutrality, the perfect, swooning consummation,   40 the timeless ecstasy. There his soul remained, at the apex of the arch,* clinched in the timeless ecstasy, consummated.

And there was no time nor life nor death, but only this, this timeless consummation, where the thrust from earth met the thrust
5 from earth and the arch was locked on the keystone of ecstasy. This was all, this was everything. Till he came to himself in the world below. Then again he gathered himself together, in transit, every jet of him strained and leaped, leaped clear in to the darkness above, to the fecundity and the unique mystery, to the touch, the clasp, the
10 consummation, the climax of eternity, the apex of the arch.*

She too was overcome, but silenced rather than tuned to the place. She loved it as a world not quite her own, she resented his transports and ecstasies.* His passion in the cathedral at first awed her, then made her angry. After all, there was the sky outside, and in here, in
15 this mysterious half-night, when his soul leapt with the pillars upwards, it was not to the stars and the crystalline dark space, but to meet and clasp with the answering impulse of leaping stone, there in the dusk and secrecy of the roof. The far-off clinching and mating of arches, the leap and thrust of the stone, carrying a great roof
20 overhead, awed and silenced her.

But yet—yet she remembered that the open sky was no blue vault, no dark dome hung with many twinkling lamps, but a space where stars were wheeling in freedom, with freedom above them always higher.
25 The cathedral roused her too. But she would never consent to the knitting of all the leaping stone in a great roof that closed her in, and beyond which was nothing, nothing, it was the ultimate confine. His soul would have liked it to be so: here, here is all, complete, eternal: motion, meeting, ecstasy, and no illusion of time, of night and day
30 passing by, but only perfectly proportioned space and movement clinching and renewing, and passion surging its way in great waves to the altar, recurrence of ecstasy.

Her soul too was carried forward to the altar, to the threshold of Eternity, in reverence and fear and joy. But ever she hung back in the
35 transit, mistrusting the culmination of the altar. She was not to be flung forward on the lift and lift of passionate flights, to be cast at last upon the altar steps as upon the shore of the unknown. There was a great joy and a verity in it. But even in the dazed swoon of the cathedral, she claimed another right. The altar was barren, its lights
40 gone out. God burned no more in that bush. It was dead matter lying

there. She claimed the right to freedom above her, higher than the roof. She had always a sense of being roofed in.

So that she caught at little things, which saved her from being swept forward headlong in the tide of passion that leaps on into the Infinite in a great mass, triumphant and flinging its own course. She wanted to get out of this fixed, leaping, forward-travelling movement, to rise from it as a bird rises with wet, limp feet from the sea, to lift herself as a bird lifts its breast and thrusts its body from the pulse and heave of a sea that bears it forward to an unwilling conclusion, tear herself away like a bird on wings, and in the open space where there is clarity, rise up above the fixed, surcharged motion, a separate speck that hangs suspended, moves this way and that, seeing and answering before it sinks again, having chosen or found the direction in which it shall be carried forward.

And it was as if she must grasp at something, as if her wings were too weak to lift her straight off the heaving motion. So she caught sight of the wicked, odd little faces* carved in stone, and she stood before them arrested.

These sly little faces peeped out of the grand tide of the cathedral like something that knew better. They knew quite well, these little imps* that retorted on man's own illusion, that the cathedral was not absolute. They winked and leered, giving suggestion of the many things that had been left out of the great concept of the church. "However much there is inside here, there's a good deal they haven't got in," the little faces mocked.

Apart from the lift and spring of the great impulse towards the altar, these little faces had separate wills, separate motions, separate knowledge,* which rippled back in defiance of the tide, and laughed in triumph of their own very littleness.

"Oh look!" cried Anna, "Oh look, how adorable, the faces! Look at her."

Brangwen looked unwillingly. This was the voice of the serpent in his Eden. She pointed him to a plump, sly, malicious little face carved in stone.

"He knew her, the man who carved her," said Anna. "I'm sure she was his wife."

"It isn't a woman at all, it's a man," said Brangwen curtly.

"Do you think so?—No! That isn't a man. That is no man's face."

Her voice sounded rather jeering. He laughed shortly, and went

on. But she would not go forward with him. She loitered about the
carvings. And he could not go forward without her. He waited,
impatient of this counteraction. She was spoiling his passionate
intercourse with the cathedral. His brows began to gather.

5   "Oh, this is good!" she cried again. "Here is the same woman—
look!—only he's made her cross! Isn't it lovely! Hasn't he made her
hideous to a degree?" She laughed with pleasure. "Didn't he hate
her? He must have been a nice man! Look at her—isn't it awfully
good—just like a shrewish woman. He must have enjoyed putting

10   her in like that. He got his own back on her, didn't he."
        "It's a man's face, no woman's at all—a monk's—clean shaven."
he said.
        She laughed with a Pouf! of laughter.
        "You hate to think he put his wife in your cathedral, don't you?"

15   she mocked, with a tinkle of profane laughter. And she laughed with
malicious triumph.
        She had got free from the cathedral, she had even destroyed the
passion he had. She was glad. He was bitterly angry. Strive as he
would, he could not keep the cathedral wonderful to him. He was

20   disillusioned. That which had been his absolute, containing all
heaven and earth, was become to him as to her, a shapely heap of
dead matter—but dead, dead.
        His mouth was full of ash, his soul was furious. He hated her for
having destroyed another of his vital illusions. Soon he would be

25   stark, stark, without one place wherein to stand, without one belief in
which to rest.
        Yet somewhere in him he responded more deeply to the sly little
face that knew better, than he had done before to the perfect surge of
his cathedral.

30   Nevertheless for the time being his soul was wretched and
homeless, and he could not bear to think of Anna's ousting him from
his beloved realities. He wanted his cathedral, he wanted to satisfy
his blind passion. And he could not any more. Something intervened.

35   They went home again, both of them altered. She had some new
reverence for that which he wanted, he felt that his cathedrals would
never again be to him as they had been. Before, he had thought them
absolute. But now he saw them crouching under the sky, with still
the dark, mysterious world of reality inside, but as a world within a

40   world, a sort of side show, whereas before they had been as a world to

him within a chaos: a reality, an order, an absolute, within a meaningless confusion.

He had felt, before, that could he but go through the great door and look down the gloom towards the far-off, concluding wonder of the altar, that then, with the windows suspended around like tablets 5 of jewel* emanating their own glory, then he had arrived. Here the satisfaction he had yearned after came near, towards this, the porch of the great Unknown, all reality gathered, and there, the altar was the mystic door, through which all and everything must move on to eternity. 10

But now, somehow, sadly and disillusioned, he realised that the doorway was no doorway. It was too narrow, it was false. Outside the cathedral were many flying spirits that could never be sifted through the jewelled gloom. He had lost his absolute.

He listened to the thrushes in the garden, and heard a note which 15 the cathedrals did not include: something free and careless and joyous. He crossed a field that was all yellow with dandelions, on his way to work, and the bath of yellow glowing was something at once so sumptuous and so fresh, that he was glad he was away from his shadowy cathedral. 20

There was life outside the church. There was much that the church did not include. He thought of God, and of the whole blue rotonda* of the day. That was something great and free. He thought of the ruins of the Grecian worship, and it seemed, a temple was never perfectly a temple, till it was ruined and mixed up with the 25 winds and the sky and the herbs.

Still he loved the church. As a symbol, he loved it. He tended it for what it tried to represent, rather than for that which it did represent. Still he loved it. The little church across his garden-wall drew him, he gave it loving attention. But he went to take charge of it, to 30 preserve it. It was as an old, sacred thing to him. He looked after the stone and wood-work, mending the organ and restoring a piece of broken carving, repairing the church furniture. Later, he became choir-master also.

His life was shifting its centre, becoming more superficial. He had 35 failed to become really articulate, failed to find real expression. He had to continue in the old form. But in spirit, he was uncreated.

Anna was absorbed in the child now, she left her husband to take his own way. She was willing now to postpone all adventure into unknown realities. She had the child, her palpable and immediate 40 future was the child. If her soul had found no utterance, her womb had.

The church that neighboured with his house became very intimate and dear to him. He cherished it, he had it entirely in his charge. If he could find no new activity, he would be happy cherishing the old, dear form of worship. He knew this little, whitewashed church. In its shadowy atmosphere he sank back into being. He liked to sink himself in its hush as a stone sinks into water.

He went across his garden, mounted the wall by the little steps, and entered the hush and peace of the church. As the heavy door clanged to behind him, his feet re-echoed in the aisle, his heart re-echoed with a little passion of tenderness and mystic peace. He was also slightly ashamed, like a man who has failed, who lapses back for his fulfilment.

He loved to light the candles at the organ, and sitting there alone in the little glow, practise the hymns and chants for the service. The whitewashed arches retreated into darkness, the sound of the organ and the organ-pedals died away upon the unalterable stillness of the church, there were faint, ghostly noises in the tower, and then the music swelled out again, loudly, triumphantly.

He ceased to fret about his life. He relaxed his will, and let everything go. What was between him and his wife was a great thing, if it was not everything. She had conquered, really. Let him wait, and abide, wait and abide. She and the baby and himself, they were one. The organ rang out his protestation. His soul lay in the darkness, as he pressed the keys of the organ.

To Anna, the baby was a complete bliss and fulfilment. Her desires sank into abeyance, her soul was in bliss over the baby. It was rather a delicate child, she had trouble to rear it. She never for a moment thought it would die. It was a delicate infant, therefore it behoved her to make it strong. She threw herself into the labour, the child was everything. Her imagination was all occupied here. She was a mother. It was enough to handle the new little limbs, the new little body, hear the new little voice crying in the stillness. All the future rang to her out of the sound of the baby's crying and cooing, she balanced the coming years of life in her hands, as she nursed the child. The passionate sense of fulfilment, of the future germinated in her, made her vivid and powerful. All the future was in her hands, in the hands of the woman. And before this baby was ten months old, she was again with child. She seemed to be in the fecund storm of

life, every moment was full and busy with productiveness to her. She
felt like the earth, the mother of everything.

Brangwen occupied himself with the church, he played the organ,
he trained the choir-boys, he taught a Sunday School class of
youths. He was happy enough. There was an eager, yearning kind of 5
happiness in him as he taught the boys on Sundays. He was all the
time exciting himself with the proximity of some secret that he had
not yet fathomed.

In the house, he served his wife and the little matriarchy. She
loved him because he was the father of her children. And she always 10
had a physical passion for him. So he gave up trying to have the
spiritual superiority and control, or even her respect for his
conscious or public life. He lived simply by her physical love for him.
And he served the little matriarchy, nursing the child and helping
with the housework, indifferent any more of his own dignity and 15
importance. But his abandoning of claims, his living isolated upon
his own interest, made him seem unreal, unimportant.

Anna was not publicly proud of him. But very soon she learned to
be indifferent to public life. He was not what is called a manly man:
he did not drink or smoke or arrogate importance. But he was her 20
man, and his very indifference to all claims of manliness set her
supreme in her own world with him. Physically, she loved him and he
satisfied her. He went alone and subsidiary always. At first it had
irritated her, the outer world existed so little to him. Looking at him
with outside eyes, she was inclined to sneer at him. But her sneer 25
changed to a sort of respect. She respected him, that he could serve
her so simply and completely. Above all, she loved to bear his
children. She loved to be the source of children.

She could not understand him, his strange, dark rages and his
devotion to the church. It was the church *building* he cared for; and 30
yet his soul was passionate for something. He laboured cleaning the
stonework, repairing the wood-work, restoring the organ, and
making the singing as perfect as possible. To keep the church fabric
and the church-ritual intact was his business; to have the intimate,
sacred building utterly in his own hands, and to make the form of 35
service complete. There was a little bright anguish and tension on
his face, and in his intent movements. He was like a lover who knows
he is betrayed, but who still loves, whose love is only the more tense.
The Church was false, but he served it the more attentively.

During the day, at his work in the office, he kept himself 40

suspended. He did not exist. He worked automatically till it was time
to go home.

He loved with a hot heart the dark-haired little Ursula, and he
waited for the child to come to consciousness. Now the mother
5 monopolised the baby. But his heart waited in its darkness. His hour
would come.

In the long run, he learned to submit to Anna. She forced him to
the spirit of her laws, whilst leaving him the letter of his own. She
combated in him his devils. She suffered very much from his
10 inexplicable and incalculable dark rages, when a blackness filled
him, and a black wind seemed to sweep out of existence everything
that had to do with him. She could feel herself, everything, being
annihilated by him.

At first she fought him. At night, in this state, he would kneel
15 down to say his prayers. She looked at his crouching figure.

"Why are you kneeling there, pretending to pray?" she said
harshly. "Do you think anybody can pray, when they are in the vile
temper you are in?"

He remained crouching by the bedside, motionless.

20 "It's horrible," she continued, "and such a pretence! What do you
pretend you are saying? Who do you pretend you are praying to?"

He still remained motionless, seething with inchoate rage, when
his whole nature seemed to disintegrate. He seemed to live with a
strain upon himself, and occasionally came these dark, chaotic rages,
25 the lust for destruction. She then fought with him, and their fights
were horrible, murderous. And then the passion between them came
just as black and awful.

But little by little, as she learned to love him better, she would put
herself aside, and when she felt one of his fits upon him, would
30 ignore him, successfully leave him in his world, whilst she remained
in her own. He had a black struggle with himself, to come back to
her. For at last he learned that he would be in hell until he came back
to her. So he struggled to submit to her, and she was afraid of the
ugly strain in his eyes. She made love to him, and took him. Then he
35 was grateful to her love, humble.

He made himself a wood-work shed, in which to restore things
which were destroyed in the church. So he had plenty to do: his wife,
his child, the church, the wood-work, and his wage-earning, all
occupying him. If only there were not some limit to him, some
40 darkness across his eyes! He had to give in to it at last himself. He

must submit to his own inadequacy, the limitation of his being. He even had to know of his own black, violent temper, and to reckon with it. But as she was more gentle with him, it became quieter.

As he sat sometimes very still, with a bright, vacant face, Anna could see the suffering among the brightness. He was aware of some 5 limit to himself, of something unformed in his very being, of some buds which were not ripe in him, some folded centres of darkness which would never develop and unfold whilst he was alive in the body. He was unready for fulfilment. Something undeveloped in him limited him, there was a darkness in him which he *could* not unfold, 10 which would never unfold in him.

Chapter VIII

The Child

From the first, the baby stirred in the young father a deep, strong emotion he dared scarcely acknowledge, it was so strong and came
5 out of the dark of him. When he heard the child cry, a terror possessed him, because of the answering echo from the unfathomed distances in himself. Must he know in himself such distances, perilous and imminent?

He had the infant in his arms, he walked backwards and forwards
10 troubled by the crying of his own flesh and blood. This was his own flesh and blood* crying! His soul rose against the voice suddenly breaking out from him, from the distances in him.

Sometimes, in the night, the child cried and cried, when the night was heavy and sleep oppressed him. And half asleep, he stretched
15 out his hand to put it over the baby's face, to stop the crying. But something arrested his hand: the very inhumanness of the intolerable, continuous crying arrested him. It was so impersonal, without human cause* or object. Yet he echoed to it directly, his soul answered its madness. It filled him with terror, almost with frenzy.
20 He learned to acquiesce to this, to submit to the awful, obliterated sources which were the origin of his living tissue. He was not what he conceived himself to be! Then he was what he was, unknown, potent, dark.

He became accustomed to the child, he knew how to lift and
25 balance the little body. The baby had a beautiful, rounded head that moved him passionately. He would have fought to the last drop to defend that exquisite, perfect round head.

He learned to know the little hands and feet, the strange, unseeing, golden-brown eyes, the mouth that opened only to cry, or
30 to suck, or to show a queer, toothless laugh. He could almost understand even the dangling legs, which at first had created in him a feeling of aversion. They could kick in their queer little way, they had their own softness.

One evening, suddenly, he saw the tiny living thing rolling naked
35 in the mother's lap, and he was sick, it was so utterly helpless and

vulnerable and extraneous; in a world of hard surfaces and varying altitudes, it lay vulnerable and naked at every point. Yet it was quite blithe. And yet, in its blind, awful crying, was there not the blind, far-off terror of its own vulnerable nakedness, the terror of being so utterly delivered over, helpless at every point. He could not bear to   5
hear it crying. His heart strained and stood on guard against the whole universe.

But he waited for the dread of these days to pass; he saw the joy coming. He saw the lovely, creamy, cool little ear of the baby, a bit of dark hair rubbed to a bronze floss, like bronze-dust. And he waited,   10
for the child to become his, to look at him and answer him.

It had a separate being, but it was his own child. His flesh and blood vibrated to it. He caught the baby to his breast with his passionate, clapping laugh. And the infant knew him.

As the newly opened, newly dawned eyes looked at him, he wanted   15
them to perceive him, to recognise him. Then he was verified. The child knew him, a queer contortion of laughter came on its face for him. He caught it to his breast, clapping with a triumphant laugh.

The golden-brown eyes of the child gradually lit up and dilated at the sight of the dark-glowing face of the youth. It knew its mother   20
better, it wanted its mother more. But the brightest, sharpest little ecstasy was for the father.

It began to be strong, to move vigorously and freely, to make sounds like words. It was a baby girl now. Already it knew his strong hands, it exulted in his strong clasp, it laughed and crowed when he   25
played with it.

And his heart grew red hot with passionate feeling for the child. She was not much more than a year old when the second baby was born. Then he took Ursula for his own. She his* first little girl. He had set his heart on her.   30

The second had dark blue eyes and a fair skin: it was more a Brangwen, people said. The hair was fair. But they forgot Anna's stiff blond fleece of childhood. They called the newcomer Gudrun.*

This time, Anna was stronger, and not so eager. She did not mind that the baby was not a boy. It was enough that she had milk and   35
could suckle her child: Oh, Oh, the bliss of the little life sucking the milk of her body! Oh, Oh, Oh the bliss, as the infant grew stronger, of the two tiny hands clutching, catching blindly yet passionately at her breast, of the tiny mouth seeking her in blind, sure, vital knowledge, of the sudden consummate peace as the little body sank,   40

the mouth and throat sucking, sucking, sucking, drinking life from
her to make a new life, almost sobbing with passionate joy of
receiving its own existence, the tiny hands clutching frantically as the
nipple was drawn back, not to be gainsaid. This was enough for
5   Anna. She seemed to pass off into a kind of rapture of motherhood,
her rapture of motherhood was everything.

So that the father had the elder baby, the weaned child; the
golden-brown, wondering, vivid eyes of the little Ursula were for
him, who had waited behind the mother till the need was for him.
10 The mother felt a sharp stab of jealousy. But she was still more
absorbed in the tiny baby. It was entirely hers, its need was direct
upon her.

So Ursula became the child of her father's heart. She was the little
blossom, he was the sun. He was patient, energetic, inventive for her.
15 He taught her all the funny little things, he filled her and roused her
to her fullest tiny measure. She answered him with her extravagant
infant's laughter and her call of delight.

Now there were two babies, a woman came in to do the housework, Anna was wholly nurse. Two babies were not too much work
20 for her. But she hated any form of work, now her children had come,
except the charge of them.

When Ursula toddled about, she was an absorbed, busy child,
always amusing herself, needing not much attention from other
people. At evening, towards six o'clock, Anna very often went across
25 the lane to the stile, lifted Ursula over into the field, with a: "Go and
meet Daddy." Then Brangwen, coming up the steep round of the
hill would see before him on the brow of the path a tiny, tottering,
wind-blown little mite with a dark head, who, as soon as she saw him,
would come running in tiny, wild, windmill fashion, lifting her arms
30 up and down to him, down the steep hill. His heart leapt up, he ran
his fastest to her, to catch her, because he knew she would fall. She
came fluttering on, wildly, with her little limbs flying. And he was
glad when he caught her up in his arms. Once she fell as she came
flying to him, he saw her pitch forward suddenly as she was running
35 with her hands lifted to him; and when he picked her up, her mouth
was bleeding. He could never bear to think of it, he always wanted to
cry, even when he was an old man and she had become a stranger to
him. How he had loved that little Ursula!—his heart had been
sharply seared for her, when he was a youth, first married.
40 When she was a little older, he would see her recklessly climbing

over the bars of the stile, in her red pinafore, swinging in peril and
tumbling over, picking herself up and flitting towards him. Sometimes she liked to ride on his shoulder, sometimes she preferred to
walk with his hand, sometimes she would fling her arms round his
legs for a moment, then race free again, whilst he went shouting and   5
calling to her, a child along with her. He was still only a tall, thin,
unsettled lad of twenty two.*

It was he who had made her her cradle, her little chair, her little
stool, her high chair. It was he who would swing her up to table or
who would make for her a doll out of an old table-leg, whilst she   10
watched him, saying:

"Make her eyes, Daddy, make her eyes!"

And he made her eyes with his knife.

She was very fond of adorning herself, so he would tie a piece of
cotton round her ear, and hang a blue bead on it underneath for an   15
ear-ring. The ear-rings varied with a red bead, and a golden bead,
and a little pearl bead. And as he came home at night, seeing her
bridling and looking very self-conscious, he took notice and said:

"So you're wearing your best golden and pearl ear-rings today?"

"Yes."   20

"I suppose you've been to see the queen?"

"Yes, I have."

"Oh, and what had she to say?"

"She said—she said—'You won't dirty your nice white frock.'"

He gave her the nicest bits from his plate, putting them into her   25
red, moist mouth. And he would make on a piece of bread-and-
butter a bird, out of jam: which she ate with extraordinary relish.

After the tea-things were washed up, the woman went away,
leaving the family free. Usually Brangwen helped in the bathing of
the children. He held long discussions with his child as she sat on his   30
knee and he unfastened her clothes. And he seemed to be talking
really of momentous things, deep moralities. Then suddenly she
ceased to hear, having caught sight of a glassie* rolled into a corner.
She slipped away, and was in no hurry to return.

"Come back here," he said, waiting. She became absorbed, taking   35
no notice.

"Come on," he repeated, with a touch of command.

An excited little chuckle came from her, but she pretended to be
absorbed.

"Do you hear, Milady!"   40

She turned with a fleeting, exulting laugh. He rushed on her and swept her up.

"Who was it that didn't come!" he said, rolling her between his strong hands, tickling her. And she laughed heartily, heartily. She
5   loved him that he compelled her with his strength and decision. He was all-powerful, the tower of strength which rose out of her sight.

When the children were in bed, sometimes Anna and he sat and talked, desultorily, both of them idle. He read very little. Anything he was drawn to read became a burning reality to him, another scene
10 outside his window. Whereas Anna skimmed through a book to see what happened, then she had enough.

Therefore they would often sit together, talking desultorily. What was really between them they could not utter. Their words were only accidents in the mutual silence. When they talked, they gossiped.
15 She did not care for sewing.

She had a beautiful way of sitting musing, gratefully, as if her heart were lit up. Sometimes she would turn to him, laughing, to tell him some little thing that had happened during the day. Then he would laugh, they would talk awhile, before the vital, physical silence was
20 between them again.

She was thin but full of colour and life. She was perfectly happy to do just nothing, only to sit with a curious, languid dignity, so careless as to be almost regal, so utterly indifferent, so confident. The bond between them was undefinable, but very strong. It kept everyone else
25 at a distance.

His face never changed whilst she knew him, it only became more intense. It was ruddy and dark in its abstraction, not very human, it had a strong, intent brightness. Sometimes, when his eyes met hers, a yellow flash from them caused a darkness to swoon over her
30 consciousness, electric, and a slight, strange laugh came on his face. Her eyes would turn languidly, then close, as if hypnotised. And they lapsed into the same potent darkness. He had the quality of a young black cat, intent, unnoticeable, and yet his presence gradually made itself felt, stealthily and powerfully took hold of her. He called, not to
35 her, but to something in her, which responded subtly, out of her unconscious darkness.

So they were together in a darkness, passionate, electric, forever haunting the back of the common day, never in the light. In the light, he seemed to sleep, unknowing. Only she knew him when the
40 darkness set him free, and he could see with his gold-glowing eyes

his intention and his desires in the dark. Then she was in a spell, then she answered his harsh, penetrating call with a soft leap of her soul, the darkness woke up, electric, bristling with an unknown, overwhelming insinuation.

By now they knew each other: she was the daytime, the daylight, he was the shadow, put aside, but in the darkness potent with an overwhelming voluptuousness.

She learned not to dread and to hate him, but to fill herself with him, to give herself to his black, sensual power, that was hidden all the daytime. And the curious rolling of the eyes, as if she were lapsing in a trance away from her ordinary consciousness became habitual with her, when something threatened and opposed her in life, the conscious life.

So they remained as separate in the light, and in the thick darkness, married. He supported her daytime authority, kept it inviolable at last. And she, in all the darkness, belonged to him, to his close, insinuating, hypnotic familiarity.

All his daytime activity, all his public life, was a kind of sleep. She wanted to be free, to belong to the day. And he ran avoiding the day in work. After tea, he went to the shed to his carpentry or his wood-carving. He was restoring the patched, degraded pulpit to its original form.

But he loved to have the child near him, playing by his feet. She was a piece of light that really belonged to him, that played within his darkness. He left the shed door on the latch. And when, with his second sense of another presence, he knew she was coming, he was satisfied, he was at rest. When he was alone with her, he did not want to take notice, to talk. He wanted to live unthinking, with her presence flickering upon him.

He always went in silence. The child would push open the shed door, and see him working by lamplight, his sleeves rolled back. His clothes hung about him, carelessly, like mere wrapping. Inside, his body was concentrated, with a flexible, charged power all of its own, isolated. From when she was a tiny child, Ursula could remember his fore-arm, with its fine black hairs and its electric flexibility, working at the bench through swift, unnoticeable movements, always ambushed in a sort of silence.

She hung a moment in the door of the shed, waiting for him to notice her. He turned, his black, curved eyebrows arching slightly.

"Hullo, Twittermiss!"

And he closed the door behind her. Then the child was happy, in the shed that smelled of sweet wood and resounded to the noise of the plane or the hammer or the saw, yet was charged with the silence of the worker. She played on, intent and absorbed, among the shavings and the little nogs of wood. She never touched him: his feet and legs were near, she did not approach them.

She liked to flit out after him when he was going to church at night. If he were going to be alone, he swung her over the wall, and let her come.

Again, she was transported when the door was shut behind them, and they two inherited the big, pale, void place. She would watch him as he lit the organ candles, wait whilst he began his practising, his tunes, then she ran foraging here and there, like a kitten playing by herself in the darkness, with eyes dilated. The ropes hung vaguely, twining on the floor, from the bells in the tower, and Ursula always wanted the fluffy, red-and-white, or blue-and-white rope-grips. But they were above her.

Sometimes her mother came to claim her. Then the child was seized with resentment. She passionately resented her mother's superficial authority. She wanted to assert her own detachment.

He, however, also gave her occasional cruel shocks. He let her play about in the church, she rifled foot-stools and hymn-books and cushions, like a bee among flowers, whilst the organ echoed away. This continued for some weeks. Then the char-woman worked herself up into a frenzy of rage, to dare to attack Brangwen, and one day descended on him like a harpy. He wilted away, and wanted to break the old beast's neck.

Instead he came glowering in fury to the house, and turned on Ursula:

"Why, you tiresome little monkey, can't you even come to church without pulling the place to bits?"

His voice was harsh and cat-like, he was blind to the child. She shrank away in childish anguish and dread. What was it, what awful thing was it?

The mother turned with her calm, almost superb manner.

"What has she done, then?"

"Done? She shall go in the church no more, pulling and littering and destroying."

The wife slowly rolled her eyes and lowered her eyelids.

"What has she destroyed, then?"

He did not know.

"I've just had Mrs Wilkinson at me," he cried, "with a list of things she's done."

Ursula withered under the contempt and anger of the "she," as he spoke of her.   5

"Send Mrs Wilkinson here to me with a list of the things she's done," said Anna. "*I* am the one to hear that.

"It's not the things the child has done," continued the mother, "that have put you out so much, it's because you can't bear being spoken to by that old woman. But you haven't the courage to turn on 10 *her* when she attacks you, you bring your rage here."

He relapsed into silence. Ursula knew that he was wrong. In the outside, upper world, he was wrong. Already came over the child the cold sense of the impersonal world. There she knew her mother was right. But still her heart clamoured after her father, for him to be 15 right, in his dark, sensuous underworld. But he was angry, and went his way in blackness and brutal silence again.

The child ran about absorbed in life, quiet, full of amusement. She did not notice things, not changes nor alterations. One day she would find daisies in the grass, another day apple-blossom would be 20 sprinkled white on the ground, and she would run among it, for pleasure because it was there. Yet again birds would be pecking at the cherries, her father would throw cherries down from the tree all round her on the garden. Then the fields were full of hay.

She did not remember what had been nor what would be, the 25 outside things were there each day. She was always herself, the world outside was accidental. Even her mother was accidental to her: a condition that happened to endure.

Only her father occupied any permanent position in the childish consciousness. When he came back, she remembered vaguely how 30 he had gone away: when he went away, she knew vaguely that she must wait for his coming back. Whereas her mother, returning from an outing, merely became present, there was no reason for connecting her with some previous departure.

The return or the departure of the father was the one event which 35 the child remembered. When he came, something woke up in her, some yearning. She knew when he was out of joint or irritable or tired: then she was uneasy, she could not rest.

When he was in the house, the child felt full and warm, rich like a creature in the sunshine. When he was gone, she was vague, 40

forgetful. When he scolded her even, she was often more aware of
him than of herself. He was her strength and her greater self.

Ursula was three years old when another baby girl was born. Then
the two small sisters were much together, Gudrun and Ursula.
5 Gudrun was a quiet child who played for hours alone, absorbed in
her fancies. She was brown haired, fair skinned, strangely placid,
almost passive. Yet her will was indomitable, once set. From the first
she followed Ursula's lead. Yet she was a thing to herself, so that to
watch the two together was strange. They were like two young
10 animals playing together but not taking real notice of each other.
Gudrun was the mother's favorite—except that Anna always lived in
her latest baby.

The burden of so many lives depending on him wore the youth
down. He had his work in the office, which was done purely by effort
15 of will: he had his barren passion for the church; he had three young
children. Also at this time his health was not good. So he was
haggard and irritable, often a pest in the house. Then he was told to
go to his wood-work, or to the church.

Between him and the little Ursula there came into being a strange
20 alliance. They were aware of each other. He knew the child was
always on his side. But in his consciousness he counted it for
nothing. She was always for him. He took it for granted. Yet his life
was based on her, even whilst she was a tiny child, on her support and
her accord.

25 Anna continued in her violent trance of motherhood, always busy,
often harassed, but always contained in her trance of motherhood.
She seemed to exist in her own violent fruitfulness, and it was as if
the sun shone tropically on her. Her colour was bright, her eyes full
of a fecund gloom, her brown hair tumbled loosely over her ears. She
30 had a look of richness. No responsibility, no sense of duty troubled
her. The outside, public life was less than nothing to her, really.

Whereas when, at twenty six, he found himself father of four
children, with a wife who lived intrinsically like the ruddiest lilies of
the field,* he let the weight of responsibility press on him and drag
35 him. It was then that his child Ursula strove to be with him. She was
with him, even as a baby of four, when he was irritable and shouted
and made the household unhappy. She suffered from his shouting,
but somehow it was not really him. She wanted it to be over, she
wanted to resume her normal connection with him. When he was
40 disagreeable, the child echoed to the crying of some need in him, and

she responded blindly. Her heart followed him as if he had some tie
with her, and some love which he could not deliver. Her heart
followed him persistently, in its love.

But there was the dim, childish sense of her own smallness and
inadequacy, a fatal sense of worthlessness. She could not do   5
anything, she was not enough. She could not be important to him.
This knowledge deadened her from the first.

Still she set towards him like a quivering needle.* All her life was
directed by her awareness of him, her wakefulness to his being. And
she was against her mother.   10

Her father was the dawn wherein her consciousness woke up. But
for him, she might have gone on like the other children, Gudrun and
Theresa and Catherine, one with the flowers and insects and
playthings, having no existence apart from the concrete object of her
attention. But her father came too near to her. The clasp of his hands   15
and the power of his breast woke her up almost in pain from the
transient unconsciousness of childhood. Wide-eyed, unseeing, she
was awake before she knew how to see. She was wakened too soon.
Too soon the call had come to her, when she was a small baby, and
her father held her close to his breast, her sleep-living heart was   20
beaten into wakefulness by the striving of his bigger heart, by his
clasping her to his body for love and for fulfilment, asking as a
magnet must always ask. From her the response had struggled dimly,
vaguely into being.

The children were dressed roughly for the country. When she was   25
little, Ursula pattered about in little wooden clogs, a blue overall over
her thick red dress, a red shawl crossed on her breast and tied behind
again. So she ran with her father to the garden.

The household rose early. He was out digging by six o'clock in the
morning, he went to his work at half past eight. And Ursula was   30
usually in the garden with him, though not near at hand.

At Eastertime one year she helped him to set potatoes. It was the
first time she had ever helped him. The occasion remained as a
picture, one of her earliest memories.* They had gone out soon after
dawn. A cold wind was blowing. He had his old trousers tucked into   35
his boots, he wore no coat nor waistcoat, his shirt-sleeves fluttered in
the wind, his face was ruddy and intent, in a kind of sleep. When he
was at work he neither heard nor saw. A long, thin man, looking still
a youth, with a line of black moustache above his thick mouth, and
his fine hair blown on his forehead, he worked away at the earth in   40

the grey first light, alone. His solitariness drew the child like a
spell.

The wind came chill over the dark-green fields. Ursula* ran up
and watched him push the setting-peg in at one side of his ready
5   earth, stride across, and push it in the other side, pulling the line taut
and clear upon the clods intervening. Then with a sharp, cutting
noise the bright spade came towards her, cutting a grip* into the new,
soft earth.

He stuck his spade upright and straightened himself.
10   "Do you want to help me?" he said.

She looked up at him from out of her little woollen bonnet.

"Ay," he said, "you can put some taters in for me. Look—like
that—these little sprits* standing up—so much apart, you see."

And stooping down he quickly, surely placed the spritted potatoes
15   in the soft grip, where they rested separate and pathetic on the heavy
cold earth.

He gave her a little basket of potatoes, and strode himself to the
other end of the line. She saw him stooping, working towards her.
She was excited, and unused. She put in one potato, then rearranged
20   it, to make it sit nicely. Some of the sprits were broken, and she was
afraid. The responsibility excited her like a string tying her up. She
could not help looking with dread at the string buried under the
heaped-back soil. Her father was working nearer, stooping, working
nearer. She was overcome by her responsibility. She put potatoes
25   quickly into the cold earth.

He came near.

"Not so close," he said, stooping over her potatoes, taking some
out and rearranging the others. She stood by with the painful
terrified helplessness of childhood. He was so unseeing and con-
30   fident, she wanted to do the thing and yet she could not. She stood by
looking on, her little blue overall fluttering in the wind, the red
woollen ends of her shawl blowing gustily. Then he went down the
row, relentlessly, turning the potatoes in with his sharp spade cuts.
He took no notice of her, only worked on. He had another world
35   from hers.

She stood helplessly, stranded on his world. He continued his
work. She knew she could not help him. A little bit forlorn, at last she
turned away, and ran down the garden, away from him, as fast as she
could go away from him, to forget him and his work.

He missed her presence, her face in her red woollen bonnet, her blue overall fluttering. She ran to where a little water ran trickling between grass and stones. That she loved.

When he came by he said to her:

"You didn't help me much." 5

The child looked at him dumbly. Already her heart was heavy because of her own disappointment. Her mouth was dumb and pathetic. But he did not notice, he went his way.

And she played on, because of her disappointment persisting even the more in her play. She dreaded work, because she could not do it 10 as he did it. She was conscious of the great breach between them. She knew she had no power. The grown-up power to work deliberately was a mystery to her.

He would smash into her sensitive child's world destructively. Her mother was lenient, careless. The children played about as they 15 would all day. Ursula was thoughtless—why should she remember things? If across the garden she saw the hedge had budded, and if she wanted these greeny-pink, tiny buds for bread-and-cheese, to play at tea-party with, over she went for them.

Then suddenly, perhaps the next day, her soul would almost start 20 out of her body as her father turned on her, shouting:

"Who's been tramplin' an' dancin' across where I've just sowed seed. I know it's you, nuisance! Can you find nowhere else to walk, but just over my seed beds? But it's like you, that is—no heed but to follow your own greedy nose." 25

It had shocked him in his intent world to see the zig-zagging lines of deep little foot-prints across his work. The child was infinitely more shocked. Her vulnerable little soul was flayed and trampled. *Why* were the foot-prints there? She had not wanted to make them. She stood dazzled with pain and shame and unreality. 30

Her soul, her consciousness seemed to die away. She became shut off and senseless, a little fixed creature whose soul had gone hard and unresponsive. The sense of her own unreality hardened her like a frost. She cared no longer.

And the sight of her face, shut and superior with self-asserting 35 indifference, made a flame of rage go over him. He wanted to break her.

"I'll break your obstinate little face," he said, through shut teeth, lifting his hand.

The child did not alter in the least. The look of indifference, 40 complete glancing indifference, as if nothing but herself existed to her, remained fixed.

Yet far away in her, the sobs were tearing her soul. And when he had gone, she would go and creep under the parlour sofa, and lie
5   clinched in the silent, hidden misery of childhood.

When she crawled out, after an hour or so, she went rather stiffly to play. She willed to forget. She cut off her childish soul from memory, so that the pain, and the insult should not be real. She asserted her self only. There was now nothing in the world but her
10   own self. So very soon, she came to believe in the outward malevolence that was against her. And very early, she learned that even her adored father was part of this malevolence. And very early, she learned to harden her soul in resistance and denial of all that was outside her, harden herself upon her own being.

15   She never felt sorry for what she had done, she never forgave those who had made her guilty. If he had said to her "Why, Ursula, did you trample my carefully-made bed?" that would have hurt her to the quick, and she would have done anything for him. But she was always tormented by the unreality of outside things. The earth was
20   to walk on. Why must she avoid a certain patch, just because it was called a seed bed. It was the earth to walk on. This was her instinctive assumption. And when he bullied her, she became hard, cut herself off from all connection, lived in the little separate world of her own violent will.

25   As she grew older, five, six, seven, the connection between her and her father was even stronger. Yet it was always straining to break. She was always relapsing on her own violent will into her own separate world of herself. This made him grind his teeth with bitterness, for he still wanted her. But she could harden herself into
30   her own self's universe, impregnable.

He was very fond of swimming, and in warm weather would take her down to the canal, to a silent place, or to a big pond or reservoir, to bathe. He would take her on his back as he went swimming, and she clung close, feeling his strong movement under her, so strong, as
35   if it would uphold all the world. Then he taught her to swim.

She was a fearless little thing, when he dared her. And he had a curious craving to frighten her, to see what she would do with him. He said, would she ride on his back whilst he jumped off the canal bridge down into the water beneath.
40   She would. He loved to feel the naked child clinging on to his

shoulders. There was a curious fight between their two wills. He mounted the parapet of the canal bridge. The water was a long way down. But the child had a deliberate will set upon his. She held herself fixed to him.

He leapt, and down they went. The crash of the water as they went 5 under struck through the child's small body, with a sort of unconsciousness. But she remained fixed. And when they came up again, and when they went to the bank, and when they sat on the grass side by side, he laughed, and said it was fine. And the dark-dilated eyes of the child looked at him wonderingly, darkly, 10 wondering from the shock, yet reserved and unfathomable, so he laughed almost with a sob.

In a moment she was clinging safely on his back again, and he was swimming in deep water. She was used to his nakedness, and to her mother's nakedness, ever since she was born. They were clinging to 15 each other, and making up to each other for the strange blow that had been struck at them. Yet still, on other days, he would leap again with her from the bridge, daringly, almost wickedly. Till at length, as he leapt, once, she dropped forward on to his head, and nearly broke his neck, so that they fell into the water in a heap, and fought for a 20 few moments with death. He saved her, and sat on the bank, quivering. But his eyes were full of the blackness of death, it was as if death had cut between their two lives, and separated them.

Still they were not separate. There was this curious taunting intimacy between them. When the fair came, she wanted to go in the 25 swingboats. He took her, and, standing up in the boat, holding on to the irons, began to drive higher, perilously higher. The child clung fast on her seat.

"Do you want to go any higher?" he said to her, and she laughed with her mouth, her eyes wide and dilated. They were rushing 30 through the air.

"Yes," she said, feeling as if she would turn into vapour, lose hold of everything, and melt away. The boat swung far up, then down like a stone, only to be caught sickeningly up again.

"Any higher?" he called, looking at her over his shoulder, his face 35 evil and beautiful to her.

She laughed with white lips.

He sent the swingboat sweeping through the air in a great semicircle, till it jerked and swayed at the high horizontal. The child clung on, pale, her eyes fixed on him. People below were calling. The 40 jerk at the top had almost shaken them both out. He had done what he could—and he was attracting censure. He sat down, and let the swingboat swing itself out.

People in the crowd cried shame on him as he came out of the
5   swingboat. He laughed. The child clung to his hand, pale and mute. In a while she was violently sick. He gave her lemonade, and she gulped a little.

"Don't tell your mother you've been sick," he said.

There was no need to ask that. When she got home, the child crept
10 away under the parlour sofa, like a sick little animal, and was a long time before she crawled out.

But Anna got to know of this escapade, and was passionately angry and contemptuous of him. His golden-brown eyes glittered, he had a strange, cruel little smile. And as the child watched him, for the first
15 time in her life a disillusion came over her, something cold and isolating. She went over to her mother. Her soul was dead towards him. It made her sick.

Still she forgot and continued to love him, but ever more coldly. He was at this time, when he was about twenty eight years old,
20 strange and violent in his being, sensual. He acquired some power over Anna, over everybody he came into contact with.

After a long bout of hostility,* Anna at last closed with him. She had now four children, all girls. For seven years she had been absorbed in wifehood and motherhood. For years he had gone on
25 beside her, never really encroaching upon her. Then gradually another self seemed to assert its being within him. He was still silent and separate. But she could feel him all the while coming near upon her, as if his breast and his body were threatening her, and he was always coming closer. Gradually he became indifferent of responsi-
30 bility. He would do what pleased him, and no more.

He began to go away from home. He went to Nottingham on Saturdays, always alone, to the football match* and to the music-hall, and all the time he was watching, in readiness. He never cared to drink. But with his hard, golden-brown eyes, so keen seeing with
35 their tiny black pupils, he watched all the people, everything that happened, and he waited.

In the Empire* one evening he sat next to two girls. He was aware of the one beside him. She was rather small, common, with a fresh complexion and an upper lip that lifted from her teeth, so that, when
40 she was not conscious, her mouth was slightly open and her lips

pressed outwards in a kind of blind appeal. She was strongly aware of
the man next to her, so that all her body was still, very still. Her face
watched the stage. Her arms went down into her lap, very self-
conscious and still.

A gleam lit up in him: should he begin with her? Should he begin
with her to live the other, the unadmitted life of his desire? Why not?
He had always been so good. Save for his wife, he was virgin. And
why, when all women were different? Why, when he would only live
once? He wanted the other life. His own life was barren, not enough.
He wanted the other.

Her open mouth, showing the small, irregular, white teeth,
appealed to him. It was open and ready. It was so vulnerable. Why
should he not go in and enjoy what was there? The slim arm that
went down so still and motionless to the lap, it was pretty. She would
be small, he would be able almost to hold her in his two hands. She
would be small, almost like a child, and pretty. Her childishness
whetted him keenly. She would be helpless between his hands.

"That was the best turn we've had," he said to her, leaning over as
he clapped his hands. He felt strong and unshakeable in himself, set
over against all the world. His soul was keen and watchful, glittering
with a kind of amusement. He was perfectly self-contained. He was
himself, the absolute, the rest of the world was the object that should
contribute to his being.

The girl started, turned round, her eyes lit up with an almost
painful flash of a smile, the colour came deeply in her cheeks.

"Yes, it was," she said, quite meaninglessly, and she covered her
rather prominent teeth with her lips. Then she sat looking straight
before her, seeing nothing, only conscious of the colour burning in
her cheek.

It pricked him with a pleasant sensation. His veins and his nerves
attended to her, she was so young and palpitating.

"It's not such a good programme as last week's," he said.

Again she half turned her face to him, and her clear, bright eyes,
bright like shallow water, filled with light, frightened, yet involuntarily lighting and shaking with response.

"Oh isn't it! I wasn't able to come last week."

He noted the common accent. It pleased him. He knew what class
she came of. Probably she was a warehouse-lass. He was glad she
was a common girl.

He proceeded to tell her about the last week's programme. She

answered at random, very confusedly. The colour burned in her
cheek. Yet she always answered him. The girl on the other side sat
remotely, obviously silent. He ignored her. All his address was for
his own girl, with her bright, shallow eyes and her vulnerably opened
5 mouth.

The talk went on, meaningless and random on her part, quite
deliberate and purposive on his. It was a pleasure to him to make this
conversation, an activity pleasant as a fine game of chance and skill.
He was very quiet and pleasant-humoured, but so full of strength.
10 She fluttered beside his steady pressure of warmth and his surety.

He saw the performance drawing to a close. His senses were alert
and wilful. He would press his advantages. He followed her and her
plain friend down the stairs to the street. It was raining.

"It's a nasty night," he said. "Shall you come and have a drink of
15 something—a cup of coffee—it's early yet."

"Oh, I don't think so," she said, looking away into the night.

"I wish you would," he said, putting himself as it were at her
mercy.

There was a moment's pause.
20 "Come to Rollins," he said.

"No—not there."

"To Carson's then?"

There was a silence. The other girl hung on. The man was the
centre of positive force.
25 "Will your friend come as well?"

There was another moment of silence, while the other girl felt her
ground.

"No thanks," she said. "I've promised to meet a friend."

"Another time, then?" he said.
30 "Oh, thanks," she replied, very awkward.

"Goodnight," he said.

"See you later," said his girl to her friend.

"Where?" said the friend.

"You know, Gertie," replied his girl.
35 "All right, Jennie."

The friend was gone into the darkness. He turned with his girl to
the tea-shop. They talked all the time. He made his sentences in
sheer, almost muscular pleasure of exercising himself with her. He
was looking at her all the time, perceiving her, appreciating her,
40 finding her out, gratifying himself with her. He could see distinct
attractions in her; her eyebrows, with their particular curve, gave him

keen æsthetic pleasure. Later on he would see her bright, pellucid eyes, like shallow water, and know those. And there remained the opened, exposed mouth, red and vulnerable. That he reserved as yet. And all the while his eyes were on the girl, estimating and handling with pleasure her young softness. About the girl herself, who or what she was, he cared nothing, he was quite unaware that she was anybody. She was just the sensual object of his attention.

"Shall we go, then?" he said.

She rose in silence, as if acting without a mind, merely physically. He seemed to hold her in his will. Outside it was still raining.

"Let's have a walk," he said. "I don't mind the rain, do you?"

"No, I don't mind it," she said.

He was alert in every sense and fibre, and yet quite sure and steady, and lit up, as if transfused. He had a free sensation of walking in his own darkness, not in anybody else's world at all. He was purely a world to himself, he had nothing to do with any general consciousness. Just his own senses were supreme. All the rest was external, insignificant, leaving him alone with this girl whom he wanted to absorb, whose properties he wanted to absorb into his own senses. He did not care about her, except that he wanted to overcome her resistance, to have her in his power, fully and exhaustively to enjoy her.

They turned into the dark streets. He held her umbrella over her, and put his arm round her. She walked as if she were unaware. But gradually, as he walked, he drew her a little closer, into the movement of his side and hip. She fitted in there very well. It was a real good fit, to walk with her like this. It made him exquisitely aware of his own muscular self. And his hand that grasped her side felt one curve of her, and it seemed like a new creation to him, a reality, an absolute, an existing tangible beauty of the absolute. It was like a star. Everything in him was absorbed in the sensual delight of this one small, firm curve in her body, that his hand, and his whole being had lighted upon.

He led her into the Park, where it was almost dark. He noticed a corner between two walls, under a great overhanging bush of ivy.

"Let us stand here a minute," he said.

He put down the umbrella, and followed her into the corner, retreating out of the rain. He needed no eyes to see. All he wanted was to know through touch. She was like a piece of palpable darkness. He found her in the darkness, put his arms round her and

his hands upon her. She was silent and inscrutable. But he did not
want to know anything about her, he only wanted to discover her.
And through her clothing, what absolute beauty he touched.

"Take your hat off," he said.

5   Silently, obediently, she took off her hat and gave herself to his
arms again. He liked her—he liked the feel of her—he wanted to
know her more closely. He let his fingers subtly seek out her cheek
and neck. What amazing beauty and pleasure, in the dark! His
fingers had often touched Anna on the face and neck like that. What
10 matter! It was one man who touched Anna, another who now
touched this girl. He liked best his new self. He was given over
altogether to the sensuous knowledge of this woman, and every
moment he seemed to be touching absolute beauty, something
beyond knowledge.

15 Very close, marvelling and exceedingly joyful in their discoveries,
his hands pressed upon her, so subtly, so seekingly, so finely and
desirously searching her out, that she too was almost swooning in the
absolute of sensual knowledge. In utter sensual delight she clenched
her knees, her thighs, her loins together.* It was an added beauty to
20 him.

But he was patiently working for her relaxation, patiently, his
whole being fixed in the smile of latent gratification, his whole body
electric with subtle, powerful, reducing force upon her. So he came
at length to kiss her, and she was almost betrayed by his insidious
25 kiss. Her open mouth was too helpless and unguarded. He knew
this, and his first kiss was very gentle, and soft, and assuring, so
assuring. So that her soft, defenceless mouth became assured, even
bold, seeking upon his mouth. And he answered her gradually,
gradually, his soft kiss sinking in softly, softly, but every more
30 heavily, more heavily yet, till it was too heavy for her to meet, and she
began to sink under it. She was sinking, sinking, his smile of latent
gratification was becoming more tense, he was sure of her. He let the
whole force of his will sink upon her to sweep her away. But it was
too great a shock for her.

35 With a sudden, horrible movement she ruptured the state that
contained them both.

"Don't—don't!"

It was a rather horrible cry that seemed to come out of her, not to
belong to her. It was some strange agony of terror crying out the

words. There was something vibrating and beside herself in the noise. His nerves ripped like silk.

"What's the matter?" he said, as if calmly, "What's the matter?"

She came back to him, but trembling, reservedly this time.

Her cry had given him gratification. But he knew he had been too 5 sudden for her. He was now careful. For a while he merely sheltered her. Also there had broken a flaw into his perfect will. He wanted to persist, to begin again, to lead up to the point where he had let himself go on her, and then manage more carefully, successfully. So far she had won. And the battle was not over yet. But another voice 10 woke in him and prompted him to let her go—let her go in contempt.

He sheltered her, and soothed her, and caressed her, and kissed her, and again began to come nearer, nearer. He gathered himself together. Even if he did not take her, he would make her relax, he would fuse away her resistance. So softly, softly, with infinite 15 caressiveness he kissed her, and the whole of his being seemed to fondle her. Till, at the verge, swooning at the breaking point, there came from her a beaten, inarticulate, moaning cry:

"Don't—oh don't."

His veins fused with extreme voluptuousness. For a moment he 20 almost lost control of himself, and continued automatically. But there was a moment of inaction, of cold suspension. He was not going to take her. He drew her to him and soothed her, and caressed her. But the pure zest had gone. She struggled to herself and realised he was not going to take her. And then, at the very last moment, 25 when his fondling had come near again, his hot living desire despising her, against his cold sensual desire, she broke violently away from him.

"Don't," she cried, harsh now with hatred, and she flung her hand across and hit him violently. "Keep off of me." 30

His blood stood still for a moment. Then the smile came again within him, steady, cruel.

"Why, what's the matter?" he said, with suave irony. "Nobody's going to hurt you."

"I know what *you* want," she said. 35

"*I* know what I want," he said. "What's the odds?"

"Well you're not going to have it off *me*."

"Aren't I? Well then I'm not. It's no use crying about it, is it?"

"No, it isn't," said the girl, rather disconcerted by his irony.

"But there's no need to have a row about it. We can kiss goodnight just the same, can't we?"

She was silent in the darkness.

"Or do you want your hat and umbrella to go home this minute?"

5   Still she was silent. He watched her dark figure as she stood there on the edge of the faint darkness, and he waited.

"Come and say goodnight nicely, if we're going to say it," he said.

Still she did not stir. He put his hand out and drew her into the
10 darkness again.

"It's warmer in here," he said; "a lot cosier."

His will yet had not relaxed from her. The moment of hatred exhilarated him.

"I'm going now," she muttered, as he closed his hand over her.

15 "See how well you fit your place," he said, as he drew her to her previous position, close upon him. "What do you want to leave it for?"

And gradually the intoxication invaded him again, the zest came back. After all, why should he not take her?

20 But she did not yield to him entirely.

"Are you a married man?" she asked at length,

"What if I am?" he said.

She did not answer.

"I don't ask you whether *you're* married or not," he said.

25 "You know jolly well I'm *not*," she answered hotly. Oh, if she could only break away from him, if only she need not yield to him.

At length her will became cold against him. She had escaped. But she hated him for her escape more than for her danger. Did he despise her so coldly. And she was in torture of adherence to him
30 still.

"Shall I see you next week—next Saturday?" he said, as they returned to the town.

She did not answer.

"Come to the Empire with me—you and Gertie," he said.

35 "I should look well, going with a married man," she said.

"I'm no less of a man for being married, am I?" he said.

"Oh, it's a different matter altogether with a married man," she said, in a ready-made speech that showed her chagrin.

"How's that?" he asked.

40 But she would not enlighten him. Yet she promised, without promising, to be at the meeting-place next Saturday evening.

So he left her. He did not even know her name. He caught a train and went home.

It was the last train, he was very late. He was not home till midnight. But he was quite indifferent. He had no real relation with his home, not this man which he now was. Anna was sitting up for 5
him. She saw the queer, absolved look on his face, a sort of latent, almost sinister smile, as if he were absolved from his "good" ties.

"Where have you been?" she asked, puzzled, interested.

"To the Empire."

"Who with?" 10

"By myself. I came home with Tom Cooper."*

She looked at him, and wondered what he had been doing. She was indifferent as to whether he lied or not.

"You have come home very strange," she said. And there was an appreciative inflexion in the speech. 15

He was not affected. As for his humble, good self, he was absolved from it. He sat down and ate heartily. He was not tired. He seemed to take no notice of her.

For Anna the moment was critical. She kept herself aloof, and watched him. He talked to her, but with a little indifference, since he 20
was scarcely aware of her. So, then she did not affect him? Here was a new turn of affairs! He was rather attractive, nevertheless. She liked him better than the ordinary mute, half-effaced, half-subdued man she usually knew him to be. So, he was blossoming out into his real self! It piqued her. Very good, let him blossom! She liked a new 25
turn of affairs. He was a strange man come home to her. Glancing at him, she saw she could not reduce him to what he had been before. In an instant, she gave it up. Yet not without a pang of rage, which would insist on their old, beloved love, their old, accustomed intimacy and her old, established supremacy. She almost rose up to 30
fight for them. But looking at him, and remembering his father, she was wary. This was the new turn of affairs!

Very good, if she could not influence him in the old way, she would be level with him in the new. Her old defiant hostility came up. Very good, she too was out on her own adventure. Her voice, her 35
manner changed, she was ready for the game. Something was liberated in her. She liked him. She liked this strange man come home to her. He was very welcome, indeed. She was very glad to welcome a stranger. She had been bored by the old husband. To his latent, cruel smile she replied with brilliant challenge. He expected 40

her to keep the moral fortress. Not she! It was much too dull a part. She challenged him back with a sort of radiance, very bright and free, opposite to him. He looked at her, and his eyes glinted. She too was out in the field.

5   His senses pricked up and keenly attended to her. She laughed, perfectly indifferent and loose as he was. He came towards her. She neither rejected him nor responded to him. In a kind of radiance, superb in her inscrutability, she laughed before him. She too could throw everything overboard, love, intimacy, responsibility. What
10 were her four children to her now? What did it matter that this man was the father of her four children?

    He was the sensual male seeking his pleasure, she was the female ready to take hers: but in her own way. A man could turn into a free lance: so then could a woman. She adhered as little as he to the moral
15 world. All that had gone before was nothing to her. She was another woman, under the instance of a strange man. He was a stranger to her, seeking his own ends. Very good. She wanted to see what this stranger would do now, what he was.

    She laughed, and kept him at arms' length, whilst apparently
20 ignoring him. She watched him undress as if he were a stranger. Indeed he was a stranger to her.

    And she roused him profoundly, violently, even before he touched her. The little creature in Nottingham had but been leading up to this. They abandoned in one motion the moral position, each was
25 seeking gratification pure and simple.

    Strange his wife was to him. It was as if he were a perfect stranger, as if she were infinitely and essentially strange to him, the other half of the world, the dark half of the moon. She waited for his touch as if he were a marauder who had come in, infinitely unknown
30 and desirable to her. And he began to discover her. He had an inkling of the vastness of the unknown sensual store of delights she was. With a passion of voluptuousness that made him dwell on each tiny beauty in a kind of frenzy of enjoyment, he lit upon her: her beauty, the beauties, the separate, several beauties of her body.

35   He was quite ousted from himself, and sensually transported by that which he discovered in her. He was another man revelling over her. There was no tenderness, no love between them any more, only the maddening, sensuous lust for discovery and the insatiable, exorbitant gratification in the sensual beauties of her body. And she
40 was a store, a store of absolute beauties that it drove him mad to

contemplate. There was such a feast to enjoy, and he with only one man's capacity.

He lived in a passion of sensual discovery with her for some time—it was a duel: no love, no words, no kisses even, only the maddening perception of beauty consummate, absolute through touch. He wanted to touch her, to discover her, maddeningly he wanted to know her. Yet he must not hurry, or he missed everything. He must enjoy one beauty at a time. And the multitudinous beauties of her body, the many little rapturous places, sent him mad with delight, and with desire to be able to know more, to have strength to know more. For all was there.

He would say during the daytime:

"Tonight I shall know the little hollow under her ankle, where the blue vein crosses." And the thought of it, and the desire for it, made a thick darkness of anticipation.

He would go all the day waiting for the night to come, when he could give himself to the enjoyment of some luxurious absolute of beauty in her. The thought of the hidden resources of her, the undiscovered beauties and ecstatic place of delight in her body, waiting, only waiting for him to discover them, sent him slightly insane. He was obsessed. If he did not discover and make known to himself these delights, they might be lost for ever. He wished he had a hundred men's energies, with which to enjoy her. He wished he were a cat, to lick her with a rough, grating, lascivious tongue. He wanted to wallow in her, bury himself in her flesh, cover himself over with her flesh.*

And she, separate, with a strange, dangerous, glistening look in her eyes received all his activities upon her as if they were expected by her, and provoked him when he was quiet to more, till sometimes he was ready to perish for sheer inability to be satisfied of her, inability to have had enough of her.

Their children became mere offspring to them, they lived in the darkness and death of their own sensual activities. Sometimes he felt he was going mad with a sense of Absolute Beauty,* perceived by him in her through his senses. It was something too much for him. And in everything, was this same, almost sinister, terrifying beauty. But in the revelations of her body through contact with his body, was the ultimate beauty, to know which was almost death in itself, and yet for the knowledge of which he would have undergone endless torture. He would have forfeited anything, anything, rather than forego his

right even to the instep of her foot, and the place from which the toes
radiated out, the little, miraculous white plain from which ran the
little hillocks of the toes and the folded, dimpling hollows between
the toes. He felt he would have died rather than forfeit this.

5   This was what their love had become, a sensuality violent and
extreme as death. They had no conscious intimacy, no tenderness of
love. It was all the lust and the infinite, maddening intoxication of the
senses, a passion of death.

He had always, all his life, had a secret dread of Absolute Beauty.
10   It had always been like a fetish to him, something to fear, really. For
it was immoral and against mankind. So he had turned to the Gothic
form, which always asserted the broken desire of mankind in its
pointed arches, escaping the rolling, absolute beauty of the round
arch.*

15   But now he had given way, and with infinite sensual violence gave
himself to the realisation of this supreme, immoral, Absolute Beauty,
in the body of woman. It seemed to him, that it came to being in the
body of woman, under his touch. Under his touch, even under his
sight, it was there. But when he neither saw nor touched the perfect
20   place, it was not perfect, it was not there. And he must make it exist.

But still the thing terrified him. Awful and threatening it was,
dangerous to a degree, even whilst he gave himself to it. It was pure
darkness, also. All the shameful things of the body revealed themselves to him now with a sort of sinister, tropical beauty. All the
25   shameful, natural and unnatural acts of sensual voluptuousness
which he and the woman partook of together, created together, they
had their heavy beauty and their delight. Shame, what was it? It was
part of extreme delight. It was that part of delight of which man is
usually afraid. Why afraid? The secret, shameful things are most
30   terribly beautiful.

They accepted shame, and were one with it in their most
unlicensed pleasures. It was incorporated. It was a bud that blossomed into beauty and heavy, fundamental gratification.

Their outward life went on much the same, but the inward life was
35   revolutionised. The children became less important, the parents
were absorbed in their own living.

And gradually, Brangwen began to find himself free to attend to
the outside life as well. His intimate life was so violently active, that it
set another man in him free. And this new man turned with interest
40   to public life, to see what part he could take in it. This would give him

scope for new activity, activity of a kind for which he was now created and released. He wanted to be unanimous with the whole of purposive mankind.

At this time Education was in the forefront as a subject of interest. There was talk of new Swedish methods,* of handwork instruction, 5 and so on. Brangwen embraced sincerely the idea of handwork in schools. For the first time, he began to take real interest in a public affair. He had at length, from his profound sensual activity, developed a real purposive self.

There was talk of night-schools, and of handicraft classes. He 10 wanted to start a wood-work class in Cossethay, to teach carpentry and joinery and wood-carving to the village boys, two night a week. This seemed to him a supremely desirable thing to be doing. His pay would be very little—and when he had it, he spent it all on extra wood and tools. But he was very happy and keen in his new public 15 spirit.

He started his night-classes in wood-work when he was thirty years old. By this time he had five children, the last a boy. But boy or girl mattered very little to him. He had a natural blood-affection for his children, and he liked them as they turned up: boys or girls. Only 20 he was fondest of Ursula. Somehow, she seemed to be at the back of his new night-school venture.

The house by the yew-trees was in connection with the great human endeavour at last. It gained a new vigour thereby.

To Ursula, a child of eight, the increase in magic was consider- 25 able. She heard all the talk, she saw the parish room* fitted up as a workshop. The parish room was a high, stone, barn-like, ecclesiastical building standing away by itself in the Brangwens' second garden, across the lane. She was always attracted by its age and its stranded obsoleteness. Now she watched preparations made, she sat 30 on the flight of stone steps that came down from the porch to the garden, and heard her father and the vicar talking and planning and working. Then an inspector* came, a very strange man, and stayed talking with her father all one evening. Everything was settled, and twelve boys enrolled their names. It was very exciting. 35

But to Ursula, everything her father did was magic. Whether he came from Ilkeston with news of the town, whether he went across to the church with his music or his tools on a sunny evening, whether he sat in his white surplice at the organ on Sundays, leading the singing with his strong tenor voice, or whether he were in the 40

workshop with the boys, he was always a centre of magic and
fascination to her, his voice, sounding out in command, cheerful,
laconic, had always a twang in it that sent a thrill over her blood, and
hypnotised her. She seemed to run in the shadow of some dark,
5   potent secret of which she would not, of whose existence even she
dared not become conscious, it cast such a spell over her, and so
darkened her mind.

Chapter IX

The Marsh and the Flood

There was always regular connection between the Yew Cottage and the Marsh, yet the two households remained separate, distinct.

After Anna's marriage, the Marsh became the home of the two 5 boys, Tom and Fred. Tom was a rather short, good-looking youth, with crisp black hair and long black eyelashes and soft, dark, possessed eyes. He had a quick intelligence. From the High School* he went to London, to study. He had an instinct for attracting people of character and energy. He gave place entirely to the other person, 10 and at the same time kept himself independent. He scarcely existed except through other people. When he was alone he was unresolved. When he was with another man, he seemed to add himself to the other, make the other bigger almost than life size. So that a few people loved him and attained a sort of fulfilment in him. He 15 carefully chose these few.

He had a subtle, quick, critical intelligence, a mind that was like a scale or balance. There was something of a woman in all this.

In London he had been the favorite pupil of an engineer,* a clever man, who became well-known at the time when Tom Brangwen had 20 just finished his studies. Through this master the youth kept acquaintance with various individual, outstanding characters. He never asserted himself. He seemed to be there to estimate and establish the rest. He was like a presence that makes us aware of our own being. So that he was while still young connected with some of 25 the most energetic scientific and mathematical people in London. They took him as an equal. Quiet and perceptive and impersonal as he was, he kept his place and learned how to value others in just degree. He was there like a judgment. Besides, he was very good-looking, of medium stature but beautifully proportioned, dark, with 30 fine colouring, always perfectly healthy.

His father allowed him a liberal pocket-money, besides which he had a sort of post as assistant to his chief. Then from time to time the young man appeared at the Marsh, curiously attractive, well dressed, reserved, having by nature a subtle, refined manner. And he set the change in the farm.

Fred, the younger brother, was a Brangwen, large-boned, blue-eyed, English. He was his father's very son, the two men, father and
5 son, were supremely at ease with one another. Fred was succeeding to the farm.

Between the elder brother and the younger existed an almost passionate love. Tom watched over Fred with a woman's poignant attention and self-less care. Fred looked up to Tom as to something
10 miraculous, that which he himself would aspire to be, were he great also.

So that after Anna's departure, the Marsh began to take on a new tone. The boys were gentlemen;* Tom had a rare nature, and had risen high, Fred was sensitive and fond of reading, he pondered
15 Ruskin and then the Agnostic writings.* Like all the Brangwens, he was very much a thing to himself, though fond of people, and indulgent to them, having an exaggerated respect for them.

There was a rather uneasy friendship between him and one of the young Hardys at the Hall. The two households were different, yet
20 the young men met on shy terms of equality.

It was young Tom Brangwen, with his dark lashes and beautiful colouring, his soft, inscrutable nature, his strange repose and his informed air, added to his position in London, who seemed to emphasize the superior, foreign element in the Marsh. When he
25 appeared, perfectly dressed, as if soft and affable and yet quite removed from everybody, he created an uneasiness in people, he was reserved in the minds of the Cossethay and Ilkeston acquaintances to a different, remote world.

He and his mother had a kind of affinity. The affection between
30 them was of a mute, distant character, but radical. His father was always uneasy and slightly deferential to his eldest son. Tom also formed the link that kept the Marsh in real connection with the Skrebenskys, now quite important people in their own district.

So a change in tone came over the Marsh. Tom Brangwen, the
35 father, as he grew older seemed to mature into a gentleman-farmer. His figure lent itself: burly and handsome. His face remained fresh and his blue eyes as full of light, his thick hair and beard had turned gradually to a silky whiteness. It was his custom to laugh a great deal, in his acquiescent, wilful manner. Things had puzzled him very
40 much, so he had taken the line of easy, good-humoured acceptance.

He was not responsible for the frame of things. Yet he was afraid of the unknown in life.

He was fairly well-off. His wife was there with him, a different being from himself, yet somewhere vitally connected with him:—who was he to understand where and how? His two sons were gentlemen. They were men distinct from himself, they had separate beings of their own, yet they were connected with himself. It was all adventurous and puzzling. Yet one remained vital within one's own existence, whatever the off-shoots.

So, handsome and puzzled, he laughed and stuck to himself, as the only thing he could stick to. His youngness and the wonder remained almost the same in him. He became indolent, he developed a luxuriant ease. Fred did most of the farm-work, the father saw to the more important transactions. He drove a good mare, and sometimes he rode his cob. He drank in the hôtels and the inns with better-class farmers and proprietors, he had well-to-do acquaintances among men. But one class suited him no better than another.

His wife, as ever, had no acquaintances. Her hair was threaded now with grey, her face grew older in form without changing in expression. She seemed the same as when she had come to the Marsh twenty five years ago, save that her health was more fragile. She seemed always to haunt the Marsh rather than to live there. She was never part of the life. Something she represented was alien there, she remained a stranger within the gates,* in some ways fixed and impervious, in some ways curiously refining. She caused the separateness and individuality of all the Marsh inmates, the friability of the household.

When young Tom Brangwen was twenty three years old there was some breach between him and his chief which was never explained, and he went away to Italy, then to America. He came home for a while, then went to Germany; always the same good-looking, carefully-dressed, attractive young man, in perfect health, yet somehow outside of everything. In his dark eyes was a deep misery which he wore with the same ease and pleasantness as he wore his close-sitting clothes.

To Ursula he was a romantic, alluring figure. He had a grace of bringing beautiful presents: a box of expensive sweets such as Cossethay had never seen; or he gave her a hair-brush and a long, slim mirror of mother-of-pearl, all pale and glimmering and exquisite; or he sent her a little necklace of rough stones, amethyst and opal

and brilliants and garnet. He spoke other languages easily and
fluently, his nature was curiously gracious and insinuating. With all
that, he was undefinably an outsider. He belonged to nowhere, to no
society.

5   Anna Brangwen had left her intimacy with her father undeveloped
since the time of her marriage. At her marriage it had been
abandoned. He and she had drawn a reserve between them. Anna
went more to her mother.

Then suddenly the father died.

10   It happened one spring-time when Ursula was about eight years
old, he, Tom Brangwen, drove off on a Saturday morning to the
market in Nottingham, saying he might not be back till late, as there
was a special show and then a meeting he had to attend. His family
understood that he would enjoy himself.

15   The season had been rainy and dreary. In the evening it was
pouring with rain. Fred Brangwen, unsettled, uneasy, did not go out,
as was his wont. He smoked and read and fidgeted, hearing always
the trickling of water outside. This wet, black night seemed to cut
him off and make him unsettled, aware of himself, aware that he
20   wanted something else, aware that he was scarcely living. There
seemed to him to be no root to his life, no place for him to get
satisfied in. He dreamed of going abroad. But his instinct knew that
change of place would not solve his problem. He wanted change,
deep, vital change of living. And he did not know how to get it.

25   Tilly, an old woman now, came in saying that the laborers who had
been suppering up said the yard and everywhere was just a slew* of
water. He heard in indifference. But he hated a desolate, raw
wetness in the world. He would leave the Marsh.

His mother was in bed. At last he shut his book, his mind was
30   blank, he walked upstairs intoxicated with depression and anger,
and, intoxicated with depression and anger, locked himself into
sleep.

Tilly set slippers before the kitchen fire, and she also went to bed,
leaving the door unlocked. Then the farm was in darkness, in the
35   rain.

At eleven o'clock it was still raining. Tom Brangwen stood in the
yard of the "Angel,"* in Nottingham, and buttoned his coat.

"Oh well," he said cheerfully, "it's rained on me before. Put 'er in,
Jack my lad, put her in—Tha'rt a rare old cock, Jacky-boy, wi' a belly
40   on thee as does credit to thy drink, if not to thy corn. Co' up, lass, let's

get off ter th' old homestead. Oh my heart, what a wetness in the night! There'll be no volcanoes after this. Hey, Jack, my beautiful young slender feller, which of us is Noah? It seems as though the water-works is bursted. Ducks and ayquatic fowl 'll be king o' the castle at this rate—dove an' olive branch* an' all. Stand up then, gel, stand up, we're not stoppin' here all night, even if you thought we was. I'm dashed if the jumping rain wouldn't make anybody think they was drunk. Hey Jack—does rain-water wash the sense in, or does it wash it out?"

And he laughed to himself at the joke.

He was always ashamed when he had to drive after he had been drinking, always apologetic to the horse. His apologetic frame made him facetious. He was aware of his inability to walk quite straight. Nevertheless his will kept stiff and attentive, in all his fuddledness.

He mounted and bowled off through the gates of the inn-yard. The mare went well, he sat fixed, the rain beating on his face. His heavy body rode motionless in a kind of sleep, one centre of attention was kept fitfully burning, the rest was dark. He concentrated his last attention on the fact of driving along the road he knew so well. He knew it so well, he watched for it attentively, with an effort of will.

He talked aloud to himself, sententious in his anxiety, as if he were perfectly sober, whilst the mare bowled along and the rain beat on him. He watched the rain before the gig-lamps, the faint gleaming of the shadowy horse's body, the passing of the dark hedges.

"It's not a fit night to turn a dog out," he said to himself, aloud. "It's high time as it did a bit of clearing up, I'll be damned if it isn't. It was a lot of use putting those ten loads of cinders on th' road. They'll be washed to kingdom-come if it doesn't alter. Well, it's our Fred's look-out, if they are. He's top-sawyer as far as those things go. I don't see why I should concern myself. They can wash to kingdom-come and back again for what I care. I suppose they *would* be washed back again some day. That's how things are. Th' rain tumbles down just to mount up in clouds again. So they say. There's no more water on the earth than there was in the year naught. That's the story, my boy, if you understand it. There's no more today than there was a thousand years ago—nor no less either. You can't wear water out. No, my boy: it'll give you the go-by. Try to wear it out, and it takes its hook* into vapour, it has its fingers at its nose to you. It turns into cloud and falleth as rain on the just and unjust.* I wonder if I'm the just or the unjust."

He started awake as the trap lurched deep into a rut. And he wakened to the point in his journey. He had travelled some distance since he was last conscious.

But at length he reached the gate, and stumbled heavily down,
5   reeling, gripping fast to the trap. He descended into several inches of water.

"Be damned!" he said angrily. "Be damned to the miserable slop."

And he led the horse washing through the gate. He was quite
10   drunk now, moving blindly, in habit. Everywhere there was water underfoot.

The raised causeway of the house and the farm-stead was dry, however. But there was a curious roar in the night which seemed to be made in the darkness of his own intoxication. Reeling, blinded,
15   almost without consciousness, he carried his parcels and the rug and cushions into the house, dropped them, and went out to put up the horse.

Now he was at home, he was a sleep-walker, waiting only for the moment of activity to stop. Very deliberately and carefully, he led the
20   horse down the slope to the cart-shed. She shied and backed.

"Why wha's amiss?" he hiccupped, plodding steadily on. And he was again in a wash of water, the horse splashed up water as she went. It was thickly dark, save for the gig-lamps, and they lit on a rippling surface of water.

25   "Well that's a knock-out," he said, as he came to the cart-shed, and was wading in six inches of water. But everything seemed to him amusing. He laughed to think of six inches of water being in the cart-shed.

He backed in the mare. She was restive. He laughed at the fun of
30   untackling the mare with a lot of water washing round his feet. He laughed because it upset her. "What's amiss, what's amiss, a drop o' water won't hurt you!" As soon as he had undone the traces, she walked quickly away.

He hung up the shafts and took the gig-lamp. As he came out of
35   the familiar jumble of shafts and wheels in the shed, the water, in little waves, came washing strongly against his legs. He staggered and almost fell.

"Well what the deuce!" he said, staring round at the running water in the black, watery night.

40   He went to meet the running flood, sinking deeper and deeper.

His soul was full of great astonishment. He *had* to go and look where
it came from, though the ground was going from under his feet. He
went on, down towards the pond, shakily. He rather enjoyed it. He
was now knee deep, and the water was pulling heavily. He stumbled,
reeled sickeningly. 5

Fear took hold of him. Gripping tightly to the lamp, he reeled, and
looked round. The water was carrying his feet away, he was dizzy.
He did not know which way to turn. The water was whirling,
whirling, the whole black night was swooping in rings. He swayed
uncertainly at the centre of all the attack, reeling in dismay. In his 10
soul, he knew he would fall.

As he staggered, something in the water struck his legs, and he
fell. Instantly he was in the turmoil of suffocation. He fought in a
black horror of suffocation, fighting, wrestling, but always borne
down, borne inevitably down. Still he wrestled and fought to get 15
himself free, in the unutterable struggle of suffocation, but he always
fell again deeper. Something struck his head, a great wonder of
anguish went over him, then the blackness covered him entirely.

In the utter darkness, the unconscious, drowning body was rolled
along, the waters pouring, washing, filling in the place. The cattle 20
woke up and rose to their feet, the dog began to yelp. And the
unconscious, drowning body was washed along in the black, swirling
darkness, passively.

Mrs Brangwen woke up and listened. With preternaturally sharp
senses she heard the movement of all the darkness that swirled 25
outside. For a moment she lay still. Then she went to the window.
She heard the sharp rain, and the deep running of water. She knew
her husband was outside.

"Fred," she called, "Fred!"

Away in the night was a hoarse, brutal roar of a mass of water 30
rushing downwards.

She went downstairs. She could not understand the multiplied
running of water. Stepping down the step into the kitchen, she put
her foot into water. The kitchen was flooded. Where did it come
from? She could not understand. 35

Water was running in out of the scullery. She paddled through
barefoot, to see. Water was bubbling fiercely under the outer door.
She was afraid. Then something washed against her, something
twined under her foot. It was the riding whip. On the table were the
rug and the cushions and the parcels from the gig. 40

He had come home.

"Tom!" she called, afraid of her own voice.

She opened the door. Water ran in with a horrid sound. Every-where was moving water, a sound of waters.

5   "Tom!" she cried, standing in her nightdress with the candle, calling into the darkness and the flood out of the doorway.

"Tom! Tom!"

And she listened. Fred appeared behind her, in trousers and shirt.

"Where is he?" he asked.

10 He looked at the flood, then at his mother. She seemed small and uncanny, elvish, in her nightdress.

"Go upstairs," he said. "He'll be in th' stable."

"To—om! To—om!" cried the elderly woman, with a long, un-natural, penetrating call that chilled her son to the marrow. He

15 quickly pulled on his boots and his coat.

"Go upstairs, mother," he said, "I'll go an' see where he is."

"To—om! To—o—om!" rang out the shrill, unearthly cry of the small woman. There was only the noise of water and the mooing of uneasy cattle, and the long yelping of the dog, clamouring in the

20 darkness.

Fred Brangwen splashed out into the flood with a lantern. His mother stood on a chair in the doorway, watching him go. It was all water, water, running, flashing under the lantern.

"Tom! Tom! To—o—om!" came her long, unnatural cry, ringing

25 over the night. It made her son feel cold in his soul.

And the unconscious, drowning body of the father rolled on below the house, driven by the black water towards the high-road.

Tilly appeared, a skirt over her nightdress. She saw her mistress clinging on the top of a chair in the open doorway, a candle burning

30 on the table.

"God's sake!" cried the old serving-woman. "The cut's* burst. That embankment's broke down. Whativer are we goin' to do!"

Mrs Brangwen watched her son, and the lantern, go along the upper causeway to the stable. Then she saw the dark figure of a

35 horse: then her son hung the lamp in the stable, and the light shone out faintly on him as he untackled the mare. The mother saw the soft blazed face of the horse thrust forward into the stable-door. The stables were still above the flood. But the water flowed strongly into the house.

40 "It's getting higher," said Tilly. "Hasn't master come in?"

Mrs Brangwen did not hear.

"Isn't he the—ere?" she called, in her far-reaching, terrifying voice.

"No," came the short answer out of the night.

"Go and loo—ok for him." 5

His mother's voice nearly drove the youth mad.

He put the halter on the horse and shut the stable door. He came splashing back through the water, the lantern swinging.

The unconscious, drowning body was pushed past the house in the deepest current. Fred Brangwen came to his mother. 10

"I'll go to th' cart-shed," he said.

"To—om—To—o—om!" rang out the strong, inhuman cry. Fred Brangwen's blood froze, his heart was very angry. He gripped his veins in a frenzy. Why was she yelling like this? He could not bear the sight of her, perched on a chair in her white nightdress in the 15 doorway, elvish and horrible.

"He's taken the mare out of the trap, so he's all right," he said, growling, pretending to be normal.

But as he descended to the cart-shed, he sank into a foot of water. He heard the rushing in the distance, he knew the canal had broken 20 down. The water was running deeper.

The trap was there all right, but no signs of his father. The young man waded down to the pond. The water rose above his knees, it swirled and forced him. He drew back.

"Is he the—e—ere?" came the maddening cry of the mother. 25

"No," was the sharp answer.

"To—om—To—o—om!" came the piercing, free, unearthly call. It seemed high and supernatural, almost pure. Fred Brangwen hated it. It nearly drove him mad. So awfully it sang out, almost like a song.

The water was flowing fuller into the house. 30

"You'd better go up to Beeby's, and bring him and Arthur down, and tell Mrs Beeby to fetch Wilkinson," said Fred to Tilly.

He forced his mother to go upstairs.

"I know your father is drowned," she said, in a curious dismay.

The flood rose through the night, till it washed the kettle off the 35 hob in the kitchen. Mrs Brangwen sat alone at a window upstairs. She called no more. The men were busy with the pigs and the cattle. They were coming with a boat for her.

Towards morning the rain ceased, the stars came out over the noise and the terrifying clucking and trickling of the water. Then 40

there was a pallor in the east, the light began to come. In the ruddy
light of the dawn she saw the waters spreading out, moving
sluggishly, the buildings rising out of a waste of water. Birds began to
sing, drowsily, and as if slightly hoarse with the dawn. It grew
5 brighter. Up the second field was the great, raw gap in the canal
embankment.

Mrs Brangwen went from window to window, watching the flood.
Somebody had brought a little boat. The light grew stronger, the red
gleam was gone off the flood-waters, day took place. Mrs Brangwen
10 went from the front of the house to the back, looking out, intent and
unrelaxing, on the pallid morning of spring.

She saw a glimpse of her husband's buff coat in the floods, as the
water rolled the body against the garden hedge. She called to the
men in the boat. She was glad he was found. They dragged him out
15 of the hedge. They could not lift him into the boat. Fred Brangwen
jumped into the water, up to his waist, and half carried the body of
his father through the flood to the road. Hay and twigs and dirt were
in the beard and hair. The youth pushed through the water crying
loudly without tears, like a stricken animal. The mother at the
20 window cried, making no trouble.

The doctor came. But the body was dead. They carried it up to
Cossethay, to Anna's house.

When Anna Brangwen heard the news, she pressed back her head
and rolled her eyes, as if something were reaching forward to bite at
25 her throat. She pressed back her head, her mind was driven back, to
sleep. Since she had married and become a mother, the girl she had
been was forgotten. Now, the shock threatened to break in upon her
and sweep away all her intervening life, make her as a girl of eighteen
again, loving her father. So she pressed back, away from the shock,
30 she clung to her present life.

It was when they brought him to her house dead and in his wet
clothes, his wet, sodden clothes, fully dressed as he came from
market, yet all sodden and inert, that the shock really broke into her,
and she was terrified. A big, soaked, inert heap, he was, who had
35 been to her the image of power and strong life.

Almost in horror, she began to take the wet things from him, to
pull off him the incongruous market-clothes of a well-to-do farmer.
The children were sent away to the vicarage, the dead body lay on
the parlour floor, Anna quickly began to undress him, laid his fob
40 and seals in a wet heap on the table. Her husband and the woman

helped her. They cleared and washed the body, and laid it on the bed.

There, it looked still and grand. He was perfectly calm in death, and, now he was laid in line, inviolable,* unapproachable. To Anna, he was the majesty of the inaccessible male, the majesty of death. It made her still and awe-stricken, almost glad.

Lydia Brangwen, the mother, also came and saw the impressive, inviolable body of the dead man. She went pale, seeing death. He was beyond change or knowledge, absolute, laid in line with the infinite. What had she to do with him? He was a majestic Abstraction,* made visible now for a moment, inviolate, absolute. And who could lay claim to him, who could speak of him, of the him who was revealed in the stripped moment of transit from life into death? Neither the living nor the dead could claim him, he was both the one and the other, inviolable, inaccessibly himself.

"I shared life with you, I belong in my own way to eternity," said Lydia Brangwen, her heart cold, knowing her own singleness.

"I did not know you in life. You are beyond me, supreme now in death," said Anna Brangwen, awe-stricken, almost glad.

It was the sons who could not bear it. Fred Brangwen went about with a set, blanched face and shut hands, his heart full of hatred and rage for what had been done to his father, bleeding also with desire to have his father again, to see him, to hear him again. He could not bear it.

Tom Brangwen only arrived on the day of the funeral. He was quiet and controlled as ever. He kissed his mother, who was still, dark-faced, inscrutable, he shook hands with his brother without looking at him, he saw the great coffin with its black handles. He even read the name-plate "Tom Brangwen, of the Marsh Farm. Born— Died—."

The good-looking, still face of the young man crinkled up for a moment in a terrible grimace, then resumed its stillness. The coffin was carried round to the church, the funeral bell tanged at intervals, the mourners carried their wreaths of white flowers. The mother, the Polish woman, went with dark, abstract face, on her son's arm. He was good-looking as ever, his face perfectly motionless and somehow pleasant. Fred walked with Anna, she strange and winsome, he with a face like wood, stiff, unyielding.

Only afterwards Ursula, flitting between the currant bushes down the garden, saw her uncle Tom standing in his black clothes, erect

and fashionable, but his fists lifted, and his face distorted, his lips
curled back from his teeth in a horrible grin, like an animal which
grimaces with torment, whilst his body panted quick, like a panting
dog's. He was facing the open distance, panting, and holding still,
5 then panting rapidly again, but his face never changing from its
almost bestial look of torture, the teeth all showing, the nose
wrinkled up, the eyes unseeing, fixed.

Terrified, Ursula slipped away. And when her uncle Tom was in
the house again, grave and very quiet, so that he seemed almost to
10 affect gravity, to pretend grief, she watched his still, handsome face,
imagining it again in its distortion. And she saw the nose was rather
thick, rather Russian, under its transparent skin, she remembered
the teeth under the carefully cut moustache were small and sharp
and spaced. She could see him, in all his elegant demeanour, bestial,
15 almost corrupt. And she was frightened. She never forgot to look for
the bestial, frightening side of him, after this.

He said "good-bye" to his mother and went away at once. Ursula
almost shrank from his kiss, now. She wanted it, nevertheless, and
the little revulsion as well.

20 At the funeral, and after the funeral, Will Brangwen was madly in
love with his wife. The death had shaken him. But death and all
seemed to gather in him into a mad, overwhelming passion for his
wife. She seemed so strange and winsome. He was almost beside
himself with desire for her.

25 And she took him, she seemed ready for him, she wanted him.

The grandmother stayed a while at the Yew Cottage, till the
Marsh was restored. Then she returned to her own rooms, quiet,
and it seemed, wanting nothing. Fred threw himself into the work of
restoring the farm. That his father was killed there seemed to make it
30 only the more intimate and the more inevitably his own place.

There was a saying that the Brangwens always died a violent
death. To them all, except perhaps Tom, it seemed almost natural.
Yet Fred went about obstinate, his heart fixed. He could never
forgive the Unknown this murder of his father.

35 After the death of the father, the Marsh was very quiet. Mrs
Brangwen was unsettled. She could not sit all the evening peacefully,
as she could before, and during the day, she was always rising to her
feet and hesitating, as if she must go somewhere, and were not quite
sure whither.

40 She was seen loitering about the garden, in her little woollen

jacket. She was often driven out in the gig, sitting beside her son and watching the countryside or the streets of the town, with a childish, candid, uncanny face, as if it all were strange to her.

The children, Ursula and Gudrun and Theresa went by the garden gate on their way to school. The grandmother would have them call in each time they passed, she would have them come to the Marsh for dinner. She wanted children about her.

Of her sons, she was almost afraid. She could see the sombre passion and desire and dissatisfaction in them, and she wanted not to see it any more. Even Fred, with his blue eyes and his heavy jaw, troubled her. There was no peace. He wanted something, he wanted love, passion, and he could not find them. But why must he trouble her? Why must he come to her with his seething and suffering and dissatisfactions? She was too old.

Tom was more restrained, reserved. He kept his body very still. But he troubled her even more. She could not but see the black depths of disintegration in his eyes, the sudden glance upon her, as if she could save him, as if he would reveal himself.

And how could age save youth? Youth must go to youth. Always the storm! Could she not lie in peace, these years, in the quiet, apart from life? No, always the swell must heave upon her and break her against the barriers. Always she must be embroiled in the seethe and rage and passion, endless, endless, going on forever. And she wanted to draw away. She wanted at last her own innocence and peace. She did not want her sons to force upon her any more the old, brutal story, of desire and offerings and deep, deep-hidden rage of unsatisfied men against women. She* wanted to be beyond it all, to know the peace and innocence of age.

She had never been a woman to work much. So that now she would stand often at the garden gate, watching the scant world go by. And the sight of children pleased her, made her happy. She had usually an apple or a few sweets in her pocket. She liked children to smile at her.

She never went to her husband's grave. She spoke of him simply, as if he were alive. Sometimes the tears would run down her face, in helpless sadness. Then she recovered, and was herself again, happy.

On wet days, she stayed in bed. Her bedroom was her city of refuge, where she could lie and muse and muse. Sometimes Fred would read to her. But that did not mean much. She had so many dreams to dream over, such an unsifted store. She wanted time.

Her chief friend at this period was Ursula. The little girl and the musing, fragile woman of sixty seemed to understand the same language. At Cossethay all was activity and passion, everything moved upon poles of passion. Then there were four children
5   younger than Ursula, a throng of babies, all the time many lives beating against each other.

So that for the eldest child, the peace of the grandmother's bedroom was exquisite. Here Ursula came as to a hushed, paradisal land, here her own existence became simple and exquisite to her as if
10 she were a flower.

Always on Saturdays she came down to the Marsh, and always clutching a little offering, either a little mat made of strips of coloured, woven paper, or a tiny basket made in the kindergarten* lesson, or a little crayon drawing of a bird.

15 When she appeared in the doorway, Tilly, ancient but still in authority, would crane her skinny neck to see who it was.

"Oh, it's you, is it?" she said. "I thought we should be seein' you. My word, that's a bobby-dazzlin'* posy you've brought!"

It was curious how Tilly preserved the spirit of Tom Brangwen,
20 who was dead, in the Marsh. Ursula always connected her with her grandfather.

This day the child had brought a tight little nosegay of pinks, white ones, with a rim of pink ones. She was very proud of it, and very shy because of her pride.

25 "Your gran'mother's in her bed. Wipe your shoes well if you're goin' up, and don't go burstin' in on her like a sky-rocket. My word, but that's a fine posy! Did you do it all by yourself, an' all?"

Tilly stealthily ushered her into the bedroom. The child entered with a strange, dragging hesitation characteristic of her when she
30 was moved. Her grandmother was sitting up in bed, wearing a little grey woollen jacket.

The child hesitated in silence near the bed, clutching the nosegay in front of her. Her childish eyes were shining. The grandmother's grey eyes shone with a similar light.

35 "How pretty!" she said. "How pretty you have made them! What a darling little bunch."

Ursula, glowing, thrust them into her grandmother's hand, saying: "I made them you."*

"That is how the peasants tied them at home," said the grand-
40 mother, pushing the pinks with her finger, and smelling them. "Just

such tight little bunches! And they make wreaths for their hair—they weave the stalks. Then they go round with wreaths in their hair, and wearing their best aprons."

Ursula immediately imagined herself in this story-land.

"Did you used to have a wreath in your hair, grandmother?" 5

"When I was a little girl, I had golden hair, something like Katie's. Then I used to have a wreath of little blue flowers, oh, so blue, that come when the snow is gone. Andrey, the coachman, used to bring me the very first."

They talked, and then Tilly brought the tea-tray, set for two. 10 Ursula had a special green and gold cup kept for herself at the Marsh. There was thin bread and butter, and cress for tea. It was all special and wonderful. She ate very daintily, with little, fastidious bites.

"Why do you have two wedding-rings, grandmother?—must 15 you?" asked the child, noticing her grandmother's ivory coloured hand with blue veins, above the tray.

"If I had two husbands, child."

Ursula pondered a moment.

"Then must you wear both the rings together?" 20

"Yes."

"Which was my grandfather's ring?"

The woman hesitated.

"This grandfather whom you knew? This was his ring, the red one. The yellow one was your other grandfather's, whom you never 25 knew."

Ursula looked interestedly at the two rings on the proffered finger.

"Where did he buy it you?" she asked.

"This one? In Warsaw, I think."

"You didn't know my own grandfather then?" 30

"Not this grandfather."

Ursula pondered this fascinating intelligence.

"Did he have white whiskers, as well?"

"No, his beard was dark. You have his brows, I think."

Ursula flushed* and became self-conscious. She wanted to go and 35 look at her brows in the mirror. She at once identified herself with her Polish grandfather.

"And did he have brown eyes?"

"Yes, dark eyes. He was a clever man, as quick as a lion. He was never still." 40

Lydia still resented Lensky. When she thought of him, she was always younger than he, she was always twenty, or twenty five, and under his domination. He incorporated her in his ideas as if she were not a person herself, as if she were just his aide-de-camp, or part of
5 his baggage, or one among his surgical appliances. She still resented it. And he was always only thirty: he had died when he was thirty four. She did not feel sorry for him. He was older than she. Yet she still ached in the thought of those days.

"Did you like my first grandfather best?" asked Ursula.
10 "I liked them both," said her grandmother.

And, thinking, she became again Lensky's girl-bride. He was of good family, of better family even than her own, for she was half German. She was a young girl in a house of insecure fortune. And he, an intellectual, a clever surgeon and physician, had loved her.
15 How she had looked up to him! She remembered her first transports when he talked to her, the important young man with the severe black beard. He had seemed so wonderful, such an authority. After her own lax household, his gravity and confident, hard authority seemed almost God-like to her. For she had never known it in
20 her life, all her surroundings had been loose, lax, disordered, a welter.

"Miss Lydia, will you marry me?" he had said to her in German, in his grave, yet tremulous voice. She had been afraid of his dark eyes upon her. They did not see her, they were fixed upon her. And he
25 was hard, confident. She thrilled with the excitement of it, and accepted. During the courtship, his kisses were a wonder to her. She always thought about them, and wondered over them. She never wanted to kiss him back. In her idea, the man kissed, and the woman examined in her soul the kisses she had received.
30 She had never quite recovered from her prostration of the first days, or nights, of marriage. He had taken her to Vienna, and she was utterly alone with him, utterly alone in another world, everything, everything foreign, even he foreign to her. Then came the real marriage, passion came to her, and she became his slave, he was her
35 lord, her lord. She was the girl-bride, the slave, she kissed his feet, she had thought it an honor to touch his body, to unfasten his boots. For two years, she had gone on as his slave, crouching at his feet, embracing his knees.

Children had come, he had followed his ideas. She was there for
40 him just to keep him in condition. She was to him one of the baser or

material conditions necessary for his welfare in prosecuting his
ideas, of nationalism, of liberty, of science.

But gradually, at twenty three, twenty four, she began to realise
that she too might consider these ideas. By his acceptance of her
self-subordination, he exhausted the feeling in her. There were 5
those of his associates who would discuss the ideas with her, though
he did not wish to do so himself. She adventured into the minds of
other men. His, then, was not the only male mind! She did not exist,
then, just as his attribute! She began to perceive the attentions of
other men. An excitement came over her. She remembered now the 10
men who had paid her court, when she was married, in Warsaw.

Then the rebellion broke out, and she was inspired too. She would
go as nurse at her husband's side. He worked like a lion, he wore his
life out. And she followed him helplessly. But she disbelieved in him.
He was so separate, he ignored so much. He counted too much on 15
himself. His work, his ideas—did nothing else matter?

Then the children were dead, and for her, everything became
remote. He became remote. She saw him, she saw him go white
when he heard the news, then frown, as if he thought "*Why* have they
died now, when I have no time to grieve?" 20

"He has no time to grieve," she had said, in her remote, awful
soul. "He has no time. It is so important, what he does! He is then so
self-important, this half-frenzied man! Nothing matters, but this
work of rebellion! He has not time to grieve, nor to think of his
children! He had not time even to beget them, really." 25

She had let him go on alone. But, in the chaos, she had worked by
his side again. And out of the chaos, she had fled with him to
London.

He was a broken, cold man. He had no affection for her nor for
anyone. He had failed in *his* work, so everything had failed. He 30
stiffened himself, and died.

She could not subscribe. He had failed, everything had failed, yet
behind the failure was the unyielding passion of life. The individual
effort might fail, but not the human joy. She belonged to the human
joy. 35

He died, and went his way, but not before there was another child.
And this little Ursula was his grandchild. She was glad of it. For she
still honored him, though he had been mistaken.

She, Lydia Brangwen, was sorry for him now. He was dead—he
had scarcely lived. He had never known her. He had lain with her, 40

but he had never known her. He had never received what she could give him. He had gone away from her empty. So, he had never lived. So, he had died and passed away. Yet there had been strength and power in him.

5 She could scarcely forgive him that he had never lived. If it were not for Anna, and for this little Ursula, who had his brows, there would be no more left of him than of a broken vessel thrown away, and just remembered.

Tom Brangwen had served her. He had come to her, and taken
10 from her. He had died and gone his way into death. But he had made himself immortal in his knowledge with her. So she had her place here, in life, and in immortality. For he had taken his knowledge of her into death, so that she had her place in death. 'In my father's house are many mansions.'*

15 She loved both her husbands. To one she had been a naked little girl-bride, running to serve him. The other she loved out of fulfilment, because he was good and had given her being, because he had served her honorably, and become her man, one with her.

She was established in this stretch of life, she had come to herself.
20 During her first marriage, she had not existed, except through him, he was the substance and she the shadow running at his feet. She was very glad she had come to her own self. She was grateful to Brangwen. She reached out to him in gratitude, into death.

In her heart, she felt a vague tenderness and pity for her first
25 husband, who had been her lord. He was so wrong when he died. She could not bear it, that he had never lived, never really become himself. And he had been her lord! Strange, it all had been! Why had he been her lord? He seemed now so far off, so without bearing on her.

30 "Which did you, grandmother?"

"What?"

"Like best."

"I liked them both. I married the first when I was quite a girl. Then I loved your grandfather when I was a woman. There is a
35 difference."

They were silent for a time.

"Did you cry when my first grandfather died?" the girl asked.

Lydia Brangwen rocked herself on the bed, thinking aloud.

"When we came to England, he hardly ever spoke, he was too
40 much concerned to take any notice of anybody. He grew thinner and

thinner, till his cheeks were hollow and his mouth stuck out. He wasn't handsome any more. I knew he couldn't bear being beaten, I thought everything was lost in the world. Only I had your mother a baby, it was no use my dying.

"He looked at me with his black eyes, almost as if he hated me, when he was ill, and said 'It only wanted this. It only wanted that I should leave you and a young child to starve in this London.' I told him we should not starve. But I was young, and foolish, and frightened, which he knew.

"He was bitter, and he never gave way. He lay beating his brains, to see what he could do. 'I don't know what you will do,' he said. 'I am no good, I am a failure from beginning to end. I cannot even provide for my wife and child.'

"But you see, it was not for him to provide for us. My life went on, though his stopped, and I married your grandfather.

"I ought to have known, I ought to have been able to say to him: 'Don't be so bitter, don't die because this has failed. You are not the beginning and the end.'* But I was too young, he had never let me become myself, I thought he was truly the beginning and the end. So I let him take all upon himself. Yet all did not depend on him. Life must go on, and I must marry your grandfather, and have your uncle Tom, and your uncle Fred. We cannot take so much upon ourselves—"

The child's heart beat fast as she listened to these things. She could not understand, but she seemed to feel far-off things. It gave her a deep, joyous thrill, to know she hailed from far off, from Poland, and that dark-bearded impressive man. Strange, her antecedents were, and she felt fate on either side of her terrible.

Almost every day, Ursula saw her grandmother, and every time, they talked together. Till the grandmother's sayings and stories, told in the complete hush of the Marsh bedroom, accumulated with mystic significance, and became a sort of Bible to the child.

And Ursula asked her deepest childish questions of her grandmother.

"Will somebody love me, grandmother?"

"Many people love you, child. We all love you."

"But when I am grown up, will somebody love me?"

"Yes, some man will love you, child, because it's your nature. And I hope it will be somebody who will love you for what you are, and not for what he wants of you. But we have a right to what we want."

Ursula was frightened, hearing these things. Her heart sank, she felt she had no ground under her feet. She clung to her grandmother. Here was peace and security. Here, from her grandmother's peaceful room, the door opened on to the greater space, the past,

5   which was so big, that all it contained seemed tiny, loves and births and deaths, tiny units and features within a vast horizon. That was a great relief, to know the tiny importance of the individual, within the great past.

Chapter X*

The Widening Circle

It was very burdensome to Ursula, that she was the eldest of the family. By the time she was eleven, she had to take to school Gudrun and Theresa and Catherine. The boy, William, always called Billy, so that he should not be confused with his father, was a lovable, rather delicate child of three, so he stayed at home as yet. There was another baby girl, called Cassandra.

The children went for a time to the little church school just near the Marsh.* It was the only place within reach, and being so small, Mrs Brangwen felt safe in sending her children there, though the village boys did nickname Ursula "Urtler," and Gudrun "Good-runner," and Theresa "Tea-pot."

Gudrun and Ursula were co-mates. The second child, with her long, sleepy body and her endless chain of fancies, would have nothing to do with realities. She was not for them, she was for her own fancies. Ursula was the one for realities. So Gudrun left all such to her elder sister, and trusted in her implicitly, indifferently. Ursula had a great tenderness for her co-mate sister.

It was no good trying to make Gudrun responsible. She floated along like a fish in the sea, perfect within the medium of her own difference and being. Other existences did not trouble her. Only she believed in Ursula, and trusted to Ursula.

The eldest child was very much fretted by her responsibility for the other young ones. Especially Theresa, a sturdy, bold-eyed thing, had a faculty for warfare.

"Our Ursula, Billy Pillins has lugged my hair."

"What did you say to him?"

"I said nothing."

Then the Brangwen girls were in for a feud with the Pillinses, or Phillipses.

"You won't pull my hair again, Billy Pillins," said Theresa, walking with her sisters, and looking superbly at the freckled, red-haired boy.

"Why shan't I?" retorted Billy Pillins.

"You won't because you dursn't," sang the tiresome Theresa.

"You come here then, Tea-pot, an' see if I dursna."

Up marched Tea-pot, and immediately Billy Pillins lugged her black, snaky locks. In a rage she flew at him. Immediately in rushed
5 Ursula and Gudrun, and little Katie, in clashed the other Phillipses, Clem* and Walter, and Eddie Anthony. Then there was a fray. The Brangwen girls were well-grown and stronger than many boys. But for pinafores and long hair, they would have carried easy victories. They went home, however, with hair lugged and pinafores torn. It
10 was a joy to the Phillips boys to rip the pinafores of the Brangwen girls.

Then there was an outcry. Mrs Brangwen *would not* have it, no she would not. All her innate dignity and stand-offishness rose up. Then there was the vicar lecturing the school. "It was a sad thing that the
15 boys of Cossethay could not behave more like gentlemen to the girls of Cossethay. Indeed, what kind of boy was it that should set upon a girl, and kick her, and beat her, and tear her pinafore. That boy deserved severe castigation, and the name of *coward*, for no boy who was not a *coward*—etc. etc."

20 Meanwhile much hang-dog fury in the Pillinses' hearts, much virtue in the Brangwen girls', particularly in Theresa's. And the feud continued, with periods of extraordinary amity, when Ursula was Clem Phillips's sweetheart, and Gudrun was Walter's, and Theresa was Billy's, and even the tiny Katie had to be Eddie Ant'ny's
25 sweetheart. There was the closest union. At every possible moment, the little gang of Brangwens and Phillipses flew together. Yet neither Ursula nor Gudrun could have any real intimacy with the Phillips boys. It was a sort of fiction to them, this alliance and this dubbing of sweethearts.

30 Again Mrs Brangwen rose up.

"Ursula, I *will* not have you raking* the roads with lads, so I tell you. Now stop it, and the rest will stop it."

How Ursula *hated* always to represent the little Brangwen club. She could never be herself, no, she was always Ursula-Gudrun-
35 Theresa-Catherine—and later even Billy was added on to her. Moreover, she did not want the Phillipses either. She was out of taste* with them.

However, the Brangwen-Pillins coalition readily broke down, owing to the unfair superiority of the Brangwens. The Brangwens
40 were rich. They had free access to the Marsh Farm. The school

teachers were almost respectful to the girls, the vicar spoke to them on equal terms. The Brangwen girls presumed, they tossed their heads.

"*You're* not ivrybody, Urtler Brangwin, ugly-mug," said Clem Phillips, his face going very red.

"I'm better than you, for all that," retorted Urtler.

"You *think* you are—wi' a face like that—Ugly-Mug,—Urtler Brangwin," he began to jeer, trying to set all the others in cry against her.

Then there was hostility again. How she *hated* their jeering. She became cold against the Phillipses. Ursula was very proud in her family. The Brangwen girls had all a curious blind dignity, even a kind of nobility in their bearing. By some result of breed and upbringing, they seemed to rush along their own lives without caring that they existed to other people. Never from the start did it occur to Ursula that other people might hold a low opinion of her. She thought that whosoever knew her, knew she was enough and accepted her as such. She thought it was a world of people like herself. She suffered bitterly if she were forced to have a low opinion of any person, and she never forgave that person.

This was maddening to many little people. All their lives, the Brangwens were meeting folk who tried to pull them down, to make them seem little. Curiously, the mother was aware of what would happen, and was always ready to give her children the advantage of the move.

When Ursula was twelve, and the common school and the companionship of the village children, niggardly and begrudging, was beginning to affect her, Anna sent her with Gudrun to the Grammar School in Nottingham.* This was a great release for Ursula. She had a passionate craving to escape from the belittling circumstances of life, the little jealousies, the little differences, the little meannesses. It was a torture to her that the Phillipses were poorer and meaner than herself, that they used mean little reservations, took petty little advantages. She wanted to be with her equals: but not by diminishing herself.* She *did* want Clem Phillips to be her equal. But by some puzzling, painful fate or other, when he was really there with her, he produced in her a tight feeling in the head. She wanted to beat her forehead, to escape.

Then she found, that the way to escape was easy. One departed from the whole circumstance. One went away to the Grammar

School, and left the little school, the meagre teachers, the Phillipses whom she had tried to love but who had made her fail, and whom she could not forgive. She had an instinctive fear of petty people, as a deer is afraid of dogs. Because she was blind, she could not calculate
5 nor estimate people. She must think that everybody was just like herself.

She measured by the standard of her own people: her father and mother, her grandmother, her uncles. Her beloved father, so utterly simple in his demeanour, yet with his strong, dark soul fixed like a
10 root in unexpressed depths that fascinated and terrified her: her mother, so strangely free of all money and convention and fear, entirely indifferent to the world, standing by herself, without connection: her grandmother, who had come from so far and was centred in so wide an horizon: people must come up to these
15 standards before they could be Ursula's people.

So even as a girl of twelve she was glad to burst the narrow boundary of Cossethay, where only limited people lived. Outside, was all vastness, and a throng of real, proud people whom she would love.

20 Going to school by train, she must leave home at a quarter to eight in the morning, and she did not arrive again till half past five at evening. Of this she was glad, for the house was small and overfull. It was a storm of movement, whence there had been no escape. She hated so much being in charge.

25 The house was a storm of movement. The children were healthy and turbulent, the mother only wanted their animal well-being. To Ursula, as she grew a little older, it became a nightmare. When she saw, later, a Rubens picture with storms of naked babies, and found this was called "Fecundity,"* she shuddered, and the word became
30 abhorrent to her. She knew as a child what it was to live amidst storms of babies, in the heat and welter of fecundity. And as a child, she was against her mother, passionately against her mother; she craved for some spirituality and stateliness.

In bad weather, home was a bedlam. Children dashed in and out
35 of the rain, to the puddles under the dismal yew-trees, across the wet flagstones of the kitchen, whilst the cleaning-woman grumbled and scolded; children were swarming on the sofa, children were kicking the piano in the parlour, to make it sound like a bee-hive, children were rolling on the hearthrug, legs in air, pulling a book in two
40 between them, children, fiendish, ubiquitous, were stealing upstairs

to find out where our Ursula was, whispering at bedroom doors, hanging on the latch, calling mysteriously "Ursula!" "Ursula!" to the girl who had locked herself in to read. And it was hopeless. The locked door excited their sense of mystery, she had to open to dispel the lure. Then children hung on to her with round-eyed, excited 5 questions.

The mother flourished amid all this.

"Better have them noisy than ill," she said.

But the growing girls, in turn, suffered bitterly. Ursula was just coming to the stage when Andersen and Grimm were being left 10 behind for the "Idylls of the King"* and romantic love-stories.

> "Elaine the fair, Elaine the lovable,
> Elaine the lily maid of Astolat,
> High in her chamber in a tower to the east
> Guarded the sacred shield of Launcelot."   15

How she loved it! How she leaned in her bedroom window with her black, rough hair on her shoulders, and her warm face all rapt, and gazed across at the churchyard and the little church, which was a turretted castell,* whence Launcelot would ride just now, would wave to her as he rode by, his scarlet cloak passing behind the dark 20 yew-trees and between the open space: whilst she, Ah she, would remain the lonely maid high up and isolated in the tower, polishing the terrible shield, weaving it a covering with a true device, and waiting, waiting, always remote and high.

At which point there would be a faint scuffle on the stairs, a 25 high-pitched whispering outside the door, and a creaking of the latch: then Billy, excited, whispering:

"It's locked—it's locked."

Then the knocking, kicking at the door with childish knees, and the urgent, childish: 30

"Ursula—our Ursula? Ursula? Eh, our Ursula?"

No reply.

"Ursula! Eh—our Ursula?" the name was shouted now.

Still no answer.

"Mother, she won't answer," came the yell. "She's dead."   35

"Go away—I'm not dead. What do you want?" came the angry voice of the girl.

"Open the door, our Ursula," came the complaining cry.

It was all over. She must open the door. She heard the screech of the bucket downstairs dragged across the flagstones as the woman washed the kitchen floor. And the children were prowling in the bedroom, asking:

"What were you doing? What had you locked the door for?"

Then she discovered the key of the parish room, and betook herself there, and sat on some sacks with her books. There began another dream.

She was the only daughter of the old lord, she was gifted with magic. Day followed day of rapt silence, whilst she wandered ghostlike in the hushed, ancient mansion, or flitted along the sleeping terraces.

Here a grave grief attacked her: that her hair was dark. She *must* have fair hair and a white skin. She was rather bitter about her black mane.

Never mind, she would dye it when she grew up, or bleach it in the sun, till it was bleached fair. Meanwhile she wore a fair white coif of pure Venetian lace.*

She flitted silently along the terraces, where jewelled lizards basked upon the stone, and did not move when her shadow fell upon them. In the utter stillness she heard the tinkle of the fountain, and smelled the roses whose blossoms hung rich and motionless. So she drifted, drifted on the wistful feet of beauty, past the water and the swans, to the noble park, where, underneath a great oak, a doe all dappled lay with four fine feet together, her fawn nestling sun-coloured beside her.

Oh, and this doe was her familiar. It would talk to her, because she was a magician, it would tell her stories as if the sunshine spoke.

Then one day, she left the door of the parish room unlocked, careless and unheeding as she always was; the children found their way in, Katie cut her finger and howled, Billy hacked notches in the fine chisels, and did much damage. There was a great commotion.

The crossness of the mother was soon finished. Ursula locked up the room again, and considered all was over. Then her father came in with the notched tools, his forehead knitted.

"Who the deuce opened the door?" he cried in anger.

"It was Ursula who opened the door," said the mother.

He had a duster in his hand. He turned and flapped the cloth hard across the girl's face. The cloth stung, for a moment the girl was as if stunned. Then she remained motionless, her face closed and stubborn. But her heart was blazing. In spite of herself the tears surged higher, in spite of her they surged higher.

In spite of her, her face broke, she made a curious gulping grimace, and the tears were falling. So she went away, desolate. But her blazing heart was fierce and unyielding. He watched her go, and a pleasurable pain filled him, a sense of triumph and easy power, followed immediately by acute pity.

"I'm sure that was unnecessary—to hit the girl across the face," said the mother coldly.

"A flip with a duster won't hurt her," he said.

"Nor will it do her any good."

For days, for weeks, Ursula's heart burned from this rebuff. She felt so cruelly vulnerable. Did he not know how vulnerable she was, how exposed and wincing? He, of all people, knew. And he wanted to do this to her. He wanted to hurt her right through her closest sensitiveness, he wanted to treat her with shame, to maim her with insult.

Her heart burnt in isolation, like a watchfire lighted. She did not forget, she did not forget, she never forgot. When she returned to her love for her father, the seed of mistrust and defiance burned unquenched, though covered up far from sight. She no longer belonged to him unquestioned. Slowly, slowly, the fire of mistrust and defiance burned in her, burned away her connection with him.

She ran a good deal alone, having a passion for all moving, active things. She loved the little brooks. Wherever she found a little running water, she was happy. It seemed to make her run and sing in spirit along with it. She could sit for hours by a brook or stream, on the roots of the alders, and watch the water hasten dancing over the stones, or among the twigs of a fallen branch. Sometimes, little fish vanished before* they had become real, like hallucinations, sometimes wagtails ran by the water's brink, sometimes other little birds came to drink. She saw a kingfisher darting blue—and then she was very happy. The kingfisher was the key to the magic world: he was witness of the order of enchantment.

But she must move out of the intricately woven illusion of her life: the illusion of a father whose life was an Odyssey in an outer world; the illusion of her grandmother, of realities so shadowy and far-off that they became as mystic symbols:—peasant-girls with wreaths of blue flowers in their hair, the sledges and the depth of winter; the dark-bearded young grandfather, marriage and war and death; then

the multitude of illusions concerning herself, how she was truly a
princess of Poland, how in England she was under a spell, she was
not really this Ursula Brangwen; then the mirage of her reading: out
of the multicoloured illusion of this her life, she must move on, to the
5   Grammar School in Nottingham.

She was shy, and she suffered. For one thing, she bit her nails, and
had a cruel consciousness in her finger-tips, a shame, an exposure.
Out of all proportion, this shame haunted her. She spent hours of
torture, conjuring how she might keep her gloves on: if she might say
10 her hands were scalded, if she might seem to forget to take off her
gloves.

For she was going to inherit her own estate, when she went to the
High School.* There, each girl was a lady. There, she was going to
walk amongst free souls, her co-mates and her equals, and all petty
15 things would be put away. Ah, if only she did not bite her nails! If
only she had not this blemish! She wanted so much to be perfect—
without spot or blemish,* living the high, noble life.

It was a grief to her that her father made such a poor introduction.
He was brief as ever, like a boy saying his errand, and his clothes
20 looked ill-fitting and casual. Whereas Ursula would have liked robes
and a ceremonial of introduction to this her new estate.

She made a new illusion of school. Miss Grey, the head-mistress,
had a certain silvery, school-mistressy beauty of character. The
school itself had been a gentleman's house. Dark, sombre lawns
25 separated it from the dark, select avenue. But its rooms were large
and of good appearance, and from the back, one looked over lawns
and shrubbery, over the trees and the grassy slope of the Arboretum,
to the town which heaped the hollow with its roofs and cupolas and
its shadows.

30 So Ursula seated herself upon the hill of learning, looking down
on the smoke and confusion and the manufacturing, engrossed
activity of the town. She was happy. Up here, in the Grammar
School, she fancied the air was finer, beyond the factory smoke. She
wanted to learn Latin and Greek and French and mathematics. She
35 trembled like a postulant when she wrote the Greek alphabet for the
first time.

She was upon another hill-slope,* whose summit she had not
scaled. There was always the marvellous eagerness in her heart, to
climb and to see beyond. A Latin verb was virgin soil to her: she
40 sniffed a new odour in it; it meant something, though she did not

know what it meant. But she gathered it up: it was significant. When she knew that:

$$x^2 - y^2 = (x+y)(x-y)$$

then she felt that she had grasped something, that she was liberated into an intoxicating air, rare and unconditioned. And she was very glad as she wrote her French exercise:

"J'ai donné le pain à mon petit frère."*

In all these things there was the sound of a bugle to her heart, exhilarating, summoning her to perfect places. She never forgot her brown "Longman's First French Grammar," nor her "Via Latina"* with its red edges, nor her little grey Algebra book. There was always a magic in them.

At learning, she was quick, intelligent, instinctive, but she was not "thorough." If a thing did not come to her intuitively, she could not learn it. And then, her mad rage of loathing for all lessons, her bitter contempt of all teachers and school-mistresses, her recoil to a fierce, animal arrogance made her detestable.

She was a free, unabateable animal, she declared in her revolts: there was no law for her, nor any rule. She existed for herself alone. Then ensued a long struggle with everybody, in which she broke down at last, when she had run the full length of her resistance, and sobbed her heart out, desolate; and afterwards, in a chastened, washed-out, bodiless state, she received the understanding that would not come before, and went her way sadder and wiser.

Ursula and Gudrun went to school together. Gudrun was a shy, quiet, wild creature, a thin slip of a thing hanging back from notice or twisting past to disappear into her own world again. She seemed to avoid all contact, instinctively, and pursued her own intent way, pursuing half formed fancies that had no relation to anyone else.

She was not clever at all. She thought Ursula clever enough for two. Ursula understood, so why should she, Gudrun, bother herself? The younger girl lived her religious, responsible life in her sister, by proxy. For herself, she was indifferent and intent as a wild animal, and as irresponsible.

When she found herself at the bottom of the class, she laughed, lazily, and was content, saying she was safe now. She did not mind her father's chagrin nor her mother's twinge of mortification.

"What do I pay for you to go to Nottingham for?" her father asked, exasperated.

"Well Dad, you know you needn't pay for me," she replied, nonchalant. "I'm ready to stop at home."

She was happy at home, Ursula was not. Slim and unwilling abroad, Gudrun was easy in her own house as a wild thing in its lair.
5   Whereas Ursula, attentive and keen abroad, at home was reluctant, uneasy, unwilling to be herself, or unable.

Nevertheless Sunday remained the maximum day of the week for both. Ursula turned passionately to it, to the sense of eternal security it gave. She suffered anguish of fears during the week-days, for she
10 felt strong powers that would not recognise her. There was upon her always a fear and a dislike of authority. She felt she could always do as she wanted if she managed to avoid a battle with Authority and the authorised Powers. But if she gave herself away, she would be lost, destroyed. There was always the menace against her.

15 This strange sense of cruelty and ugliness always imminent, ready to seize hold upon her, this feeling of the grudging power of the mob lying in wait for her, who was the exception, formed one of the deepest influences of her life. Wherever she was, at school, among friends, in the street, in the train, she instinctively abated
20 herself, made herself smaller, feigned to be less than she was, for fear that her undiscovered self should be seen, pounced upon, attacked by brutish resentment of the commonplace, the average Self.

She was fairly safe at school, now. She knew how to take her place
25 there, and how much of herself to reserve. But she was free only on Sundays. When she was but a girl of fourteen, she began to feel a resentment growing against her in her own home. She knew she was the disturbing influence there. But as yet, on Sundays, she was free, really free, free to be herself, without fear or misgiving.

30 Even at its stormiest, Sunday was a blessed day. Ursula woke to it with a feeling of immense relief. She wondered why her heart was so light. Then she remembered:—it was Sunday. A gladness seemed to burst out around her, a feeling of great freedom. The whole world was for twenty four hours revoked, put back. Only the Sunday world
35 existed.

She loved the very confusion of the household. It was lucky if the children slept till seven o'clock. Usually, soon after six, a chirp was heard, a voice, an excited chirrup began, announcing the creation of a new day, there was a thudding of quick little feet, and the children
40 were up and about, scampering in their shirts, with pink legs and

glistening, flossy hair all clean from the Saturday night's bathing, their souls excited by their bodies' cleanliness.

As the house began to teem with rushing, half naked clean children, one of the parents rose, either the mother, easy and slatternly, with her thick, dark hair loosely coiled and slipping over one ear, or the father, warm and comfortable, with ruffled black hair and shirt unbuttoned at the neck.

Then the girls upstairs heard the continual:

"Now then Billy, what are you up to?" in the father's strong, vibrating voice; or the mother's dignified:

"I have said, Cassie, I will not have it."

It was amazing how the father's voice could ring out like a gong, without his being in the least moved, and how the mother could speak like a queen holding an audience, though her blouse was sticking out all round and her hair was not fastened up and the children were yelling a pandemonium.

Gradually breakfast was produced, and the elder girls came down into the babel, whilst half naked children flitted round like the wrong ends of cherubs, as Gudrun said, watching the bare little legs and the chubby tails appearing and disappearing.

Gradually the young ones were captured, and nightdresses finally removed, ready for the clean Sunday shirt. But before the Sunday shirt was slipped over the fleecy head, away darted the naked body, to wallow in the sheep-skin which formed the parlour rug, whilst the mother walked after, protesting sharply, holding the shirt like a noose, and the father's bronze voice rang out, and the naked child wallowing on its back in the deep sheep-skin announced gleefully:

"I'm bading in the sea, mother."

"Why should I walk after you with your shirt?" said the mother. "Get up now."

"I'm bading in the sea, mother," repeated the wallowing, naked figure.

"We say bathing, not bading," said the mother, with her strange, indifferent dignity. "I am waiting here with your shirt."

At length shirts were on, and stockings were paired, and little trousers buttoned and little petticoats tied behind. The besetting cowardice of the family was its shirking of the garter question.

"Where are your garters, Cassie?"

"I don't know."

"Well look for them."

But not one of the elder Brangwens would really face the situation. After Cassie had grovelled under all the furniture and blacked up all her Sunday cleanliness, to the infinite grief of everybody, the garter was forgotten in the new washing of the young face and hands.

5   Later, Ursula would be indignant to see Miss Cassie marching into church from Sunday school with her stocking sluthered* down to her ankle, and a grubby knee showing.

"It's disgraceful!" cried Ursula at dinner. "People will think we're pigs, and the children are *never* washed."

10   "Never mind what people think," said the mother superbly. "*I* see that the child is bathed properly, and if I satisfy myself I satisfy everybody. She can't keep her stocking up and no garter, and it isn't the child's fault she was let to go without one."

The garter trouble continued in varying degrees, but till each
15 child wore long skirts or long trousers, it was not removed.

On this day of decorum, the Brangwen family went to church by the high-road, making a detour outside all the garden-hedge, rather than climb the wall into the churchyard. There was no law of this, from the parents. The children themselves were the wardens of the
20 Sabbath decency, very jealous and instant with each other.

It came to be, gradually, that after church on Sundays the house was really something of a sanctuary, with peace breathing like a strange bird alighted in the rooms. Indoors, only reading and tale-telling and quiet pursuits, such as drawing, were allowed. Out of
25 doors, all playing was to be carried on unobtrusively. If there were noise, yelling and shouting, then some fierce spirit woke up in the father and the elder children, so that the younger were subdued, afraid of being excommunicated.

The children themselves preserved the Sabbath. If Ursula in her
30 vanity sang:

"Il était un' bergère
Et ron-ron-ron petit patapon,"*

Theresa was sure to cry:
"*That's* not a Sunday song, our Ursula."
35   "You don't know," replied Ursula, superior. Nevertheless, she wavered. And her song faded down before she came to the end.

Because, though she did not know it, her Sunday was very precious to her. She found herself in a strange, undefined place, where her spirit could wander in dreams, unassailed.

The white-robed spirit of Christ passed between olive trees.* It was a vision, not a reality. And she herself partook of the visionary being. There was a voice in the night calling "Samuel, Samuel!"* And still the voice called in the night. But not this night, nor last night, but in the unfathomed night of Sunday, of the Sabbath silence.

There was Sin, the serpent, in whom was also wisdom. There was Judas with the money and the kiss.*

But there was no *actual* Sin. If Ursula slapped Theresa across the face, even on a Sunday, that was not Sin, the everlasting. It was misbehaviour. If Billy played truant from Sunday school, he was bad, he was wicked, but he was not a Sinner.

Sin was absolute and everlasting: wickedness and badness were temporary and relative. When Billy, catching up the local jargon, called Cassie a "sinner," everybody detested him. Yet when there came to the Marsh a flippetty-floppetty fox-hound puppy, he was mischievously christened "Sinner."

The Brangwens shrank from applying their religion to their own immediate actions. They wanted the sense of the eternal and immortal, not a list of rules for everyday conduct. Therefore they were badly-behaved children, head-strong and arrogant, though their feelings were generous. They had moreover—intolerable to their ordinary neighbours—a proud gesture, that did not fit with the jealous idea of the democratic Christian.* So that they were always extraordinary, outside of the ordinary.

How bitterly Ursula resented her first acquaintance with evangelical teachings.* She got a peculiar thrill from the application of salvation to her own personal case. "Jesus died for *me*, He suffered for me." There was a pride and a thrill in it, followed almost immediately by a sense of dreariness. Jesus with holes in His hands and feet: it was distasteful to her. The shadowy Jesus with the Stigmata: that was her own vision. But Jesus the actual man, talking with teeth and lips, telling one to put one's finger into His wounds,* like a villager gloating in his sores, repelled her. She was enemy of those who insisted on the humanity of Christ. If He were just a man, living in ordinary human life, then she was indifferent.

But it was the jealousy of vulgar people which must insist on the humanity of Christ. It was the vulgar mind which would allow nothing extra-human, nothing beyond itself to exist. It was the dirty, desecrating hands of the revivalists* which wanted to drag Jesus into this everyday life, to dress Jesus up in trousers and frock coat, to compel Him to a vulgar equality of footing. It was the impudent suburban soul which would ask, "What would Jesus do, if He were in my shoes?"

5   Against all this, the Brangwens stood at bay. If anyone, it was the mother who was caught by, or who was most careless of the vulgar clamour.* She would have nothing extra-human. She never really subscribed, all her life, to Brangwen's mystical passion.

But Ursula was with her father. As she became adolescent,
10 thirteen, fourteen, she set more and more against her mother's practical indifference. To Ursula, there was something callous, almost wicked in her mother's attitude. What did Anna Brangwen, in these years, care for God or Jesus or Angels? She was the immediate life of today. Children were still being born to her, she was throng*
15 with all the little activities of her family. And almost instinctively she resented her husband's slavish service to the Church, his dark, subject hankering to worship an unseen God. What did the unrevealed God matter, when a man had a young family that needed fettling* for? Let him attend to the immediate concerns of his life, not
20 go projecting himself towards the ultimate.

But Ursula was all for the ultimate. She was always in revolt against babies and muddled domesticity. To her, Jesus was another world, He was not of this world. He did not thrust His hands under her face and, pointing to the wounds, say:
25 "Look, Ursula Brangwen, I got these for your sake. Now do as you're told."

To her, Jesus was beautifully remote, shining in the distance, like a white moon at sunset, a crescent moon beckoning as it follows the sun, out of our ken. Sometimes dark clouds standing very far off,
30 pricking up into a clear yellow band of sunset, of a winter evening, reminded her of Calvary,* sometimes the full moon rising blood-red upon the hill terrified her with the knowledge that Christ was now dead, hanging heavy and dead on the Cross.

On Sundays, this visionary world came to pass. She heard the long
35 hush, she knew the marriage of dark and light was taking place. In church, the Voice sounded re-echoing not from this world, as if the church itself were a shell that still spoke the language of creation.

"The Sons of God saw the daughters of men that they were fair; and they took them wives of all which they chose.
40 "And the Lord said, My spirit shall not always strive with Man, for

that he also is flesh; yet his days shall be an hundred and twenty years.

"There were giants in the earth in those days; and also after that, when the Sons of God came in unto the daughters of men, and they bare children unto them, the same became mighty men which were 5 of old, men of renown."*

Over this Ursula was stirred as by a call from far off. In those days, would not the Sons of God have found her fair, would she not have been taken to wife by one of the Sons of God? It was a dream that frightened her, for she could not understand it. 10

Who were the sons of God? Was not Jesus the only begotten Son?* Was not Adam the only man created from God? Yet there were men not begotten by Adam. Who were these, and whence did they come? They too must derive from God. Had God many offspring, besides Adam and besides Jesus, children whose origin the children of 15 Adam cannot recognise? And perhaps these children, these sons of God, had known no expulsion, no ignominy of the fall.

These came on free feet to the daughters of men, and saw they were fair, and took them to wife, so that the women conceived and brought forth men of renown. This was a genuine fate. She moved 20 about in the essential days, when the Sons of God came in unto the daughters of men.

Nor would any comparison of myths* destroy her passion in the knowledge. Jove had become a bull, or a man, in order to love a mortal woman. He had begotten in her a giant, a hero.* 25

Very good, so he had, in Greece. For herself, she was no Grecian woman. Not Jove nor Pan nor any of those gods, not even Bacchus nor Apollo, could come to her. But the Sons of God who took to wife the daughters of men, these were such as should take her to wife. 30

She clung to the secret hope, the aspiration. She lived a dual life, one where the facts of daily life encompassed everything, being legion, and the other wherein the facts of daily life were superseded by the eternal truth. So utterly did she desire the Sons of God should come to the daughters of men; and she believed more in her desire 35 and its fulfilment than in the obvious facts of life. The fact that a man was a man, did not state his descent from Adam, did not exclude that he was also one of the unhistoried, unaccountable Sons of God. As yet, she was confused, but not denied.

Again she heard the Voice: 40

"It is easier for a camel to go through the eye of a needle, than for a rich man to enter into heaven."*

But it was explained, the needle's eye was a little gateway for foot-passengers, through which the great, humped camel with his load could not possibly squeeze himself: or perhaps, at a great risk, if he were a little camel, he might get through. For one could not absolutely exclude the rich man from heaven, said the Sunday School teacher.

It pleased her also to know, that in the East one must use hyperbole, or else remain unheard; because the Eastern man must see a thing swelling to fill all heaven, or dwindled to a mere nothing, before he is suitably impressed. She immediately sympathised with this Eastern mind.

Yet the words continued to have a meaning that was untouched either by the knowledge of gateways or hyperboles. The historical, or local, or psychological interest in the words was another thing. There remained unaltered the inexplicable value of the saying. What was this relation between a needle's eye, a rich man, and heaven? What sort of a needle's eye, what sort of a rich man, what sort of heaven? Who knows? It means the Absolute World, and can never be more than half interpreted in terms of the relative world.

But must one apply the speech literally? Was her father a rich man? Couldn't he get to heaven? Or was he only a half-rich man? Or was he nearly a poor man? At any rate, unless he gave everything away to the poor,* he would find it much harder to get to heaven. The needle's eye would be tight for him. She almost wished he were penniless poor. If one were coming to the base of it, any man was rich who was not as poor as the poorest.

She had her qualms, when in imagination she saw her father giving away their piano and the two cows, and the capital at the bank, to the laborers of the district, so that they, the Brangwens, should be as poor as the Wherrys. And she did not want it. She was impatient.

"Very well," she thought, "we'll forego that heaven,* that's all—at any rate the needle's eye sort." And she dismissed the problem. She was *not* going to be as poor as the Wherrys, not for all the sayings on earth—the miserable squalid Wherrys.

So she reverted to the non-literal application of the scriptures.

Her father very rarely read, but he had collected many books of reproductions, and he would sit and look at these, curiously intent, like a child, yet with a passion that was not childish. He loved the early Italian painters, but particularly Giotto and Fra Angelico and Filippo Lippi. The great compositions cast a spell over him. How many times had he turned to Raphael's "Dispute of the Sacrament" or Fra Angelico's "Last Judgment"* or the beautiful, complicated renderings of the Adoration of the Magi,* and always, each time, he 5 received the same gradual fulfilment of delight. It had to do with the establishment of a whole mystical, architectural conception which used the human figure as a unit. Sometimes he had to hurry home, and go to the Fra Angelico "Last Judgment." The pathway of open graves, the huddled earth on either side, the seemly heaven arrayed 10 above, the singing progress to paradise on the one hand, the stuttering descent to hell on the other, completed and satisfied him. He did not care whether or not he believed in devils or angels. The whole conception gave him the deepest satisfaction, and he wanted nothing more. 15

Ursula, accustomed to these pictures from her childhood, hunted out their detail. She adored Fra Angelico's flowers and light and angels, she liked the demons and enjoyed the hell. But the representation of the encircled God, surrounded by all the angels on high, suddenly bored her. The figure of the Most High bored her, and 20 roused her resentment. Was this the culmination and the meaning of it all, this draped, null figure? The angels were so lovely, and the light so beautiful. And only for this, to surround such a banality for God!

She was dissatisfied, but not fit as yet to criticise. There was yet so much to wonder over. Winter came, pine branches were torn down 25 in the snow, the green pine needles looked rich upon the ground. There was the wonderful, starry, straight track of a pheasant's foot-steps across the snow, imprinted so clear; there was the lobbing mark of the rabbit, two holes abreast, two holes following behind; the hare shoved deeper shafts, slanting, and his two hind feet came down 30 together and made one large pit; the cat podded little holes, and birds made a lacy pattern.

Gradually there gathered the feeling of expectation. Christmas was coming. In the shed, at nights, a secret candle was burning, a sound of veiled voices was heard. The boys were learning the old 35 mystery play of St George and Beelzebub. Twice a week, by lamplight, there was choir practice in the church, for the learning of old carols Brangwen wanted to hear. The girls went to these practices. Everywhere was a sense of mystery and rousedness. Everybody was preparing for something. 40

The time came near, the girls were decorating the church, with cold fingers binding holly and fir and yew about the pillars, till a new spirit was in the church, the stone broke out into dark, rich leaf, the arches put forth their buds, and cold flowers rose to blossom in the
5   dim, mystic atmosphere. Ursula must weave mistletoe over the door, and over the screen, and hang a silver dove from a sprig of yew, till dusk came down, and the church was like a grove.

In the cow-shed the boys were blacking their faces for a dress-rehearsal; the turkey hung dead, with opened, speckled wings, in the
10 dairy. The time was come to make pies, in readiness.

The expectation grew more tense. The star was risen* into the sky, the songs, the carols were ready to hail it. The star was the sign in the sky. Earth too should give a sign. As evening drew on, hearts beat fast with anticipation, hands were full of ready gifts. There were the
15 tremulously expectant words of the church service, the night was past and the morning was come, the gifts were given and received, joy and peace made a flapping of wings in each heart, there was a great burst of carols, the Peace of the World* had dawned, strife had passed away, every hand was linked in hand, every heart was singing.
20   It was bitter, though, that Christmas day, as it drew on to evening, and night, became a sort of bank holiday,* flat and stale. The morning was so wonderful, but in the afternoon and evening the ecstasy perished like a nipped thing, like a bud in a false spring. Alas, that Christmas was only a domestic feast, a feast of sweetmeats and
25 toys! Why did not the grown-ups also change their everyday hearts, and give way to ecstasy? Where was the ecstasy?

How passionately the Brangwens craved for it, the ecstasy. The father was troubled, dark-faced and disconsolate, on Christmas night, because the passion was not there, because the day was
30 become as every day, and hearts were not aflame. Upon the mother was a kind of absentness, as ever, as if she were exiled for all her life. Where was the fiery heart of joy, now the coming was fulfilled; where was the star, the Magis' transport,* the thrill of new being that shook the earth?
35   Still it was there, even if it were faint and inadequate. The cycle of creation still wheeled in the Church year. After Christmas, the ecstasy slowly sank and changed. Sunday followed Sunday, trailing a fine movement, a finely developed transformation over the heart of the family. The heart that was big with joy, that had seen the star and
40 had followed to the inner walls of the Nativity, that there had

swooned in the great light,* must now feel the light slowly withdraw-
ing, a shadow falling, darkening. The chill crept in, silence came
over the earth, and then all was darkness. The veil of the temple was
rent, each heart gave up the ghost,* and sank dead.

They moved quietly, a little wanness on the lips of the children, at 5
Good Friday, feeling the shadow upon their hearts. Then, pale with
a deathly scent, came the lilies of resurrection, that shone coldly till
the Comforter was given.*

But why the memory of the wounds and the death? Surely Christ
rose with healed hands and feet, sound and strong and glad? Surely 10
the passage of the cross and the tomb was forgotten? But no—always
the memory of the wounds, always the smell of grave-cloths? A small
thing was Resurrection, compared with the Cross and the death, in
this cycle.

So the children lived the year of Christianity, the epic of the soul 15
of mankind. Year by year the inner, unknown drama went on in
them, their hearts were born and came to fulness, suffered on the
cross, gave up the ghost, and rose again to unnumbered days,
untired, having at least this rhythm of eternity in a ragged, inconsequential life. 20

But it was becoming a mechanical action now, this drama: birth at
Christmas for death at Good Friday. On Easter Sunday the life-
drama was as good as finished. For the Resurrection was shadowy
and overcome by the shadow of death, the Ascension* was scarce
noticed, a mere confirmation of death. 25

What was the hope and the fulfilment? Nay, was it all only a
useless after-death, a wan, bodiless after-death? Alas, and alas for
the passion of the human heart, that must die so long before the body
was dead.

For from the grave, after the passion and the trial of anguish, the 30
body rose torn and chill and colourless. Did not Christ say 'Mary!'
and when she turned with outstretched hands to Him, did He not
hasten to add 'Touch me not; for I am not yet ascended to my
father.'*

Then how could the hands rejoice, or the heart be glad, seeing 35
themselves repulsed. Alas, for the resurrection of the dead body!
Alas, for the wavering, glimmering appearance of the risen Christ.
Alas, for the Ascension into heaven, which is a shadow within death,
a complete passing away.

Alas, that so soon the drama is over; that life is ended at thirty 40

three;* that the half of the year of the soul is cold and historiless! Alas
that a risen Christ has no place with us! Alas, that the memory of the
passion of Sorrow and Death and the Grave holds triumph over the
pale fact of Resurrection!

5   But why? Why shall I not rise with my body whole and perfect,
shining with strong life? Why, when Mary says: Rabboni,* shall I not
take her in my arms and kiss her and hold her to my breast? Why is
the risen body deadly, and abhorrent with wounds?

The Resurrection is to life, not to death.* Shall I not see those who
10   have risen again walk here among men perfect in body and spirit,
whole and glad in the flesh, living in the flesh, loving in the flesh,
begetting children in the flesh, arrived at last to wholeness, perfect
without scar or blemish, healthy without fear of ill-health? Is this not
the period of manhood and of joy and fulfilment, after the Resurrec-
15   tion? Who shall be shadowed by Death and the Cross, being risen,
and who shall fear the mystic, perfect flesh that belongs to heaven?

Can I not, then, walk this earth in gladness,* being risen from
sorrow? Can I not eat with my brother happily, and with joy kiss my
beloved, after my resurrection, celebrate my marriage in the flesh
20   with feastings, go about my business eagerly, in the joy of my fellows?
Is heaven impatient for me, and bitter against this earth, that I should
hurry off, or that I should linger pale and untouched? Is the flesh
which was crucified become as poison to the crowds in the street, or
is it as a strong gladness and hope to them, as the first flower
25   blossoming out of the earth's humus?

Chapter XI

First Love

As Ursula passed from girlhood towards womanhood, gradually the
cloud of self-responsibility gathered upon her. She became aware of
herself, that she was a separate entity in the midst of an unseparated
obscurity, that she must go somewhere, she must become something. And she was afraid, troubled. Why, oh why must one grow up,
why must one inherit this heavy, numbing responsibility of living an
undiscovered life? Out of the nothingness and the undifferentiated
mass, to make something of oneself! But what? In the obscurity and
pathlessness, to take a direction! But whither? How take even one
step? And yet, how stand still? This was torment indeed, to inherit
the responsibility of one's own life.

The religion which had been another world for her, a glorious sort
of play-world, where she lived, climbing the tree with the short-
statured man, walking shakily on the sea like the disciple, breaking
the bread into five thousand portions, like the Lord,* giving a great
picnic to five thousand people, now fell away from reality, and
became a tale, a myth, an illusion, which, however much one might
assert it to be true in historical fact, one knew was not true—at least,
for this present-day life of ours. There could, within the limits of this
life we know, be no Feeding of Five Thousand. And the girl had
come to the point where she held that that which one cannot
experience in daily life is not true for oneself.

So, the old duality of life, wherein there had been a week-day
world of people and trains and duties and reports, and besides that a
Sunday world of absolute truth and living mystery, of walking upon
the waters and being blinded by the face of the Lord,* of following
the pillar of cloud across the desert and watching the bush that
crackled yet did not burn away, this old, unquestioned duality
suddenly was found to be broken apart. The week-day world had
triumphed over the Sunday world. The Sunday world was not real,
or at least, not actual. And one lived by action.

Only the week-day world mattered. She herself, Ursula
Brangwen, must know how to take the week-day life. Her body must

263

be a week-day body, held in the world's estimate. Her soul must have a week-day value, known according to the world's knowledge.

Well then, there was a week-day life to live, of action and deeds. And so there was a necessity to choose one's action and one's deeds.
5 One was responsible to the world for what one did.

Nay, one was more than responsible to the world. One was responsible to oneself. There was some puzzling, tormenting residue of the Sunday world within her, some persistent Sunday self, which insisted upon a relationship with the now shed-away vision
10 world. How could one keep up a relationship with that which one denied? Her task was now to learn the week-day life.

How to act, that was the question? Whither to go, how to become oneself? One was not oneself, one was merely a half-stated question. How to become oneself, how to know the question and the answer of
15 oneself, when one was merely an unfixed something-nothing, blowing about like the winds of heaven, undefined, unstated.

She turned to the visions, which had spoken far-off words that ran along the blood like ripples of an unseen wind, she heard the words again, she denied the vision, for she must be a week-day person, to
20 whom visions were not true, and she demanded only the week-day meaning of the words.

There *were* words spoken by the vision: and words must have a week-day meaning, since words were week-day stuff. Let them speak now: let them bespeak themselves in week-day terms. The
25 vision should translate itself into week-day terms.

"Sell all thou hast, and give to the poor,"* she heard on Sunday morning. That was plain enough, plain enough for Monday morning too. As she went down the hill to the station, going to school, she took the saying with her.
30 "Sell all thou hast, and give to the poor."

Did she want to do that? Did she want to sell her pearl-backed brush and mirror, her silver candlestick, her pendant, her lovely little necklace, and go dressed in drab like the Wherrys: the unlovely, uncombed Wherrys, who were "the poor" to her? She did not.
35 She walked this Monday morning on the verge of misery. For she *did* want to do what was right. And she *didn't* want to do what the gospels said. She didn't want to be poor—really poor. The thought was a horror to her: to live like the Wherrys, so ugly, to be at the mercy of everybody!
40 "Sell that thou hast, and give to the poor."

One could not do it, in real life. How dreary and hopeless it made her!

Nor could one turn the other cheek.* Theresa slapped Ursula on the face. Ursula, in a mood of Christian humility, silently presented the other side of her face. Which Theresa, in exasperation at the challenge, also hit. Whereupon Ursula, with boiling heart, went meekly away.

But anger and deep, writhing shame tortured her, so she was not easy till she had again quarrelled with Theresa and had almost shaken her sister's head off.

"That'll teach *you*," she said grimly.

And she went away, unChristian but clean.

There was something unclean and degrading about this humble side of Christianity. Ursula suddenly revolted to the other extreme.

"I hate the Wherrys, and I wish they were dead. Why does my father leave us in the lurch like this, making us be poor and insignificant? Why is he not more? If we had a father as he ought to be, he would be Earl William Brangwen, and I should be the Lady Ursula. What right have *I** to be poor, crawling along the lane like vermin? If I had my rights, I should be seated on horseback in a green riding-habit, and my groom would be behind me. And I should stop at the gates of the cottages, and inquire of the cottage woman who came out with a child in her arms, how did her husband, who had hurt his foot. And I would pat the flaxen head of the child, stooping from my horse, and I would give her a shilling from my purse, and order nourishing food to be sent from the hall to the cottage."

So she rode in her pride. And sometimes, she dashed into flames to rescue a forgotten child; or she dived into the canal locks, and supported a boy who was seized with cramp; or she swept up a toddling infant from the feet of a runaway horse: always imaginatively, of course.

But in the end there returned the poignant yearning from the Sunday world. As she went down in the morning from Cossethay, and saw Ilkeston smoking blue and tender upon its hill, then her heart surged with far-off words:

"Oh Jerusalem Jerusalem—how often would I have gathered thy children together as a hen gathereth her chickens under her wings, and ye would not—"*

The passion rose in her, for Christ, for the gathering under the wings of security and warmth. But how did it apply to the week-day

world? What could it mean, but that Christ should clasp her to his
breast, as a mother clasps her child? And Oh, for Christ, for him who
could hold her to his breast and lose her there. Oh, for the breast of
Man, where she should have refuge and bliss for ever! All her senses
5 quivered with passionate yearning.

Vaguely, she knew that Christ meant something else: that in the
vision world, He* spoke of Jerusalem, something that did not exist in
the everyday world. It was not houses and factories He would hold in
His bosom: nor householders nor factory-workers nor poor people:
10 but something that had no part in the week-day world, not seen nor
touched with week-day hands and eyes.

Yet she *must* have it in week-day terms—she must. For all her life
was a week-day life, now, this was the whole. So he must gather her
body to his breast, that was strong with a broad bone, and which
15 sounded with the beating of the heart, and which was warm with this
life of which she partook, the life of the running blood.

So she craved for the breast of the Son of Man,* to lie there. And
she was ashamed in her soul, ashamed. For whereas Christ spoke for
the Vision to answer, she answered from the week-day fact. It was a
20 betrayal, a transference of meaning, from the vision world, to the
matter-of-fact world. So she was ashamed of her religious ecstasy,
and dreaded lest anyone should see it.

Early in the year, when the lambs came, and shelters were built of
straw, and on her uncle's farm the men sat at night with a lantern and
25 a dog, then again there swept over her this passionate confusion
between the vision world and the week-day world. Again she felt
Jesus in the countryside. Ah, he would lift up the lambs in his arms!*
Ah, and she was the lamb. Again, in the morning, going down the
lane, she heard the ewe call, and the lambs came running, shaking
30 and twinkling with new-born bliss. And she saw them stooping,
nuzzling, groping to the udder, to find the teats, whilst the mother
turned her head gravely and sniffed her own. And they were sucking,
vibrating with bliss on their little, long legs, their throats stretched
up, their new bodies quivering to the stream of blood-warm, loving
35 milk.

Oh, and the bliss, the bliss! She could scarcely tear herself away to
go to school. The little noses nuzzling at the udder, the little bodies
so glad and sure, the little black legs crooked, the mother standing
still, yielding herself to their quivering attraction—then the mother
40 walked calmly away.

Jesus—the vision world—the everyday world—all mixed inextric-
ably in a confusion of pain and bliss. It was almost agony, the
confusion, the inextricability. Jesus, the vision, speaking to her, who
was non-visionary! And she would take His words of the spirit and
make them to pander to her own carnality.   5

This was a shame to her. The confusing of the spirit world with
the material world, in her own soul, degraded her. She answered the
call of the spirit in terms of immediate, everyday desire.

"Come unto me, all ye that labour and are heavy laden, and I will
give you rest."*   10

It was the temporal answer she gave. She leapt with sensuous
yearning, to respond to Christ. If she could go to him really, and lay
her head on his breast, to have comfort, to be made much of,
caressed like a child!

All the time she walked in a confused heat of religious yearning.   15
She wanted Jesus to love her deliciously, to take her sensuous
offering, to give her sensuous response. For weeks she went in a
muse of enjoyment.

And all the time she knew underneath that she was playing false,
accepting the passion of Jesus for her own physical satisfaction. But   20
she was in such a daze, such a tangle. How could she get free?

She hated herself, she wanted to trample on herself, destroy
herself. How could one become free? She hated religion, because it
lent itself to her confusion. She abused everything. She wanted to
become hard, indifferent, brutally callous to everything but just the   25
immediate need, the immediate satisfaction. To have a yearning
towards Jesus, only that she might use him to pander to her own soft
sensation, use him as a means of re-acting upon herself, maddened
her in the end. There was then no Jesus, no sentimentality. With all
the bitter hatred of helplessness she hated sentimentality.   30

At this period came the young Skrebensky. She was nearly sixteen
years old, a slim, smouldering girl, deeply reticent, yet lapsing into
unreserved expansiveness now and then, when she seemed to give
away her whole soul, but when in fact she only made another
counterfeit of her soul for outward presentation. She was sensitive in   35
the extreme, always tortured, always affecting a callous indifference
to screen herself.

She was at this time a nuisance on the face of the earth, with her
spasmodic passion and her slumberous torment. She seemed to go
with all her soul in her hands, yearning, to the other person. Yet all   40

the while, deep at the bottom of her, was a childish antagonism of mistrust. She thought she loved everybody and believed in everybody. But because she could not love herself nor believe in herself, she mistrusted everybody with the mistrust of a serpent or a captured
5 bird.* Her starts of revulsion and hatred were more inevitable than her impulses to love.

So she wrestled through her dark days of confusion, soulless, uncreated, unformed.

One evening, as she was studying in the parlour, her head buried
10 in her hands, she heard new voices in the kitchen speaking. At once, from its apathy, her excitable spirit started and strained to listen. It seemed to crouch, to lurk under cover, tense, glaring forth unwilling to be seen.

There were two strange men's voices, one soft and candid, veiled
15 with soft candour, the other veiled with easy mobility, running quickly. Ursula sat quite tense, shocked out of her studies, lost. She listened all the time to the sound of the voices, scarcely heeding the words.

The first speaker was her uncle Tom. She knew the naïve candour
20 covering the girding and savage misery of his soul. Who was the other speaker, whose voice ran on so easy, yet with an inflamed pulse? It seemed to hasten and urge her forward, that other voice.

"I remember you," the young man's voice was saying. "I remember you from the first time I saw you, because of your dark eyes and
25 fair face."

Mrs Brangwen laughed, shy and pleased.

"You were a curly-headed little lad," she said.

"Was I? Yes, I know. They were very proud of my curls."

And a laugh ran to silence.

30 "You were a very well-mannered lad, I remember," said her father.

"Oh! Did I ask you to stay the night? I always used to ask people to stay the night. I believe it was rather trying for my mother."

There was a general laugh. Ursula rose. She had to go.

35 At the click of the latch everybody looked round. The girl hung in the doorway, seized with a moment's fierce confusion. She was going to be good-looking. Now, she had an attractive gawkiness, as she hung a moment, not knowing how to carry her shoulders. Her dark hair was tied behind, her yellow-brown eyes shone without direction.

Behind her, in the parlour, was the soft light of a lamp upon open books.

A superficial readiness took her to her uncle Tom, who kissed her, greeting her with warmth, making a show of intimate possession of her, and at the same time leaving evident his own complete detach- 5 ment.

But she wanted to turn to the stranger. He was standing back a little, waiting. He was a young man with very clear greyish eyes that waited until they were called upon, before they took expression. 10

Something in his self-possessed waiting moved her, and she broke into a confused, rather beautiful laugh as she gave him her hand, catching her breath like an excited child. His hand closed over hers very close, very near, he bowed, and his eyes were watching her with some attention. She felt proud, her spirit leapt to life. 15

"You don't know Mr Skrebensky, Ursula," came her uncle Tom's intimate voice. She lifted her face with an impulsive flash to the stranger, as if to declare a knowledge, laughing her palpitating, excited laugh.

His eyes became confused with roused lights, his detached 20 attention changed to a readiness for her. He was a young man of twenty one, with a slender figure and soft brown hair brushed up in the German fashion straight from his brow.

"Are you staying long?" she asked.

"I've got a month's leave," he said, glancing at Tom Brangwen. 25 "But I've various places I must go to—put in some time here and there."

He brought her a strong sense of the outer world. It was as if she were set on a hill and could feel, vaguely, the whole world lying spread before her. 30

"What have you a month's leave from?" she asked.

"I'm in the Engineers*—in the army."

"Oh!" she exclaimed, glad.

"We're taking *you* away from your studies," said her uncle Tom.

"Oh no," she replied quickly. 35

Skrebensky laughed, young and inflammable.

"She won't wait to be taken away," said her father.

But that seemed clumsy. She wished he would leave her to say her own things.

"Don't you like study?" asked Skrebensky, turning to her, putting the question from his own case.

"I like some things," said Ursula. "I like Latin and French—and grammar."

5 He watched her, and all his being seemed attentive to her, then he shook his head.

"I don't," he said. "They say all the brains of the army are in the Engineers. I think that's why I joined them—to get the credit of other people's brains."

10 He said this quizzically and with chagrin. And she became alert to him. It interested her. Whether he had brains or not, he was interesting. His directness attracted her, his independent motion. She was aware of the movement of his life over against her.

"I don't think brains matter," she said.

15 "What does matter then?" came her uncle Tom's intimate, caressing, half-jeering voice.

She turned to him.

"It matters whether people have courage or not," she said.

"Courage for what?" asked her uncle.

20 "For everything."

Tom Brangwen gave a sharp little laugh. The mother and father sat silent, with listening faces. Skrebensky waited. She was speaking for him.

"Everything's nothing," laughed her uncle.

25 She disliked him at that moment.

"She doesn't practise what she preaches," said her father, stirring in his chair and crossing one leg over the other. "She has courage for mighty little."

But she would not answer. Skrebensky sat still, waiting. His face
30 was irregular, almost ugly, flattish, with a rather thick nose. But his eyes were pellucid, strangely clear, his brown hair was soft and thick as silk, he had a slight moustache. His skin was fine, his figure slight, beautiful. Beside him, her uncle Tom looked full-blown, her father seemed uncouth. Yet he reminded her of her father, only he was
35 finer, and he seemed to be shining. And his face was almost ugly.

He seemed simply acquiescent in the fact of his own being, as if he were beyond any change or question. He was himself. There was a sense of fatality about him that fascinated her. He made no effort to prove himself to other people. Let it be accepted for what it was, his
40 own being. In its isolation it made no excuse or explanation for itself.

So he seemed perfectly, even fatally established, he did not ask to be rendered before he could exist, before he could have relationship with another person.

This attracted Ursula very much. She was so used to unsure people who took on a new being with every new influence. Her uncle 5 Tom was always more or less what the other person would have him. In consequence, one never knew the real uncle Tom, only a fluid, unsatisfactory flux with a more or less consistent appearance.

But, let Skrebensky do what he would, betray himself entirely, he betrayed himself always upon his own responsibility. He permitted 10 no question about himself. He was irrevocable in his isolation.

So Ursula thought him wonderful, he was so finely constituted, and so distinct, self-contained, self-supporting. This, she said to herself, was a gentleman, he had a nature like fate, the nature of an aristocrat.* 15

She laid hold on him at once for her dreams. Here was one such as those Sons of God who saw the daughters of men, that they were fair. He was no son of Adam. Adam was servile. Had not Adam been driven cringing* out of his native place, had not the human race been a beggar ever since, seeking its own being. But Anton Skrebensky 20 could not beg. He was in possession of himself, of that, and no more. Other people could not really give him anything nor take anything from him. His soul stood alone.

She knew that her mother and father acknowledged him. The house was changed. There had been a Visit paid to the house. Once 25 three angels stood in Abraham's doorway,* and greeted him, and stayed and ate with him, leaving his household enriched for ever when they went.

The next day she went down to the Marsh according to invitation. The two men were not come home. Then, looking through the 30 window, she saw the dog-cart drive up and Skrebensky leapt down. She saw him draw himself together, jump, laugh to her uncle, who was driving, then come towards her, to the house. He was so spontaneous and revealed in his movements. He was isolated within his own clear, fine atmosphere, and as still as if fated. 35

His resting in his own fate gave him an appearance of indolence, almost of languor: he made no exuberant movement. When he sat down, he seemed to go loose, languid.

"We are a little late," he said.

"Where have you been?" 40

"We went to Derby to see a friend of my father's."

"Who?"

It was an adventure to her to put direct questions and get plain answers. She knew she might do it with this man.

5   "Why, he is a clergyman too—he is my guardian—one of them."

Ursula knew that Skrebensky was an orphan.

"Where is really your home, now?" she asked.

"My home?—I wonder. I am very fond of my colonel—Colonel Hepburn: then there are my aunts: but my real home, I suppose, is

10   the army."

"Do you like being on your own?"

His clear, greenish grey eyes rested on her a moment, and, as he considered, he did not see her.

"I suppose so," he said. "You see my father—well, he was never

15   acclimatised here. He wanted—I don't know what he wanted, but it was a strain. And my mother—I always knew she was too good to me. I could feel her being too good to me—my mother! Then I went away to school so early. And I must say, the outside world was always more naturally a home to me than the vicarage—I don't know why."

20   "Do you feel like a bird blown out of its own latitude?"* she asked, using a phrase she had met.

"No—no. I find everything very much as I like it."

He seemed more and more to give her a sense of the vast world, a sense of distances and large masses of humanity. It drew her as a

25   scent draws a bee from afar. But also it hurt her.

It was summer, and she wore cotton frocks. The third time he saw her she had on a dress with fine blue and white stripes, with a white collar, and a large white hat. It suited her golden, warm complexion.

"I like you best in that dress," he said, standing with his head

30   slightly on one side, and appreciating her in a perceiving, critical fashion.

She was thrilled with a new life. For the first time, she was in love with a vision of herself: she saw as it were a fine little reflection of herself in his eyes. And she must act up to this: she must be

35   beautiful. Her thoughts turned swiftly to clothes, her passion was to make a beautiful appearance. Her family looked on in amazement at the sudden transformation of Ursula. She became elegant, really elegant, in figured cotton frocks she made for herself, and hats she bent to her fancy. An inspiration was upon her.

40   He sat with a sort of languor in her grandmother's rocking chair,

rocking slowly, languidly backward and forward, as Ursula talked to him.

"You are not poor, are you?" she said.

"Poor in money? I have about a hundred and fifty a year of my own—so I am poor or rich, as you like. I am poor enough, in fact." 5

"But you will earn money?"

"I shall have my pay—I have my pay now. I've got my commission. That is another hundred and fifty."

"You will have more though."

"I shan't have more than £200 a year for ten years to come. I shall 10 always be poor, if I have to live on my pay."

"Do you mind?"

"Being poor? Not now—not very much. I may later. People—the officers, are good to me. Colonel Hepburn has a sort of fancy for me—he is a rich man, I suppose." 15

A chill went over Ursula. Was he going to sell himself, in some way?

"Is Colonel Hepburn married?"

"Yes—with two daughters."

But she was too proud at once to care whether Colonel Hepburn's 20 daughter wanted to marry him or not.

There came a silence. Gudrun entered, and Skrebensky still rocked languidly in the chair.

"You look very lazy," said Gudrun.

"I am lazy," he answered. 25

"You look really floppy," she said.

"I am floppy," he answered.

"Can't you stop?" asked Gudrun.

"No—it's the *perpetuum mobile.*"*

"You look as if you hadn't a bone in your body." 30

"That's how I like to feel."

"I don't admire your taste."

"That's my misfortune."

And he rocked on.

Gudrun seated herself behind him, and as he rocked back, she 35 caught his hair between her finger and thumb, so that it tugged him as he swung forward again. He took no notice. There was only the sound of the rockers on the floor. In silence, like a crab, Gudrun caught a strand of his hair each time he rocked back. Ursula flushed, and sat in some pain. She saw the irritation gathering on his brow. 40

At last he leapt up, suddenly, like a steel spring going off, and stood on the hearthrug.

"Damn it, *why* can't I rock?" he asked petulantly, fiercely.

Ursula loved him for his sudden, steel-like start out of the languor.

5   He stood on the hearthrug fuming, his eyes gleaming with anger.

Gudrun laughed in her deep, mellow fashion.

"Men don't rock themselves," she said.

"Girls don't pull men's hair," he said.

Gudrun laughed again.

10 Ursula sat amused, but waiting. And he knew Ursula was waiting for him. It roused his blood. He had to go to her, to follow her call.

Once he drove her to Derby in the dog-cart. He belonged to the horsey set of the sappers.* They had lunch in an inn, and went through the market, pleased with everything. He bought her a copy

15 of "Wuthering Heights"* from a book-stall. Then they found a little fair in progress, and she said:

"My father used to take me in the swingboats."

"Did you like it?" he asked.

"Oh, it was fine!" she said.

20 "Would you like to go now?"

"Love it," she said, though she was afraid. But the prospect of doing an unusual, exciting thing was too attractive for her.

He went straight to the stand, paid the money, and helped her to mount. He seemed to ignore everything but just what he was doing.

25 Other people were mere objects of indifference to him. She would have liked to hang back, but she was more ashamed to retreat from him than to expose herself to the crowd or to dare the swingboat. His eyes laughed, and standing before her with his sharp, sudden figure, he set the boat swinging. She was not afraid, she was thrilled. His

30 colour flushed, his eyes shone with a roused light, and she looked up at him, her face like a flower in the sun, so bright and attractive. So they rushed through the bright air, up at the sky as if flung from a catapult, then falling terribly back. She loved it. The motion seemed to fan their blood to fire, they laughed, feeling like flames.

35 After the swingboats, they went on the roundabouts to calm down, he twisting astride on his jerky wooden steed, towards her, and always seeming at his ease, enjoying himself. A zest of antagonism to the convention made him fully himself. As they sat on the whirling carousel, with the music grinding out, she was aware of the people on

40 the earth outside, and it seemed that he and she were riding

carelessly over the faces of the crowd, riding forever buoyantly, proudly, gallantly over the upturned faces of the crowd, moving on a higher level, spurning the common mass.

When they must descend and walk away, she was unhappy, feeling like a giant suddenly cut down to ordinary level, at the mercy of the 5 mob.

They left the fair, to return for the dog-cart. Passing the large church,* Ursula must look in. But the whole interior was filled with scaffolding, fallen stone and rubbish were heaped on the floor, bits of plaster crunched underfoot, and the place re-echoed to the calling of 10 secular voices and to blows of the hammer.

She had come to plunge in the utter gloom and peace for a moment, bringing all her yearning, that had returned on her uncontrolled after the reckless riding over the face of the crowd, in the fair. After pride, she wanted comfort, solace, for pride and scorn 15 seemed to hurt her most of all.

And she found the immemorial gloom full of bits of falling plaster and dust of floating plaster, smelling of old lime, having scaffolding and rubbish heaped about, dust cloths over the altar.

"Let us sit down a minute," she said. 20

They sat unnoticed in the back pew, in the gloom, and she watched the dirty, disorderly work of bricklayers and plasterers. Workmen in heavy boots walked grinding down the aisles, calling out in a vulgar accent:

"Hi, mate, has them corner mouldin's come?" 25

There were shouts of coarse answer from the roof of the church. The place echoed desolate.

Skrebensky sat close to her. Everything seemed wonderful, if dreadful, to her, the world tumbling into ruins, and she and he clambering unhurt, lawless over the face of it all. He sat close to her, 30 touching her, and she was aware of his influence upon her. But she was glad. It excited her to feel the press of him upon her, as if his being were urging her to something.

As they drove home, he sat near to her. And when he swayed to the cart, he swayed in a voluptuous, lingering way, against her, lingering 35 as he swung away to recover balance. Without speaking, he took her hand across, under the wrap, and with his unseeing face lifted to the road, his soul intent, he began with his one hand to unfasten the buttons of her glove, to push back her glove from her hand, carefully, laying bare her hand. And the close-working, instinctive subtlety of 40

his fingers upon her hand sent the young girl mad with voluptuous
delight. His hand was so wonderful, intent as a living creature
skilfully pushing and manipulating in the dark underworld, removing her glove and laying bare her palm, her fingers. Then his hand
5 closed over hers, so firm, so close, as if the flesh knitted to one thing,
his hand and hers. Meanwhile his face watched the road and the ears
of the horse, he drove with steady attention through the villages, and
she sat beside him, rapt, glowing, blinded with a new light. Neither
of them spoke. In outward attention they were entirely separate. But
10 between them was the compact of his flesh with hers, in the hand-
clasp.

Then, in a strange voice, affecting nonchalance and superficiality,
he said to her:

"Sitting in the church there reminded me of Ingram."

15 "Who is Ingram?" she asked.

She also affected calm superficiality. But she knew that something
forbidden was coming.

"He is one of the other men with me down at Chatham—a
subaltern—but a year older than I am."

20 "And why did the church remind you of him?"

"Well—he had a girl in Rochester, and they always sat in a
particular corner in the cathedral for their love-making."

"How nice!" she cried impulsively.

They misunderstood each other.

25 "It had its disadvantages, though. The verger made a row about
it."

"What a shame! Why shouldn't they sit in a cathedral?"

"I suppose they all think it a profanity—except you and Ingram
and the girl."

30 "I don't think it a profanity—I think it's right, to make love in a
cathedral."

She said this almost defiantly, in despite of her own soul.

He was silent.

"And was she nice?"

35 "Who, Emily? Yes, she was rather nice. She was a milliner, and
she wouldn't be seen in the streets with Ingram. It was rather sad,
really, because the verger spied on them, and got to know their
names, and then made a regular row. It was a common tale
afterwards."

40 "What did she do?"

"She went to London, into a big shop. Ingram still goes up to see her."

"Does he love her?"

"It's a year and a half he's been with her now."

"What was she like?"

"Emily? Little, shy-violet sort of girl with nice eyebrows."

Ursula meditated this. It seemed like real romance of the outer world.

"Do all the men have lovers?" she asked, amazed at her own temerity. But her hand was still fastened with his, and his face still had the same unchanging fixity of outward calm.

"They're always mentioning some amazing fine woman or other, and getting drunk to talk about her. Most of them dash up to London the moment they are free."

"What for?"

"To some amazing fine woman or other."

"What sort of women?"

"Various. Her name changes pretty frequently, as a rule. One of the fellows is a perfect maniac. He keeps a suit-case always ready, and the instant he is at liberty, he bolts with it to the station, and changes in the train. No matter who is in the carriage, off he whips his tunic, and performs at least the top half of his toilet."

Ursula quivered, and wondered.

"Why is he in such a hurry?" she asked.

Her throat was becoming hard and difficult.

"He's got a woman in his mind, I suppose."

She was chilled, hardened. And yet this world of passions and lawlessness was fascinating to her. It seemed to her a splendid recklessness. Her adventure in life was beginning. It seemed very splendid.

That evening she stayed at the Marsh till after dark, and Skrebensky escorted her home. For she could not go away from him. And she was waiting, waiting for something more.

In the warm of the early night, with the shadows new about them, she felt in another, harder, more beautiful, less personal world. Now a new state should come to pass.

He walked near to her, and with the same silent, intent approach, put his arm round her waist, and softly, very softly, insidiously, drew her to him, till his arm was hard and pressed in upon her; she seemed to be carried along, floating, her feet scarce touching the ground,

borne upon the firm, moving surface of his body, upon whose side she seemed to lie, in a delicious swoon of motion. And whilst she swooned, his face bent nearer to her, her head was leaned on his shoulder, she felt his warm breath on her face. Then softly, oh softly,
5 so softly that she seemed to faint away, his lips touched her cheek, and she drifted through strands of heat and darkness.

Still, she waited, in her swoon and her drifting, waited, like the Sleeping Beauty in the story. She waited, and again his face was bent to hers, his lips came warm on her face, their footsteps lingered and
10 ceased, they stood still under the trees, whilst his lips waited on her face, waited like a butterfly that does not move on a flower. She pressed her breast a little nearer to him, he moved, put both his arms round her, and drew her close.

And then, in the darkness, he bent to her mouth, softly, and
15 touched her mouth with his mouth. She was afraid, she lay still on his arms, feeling his lips on her lips. She kept still, helpless. Then his mouth drew near, pressing open her mouth, a hot, drenching surge rose within her, she opened her lips to him, in pained, poignant eddies she drew him nearer, she let him come further, his lips came
20 and surging, surging, soft, oh soft, yet oh, like the powerful surge of water, irresistible, till with a little blind cry, she broke away.

She heard him breathing heavily, strangely, beside her. A terrible and magnificent sense of his strangeness possessed her. But she shrank a little now, within herself. Hesitating, they continued to walk
25 on, quivering like shadows under the ash-trees of the hill, where her grandfather had walked with his daffodils to make his proposal, and where her mother had gone with her young husband, walking close upon him as Ursula was now walking upon Skrebensky.

Ursula was aware of the dark limbs of the trees stretching over-
30 head, clothed with leaves, and of fine ash-leaves tressing the summer night.

They walked with their bodies moving in complex unity, close together. He held her hard, and they went the long way round by the road, to be further. Always she felt as if she were supported off her
35 feet, as if her feet were light as little breezes in motion.

He would kiss her again—but not again that night with the same, deep-reaching kiss. She was aware now, aware of what a kiss might be. And so, it was more difficult to come to him.

She went to bed feeling all warm with electric warmth, as if the
40 gush of dawn were within her, upholding her. And she slept deeply,

sweetly, oh, so sweetly. In the morning she felt sound as an ear of wheat, fragrant and firm and full.

They continued to be lovers, in the first, wondering state of unrealisation. Ursula told nobody: she was entirely lost in her own world.

Yet some strange affectation made her seek for a spurious confidence. She had at school a quiet, meditative, serious-souled friend called Ethel, and to Ethel must Ursula confide the story. Ethel listened absorbedly, with bowed, unbetraying head, whilst Ursula told her secret. Oh, it was so lovely, his gentle, delicate way of making love! Ursula talked like a practised lover.

"Do you think," asked Ursula, "it is wicked to let a man kiss you—*real* kisses, not flirting?"

"I should think," said Ethel, "it depends."

"He kissed me under the ash-trees on Cossethay hill—do you think it was wrong?"

"When?"

"On Thursday night when he was seeing me home—but real kisses—real—. He is an officer in the army."

"What time was it?" asked the deliberate Ethel.

"I don't know—about half past nine."

There was a pause.

"*I* think it's wrong," said Ethel, lifting her head with impatience. "You don't *know* him."

She spoke with some contempt.

"Yes I do. He is half a Pole, and a Baron too. In England he is equivalent to a Lord. My grandmother was his father's friend."

But the two friends were hostile. It was as if Ursula *wanted* to divide herself from her acquaintances, in asserting her connection with Anton, as she now called him.

He came a good deal to Cossethay, because her mother was fond of him. Anna Brangwen became something of a *grande dame* with Skrebensky, very calm, taking things for granted.

"Aren't the children in bed?" cried Ursula petulantly as she came in with the young man.

"They will be in bed in half an hour," said her mother.

"There is *no* peace," cried Ursula.

"The children must *live*, Ursula," said her mother.

And Skrebensky was against Ursula in this. Why should she be so insistent?

But then, as Ursula knew, he did not have the perpetual tyranny of young children about him. He treated her mother with great courtliness, to which Mrs Brangwen returned an easy, friendly hospitality. Something pleased the girl in her mother's calm assump-

5   tion of state. It seemed impossible to abate Mrs Brangwen's position. She could never be beneath anyone in public relation. Between Brangwen and Skrebensky there was an unbridgeable silence. Sometimes the two men made a slight conversation, but there was no interchange. Ursula rejoiced to see her father retreating into himself

10   against the young man.

She was proud of Skrebensky in the house. His lounging, languorous indifference irritated her and yet cast a spell over her. She knew it was the outcome of a spirit of *laisser-aller* combined with profound young vitality. Yet it irritated her deeply.

15   Notwithstanding, she was proud of him as he lounged in his lambent fashion in her home, he was so attentive and courteous to her mother and to herself all the time. It was wonderful to have his awareness in the room. She felt rich and augmented by it, as if she were the positive attraction and he the flow towards her. And his

20   courtesy and his agreement might be all her mother's, but the lambent flicker of his body was for herself. She held it.

She must even prove her power.

"I meant to show you my little wood-carving," she said.

"I'm sure it's not worth showing, that," said her father.

25   "Would you like to see it?" she asked, leaning towards the door.

And his body had risen from the chair, though his face seemed to want to agree with her parents.

"It is in the shed," she said.

And he followed her out of the door, whatever his feelings might

30   be.

In the shed they played at kisses, really played at kisses. It was a delicious, exciting game. She turned to him, her face all laughing, like a challenge. And he accepted the challenge at once. He twined his hand full of her hair, and gently, with his hand wrapped round

35   with hair behind her head, gradually brought her face nearer to his, whilst she laughed breathless with challenge, and his eyes gleamed with answer, with enjoyment of the game. And he kissed her, asserting his will over her, and she kissed him back, asserting her deliberate enjoyment of him. Daring and reckless and dangerous

40   they knew it was, their game, each playing with fire, not with love. A

sort of defiance of all the world possessed her in it—she would kiss him just because she wanted to. And a dare-devilry in him, like a cynicism, a cut at everything he pretended to serve, retaliated in him.

She was very beautiful then, so wide opened, so radiant, so palpitating, exquisitely vulnerable and poignantly, wrongly throwing herself to risk. It roused a sort of madness in him. Like a flower shaking and wide opened in the sun, she tempted him and challenged him, and he accepted her challenge, something went fixed in him. And under all her laughing, poignant, reckless, was the quiver of tears. That almost sent him mad, mad with desire, with pain, whose only issue was through possession of her body.

So, shaken, afraid, they went back to her parents in the kitchen, and dissimulated. But something was roused in both of them that they could not now allay. It intensified and heightened their senses, they were more vivid and powerful in their being. But under it all, was a poignant sense of transience. It was a magnificent self-assertion on the part of both of them, he asserted himself before her, he felt himself infinitely male and infinitely irresistible, she asserted herself before him, she knew herself infinitely desirable and hence infinitely strong. And after all, what could either of them get from such a passion but a sense of his or of her own maximum self, in contradistinction to all the rest of life? Wherein was something finite and sad, for the human soul at its maximum wants a sense of the infinite.

Nevertheless, it was begun, now, this passion, and must go on, the passion of Ursula to know her own maximum self, limited and so defined against him. She could limit and define herself against him, the male, she could be her maximum self, female, oh female, triumphant for one moment in exquisite assertion against the male, in supreme contradistinction to the male.

The next afternoon, when he came, prowling, she went with him across to the church. Her father was gradually gathering in anger against him, her mother was hardening in anger against her. But the parents were naturally tolerant in action.

They went together across the churchyard, Ursula and Skrebensky, and ran to hiding in the church. It was dimmer in there than the sunny afternoon outside, but the mellow glow among the bowed stone was very sweet. The windows burned in ruby and in blue, they made magnificent arras to their bower of secret stone.

"What a perfect place for a *rendez-vous*," he said, in a hushed voice, glancing round.

She too glanced round the familiar interior. The dimness and stillness chilled her. But her eyes lit up with daring. Here, here she
5 would assert her indomitable, gorgeous female self, here. Here she would open her female flower like a flame, in this dimness that was more passionate than light.

They hung apart a moment, then wilfully turned to each other for the desired contact. She put her arms round him, she cleaved her
10 body to his, and with her hands pressed upon his shoulders, on his back, she seemed to feel right through him, to know his young, tense body right through. And it was so fine, so hard, yet so exquisitely subject and under her control. She reached him her mouth and drank his full kiss, drank it fuller and fuller.

15 And it was good, it was very, very good. She seemed to be filled with his kiss, filled as if she had drunk strong, glowing sunshine. She glowed all inside, the sunshine seemed to beat upon her heart underneath, she had drunk so beautifully.

She drew away, and looked at him radiant, exquisitely, glowingly
20 beautiful, and satisfied, but radiant as an illumined cloud.

To him this was bitter, that she was so radiant and satisfied. She laughed upon him, blind to him, so full of her own bliss, never doubting but that he was the same as she was. And radiant as an angel she went with him out of the church, as if her feet were beams
25 of light that walked on flowers for footsteps.

He went beside her, his soul clenched, his body unsatisfied. Was she going to make this easy triumph over him? For him, there was now no self-bliss, only pain and confused anger.

It was high summer, and the hay-harvest was almost over. It would
30 be finished on Saturday. On Saturday however Skrebensky was going away. He could not stay any longer.

Having decided to go, he became very tender and loving to her, kissing her gently, with such soft, sweet, insidious closeness that they were both of them intoxicated.

35 The very last Friday of his stay, he met her coming out of school and took her to tea in the town. Then he had a motor-car to drive her home.

Her excitement at riding in a motor-car was greatest of all. He too was very proud of this last *coup*.* He saw Ursula kindle and flare up to the romance of the situation, she raised her head like a young horse snuffing with wild delight.

The car swerved round a corner, and Ursula was swung against Skrebensky. The contact made her aware of him. With a swift, foraging impulse she sought for his hand and clasped it in her own, so close, so combined, as if they were two children. But they were more than two children.

The wind blew in on Ursula's face, the mud flew in a soft, wild rush from the wheels, the country was blackish green, with the silver of new hay here and there, and masses of trees under a silver-gleaming sky.

Her hand tightened on his with a new consciousness, troubled. They did not speak for some time but sat, handfast, with averted, shining faces.

And every now and then the car swung her against him. And they waited for the motion to bring them together. Yet they stared out of the windows, mute.

She saw the familiar country racing by. But now, it was no familiar country, it was wonderland. There was the Hemlock Stone* standing on its grassy hill. Strange, it looked, on this wet, early summer evening, remote, in a magic land. Some rooks were flying out of the trees.

Ah, if only she and Skrebensky could get out, dismount into this enchanted land where nobody had ever been before! Then they would be enchanted people, they would put off the dull, customary self. If she were wandering there, on that hill-slope under a silvery, changing sky, in which many rooks melted like hurrying showers of blots! If they could walk past the wetted hay-swaths, smelling the early evening, and pass in to the wood where the honeysuckle scent was sweet on the cold tang of the air, and showers of drops fell when one brushed a bough, cold and lovely on the face!

But she was here with him in the car, close to him, and the wind was rushing on her lifted, eager face, blowing back the hair. He turned and looked at her, at her face clean as a chiselled thing, her hair chiselled back by the wind, her fine nose keen and lifted.

It was agony to him, seeing her swift and clean-cut and virgin. He wanted to kill himself, and throw his detested carcase at her feet. His desire to turn round on himself and rend himself was an agony to him.

Suddenly she glanced at him. He seemed to be crouching towards her, reaching, he seemed to wince between the brows. But instantly, seeing her lighted eyes and radiant face, his expression changed, his old, reckless laugh shone to her. She pressed his hand in utter
5   delight, and he abided. And suddenly she stooped and kissed his hand, bent her head and caught it to her mouth, in generous homage. And the blood burned in him. Yet he remained still, he made no move.

She started. They were swinging into Cossethay. Skrebensky was
10 going to leave her. But it was all so magic, her cup was so full of bright wine, her eyes could only shine.

He tapped, and spoke to the man. The car swung up by the yew-trees. She gave him her hand and said goodbye, naïve and brief as a school-girl. And she stood watching him go, her face shining.
15 The fact of his driving on meant nothing to her, she was so filled by her own bright ecstasy. She did not see him go, for she was filled with light, which was of him. Bright with an amazing light as she was, how could she miss him?

In her bedroom she threw her arms in the air in clear pain of
20 magnificence. Oh, it was her transfiguration, she was beyond herself. She wanted to fling herself into all the hidden brightness of the air. It was there, it was there! If she could but meet it.

But the next day, she knew he had gone. Her glory had partly died down—but never from her memory. It was too real. Yet it was gone
25 by, leaving a wistfulness. A deeper yearning came into her soul, a new reserve.

She shrank from touch and question. She was very proud, but very new, and very sensitive. Oh, that no-one should lay hands on her!
30 She was happiest running on by herself. Oh, it was a joy to run along the lanes without seeing things, yet being with them. It was such a joy to be alone with all one's riches.

The holidays came, when she was free. She spent most of her time running on by herself, curled up in a squirrel-place in the garden,
35 lying in a hammock in the coppice, while the birds came near—near,—so near. Or, in rainy weather, she flitted to the Marsh, and lay hidden with her book in a hay-loft.

All the time, she dreamed of him, sometimes definitely, but when she was happiest, only vaguely. He was the warm colouring to her
40 dreams, he was the hot blood beating within them.

When she was less happy, out of sorts, she pondered over his appearance, his clothes, the button with his regimental badge, which he had given her. Or she tried to imagine his life in barracks. Or she conjured up a vision of herself as she appeared in his eyes.

His birthday was in August, and she spent some pains on making him a cake. She felt that it would not be in good taste for her to give him a present.

Their correspondence was brief, mostly an exchange of post-cards, not at all frequent. But with her cake she must send him a letter.

"Dear Anton—The sunshine has come back specially for your birthday, I think.

I made the cake myself, and wish you many happy returns of the day. Don't eat it if it isn't good. Mother hopes you will come and see us when you are near enough,

I am

Your sincere friend

Ursula Brangwen."

It bored her to write a letter even to him. After all, writing words on paper had nothing to do with him and her.

The fine weather had set in, the cutting machine went on from dawn till sunset, chattering round the fields. She heard from Skrebensky; he too was on duty in the country, on Salisbury Plain.* He was now a second lieutenant in a Field Troop. He would have a few days off shortly, and would come to the Marsh for the wedding.

Fred Brangwen was going to marry a school-mistress out of Ilkeston, as soon as corn-harvest was at an end.

The dim, blue-and-gold of a hot, sweet autumn saw the close of the corn-harvest. To Ursula, it was as if the world had opened its softest, purest flower, its chicory flower, its meadow saffron. The sky was blue and sweet, the yellow leaves down the lane seemed like free, wandering flowers as they chittered round the feet, making a keen, poignant, almost unbearable music to her heart. And the scents of autumn were like a summer madness to her. She fled away from the little, purple-red button-chrysanthemums like a frightened dryad, the bright yellow little chrysanthemums smelled so strong her feet seemed to dither in a drunken dance.

Then her uncle Tom appeared, always like the cynical Bacchus in

the picture.* He would have a jolly wedding, a harvest supper and a
wedding feast in one: a tent in the home close, and a band for
dancing, and a great feast out of doors.

Fred demurred, but Tom must be satisfied. Also Laura, a
5 handsome, clever girl, the bride, she also must have a great and jolly
feast. It appealed to her educated sense. She had been to Salisbury
Training College,* knew folk-songs and morris-dancing.

So the preparations were begun, directed by Tom Brangwen. A
marquee was set up on the home close, two large bon-fires were
10 prepared. Musicians were hired, a feast made ready.

Skrebensky was to come, arriving in the morning. Ursula had a
new white dress of soft crape, and a white hat. She liked to wear
white. With her black hair and clear, golden skin, she looked
southern, or rather tropical, like a Creole. She wore no colour
15 whatsoever.

She trembled that day as she prepared to go down to the wedding.
She was to be a bridesmaid. Skrebensky would not arrive till
afternoon. The wedding was at two o'clock.

As the wedding party returned home, Skrebensky stood in the
20 parlour at the Marsh. Through the window he saw Tom Brangwen,
who was best man, coming up the garden path most elegant in
cut-away coat and white slip* and spats, with Ursula laughing on his
arm. Tom Brangwen was handsome, with his womanish colouring
and dark eyes and black, close-cut moustache. But there was
25 something subtly coarse and suggestive about him, for all his beauty:
his strange, bestial nostrils, opened so hard and wide, and his
well-shaped head almost disquieting in its nakedness, rather bald
from the front, and all its soft fulness betrayed.

Skrebensky saw the man rather than the woman. She was brilliant
30 with a curious, wordless, distracted animation which she always felt
when with her uncle Tom, always confused in herself.

But when she met Skrebensky everything vanished. She saw only
the slender, unchangeable youth waiting there inscrutable, like her
fate. He was beyond her, with his loose, slightly horsey appearance,
35 that made him seem very manly and foreign. Yet his face was smooth
and soft and impressionable. She shook hands with him, and her
voice was like the rousing of a bird startled by the dawn.

"Isn't it nice," she cried, "to have a wedding!"

There were bits of coloured confetti lodged in her dark hair.

40 Again the confusion came over him, as if he were losing himself

and becoming all vague, undefined, inchoate. Yet he wanted to be
hard, manly, horsey. And he followed her.

There was a light tea, and the guests scattered. The real feast was
for the evening. Ursula walked out with Skrebensky through the
stackyard to the fields, and up the embankment to the canal-side.   5

The new corn-stacks were big and golden as they went by, an
army of white geese marched aside in braggart protest. Ursula was
light as a white ball of down, Skrebensky drifted beside her,
indefinite, his old form loosened, and another self, grey, vague,
drifting out, as from a bud. They talked lightly, of nothing.   10

The blue way of the canal wound softly between the autumn
hedges, on towards the greenness of a small hill. On the left was the
whole black agitation of colliery and railway and the town which rose
on its hill, the church-tower topping all. The round white dot of the
clock on the tower was distinct in the evening light.   15

That way, Ursula felt, was the way to London, through the grim,
alluring seethe of the town. On the other hand was the evening,
mellow over the green water-meadows and the winding alder trees
beside the river, and the pale stretches of stubble beyond. There the
evening glowed softly, and even a pee-wit was flapping in solitude   20
and peace.

Ursula and Anton Skrebensky walked along the ridge of the canal
between. The berries on the hedges were crimson and bright red,
above the leaves. The glow of evening and the wheeling of the
solitary pee-wit and the faint cry of the birds came to meet the   25
shuffling noise of the pits, the dark, fuming stress of the town
opposite, and they two walked the blue strip of water-way, the ribbon
of sky between.

He was looking, Ursula thought, very beautiful, because of a flush
of sunburn on his hands and face. He was telling her how he had   30
learned to shoe horses and select cattle fit for killing.

"Do you like to be a soldier?" she asked.

"I am not exactly a soldier," he replied.

"But you only do things for wars," she said.

"Yes."   35

"Would you like to go to war?"

"I? Well, it would be exciting. If there were a war, I would want
to go."

A strange, distracted feeling came over her, a sense of potent
unrealities.   40

"Why would you want to go?"

"I should be doing something, it would be genuine. It's a sort of toy-life, as it is."

"But what would you be doing if you went to war?"

5 "I would be making railways or bridges, working like a nigger."

"But you'd only make them to be pulled down again when the armies had done with them. It seems just as much a game."

"If you call war a game."

"What is it?"

10 "It's about the most serious business there is, fighting."

A sense of hard separateness came over her.

"Why is fighting more serious than anything else?" she asked.

"You either kill or get killed—and I suppose it is serious enough, killing."*

15 "But when you're dead, you don't matter any more," she said.

He was silenced for a moment.

"But the result matters," he said. "It matters whether we settle the Mahdi or not."

"Not to you—nor me—we don't care about Khartoum."*

20 "You want to have room to live in: and somebody has to make room."

"But I don't want to live in the desert of Sahara—do you?" she replied, laughing with antagonism.

"*I* don't—but we've got to back up those who do."

25 "Why have we?"

"Where is the nation, if we don't?"

"But we aren't the nation. There are heaps of other people who are the nation."

"They might say *they* weren't, either."

30 "Well, if everybody said it, there wouldn't be a nation. But I should still be myself,"* she asserted, brilliantly.

"You wouldn't be yourself, if there were no nation."

"Why not?"

"Because you'd just be a prey to everybody or anybody."

35 "How a prey?"

"They'd come and take everything you've got."

"Well, they couldn't take much even then. I don't care what they take. I'd rather have a robber who carried me off than a millionaire who gave me everything you can buy."

40 "That's because you are a romanticist."

"Yes I am. I want to be romantic. I hate houses that never go away, and people just living in the houses. It's all so stiff and stupid. I hate soldiers, they are stiff and wooden. What do you fight for, really?"

"I would fight for the nation." 5

"For all that, you aren't the nation. What would you do for yourself?"

"I belong to the nation and must do my duty by the nation."

"But when it didn't need your services in particular—when there *is* no fighting? What would you do then?" 10

He was irritated.

"I would do what everybody else does."

"What?"

"Nothing. I would be in readiness for when I was needed."

The answer came in exasperation. 15

"It seems to me," she answered, "as if you weren't anybody—as if there weren't anybody there, where you are. Are you anybody, really? You seem like nothing to me."

They had walked till they reached a wharf, just above a lock. There an empty barge, painted with a red and yellow cabin hood, but 20 with a long, coal-black hold, was lying moored. A man, lean and grimy, was sitting on a box against the cabin-side by the door, smoking, and nursing a baby that was wrapped in a drab shawl, and looking into the glow of evening. A woman bustled out, sent a pail dashing into the canal, drew her water and bustled in again. 25 Children's voices were heard. A thin blue smoke ascended from the cabin chimney, there was a smell of cooking.

Ursula, white as a moth, lingered to look. Skrebensky lingered by her. The man glanced up.

"Good-evening," he called, half impudent, half attracted. 30

He had blue eyes which glanced impudently from his grimy face.

"Good-evening," said Ursula, delighted. "*Isn't* it nice now!"

"Ay," said the man, "very nice."

His mouth was red under his ragged, sandy moustache, his teeth were white as he laughed. 35

"Oh but—" stammered Ursula, laughing. "it *is*. Why do you say it as if it weren't?"

"''Appen* for them as is childt-nursin' it's none so rosy."

"May I look inside your barge?" asked Ursula.

"There's nobody'll stop you; you come if you like." 40

The barge lay at the opposite bank, at the wharf. It was the
"Annabel," belonging to J. Ruth of Loughborough.* The man
watched Ursula closely from his keen, twinkling eyes. His fair hair
was wispy on his grimed forehead. Two dirty children appeared, to
5   see who was talking.

Ursula glanced at the great lock gates. They were shut, and the
water was sounding, spurting and trickling down in the gloom
beyond. On this side the bright water was almost to the top of the
gate. She went boldly across, and round to the wharf.

10   Stooping from the bank, she peeped into the cabin, where was a
red glow of fire and the shadowy figure of a woman. She *did* want to
go down.

"You'll mess your frock," said the man, warningly.

"I'll be careful," she answered. "May I come?"

15   "Ay, come if you like."

She gathered her skirts, lowered her foot to the side of the boat,
and leapt down, laughing. Coal-dust flew up.

The woman came to the door. She was plump and sandy haired,
young, with an odd, stubby nose.

20   "Oh you *will* make a mess of yourself," she cried, surprised and
laughing with a little wonder.

"I did want to see. Isn't it lovely living on a barge?" asked Ursula.

"I don't live on one altogether," said the woman cheerfully.

"She's got her parlour an' her plush suite in Loughborough," said
25   her husband, with just pride.

Ursula peeped into the cabin, where saucepans were boiling and
some dishes were on the table. It was very hot. Then she came out
again. The man was talking to the baby. It was a blue-eyed,
fresh-faced thing with floss of red-gold hair.

30   "Is it a boy or a girl?" she asked.

"It's a girl—aren't you a girl, eh?" he shouted at the infant,
shaking his head. Its little face wrinkled up into the oddest, funniest
smile.

"Oh!" cried Ursula, "Oh, the dear! Oh, how nice, when she
35   laughs!"

"She'll laugh hard enough," said the father.

"What is her name?" asked Ursula.

"She hasn't got a name, she's not worth one," said the man. "Are
you, you fag-end o' nothing," he shouted to the baby.

40   The baby laughed.

"No, we've been that busy, we've never took her to th' registry office," came the woman's voice. "She was born on th' boat here."

"But you know what you're going to call her?" asked Ursula.

"We did think of Gladys Em'ly," said her mother.

"We thought of nowt o' th' sort," said the father. 5

"Hark at him! What *do* you want?" cried the mother in exasperation.

"She'll be called Annabel, after th' boat she was born on."

"She's not, so there," said the mother, viciously defiant.

The father sat in humorous malice, grinning. 10

"Well, you'll see," he said.

And Ursula could tell, by the woman's vibrating exasperation, that he would never give way.

"They're all nice names," she said. "Call her Gladys Annabel Emily." 15

"Nay, that's heavy-laden if you like," he answered.

"You see!" cried the woman. "He's that *pig-headed*!"

"And she's so nice, and she laughs, and she hasn't even got a name," crooned Ursula to the child.

"Let me hold her," she added. 20

He yielded her the child, that smelt of babies. But it had such blue, wide, china eyes, and it laughed so oddly, with such a taking grimace, Ursula loved it. She cooed and talked to it. It was such an odd, exciting child.

"What's *your* name?" the man suddenly asked of her. 25

"My name is Ursula—Ursula Brangwen," she replied.

"Ursula!" he exclaimed, dumb-founded.

"There was a Saint Ursula. It's a very old name," she added hastily, in justification.

"Hey, mother!" he called. 30

There was no answer.

"Pem!" he called, "can't y' hear?"

"What?" came the short answer.

"What about 'Ursula'?" he grinned.

"What about *what*?" came the answer, and the woman appeared in 35 the doorway, ready for combat.

"Ursula—it's the lass's name there," he said gently.

The woman looked the young girl up and down. Evidently she was attracted by her slim, graceful, new beauty, her effect of white elegance, and her tender way of holding the child. 40

"Why, how do you write it?" the mother asked, awkward now she was touched.

Ursula spelled out her name. The man looked at the woman. A bright, confused flush came over the mother's face, a sort of luminous shyness.

"It's not a *common* name, is it!" she exclaimed, excited as by an adventure.

"Are you goin' to have it then?" he asked.

"I'd rather have it than Annabel," she said, decisively.

"An' I'd rather have it than Gladys Em'ler," he replied.

There was a silence. Ursula looked up.

"Will you really call her Ursula?" she asked.

"Ursula Ruth," replied the man, laughing vainly, as pleased as if he had found something.

It was now Ursula's turn to be confused.

"It *does* sound *awfully* nice," she said. "I *must* give her something. And I haven't got anything at all."

She stood in her white dress, wondering, down there in the barge. The lean man sitting near to her watched her as if she were a strange being, as if she lit up his face. His eyes smiled on her, boldly and yet with exceeding admiration underneath.

"Could I give her my necklace?" she said.

It was the little necklace made of pieces of amethyst and topaz and pearl and crystal, strung at intervals on a little golden chain, which her uncle Tom had given her. She was very fond of it. She looked at it lovingly, when she had taken it from her neck.

"Is it valuable?" the man asked her, curiously.

"I think so," she replied.

"The stones and pearl are real: it is worth three or four pounds," said Skrebensky from the wharf above. Ursula could tell he disapproved of her.

"I *must* give it to your baby—may I?" she said to the bargee.

He flushed, and looked away into the evening.

"Nay," he said, "it's not for me to say."

"What would your father and mother say?" cried the woman curiously, from the door.

"It is my own," said Ursula, and she dangled the little glittering string before the baby. The infant spread its little fingers. But it could not grasp. Ursula closed the tiny hand over the jewel. The baby waved the bright ends of the string. Ursula had given her necklace away. She felt sad. But she did not want it back.

The jewel swung from the baby's hand and fell in a little heap on
the coal-dusty bottom of the barge. The man groped for it, with a
kind of careful reverence. Ursula noticed the coarsened, blunted
fingers groping at the little jewelled heap. The skin was red on the
back of the hand, the fair hairs glistened stiffly. It was a thin, sinewy,
capable hand nevertheless, and Ursula liked it. He took up the
necklace, carefully, and blew the coal-dust from it, as it lay in the
hollow of his hand. He seemed still and attentive. He held out his
hand with the necklace shining small in its hard, black hollow.

"Take it back," he said.

Ursula hardened with a kind of radiance.

"No," she said, "It belongs to little Ursula."

And she went to the infant and fastened the necklace round its
warm, soft, weak little neck.

There was a moment of confusion, then the father bent over his
child:

"What do you say?" he said. "Do you say thank you? Do you say
thank you, Ursula?"

"Her name's Ursula *now*," said the mother, smiling a little bit
ingratiatingly from the door. And she came out to examine the jewel
on the child's neck.

"It *is* Ursula, isn't it?" said Ursula Brangwen.

The father looked up at her, with an intimate, half gallant, half
impudent, but wistful look. His captive soul loved her: but his soul
was captive, he knew, always.

She wanted to go. He set a little ladder for her to climb up to the
wharf. She kissed the child, which was in its mother's arms, and then
she turned away. The mother was effusive. The man stood silent by
the ladder. Ursula joined Skrebensky. The two young figures
crossed the lock above the shining yellow water. The barge-man
watched them go.

"I *loved* them," she was saying. "He was so gentle—oh, so gentle!
And the baby was such a dear!"

"Was he gentle?" said Skrebensky. "The woman had been a
servant, I'm sure of that."

Ursula winced.

"But I loved his impudence—it was so gentle underneath."

She went hastening on, gladdened by having met the grimy, lean
man with the ragged moustache. He gave her a pleasant, warm
feeling. He made her feel the richness of her own life. Skrebensky,

somehow, had created a deadness round her, a sterility, as if the
world were ashes.

They said very little as they hastened home to the big supper. He
was envying the lean father of three children, for his impudent
5 directness and his worship of the woman in Ursula, a worship of
body and soul together, the man's body and soul wistful and
worshipping the body and spirit of the girl, with a desire that knew
the inaccessibility of its object, but was only glad to know that the
perfect thing existed, glad to have had a moment of communion.
10 Why could not he himself desire a woman so? Why did he never
really want a woman, not with the whole of him: never loved, never
worshipped, only just physically wanted her.

But he would want her with his body, let his soul do as it would. A
kind of flame of physical desire was gradually beating up in the
15 Marsh, kindled by Tom Brangwen, and by the fact of the wedding of
Fred, the shy, fair, stiff-set farmer with the handsome, half-educated
girl. Tom Brangwen, with all his secret power, seemed to fan the
flame that was rising. The bride was strongly attracted by him, and
he was exerting his influence on another beautiful, fair girl, chill and
20 burning as the sea, who said witty things which he appreciated,
making her glint with more, like phosphorescence. And her greenish
eyes seemed to rock a secret, and her hands like mother-of-pearl
seemed luminous, transparent, as if the secret were burning visible
in them.

25 At the end of supper, during dessert, the music began to play,
violins and flutes. Everybody's face was lit up. A glow of excitement
prevailed. When the little speeches were over, and the port remained
unreached-for any more, those who wished were invited out to the
open for coffee. The night was warm.

30 Bright stars were shining, the moon was not yet up. And under the
stars burned two great, red, flameless fires, and round these, lights
and lanterns hung, the marquee stood open before a fire, with its
lights inside.

The young people flocked out into the mysterious night. There
35 was sound of laughter and voices, and a scent of coffee. The
farm-buildings loomed dark in the background. Figures, pale and
dark, flitted about, intermingling. The red fire glinted on a white or a
silken skirt, the lanterns gleamed on the transient heads of the
wedding guests.

40 To Ursula, it was wonderful. She felt she was a new being. The

darkness seemed to breathe like the sides of some great beast, the hay-stacks loomed half-revealed, a crowd of them, a dark, fecund lair just behind. Waves of delirious darkness ran through her soul. She wanted to let go. She wanted to reach and be amongst the flashing stars, she wanted to race with her feet and be beyond the confines of this earth. She was mad to be gone. It was as if a hound were straining on the leash, ready to hurl itself after a nameless quarry, into the dark. And she was the quarry, and she was also the hound. The darkness was passionate and breathing with immense, unperceived heaving. It was waiting to receive her in her flight. And how could she start—and how could she let go? She must leap from the known into the unknown. Her hands and feet beat like a madness, her breast strained as if in bonds.

The music began, and the bonds began to slip. Tom Brangwen was dancing with the bride, quick and fluid and as if in another element, inaccessible as the creatures that move in the water. Fred Brangwen went in with another partner. The music came in waves. One couple after another was washed and absorbed into the deep underwater of the dance.

"Come," said Ursula to Skrebensky, laying her hand on his arm.

At the touch of her hand on his arm, his consciousness melted away from him. He took her into his arms, as if into the sure, subtle power of his will, and they became one movement, one dual movement, dancing on the slippery grass. It would be endless, this movement, it would continue for ever. It was his will and her will locked in a trance of motion, two wills locked in one motion, yet never fusing, never yielding one to the other. It was a glaucous,* intertwining, delicious flux and contest in flux.

They were both absorbed into a profound silence, into a deep, fluid, underwater energy that gave them unlimited strength. All the dancers were waving intertwined in the flux of music. Shadowy couples passed and re-passed before the fire, the dancing feet danced silently by into the darkness, it was a vision of the depths of the underworld, under the great flood.

There was a wonderful rocking of the darkness, slowly, a great, slow swinging of the whole night, with the music playing lightly on the surface, making the strange, ecstatic rippling on the surface of the dance, but underneath only one great flood heaving slowly backwards to the verge of oblivion, slowly forward to the other verge, the heart sweeping along each time, and tightening with anguish as the limit was reached, and the movement, at crisis, turned and swept back.

As the dance surged heavily on, Ursula was aware of some influence looking-in upon her. Something was looking at her. Some
5 powerful, glowing sight was looking right into her, not upon her, but right at her. Out of the great distance, and yet imminent, the powerful, overwhelming watch was kept upon her. And she danced on and on with Skrebensky, while the great, white watching continued, balancing all in its revelation.

10 "The moon has risen," said Anton, as the music ceased and they found themselves suddenly stranded, like bits of jetsam on a shore. She turned, and saw a great white moon looking at her over the hill. And her breast opened to it, she was cleaved like a transparent jewel to its light. She stood filled with the full moon, offering herself. Her
15 two breasts opened to make way for it, her body opened wide like a quivering anemone, a soft, dilated invitation touched by the moon. She wanted the moon to fill in to her, she wanted more, more communion with the moon, consummation. But Skrebensky put his arm round her and led her away. He put a big, dark cloak round her,
20 and sat holding her hand, whilst the moonlight streamed above the glowing fires.

She was not there. Patiently she sat, under the cloak, with Skrebensky holding her hand. But her naked self was away there beating upon the moonlight, dashing the moonlight with her breasts
25 and her belly and her thighs and her knees, in meeting, in communion. She half started, to go in actuality, to fling away her clothing and flee away, away from this dark confusion and chaos of people to the hill and the moon. But the people stood round her like stones, like magnetic stones, and she could not go, in actuality. Skrebensky,
30 like a loadstone weighed on her, the weight of his presence detained her. She felt the burden of him, the blind, persistent, inert burden. He was inert, and he weighed upon her. She sighed in pain. Oh for the coolness and entire liberty and brightness of the moon. Oh for the cold liberty to be herself, to do entirely as she liked. She wanted
35 to get right away. She felt like bright metal weighted down by dark, impure magnetism. He was the dross, people were the dross. If she could but get away to the clean free moonlight.

"Don't you like me tonight?" said his low voice, the voice of the shadow over her shoulder. She clenched her hands in the dewy
40 brilliance of the moon, as if she were mad.

"Don't you like me tonight?" repeated the soft voice.

And she knew that, if she turned, she would die. A strange rage filled her, a rage to tear things asunder. Her hands felt destructive, like metal blades of destruction.

"Let me alone," she said. 5

A darkness, an obstinacy settled on him too, in a kind of inertia. He sat inert beside her. She threw off her cloak and walked towards the moon, silver white herself. He followed her closely.

The music began again, and the dance. He appropriated her. There was a fierce, white, cold passion in her heart. But he held her 10 close, and danced with her. Always present, like a soft weight upon her, bearing her down, was his body against her as they danced. He held her very close, so that she could feel his body, the weight of him sinking, settling upon her, overcoming her life and energy, making her inert along with him, she felt his hands pressing behind her, 15 upon her. But still in her body was the subdued, cold, indomitable passion. She liked the dance: it eased her, put her into a sort of trance. But it was only a kind of waiting, of using up the time that intervened between her and her pure being. She left herself against him, she let him exert all his power over her, as if he would gain 20 power over her, to bear her down. She received all the force of his power. She even wished he might overcome her. She was cold and unmoved as a pillar of salt.*

His will was set and straining with all its tension to encompass her and compel her. If he could only compel her. He seemed to be 25 annihilated. She was cold and hard and compact of brilliance as the moon itself, and beyond him as the moonlight was beyond him, never to be grasped or known. If he could only set a bond round her and compel her!

So they danced four or five dances, always together, always his will 30 becoming more tense, his body more subtle, playing upon her. And still he had not got her, she was hard and bright as ever, intact. But he must weave himself round her, enclose her, enclose her in a net of shadow, of darkness, so she would be like a bright creature gleaming in a net of shadows, caught. Then he would have her, he would enjoy 35 her. How he would enjoy her, when she was caught.

At last, when the dance was over, she would not sit down, she walked away. He came with his arm round her, keeping her upon the movement of his walking. And she seemed to agree. She was bright as a piece of moonlight, as bright as a steel blade, he seemed 40 to be clasping a blade that hurt him. Yet he would clasp her, if it killed him.

They went towards the stackyard. There he saw, with something like terror, the great new stacks of corn glistening and gleaming
5   transfigured, silvery and present under the night-blue sky, throwing dark, substantial shadows, but themselves majestic and dimly present. She, like glimmering gossamer, seemed to burn among them, as they rose like cold fires to the silvery-bluish air. All was intangible, a burning of cold, glimmering, whitish-steely fires. He
10 was afraid of the great moon-conflagration* of the corn-stacks rising above him. His heart grew smaller, it began to fuse like a bead. He knew he would die.

She stood for some moments out in the overwhelming luminosity of the moon. She seemed a beam of gleaming power. She was afraid
15 of what she was. Looking at him, at his shadowy, unreal, wavering presence a sudden lust seized her, to lay hold of him and tear him and make him into nothing. Her hands and wrists felt immeasurably hard and strong, like blades. He waited there beside her like a shadow which she wanted to dissipate, destroy as the moonlight
20 destroys a darkness, annihilate, have done with. She looked at him and her face gleamed bright and inspired. She tempted him.

And an obstinacy in him made him put his arm round her and draw her to the shadow. She submitted: let him try what he could do. Let him try what he could do. He leaned against the side of the stack,
25 holding her. The stack stung him keenly with a thousand cold, sharp flames. Still obstinately he held her.

And temerously, his hands went over her, over the salt, compact brilliance of her body. If he could but have her, how he would enjoy her! If he could but net her brilliant, cold, salt-burning body in the
30 soft iron of his own hands, net her, capture her, hold her down, how madly he would enjoy her. He strove subtly, but with all his energy, to enclose her, to have her. And always she was burning and brilliant and hard as salt, and deadly. Yet obstinately, all his flesh burning and corroding, as if he were invaded by some consuming, scathing
35 poison, still he persisted, thinking at last he might overcome her. Even, in his frenzy, he sought for her mouth with his mouth, though it was like putting his face into some awful death. She yielded to him, and he pressed himself upon her in extremity, his soul groaning over and over:
40   "Let me come—let me come."*

She took him in the kiss, hard her kiss seized upon him, hard and fierce and burning corrosive as the moonlight. She seemed to be destroying him. He was reeling, summoning all his strength to keep his kiss upon her, to keep himself in the kiss.

But hard and fierce she had fastened upon him, cold as the moon and burning as a fierce salt. Till gradually his warm, soft iron yielded, yielded, and she was there fierce, corrosive, seething with his destruction, seething like some cruel, corrosive salt around the last substance of his being, destroying him, destroying him in the kiss. And her soul crystallised with triumph, and his soul was dissolved with agony and annihilation. So she held him there, the victim, consumed, annihilated. She had triumphed:* he was not any more.

Gradually she began to come to herself. Gradually a sort of daytime consciousness came back to her. Suddenly the night was struck back into its old, accustomed, mild reality. Gradually she realised that the night was common and ordinary, that the great, blistering, transcendent night did not really exist. She was overcome with slow horror. Where was she? What was this nothingness she felt? The nothingness was Skrebensky. Was he really there?—who was he? He was silent, he was not there. What had happened? Had she been mad. What horrible thing had possessed her? She was filled with overpowering fear of herself, overpowering desire that it should not be, that other burning, corrosive self. She was seized with a frenzied desire that what had been should never be remembered, never be thought of, never be for one moment allowed possible. She denied it with all her might. With all her might she turned away from it. She was good, she was loving. Her heart was warm, her blood was dark and warm and soft. She laid her hand caressively on Anton's shoulder.

"Isn't it lovely?" she said, softly, coaxingly, caressingly.

And she began to caress him to life again. For he was dead. And she intended that he should never know, never become aware of what had been. She would bring him back from the dead without leaving him one trace of fact to remember his annihilation by.

She exerted all her ordinary, warm self, she touched him, she did him homage of loving awareness. And gradually he came back to her, another man. She was soft and winning and caressing. She was his servant, his adoring slave. And she restored the whole shell of him. She restored the whole form and figure of him. But the core was

gone. His pride was bolstered up, his blood ran once more in pride. But there was no core to him: as a distinct male he had no core. His triumphant, flaming, overweening heart of the intrinsic male would never beat again. He would be subject now, reciprocal, never the
5 indomitable thing with a core of overweening, unabateable fire. She had abated that fire, she had broken him.

But she caressed him. She would not have him remember what had been. She would not remember herself.

"Kiss me, Anton, kiss me," she pleaded.
10 He kissed her, but she knew he could not touch her. His arms were round her, but they had not got her. She could feel his mouth upon her, but she was not at all compelled by it.

"Kiss me," she whispered, in acute distress, "kiss me."

And he kissed her as she bade him, but his heart was hollow. She
15 took his kisses, outwardly. But her soul was empty and finished.

Looking away, she saw the delicate glint of oats dangling from the side of the stack, in the moonlight, something proud and royal, and quite impersonal. She had been proud with them, where they were, she had been also. But in this temporary warm world of the common-
20 place, she was a kind, good girl. She reached out yearningly for goodness and affection. She wanted to be kind and good.

They went home through the night that was all pale and glowing around, with shadows and glimmerings and presences. Distinctly, she saw the flowers in the hedge-bottoms, she saw the thin, raked
25 sheaves flung white upon the thorny hedge.

How beautiful, how beautiful it was! She thought with anguish how wildly happy she was tonight, since he had kissed her. But as he walked with his arm round her waist, she turned with a great offering of herself to the night that glistened tremendous, a magnificent godly
30 moon white and candid as a bridegroom, flowers silvery and transformed filling up the shadows.

He kissed her again, under the yew-trees at home, and she left him. She ran from the intrusion of her parents at home, to her bedroom, where, looking out on the moonlit country, she stretched
35 up her arms, hard, hard, in bliss, agony, offering herself to the blond, debonair presence of the night.

But there was a wound of sorrow, she had hurt herself, as if she had bruised herself, in annihilating him. She covered up her two young breasts with her hands, covering them to herself; and covering
40 herself with herself, she crouched in bed, to sleep.

In the morning the sun shone, she got up strong and dancing. Skrebensky was still at the Marsh. He was coming to church. How lovely, how amazing life was! On the fresh Sunday morning she went out to the garden, among the yellows and the deep-vibrating reds of autumn, she smelled the earth and felt the gossamer, the cornfields 5 across the country were pale and unreal, everywhere was the intense silence of the Sunday morning, filled with unacquainted noises. She smelled the body of the earth, it seemed to stir its powerful flank beneath her as she stood. Into the bluish air came the powerful exudation, the peace was the peace of strong, exhausted breathing, 10 the reds and yellows and the white gleam of stubble were the quivers and motion of the last subsiding transports and clear bliss of fulfilment.

The church bells were ringing when he came. She looked up in keen anticipation at his entry. But he was troubled and his pride was 15 hurt. He seemed very much clothed, she was conscious of his tailored suit.

"Wasn't it lovely, last night?" she whispered to him.

"Yes," he said. But his face did not open nor become free.

The service and the singing in church that morning passed 20 unnoticed by her. She saw the coloured glow of the windows, the forms of the worshippers. Only she glanced at the book of Genesis, which was her favorite book in the Bible.

"And God blessed Noah and his sons, and said unto them, Be fruitful and multiply and replenish the earth. 25

"And the fear of you and the dread of you shall be upon every beast of the earth, and upon every fowl of the air, upon all that moveth upon the earth, and upon all the fishes in the sea; into your hand are they delivered.

"Every moving thing that liveth shall be meat for you; even as the 30 green herb have I given you all things."*

But Ursula was not moved by the history this morning, Multiplying and replenishing the earth bored her. Altogether it seemed merely a vulgar and stock-raising sort of business. She was left quite cold by man's stock-breeding lordship over beast and fishes. 35

"And you, be ye fruitful and multiply: bring forth abundantly in the earth, and multiply therein."

In her soul she mocked at this multiplication, every cow becoming two cows, every turnip ten turnips.

"And God said: This is the token of the covenant which I make 40

between me and you and every living creature that is with you, for
perpetual generations:

"I do set my bow in the cloud, and it shall be a token of a covenant
between me and the earth.

5 "And it shall come to pass, when I bring a cloud over the earth,
that a bow shall be seen in the cloud:

"And I will remember my covenant, which is between me and you
and every living creature of all flesh; and the waters shall no more
become a flood to destroy all flesh."*

10 "Destroy all flesh," why "flesh" in particular? Who was this lord of
flesh? After all, how big was the Flood? Perhaps a few dryads and
fauns had just run into the hills and the further valleys and woods,
frightened, but most had gone on blithely unaware of any flood at all,
unless the nymphs should tell them. It pleased Ursula to think of the
15 naiads in Asia Minor meeting the nereids at the mouth of the
streams, where the sea washed against the fresh, sweet tide, and
calling to their sisters the news of Noah's Flood. They would tell
amusing accounts of Noah in his ark. Some nymphs would relate
how they had hung on the side of the ark, peeped in, and heard Noah
20 and Shem and Ham and Japheth,* sitting in their place under the
rain, saying, how they four were the only men on earth now, because
the Lord had drowned all the rest, so that they four would have
everything to themselves and be masters of every thing, sub-tenants
under the great Proprietor.

25 Ursula wished she had been a nymph. She would have laughed
through the window of the ark, and flicked drops of the flood at
Noah, before she drifted away to people who were less important in
their Proprietor and their Flood.

What was* God, after all? If maggots in a dead dog* be but God
30 kissing carrion, what then is not God? She was surfeited of this God.
She was weary of the Ursula Brangwen who felt troubled about God.
Whatever God was, He was, and there was no need for her to trouble
about Him. She felt she had now all licence.

Skrebensky sat beside her, listening to the sermon, to the voice of
35 law and order. "The very hairs of your head are all numbered."* He
did not believe it. He believed his own things were quite at his own
disposal. You could do as you liked with your own things, so long as
you left other people's alone.

Ursula caressed him and made love to him. Nevertheless he knew
40 she wanted to react upon him and to destroy his being. She was not

with him, she was against him. But her making love to him, her complete admiration of him, in open life, gratified him.

She caught him out of himself, and they were lovers, in a young, romantic, almost fantastic way. He gave her a little ring. They put it in Rhine wine, in their glass, and she drank, then he drank. They 5 drank till the ring lay exposed in the bottom of the glass. Then she took the simple jewel, and tied it on a thread round her neck, where she wore it.

He asked her for a photograph, when he was going away. She went in great excitement to the photographer, with five shillings. The 10 result was an ugly little picture of herself with her mouth on one side. She wondered over it and admired it.

He saw only the live face of the girl. The picture hurt him. He kept it, he always remembered it, but he could scarcely bear to see it. There was a hurt to his soul in the clear, fearless face that was 15 touched with abstraction. Its abstraction was certainly away from him.

Then war was declared with the Boers in South Africa,* and everywhere was a fizz of excitement. He wrote that he might have to go. And he sent her a box of sweets. 20

She was slightly dazed at the idea of his going to the war, not knowing how to feel. It was a sort of romantic situation that she knew so well in fiction she hardly understood it in fact. Underneath a top elation was a sort of dreariness, deep, ashy disappointment.

However she secreted the sweets under her bed, and ate them all 25 herself,* when she went to bed and when she woke in the morning. All the time she felt very guilty and ashamed, but she simply did not want to share them.

That box of sweets remained stuck in her mind afterwards. Why had she secreted them and eaten them every one? Why? She did not 30 feel guilty—she only knew she ought to feel guilty. And she could not make up her mind. Curiously monumental that box of sweets stood up, now it was empty. It was a crux for her. What was she to think of it?

The idea of war altogether made her feel uneasy, uneasy. When 35 men began organised fighting with each other it seemed to her as if the poles of the universe were cracking, and the whole might go tumbling into the bottomless pit. A horrible bottomless feeling she had. Yet of course there was the minted superscription of romance and honor and even religion about war. She was very confused. 40

Skrebensky was busy, he could not come to see her. She asked for
no assurance, no security. What was between them, was, and could
not be altered by avowals. She knew that by instinct, she trusted to
the intrinsic reality.

5   But she felt an agony of helplessness. She could do nothing.
Vaguely she knew the huge powers of the world rolling and crashing
together, darkly, clumsily, stupidly, yet colossal, so that one was
brushed along almost as dust. Helpless, helpless, swirling like dust!
Yet she wanted so hard to rebel, to rage, to fight. But with what?

10   Could she with her hands fight the face of the earth, beat the hills
in their places? Yet her breast wanted to fight, to fight the whole
world. And these two small hands were all she had to do it with.

The months went by, and it was Christmas—the snowdrops came.
There was a little hollow in the wood near Cossethay, where
15   snowdrops* grew wild. She sent him some in a box, and he wrote her
a quick little note of thanks—very grateful and wistful he seemed.
Her eyes grew childlike and puzzled. Puzzled, from day to day she
went on, helpless, carried along by all that must happen.

He went about at his duties, giving himself up to them. At the
20   bottom of his heart his self, the soul that aspired and had true hope of
self-effectuation lay as dead, still-born, a dead weight in his womb.
Who was he, to hold important his personal connections? What did a
man matter, personally? He was just a brick in the whole great social
fabric, the nation, the modern humanity. His personal movements
25   were small, and entirely subsidiary. The whole form must be
ensured, not ruptured, for any personal reason whatsoever, since no
personal reason could justify such a breaking. What did personal
intimacy matter? One had to fill one's place in the whole, the great
scheme of man's elaborate civilisation, that was all. The Whole
30   mattered—but the unit, the person, had no importance, except as he
represented the Whole.

So Skrebensky left the girl out and went his way, serving what he
had to serve, and enduring what he had to endure, without remark.
To his own intrinsic life, he was dead. And he could not rise again
35   from the dead. His soul lay in the tomb. His life lay in the established
order of things. He had his five senses too. They were to be gratified.
Apart from this, he represented the great, established, extant Idea of
life, and as this he was important and beyond question.

The good of the greatest number was all that mattered. That
40   which was the greatest good for them all, collectively, was the

greatest good for the individual. And so, every man must give himself to support the State, and so labour for the greatest good of all. One might make improvements in the State, perhaps, but always with a view to preserving it intact.*

No highest good of the community would, however, give him the 5 vital fulfilment of his soul. He knew this. But he did not consider the soul of the individual sufficiently important. He believed a man was important in so far as he represented all humanity.

He could not see, it was not born in him to see, that the highest good of the community as it stands is no longer the highest good of 10 even the average individual. He thought that, because the community represents millions of people, therefore it must be millions of times more important than any individual, forgetting that the community is an abstraction from the many, and is not the many themselves. Now when the statement of the abstract good for the 15 community has become a formula lacking in all inspiration or value to the average intelligence, then the "common good" becomes a general nuisance, representing the vulgar, conservative materialism at a low level.

And by the highest good of the greatest number* is chiefly meant 20 the material prosperity of all classes. Skrebensky did not really care about his own material prosperity. If he had been penniless—well, he would have taken his chances. Therefore how could he find his highest good in giving up his life for the material prosperity of everybody else? What he considered an unimportant thing for 25 himself he could not think worthy of every sacrifice on behalf of other people. And that which he would consider of the deepest importance to himself as an individual—oh, he said, you mustn't consider the community from that standpoint. No—no—we know what the community wants; it wants something solid, it wants good 30 wages, equal opportunities, good conditions of living, that's what the community wants. It doesn't want anything subtle or difficult. Duty is very plain—keep in mind the material, the immediate welfare of every man, that's all.

So there came over Skrebensky a sort of nullity, which more and 35 more terrified Ursula. She felt there was something hopeless which she had to submit to. She felt a great sense of disaster impending. Day after day was made inert with a sense of disaster. She became morbidly sensitive, depressed, apprehensive. It was anguish to her when she saw one rook slowly flapping in the sky. That was a sign of 40

ill-omen.* And the foreboding became so black and so powerful in
her, that she was almost extinguished.

    Yet what was the matter? At the worst he was only going away.
Why did she mind, what was it she feared? She did not know. Only
5 she had a black dread possessing her. When she went at night and
saw the big, flashing stars they seemed terrible, by day she was always
expecting some charge to be made against her.

    He wrote in March to say that he was going to South Africa in a
short time, but before he went, he would snatch a day at the Marsh.
10 As if in a painful dream, she waited suspended, unresolved. She
did not know, she could not understand. Only she felt that all the
threads of her fate were being held taut, in suspense. She only wept
sometimes as she went about, saying blindly:

    "I am so fond of him, I am so fond of him."

15 He came. But why did he come? She looked at him for a sign. He
gave no sign. He did not even kiss her. He behaved as if he were an
affable, usual acquaintance. This was superficial, but what did it
hide? She waited for him, she wanted him to make some sign.

    So the whole of the day they wavered and avoided contact, until
20 evening. Then, laughing, saying he would be back in six months'
time and would tell them all about it, he shook hands with her
mother and took his leave.

    Ursula accompanied him into the lane. The night was windy, the
yew-trees seethed and hissed and vibrated. The wind seemed to rush
25 about among the chimneys and the church-tower. It was dark.

    The wind blew Ursula's face, and her clothes cleaved to her limbs.
But it was a surging, turgid wind, instinct with compressed vigour of
life. And she seemed to have lost Skrebensky. Out there in the
strong, urgent night she could not find him.

30 "Where are you?" she asked.

    "Here!" came his bodiless voice.

    And groping, she touched him. A fire like lightning drenched
them.

    "Anton?" she said.

35 "What?" he answered.

    She held him with her hands in the darkness, she felt his body
again with hers.

    "Don't leave me—come back to me," she said.

    "Yes," he said, holding her in his arms.

40 But the male in him was scotched by the knowledge that she was

not under his spell nor his influence. He wanted to go away from her. He rested in the knowledge that tomorrow he was going away, his life was really elsewhere. His life was elsewhere—his life was elsewhere—the centre of his life was not what she would have. She was different—there was a breach between them. They were hostile 5 worlds.

"You will come back to me?" she reiterated.

"Yes," he said. And he meant it. But as one keeps an appointment, not as a man returning to his fulfilment.

So she kissed him, and went indoors, lost. He walked down to the 10 Marsh abstracted. The contact with her hurt him and threatened him. He shrank, he had to be free of her spirit. For she would stand before him, like the angel before Balaam,* and drive him back with a sword from the way he was going, into a wilderness.

The next day she went to the station to see him go. She looked at 15 him, she turned to him, but he was always so strange and null—so null. He was so collected. She thought it was that which made him null. Strangely nothing he was.

Ursula stood near to him with a mute, pale face which he would rather not see. There seemed some shame at the very root of life, 20 cold, dead shame for her.

The three made a noticeable group on the station: the girl in her fur cap and tippet and her olive green costume, pale, tense with youth, isolated, unyielding; the soldierly young man in a crush hat* and a heavy over-coat, his face rather pale and reserved 25 above his purple scarf, his whole figure neutral; then the elder man, a fashionable bowler hat pressed low over his dark brows, his face warm-coloured and calm, his whole figure curiously suggestive of full-blooded indifference; he was the eternal audience, the chorus, the spectator at the drama; in his own life he would have 30 no drama.

The train was rushing up. Ursula's heart heaved, but the ice was frozen too strong upon it.

"Good-bye," she said, lifting her hand, her face laughing with her peculiar blind, almost dazzling laugh. She wondered what he was 35 doing, when he stooped and kissed her. He should be shaking hands and going.

"Goodbye," she said again.

He picked up his little bag and turned his back on her. There was a hurry along the train. Ah, here was his carriage. He took his seat. 40

Tom Brangwen shut the door, and the two men shook hands as the whistle went.

"Good-bye—and good luck," said Brangwen.

"Thank you—good-bye."

5   The train moved off. Skrebensky stood at the carriage window, waving, but not really looking to the two figures, the girl and the warm-coloured, almost effeminately-dressed man. Ursula waved her handkerchief. The train gathered speed, it grew smaller and smaller. Still it ran in a straight line. The speck of white vanished.

10 The rear of the train was small in the distance. Still she stood on the platform, feeling a great emptiness about her. In spite of herself her mouth was quivering: she did not want to cry: her heart was dead cold.

Her uncle Tom had gone to an automatic machine, and was
15 getting matches.

"Would you like some sweets," he said, turning round.

Her face was covered with tears, she made curious, downward grimaces with her mouth, to get control. Yet her heart was not crying—it was cold and earthy.

20 "What kind would you like—any?" persisted her uncle.

"I should love some peppermint drops," she said, in a strange, normal voice, from her distorted face. But in a few moments she had gained control of herself, and was still, detached.

"Let us go into the town," he said, and he rushed her into a train
25 moving to the town station. They went to a café to drink coffee, she sat looking at the people in the street, and a great wound was in her breast, a cold imperturbability in her soul.

This cold imperturbability of spirit continued in her now. It was as if some disillusion had frozen upon her, a hard disbelief. Part of her
30 had gone cold, apathetic. She was too young, too baffled to understand, or even to know that she suffered much. And she was too deeply hurt to submit.

She had her blind agonies, when she wanted him, she wanted him. But from the moment of his departure, he had become a visionary
35 thing of her own. All her roused torment and passion and yearning she turned to him.

She kept a diary, in which she wrote impulsive thoughts. Seeing the moon in the sky, her own heart surcharged, she went and wrote:

"If I were the moon,* I know where I would fall down."

40 It meant so much to her, that sentence—she put into it all the

anguish of her youth and her young passion and yearning. She called
to him from her heart wherever she went, her limbs vibrated with
anguish towards him wherever she was, radiating force of her soul
seemed to travel to him, endlessly, endlessly, and in her soul's own
creation, find him.   5

But who was he, and where did he exist? In her own desire only.

She received a post-card from him, and she put it in her bosom. It
did not mean much to her, really. The second day, she lost it, and
never even remembered she had had it, till some days afterwards.

The long weeks went by. There came the constant bad news of the   10
war.* And she felt as if all, outside there in the world, were a hurt, a
hurt, a hurt against her. And something in her soul remained cold,
apathetic, unchanging.

Her life was always only partial at this time, never did she live
completely. There was the cold, unliving part of her. Yet she was   15
madly sensitive. She could not bear herself. When a dirty, red-eyed
old woman came begging of her in the street, she started away as
from an unclean thing. And then, when the old woman shouted acrid
insults after her, she winced, her limbs palpitated with insane
torment, she could not bear herself. Whenever she thought of the   20
red-eyed old woman, a sort of madness ran in inflammation over her
flesh and her brain, she almost wanted to kill herself.

And in this state, her sexual life flamed into a kind of disease
within her. She was so overwrought and sensitive, that the mere
touch of coarse wool seemed to tear her nerves.*   25

Chapter XII

Shame*

Ursula had only two more terms at school. She was studying for her matriculation examination.* It was dreary work, for she had very little intelligence when she was disjointed from happiness. Stubbornness and a consciousness of impending fate kept her half-heartedly pinned to it. She knew that soon she would want to become a self-responsible person, and her dread was, that she would be prevented. An all-containing will in her for complete independence, complete social independence, complete independence from any personal authority, kept her dullishly at her studies. For she knew that she had always her price of ransom—her femaleness. She was always a woman, and what she could not get because she was a human being, fellow to the rest of mankind, she would get because she was a female, other than the man. In her femaleness she felt a secret riches, a reserve, she had always the price of freedom.

However, she was sufficiently reserved about this last resource. The other things should be tried first. There was the mysterious man's world to be adventured upon, the world of daily work and duty and existence as a working member of the community. Against this she had a subtle grudge. She wanted to make her conquest also of this man's world.

So she ground away at her work, never giving herself, never giving it up. Some things she liked. Her subjects were English, Latin, French, mathematics and history. Once she knew how to read French and Latin, the syntax bored her. Most tedious was the close study of English literature. Why should one remember the things one read? Something in mathematics, their cold absoluteness, fascinated her, but the actual practice was tedious. Some people in history puzzled her and made her ponder, but the political parts angered her, and she hated ministers. Only in odd streaks did she get a poignant sense of acquisition and enrichment and enlarging, from her studies: one afternoon, reading "As You Like It"; once when, with her blood, she heard a passage of Latin, and she knew how the blood beat in a Roman's body, so that ever after she felt she knew the

Romans, by contact; she enjoyed the vagaries of English Grammar, because it gave her pleasure to detect the live movements of words and sentences; and mathematics, the very sight of the letters in Algebra, had a real lure for her.

She felt so much and so confusedly at this time, that her face got a queer, wondering, half-scared look, as if she were not sure what might seize upon her at any moment out of the unknown.

Odd little bits of information stirred unfathomable passion in her. When she knew that in the tiny brown buds of autumn were folded, minute and complete, the finished flowers of the summer nine months hence, tiny, folded up, and left there waiting, a flash of triumph and love went over her.

"I could never die while there was a tree," she said passionately, sententiously, standing before a great ash, in worship.

It was the people who, somehow, walked as an upright menace to her. Her life at this time was unformed, palpitating, essentially shrinking from all touch. She gave something to other people, but she was never herself, since she *had* no self. She was not afraid nor ashamed before trees and birds and the sky. But she shrank violently from people, ashamed she was not as they were, fixed, emphatic, but a wavering, undefined sensibility only, without form or being.

Gudrun was at this time a great comfort and shield to her. The younger girl was a lithe, farouche* animal who mistrusted all approach, and would have none of the petty secrecies and jealousies of school-girl intimacy. She would have no truck with the tame cats, nice or not, because she believed that they were all only untamed cats with a nasty, untrustworthy habit of tameness.

This was a great stand-back* to Ursula, who suffered agonies when she thought a person disliked her, no matter how much she despised that person. How could anyone *dislike her*, Ursula Brangwen? The question terrified her and was unanswerable. She sought refuge in Gudrun's natural, proud indifference.

It had been discovered that Gudrun had a talent for drawing. This solved the problem of the girl's indifference to all study. It was said of her "She can draw marvellously."

Suddenly Ursula found a queer awareness existed between herself and her class-mistress, Miss Inger. The latter was a rather beautiful woman of twenty eight, a fearless-seeming, clean type of modern girl whose very independence betrays her to sorrow. She was clever, and expert in what she did, accurate, quick, commanding.

To Ursula she had always given pleasure, because of her clear, decided, yet graceful appearance. She carried her head high, a little thrown back, and, Ursula thought, there was a look of nobility in the way she twisted her smooth brown hair upon her head. She always 5 wore clean, attractive, well-fitting blouses, and a well-made skirt. Everything about her was so well-ordered, betraying a fine, clear spirit, that it was a pleasure to sit in her class.

Her voice was just as ringing and clear, and with unwavering, finely-touched modulation. Her eyes were blue, clear, proud, she 10 gave one altogether the sense of a fine-mettled, scrupulously groomed person and of an unyielding mind. Yet there was an infinite poignancy about her, a great pathos in her lonely, proudly closed mouth.

It was after Skrebensky had gone that there sprang up between the 15 mistress and the girl that strange awareness, then the unspoken intimacy that sometimes connects two people who may never even make each other's acquaintance. Before, they had always been good friends, in the undistinguished way of the classroom, with the professional relationship of mistress and scholar always present. 20 Now, however, another thing came to pass. When they were in the room together, they were aware of each other, almost to the exclusion of everything else. Winifred Inger felt a hot delight in the lessons when Ursula was present, Ursula felt her whole life begin when Miss Inger came into the room. Then, with the beloved, 25 subtly-intimate teacher present, the girl sat as within the rays of some enrichening sun, whose intoxicating heat poured straight into her veins.

The state of bliss, when Miss Inger was present, was supreme in the girl, but always eager, eager. As she went home, Ursula dreamed 30 of the school-mistress, made infinite dreams of things she could give her, of how she might make the elder woman adore her.

Miss Inger was a Bachelor of Arts who had studied at Newnham.* She was a clergyman's daughter, of good family. But what Ursula adored so much was her fine, upright, athletic bearing and her 35 indomitably proud nature. She was proud and free as a man, yet exquisite as a woman.

The girl's heart burned in her breast as she set off for school in the morning. So eager was her breast, so glad her feet, to travel towards the beloved. Ah, Miss Inger, how straight and fine was her back, how 40 strong her loins, how clean and free her limbs!

Ursula craved ceaselessly to know if Miss Inger cared for her. As yet no definite signs had been passed between the two. Yet surely, surely Miss Inger loved her too, was fond of her, liked her at least more than the rest of the scholars in the class. Yet she was never certain. It might be that Miss Inger cared nothing for her. And yet, and yet, with blazing heart, Ursula felt that if only she could speak to her, touch her, she would know.

The summer term came, and with it the swimming class. Miss Inger was to take the swimming class. Then Ursula trembled and was dazed with passion. Her hopes were soon to be realised. She would see Miss Inger in her bathing dress.

The day came. In the great bath the water was glimmering pale emerald-green, a lovely, glimmering mass of colour within the whitish, marble-like confines. Overhead the light fell softly and the great green body of pure water moved under it as someone dived from the side.

Ursula, trembling, hardly able to contain herself, pulled off her clothes, put on her tight bathing suit, and opened the door of her cabin. Two girls were in the water. The mistress had not appeared. She waited. A door opened, Miss Inger came out, dressed in a rust-red tunic like a Greek girl's, tied round the waist, and a red silk handkerchief round her head. How lovely she looked. Her knees were so white and strong and proud, she was firm-bodied as Diana.* She walked simply to the side of the bath, and with a negligent movement, flung herself in. For a moment Ursula watched the white, smooth, strong shoulders and the easy arms swimming. Then she too dived into the water.

Now, ah now she was swimming in the same water with her dear mistress. The girl moved her limbs voluptuously, and swam by herself, deliciously, yet with a craving of unsatisfaction. She wanted to touch the other, to touch her, to feel her.

"I will race you, Ursula," came the well-modulated voice.

Ursula started violently. She turned to see the warm, unfolded face of her mistress looking at her, to her. She was acknowledged. Laughing her own beautiful, startled laugh, she began to swim. The mistress was just ahead, swimming with easy strokes. Ursula could see the head put back, the water flickering upon the white shoulders, the strong legs kicking shadowily. And she swam blinded with passion. Ah, the beauty of the firm, white, cool flesh! Ah, the wonderful firm limbs. If she could but hold them, hug them, press

them between her own small breasts!* Ah, if she did not so despise
her own thin, dusky fragment of a body, if only she too were fearless
and capable.

5   She swam on, eagerly, not wanting to win, only wanting to be
near her mistress, to swim in a race with her. They neared the end
of the bath—the deep end. Miss Inger touched the pipe, swung
herself round, and caught Ursula round the waist, in the water, and
held her for a moment against herself. The bodies of the two women
touched, heaved against each other for a moment, then were
10 separate.*

    "I won," said Miss Inger, laughing.

    There was a moment of suspense. Ursula's heart was beating so
fast, she clung to the rail, and could not move. Her dilated, warm,
unfolded, glowing face turned to the mistress, as if to her very sun.

15   "Goodbye," said Miss Inger, and she swam away to the other
pupils, taking professional interest in them.

    Ursula was dazed. She could still feel the touch of the mistress's
body against her own—only this, only this. The rest of the swimming
time passed like a trance. When the call was given to leave the water,
20 Miss Inger walked down the bath towards Ursula. Her rust-red, thin
tunic was clinging to her, the whole body was defined, firm and
magnificent, as it seemed to the girl.

    "I enjoyed our race, Ursula," said Miss Inger. "Did you?"

    The girl could only laugh with revealed, open, glowing face.

25   The love was now tacitly confessed. But it was some time before
any further progress was made. Ursula continued in suspense, in
inflamed bliss.

    Then one day, when she was alone, the mistress came near to her,
and touching her cheek with her fingers, said, with some difficulty:
30   "Would you like to come to tea with me on Saturday, Ursula?"

    The girl flushed all gratitude.

    "We'll go to a lovely little bungalow on the Soar,* shall we. I stay
the week-ends there sometimes."

    Ursula was beside herself. She could not endure till the Saturday
35 came, her thoughts burned up like a fire. If only it were Saturday, if
only it were Saturday.

    Then Saturday came, and she set out. Miss Inger met her in
Sawley,* and they walked about three miles to the bungalow. It was a
moist, warm, cloudy day.

40   The bungalow was a tiny, two-roomed shanty set on a steep bank.

Everything in it was exquisite. In delicious privacy, the two girls made tea, and then they talked. Ursula need not be home till about ten o'clock.

The talk was led, by a kind of spell, to love. Miss Inger was telling Ursula of a friend, how she had died in childbirth, and what she had suffered: then she told of a prostitute, and of some of her experiences with men.

As they talked thus, on the little verandah of the bungalow, the night fell, there was a little warm rain.

"It is really stifling," said Miss Inger.

They watched a train, whose lights were pale in the lingering twilight, rushing across the distance.

"It will thunder," said Ursula.

The electric suspense continued, the darkness sank, they were eclipsed.

"I think I shall go and bathe," said Miss Inger, out of the cloud-black darkness.

"At night?" said Ursula.

"It is best at night. Will you come?"

"I should like to"

"It is quite safe—the grounds are private. We had better undress in the bungalow, for fear of the rain, then run down."

Shyly, stiffly, Ursula went into the bungalow and began to remove* her clothes. The lamp was turned low, she stood in the shadow. By another chair Winifred Inger was undressing.

Soon the naked, shadowy figure of the elder girl came to the younger.

"Are you ready?" she said.

"One moment."

Ursula could hardly speak. The other naked woman stood by, stood near, silent. Ursula was ready.

They ventured out into the darkness, feeling the soft air of night upon their skins.

"I can't see the path," said Ursula.

"It is here," said the voice, and the wavering, pallid figure was beside her, a hand grasping her arm. And the elder held the younger close against her, close, as they went down, and by the side of the water, she put her arms round her, and kissed her. And she lifted her in her arms, close, saying softly:

"I shall carry you into the water."

Ursula lay still in her mistress's arms, her forehead against the beloved, maddening breast.

"I shall put you in," said Winifred.

But Ursula twined her body about her mistress.*

5 After a while the rain came down on their flushed, hot limbs, startling, delicious. A sudden, ice-cold shower burst in a great weight upon them. They stood up to it with pleasure. Ursula received the stream of it upon her breasts and her belly and her limbs. It made her cold, and a deep, bottomless silence welled up in 10 her, as if bottomless darkness were returning upon her.

So the heat vanished away, she was chilled, as if from a waking up. She ran indoors, a chill, non-existent thing, wanting to get away. She wanted the light, the presence of other people, the external connection with the many. Above all she wanted to lose herself among 15 natural surroundings.

She took her leave of her mistress and returned home. She was glad to be on the station with a crowd of Saturday-night people, glad to sit in the lighted, crowded railway carriage. Only she did not want to meet anybody she knew. She did not want to talk. She was alone, 20 immune.

All this stir and seethe of lights and people was but the rim, the shores of a great inner darkness and void. She wanted very much to be on the seething, partially illuminated shore, for within her was the void reality of dark space.

25 For a time, Miss Inger, her mistress, was gone; she was only a dark void, and Ursula was free as a shade walking in an underworld of extinction, of oblivion. Ursula was glad, with a kind of motionless, lifeless gladness, that her mistress was extinct, gone out of her.

In the morning, however, the love was there again, burning, 30 burning. She remembered yesterday, and she wanted more, always more. She wanted to be with her mistress. All separation from her mistress was a restriction from living. Why could she not go to her today, today? Why must she pace about revoked at Cossethay, whilst her mistress was elsewhere? She sat down and wrote a burning, 35 passionate love-letter: she could not help it.

The two women became intimate. Their lives suddenly seemed to fuse into one, inseparable. Ursula went to Winifred's lodging, she spent there her only living hours. Winifred was very fond of water—of swimming, or rowing. She belonged to various athletic 40 clubs. Many delicious afternoons the two girls spent in a light boat on the river, Winifred always rowing. Indeed, Winifred seemed to delight in having Ursula in her charge, in giving things to the girl, in filling and enrichening her life.

So that Ursula developed rapidly during the few months of her intimacy with her mistress. Winifred had had a scientific education. She had known many clever people. She wanted to bring Ursula to her own position of thought.

They took religion and rid it of its dogmas, its falsehoods. Winifred humanised it all. Gradually it dawned upon Ursula that all the religion she knew was but a particular clothing to a human aspiration. The aspiration was the real thing—the clothing was a matter almost of national taste or need. The Greeks had a naked Apollo, the Christians a white-robed Christ, the Buddhists a royal prince, the Egyptians their Osiris.* Religions were local and religion was universal. Christianity was a local branch. There was as yet no assimilation of local religions into universal religion.

In religion, there were the two great motives of fear and love. The motive of fear was as great as the motive of love. Christianity accepted crucifixion to escape from fear: "do your worst to me, that I may have no more fear of the worst." But that which was feared was not necessarily all evil, and that which was loved not necessarily all good. Fear shall become reverence, and reverence is submission in identification; love shall become triumph, and triumph is delight in identification.

So much she talked of religion, getting the gist of many writings. In philosophy she was brought to the conclusion that the human desire is the criterion of all truth and all good. Truth does not lie beyond humanity, but is one of the products of the human mind and feeling. There is really nothing to fear. The motive of fear in religion is base, and must be left to the ancient worshippers of power, worship of Moloch.* We do not worship power, in our enlightened souls. Power is degenerated to money and Napoleonic stupidity.

Ursula could not help dreaming of Moloch. Her God was not mild and gentle, neither Lamb nor Dove. He was the lion and the eagle.* Not because the lion and the eagle had power, but because they were proud and strong; they were themselves, they were not passive subjects of some shepherd, or pets of some loving woman, or sacrifices of some priest. She was weary to death of mild, passive lambs and monotonous doves. If the lamb might lie down with the lion, it would be a great honor to the lamb, but the lion's powerful

heart would suffer no diminishing. She loved the dignity and
self-possession of lions.

She did not see how lambs could love. Lambs could only be loved.
They could only be afraid, and tremblingly submit to fear, and
5 become sacrificial; or they submit to love, and become beloveds. In
both they were passive. Raging, destructive lovers, seeking the
moment when fear is greatest and triumph is greatest, the fear not
greater than the triumph, the triumph not greater than the fear, these
were no lambs nor doves. She stretched her own limbs like a lion or a
10 wild horse, her heart was relentless in its desires. It would suffer a
thousand deaths, but it would still be a lion's heart when it rose from
death, a fiercer lion she would be, a surer, knowing herself different
from and separate from the great, conflicting universe that was not
herself.

15 Winifed Inger was also interested in the Women's Movement.*

"The men will do no more—they have lost the capacity for doing,"
said the elder girl. "They fuss, and talk, but they are really inane.
They make everything fit into an old, inert idea. Love is a dead idea
to them. They don't come to one and love one, they come to an idea,
20 and they say 'You are my idea,' so they embrace themselves.* As if I
were any man's idea! As if I exist because a man has an idea of me! As
if I will be betrayed by him, lend him my body as an instrument for
his idea, to be a mere apparatus of his dead theory. But they are too
fussy to be able to act: they are all impotent, they can't *take* a woman.
25 They come to their own idea every time, and take that. They are like
serpents trying to swallow themselves* because they are hungry."

Ursula was introduced by her friend to various women and men,
educated, unsatisfied people, who still moved within the smug
provincial society as if they were nearly as tame as their outward
30 behaviour showed, but who were inwardly raging and mad.

It was a strange world the girl was swept into, like a chaos, like the
end of the world. She was too young to understand it all. Yet the
inoculation passed into her, through her love for her mistress.

The examination came, and then school was over. It was the long
35 vacation. Winifred Inger went away to London. Ursula was left alone
in Cossethay. A terrible outcast, almost poisonous despair possessed
her. It was no use doing anything or being anything. She had no connection with other people. Her lot was isolated and deadly. There
was nothing for her anywhere, but this black disintegration. Yet,
40 within all the great attack of disintegration upon her, she remained

herself. It was the terrible core of all her suffering, that she was always herself. Never could she escape that: she could not put off being herself.

She still adhered to Winifred Inger. But a sort of nausea was coming over her. She loved her mistress. But a heavy, clogged sense 5 of deadness began to gather upon her, from the other woman's contact. And sometimes she thought Winifred was ugly, clayey. Her female hips seemed big and earthy, her ankles and her arms were too thick. She wanted some fine intensity, instead of this heavy cleaving of moist clay, that cleaves because it has no life of its own. 10

Winifred still loved Ursula. She had a passion for the fine flame of the girl, she served her endlessly, would have done anything for her.

"Come with me to London," she pleaded to the girl. "I will make it nice for you—you shall do lots of things you will enjoy."

"No," said Ursula stubbornly and dully. "No, I don't want to go to 15 London, I want to be by myself."

Winifred knew what this meant. She knew that Ursula was beginning to reject her. The fine, unquenchable flame of the younger girl would consent no more to mingle with the perverted life of the elder woman. Winifred knew it would come. But she was too 20 proud. At the bottom of her was a black pit of despair. She knew perfectly well that Ursula would cast her off.

And that seemed like the end of her life. But she was too hopeless to rage. Wisely, economising what was left of Ursula's love, she went away to London, leaving the beloved girl alone. 25

And after a fortnight, Ursula's letters became tender again, loving. Her uncle Tom had invited her to go and stay with him. He was managing a big new colliery in Yorkshire.* Would Winifred come too?

For now Ursula was imagining marriage for Winifred. She wanted 30 her to marry her uncle Tom. Winifred knew this. She said she would come to Wiggiston. She would now let fate do as it liked with her, since there was nothing remaining to be done. Tom Brangwen also saw Ursula's intention. He too was at the end of his desires. He had done the things he had wanted to. They had all ended in a 35 disintegrated lifelessness of soul, which he hid under an utterly tolerant good-humour. He no longer cared about anything on earth, neither man nor woman nor God nor humanity. He had come to a stability of nullification. He did not care any more, neither about his body nor about his soul. Only he would preserve intact his own life. 40

Only, the simple, superficial fact of living persisted. He was still healthy. He lived. Therefore he would fill each moment. That had always been his creed. It was not instinctive easiness: it was the inevitable outcome of his nature. When he was in the absolute
5 privacy of his own life, he did as he pleased, unscrupulous, without any ulterior thought. He believed neither in good nor evil. Each moment was like a separate little island, isolated from time, and blank, unconditioned by time.

He lived in a large new house of red-brick standing outside a mass
10 of homogeneous red-brick dwellings called Wiggiston. Wiggiston was only seven years old. It had been a hamlet of eleven houses on the edge of healthy, half-agricultural country. Then the great seam of coal had been opened. In a year Wiggiston appeared, a great mass of pinkish rows of thin, unreal dwellings of five rooms each. The
15 streets were like visions of pure ugliness: a grey-black, macadamised road, asphalt causeways, held in between a flat succession of wall, window and door, a new-brick channel that began nowhere and ended nowhere. Everything was amorphous, yet everything repeated itself endlessly. Only now and then, in one of the house-windows,
20 vegetables or small groceries were displayed for sale.

In the middle of the town was a large, open, shapeless space, or market-place of black, trodden earth, surrounded by the same flat material of dwellings, new red-brick becoming grimy, small oblong windows and oblong doors repeated endlessly, with just, at one
25 corner, a great and gaudy public-house, and somewhere lost on one of the sides of the square, a large window opaque and darkish green, which was the post-office.

The place had the strange desolation of a ruin. Colliers hanging about in gangs and groups, or passing along the asphalt pavements
30 heavily to work, seemed not like living people, but like spectres. The rigidity of the blank streets, the homogeneous amorphous sterility of the whole suggested death rather than life. There was no meeting place, no centre, no artery, no organic formation. There it lay, like the new foundations of a red-brick confusion rapidly spreading, like
35 a skin-disease.

Just outside of this, on a little hill, was Tom Brangwen's big, red-brick house. It looked from the front upon the edge of the place, a meaningless squalor of ash-pits and closets and irregular rows of the backs of houses, each with its small activity made sordid by
40 barren cohesion with the rest of the small activities. Further off was

the great colliery that went night and day. And all around was the country, green with two winding streams, ragged with gorse, and heath, the darker woods in the distance.

The whole place was just unreal, just unreal. Even now, when he had been there for two years, Tom Brangwen did not believe in the actuality of the place. It was like some gruesome dream, some ugly, dead, amorphous mood become concrete.

Ursula and Winifred were met by the motor-car at the raw little station, and drove through what seemed to them like the horrible raw beginnings of something. The place was a moment of chaos perpetuated, persisting, chaos fixed and rigid. Ursula was fascinated by the many men who were there—groups of men standing in the streets, four or five men walking in a gang together, their dogs running behind or before. They were all decently dressed, and most of them rather gaunt. The terrible gaunt repose of their bearing fascinated her. Like creatures with no more hope, but which still live and have passionate being, within some utterly unliving shell, they passed meaninglessly along, with strange, isolated dignity. It was as if a hard, horny* shell enclosed them all.

Shocked and startled, Ursula was carried to her uncle Tom's house. He was not yet at home. His house was simply but well furnished. He had taken out a dividing wall, and made the whole front of the house into a large library, with one end devoted to his science. It was a handsome room, appointed as a laboratory and reading room, but giving the same sense of hard, mechanical activity, activity mechanical yet inchoate, and looking out on the hideous abstraction of the town, and at the green meadows and rough country beyond, and at the great, mathematical colliery* on the other side.

They saw Tom Brangwen walking up the curved drive. He was getting stouter, but, with his bowler hat worn well set down on his brows, he looked manly, handsome, curiously like any other man of action. His colour was as fresh, his health as perfect as ever, he walked like a man rather absorbed.

Winifred Inger was startled when he entered the library, his coat fastened close and correct, his head bald to the crown, but not shiny, rather like something naked that one is accustomed to see covered, and his dark eyes liquid and formless. He seemed to stand in the shadow, like a thing ashamed. And the clasp of his hand was so soft and yet so forceful, that it chilled the heart. She was afraid of him, repelled by him, and yet attracted.

He looked at the athletic, seemingly fearless girl, and he detected in her a kinship with his own dark corruption. Immediately, he knew they were akin.

His manner was polite, almost foreign, and rather cold. He still
5 laughed in his curious, animal fashion, suddenly wrinkling up his wide nose and showing his sharp teeth. The fine beauty of his skin and his complexion, some almost waxen quality, hid the strange, repellent grossness of him, the slight sense of putrescence, the commonness which revealed itself in his rather fat thighs and loins.
10 Winifred saw at once the deferential, slightly servile, slightly cunning regard he had for Ursula, which made the girl at once so proud and so perplexed.

"But is this place as awful as it looks?" the young girl asked, a strain in her eyes.
15 "It is just what it looks," he said. "It hides nothing."

"Why are the men so sad?"

"Are they sad?" he replied.

"They seem unutterably, unutterably sad," said Ursula, out of a passionate throat.
20 "I don't think they are that. They just take it for granted."

"What do they take for granted?"

"This—the pits and the place altogether."

"Why don't they alter it?" she passionately protested.

"They believe they must alter themselves to fit the pits* and the
25 place, rather than alter the pits and the place to fit themselves. It is easier," he said.

"And you agree with them," burst out his niece, unable to bear it. "You think like they do—that living human beings must be taken and adapted to all kinds of horrors. We could easily do without the
30 pits."

He smiled, uncomfortably, cynically. Ursula felt again the revolt of hatred from him.

"I suppose their lives are not really so bad," said Winifred Inger, superior to the Zolaesque tragedy.*
35 He turned with his polite, distant attention.

"Yes, they are pretty bad. The pits are very deep, and hot, and in some places wet. The men die of consumption fairly often. But they earn good wages."

"How gruesome!" said Winifred Inger.
40 "Yes," he replied, gravely. It was his grave, solid, self-

contained manner which made him so much respected as a colliery-
manager.

The servant came in to ask where they would have tea.

"Put it in the summer house, Mrs Smith," he said.

The fair-haired, good-looking young woman went out.

"Is she married and in service?" asked Ursula.

"She is a widow. Her husband died of consumption a little while
ago." Brangwen gave a sinister little laugh. "He lay there in the
house-place at her mother's, and five or six other people in the
house, and died very gradually. I asked her if his death wasn't a great
trouble to her. 'Well,' she said, 'he was very fretful towards the last,
never satisfied, never easy, always fret-fretting, an' never knowing
what would satisfy him. So in one way it was a relief when it was
over—for him and for everybody.'—They had only been married
two years, and she has one boy. I asked her if she hadn't been very
happy. 'Oh, yes Sir, we was very comfortable at first, till he took
bad—oh, we was very comfortable—oh yes—! But you see—you get
used to it. I've had my father an' two brothers go off just the same.
You get used to it.'"

"It's a horrible thing to get used to," said Winifred Inger, with a
shudder.

"Yes," he said, still smiling. "But that's how they are. She'll be
getting married again directly. One man or another—it doesn't
matter very much. They're all colliers."

"What do you mean?" asked Ursula, "—'they're all colliers'?"

"It is with the women as with us," he replied. "Her husband was
John Smith, loader. We reckoned him as a loader, he reckoned
himself as a loader, and so she knew he represented his job.
Marriage and home is a little side-show. The women know it right
enough, and take it for what it's worth. One man or another, it
doesn't matter all the world. The pit matters. Round the pit there
will always be the side-shows, plenty of 'em."—He looked round
at the red chaos, the rigid, amorphous confusion of Wiggiston.—
"Every man his own little side-show, his home, but the pit owns
every man. The women have what is left. What's left of this man, or
what is left of that—it doesn't matter altogether. The pit takes all that
really matters."

"It is the same everywhere," burst out Winifred. "It is the
office, or the shop or the business that gets the man, the woman gets
the bit the shop can't digest. What is he, at home, a man? He

is a meaningless lump—a standing machine, a machine out of work."

"They know they are sold," said Tom Brangwen. "That's where it is. They know they are sold to their job. If a woman talks her throat
5 out, what difference can it make? The man is sold to his job. So the women don't bother. They take what they can catch—and *vogue la galère*."*

"Aren't they very strict here?" asked Miss Inger.

"Oh no. Mrs Smith has two sisters who have changed husbands.
10 They're not very particular—neither are they very interested. They go dragging along what is left from the pits. They're not interested enough to be very immoral—it all amounts to the same thing, moral or immoral—just a question of pit-wages. The most moral duke in England makes two hundred thousand a year out of these pits. He
15 keeps the morality end up."

Ursula sat black-souled and very bitter, hearing the two of them talk. There seemed something ghoulish even in their very deploring of the state of things. They seemed to take a ghoulish satisfaction in it. The pit was the great mistress. Ursula looked out the window and
20 saw the proud, demon-like colliery with her wheels twinkling in the heavens, the formless, squalid mass of the town lying aside. It was the squalid heap of side-shows. The pit was the main show, the *raison d'être* of all.

How terrible it was! There *was* a horrible fascination in it—human
25 bodies and lives subjected in slavery to that symmetric monster of the colliery. There was a swooning, perverse satisfaction in it. For a moment she was dizzy.

Then she recovered, felt herself in a great loneliness, wherein she was sad but free. She had departed. No more would she subscribe to
30 the great colliery, to the great machine which has taken us all captives. In her soul, she was against it, she disowned even its power. It had only to be forsaken to be inane, meaningless. And she knew it was meaningless. But it needed a great, passionate effort of will on her part, seeing the colliery, still to maintain her knowledge that it
35 was meaningless.

But her uncle Tom and her mistress remained there among the horde, cynically reviling the monstrous state and yet adhering to it, like a man who reviles his mistress yet who is in love with her. She knew her uncle Tom perceived what was going on. But she knew
40 moreover that in spite of his criticism and condemnation, he still

wanted the great machine. His only happy moments, his only moments of pure freedom, were when he was serving the machine. Then, and then only, when the machine caught him up, was he free from the hatred of himself, could he act wholely, without cynicism and unreality.

His real mistress was the machine, and the real mistress of Winifred was the machine. She too, Winifred, worshipped the impure abstraction, the mechanisms of matter. There, there, in the machine, in service of the machine, was she free from the clog and degradation of human feeling. There, in the monstrous mechanism that held all matter, living or dead, in its service, did she achieve her consummation and her perfect unison, her immortality.

Hatred sprung up in Ursula's heart. If she could she would smash the machine. Her soul's action should be the smashing of the great machine. If she could destroy the colliery, and make all the men of Wiggiston out of work, she would do it. Let them starve and grub in the earth for roots, rather than serve such a Moloch as this.

She hated her uncle Tom, she hated Winifred Inger. They went down to the summer house for tea. It was a pleasant place among a few trees, at the end of a tidy garden, on the edge of a field. Her uncle Tom and Winifred seemed to jeer at her, to cheapen her. She was miserable and desolate. But she would never give way.

Her coldness for Winifred should never cease. She knew it was over between them. She saw gross, ugly movements in her mistress, she saw a clayey, inert, unquickened flesh, that reminded her of the great prehistoric lizards. One day her uncle Tom came in out of the broiling sunshine, heated from walking. Then the perspiration stood out upon his head and brow, his hand was wet and hot and suffocating in its clasp. He too had something marshy about him—the succulent moistness and turgidity, and the same brackish,* nauseating effect of a marsh,* where life and decaying are one.

He was repellent to her, who was so dry and fine in her fire. Her very bones seemed to bid him keep his distance from her.

It was in these weeks that Ursula grew up. She stayed two weeks at Wiggiston, and she hated it. All was grey, dry ash, cold and dead and ugly. But she stayed. She stayed also to get rid of Winifred. The girl's hatred and her sense of repulsiveness in her mistress and in her uncle seemed to throw the other two together. They drew together as if against her.

In hardness and bitterness of soul, Ursula knew that Winifred was

become her uncle's lover. She was glad. She had loved them both. Now she wanted to be rid of them both. Their marshy, bitter-sweet corruption came sick and unwholesome in her nostrils. Anything, to get out of the fœtid air. She would leave them both for ever, leave for
5   ever their strange, soft, half corrupt element. Anything to get away.

One night Winifred came all burning into Ursula's bed, and put her arms round the girl, holding her to herself in spite of unwillingness, and said:

"Dear, my dear—shall I marry Mr Brangwen—shall I?"
10 The clinging, heavy, muddy question weighed on Ursula intolerably.

"Has he asked you?" she said, using all her might of hard resistance.

"He's asked me," said Winifred. "Do you want me to marry him,
15 Ursula?"

"Yes," said Ursula.

The arms tightened more on her.

"I knew you did, my sweet—and I will marry him. You're *fond* of him, aren't you?"
20 "I've been *awfully* fond of him—ever since I was a child."

"I know—I know. I can see what you like in him. He *is* a man by himself, he has something apart from the rest."

"Yes," said Ursula.

"But he's not like you, my dear—ha, he's not as good as you.
25 There's something even objectionable in him—his thick thighs—"*
Ursula was silent.

"But I'll marry him, my dear—it will be best. Now say you love me."

A sort of profession was extorted out of the girl. Nevertheless her
30 mistress went away sighing, to weep in her own chamber.

In two days' time Ursula left Wiggiston. Miss Inger went to Nottingham. There was an engagement between her and Tom Brangwen, which the uncle seemed to vaunt as if it were an assurance of his validity.
35 Brangwen and Winifred Inger continued engaged for another term. Then they married. Brangwen had reached the age when he wanted children. He wanted children. Neither marriage nor the domestic establishment meant anything to him. He wanted to propagate himself. He knew what he was doing. He had the instinct
40 of a growing inertia, of a thing that chooses its place of rest in which

to lapse into apathy, complete, profound indifference. He would let
the machinery carry him: husband, father, pit-manager, warm clay
lifted through the recurrent action of day after day by the great
machine from which it derived its motion. As for Winifred, she was
an educated woman, and of the same sort as himself. She would   5
make a good companion. She was his mate.*

Chapter XIII

The Man's World

Ursula came back to Cossethay to fight with her mother. Her school-days were over. She had passed the matriculation examination. Now she came home to face that empty period between school and possible marriage.

At first she thought it would be just like holidays all the time, she would feel just free. Her soul was in chaos, blinded, suffering, maimed. She had no will left to think about herself. For a time she must just lapse.

But very shortly, she found herself up against her mother. Her mother had, at this time, the power to irritate and madden the girl continuously. There were already seven children, yet Mrs Brangwen was again with child, the ninth she had borne. One had died of diphtheria in infancy.

Even this fact of her mother's pregnancy enraged the eldest girl. Mrs Brangwen was so complacent, so utterly fulfilled in her breeding. She would not have the existence at all of anything but the immediate, physical, common things. Ursula, inflamed in soul, was suffering all the anguish of youth's reaching for some unknown ideal, that it can't grasp, can't even distinguish or conceive. Maddened, she was fighting all the darkness she was up against. And part of this darkness was her mother. To limit, as her mother did, everything to the ring of physical considerations, and complacently to reject the reality of anything else, was horrible. Not a thing did Mrs Brangwen care about, but the children, the house, and a little local gossip. And she *would not* be touched, she would let nothing else live near her. She went about, big with child, slovenly, easy, having a certain lax dignity, taking her own time, pleasing herself, always, always doing things for the children, and feeling that thereby she fulfilled the whole of womanhood.

This long trance of complacent child-bearing had kept her young and undeveloped. She was scarcely a day older than when Gudrun was born. All these years, nothing had happened save the coming of the children, nothing had mattered but the bodies of her babies. As her children came into consciousness, as they began to suffer their own fulfilment, she cast them off. But she remained dominant in the house. Brangwen continued in a kind of rich drowse of physical heat, in connection with his wife. They were neither of them quite personal, quite defined as individuals, so much were they pervaded by the physical heat of breeding and rearing their young.

How Ursula resented it, how she fought against the close, physical, limited life of herded domesticity. Calm, placid, unshakeable as ever, Mrs Brangwen went about in her dominance of physical maternity.

There were battles. Ursula would fight for things that mattered to her. She would have the children less rude and tyrannical, she *would* have a place in the house. But her mother pulled her down, pulled her down. With all the cunning instinct of a breeding animal, Mrs Brangwen ridiculed and held cheap Ursula's passions, her ideas, her pronunciations. Ursula would try to insist, in her own home, on the right of women to take equal place with men in the field of action and work.

"Ay," said the mother, "there's a good crop of stockings lying ripe for mending. Let that be your field of action."

Ursula disliked mending stockings, and this retort maddened her. She hated her mother bitterly. After a few weeks of enforced domestic life, she had had enough of her home. The commonness, the triviality, the immediate meaninglessness of it all drove her to frenzy. She talked and stormed ideas, she corrected and nagged at the children, she turned her back in silent contempt on her breeding mother, who treated her with supercilious indifference, as if she were a pretentious child not to be taken seriously.

Brangwen was sometimes dragged into the trouble. He loved Ursula, therefore he always had a sense of shame, almost of betrayal, when he turned on her. So he turned fiercely and scathingly and with a wholesale brutality that made Ursula go white, mute, and numb. Her feelings seemed to be becoming deadened in her, her temper hard and cold.

Brangwen himself was in one of his states of flux. After all these years, he began to see a loop-hole of freedom. For twenty years he had gone on at his office as a draughtsman, doing work in which he had no interest, because it seemed his allotted work. The growing up of his daughters, their developing rejection of old forms set him also free.

He was a man of ceaseless activity. Blindly, like a mole, he pushed
his way out of the earth that covered him, working always away from
the physical element in which his life was captured. Slowly, blindly,
gropingly, with what initiative was left to him, he made his way
5 towards individual expression and individual form.

At last, after twenty years, he came back to his wood-carving,
almost to the point where he had left off his Adam and Eve panel
when he was courting. But now he had knowledge and skill without
vision. He saw the puerility of his young conceptions, he saw the
10 unreal world in which they had been conceived. He now had a new
strength in his sense of reality. He felt as if he were real, as if he
handled real things. He had worked for many years at Cossethay,
building the organ for the church, restoring the wood-work, gradually coming to a knowledge of beauty in the plain labours. Now he
15 wanted again to carve things that were utterances of himself.

But he could not quite hitch on—always he was too busy, too
uncertain, confused. Wavering, he began to study modelling. To his
surprise he found he could do it. Modelling in clay, in plaster, he
produced beautiful reproductions, really beautiful. Then he set-to to
20 make a head of Ursula, in high relief, in the Donatello manner.* In
his first passion, he got a beautiful suggestion of his desire. But the
pitch of concentration would not come. With a little ash in his
mouth, he gave up. He continued to copy, or to make designs by
selecting motives from classic stuff. He loved the Della Robbia* and
25 Donatello as he had loved Fra Angelico when he was a young man.
His work had some of the freshness, the naïve alertness of the early
Italians. But it was only reproduction.

Having reached his limit in modelling, he turned to painting. But
he tried water-colour painting after the manner of any other
30 amateur. He got his results but was not much interested. After one
or two drawings of his beloved church, which had the same alertness
as his modelling, but seemed to be incongruous with the modern
atmospheric way of painting, so that his church-tower stood up,
really stood and asserted its standing, but was ashamed of its own
35 lack of meaning, he turned away again.

He took up jewellery, read Benvenuto Cellini,* pored over
reproductions of ornament, and began to make pendants in silver
and pearl and matrix. The first things he did, in his start of discovery,
were really beautiful. Those later were more imitative. But, starting

with his wife, he made a pendant each for all his women folk. Then
he made rings and bracelets.

Then he took up beaten and chiselled metal work. When Ursula
left school, he was making a silver bowl of lovely shape. How he
delighted in it, almost lusted after it.

All this time, his only connection with the real outer world was
through his winter evening classes, which brought him into contact
with state education. So that he did read papers in education, he did
actually watch the politics of education. About all the rest, he was
oblivious and entirely indifferent—even about the war. The nation
did not exist to him. He was in a private retreat of his own, that had
neither nationality nor any great adherent.

Ursula watched the newspapers, vaguely, concerning the war in
South Africa. They made her miserable, and she tried to have as
little to do with them as possible. But Skrebensky was out there. He
sent her an occasional post-card. But it was as if she were a blank
wall in his direction, without windows or out-going. She adhered to
the Skrebensky of her memory.

Her love for Winifred Inger had wrenched her life as it seemed
from the roots and native soil where Skrebensky had belonged to it,
and she was aridly transplanted. He was really only a memory. She
revived his memory with strange passion, after the departure of
Winifred. He was to her almost the symbol of her real life. It was as
if, through him, in him, she might return to her own self, which she
was before she had loved Winifred, before this deadness had come
upon her, this pitiless transplanting. But even her memories were the
work of her imagination.

She dreamed of him and her as they had been together. She could
not dream of him progressively, of what he was doing now, of what
relation he would have to her now. Only sometimes she wept to think
how cruelly she had suffered when he left her—ah, *how* she had
suffered! She remembered what she had written in her diary:

"If I were the moon, I know where I would fall down."

Ah, it was a dull agony to her to remember what she had been
then. For it was remembering a dead self. All that was dead after
Winifred. She knew the corpse of her young, loving self, she knew its
grave. And the young loving self she mourned for had scarcely
existed, it was the creature of her imagination.

Deep within her a cold despair remained unchanging and

unchanged. No-one would ever love her now—she would love no-one. The body of love was killed in her after Winifred, there was something of the corpse in her. She would live, she would go on, but she would have no lovers, no lover would want her any more. She herself would want no lover. The vividest little flame of desire was extinct in her for ever. The tiny, vivid germ that contained the bud of her real self, her real love, was killed, she would go on growing as a plant, she would do her best to produce her minor flowers, but her leading flower was dead before it was born, all her growth was the conveying of a corpse of hope.

The miserable weeks went on, in the poky house crammed with children. What was her life—a sordid, formless, disintegrated nothing: Ursula Brangwen, a person without worth or importance, living in the mean village of Cossethay, within the sordid scope of Ilkeston. Ursula Brangwen, at seventeen worthless and unvalued, neither wanted nor needed by anybody, and conscious herself of her own dead value. It would not bear thinking of.

But still her dogged pride held its own. She might be defiled, she might be a corpse that should never be loved, she might be a core-rotten stalk living upon the food that others provided: yet she would give in to nobody.

Gradually she became conscious that she could not go on living at home as she was doing, without place or meaning or worth. The very children that went to school held her uselessness in contempt. She must do something.

Her father said she had plenty to do to help her mother. From her parents she would never get more than a hit in the face. She was not a practical person. She thought of wild things, of running away and becoming a domestic servant, of asking some man to take her.

She wrote to the mistress of the High School for advice.

"I cannot see very clearly what you should do, Ursula," came the reply, "unless you are willing to become an elementary school-teacher. You have matriculated, and that qualifies you to take a post as uncertificated teacher in any school, at a salary of about fifty pounds a year.

"I cannot tell you how deeply I sympathise with you in your desire to do something. You will learn that mankind is a great body of which you are one useful member, you will take your own place at the great task which humanity is trying to fulfil. That will give you a satisfaction and a self-respect which nothing else could give."

Ursula's heart sank. It was a cold, dreary satisfaction to think of. Yet her cold will acquiesced. This was what she wanted.

"You have an emotional nature," the letter went on, "a quick, natural response. If only you could learn patience and self-discipline, I do not see why you should not make a good teacher. The least you could do is to try. You need only serve a year, or perhaps two years, as uncertificated teacher. Then you would go to one of the training colleges, where I hope you would take your degree. I most strongly urge and advise you to keep up your studies always with the intention of taking a degree. That will give you a qualification and a position in the world, and will give you more scope to choose your own way.

"I shall be proud to see one of my girls win her own economical independence, which means so much more than it seems. I shall be glad indeed to know that one more of my girls has provided for herself the means of freedom to choose for herself."

It all sounded grim and desperate. Ursula rather hated it. But her mother's contempt and her father's harshness had made her raw at the quick, she knew the ignominy of being a hanger-on, she felt the festering thorn of her mother's animal estimation.

At length she had to speak. Hard and shut down and silent within herself, she slipped out one evening to the work-shed. She heard the tap-tap-tap of the hammer upon the metal. Her father lifted his head as the door opened. His face was ruddy and bright with instinct, as when he was a youth, his black moustache was cut close over his wide mouth, his black hair was fine and close as ever. But there was about him an abstraction, a sort of instrumental detachment from human things. He was a worker. He watched his daughter's hard, expressionless face. A hot anger came over his breast and belly.

"What now?" he said.

"Can't I," she answered, looking aside, not looking at him, "can't I go out to work?"

"Go out to work, what for?"

His voice was so strong and ready and vibrant. It irritated her.

"I want some other life than this."

A flash of strong rage arrested all his blood for a moment.

"Some other life!" he repeated. "Why what other life do you want?"

She hesitated.

"Something else besides housework and hanging about. And I want to earn something."

Her curious, brutal hardness of speech, and the fierce invincibility of her youth, which ignored him, made him also harden with anger.

"And how do you think *you're* going to earn anything?" he asked.

5   "I can become a teacher—I'm qualified by my matric."

He wished her matric. in hell.

"And how much are you qualified to earn, by your matric?" he asked, jeering.

"Fifty pounds a year," she said.

10   He was silent, his power taken out of his hand.

He had always hugged a secret pride in the fact that his daughters need not go out to work. With his wife's money and his own, they had four hundred a year. They could draw on the capital if need be, later on. He was not afraid for his old age. His daughters might be ladies.

15   Fifty pounds a year was a pound a week—which was enough for her to live on independently.

"And what sort of a teacher do you think *you'd* make? You haven't the patience of a Jack-gnat* with your own brothers and sisters, let alone with a class of children. And I thought you didn't like 'dirty,

20   board-school* brats.'"

"They're not all dirty."

"You'd find they're not all clean."

There was silence in the work-shop. The lamp-light fell on the burned silver bowl that lay before him, on mallet and furnace and

25   chisels. Brangwen stood with a queer, cat-like light on his face, almost like a smile. But it was no smile.

"Can I try?" she said.

"You can do what the deuce you like, and go where you like."

Her face was fixed and expressionless and indifferent. It always

30   sent him to a pitch of frenzy to see it like that. He kept perfectly still.

Cold, without any betrayal of feeling, she turned and left the shed. He worked on, with all his nerves jangled. Then he had to put down his tools and go into the house.

In a bitter tone of anger and contempt, he told his wife. Ursula was

35   present. There was a brief altercation, closed by Mrs Brangwen's saying, in a tone of biting superiority and indifference:

"Let her find out what it's like. She'll soon have had enough."

The matter was left there. But Ursula considered herself free to act. For some days she made no move. She was reluctant to take the

cruel step of finding work, for she shrank with extreme sensitiveness
and shyness from new contact, new situations. Then at length a sort
of doggedness drove her. Her belly was full of bitterness.

She went to the Free Library in Ilkeston, copied out addresses
from the "Schoolmistress,"* and wrote for application forms. After 5
two days she rose early to meet the postman. As she expected, there
were three long envelopes.

Her heart beat painfully as she went up with them to her bedroom.
Her fingers trembled, she could hardly force herself to look at the
long, official forms she had to fill in. The whole thing was so cruel, so 10
impersonal. Yet it must be done.

"Name (surname first): _____."

In a trembling hand she wrote "Brangwen—Ursula."

"Age and Date of Birth: _____."

After a long time considering, she filled in that line. 15

"Qualifications, with Dates of Examinations: _____."

With a little pride she wrote:

"London Matriculation Examination. June 1900."*

"Previous Experience and Where Obtained: _____."

Her heart sank as she wrote: 20

"None."

Still there was much to answer. It took her two hours to fill in the
three forms. Then she had to copy her testimonials from her
head-mistress and from the clergyman.

At last, however, it was finished. She had sealed the three long 25
envelopes. In the afternoon she went down to Ilkeston to post them.
She said nothing of it all to her parents. As she stamped her long
letters, and put them into the box at the main post-office, she felt as if
already she was out of the reach of her father and mother, as if she
had connected herself with the outer, greater world of activity, the 30
man-made world.

As she returned home, she dreamed again in her own fashion her
old, gorgeous dreams. One of her applications was to Gillingham, in
Kent, one to Kingston-on-Thames, and one to Swanwick in Derbyshire. 35

"Gillingham" was such a lovely name,* and Kent was the Garden
of England. So that, in Gillingham, an old, old village by the hopfields, where the sun shone softly, she came out of school in the
afternoon into the shadow of the plane-trees by the gate, and turned

down the sleepy road towards the cottage where corn-flowers poked their blue heads through the old wooden fence, and phlox stood built up of blossom, beside the path.

A delicate, silver-haired lady rose with delicate, ivory hands
5 uplifted as Ursula entered the room, and:

"Oh my dear, what do you think!"

"What is it, Mrs Wetherall?"

Frederick had come home. Nay, his manly step was heard on the stair, she saw his strong boots, his blue trousers, his uniformed
10 figure, and then his face, clean and keen as an eagle's, and his eyes lit up with the glamour of strange seas, ah, strange seas that had woven through his soul, as he descended into the kitchen.

This dream, with its amplifications, lasted her a mile of walking. Then she went to Kingston-on-Thames.

15 Kingston-on-Thames was an old, historic place just south of London. There lived the well-born, dignified souls who belonged to the metropolis but who loved peace. There she met a wonderful family of girls, living in a large, old, Queen-Anne house whose lawns sloped to the river, and, in an atmosphere of stately peace, she found
20 herself among her soul's intimates. They loved her as sisters, they shared with her all noble thoughts.

She was happy again. In her musings she spread her poor, clipped wings, and flew into the pure empyrean.

Day followed day. She did not speak to her parents. There came
25 the return of her testimonials from Gillingham. She was not wanted—neither at Swanwick. The bitterness of rejection followed the sweets of hope. Her bright feathers were in the dust again.

Then, suddenly, after a fortnight, came an intimation from Kingston-on-Thames. She was to appear at the Education Office of
30 that town on the following Thursday, for an interview with the Committee. Her heart stood still. She knew she would make the Committee accept her. Now, she was afraid, now that her removal was imminent. Her heart quivered with fear and reluctance. But underneath, her purpose was fixed.

35 She passed shadowily through this day, unwilling to tell her news to her mother, waiting for her father. Suspense and fear were strong upon her. She dreaded going to Kingston. Her easy dreams disappeared from the grasp of reality.

And yet, as the afternoon wore away, the sweetness of the dream
40 returned again. Kingston-on-Thames—there was such sound of

dignity to her. The shadow of history and the glamour of stately
progress enveloped her. The palaces would be old and darkened, the
place of kings obscured. Yet it was a place of kings for her—Richard
and Henry and Wolsey and Queen Elizabeth. She divined great
lawns with noble trees, and terraces whose steps the water washed   5
softly, where the swans sometimes came to earth. Still she must see
the stately, gorgeous barge of the Queen float down, the crimson
carpet put upon the landing stairs, the gentlemen in their purple-
velvet cloaks bare-headed, standing in the sunshine grouped on
either side, waiting.   10
   "Sweet Thames run softly till I end my song—."*
Evening came, her father returned home, sanguine and alert
and detached as ever. He was less real than her fancies. She waited
whilst he ate his tea. He took big mouthfuls, big bites, and ate
unconsciously, with the same abandon an animal gives to its food.   15
   Immediately after tea he went over to the church. It was choir-
practice, and he wanted to try the tunes, on his organ.
   The latch of the big door clicked loudly as she came after him, but
the organ rolled more loudly still, he was unaware. He was practising
the anthem. She saw his small, jet-black head and alert face between 20
the candle-flames, his slim body sagged on the music stool. His face
was so luminous and fixed, the movement of his limbs seemed
strange, apart from him. The sound of the organ seemed to belong to
the very stone of the pillars, like sap running in them.
   Then there was a close of music, and silence.   25
   "Father!" she said.
   He looked round as if at an apparition. Ursula stood shadowily
within the candle-light.
   "What now?" he said, not coming to earth.
   It was difficult to speak to him.   30
   "I've got a situation," she said, forcing herself to speak.
   "You've got what?" he answered, unwilling to come out of his
mood of organ-playing. He closed the music before him.
   "I've got a situation to go to."
   Then he turned to her, still abstracted, unwilling.   35
   "Oh, where's that?" he said.
   "At Kingston-on-Thames. I must go on Thursday for an inter-
view with the Committee."
   "You must go on Thursday?"
   "Yes."   40

And she handed him the letter. He read it by the light of the candles:

"Ursula Brangwen, Yew Tree Cottage, Cossethay, Derbyshire.

"Dear Madam, You are requested to call at the above offices on
5 Thursday next, the 10th., at 11.30 a.m., for an interview with the committee, referring to your application for the post of assistant mistress at the Wellingborough Green School."

It was very difficult for Brangwen to take in this remote and official information, glowing as he was within the quiet of his church and his
10 anthem music.

"Well you needn't bother me with it now, need you?" he said impatiently, giving her back the letter.

"I've got to go on Thursday," she said.

He sat motionless. Then he reached more music, and there was a
15 rushing sound of air, then a long, emphatic, trumpet-note of the organ as he laid his hands on the keys. Ursula turned and went away.

He tried to give himself again to the organ. But he could not. He could not get back. All the time a sort of string was tugging, tugging
20 him elsewhere, miserably.

So that when he came into the house after choir-practice his face was dark and his heart black. He said nothing, however, until all the younger children were in bed. Ursula, however, knew what was brewing.

25 At length he asked:

"Where's that letter?"

She gave it to him. He sat looking at it. "You are requested to call at the above offices on Thursday next—" It was a cold, official notice to Ursula herself, and had nothing to do with him. So! She existed
30 now as a separate social individual. It was for her to answer this note without regard to him. He had even no right to interfere. His heart was hard and angry.

"You had to do it behind our backs, had you?" he said with a sneer. And her heart leapt with hot pain. She knew she was
35 free—she had broken away from him. He was beaten.

"You said 'let her try,'" she retorted, almost apologising to him.

He did not hear. He sat looking at the letter.

"Education Office, Kingston-on-Thames"—and then the type-written "Miss Ursula Brangwen—Yew Tree Cottage—Cossethay."
40 It was all so complete and so final. He could not but feel the new

position Ursula held, as recipient of that letter. It was an iron in his soul.

"Well," he said at length, "you're not going."

Ursula started and could find no words to clamour her revolt.

"If you think you're going dancing off to th' other side of London, you're mistaken."

"Why not?" she cried, at once hard fixed in her will to go.

"That's why not," he said.

And there was silence till Mrs Brangwen came downstairs.

"Look here, Anna," he said, handing her the letter.

She put back her head, seeing a type-written letter, anticipating trouble from the outside world. There was the curious sliding motion of her eyes, as if she shut off her sentient, maternal self, and a kind of hard trance, meaningless, took its place. Thus, meaningless, she glanced over the letter, careful not to take it in. She apprehended the contents with her callous, superficial mind. Her feeling self was shut down.

"What post is it?" she asked.

"She wants to go and be a teacher in Kingston-on-Thames, at fifty pounds a year."

"Oh indeed."

The mother spoke as if it were a hostile fact concerning some stranger. She would have let her go, out of callousness. Mrs Brangwen would begin to grow up again only with her youngest child. Her eldest girl was in the way now.

"She's not going all that distance," said the father.

"I have to go where they want me," cried Ursula. "And it's a *good* place to go to."

"What do *you* know about the place?" said her father harshly.

"And it doesn't matter whether they want you or not, if your father says you are not to go," said the mother calmly.

How Ursula hated her!

"You said I was to try," the girl cried. "Now I've got a place, and I'm going to go."

"You're not going all that distance," said her father.

"Why don't you get a place at Ilkeston, where you can live at home?" asked Gudrun, who hated conflicts, who could not understand Ursula's uneasy way, yet who must stand by her sister.

"There aren't any places in Ilkeston," cried Ursula. "And I'd rather go right away."

"If you'd asked about it, a place could have been got for you in Ilkeston. But you had to play Miss High-an'-mighty, and go your own way," said her father.

"I've no doubt you'd rather go right away," said her mother, very caustic. "And I've no doubt you'd find other people didn't put up with you for very long, either. You've too much opinion of yourself, for your good."

Between the girl and her mother was a feeling of pure hatred. There came a stubborn silence. Ursula knew she must break it.

"Well, they've written to me, and I s'll have to go," she said.

"Where will you get the money from?" asked her father.

"Uncle Tom will give it me," she said.

Again there was silence. This time she was triumphant.

Then at length her father lifted his head. His face was abstracted, he seemed to be abstracting himself, to make a pure statement.

"Well, you're not going all that distance away," he said. "I'll ask Mr Burt about a place here. I'm not going to have you by yourself at the other side of London."

"But I've *got* to go to Kingston," said Ursula. "They've sent for me."

"They'll do without you," he said.

There was a trembling silence, when she was on the point of tears.

"Well," she said, low and tense, "you can put me off this, but I'm *going* to have a place. I'm *not* going to stop at home."

"Nobody wants you to stop at home," he suddenly shouted, going livid with rage.

She said no more. Her nature had gone hard and smiling in its own arrogance, in its own antagonistic indifference to the rest of them. This was the state in which he wanted to kill her. She went singing into the parlour:

> "C'est la mère Michel qui a perdu son chat
> Qui cri par la fenêtre qu'est-ce qui le lui rendra—"*

During the next days Ursula went about bright and hard, singing to herself, making love to the children, but her soul hard and cold with regard to her parènts. Nothing more was said.

The hardness and brightness lasted for four days. Then it began to break up. So at evening she said to her father:

"Have you spoken about a place for me?"

"I spoke to Mr Burt."

"What did he say?"

"There's a committee meeting tomorrow. He'll tell me on Friday."

So she waited till Friday. Kingston-on-Thames had been an exciting dream. Here she could feel the hard, raw reality. So she knew that this would come to pass. Because nothing was ever fulfilled, she found, except in the hard, limited reality. She did not want to be a teacher in Ilkeston, because she knew Ilkeston, and hated it. But she wanted to be free, so she must take her freedom where she could.

On Friday her father said there was a place vacant in Brinsley Street school. This could most probably be secured for her at once, without the trouble of application.

Her heart halted. Brinsley Street was a school in a poor quarter, and she had had a taste of the common children of Ilkeston. They had shouted after her and thrown stones. Still, as a teacher, she would be in authority. And it was all unknown. She was excited. The very forest of dry, sterile brick had some fascination for her. It was so hard and ugly, so relentlessly ugly, it would purge her of some of her floating sentimentality.

She dreamed how she would make the little, ugly children love her. She would be so *personal*. Teachers were always so hard and impersonal. There was no vivid relationship. She would make everything personal and vivid, she would give herself, she would give, give, give all her great stores of wealth to her children, she would make them *so* happy, and they would prefer her to any teacher on the face of the earth.

At Christmas she would choose such fascinating Christmas cards for them, and she would give them such a happy party in one of the classrooms.

The head-master, Mr Harby, was a short, thick-set, rather common man, she thought. But she would hold before him the light of grace and refinement, he would have her in such high esteem, before long; she would be the gleaming sun of the school, the children would blossom like little weeds, the teachers like tall, hard plants would burst into rare flower.

The Monday morning came. It was the end of September, and a drizzle of fine rain like veils round her, making her seem intimate, a world to herself. She walked forward to the new land. The old was blotted out. The veil would be rent that hid the new world. She was gripped hard with suspense as she went down the hill in the rain, carrying her dinner bag.

Through the thin rain she saw the town, a black, extensive mount. She must enter in upon it. She felt at once a feeling of repugnance and of excited fulfilment. But she shrank.

She waited at the terminus for the tram.* Here it was beginning. Behind her* was the station to Nottingham, whence Theresa had gone to school half an hour before: behind her was the little church school she had attended when she was a child, when her grandmother was alive. Her grandmother had been dead two years now. There was a strange woman at the Marsh, with her uncle Fred, and a small baby. Behind her was Cossethay, and blackberries were ripe on the hedges.

As she waited at the tram-terminus she reverted swiftly to her childhood: her teasing grandfather with his fair beard and blue eyes and his big, monumental body; he had got drowned: her grandmother, whom Ursula would sometimes say she had loved more than anyone else in the world: the little church school, the Phillips boys; one was a soldier in the Life Guards now, one was a collier. With a passion she clung to the past.

But as she dreamed of it, she heard the tram-car grinding round a bend, rumbling dully, she saw it draw into sight, and hum nearer. It sidled round the loop at the terminus, and came to a standstill, looming above her. Some shadowy grey people stepped from the far end, the conductor was walking in the puddles, swinging round the pole.*

She mounted into the wet, comfortless tram, whose floor was dark with wet, whose windows were all steamed, and she sat in suspense. It had begun, her new existence.

One other passenger mounted—a sort of char-woman with a drab, wet coat. Ursula could not bear the waiting of the tram. The bell clanged, there was a lurch forward. The car moved cautiously down the wet street. She was being carried forward, into her new existence. He heart burned with pain and suspense, as if something were cutting her living tissue.

Often, oh often the tram seemed to stop, and wet, cloaked people mounted and sat mute and grey, in stiff rows opposite her, their umbrellas between their knees. The windows of the tram grew more steamy, opaque. She was shut in with those unliving, spectral people. Even yet it did not occur to her that she was one of them. The

conductor came down issuing tickets. Each little ring of his clipper
sent a pang of dread through her. But her ticket surely was different
from the rest.

They were all going to work; she also was going to work. Her ticket
was the same. She sat trying to fit in with them. But fear was at her 5
bowels, she felt an unknown, terrible grip upon her.

At Bath Street she must dismount and change trams. She looked
uphill. It seemed to lead to freedom. She remembered the many
Saturday afternoons she had walked up to the shops. How free and
careless she had been. 10

Ah, her tram was sliding gingerly downhill. She dreaded every
yard of her conveyance. The car halted, she mounted hastily.

She kept turning her head as the car ran on, because she was
uncertain of the street. At last, her heart a flame of suspense,
trembling, she rose. The conductor rang the bell brusquely. 15

She was walking down a small, mean, wet street, empty of people.
The school squatted low within its railed, asphalt yard, that shone
black with rain. The building was grimy, and horrible, dry plants
were shadowily looking through the windows.

She entered the arched doorway of the porch. The whole place 20
seemed to have a threatening expression, imitating the church's
architecture for the purpose of domineering, like a gesture of vulgar
authority. She saw* that one pair of feet had paddled across the
flagstone floor of the porch. The place was silent, deserted, like an
empty prison, waiting the return of tramping feet. 25

Ursula went forward, to the teachers' room that burrowed in a
gloomy hole. She knocked timidly.

"Come in!" called a surprised man's voice, as from a prison cell.
She entered the dark little room, that never got any sun. The gas was
lighted naked and raw. At the table, a thin man in shirt-sleeves was 30
rubbing a paper on a jelly-tray.* He looked up at Ursula with his
narrow, sharp face, said "Good morning," then turned away again,
and stripped the paper off the tray, glancing at the violet-coloured
writing transferred, before he dropped the curled sheet aside, among
a heap. 35

Ursula watched him fascinated. In the gas-light and gloom and
the narrowness of the room, all seemed unreal.

"Isn't it a nasty morning?" she said.

"Yes," he said. "It's not much of weather."

But in here, it seemed that neither morning nor weather really 40

existed. This place was timeless. He spoke in an occupied voice, like
an echo. Ursula did not know what to say. She took off her
waterproof.

"Am I early?" she asked.

5 The man looked first at a little clock, then at her. His eyes seemed
to be sharpened to needle-points of vision.

"Twenty five past," he said. "You're the second to come. I'm first
this morning."

Ursula sat down gingerly on the edge of a chair, and watched his
10 thin red hands rubbing away on the white surface of the paper, then
pausing, pulling up a corner of the sheet, peering, and rubbing away
again. There was a great heap of curled, white and scribbled sheets
on the table.

"Must you do so many?" asked Ursula.

15 Again the man glanced up sharply. He was about thirty or thirty
three years old, thin, greenish, with a long nose and a sharp face. His
eyes were blue, and sharp as points of steel, rather beautiful, the girl
thought.

"Sixty three," he answered.

20 "So many!" she said, gently. Then she remembered.

"But they're not all for your class, are they?" she added.

"Why aren't they?"* he replied, a fierceness in his voice. Ursula
was rather frightened by his mechanical ignoring of her and his
directness of statement. It was something new to her. She had never
25 been treated like this before, as if she did not count, as if she were
addressing a machine.

"It is too many," she said sympathetically.

"You'll get about the same," he said.

That was all she received. She sat rather blank, not knowing how
30 to feel. Still she liked him. He seemed so cross. There was a queer,
sharp, keen-edge feeling about him that attracted her and frightened
her at the same time. It was so cold, and against his nature.

The door opened, and a short, neutral-tinted young woman of
about twenty eight appeared.

35 "Oh Ursula!" the newcomer exclaimed. "You *are* here early! My
word, I'll warrant you don't keep it up.—That's Mr Williamson's
peg—*This* is yours. Standard Five Teacher always has this. Aren't
you going to take your hat off?"

Miss Violet Harby removed Ursula's waterproof from the peg on
40 which it was hung, to one a little further down the row. She had

already snatched the pins from her own stuff hat,* and jammed them through her coat. She turned to Ursula, as she pushed up her frizzed, flat, dun-coloured hair.

"Isn't it a beastly morning!" she exclaimed, "beastly! And if there's one thing I hate above another, it's a wet Monday morning; 5 —pack of kids trailing in anyhow-nohow, and no holding 'em—"

She had taken a black pinafore from a newspaper package, and was tying it round her waist.

"You've brought an apron, haven't you?" she said jerkily, glancing at Ursula. "Oh—you'll want one. You've no idea what a sight you'll 10 look before half past four, what with chalk and ink and kids' dirty feet.—Well I can send a boy down to Mamma's for one."

"Oh, it doesn't matter," said Ursula.

"Oh, yes—I can send, easily," cried Miss Harby.

Ursula's heart sank. Everybody seemed so cock-sure, and so 15 bossy. How was she going to get on with such jolty, jerky, bossy people. And Miss Harby had not spoken a word to the man at the table. She simply ignored him. Ursula felt the callous, crude rudeness between the two teachers.

The two girls went out into the passage. A few children were 20 already clattering in the porch.

"Jim Richards," called Miss Harby, hard and authoritative. A boy came sheepishly forward.

"Shall you go down to our house for me, eh?" said Miss Harby, in a commanding, condescending, coaxing voice. She did not wait for 25 an answer. "Go down and ask Mamma to send me one of my school pinas, for Miss Brangwen—shall you?"

The boy muttered a sheepish "Yes, Miss," and was moving away.

"Hey!" called Miss Harby. "Come here—Now what are you 30 going for:—what shall you say to Mamma?"

"A school pina—" muttered the boy.

"'Please, Mrs Harby, Miss Harby says will you send her another school pinafore for Miss Brangwen, because she's come without one.'" 35

"Yes Miss," muttered the boy, head ducked, and was moving off. Miss Harby caught him back, holding him by the shoulder.

"What are you going to say?"

"Please Mrs Harby, Miss Harby wants a pinny for Miss Brang-win," muttered the boy very sheepishly. 40

"Miss *Brangwen*!" laughed Miss Harby, pushing him away. "Here, you'd better have my umbrella—wait a minute."

The unwilling boy was rigged up with Miss Harby's umbrella, and set off.

5 "Don't take long over it," called Miss Harby after him. Then she turned to Ursula, and said brightly:

"Oh, he's a caution,* that lad—but not bad you know."

"No," Ursula agreed, weakly.

The latch of the door clicked, and they entered the big room.
10 Ursula glanced down the place. Its rigid, long silence was official and chilling. Halfway down was a glass partition, the doors of which were open. A clock ticked re-echoing, and Miss Harby's voice sounded double as she said:

"This is the big room—Standard Five-Six-and-Seven.—Here's
15 your place—Five—"

She stood in the near end of the great room. There was a small high teacher's desk facing a squadron of long benches, two high windows in the wall opposite.

It was fascinating and horrible to Ursula. The curious, unliving
20 light in the room changed her character. She thought it was the rainy morning. Then she looked up again, because of the horrid feeling of being shut in a rigid, inflexible air, away from all feeling of the ordinary day; and she noticed that the windows were of ribbed, suffused glass.

25 The prison was round her now! She looked at the walls, colour washed, pale green and chocolate, at the large windows with frowsy geraniums against the pale glass, at the long rows of desks, arranged in a squadron, and dread filled her. This was a new world, a new life, with which she was threatened. But still excited, she climbed into her
30 chair at her teacher's desk. It was high, and her feet could not reach the ground, but must rest on the step. Lifted up there, off the ground, she was in office. How queer, how queer it all was! How different it was from the mist of rain blowing over Cossethay. As she thought of her own village, a spasm of yearning crossed her, it
35 seemed so far off, so lost to her.

She was here in this hard, stark reality—*reality*. It was queer that she should call this the reality, which she had never known till today, and which now so filled her with dread,* that she wished she might go away. This was the reality—and Cossethay, her beloved, beautiful,
40 well-known Cossethay, which was as herself unto her, that was

minor reality. This prison of a school was reality. Here, then, she would sit in state, the queen of scholars! Here she would realise her dream of being the beloved teacher bringing light and joy to her children! But the desks before her had an abstract angularity that bruised her sentiment and made her shrink. She winced, feeling she had been a fool in her anticipations. She had brought her feelings and her generosity to where neither generosity nor emotion were wanted. And already she felt rebuffed, troubled by the new atmosphere, out of place.

She slid down, and they returned to the teachers' room. It was queer to feel that one ought to alter one's personality. She was nobody, there was no reality in herself, the reality was all outside of her, and she must apply herself to it.

Mr Harby was in the teachers' room, standing before a big, open cupboard, in which Ursula could see piles of pink blotting paper, heaps of shiny new books, boxes of chalk and bottles of coloured inks. It looked a treasure store.

The school-master was a short, sturdy man, with a fine head, and a heavy jowl. Nevertheless he was good-looking, with his shapely brows and nose, and his great, hanging moustache. He seemed absorbed in his work, and took no notice of Ursula's entry. There was something insulting in the way he could be so actively unaware of another person, so occupied.

When he had a moment of absence, he looked up from the table and said good-morning to Ursula. There was a pleasant light in his brown eyes. He seemed very manly and incontrovertible, like something she wanted to push over.

"You had a wet walk," he said to Ursula.

"Oh, I don't mind, I'm used to it," she replied, with a nervous little laugh.

But already he was not listening. Her words sounded ridiculous and babbling. He was taking no notice of her.

"You will sign your name here," he said to her, as if she were some child—"and the time when you come and go."

Ursula signed her name in the time book and stood back. No-one took any further notice of her. She beat her brains for something to say, but in vain.

"I'd let them in now," said Mr Harby to the thin man, who was very hastily arranging his papers.

The assistant teacher made no sign of acquiescence, and went on

with what he was doing. The atmosphere in the room grew tense. At
the last moment, Mr Brunt slipped into his coat.

"You will go to the girls' lobby," said the school-master to Ursula,
with a fascinating, insulting geniality, purely official and domin-
5   eering.

She went out and found Miss Harby, and another girl teacher, in
the porch. On the asphalt yard the rain was failling. A toneless bell
tang-tang-tanged drearily overhead, monotonously, insistently. It
came to an end. Then Mr Brunt was seen, bare-headed, standing at
10   the other gate of the school yard, blowing shrill blasts on a whistle
and looking down the rainy, dreary street.

Boys in gangs and streams came trotting up, running past the
master and with a loud clatter of feet and voices, over the yard to the
boys' porch. Girls were running and walking through the other
15   entrance.

In the porch where Ursula stood there was a great noise of girls
who were tearing off their coats and hats, and hanging them on the
racks bristling with pegs. There was a smell of wet clothing, a tossing
out of wet, draggled hair, a noise of voices and feet.

20   The mass of girls grew greater, the rage around the pegs grew
steadier, the scholars tended to fall into little noisy gangs in the
porch. Then Violet Harby clapped her hands, clapped them louder,
with a shrill "Quiet girls, quiet!"

There was a pause. The hubbub died down, but did not cease.

25   "What did I say?" cried Miss Harby shrilly.

There was almost complete silence. Sometimes a girl, rather late,
whirled into the porch and flung off her things.

"Leaders—in place," commanded Miss Harby shrilly.

Pairs of girls in pinafores and long hair stood separate in the
30   porch.

"Standard Four, Five and Six—fall in," cried Miss Harby.

There was a hubbub, which gradually resolved itself into three
columns of girls, two and two, standing smirking in the passage. In
among the peg-racks, other teachers were putting the lower classes
35   into ranks.

Ursula stood by her own Standard Five. They were jerking their
shoulders, tossing their hair, nudging, writhing, staring, grinning,
whispering and twisting.

A sharp whistle was heard, and Standard Six, the biggest girls, set
40   off, led by Miss Harby. Ursula, with her Standard Five, followed

after. She stood beside a smirking, grinning row of girls, waiting in a narrow passage. What she was herself, she did not know.

Suddenly the sound of a piano was heard, and Standard Six set off hollowly down the big room. The boys had entered by another door. The piano played on, a march tune. Standard Five followed to the 5 door of the big room. Mr Harby was seen away beyond at his desk. Mr Brunt guarded the other door of the room. Ursula's class pushed up. She stood near them. They glanced and smirked and shoved.

"Go on," said Ursula.

They tittered. 10

"Go on," said Ursula, for the piano continued.

The girls broke loosely into the room. Mr Harby, who had seemed immersed in some occupation, away at his desk, lifted his head and thundered,

"Halt!" 15

There was a halt, the piano stopped. The boys who were just starting through the other door, pushed back. The harsh, subdued voice of Mr Brunt was heard, then the booming shout of Mr Harby, from far down the room:

"Who told Standard Five girls to come in like that?" 20

Ursula crimsoned. Her girls were glancing up at her, smirking their accusation.

"I sent them in, Mr Harby," she said, in a clear, struggling voice. There was a moment of silence. Then Mr Harby roared from the distance: 25

"Go *back* to your places, Standard Five girls."

The girls glanced up at Ursula, accusing, rather jeering, furtive. They pushed back. Ursula's heart hardened with ignominious pain.

"Forward—march," came Mr Brunt's voice, and the girls set off, keeping time with the ranks of boys. 30

Ursula faced her class, some fifty five boys and girls who stood filling the ranks of the desks. She felt utterly non-existent. She had no place nor being there. She faced the block of children.

Down the room she heard the rapid firing of questions. She stood before her class not knowing what to to. She waited painfully. Her 35 block of children, fifty unknown faces, watched her, hostile, ready to jeer. She felt as if she were in torture over a fire of faces. And on every side she was naked to them. Of unutterable length and torture the seconds went by.

Then she gathered courage. She heard Mr Brunt asking ques- 40

tions in mental arithmetic. She stood near to her class, so that her
voice need not be raised too much, and faltering, uncertain, she said:
    "Seven hats at two-pence ha'penny each?"
    A grin went over the face of the class, seeing her commence. She
5 was red and suffering. Then some hands shot up like blades, and she
asked for the answer.
    The day passed incredibly slowly. She never knew what to do,
there came horrible gaps, when she was merely exposed to the
children; and when, relying on some pert little girl for information,
10 she had started a lesson, she did not know how to go on with it
properly. The children were her masters. She deferred to them. She
could always hear Mr Brunt. Like a machine, always in the same
hard, high, inhuman voice he went on with his teaching, oblivious of
everything. And before this inhuman number of children she was
15 always at bay. She could not get away from it. There it was, this class
of fifty collective children, depending on her for command, for
command it hated and resented. It made her feel she could not
breathe: she must suffocate, it was so inhuman. They were so many,
that they were not children. They were a squadron. She could not
20 speak as she would to a child, because they were not individual
children, they were a collective inhuman thing.
    Dinner-time came, and stunned, bewildered, solitary, she went
into the teachers' room for dinner. Never had she felt such a stranger
to life before. It seemed to her she had just disembarked from some
25 strange horrible state where everything was as in hell, a condition of
hard, malevolent system. And she was not really free. The afternoon
ahead drew at her like some bondage.
    The first week passed in a blind confusion. She did not know how
to teach, and she felt she never would know. Mr Harby came down
30 every now and again to her class, to see what she was doing. She felt
so incompetent as he stood by, bullying and threatening, so unreal,
that she wavered, became neutral and non-existent. But he stood
there watching with that listening-genial smile of the eyes, that was
really threatening; he said nothing, he made her go on teaching, she
35 felt she had no soul in her body. Then he went away, and his going
was like a derision. The class was his class. She was a wavering
substitute. He thrashed and bullied, he was hated. But he was
master. Though she was gentle and always considerate of her class,
yet they belonged to Mr Harby, and they did not belong to her. Like
40 some invincible source of the mechanism he kept all power to

himself. And the class owned his power. And in school, it was power and power alone that mattered.

Soon Ursula came to dread him, and at the bottom of her dread was a seed of hate, for she despised him, yet he was master of her. Then she began to get on. All the other teachers hated him, and fanned their hatred among themselves. For he was master of them and the children, he stood like a bull* to make absolute his authority over the herd. That seemed to be his one reason in life, to hold blind authority over the school. His teachers were his subjects as much as the pupils. Only, because they had some authority, his instinct was to detest them.

Ursula could not make herself a favorite with him. From the first moment she set hard against him. She set against Violet Harby also, even though she did not dislike her. Mr Harby was, however, too much for her, he was something she could not come to grips with, something too strong for her. She tried to approach him as a young bright girl usually approaches a man, expecting a little chivalrous courtesy. But the fact that she was a girl, a woman, was ignored or used as a matter for contempt against her. She did not know what she was, nor what she must be. She wanted to remain her own responsive, personal self.

So she taught on. She made friends with the Standard Three teacher, Maggie Schofield. Miss Schofield was about twenty years old, a subdued girl who held aloof from the other teachers. She was rather beautiful, meditative, and seemed to live in another, lovelier world.

Ursula took her dinner to school, and during the second week ate it in Miss Schofield's room. Standard Three classroom stood by itself and had windows on two sides, looking on to the playground. It was a passionate relief to find such a retreat in the jarring school. For there were pots of chrysanthemums and coloured leaves, and a big jar of berries: there were pretty little pictures on the wall, photogravure reproductions from Greuze and Reynolds's "Age of Innocence,"* giving an air of intimacy; so that the room, with its window space, its smaller, tidier desks, its touch of pictures and flowers, made Ursula at once glad. Here at last was a little personal touch, to which she could respond.

It was Monday. She had been at school a week and was getting used to the surroundings, though she was still an entire foreigner in herself. She looked forward to having dinner with Maggie. That was the bright spot in the day. Maggie was so strong and remote, walking with slow, sure steps down a hard road, carrying the dream within her. Ursula went through the class-teaching as through a meaningless daze.

5   Her class tumbled out at midday in haphazard fashion. She did not yet realise what host she was gathering against herself by her superior tolerance, her kindness and her *laisser-aller*. They were gone, and she was rid of them, and that was all. She hurried away to the teachers' room.

10   Mr Brunt was crouching at the small stove, putting a little rice-pudding into the oven. He rose then, and attentively poked in a small saucepan on the hob with a fork. Then he replaced the saucepan lid.

"Aren't they done?" asked Ursula gaily, breaking in on his tense
15 absorption.

She always kept a bright, blithe manner and was pleasant to all the teachers. For she felt like the swan among the geese, of superior heritage and belonging. And her pride at being the swan in this ugly school was not yet abated.

20   "Not yet," replied Mr Brunt, laconic.

"I wonder if my dish is hot," she said, bending down at the oven. She half expected him to look for her, but he took no notice. She was hungry, and she poked her finger eagerly in the pot, to see if her brussels sprouts and potatoes and meat were ready. They were not.

25   "Don't you think it's rather jolly, bringing dinner?" she said to Mr Brunt.

"I don't know as I do," he said, spreading a serviette on a corner of a table, and not looking at her.

"I suppose it is too far for you to go home?"

30   "Yes," he said. Then he rose and looked at her. He had the bluest, fiercest, most pointed eyes that she had ever met. He stared at her with growing fierceness.

"If I were you, Miss Brangwen," he said, menacingly, "I should get a bit tighter hand over my class."

35   Ursula shrank.

"Would you?" she asked, sweetly, yet in terror. "Aren't I strict enough?"

"Because!" he repeated, taking no notice of her, "they'll get you down if you don't tackle 'em pretty quick. They'll pull you down, and
40 worry you, till Harby gets you shifted—that's how it'll be ... you

won't be here another six weeks—" and he filled his mouth with food—"if you don't tackle 'em, and tackle 'em quick."

"Oh but—" Ursula said, resentfully, ruefully. The terror was deep in her.

"Harby'll not help you. This is what he'll do—he'll let you go on, 5 getting worse and worse, till either you clear out or he clears you out.—It doesn't matter to me, except that you'll leave a class behind you as I hope *I* shan't have to cope with—"

She heard the accusation in the man's voice, and felt condemned. But still, school had not yet become a definite reality to her. 10 She was shirking it. It was reality, but it was all outside her. And she fought against Mr Brunt's representation. She did not want to realise.

"Will it be so terrible?" she said, quivering, rather beautiful, but with a slight touch of condescension, because she would not betray 15 her own trepidation.

"Terrible?" said the man, turning to his potatoes again. "I dunno about terrible."

"I *do* feel frightened," said Ursula. "The children seem so—."

"What?" said Miss Harby, entering at that moment. 20

"Why," said Ursula, "Mr Brunt says I ought to tackle my class," and she laughed uneasily.

"Oh, you have to keep order if you want to teach," said Miss Harby, hard, superior, trite.

Ursula did not answer. She felt non valid before them. 25

"If you want to be let to *live*, you have," said Mr Brunt.

"Well if you can't keep order, what good *are* you?" said Miss Harby.

"An' you've got to do it by yourself,"—his voice rose like the bitter cry of the prophets. "You'll get no *help* from anybody." 30

"Oh indeed!" said Miss Harby. "Some people can't be helped." And she departed.

The air of hostility and disintegration, of wills working in antagonistic subordination, was hideous. Mr Brunt, subordinate, afraid, acid with shame, frightened her. Ursula wanted to run. She only 35 wanted to clear out, not to understand.

Then Miss Schofield came in, and with her another, more restful note. Ursula at once turned for confirmation to the newcomer. Maggie remained personal within all this unclean system of authority. 40

"Is the big Anderson here?" she asked of Mr Brunt. And they spoke of some affair about two scholars, coldly, officially.

Miss Schofield took her brown dish, and Ursula followed with her own. The cloth was laid in the pleasant Standard Three room, there
5 was a jar with two or three monthly roses* on the table.

"It is so nice in here, you *have* made it different," said Ursula, gaily. But she was afraid. The atmosphere of the school was upon her.

"The big room," said Miss Schofield; "ha, it's misery to be in it!"
10 She too spoke with bitterness. She too lived in the ignominious position of an upper servant hated by the master above and the class beneath. She was, she knew, liable to attack from either side at any minute, or from both at once, for the authorities would listen to the complaints of parents, and both would turn round on the mongrel
15 authority, the teacher.

So there was a hard, bitter withholding in Maggie Schofield even as she poured out her savoury mess of big, golden beans and brown gravy.

"It is a vegetarian hot-pot," said Miss Schofield. "Would you like
20 to try it?"

"I should love to," said Ursula.

Her own dinner seemed coarse and ugly beside this savoury, clean dish.

"I've never eaten vegetarian things," she said. "But I should think
25 they can be good."

"I'm not really a vegetarian," said Maggie, "I don't like to bring meat to school."

"No," said Ursula, "I don't think I do either."

And again her soul rang an answer to a new refinement, a new
30 liberty. If all vegetarian things were as nice as this, she would be glad to escape the slight uncleanness of meat.

"How good!" she cried.

"Yes," said Miss Schofield, and she proceeded to tell her the receipt. The two girls passed on to talk about themselves. Ursula told
35 all about the High School and about her matriculation, bragging a little. She felt so poor, here, in this ugly place. Miss Schofield listened with brooding, handsome face, rather gloomy.

"Couldn't you have got to some better place than this?" she asked at length.
40 "I didn't know what it was like," said Ursula, doubtfully.

"Ah!" said Miss Schofield, and she turned aside her head with a bitter motion.

"Is it as horrid as it seems?" asked Ursula, frowning lightly, in fear.

"It *is*," said Miss Schofield bitterly. "Ha!—it is *hateful!*"   5

Ursula's heart sank, seeing even Miss Schofield in the deadly bondage.

"It is Mr Harby," said Maggie Schofield, breaking forth. "I don't think I *could* live again in the big room.—Mr Brunt's voice and Mr Harby—ah—"   10

She turned aside her head with a deep hurt. Some things she could not bear.

"Is Mr Harby really horrid?" asked Ursula, venturing into her own dread.

"He!—why, he's just a bully," said Miss Schofield, raising her   15
shamed dark eyes, that flamed with tortured contempt. "He's not bad as long as you keep in with him, and refer to him, and do everything in his way—but—it's all so *mean*! It's just a question of fighting on both sides—and those great *louts*—"

She spoke with difficulty, and with increased bitterness. She had   20
evidently suffered. Her soul was raw with ignominy. Ursula suffered in response.

"But why is it so horrid?" she asked, helplessly.

"You can't do *anything*," said Miss Schofield. "*He's* against you on one side, and he sets the children against you on the other. The   25
children are simply awful. You've got to *make* them do everything. Everything, everything has got to come out of you. Whatever they learn, you've got to force it into them—and that's how it is."

Ursula felt her heart faint inside her. Why must she grasp all this, why must she force learning on fifty five reluctant children, having all   30
the time an ugly, rude jealousy behind her, ready to throw her to the mercy of the herd of children, who would like to rend her as a weaker representative of authority. A great dread of her task possessed her. She saw Mr Brunt, Miss Harby, Miss Schofield, all the school-teachers, drudging unwillingly at the graceless task of compelling   35
many children into one disciplined, mechanical set, reducing the whole set to an automatic state of obedience and attention, and then of commanding their acceptance of various pieces of knowledge. The first great task was to reduce sixty children to one state of mind, or being. This state must be produced automatically, through the   40

will of the teacher and the will of the whole school authority, imposed
upon the will of the children. The point was that the head-master
and the teachers should have one will in authority, which should
bring the will of the children into accord. But the head-master was
5   narrow and exclusive. The will of the teachers could not agree with
his, their separate wills refused to be so subordinated. So there was a
state of anarchy, leaving the final judgment to the children themselves, which authority should exist.

   So there existed a set of separate wills, each straining itself to the
10 utmost to exert its own authority. Children will never naturally
acquiesce to sitting in a class and submitting to knowledge. They
must be compelled by a stronger, wiser will. Against which will they
must always strain to revolt. So that the first great effort of every
teacher of a large class must be to bring the will of the children into
15 accordance with his own will. And this he can only do through an
abnegation of his personal self, and an application of a system of
laws, for the purpose of achieving a certain calculable result, the
imparting of certain knowledge. Whereas Ursula thought she was
going to become the first wise teacher, by making the whole business
20 personal, and using no compulsion. She believed entirely in her own
personality.

   So that she was in a very deep mess. In the first place she was
offering to a class a relationship which only one or two of the
children were sensitive enough to appreciate, so that the mass were
25 left outsiders, therefore against her. Secondly she was placing
herself in passive antagonism to the one fixed authority of Mr Harby,
so that the scholars could more safely harry her. She did not know,
but her instinct gradually warned her. She was tortured by the voice
of Mr Brunt. On it went, jarring, harsh, full of hate, but so
30 monotonous, it nearly drove her mad: always the same set, harsh
monotony. The man was become a mechanism working on and on
and on. But the personal man was in subdued friction all the time. It
was horrible—all hate! Must she be like this? She could feel the
ghastly necessity. She must become the same—put away her
35 personal self, become an instrument, an abstraction, working upon a
certain material, the class, to achieve a set purpose of making them
know so much each day. And she could not submit. Yet gradually she
felt the invincible iron closing upon her. The sky was being blocked
out. Often, when she went out at playtime and saw a luminous blue
40 sky with changing clouds, it seemed just a fantasy, like a piece of

painted scenery. Her heart was so black and tangled in the teaching, her personal self was shut in prison, abolished, she was subjugate to a bad, destructive will. How then could the sky be shining? There was no sky, there was no luminous atmosphere of out-of-doors. Only the inside of the school was real—hard, concrete, real and vicious. 5

She would not yet, however, let school quite overcome her. She always said "It is not a permanency, it will come to an end." She could always see beyond the place, see the time when she had left it. On Sundays, and on holidays, when she was away at Cossethay or in the woods where the beech-leaves were fallen, she could think of St 10 Philips* Church School, and by an effort of will put it in the picture as a dirty little low-squatting building that made a very tiny mound under the sky, while the great beech woods spread immense about her, and the afternoon was spacious and wonderful. Moreover the children, the scholars, they were insignificant little objects far away, 15 oh far away. And what power had they over her free soul? A fleeting thought of them, as she kicked her way through the beech-leaves, and they were gone! But her will was tense against them all the time.

All the while, they pursued her. She had never had such a passionate love of the beautiful things about her. Sitting on top of the 20 tram-car, at evening, sometimes school was swept away as she saw a magnificent sky settling down. And her breast, her very hands clamoured for the lovely flare of sunset. It was poignant almost to agony, her reaching for it. She almost cried aloud, seeing the sundown so lovely. 25

For she was held away. It was no matter how she said to herself that school existed no more once she had left it. It existed. It was within her like a dark weight, controlling her movement. It was in vain the high-spirited, proud young girl flung off the school and its association with her. She was Miss Brangwen, she was Standard 30 Five Teacher, she had her most important being in her work now.

Constantly haunting her, like a darkness hovering over her heart and threatening to swoop down on it at every moment, was the sense that somehow, somehow she was brought down. Bitterly she denied unto herself that she was really a school-teacher. Leave that to the 35 Violet Harbys. She herself would stand clear of the accusation.—It was in vain she denied it.

Within herself some recording hand seemed to point mechanically to a negation. She was incapable of fulfilling her task. She could never for a moment escape from the fatal weight of the knowledge. 40

And so she felt inferior to Violet Harby. Miss Harby was a
splendid teacher. She could keep order and inflict knowledge on a
class with remarkable efficiency. It was no good Ursula's protesting
to herself that she was infinitely, infinitely the superior of Violet
5 Harby. She knew that Violet Harby succeeded where she failed, and
this in a task which was almost a test of her. She felt something all the
time wearing upon her, wearing her down. She went about in these
first weeks trying to deny it, to say she was free as ever. She tried not
to feel at a disadvantage before Miss Harby, tried to keep up the
10 effect of her own superiority. But a great weight was on her, which
Violet Harby could bear, and she herself could not.

Though she did not give in, she never succeeded. Her class was
getting in worse condition, she knew herself less and less secure in
teaching it. Ought she to withdraw and go home again? Ought she to
15 say she had come to the wrong place, and so retire? Her very life was
at test.

She went on rather doggedly, blindly, waiting for a crisis. Mr
Harby had now begun to persecute her. Her dread and hatred of him
grew and loomed larger and larger. She was afraid he was going to
20 bully her and destroy her. He began to persecute her because she
could not keep her class in proper condition, because her class was
the weak link in the chain which made up the school.

One of the offences was that her class was noisy and disturbed Mr
Harby, as he took Standard Seven at the other end of the room. She
25 was taking composition on a certain morning, walking in among the
scholars. Some of the boys had dirty ears and necks, their clothing
smelled unpleasantly, but she could ignore it. She corrected the
writing as she went.

"When you say 'their fur is brown,' how do you write 'their'?" she
30 asked.

There was a little pause: the boys were always jeeringly backward
in answering. They had begun to jeer at her authority altogether.

"Please Miss, t-h-e-i-r," spelled a lad, loudly, with a note of
mockery.

35 At that moment Mr Harby was passing.

"Stand up Hill!" he called, in a big voice.

Everybody started. Ursula watched the boy. He was evidently
poor, and rather cunning. A stiff bit of hair stood straight off his
forehead, the rest fitted close to his meagre head. He was pale and
40 colourless.

"Who told you to call out?" thundered Mr Harby.

The boy looked up and down, with a guilty air, and a cunning, cynical reserve.

"Please Sir, I was answering," he replied, with the same humble insolence.

"Go to my desk."

The boy set off down the room, the big black jacket hanging in dejected folds about him, his thin legs, rather knocked at the knees, going already with the pauper's crawl, his feet in their big boots scarcely lifted. Ursula watched him in his crawling, slinking progress down the room. He was one of *her* boys! When he got to the desk, he looked round, half furtively, with a sort of cunning grin and pathetic leer, at the big boys of Standard VII. Then, pitiable, pale, in his dejected garments, he lounged under the menace of the head-master's desk, with one thin leg crooked at the knee and the foot stuck out sideways, his hands in the low-hanging pockets of his man's jacket.

Ursula tried to get her attention back to the class. The boy gave her a little horror, and she was at the same time hot with pity for him. She felt she wanted to scream. She was responsible for the boy's punishment. Mr Harby was looking at her handwriting on the board. He turned to the class.

"Pens down."

The children put down their pens and looked up.

"Fold arms."

They pushed back their books and folded arms.

Ursula, stuck among the back forms, could not extricate herself.

"*What* is your composition about?" asked the head-master. Every hand shot up. "The—" stuttered some voice in its eagerness to answer.

"I wouldn't advise you to call out," said Mr Harby. He would have a pleasant voice, full and musical, but for the detestable menace that always tailed in it. He stood unmoved, his eyes twinkling under his bushy black brows, watching the class. There was something fascinating in him, as he stood, and again she wanted to scream. She was all jarred, she did not know what she felt.

"Well, Alice?" he said.

"The rabbit," piped a girl's voice.

"A very easy subject for Standard Five."

Ursula felt a slight shame of incompetence. She was exposed

before the class. And she was tormented by the contradictoriness of
everything. Mr Harby stood so strong, and so male, with his black
brows and clear forehead, the heavy jaw, the big, overhanging
moustache: such a man, with strength and male power, and a certain
5   blind, native beauty. She might have liked him as a man. And here he
stood in some other capacity, bullying over such a trifle as a boy's
speaking out without permission. Yet he was not a little, fussy man.
He seemed to have some cruel, stubborn, evil spirit, he was
imprisoned in a task too small and petty for him, which yet, in a
10 servile acquiescence, he would fulfil, because he had to earn his
living. He had no finer control over himself, only this blind, dogged,
wholesale will. He would keep the job going, since he must. And his
job was to make the children spell the word "caution" correctly, and
put a capital letter after a full-stop. So at this he hammered with his
15 suppressed hatred, always suppressing himself, till he was beside
himself. Ursula suffered bitterly as he stood, short and handsome
and powerful, teaching her class. It seemed such a miserable thing
for him to be doing. He had a decent, powerful, rude soul. What did
he care about the composition on "The Rabbit"? Yet his will kept
20 him there before the class, threshing the trivial subject. It was habit
with him now, to be so little and vulgar, out of place. She saw the
shamefulness of his position, felt the fettered wickedness in him
which would blaze out into evil rage in the long run, so that he was
like a persistent, strong creature tethered. It was really intolerable.
25 The jarring was torture to her. She looked over the silent, attentive
class that seemed to have crystallised into order and rigid, neutral
form. This he had it in his power to do, to crystallise the children into
hard, mute fragments, fixed under his will: his brute will, which fixed
them by sheer force. She too must learn to subdue them to her will:
30 she must. For it was her duty, since the school was such. He had
crystallised the class into order. But to see him, a strong, powerful
man, using all his power for such a purpose, seemed almost horrible.
There was something hideous about it. The strange, genial light in
his eye was really vicious, and ugly, his smile was one of torture. He
35 could not be impersonal. He could not have a clear, pure purpose, he
could only exercise his own brute will. He did not believe in the least
in the education he kept inflicting year after year upon the children.
So he must bully, only bully, even while it tortured his strong,
wholesome nature with shame like a spur always galling. He was so

blind and ugly and out of place. Ursula could not bear it as he stood there. The whole situation was wrong and ugly.

The lesson was finished, Mr Harby went away. At the far end of the room, she heard the whistle and thud of the cane. Her heart stood still within her. She could not bear it, no, she could not bear it when the boy was beaten. It made her sick. She felt that she must go out of his school, this torture-place. And she hated the school-master, thoroughly and finally. The brute, had he no shame? He should never be allowed to continue the atrocity of this bullying cruelty. Then Hill came crawling back, blubbering piteously. There was something desolate about his blubbering that nearly broke her heart. For after all, if she had kept her class in proper discipline, this would never have happened, Hill would never have called out, and been caned.

She began the arithmetic lesson. But she was distracted. The boy Hill sat away on the back desk, huddled up, blubbering and sucking his hand. It was a long time. She dared not go near, nor speak to him. She felt ashamed before him. And she felt she could not forgive the boy for being the huddled, blubbering object, all wet and snivelled, which he was.

She went on correcting the sums. But there were too many children. She could not get round the class. And Hill was on her conscience. At last he had stopped crying, and sat bunched over his hands, playing quietly. Then he looked up at her. His face was dirty with tears, his eyes had a curious washed look, like the sky after rain, a sort of wanness. He bore no malice. He had already forgotten, and was waiting to be restored to the normal position.

"Go on with your work Hill," she said.

The children were playing over their arithmetic, and, she knew, cheating thoroughly. She wrote another sum on the blackboard. She could not get round the class. She went again to the front to watch. Some were ready. Some were not. What was she to do?

At last it was time for recreation. She gave the order to cease working, and in some way or other got her class out of the room. Then she faced the disorderly litter of blotted, uncorrected books, of broken rulers and chewed pens. And her heart sank in sickness. The misery was getting deeper.

The trouble went on and on, day after day. She had always piles of books to mark, myriads of errors to correct, a heart-wearying task

that she loathed. And the work got worse and worse. When she tried
to flatter herself that the composition grew more alive, more
interesting, she had to see that the handwriting grew more and more
slovenly, the books more filthy and disgraceful. She tried what she
5 could, but it was of no use. But she was not going to take it seriously.
Why should she? Why should she say to herself, that it mattered, if
she failed to teach a class to write perfectly neatly? Why should she
take the blame unto herself?

Pay day came, and she received four pounds two shillings and one
10 penny. She was very proud that day. She had never had so much
money before. And she had earned it all herself. She sat on the top of
the tram-car fingering the gold* and fearing she might lose it. She
felt so established and strong, because of it. And when she got home,
she said to her mother:

15   "It is pay day today, mother."

"Ay," said her her mother coolly.

Then Ursula put down fifty shillings on the table.

"That is my board," she said.

"Ay," said her mother, letting it lie.

20 Ursula was hurt. Yet she had paid her scot. She was free. She paid
for what she had. There remained moreover thirty two shillings of
her own. She would not spend any, she who was naturally a
spendthrift, because she could not bear to damage her fine gold.

She had a standing ground now apart from her parents. She was
25 something else besides the mere daughter of William and Anna
Brangwen. She was independent. She earned her own living. She
was an important member of the working community. She was sure
that fifty shillings a month quite paid for her keep. If her mother
received fifty shillings a month for each of the children, she would
30 have twenty pounds a month and no clothes to provide. Very well
then.

Ursula was independent of her parents. She now adhered elsewhere. Now, the "Board of Education" was a phrase that rang
significant to her, and she felt Whitehall* far beyond her as her
35 ultimate home. In the government, she knew which minister had
supreme control over Education, and it seemed to her that, in some
way, he was connected with her, as her father was connected with
her.

She had another self, another responsibility. She was no longer
40 only Ursula Brangwen, daughter of William Brangwen. She was also

Standard Five Teacher in St Philips School. And it was a case now of being Standard Five Teacher, and nothing else. For she could not escape.

Neither could she succeed. That was her horror. As the weeks passed on, there was no Ursula Brangwen, free and jolly. There was only a girl of that name obsessed by the fact that she could not manage her class of children. At week-ends there came days of passionate reaction, when she went mad with the taste of liberty, when merely to be free in the morning, to sit down at her embroidery and stitch the coloured silks was a passion of delight. For the prison house was always awaiting her!—this was only a respite. As her chained heart knew well. So that she seized hold of the swift hours of the week-end, and wrung the last drop of sweetness out of them, in a little, cruel frenzy.

She did not tell anybody how this state was a torture to her. She did not confide, either to Gudrun or to her parents, how horrible she found it, to be a school-teacher. But when Sunday night came, and she felt the Monday morning at hand, she was strung up tight with dreadful anticipation, because the strain and the torture was near again.

She did not believe she could ever teach that great, brutish class, in that brutal school: ever, ever. And yet, if she failed, she must in some way go under. She must admit that the man's world was too strong for her, she could not take her place in it; she must go down before Mr Harby. And all her life henceforth, she must go on, never having freed herself of the man's world, never having achieved the freedom of the great world of responsible work. Maggie had taken her place there, she had even stood level with Mr Harby, and got free of him; and her soul was always wandering in far-off alleys and glades of poetry. Maggie was free. Yet there was something like subjection in Maggie's very freedom. Mr Harby, the man, disliked the reserved woman, Maggie. Mr Harby, the school-master, respected his teacher, Miss Schofield.

For the present, however, Ursula only envied and admired Maggie. She herself had still to get where Maggie had got. She had still to make her footing. She had taken up a position on Mr Harby's ground, and she must keep it. For now he was beginning a regular attack on her, to drive her away out of his school. She could not keep order. Her class was a turbulent crowd, and the weak spot in the school's work. Therefore she must go, and some-

one more useful must come in her place, someone who could keep
discipline.

The head-master had worked himself into an obsession of fury
against her. He only wanted her gone. She had come, she had got
5   worse as the weeks went on, she was absolutely no good. His system,
which was his very life in school, the outcome of his bodily
movement, was attacked and threatened at the point where Ursula
was included. She was the danger that threatened his body with a
blow, a fall. And blindly, thoroughly, moving from strong instinct of
10   opposition, he set to work to expel her.

When he punished one of her children as he had punished the boy
Hill, for an offence against *himself*, he made the punishment extra
heavy with the significance that the extra stroke came in because of
the weak teacher who allowed all these things to be. When he
15   punished for an offence against *her*, he punished lightly, as if
offences against her were not significant. Which all the children
knew, and they behaved accordingly.

Every now and again Mr Harby would swoop down to examine
exercise books. For a whole hour, he would be going round the class,
20   taking book after book, comparing page after page, whilst Ursula
stood aside for all the remarks and fault-finding to be pointed at her
through the scholars. It was true, since she had come, the composition books had grown more and more untidy, disorderly, filthy.
Mr Harby pointed to the pages done before her régime, and to those
25   done after, and fell into a passion of rage. Many children he sent out
to the front with their books. And after he had thoroughly gone
through the silent and quivering class, he caned the worst offenders
well, in front of the others, thundering in real passion of anger and
chagrin:

30   "Such a condition in a class, I can't believe it! It is simply
disgraceful! I can't think how you have been let to get like this! Every
Monday morning I shall come down and examine these books. So
don't think that because there is nobody paying any attention to you,
that you are free to unlearn everything you ever learnt and go back till
35   you are not fit for Standard Three. I shall examine all books every
Monday—"

Then in a rage, he went away with his cane, leaving Ursula to
confront a pale, quivering class, whose childish faces were shut in
blank resentment, fear, and bitterness, whose souls were full of
40   anger and contempt of *her* rather than of the master, whose eyes

looked at her with the cold, inhuman accusation of children. And she could hardly make mechanical words to speak to them. When she gave an order, they obeyed with an insolent off-handedness, as if to say: "As for you, do you think we would obey *you*, but for the master?" She sent the blubbering, caned boys to their seats, knowing that they too jeered at her and her authority, holding her weakness responsible for what punishment had overtaken them. And she knew the whole position, so that even her horror of physical beating and suffering sank to a deeper pain, and became a moral judgment upon her, worse than any hurt.

She must, during the next week, watch over her books, and punish any fault. Her soul decided it coldly. Her personal desire was dead for that day at least. She must have nothing more of herself in school. She was to be Standard Five Teacher only. That was her duty. In school, she was nothing but Standard Five Teacher. Ursula Brangwen must be excluded.

So that, pale, shut, at last distant and impersonal, she saw no longer the child, how his eyes danced, or how he had a queer little soul that could not be bothered with shaping handwriting so long as he dashed down what he thought. She saw no children, only the task that was to be done. And keeping her eyes there, on the task and not on the child, she was impersonal enough to punish where she could otherwise only have sympathised, understood, and condoned, to approve where she would have been merely uninterested before. But her interest had no place any more.

It was agony to the impulsive, bright girl of seventeen* to become distant and official, having no personal relationship with the children. For a few days, after the agony of the Monday, she succeeded, and had some success with her class. But it was a state not natural to her, and she began to relax.

Then came another infliction. There were not enough pens to go round the class. She sent to Mr Harby for more. He came in person.

"Not enough pens, Miss Brangwen?" he said, with the smile and calm of exceeding rage against her.

"No, we are six short," she said, quaking.

"Oh, how is that?" he said, menacingly. Then, looking over the class, he asked:

"How many are there here today?"

"Fifty two," said Ursula, but he did not take any notice, counting for himself.

"Fifty two," he said. "And how many pens are there, Staples?"

Ursula was now silent. He would not heed her if she answered, since he had addressed the monitor.

"That's a very curious thing," said Mr Harby, looking over the
5   silent class with a slight grin of fury. All the childish faces looked up at him blank and exposed.

"A few days ago," the master went on, "there were sixty pens for this class—now there are forty eight. What is forty eight from sixty, Williams?" There was a sinister suspense in the question. A thin,
10 ferret-faced boy in a sailor suit started up exaggeratedly.

"Please Sir!" he said. Then a slow, sly grin came over his face. He did not know. There was a tense silence. The boy dropped his head. Then he looked up again, a little cunning triumph in his eyes. "Twelve," he said.

15 "I would advise you to attend," said the head-master dangerously. The boy sat down.

"Forty eight from sixty is twelve: so there are twelve pens to account for. Have you looked for them, Staples?"

"Yes Sir."

20 "Then look again."

The scene dragged on. Two pens were found: ten were missing. Then the storm burst.

"Am I to have you thieving, besides your dirt and bad work and bad behaviour?" the head-master began. "Not content with being
25 the worst-behaved and dirtiest class in the school, you are thieves into the bargain, are you? It is a very funny thing! Pens don't melt into the air: pens are not in the habit of mizzling away into nothing. What has become of them? For they must be found, and found by Standard Five. They were lost by Standard Five, and they must be
30 found."

Ursula stood and listened, her heart hard and cold. She was so much upset, that she felt almost mad. Something in her tempted her to turn on the head-master and tell him to stop, about the miserable pens. But she did not. She could not.

35 After every session, morning and evening, she had the pens counted. Still they were missing. And pencils and indiarubbers disappeared. She kept the class staying behind, till the things were found. But as soon as Mr Harby had gone out of the room, the boys began to jump about and shout, and at last they bolted in a body from
40 the school.

This was drawing near a crisis. She could not tell Mr Harby because, while he would punish the class, he would make her the cause of the punishment, and her class would pay her back with disobedience and derision. Already there was a deadly hostility grown up between her and the children. After keeping in the class, at evening, to finish some work, she would find boys dodging behind her, calling after her:

"Brangwen, Brangwen—Proud-arse."*

When she went into Ilkeston of a Saturday morning with Gudrun she heard again the voices yelling after her:

"Brangwen, Brangwen."

She pretended to take no notice, but she coloured with shame at being held up to derision in the public street. She, Ursula Brangwen of Cossethay, could not escape from the Standard Five Teacher which she was. In vain she went out to buy ribbon for her hat. They called after her, the boys she tried to teach.

And one evening, as she went from the edge of the town into the country, stones came flying at her. Then the passion of shame and anger surpassed her. She walked on unheeding, beside herself. Because of the darkness, she could not see who were those that threw. But she did not want to know.

Only in her soul a change took place. Never more, and never more would she give herself as individual to her class. Never more would she, Ursula Brangwen, the girl she was, the person she was, come into contact with those boys. She would be Standard Five Teacher, as far away personally from her class as if she had never set foot in St Philips School. She would just obliterate them all, and keep herself apart, take them as scholars only.

So her face grew more and more shut, and over her flayed, exposed soul of a young girl who had gone open and warm to give herself to the children, there set a hard, insentient thing, that worked mechanically according to a system imposed.

It seemed she scarcely saw her class the next day. She could only feel her will, and what she would have of this class which she must grasp into subjection. It was no good, any more, to appeal, to play upon the better feelings of the class. Her swift-working soul realised this.

She, as teacher, must bring them all, as scholars, into subjection. And this she was going to do. All else she would forsake.* She had become hard and impersonal, almost avengeful on herself as well as on them, since the stone-throwing. She did not want to be a person, to be herself any more, after such humiliation. She would assert herself for mastery, be only teacher. She was set now. She was going to fight and subdue.

5 She knew by now her enemies in the class. The one she hated most was Williams. He was a sort of defective, not bad enough to be so classed. He could read with fluency, and had plenty of cunning intelligence. But he could not keep still. And he had a kind of sickness very repulsive to a sensitive girl, something cunning and
10 etiolated and degenerate. Once he had thrown an inkwell at her, in one of his mad little rages. Twice he had run home out of class. He was a well-known character.

And he grinned up his sleeve at this girl-teacher, sometimes hanging round her to fawn on her. But this made her dislike him the
15 more. He had a kind of leech-like power.

From one of the children she took a supple cane, and this she determined to use when real occasion came. One morning, at composition, she said to the boy Williams:

"Why have you made this blot?"

20 "Please Miss, it fell off my pen," he whined out, in the mocking voice that he was so clever in using. The boys near snorted with laughter. For Williams was an actor. He could tickle the feelings of his hearers subtly. Particularly he could tickle the children with him into ridiculing his teacher, or indeed, any authority of which he was
25 not afraid. He had that peculiar gaol instinct.

"Then you must stay in and finish another page of composition," said the teacher.

This was against her usual sense of justice, and the boy resented it derisively. At twelve o'clock, she caught him slinking out.

30 "Williams, sit down," she said.

And there she sat, and there he sat, alone, opposite to her, on the back desk, looking up at her with his furtive eyes every minute.

"Please Miss, I've got to go an errand," he called out insolently.

"Bring me your book," said Ursula.

35 The boy came out, flapping his book along the desks. He had not written a line.

"Go back and do the writing you have to do," said Ursula.

And she sat at her desk trying to correct books. She was trembling and upset. And for an hour the miserable boy writhed and grinned
40 in his seat. At the end of that time he had done five lines.

"As it is so late now," said Ursula, "you will finish the rest this evening."

The boy kicked his way insolently down the passage.

The afternoon came again. Williams was there, glancing at her, and her heart beat thick for she knew it was a fight between them. She watched him.

During the geography lesson, as she was pointing to the map with her cane, the boy continually ducked his whitish head under the desk, and attracted the attention of other boys.

"Williams," she said, gathering her courage, for it was critical now to speak to him, "what are you doing?"

He lifted his face, the sore-rimmed eyes half smiling. There was something intrinsically indecent about him. Ursula shrank away.

"Nothing," he replied, feeling a triumph.

"What are you doing?" she repeated, her heart-beat suffocating her.

"Nothing," replied the boy, insolently, aggrieved, comic.

"If I speak to you again, you must go down to Mr Harby," she said.

But this boy was a match even for Mr Harby. He was so persistent, so cringing and flexible, he howled so when he was hurt, that the master hated more the teacher who sent him than he hated the boy himself. For of the boy he was sick of the sight. Which Williams knew. He grinned visibly.

Ursula turned to the map again, to go on with the geography lesson. But there was a little ferment in the class. Williams' spirit infected them all. She heard a scuffle, and then she trembled inwardly. If they all turned on her this time, she was beaten.

"Please Miss—" called a voice in distress.

She turned round. One of the boys she liked was ruefully holding out a torn celluloid collar. She heard the complaint, feeling futile.

"Go in front, Wright," she said.

She was trembling in every fibre. A big, sullen boy, not bad but very difficult, slouched out to the front. She went on with the lesson, aware that Williams was making faces at Wright, and that Wright was grinning behind her. She was afraid. She turned to the map again. And she was afraid.

"Please Miss, Williams—" came a sharp cry, and a boy on the back row was standing up, with drawn, pained brows, half a mocking grin on his pain, half real resentment against Williams—"Please Miss, he's nipped me,"—and he rubbed his leg ruefully.

"Come in front, Williams," she said.

The rat-like boy sat with his pale smile and did not move.

"Come in front," she repeated, definite now.

"I shan't," he cried, snarling, rat-like, grinning.

5 Something went click in Ursula's soul. Her face and eyes set, she went through the class, straight. The boy cowered before her glowering, fixed eyes. But she advanced on him, seized him by the arm, and dragged him from his seat. He clung to the form. It was the battle between him and her. Her instinct had suddenly become calm
10 and quick. She jerked him from his grip, and dragged him, struggling and kicking, to the front. He kicked her several times, and clung to the forms as he passed, but she went on. The class was on its feet in excitement. She saw it, but made no move.

She knew if she let go the boy he would dash to the door. Already
15 he had run home once out of her class. So she snatched her cane from the desk, and brought it down on him. He was writhing and kicking. She saw his face beneath her, white, with eyes like the eyes of a fish, stony, yet full of hate and horrible fear. And she loathed him, the hideous writhing thing that was nearly too much for her. In
20 horror lest he should overcome her, and yet at the heart quite calm,
• she brought down the cane again and again, whilst he struggled making inarticulate noises, and lunging vicious kicks at her. With one hand she managed to hold him, and now and then, the cane came down on him. He writhed, like a mad thing. But the pain of the
25 strokes cut through his writhing, vicious, coward's courage, bit deeper, till at last, with a long whimper that became a yell, he went limp. She let him go, and he rushed at her, his teeth and eyes glinting. There was a second of agonised terror in her heart: he was a beast thing. Then she caught him, and the cane came down on him.
30 A few times, madly, in a frenzy, he lunged and writhed, to kick her. But again the cane broke him, he sank with a howling yell on the floor, and like a beaten beast lay there yelling.

Mr Harby had rushed up towards the end of this performance.

"What's the matter?" he roared.

35 Ursula felt as if something were going to break in her.

"I've thrashed him," she said, her breast heaving, forcing out the words on the last breath. The head-master stood choked with rage, helpless. She look at the writhing, howling figure on the floor.

"Get up," she said. The thing writhed away from her. She took a step forward. She had realised the presence of the head-master for one second, and then she was oblivious of it again.

"Get up," she said. And with a little dart, the boy was on his feet. His yelling dropped to a mad blubber. He had been in a frenzy.

"Go and stand by the radiator," she said. 5

As if mechanically, blubbering, he went.

The head-master stood robbed of movement or speech. His face was yellow, his hands twitched convulsively. But Ursula stood stiff not far from him. Nothing could touch her now: she was beyond Mr Harby. She was as if violated to death. 10

The head-master muttered something, turned, and went down the room, whence, from the far end, he was heard roaring in mad rage at his own class.

The boy blubbered wildly by the radiator. Ursula looked at the class. There were fifty pale, still faces watching her, a hundred round 15 eyes fixed on her in an attentive, expressionless stare.

"Give out history readers," she said to the monitors.

There was dead silence. As she stood there, she could hear again the ticking of the clock, and the chock of piles of books taken out of the low cupboard. Then came the faint flap of books on the desks. 20 The children passed in silence, their hands working in unison. They were no longer a pack, but each one separated into a silent, closed thing.

"Take page 125, and read that chapter," said Ursula.

There was a click of many books opened. The children found the 25 page, and bent their heads obediently to read. And they read, mechanically.

Ursula, who was trembling violently, went and sat in her high chair. The blubbering of the boy continued. The strident voice of Mr Brunt, the roar of Mr Harby, came muffled through the glass 30 partition. And now and then a pair of eyes rose from the reading book, rested on her a moment, watchful, as if calculating impersonally, then sank again.

She sat still without moving, her eyes watching the class, unseeing. She was quite still, and weak. She felt she could not raise her hand 35 from the desk. If she sat there forever, she felt she could not move again, nor utter a command. It was a quarter past four. She almost dreaded the closing of the school, when she would be alone.

The class began to recover its ease, the tension relaxed. Williams was still crying. Mr Brunt was giving orders for the closing of the lesson. Ursula got down.

"Take your place, Williams," she said.

He dragged his feet across the room, wiping his face on his sleeve. As he sat down, he glanced at her furtively, his eyes still redder. Now he looked like some beaten rat.

At last the children were gone. Mr Harby trod by heavily, without looking her way, or speaking. Mr Brunt hesitated as she was locking her cupboard.

"If you settle Clarke and Letts in the same way, Miss Brangwen, you'll be all right," he said, his blue eyes glancing down in strange fellowship, his long nose pointing at her.

"Shall I?" she laughed nervously. She did not want anybody to talk to her.

As she went along the street, clattering on the granite pavement, she was aware of boys dodging behind her. Something struck her hand that was carrying her bag, bruising her. As it rolled away she saw* it was a potato. Her hand was hurt, but she gave no sign. Soon she would take the tram.

She was afraid, and strange. It was to her quite strange and ugly, like some dream where she was degraded. She would have died rather than admit it to anybody. She could not look at her swollen hand. Something had broken in her; she had passed a crisis. Williams was beaten, but at a cost.

Feeling much too upset to go home, she rode a little further into the town, and got down from the tram at a small tea-shop. There, in the dark little place behind the shop, she drank her tea and ate the bread and butter. She did not taste anything. The taking tea was just a mechanical action, to cover over her existence. There she sat in the dark, obscure little place, without knowing. Only unconsciously she nursed the back of her hand, which was bruised.

When finally she took her way home, it was sunset red across the west. She did not know why she was going home. There was nothing for her there. She had, true, only to pretend to be normal. There was nobody she could speak to, nowhere to go for escape. But she must keep on, under this red sunset, alone, knowing the horror in humanity, that would destroy her, and with which she was at war. Yet it had to be so.

In the morning again she must go to school. She got up and went without murmuring even to herself. She was in the hands of some bigger, stronger, coarser will.

School was fairly quiet. But she could feel the class watching her, ready to spring on her. Her instinct was aware of the class instinct, to catch her if she were weak. But she kept cold and was guarded.

Williams was absent from school. In the middle of the morning, there was a knock at the door: someone wanted the head-master. Mr Harby went out, heavily, angrily, nervously. He was afraid of irate parents. After a moment in the passage, he came again into school.

"Sturgess," he called to one of his larger boys.—"Stand in front of the class and write down the name of anyone who speaks. Will you come this way, Miss Brangwen."

He seemed vindictively to seize upon her.

Ursula followed him, and found in the lobby a thin woman with a whitish skin, not ill dressed in a grey costume and a purple hat.

"I called about Vernon," said the woman, speaking in a refined accent. There was about the woman altogether an appearance of refinement and of cleanliness, curiously contradicted by her half beggar's deportment, and a sense of her being unpleasant to touch, like something going bad inside. She was neither a lady nor an ordinary working man's wife, but a creature separate from society. By her dress, she was not poor.

Ursula knew at once that she was Williams' mother, and that he was Vernon. She remembered that he was always clean, and well dressed, in a sailor suit. And he had this same peculiar, half transparent unwholesomeness, rather like a corpse.

"I wasn't able to send him to school today," continued the woman, with a false grace of manner. "He came home last night *so* ill—he was violently sick—I thought I should have to send for the doctor. —You know he has a weak heart."

The woman looked at Ursula with her pale, dead eyes.

"No," replied the girl, "I did not know."

She stood still with repulsion and uncertainty. Mr Harby, large and male, with his overhanging moustache, stood by with a slight, ugly smile at the corner of his eyes. The woman went on insidiously, not quite human:

"Oh yes. He has had heart-disease ever since he was a child. That is why he isn't very regular at school. And it is very bad to beat him.

He was awfully ill this morning—I shall call on the doctor as I go back."

"Who is staying with him now, then?" put in the deep voice of the school-master, cunningly.

"Oh I left him with a woman who comes in to help me—and who understands him. But I shall call in the doctor on my way home."

Ursula stood still. She felt vague threats in all this. But the woman was so utterly strange to her, that she did not understand.

"He told me he had been beaten," continued the woman, "and when I undressed him to put him to bed, his body was covered with marks—I could show them to any doctor."

Mr Harby looked at Ursula to answer. She began to understand. The woman was threatening to take out a charge of assault on her son, against her. Perhaps she wanted money.

"I caned him," she said. "He was so much trouble."

"I'm sorry if he was troublesome," said the woman, "but he must have been shamefully beaten. I could show the marks to any doctor. I'm sure it isn't allowed, if it was known."

"I caned him while he kept kicking me," said Ursula, getting angry because she was half excusing herself, Mr Harby standing there with the twinkle at the side of his eyes, enjoying the dilemma of the two women.

"I'm sure I'm sorry if he behaved badly," said the woman. "But I can't think he deserved treating as he has been. I can't send him to school, and really can't afford to pay the doctor—Is it allowed for the teachers to beat the children like that, Mr Harby?"

The head-master refused to answer. Ursula loathed herself, and loathed Mr Harby with his twinkling cunning and malice on the occasion. The other miserable woman watched her chance.

"It is an expense to me, and I have a great struggle to keep my boy decent."

Ursula still would not answer. She looked out on the asphalt yard, where a dirty rag of paper was blowing.

"And it isn't allowed to beat a child like that, I am sure, especially when he is delicate."

Ursula stared with a set face on the yard, as if she did not hear. She loathed all this, and had ceased to feel or to exist.

"Though I know he is troublesome sometimes—but I think it was too much. His body is covered with marks."

Mr Harby stood sturdy and unmoved, waiting now to have done, with the twinkling, tiny wrinkles of an ironical smile at the corners of his eyes. He felt himself master of the situation.

"And he was violently sick. I couldn't possibly send him to school today. He couldn't keep his head up."

Yet she had no answer.

"You will understand, Sir, why he is absent," she said, turning to Mr Harby.

"Oh yes," he said, rough and off-hand. Ursula detested him, for his male triumph. And she loathed the woman. She loathed everything.

"You will try to have it remembered, Sir, that he has a weak heart. He *is* so sick after these things."

"Yes," said the head-master, "I'll see about it."

"I know he is troublesome,"—the woman only addressed herself to the male now—"but if you could have him punished without beating—he is really delicate."

Ursula was beginning to feel upset. Harby stood in rather superb mastery, the woman cringing to him tickled him as one tickles trout.

"I had to come to explain why he was away this morning, Sir. You will understand."

She held out her hand. Harby took it and let it go, surprised and angry.

"Good morning," she said, and she gave her gloved, seedy hand to Ursula. She was not ill looking, and had a curious insinuating way, very distasteful yet effective.

"Good morning, Mr Harby, and thank you."

The figure in the grey costume and the purple hat was going across the school yard with a curious lingering walk. Ursula felt a strange pity for her, and revulsion from her. She shuddered. She went into the school again.

The next morning Williams turned up, looking paler than ever, very neat and nicely dressed in his sailor blouse. He glanced at Ursula with a half-smile: cunning, subdued, ready to do as she told him. There was something about him that made her shiver. She loathed the idea of having laid hands on him. His elder brother was standing outside the gate at playtime, a youth of about fifteen, tall and thin and pale. He raised his hat, almost like a gentleman. But there was something subdued, insidious about him too.

"Who is it?" said Ursula.

"It's the big Williams," said Violet Harby roughly. "*She* was here yesterday, wasn't she?"

"Yes."

"It's no good her coming—her character's not good enough for
5 her to make any trouble.—"

Ursula shrank from the scandal and the brutality. But it had some vague, horrid fascination. How sordid everything seemed! She felt sorry for the queer woman with the lingering walk, and those queer, insidious boys. The Williams in her class was wrong somewhere.
10 How nasty is was altogether.

So* the battle went on till her heart was sick. She had several more boys to subjugate before she could establish herself. And Mr Harby hated her almost as if she were a man. She knew now that nothing but a thrashing would settle some of the big louts who wanted to play
15 cat and mouse with her. Mr Harby would not give them the thrashing if he could help it. For he hated the teacher, the stuck-up, insolent high-school miss with her independence.

"Now Wright, what have you done this time?" he would say genially to the boy who was sent to him from Standard Five for
20 punishment. And he left the lad standing, lounging, wasting his time.

So that Ursula would appeal no more to the head-master, but, when she was driven wild, she seized her cane, and with fixed, desperate eyes gleaming almost cold with anger, she slashed the boy who was insolent to her, over head and ears and hands. And at length
25 they were afraid of her, she had them in order.

But she had paid a great price out of her own soul to do this. It seemed as if a great flame had gone through her and burnt her sensitive tissue. She, who shrank from the thought of physical suffering in any form, had been forced to fight and beat with a cane
30 and rouse all her instincts to hurt. And afterwards she had been forced to endure the sound of their blubbering and desolation, when she had broken them to order.

Oh, and sometimes she felt as if she would go mad. What did it matter, what did it matter if their books were dirty and they did not
35 obey? She would rather, in reality, that they disobeyed the whole rules of the school, than that they should be beaten, broken, reduced to this crying, hopeless state. She would rather bear all their insults and insolences a thousand times than reduce herself and them to this. Bitterly she repented having got beside herself, and having
40 tackled the boy she had beaten.

Yet it had to be so. She did not want to do it. Yet she had to. Oh why, why had she leagued herself to this evil system where she must brutalise herself to live? Why had she become a school-teacher, why, why?

The children had forced her to the beatings. No, she did not pity them. She had come to them full of kindness and love, and they would have torn her to pieces. They chose Mr Harby. Well then, they must know her as well as Mr Harby, they must first be subjugate to her. For she was not going to be made nought, no, neither by them, nor by Mr Harby, nor by all the system around her. She was not going to be put down, prevented from standing free. It was not to be said of her, she could not take her place and carry out her task. She would fight and hold her place in this state also, in the world of work and of man's convention.

She was isolated now from the life of her childhood, a foreigner in a new life, of work and mechanical consideration. She and Maggie, in their dinner hours and their occasional teas at the little restaurant, discussed life and ideas. Maggie was a great suffragette, trusting in the vote.* To Ursula the vote was never a reality. She had within her the strange, passionate knowledge of religion and living far transcending the limits of the automatic system that contained the vote. But her fundamental, organic-knowledge had as yet to take form and rise to utterance.

For her, as for Maggie, the liberty of woman meant something real and deep. She felt that somewhere, in something, she was not free. And she wanted to be. She was in revolt. For once she were free she could get somewhere. Ah, the wonderful, real somewhere that was beyond her, the somewhere that she felt deep, deep inside her.

In coming out and earning her own living she had made a strong, cruel move towards freeing herself. But having more freedom, she only became more profoundly aware of the big want. She wanted so many things. She wanted to read great, beautiful books, and be rich with them; she wanted to see beautiful things, and have the joy of them for ever; she wanted to know big, free people; and there remained always the want she could put no name to.

It was so difficult! There were so many things, so much to meet and surpass. And one never knew where one was going. It was a blind fight. She had suffered bitterly in this school of St Philips. She was like a young filly that has been broken in to the shafts, and has lost its freedom. And now she was suffering bitterly from the agony of the shafts. The agony, the galling, the ignominy of her breaking in. This wore into her soul. But she would never submit. To shafts like these, she would never submit for long. But she would know them. She would serve them, that she might destroy them.

5   She and Maggie went to all kinds of places together, to big suffrage meetings in Nottingham, to concerts, to theatres, to exhibitions of pictures. Ursula saved her money and bought a bicycle,* and the two girls rode to Lincoln, to Southwell, and into Derbyshire. They had an endless wealth of things to talk about. And it was a great
10   joy, finding, discovering.

But Ursula never told about Winifred Inger. That was a sort of secret side-show to her life, never to be opened. She did not even think of it. It was the closed door she had not strength to open.

Once she was broken in to her teaching, Ursula began gradually to
15   have a new life of her own again. She was going to college in eighteen months' time. Then she would take her degree, and she would—ah, she would perhaps be a big woman, and lead a movement. Who knows?—At any rate, she would go to college in eighteen months' time. All that mattered now was work, work.

20   And till college, she must go on with this teaching in St Philips School, which was always destroying her, but which she could now manage, without spilling all her life. She would submit to it for a time, since the time had a definite limit.

The class-teaching itself at last became almost mechanical. It was
25   a strain on her, an exhausting wearying strain, always unnatural. But there was a certain amount of pleasure in the sheer oblivion of teaching, so much work to do, so many children to see after, so much to be done, that one's self was forgotten. When the work had become like habit to her, and her individual soul was left out, had its growth
30   elsewhere, then she could be almost happy.

Her real, individual self drew together and became more coherent during these two years of teaching, during the struggle against the odds of class-teaching. It was always a prison to her, the school. But it was a prison where her wild, chaotic soul became hard and
35   independent. When she was well enough, and not tired, then she did not hate the teaching. She enjoyed getting into the swing of work of a morning, putting forth all her strength, making the thing go. It was for her a strenuous form of exercise. And her soul was left to rest, it had the time of torpor in which to gather itself together in strength
40   again. But the teaching hours were too long, the tasks too heavy, and

the disciplinary condition of the school too unnatural for her. She
was worn very thin and quivering.

She came to school in the morning seeing the hawthorn flowers
wet, the little, rosy grains swimming in a bowl of dew. The larks
quivered their song up into the new sunshine, and the country was so   5
glad. It was a violation to plunge into the dust and greyness of the
town.

So that she stood before her class unwilling to give herself up to
the activity of teaching, to turn her energy, that longed for the
country and for joy of early summer, into the dominating of fifty   10
children and the transferring to them some morsels of arithmetic.
There was a little absentness about her. She could not force herself
into forgetfulness. A jar of buttercups and fool's-parsley in the
window-bottom kept her away in the meadows, where in the lush
grass the moon-daisies were half submerged, and a spray of pink   15
ragged robin. Yet before her were faces of fifty children. They were
almost like big daisies in a dimness of the grass.

A brightness was on her face, a little unreality in her teaching. She
could not quite see her children. She was struggling between two
worlds, her own world of young summer and flowers, and this other   20
world of work. And the glimmer of her own sunlight was between her
and her class.

Then the morning passed with a strange far-awayness and
quietness. Dinner-time came, when she and Maggie ate joyously,
with all the windows open. And then they went out into St Philips   25
churchyard, where was a shadowy corner under red hawthorn trees.
And there they talked and read Shelley or Browning or some work
about "Woman and Labour."*

And when she went back to school, Ursula lived still in the
shadowy corner of the graveyard, where pink-red petals lay scattered   30
from the hawthorn tree, like myriad tiny shells on a beach, and a
church bell sometimes rang sonorously, and sometimes a bird called
out, whilst Maggie's voice went on low and sweet.

These days she was happy in her soul: oh, she was so happy, that
she wished she could take her joy and scatter it in armfuls broad-   35
cast. She made her children happy too, with a little tingling of
delight. But to her, the children were not a school class this
afternoon. They were flowers, birds, little bright animals, children,
anything. They only were not Standard Five. She felt no responsibility for them. It was for once a game, this teaching. And if they got   40

their sums wrong—what matter? And she would take a pleasant bit of reading. And instead of history with dates, she would tell a lovely tale. And for grammar, they could have a bit of written analysis that was not difficult, because they had done it before:

5   "She shall be sportive as a fawn
           That wild with glee across the lawn
           Or up the mountain springs."*

She wrote that, from memory, because it pleased her.

So the golden afternoon passed away, and she went home happy.
10 She had finished her day of school, and was free to plunge into the glowing evening of Cossethay. And she loved walking home. But it had not been school. It had been playing at school beneath red hawthorn blossom.

She could not go on like this. The quarterly examination was
15 coming, and her class was not ready. It irritated her that she must drag herself away from her happy self, and exert herself with all her strength to force, to compel this heavy class of children to work hard at arithmetic. They did not to work, she did not want to compel them. And yet, some second conscience gnawed at her, telling her
20 the work was not properly done. It irritated her almost to madness, and she let loose all the irritation in the class. Then followed a day of battle and hate and violence, when she went home raw, feeling the golden evening taken away from her, herself incarcerated in some dark, heavy place, and chained there with a consciousness of having
25 done badly at work.

What good was it that it was summer, that right till evening, when the corncrakes called, the larks would mount up into the light, to sing once more before nightfall. What good was it all, when she was out of tune, when she must only remember the burden and shame of school
30 that day.

And still, she hated school. Still she cried, she did not believe in it. Why should the children learn, and why should she teach them? It was all so much milling the wind. What folly was it, that made life into this, the fulfilling of some stupid, factitious duty? It was all so
35 made up, so unnatural. The school, the sums, the grammar, the quarterly examinations, the register—it was all a barren nothing.*

Why should she give her allegiance to this world, and let it so dominate her, that her own world of warm sun and growing, sap-filled life was turned into nothing? She was not going to do it. She

was not going to be prisoner in the dry, tyrannical man-world. She
was not going to care about it. What did it matter if her class did ever
so badly in the quarterly examination. Let it—what did it matter?

Nevertheless, when the time came, and the report on her class was
bad, she was miserable, and the joy of the summer was taken away 5
from her, she was shut up in gloom. She could not really escape from
this world of system and work, out into her fields where she was
happy. She must have her place in the working world, be a
recognised member with full rights there. It was more important to
her than fields and sun and poetry, at this time. But she was only the 10
more its enemy.

It was a very difficult thing, she thought, during the long hours of
intermission in the summer holidays, to be herself, her happy self
that enjoyed so much to lie in the sun, to play and swim and be
content, and also to be a school-teacher getting results out of a class 15
of children. She dreamed fondly of the time when she need not be a
teacher any more. But vaguely, she knew that responsibility had
taken place in her for ever. And as yet, her prime business was to
work.

The autumn passed away, the winter was at hand. And Ursula 20
became more and more an inhabitant of the world of work, and of
what is called life. She could not see her future, but a little way off
was college, and to the thought of this she clung fixedly. She would
go to college, and get her two or three years training, free of cost.
Already she had applied, and had her place appointed for the coming 25
year.

So she continued to study for her degree. She would take French,
Latin, English, Mathematics and Botany. She went to classes in
Ilkeston,* she studied at evening. For there was this world to
conquer, this knowledge to acquire, this qualification to attain. And 30
she worked with intensity, because of a want inside her that drove
her on. Almost everything was subordinated now to this one desire
to take her place in the world. What kind of place it was to be she did
not ask herself. The blind desire drove her on. She must take her
place. 35

She knew she would never be much of a success as an elementary
school-teacher. But neither had she failed. She hated it, but she had
managed it.

Maggie had left St Philips School, and had found a more
congenial post. The two girls remained friends. They met at evening 40

classes, they studied and somehow encouraged a firm hope each in the other. They did not know whither they were making, nor what they ultimately wanted. But they knew they wanted now to learn, to know, and to do.

5   They talked of love and marriage, and the position of woman in marriage. Maggie said that love was the flower of life, and blossomed unexpectedly and without law, and must be plucked where it was found, and enjoyed for the brief hour of its duration.

To Ursula this was unsatisfactory. She thought she still loved 10 Anton Skrebensky. But she did not forgive him that he had not been strong enough to acknowledge her. He had denied her.* How then could she love him? How then was love so absolute? She did not believe it. She believed that love was a way, a means, not an end in itself, as Maggie seemed to think. And always the way of love would 15 be found. But whither did it lead?

"I believe there are many men in the world one might love—there is not only one man," said Ursula.

She was thinking of Skrebensky. Her heart was hollow with the knowledge of Winifred Inger.

20   "But you must distinguish between love and passion," said Maggie, adding, with a touch of contempt: "Men will easily have a passion for you, but they won't love you."

"Yes," said Ursula, vehemently, the look of suffering, almost of fanaticism, on her face. "Passion is only part of love. And it seems so 25 much because it knows it can't last. That is why passion is never happy."

She was staunch for joy, for happiness, and permanency, in contrast with Maggie, who was for sadness, and the inevitable passing-away of things. Ursula suffered bitterly at the hands of life, 30 Maggie was always single, always withheld, so she went in a heavy, brooding sadness that was almost meat to her. In Ursula's last winter at St Philips the friendship of the two girls came to its climax. It was during this winter that Ursula suffered and enjoyed most keenly Maggie's fundamental sadness of enclosure.* Maggie enjoyed and 35 suffered Ursula's struggles against the confines of her life. And then the two girls began to drift apart, as Ursula broke from that form of life wherein Maggie must remain enclosed.

Chapter XIV

The Widening Circle

Maggie's people, the Schofields, lived in the large gardener's cottage, that was half a farm, behind Belcote Hall.* The hall was too damp to live in, so the Schofields were caretakers, gamekeepers, gardeners, farmers, all in one. The father was gamekeeper and stock-breeder, the eldest son was market-gardener, using the big hall gardens, the second son was farmer and gardener. There was a large family, as at Cossethay.

Ursula loved to stay at Belcote, to be treated as a grand lady by Maggie's brothers. They were good-looking men. The eldest was twenty six years old. He was the gardener, a man not very tall but strong and well-made, with brown, sunny, easy eyes and a face handsomely hewn, brown, with a long, fair moustache which he pulled as he talked to Ursula.

The girl was excited because these men attended to her when she came near. She could make their eyes light up and quiver, she could make Anthony, the eldest, twist and twist his moustache. She knew she could move them almost at will with her light laughter and chatter. They loved her ideas, watched her as she talked vehemently about politics or economics. And she, while she talked, saw the golden-brown eyes of Anthony gleam like the eyes of a satyr* as they watched her. He did not listen to her words, he listened to her. It excited her.

He was like a faun, pleased, when she would go with him over his hot-houses, to look at the green and pretty plants, at the pink primulas nodding among their leaves, and cinerarias flaunting purple and crimson and white. She asked about everything, and he told her very exactly and minutely, in a queer, pedantic way that made her want to laugh. Yet she was really interested in what he did. And he had the curious light in his face, like the light in the eyes of the goat that was tethered by the farm-yard gate.

She went down with him into the warmish cellar, where already, in the darkness, the little yellow knobs of rhubarb were coming. He held the lantern down to the dark earth. She saw the shiny knob-end

383

of the rhubarb thrusting upwards, upon the thick red stem, thrusting itself like a knob of flame through the soft soil. His face was turned up to her, the light glittered on his eyes and his teeth as he laughed, with a faint, musical neigh. He looked handsome. And she heard a
5 new sound in her ears, the faintly-musical, neighing laugh of Anthony, whose moustache twisted up and whose eyes were luminous with a cold, steady, arrogant-laughing glare. There seemed a little prance of triumph in his movement, she could not rid herself of a movement of acquiescence, a touch of acceptance. Yet he was so
10 humble, his voice was so caressing. He held his hand for her to step on when she must climb a wall. And she stepped on the living firmness of him, that quivered firmly under her weight.

She was aware of him as if in a mesmeric state. In her ordinary sense, she had nothing to do with him. But the peculiar ease and
15 unnoticeableness of his entering the house, the power of his cold, gleaming light on her when he looked at her, was like a bewitchment. In his eyes, as in the pale grey eyes of a goat, there seemed some of that steady, hard fire of moonlight which has nothing to do with the day. It made her alert, and yet her mind went out like an extinguished
20 thing. She was all senses, all her senses were alive.

Then she saw him on Sunday, dressed up in Sunday clothes, trying to impress her. And he looked ridiculous. She clung to the ridiculous effect of his stiff Sunday clothes.

She was always conscious of some unfaithfulness to Maggie, on
25 Anthony's score. Poor Maggie stood apart as if betrayed. Maggie and Anthony were enemies by instinct. Ursula had to go back to her friend brimming with affection and a poignancy of pity. Which Maggie received with a little stiffness. Then poetry and books and learning took the place of Anthony, with his goats' movements and
30 his cold, gleaming humour.

While Ursula was at Belcote, the snow fell. In the morning, a covering of snow weighed on the rhododendron bushes.

"Shall we go out?" said Maggie.

She had lost some of her leader's sureness, and was now tentative,
35 a little in reserve from her friend.

They took the key of the gate and wandered into the park. It was a white world on which dark trees and tree masses stood under a sky keen with frost. The two girls went past the hall, that was shuttered and silent, their foot-prints marking the snow on the drive. Down the park, a long way off, a man was carrying armfuls of hay across the snow. He was a small, dark figure, like an animal moving in its unawareness.

Ursula and Maggie went exploring, down to a tinkling, chilly brook that had worn the snow away in little scoops, and ran dark   5
between. They saw a robin glance its bright eyes and burst scarlet and grey into the hedge, then some pertly-marked blue-tits scuffled. Meanwhile the brook slid on coldly, chuckling to itself.

The girls wandered across the snowy grass to where the artificial fish-ponds lay under thin ice. There was a big tree with a thick trunk   10
twisted with ivy, that hung almost horizontal over the ponds. Ursula climbed joyfully into this, and sat amid bosses of bright ivy and dull berries. Some ivy leaves were like green spears held out, and tipped with snow. The ice was seen beneath them.

Maggie took out a book, and, sitting lower down the trunk, began   15
to read Coleridge's "Christabel."* Ursula half listened. She was wildly thrilled. Then she saw Anthony coming across the snow, with his confident, slightly strutting stride. His face looked brown and hard against the snow, smiling with a sort of tense confidence.

"Hello!" she called to him.   20

A response went over his face, his head was lifted in an answering, jerking gesture.

"Hello!" he said. "You're like a bird in there!"*

And Ursula's laugh rang out. She answered to the peculiar reedy twang in his penetrating voice.   25

She did not think of Anthony, yet she lived in a sort of connection with him, in his world. One evening she met him as she was coming down the lane, and they walked side by side.

"I think it's so *lovely* here," she cried.

"Do you?" he said. "I'm glad you like it."   30

There was a curious confidence in his voice.

"Oh I love it. What more does one want than to live in this beautiful place, and make things grow in your garden. It is like the Garden of Eden."

"Is it?" he said, with a little laugh. "Yes—well, it's not so bad—"   35
he was hesitating. The pale gleam was strong in his eyes, he was looking at her steadily, watching her, as an animal might. Something leaped in her soul. She knew he was going to suggest to her that she should be as he was.

"Would you like to stay here with me?" he asked, tentatively.

She blenched with fear and with the intense sensation of proffered licence suggested to her.

They had come to the gate.

5 "How?" she asked. "You aren't alone here."

"We could marry," he answered, in the strange, coldly-gleaming, insinuating tone that chilled the sunshine into moonlight. All substantial things seemed transformed. Shadows and dancing moonlight were real, and all cold, inhuman, gleaming sensations.

10 She realised with something like terror that she was going to accept this. She was going inevitably to accept him. His hand was reaching out to the gate before them. She stood still. His flesh was brown and hard and final. She seemed to be in the grip of some insult.

"I couldn't," she answered involuntarily.

15 He gave the same brief, neighing little laugh, very sad and bitter now, and slotted back the bar of the gate. Yet he did not open. For a moment they both stood looking at the fire of sunset that quivered among the purple twigs of the trees. She saw his brown, hard, well-hewn face gleaming with anger and humiliation and sub-

20 mission. He was an animal that knows that it is subdued. Her heart flamed with sensation of him, of the fascinating thing he offered her, and with sorrow, and with an inconsolable sense of loneliness. Her soul was an infant crying in the night.* He had no soul. Oh, and why had she? He was the cleaner.

25 She turned away, she turned round from him, and saw the east flushed strangely rose, the moon coming yellow and lovely upon a rosy sky, above the darkening, bluish snow. All this so beautiful, all this so lovely! He did not see it. He was one with it. But she saw it, and was one with it. Her seeing separated them infinitely.*

30 They went on in silence down the path, following their different fates. The trees grew darker and darker, the snow made only a dimness in an unreal world. And like a shadow, the day had gone into a faintly luminous, snowy evening, while she was talking aimlessly to him, to keep him at a distance, yet to keep him near her, and he

35 walked heavily. He opened the garden gate for her quietly, and she felt she was entering into her own pleasaunces, leaving him outside the gate.

Then even whilst she was escaping, or trying to escape, this feeling of pain, came Maggie the next day, saying:

"I wouldn't make Anthony love you, Ursula, if you don't want him.—It is not nice."

"But Maggie, I never made him love me," cried Ursula, dismayed and suffering, and feeling as if she had done something base.

She liked Anthony, though. All her life, at intervals, she returned 5 to the thought of him and of that which he offered. But she was a traveller, she was a traveller on the face of the earth, and he was an isolated creature living in the fulfilment of his own senses.

She could not help it, that she was a traveller. She knew Anthony, that he was not one. But oh, ultimately and finally, she must go on 10 and on, seeking the goal that she knew she did draw nearer to.

She was wearing away her second and last cycle at St Philips. As the months went, she ticked them off, first October, then November, December, January. She was careful always to subtract a month from the remainder, for the summer holidays. She saw herself 15 travelling round a circle, only an arc of which remained to complete. Then, she was in the open, like a bird tossed into mid-air, a bird that had learned in some measure to fly.

There was college ahead; that was her mid-air, unknown, spacious. Come college, and she would have broken from the confines 20 of all the life she had known. For her father also was going to move. They were all going to leave Cossethay.

Brangwen had kept his carelessness about his circumstances. He knew his work in the lace designing meant little to him personally, he just earned his wage by it. He did not know what meant much to him. 25 Living close to Anna Brangwen, his mind was always suffused through with physical heat, he moved from instinct to instinct, groping, always groping on.

When it was suggested to him that he might apply for one of the posts as handwork instructor, posts about to be created by the 30 Nottingham Education Committee, it was as if a space had been given to him, into which he could remove from his hot, dusky enclosure. He sent in his application, confidently, expectantly. He had a sort of belief in his supernatural fate. The inevitable weariness of his daily work had stiffened some of his muscles, and made a slight 35 deadness in his ruddy, alert face. Now he might escape.

He was full of the new possibilities, and his wife was acquiescent. She was willing now to have a change. She too was tired of Cossethay. The house was too small for the growing children. And

since she was nearly forty years old, she began to come awake from
her sleep of motherhood, her energy moved more outwards. The din
of growing lives roused her from her apathy. She too must have her
hand in making life. She was quite ready to move, taking all her
5   brood. It would be better now if she transplanted them. For she had
borne her last child, it would be growing up.

So that in her easy, unused fashion, she talked plans and
arrangements with her husband, indifferent really as to the method
of the change, since a change was coming; even if it did not come in
10 this way, it would come in another.

The house was full of ferment. Ursula was wild with excitement.
At last her father was going to be something, socially. So long, he had
been a social cypher, without form or standing. Now he was going to
be Art and Handwork Instructor for the County of Nottingham.*
15 That was really a status. It was a position. He would be a specialist in
his way. And he was an uncommon man. Ursula felt they were all
getting foothold at last. He was coming to his own. Who else that she
knew could turn out from his own fingers the beautiful things her
father could produce? She felt he was certain of this new job.

20   They would move. They would leave this cottage at Cossethay
which had grown too small for them; they would leave Cossethay,
where the children had all been born, and where they were always
kept to the same measure. For the people who had known them as
children along with the other village boys and girls would never,
25   could never understand that they should grow up different. They
had held "Urtler Brangwen" one of themselves, and had given her
her place in her native village, as in a family. And the bond was
strong. But now, when she was growing to something beyond what
Cossethay would allow or understand, the bond between her and her
30   old associates was becoming a bondage.

"'Ello Urs'ler, 'ow are yer goin' on?" they said when they met her.
And it demanded of her in the old voice the old response. And
something in her must respond and belong to people who knew her.
But something else denied bitterly. What was true of her ten years
35   ago was not true now. And something else which she was, and must
be, they could neither see nor allow. They felt it there nevertheless,
something beyond them, and they were injured. They said she was
proud and conceited, that she was too big for her shoes nowadays.
They said, she needn't pretend, because they knew what she was.
40   They had known her since she was born. They quoted this and that

about her. And she was ashamed because she really did feel different from the people she had lived amongst. It hurt her that she could not be at her ease with them any more. And yet—and yet—one's kite will rise on the wind as far as ever one has string to let it go. It tugs and tugs and will go, and one is glad the further it goes, even if everybody 5 else is nasty about it. So Cossethay hampered her, and she wanted to go away, to be free to fly her kite as high as she liked. She wanted to go away, to be free to stand straight up to her own height.

So that when she knew that her father had the new post, and that the family would move, she felt like skipping on the face of the earth 10 and making psalms of joy. The old, bound shell of Cossethay was to be cast off, and she was to dance away into the blue air. She wanted to dance and sing.

She made dreams of the new place she would live in, where stately cultured people of high feeling would be friends with her, and she 15 would live with the noble in the land, moving to a large freedom of feeling. She dreamed of a rich, proud, simple girl-friend, who had never known Mr Harby and his like, nor ever had a note in her voice, of bondaged contempt and fear, as Maggie had.

And she gave herself to all that she loved in Cossethay, pas- 20 sionately, because she was going away now. She wandered about to her favorite spots. There was a place where she went trespassing to find the snowdrops that grew wild. It was evening and the winter-darkened meadows were full of mystery. When she came to the woods, an oak-tree had been newly chopped down in the dell. Pale 25 drops of flowers glimmered many under the hazels, and by the sharp, golden splinters of wood that were splashed about, the grey-green blades of snowdrop leaves pricked unheeding, the drooping still little flowers were without heed.

Ursula picked some lovingly, in an ecstasy. The golden chips of 30 wood shone yellow like sunlight, the snowdrops in the twilight were like the first stars of night. And she, alone amongst them, was wildly happy to have found her way into such a glimmering dusk, to the intimate little flowers and the splash of wood chips like sunshine over the twilight of the ground. She sat down on the felled tree and 35 remained awhile remote.

Going home, she left the purplish dusk of the trees for the open lane, where the puddles shone long and jewel-like in the ruts, the land about her was darkened, and the sky a jewel overhead. Oh, how amazing it was to her! It was almost too much. She wanted to run, 40

and sing, and cry out for very wildness and poignancy, but she could
not run and sing and cry out in such a way as to cry out the deep
things in her heart, so she was still, and almost sad with loneliness.

5   At Easter she went again to Maggie's home, for a few days. She
was, however, shy and fugitive. She saw Anthony, how suggestive he
was to look on, and how his eyes had a sort of supplicating light, that
was rather beautiful. She looked at him, and she looked again, for
him to become real to her. But it was her own self that was occupied
elsewhere. She seemed to have some other being.*

10   And she turned to spring and the opening buds. There was a large
pear-tree by a wall, and it was full, thronged with tiny, grey-green
buds, myriads. She stood before it arrested with delight, and a
realisation went deep into her heart. There was so great a host in
array behind the cloud of pale, dim green, so much to come

15   forth—so much sunshine to pour down.

So the weeks passed on, trance-like and pregnant. The pear-tree
at Cossethay burst into bloom against the cottage-end, like a wave
burst into foam. Then gradually the bluebells came, blue as water
standing thin in the level places under the trees and bushes, flowing

20   in more and more, till there was a flood of azure, and pale green
leaves burning, and tiny birds with fiery little song and flight. Then
swiftly, the flood sank and was gone, and it was summer.

There was to be no going to the seaside this year for a holiday. The
holiday was the removal from Cossethay.

25   They were going to live near Willey Green,* which place was most
central for Brangwen. It was an old, quiet village on the edge of the
thronged colliery-district. So that it served, in its quaintness of odd,
old cottages lingering in their sunny gardens, as a sort of bower or
pleasaunce to the sprawling colliery-townlet of Beldover, a pleasant

30   walk-round for the colliers on Sunday morning, before the public-
houses opened.

In Willey Green stood the Grammar School where Brangwen was
occupied for two days during the week, and where experiments in
education were being carried on.

35   Ursula wanted to live in Willey Green, on the remoter side,
towards Southwell, and Sherwood Forest. There it was so lovely and
romantic. But out into the world meant out into the world. Will
Brangwen must become modern.

He bought, with his wife's money, a fairly large house in the new,

40   red-brick part of Beldover. It was a villa built by the widow of the late

colliery-manager, and stood in a quiet, new little side-street near the
large church.

Ursula was rather sad. Instead of having arrived at distinction,
they had come to new red-brick suburbia in a grimy, small town.

Mrs Brangwen was happy. The rooms were splendidly large—a 5
splendid dining-room, drawing room, and kitchen, besides a very
pleasant study, downstairs. Everything was admirably appointed.
The widow had settled herself in lavishly. She was a native of
Beldover, and had intended to reign almost queen. Her bath-room
was white and silver, her stairs were of oak, her chimney-pieces were 10
massive and oaken, with bulging, columnar supports.

"Good and substantial," was the keynote. But Ursula resented the
stout, inflated prosperity implied everywhere. She made her father
promise to chisel down the bulging oaken chimney-pieces, chisel
them flat. That sort of important paunch was very distasteful to her. 15
Her father was himself long and loosely built. What had he to do with
so much "good and substantial" importance?

They bought a fair amount, also, of the widow's furniture. It was in
common good taste—the great Wilton carpet, the large round table,
the chesterfield* covered with glossy chintz in roses and birds. It was 20
all really very sunny and nice, with large windows, and a view right
across the shallow valley.

After all, they would be, as one of their acquaintances said, among
the *élite* of Beldover. They would represent culture. And as* there
was no-one of higher social importance than the doctors, the 25
colliery-managers, and the chemists, they would shine, with their
Della Robbia, beautiful Madonna, their lovely reliefs from
Donatello,* their reproductions from Botticelli. Nay, the large
photographs of the Primavera and the Aphrodite and the Nativity* in
the dining-room, the ordinary reception room, would make dumb 30
the mouth of Beldover.

And after all, it is better to be princess in Beldover than a vulgar
nobody in the country.

There was great preparation made for the removal of the whole
Brangwen family, ten in all. The house in Beldover was prepared, 35
the house in Cossethay was dismantled. Come the end of school-
term, the removal would begin.

Ursula left school at the end of July, when the summer holiday
commenced. The morning outside was bright and sunny, and the
freedom got inside the school-room this last day. It was as if the walls 40

of the school were going to melt away. Already they seemed shadowy
and unreal. It was breaking-up morning. Soon, scholars and teachers would be outside, each going his own way. The irons were struck
off, the sentence was expired, the prison was a momentary shadow
5 halting about them. The children were carrying away books and
inkwells, and rolling up maps. All their faces were bright with
gladness and goodwill. There was a bustle of cleaning and clearing
away all marks of this last term of imprisonment. They were all
breaking free. Busily, eagerly, Ursula made up her totals of atten-
10 dances in the register. With pride, she wrote down the thousands: to
so many thousands of children had she given another session's
lesson. It looked tremendous. The excited hours passed slowly in
suspense. Then at last it was over. For the last time, she stood before
her children whilst they said their prayers and sang a hymn. Then it
15 was all over.

"Goodbye, children," she said. "I shall not forget you, and you
must not forget me."

"No Miss," cried the children in chorus, with shining faces.

She stood smiling on them, moved, as they filed out. Then she
20 gave her monitors their term sixpences, and they too departed.
Cupboards were locked, blackboards washed, inkwells and dusters
removed. The place stood bare and vacated. She had triumphed over
it. It was a shell now. She had fought a good fight* here, and it had
not been altogether unenjoyable. She owed some gratitude even to
25 this harsh, vacant place, that stood like a memorial or a trophy. So
much of her life had been fought for and won and lost here.
Something of this school would always belong to her, something of
her to it. She acknowledged it. And now came the leave-taking.

In the teachers' room the teachers were chatting and loitering,
30 talking excitedly of where they were going: to the Isle of Man, to
Llandudno, to Yarmouth. They were eager, and attached to each
other, like comrades leaving a ship.

Then it was Mr Harby's turn to make a speech to Ursula. He
looked handsome, with his silver-grey temples and black brows, and
35 his imperturbable, male solidity.

"Well," he said, "we must say goodbye to Miss Brangwen and
wish her all good fortune for the future. I suppose we shall see her
again some time, and hear how she is getting on."

"Oh yes," said Ursula, stammering, blushing, laughing. "Oh yes,
40 I shall come and see you."

Then she realised that this sounded too personal, and she felt foolish.

"Miss Schofield suggested these two books," he said, putting a couple of volumes on the table: "I hope you will like them."

Ursula, feeling very shy, picked up the books. There was a volume 5
of Swinburne's poetry, and a volume of Meredith's.*

"Oh I shall love them," she said. "Thank you very much—thank you all so much—it is so—"

She stuttered to an end, and very red, turned the leaves of the books nervously, pretending to be taking the first pleasure, but really 10
seeing nothing.

Mr Harby's eyes were twinkling. He alone was at his ease, master of the situation. It was pleasing to him to make Ursula the gift, and for once extend good feeling to his teachers. As a rule, it was so difficult, each one was so strained in resentment under his 15
rule.

"Yes," he said, "we hoped you would like the choice—"

He looked with his peculiar challenging smile, for a moment, then returned to his cupboards.

Ursula felt very confused. She hugged her books, loving them. 20
And she felt she loved all the teachers, and Mr Harby. It was very confusing.

At last she was out. She cast one hasty glance over the school buildings squatting on the asphalt yard in the hot, glistening sun, one look down the well-known road, and turned her back on it all. 25
Something strained in her heart. She was going away.

"Well, good luck," said the last of the teachers, as she shook hands at the end of the road. "We'll expect you back some day."

He spoke in irony. She laughed, and broke away. She was free. As she sat on the top of the tram in the sunlight, she looked round her 30
with tremulous delight. She had left something which had meant much to her. She would not go to school any more, and do the familar things. Queer! There was a little pang amid her exultation, of fear, not of regret. Yet how she exulted this morning!

She was tremulous with pride and joy. She loved the two books. 35
They were tokens to her, representing the fruit and trophies of her two years which, thank God, were over.

"To Ursula Brangwen, with best wishes for her future and in warm memory of the time she spent in St Philips School," was written in the head-master's neat, scrupulous handwriting. She 40 could see the careful hand holding the pen, the thick fingers with tufts of black hair on the back of each one.

He had signed, all the teachers had signed. She liked having all their signatures. She felt she loved them all, they were her fellow-
5   workers. She carried away from the school a pride she could never lose. She had her place as comrade and sharer in the work of school, her fellow teachers had signed to her, as one of them. And she was one of all workers, she had put in her tiny brick to the fabric man was building, she had qualified herself as co-builder.

10 Then the day for the home removal came. Ursula rose early, to pack up the remaining goods. The carts arrived, lent by her uncle at the Marsh, in the lull between hay and corn harvest. The goods roped in the cart, Ursula mounted her bicycle and sped away to Beldover.

15 The house was hers. She entered its clean-scrubbed silence. The dining-room had been covered with a thick rush matting, hard and of the beautiful, luminous, clean colour of sun-dried reeds. The walls were pale grey, the doors were darker grey. Ursula admired it very much, as the sun came through the large windows, streaming in.

20 She flung open doors and windows to the sunshine. Flowers were bright and shining round the small lawn, which stood above the road looking over the raw field opposite, which would later be built upon. No-one came. So she wandered down the garden at the back, to the wall. The eight bells of the church rang the hour. She could hear the
25 many sounds of the town about her.

At last, the cart was seen coming round the corner, familiar furniture piled undignified on top, Tom, her brother, and Theresa, marching on foot beside the mass, proud of having walked ten miles or more, from the tram terminus. Ursula poured out beer, and the
30 man drank thirstily, by the door. A second cart was coming. Her father appeared on his motor bicycle.* There was the staggering transport of furniture up the steps to the little lawn, where it was deposited all pell-mell in the sunshine, very queer and discomfort- ing.

35 Brangwen was a pleasant man to work with, cheerful and easy. Ursula loved deciding him where the heavy things should stand. She watched anxiously the struggle up the steps and through the doorways. Then the big things were in, the carts set off again. Ursula and her father worked away carrying in all the light things that

remained upon the lawn, and putting them in place. Dinner-time
came. They ate bread and cheese in the kitchen.

"Well, we're getting on," said Brangwen cheerfully.

Two more loads arrived. The afternoon passed away in a struggle
with the furniture, upstairs. Towards five o'clock, appeared the last 5
loads, consisting also of Mrs Brangwen and the younger children,
driven by uncle Fred in the trap. Gudrun had walked with Margaret
from the station. The whole family* had come.

"There!" said Brangwen, as his wife got down from the cart:
"Now we're all here." 10

"Ay," said his wife pleasantly.

And the very brevity, the silence of intimacy between the two
made a home in the hearts of the children, who clustered round
feeling strange in the new place.

Everything was at sixes and sevens. But a fire was made in the 15
kitchen, the hearthrug put down, the kettle set on the hob, and Mrs
Brangwen began towards sunset to prepare the first meal. Ursula
and Gudrun were slaving in the bedrooms, candles were rushing
about. Then from the kitchen came the smell of ham and eggs and
coffee, and in the gaslight, the scrambled meal began. The family 20
seemed to huddle together like a little camp in a strange place.
Ursula felt a load of responsibility upon her, caring for the half-little
ones. The smallest kept near the mother.

It was dark, and the children went sleepy but excited to bed. It was
a long time before the sound of voices died out. There was a 25
tremendous sense of adventure.

In the morning, everybody was awake soon after dawn, the
children crying:

"When I wakened up, I didn't know where I was."

There were the strange sounds of the town, and the repeated 30
chiming of the big church bells, so much harsher and more insistent
than the little bells of Cossethay. They looked through the windows,
past the other new red houses, to the wooded hill across the valley.
They had all a delightful sense of space and liberation, space, and
light and air. 35

But gradually all set to work. They were a careless, untidy family.
Yet when once they set about to get the house in order, the thing
went with felicity and quickness. By evening, the place was roughly
established.

They would not have a servant to live in the house, only a woman who could go home at night. And they would not even have the woman yet. They wanted to do as they liked in their own home, with* no stranger in the midst.

Chapter XV

The Bitterness of Ecstasy*

A storm of industry raged on in the house. Ursula did not go to college till October. So, with a distinct feeling of responsibility, as if she must express herself in this house, she laboured arranging, 5 re-arranging, selecting, contriving.

She could use her father's ordinary tools, both for wood-work and metal work, so she hammered and tinkered. Her mother was quite content to have the thing done. Brangwen was interested. He had a ready belief in his daughter. He himself was at work putting up his 10 work-shed in the garden.

At last she had finished for the time being. The drawing room was big and empty. It had the good Wilton carpet, of which the family was so proud, and the large couch and large chairs covered with shiny chintz, and the piano, a little sculpture in plaster that Brangwen had 15 done, and not very much more. It was too large and empty-feeling for the family to occupy very much. Yet they liked to know it was there, large and empty.

The home was the dining-room. There the hard rush floor-covering made the ground light, reflecting light upon the bottom of 20 their hearts; in the window-bay was a broad, sunny seat, the table was so solid one could not jostle it, and the chairs so strong one could knock them over without hurting them. The familiar organ that Brangwen had made stood on one side, looking peculiarly small, the sideboard was comfortably reduced to normal proportion. This was 25 the family living-room.

Ursula had a bedroom to herself. It was really a servant's bedroom, small and plain. Its window looked over the back garden at other back gardens, some of them old and very nice, some of them littered with packing-cases, then at the backs of the houses whose 30 fronts were the shops in High Street, or the genteel homes of the under-manager or the chief cashier, facing the chapel.

She had six weeks still before going to college. In this time she nervously read over some Latin and some Botany, and fitfully worked at some mathematics. She was going into college as a 35

teacher, for her training. But, having already taken her matriculation examination, she was entered for a university course.* At the end of a year she would sit for the Intermediate Arts, then two years after for her B.A. So her case was not that of the ordinary school-teacher.
5   She would be working among the private students who came only for pure education, not for mere professional training. She would be of the elect.

For the next three years she would be more or less dependent on her parents again. Her training was free. All college fees were paid
10 by the government, she had moreover a few pounds grant every year. This would just pay for her train-fares and her clothing. Her parents would only have to feed her. She did not want to cost them much. They would not be well-off. Her father would earn only two hundred a year, and a good deal of her mother's capital was spent
15 in buying the house. Still, there was enough to get along with.

Gudrun was attending the Art School in Nottingham.* She was working particularly at sculpture. She had a gift for this. She loved making little models in clay, of children or of animals. Already some of these had appeared in the Students' Exhibition in the Castle,* and
20 Gudrun was a distinguished person. She was chafing at the Art School, and wanted to go to London. But there was not enough money. Neither would her parents let her go so far.

Theresa had left the High School. She was a great, strapping, bold hussy, indifferent to all higher claims. She would stay at home. The
25 others were at school, except the youngest. When term started, they would all be transferred to the Grammar School at Willey Green.

Ursula was excited at making acquaintances in Beldover. The excitement soon passed. She had tea at the clergyman's, at the Chemist's, at the other chemists',* at the three doctors', at the
30 under-manager's—then she knew practically everybody. She could not take people very seriously, though at the time she wanted to.

She wandered the country, on foot and on her bicycle, finding it very beautiful in the forest direction, between Mansfield and Southwell and Worksop. But she was here only skirmishing for
35 amusement. Her real exploration would begin in college.

Term began. She went into town each day by train. The cloistered quiet of the college began to close around her.

She was not at first disappointed. The big college built of stone,* standing in the quiet street, with a rim of grass and lime-trees all so
40 peaceful: she felt it remote, a magic-land. Its architecture was

foolish, she knew from her father. Still, it was different from that of all other buildings. Its rather pretty, plaything, Gothic form was almost a style, in the dirty industrial town.

She liked the hall, with its big stone chimney-piece and its Gothic arches supporting the balcony above. To be sure the arches were 5 ugly, the chimney-piece of cardboard-like carved stone, with its armorial decoration, looked silly just opposite the bicycle stand and the radiator, whilst the great notice-board with its fluttering papers seemed to slam away all sense of retreat and mystery from the far wall. Nevertheless, amorphous as it might be, there was in it a 10 reminiscence of the wondrous, cloistral origin of education. Her soul flew straight back to the mediæval times, when the monks of God held the learning of men and imparted it within the shadow of religion. In this spirit she entered college.

The harshness and vulgarity of the lobbies and cloak-rooms hurt 15 her at first. Why was it not all beautiful? But she could not openly admit her criticism. She was on holy ground.

She wanted all the students to have a high, pure spirit, she wanted them to say only the real, genuine things, she wanted their faces to be still and luminous as the nuns' and the monks' faces. 20

Alas, the girls chattered and giggled and were nervous, they were dressed up and frizzed, the men looked mean and clownish.

Still, it was lovely to pass along the corridor with one's books in one's hand, to push the swinging, glass-panelled door, and enter the big room where the first lecture would be given. The windows were 25 large and lofty, the myriad brown students' desks stood waiting, the great blackboard was smooth behind the rostrum.

Ursula sat beside her window, rather far back. Looking down, she saw the lime-trees turning yellow, the tradesman's boy passing silent down the still, autumn-sunny street. There was the world, remote, 30 remote.

Here, within the great, whispering sea-shell, that whispered all the while with reminiscence of all the centuries, time faded away, and the echo of knowledge filled the timeless silence.

She listened, she scribbled her notes with joy, almost with ecstasy, 35 never for a moment criticising what she heard. The lecturer was a mouth-piece, a priest. As he stood, black-gowned, on the rostrum, some strands of the whispering confusion of knowledge that filled the whole place seemed to be singled out and woven together by him, till they became a lecture. 40

At first, she preserved herself from criticism. She would not consider the professors as men, ordinary men who ate bacon and pulled on their boots before coming to college. They were the black-gowned priests of knowledge, serving forever in a remote, 5 hushed temple. They were the initiated, and the beginning and end of the mystery was in their keeping.

Curious joy she had of the lectures. It was a joy to hear the theory of education, there was such freedom and pleasure in ranging over the very stuff of knowledge, and seeing how it moved and lived and 10 had its being.* How happy Racine* made her! She did not know why. But as the big lines of the drama unfolded themselves, so steady, so measured, she felt a thrill as of being in the realm of the reality. Of Latin, she was doing Livy and Horace.* The curious, intimate, gossiping tone of the Latin class suited Horace. Yet she never cared 15 for him, nor even for Livy. There was an entire lack of sternness in the gossipy classroom. She tried hard to keep her old grasp of the Roman Spirit. But gradually the Latin became mere gossip-stuff and artificiality to her, a question of manners and verbosities.

Her terror was the mathematics class. The lecturer went so fast, 20 her heart beat excitedly, she seemed to be straining every nerve. And she struggled hard, during private study, to get the stuff under control.

Then came the lovely, peaceful afternoons in the Botany laboratory. They were few students. How she loved to sit on her high stool 25 before the bench, with her pith and her razor and her material, carefully mounting her slides, carefully bringing her microscope into focus, then turning with joy to record her observation, drawing joyfully in her book, if the slide were good.

She soon made a college-friend, a girl who had lived in Florence, 30 a girl who wore a wonderful purple or figured scarf draped over a plain, dark dress. She was Dorothy Russell, daughter of a south-country advocate. Dorothy lived with a maiden aunt in Nottingham, and spent her spare moments slaving for the Women's Social and Political Union.* She was quiet and intense, with an ivory face and 35 dark hair looped plain over her ears. Ursula was very fond of her, but afraid of her. She seemed so old and so relentless towards herself. Yet she was only twenty two. Ursula always felt her to be a creature of fate, like Cassandra.*

The two girls had a close, stern friendship. Dorothy worked at all 40 things with the same passion, never sparing herself. She came closest to Ursula during the Botany hours. For she could not draw. Ursula made beautiful and wonderful drawings of the sections under the microscope, and Dorothy always came to learn the manner of the drawing.

So the first year went by, in magnificent seclusion and activity of learning. It was strenuous as a battle, her college life, yet remote as peace.

She came to Nottingham in the morning with Gudrun. The two sisters were distinguished wherever they went, slim, strong girls, eager and extremely sensitive. Gudrun was the more beautiful of the two, with her sleepy, half languid girlishness that looked so soft, and yet was balanced and inalterable underneath. She wore soft, easy clothing, and hats which fell by themselves into a careless grace.

Ursula was much more carefully dressed, but she was self-conscious, always falling into depths of admiration of somebody else, and modelling herself upon this other, and so producing a hopeless incongruity. When she dressed for practical purposes, she always looked well. In winter, wearing a tweed coat-and-skirt and a small hat of black fur pulled over her eager, palpitant face, she seemed to move down the street in a drifting motion of suspense and exceeding sensitive receptivity.

At the end of the first year Ursula got through her Intermediate Arts examination, and there came a lull in her eager activities. She slackened off, she relaxed altogether. Worn nervous and inflammable by the excitement of the preparation for the examination, and by the sort of exaltation which carried her through the crisis itself, she now fell into a quivering passivity, her will all loosened.

The family went to Scarborough for a month. Gudrun and the father were busy at the handicraft holiday school* there, Ursula was left a good deal with the children. But when she could, she went off by herself.

She stood and looked out over the shining sea. It was very beautiful to her. The tears rose hot in her heart.

Out of the far, far space there drifted slowly in to her a passionate, unborn yearning. "There are so many dawns that have not yet risen."* It seemed as if, from over the edge of the sea, all the unrisen dawns were appealing to her, all her unborn soul was crying for the unrisen dawns.

As she sat looking out at the tender sea, with its lovely, swift glimmer, the sob rose in her breast, till she caught her lip suddenly under her teeth, and the tears were forcing themselves from her. And in her very sob, she laughed. Why did she cry? She did not want to cry. It was so beautiful, that she laughed. It was so beautiful, that she cried.

5   She glanced apprehensively round, hoping no-one would see her in this state.

Then came a time when the sea was rough.* She watched the water travelling in to the coast, she watched a big wave running unnoticed, to burst in a shock of foam against a rock, enveloping all
10 in a great white beauty, to pour away again, leaving the rock emerged black and teeming. Oh, and if, when the wave burst into whiteness, it were only set free!

Sometimes she loitered along the harbour, looking at the sea-browned sailors, who, in their close blue jerseys, lounged on the
15 harbour-wall and laughed at her with impudent, communicative eyes.

There was established a little relation between her and them. She would never speak to them or know any more of them. Yet as she walked by and they leaned on the sea-wall, there was something
20 between her and them, something keen and delightful and painful. She liked best the young one whose fair, salty hair tumbled over his blue eyes. He was *so* new and fresh and salt and not of this world.

From Scarborough she went to her uncle Tom's. Winifred had a small baby, born at the end of the summer. She had become strange
25 and alien to Ursula. There was an unmentionable reserve between the two women. Tom Brangwen was an attentive father, a very domestic husband. But there was something spurious about his domesticity, Ursula did not like him any more. Something ugly, blatant in his nature had come out now, making him shift everything
30 over to a sentimental basis. A materialistic unbeliever, he carried it all off by becoming full of human feeling, a warm, attentive host, a generous husband, a model citizen. And he was clever enough to rouse admiration everywhere, and to take in his wife sufficiently. She did not love him. She was glad to live in a state of complacent
35 self-deception with him, she worked according to him.

Ursula was relieved to go home. She had still two peaceful years before her. Her future was settled for two years. She returned to college to prepare for her final examination.

But during this year, the glamour began to depart from college.*
40 The professors were not priests initiated into the deep mysteries of

life and knowledge. After all, they were only middle-men handling wares they had become so accustomed to that they were oblivious of them. What was Latin?—so much dry goods of knowledge. What was the Latin class altogether but a sort of second-hand curio shop, where one bought curios and learned the market value of curios: dull curios too, on the whole. She was as bored by the Latin curiosities as she was by Chinese and Japanese curiosities in the antique shops. "Antiques"—the very word made her soul fall flat and dead.

The life went out of her studies, why, she did not know. But the whole thing seemed sham, spurious: spurious Gothic arches, spurious peace, spurious Latinity, spurious dignity of France, spurious naïveté of Chaucer. It was a second-hand dealer's shop, and one bought an equipment for an examination. This was only a little side-show to the factories of the town. Gradually the perception stole into her. This was no religious retreat, no seclusion of pure learning. It was a little apprentice-shop where one was further equipped for making money. The college itself was a little, slovenly laboratory for the factory.

A harsh and ugly disillusion came over her again, the same darkness and bitter gloom from which she was never safe now, the realisation of the permanent substratum of ugliness under every-thing. As she came to the college in the afternoon, the lawns were frothed with daisies, the lime-trees hung tender and sunlit and green; and oh, the deep, white froth of the daisies was anguish to see.

For inside, inside the college, she knew she must enter the sham workshop. All the while, it was a sham store, a sham warehouse, with a single motive of material gain, and no productivity. It pretended to exist by the religious virtue of knowledge. But the religious virtue of knowledge was become a flunkey to the god of material success.

A sort of inertia came over her. Mechanically, from habit, she went on with her studies. But it was almost hopeless. She could scarcely attend to anything. At the Anglo-Saxon lecture, in the afternoon, she sat looking down, out of the window, hearing no word of Beowulf or of anything else. Down below, in the street, the sunny grey pavement went beside the palisade. A woman in a pink frock, with a scarlet sunshade, crossed the road, a little white dog running like a fleck of light about her. The woman with the scarlet sunshade came over the road, a lilt in her walk, a little shadow attending her. Ursula watched spell-bound. The woman with the scarlet sunshade and the flickering terrier was gone—and whither? Whither?

In what world of reality was the woman in the pink dress walking? To what warehouse of dead unreality was she herself confined?

What good was this place, this college? What good was Anglo-Saxon, when one only learned it in order to answer examination
5   questions, in order that one should have a higher commercial value later on? She was sick with this long service at the inner commercial shrine. Yet what else was there? Was life all this, and this only? Everywhere, everything was debased to the same service. Everything went to produce vulgar things, to encumber material life.
10   Suddenly she threw over French. She would take honors in Botany. This was the one study that lived* for her. She had entered into the life of the plants. She was fascinated by the strange laws of the vegetable world. She had here a glimpse of something working entirely apart from the purpose of the human world.
15   College was barren, cheap, a temple converted to the most vulgar, petty commerce. Had she not come to hear the echo of learning pulsing back to the source of the mystery?—The source of mystery! And barrenly, the professors in their gowns offered commercial commodity that could be turned to good account in the examination
20   room; ready-made stuff, too, and not really worth the money it was intended to fetch;—which they all knew.

All the time in the college, now, save when she was labouring in her Botany laboratory, for there the mystery still glimmered, she felt she was degrading herself in a kind of trade of sham gewgaws.
25   Angry and stiff, she went through her last terms. She would rather be out again earning her own living. Even Brinsley Street and Mr Harby seemed real in comparison. Her violent hatred of the Ilkeston school was nothing compared with the sterile degradation of college. But she was not going back to Brinsley Street, either. She would take
30   her B.A., and become a mistress in some Grammar School for a time.

The last year of her college career was wheeling slowly round. She could see ahead her examination and her departure. She had the ash of disillusion gritting under her teeth. Would the next move turn out
35   the same? Always the shining doorway ahead: and then, upon approach, always the shining doorway was a gate into another ugly yard, dirty and active and dead.* Always the crest of the hill gleaming ahead under heaven: and then, from the top of the hill, only another sordid valley full of amorphous, squalid activity.
40   No matter! Every hill-top was a little different, every valley was

somehow new. Cossethay and her childhood with her father; the Marsh and the little church school near the Marsh, and her grandmother and her uncles; the High School at Nottingham and Anton Skrebensky; Anton Skrebensky and the dance in the moonlight between the fires; then the time she could not think of without feeling blasted, Winifred Inger, and the months before becoming a school-teacher; then the horrors of Brinsley Street, lapsing into comparative peacefulness; Maggie, and Maggie's brother, whose influence she could still feel in her veins, when she conjured him up; then college, and Dorothy Russell, who was now in France; then the next move, into the world again!

Already it was a history. In every phase she was so different. Yet she was always Ursula Brangwen.* But what did it mean, Ursula Brangwen? She did not know what she was. Only she was full of rejection, of refusal. Always, always she was spitting out of her mouth the ash and grit of disillusion, of falsity. She could only stiffen in rejection, in rejection. She seemed always negative in her action.

That which she was, positively, was dark and unrevealed, it could not come forth. It was like a seed buried in dry ash. This world in which she lived was like a circle lighted by a lamp. This lighted area, lit up by man's completest consciousness, she thought was all the world: that here all was disclosed for ever. Yet all the time, within the darkness she had been aware of points of light, like the eyes of wild beasts,* gleaming, penetrating, vanishing. And her soul had acknowledged in a great heave of terror, only the outer darkness. This inner circle of light in which she lived and moved, wherein the trains rushed and the factories ground out their machine-produce and the plants and the animals worked by the light of science and knowledge, suddenly it seemed like the area under an arc-lamp,* wherein the moths and children played in the security of blinding light, not even knowing there was any darkness, because they stayed in the light.

But she could see the glimmer of dark movement just out of range, she saw the eyes of the wild beast gleaming from the darkness, watching the vanity of the camp fire and the sleepers; she felt the strange, foolish vanity of the camp, which said "Beyond our light and our order there is nothing," turning their faces always inward towards the sinking fire of illuminating consciousness, which comprised sun and stars, and the Creator, and the System of Righteousness, ignoring always the vast darkness that wheeled round about, with half-revealed shapes lurking on the edge.

Yea, and no man dared even throw a firebrand into the darkness. For if he did, he was jeered to death by the others, who cried "Fool, anti-social knave, why would you disturb us with bogeys? There *is* no darkness. We move and live and have our being within the light, and unto us is given the eternal light of knowledge, we comprise and comprehend the innermost core and issue of knowledge. Fool and knave, how dare you belittle us with the darkness?"

Nevertheless the darkness wheeled round about, with grey shadow-shapes of wild beasts, and also with dark shadow-shapes of the angels, whom the light fenced out, as it fenced out the more familiar beasts of darkness. And some, having for a moment seen the darkness, saw it bristling with the tufts of the hyena and wolf; and some, having given up their vanity of the light, having died in their own conceit, saw the gleam in the eyes of the wolf and the hyena, that it was the flash of the sword of angels, flashing at the door to come in, that the angels in the darkness were lordly and terrible and not to be denied, like the flash of fangs.

It was a little while before Easter, in her last year of college, when Ursula was twenty two years old, that she heard again from Skrebensky. He had written to her once or twice from South Africa, during the first months of his service out there in the war, and since had sent her a post-card every now and then, at ever longer intervals. He had become a first lieutenant, and had stayed out in Africa. She had not heard of him now for more than two years.

Often her thoughts returned to him. He seemed like the gleaming dawn, yellow, radiant, of a long, grey, ashy day. The memory of him was like the thought of the first radiant hours of morning. And here was the blank grey ashiness of later daytime. Ah, if he had only remained true to her, she might have known the sunshine, without all this toil and hurt and degradation of a spoiled day. He would have been her angel. He held the keys of the sunshine. Still he held them. He could open to her the gates of succeeding freedom and delight. Nay, if he had remained true to her, he would have been the doorway to her, into the boundless sky of happiness and plunging, inexhaustible freedom which was the paradise of her soul. Ah the great range he would have opened to her, the illimitable, endless space for self-realisation and delight for ever.

The one thing she believed in, was in the love she had held for

him. It remained shining and complete, a thing to hark back to. And
she said to herself, when present things seemed a failure:
"Ah, I *was* fond of him,"
as if with him the leading flower of her life had died.

Now she heard from him again. The chief effect was pain. The   5
pleasure, the spontaneous joy was not there any longer. But her *will*
rejoiced. Her will had fixed itself to him. And the old excitement of
her dreams stirred and woke up. He was come, the man with the
wondrous lips that could send the kiss wavering to the very end of all
space. Was he come back to her? She did not believe.   10

"My dear Ursula, I am back in England again for a few months
before going out again, this time to India. I wonder if you still keep
the memory of our times together. I have still got the little
photograph of you. You must have changed since then, for it is about
six years ago. I am fully six years older, I have lived through another   15
life since I knew you at Cossethay: I wonder if you would care to see
me. I shall come up to Derby next week, and I would call in
Nottingham, and we might have tea together. Will you let me know?
I shall look for your answer—Anton Skrebensky."

Ursula had taken this letter from the rack in the hall at college, and   20
torn it open as she crossed to the Women's room. The world seemed
to dissolve away from around her, she stood alone in clear air.

Where could she go to, to be alone? She fled away, upstairs, and
through the private way to the reference library. Seizing a book, she
sat down and pondered the letter. Her heart beat, her limbs   25
trembled. As in a dream, she heard one gong sound in the college,
then strangely, another. The first lecture had gone by.

Hurriedly she took one of her note books and began to write.

"Dear Anton, Yes, I still have the ring. I should be very glad to see
you again. You can come here to college for me, or I will meet you   30
somewhere in the town. Will you let me know? Your sincere
friend—"

Trembling, she asked the librarian, who was her friend, if he
would give her an envelope. She sealed and addressed her letter, and
went out, bare-headed, to post it. When it was dropped into the   35
pillar-box, the world became a very still, pale place, without confines. She wandered back to college, to her pale dream, like a first
wan light of dawn.

Skrebensky came one afternoon in the following week. Day after
day, she had hurried swiftly to the letter-rack, on her arrival at   40

college in the morning, and during the intervals between lectures.
Several times, swiftly, with secretive fingers, she had plucked his
letter down from its public prominence, and fled across the hall
holding it fast and hidden. She read her letters in the Botany
5 laboratory, where her corner was always reserved for her.

Several letters, and then, he was coming. It was Friday afternoon
he appointed. She worked over her microscope with feverish activity,
able to give only half her attention, yet working closely and rapidly.
She had on her slide some special stuff* come up from London that
10 day, and the professor was fussy and excited about it. At the same
time, as she focussed the light on her field, and saw the plant-animal
lying shadowy in a boundless light, she was fretting over a conversation she had had a few days before, with Dr. Frankstone,* who was
a woman doctor of physics in the college.

15 "No really," Dr. Frankstone had said, "I don't see why we should
attribute some special mystery to life—do you? We don't understand
it as we understand electricity, even, but that doesn't warrant our
saying it is something special, something different in kind and
distinct from everything else in the universe—do you think it does?
20 May it not be that life consists in a complexity of physical and
chemical activities, of the same order as the activities we already
know in science? I don't see, really, why we should imagine there is a
special order for life, and life alone— — — —"

The conversation had ended on a note of uncertainty, indefinite,
25 wistful. But the purpose, what was the purpose? Electricity had no
soul, light and heat had no soul. Was she herself an impersonal force,
or conjunction of forces, like one of these? She looked still at the
unicellular shadow that lay within the field of light, under her
microscope. It was alive. She saw it move—she saw the bright mist of
30 its ciliary activity, she saw the gleam of its nucleus, as it slid across
the plane of light. What then was its will? If it was a conjunction of
forces, physical and chemical, what held these forces unified, and for
what purpose were they unified?

For what purpose were the incalculable physical and chemical
35 activities nodalised in this shadowy, moving speck under her microscope? What was the will which nodalised them and created the one
thing she saw? What was its intention? To be itself? Was its purpose
just mechanical and limited to itself?

It intended to be itself. But what self? Suddenly in her mind* the
40 world gleamed strangely, with an intense light, like the nucleus of the

creature under the microscope. Suddenly she had passed away into
an intensely-gleaming light of knowledge. She could not understand
what it all was. She only knew that it was not limited mechanical
energy, nor mere purpose of self-preservation and self-assertion. It
was a consummation, a being infinite. Self was a oneness with the 5
infinite. To be oneself was a supreme, gleaming triumph of infinity.

Ursula sat abstracted over her microscope, in suspense. Her soul
was busy, infinitely busy, in the new world. In the new world,
Skrebensky was waiting for her—he would be waiting for her. She
could not go yet, because her soul was engaged. Soon she would 10
go.

A stillness, like passing away, took hold of her. Far off, down the
corridors, she heard the gong booming five o'clock. She must go. Yet
she sat still.

The other students were pushing back their stools and putting 15
their microscopes away. Everything broke into turmoil. She saw,
through the window, students going down the steps, with books
under their arms, talking, all talking.

A great craving to depart came upon her. She wanted also to be
gone. She was in dread of the material world, and in dread of her 20
own transfiguration. She wanted to run to meet Skrebensky—the
new life, the reality.

Very rapidly she wiped her slides and put them back, cleared her
place at the bench, active, active, active. She wanted to run to meet
Skrebensky—hasten—hasten. She did not know what she was to 25
meet. But it would be a new beginning. She must hurry.

She flitted down the corridor on swift feet, her razor and note
books and pencil in one hand, her pinafore over her arm. Her face
was lifted and tense with eagerness. He might not be there.

Issuing from the corridor, she saw him at once. She knew him at 30
once. Yet he was so strange. He stood with the curious self-effacing
diffidence which so frightened her in well-bred young men whom
she knew. He stood as if he wished to be unseen. He was very
well-dressed. She would not admit to herself the chill like a sunshine
of frost that came over her. This was he, the key, the nucleus to the 35
new world.

He saw her coming swiftly across the hall, a slim girl in a white
flannel blouse and dark skirt, with some of the abstraction and gleam
of the unknown upon her, and he started, excited. He was very
nervous. Other students were loitering about the hall. 40

She laughed, with a blind, dazzled face, as she gave him her hand. He too could not perceive her.

In a moment, she was gone, to get her outdoor things. Then again, as when she had been at school, they walked out into the town to tea. And they went to the same tea-shop.

She knew a great difference in him. The kin-ship was there, the old kin-ship, but he had belonged to a different world from hers. It was as if they had cried a state of truce between him and her, and in this truce they had met. She knew, vaguely, in the first minute, that they were enemies come together in a truce. Every movement and word of his was alien to her being.

Yet still she loved the fine texture of his face, of his skin. He was rather browner, physically stronger. He was a man now. She thought his manliness made the strangeness in him. When he was only a youth, fluid, he was nearer to her. She thought a man must inevitably set into this strange separateness, cold otherness of being. He talked, but not to her. She tried to speak to him, but she could not reach him.

He seemed so balanced and sure, he made such a confident presence. He was a great rider, so there was about him some of a horseman's sureness and habitual definiteness of decision, also some of the horseman's animal darkness. Yet his soul was only the more wavering, vague. He seemed made up of a set of habitual actions and decisions. The vulnerable, variable quick of the man was inaccessible. She knew nothing of it. She could only feel the dark, heavy fixity of his animal desire.

This dumb desire on his part had brought him to her. She was puzzled, hurt by some hopeless fixity in him, that terrified her with a cold feeling of despair. What did he want? His desires were so underground. Why did he not admit himself? What did he want? He wanted something that should be nameless. She shrank in fear.

Yet she flashed with excitement. In his dark, subterranean, male soul, he was kneeling before her, darkly exposing himself. She quivered, the dark flame ran over her. He was waiting at her feet. He was helpless, at her mercy. She could take or reject. If she rejected him, something would die in him. For him it was life or death. And yet, all must be kept so dark, the consciousness must admit nothing.

"How long," she said, "are you staying in England?"

"I am not sure—but not later than July, I believe."

Then they were both silent. He was here, in England, for six months. They had a space of six months between them. He waited. The same iron rigidity, as if the world were made of steel, possessed her again. It was no use turning with flesh and blood to this arrangement of forged metal.

Quickly, her imagination adjusted itself to the situation.   5

"Have you an appointment in India?" she asked.

"Yes—I have just the six months leave."

"Will you like being out there?"

"I think so—There's a good deal of social life, and plenty going on—hunting, polo—and always a good horse—and plenty of 10 work—any amount of work."

He was always side-tracking, always side-tracking his own soul. She could see him so well out there, in India—one of the governing class, superimposed upon an old civilisation, lord and master of a clumsier civilisation than his own. It was his choice. He would 15 become again an aristocrat, invested with authority and responsibility, having a great helpless populace beneath him. One of the ruling class, his whole being would be given over to the fulfilling and the executing of the better idea of the state. And in India, there would be real work to do. The country did need the civilisation 20 which he himself represented: it did need his roads and bridges, and the enlightenment of which he was part. He would go to India. But that was not her road.

Yet she loved him, the body of him, whatever his decisions might be. He seemed to want something of her. He was waiting for her to 25 decide of him. It had been decided in her long ago, when he had kissed her first. He was her lover, though good and evil should cease. Her will never relaxed, though her heart and soul must be imprisoned and silenced. He waited upon her, and she accepted him. For he had come back to her.   30

A glow came into his face, into his fine, smooth skin, his eyes, gold grey, glowed intimately to her. He burned up, he caught fire and became splendid, royal, something like a tiger. She caught his brilliant, burnished glamour. Her heart and her soul were shut away fast down below, hidden. She was free of them. She was to have her 35 satisfaction.

She became proud and erect, like a flower putting itself forth in its proper strength. His warmth invigorated her. His beauty of form, which seemed to glow out in contrast with the rest of people, made her proud. It was like deference to her, and made her feel as if she 40

represented before him all the grace and flower of humanity. She
was no mere Ursula Brangwen. She was Woman, she was the whole
of Woman in the human order. All-containing, universal, how
should she be limited to individuality?

5   She was exhilarated, she did not want to go away from him. She
had her place by him. Who should take her away.

They came out of the café.

"Is there anything you would like to do?" he said. "Is there
anything we *can* do?"

10   It was a dark, windy night in March.

"There is nothing to do," she said.

Which was the answer he wanted.

"Let us walk then—where shall we walk?" he asked.

"Shall we go to the river?" she suggested, timidly.

15   In a moment they were on the tram, going down to Trent Bridge.
She was so glad. The thought of walking in the dark, far-reaching
water-meadows, beside the full river, transported her. Dark water
flowing in silence through the big, restless night made her feel wild.

They crossed the bridge, descended, and went away from the
20   lights. In an instant, in the darkness, he took her hand and they went
in silence, with subtle feet treading the darkness. The town fumed
away on their left, there were strange lights and sounds, the wind
rushed against the trees and under the bridge. They walked close
together, powerful in unison. He drew her very close, held her with a
25   subtle, stealthy, powerful passion, as if they had a secret agreement
which held good in the profound darkness. The profound darkness
was their universe.

"It is like it was before," she said.

Yet it was not in the least as it was before. Nevertheless his heart
30   was perfectly in accord with her. They thought one thought.

"I knew I should come back," he said at length.

She quivered.

"Did you always love me?" she asked.

The directness of the question overcame him, submerged him for
35   a moment. The darkness travelled massively along.

"I had to come back to you," he said, as if hypnotised. "You were
always at the back of everything."

She was silent with triumph, like fate.

"I loved you," she said, "always."

40   The dark flame leaped up in him. He must give her himself. He

must give her the very foundations of himself. He drew her very close, and they went on in silence.

She started violently, hearing voices. They were near a stile across the dark meadows.

"It's only lovers," he said to her, softly.   5

She looked to see the dark figures against the fence, wondering that the darkness was inhabited.

"Only lovers will walk here tonight," he said.

Then in a low, vibrating voice he told her about Africa, the strange darkness, the strange, blood fear.   10

"I am not afraid of the darkness in England," he said. "It is soft, and natural to me, it is my medium, especially when you are here. But in Africa it seems massive and fluid with terror—not fear of anything—just fear. One breathes it, like a smell of blood. The blacks know it. They worship it, really, the darkness. One almost 15
likes it—the fear—something sensual."

She thrilled again to him. He was to her a voice out of the darkness. He talked to her all the while, in low tones, about Africa, conveying something strange and sensual to her: the negro, with his loose, soft passion that could envelop one like a bath. Gradually he 20
transferred to her the hot, fecund darkness that possessed his own blood. He was strangely secret. The whole world must be abolished. He maddened her with his soft, cajoling, vibrating tones. He wanted her to answer, to understand. A turgid, teeming night, heavy with fecundity in which every molecule of matter grew big with increase, 25
secretly urgent with fecund desire, seemed to come to pass. She quivered, taut and vibrating, almost pained. And gradually, he ceased telling her of Africa, there came a silence, whilst they walked the darkness beside the massive river. Her limbs were rich and tense, she felt they must be vibrating with a low, profound vibration. She 30
could scarcely walk. The deep vibration of the darkness could only be felt, not heard.

Suddenly, as they walked, she turned to him and held him fast, as if she were turned to steel.

"*Do* you love me?" she cried in anguish.   35

"Yes," he said, in a curious, lapping voice, unlike himself. "Yes, I love you."

He seemed like the living darkness upon her, she was in the embrace of the strong darkness. He held her enclosed, soft, unutterably soft, and with the unrelaxing softness of fate, the 40

relentless softness of fecundity. She quivered, and quivered, like a tense thing that is struck. But he held her all the time, soft, unending, like darkness closed upon her, omnipresent as the night. He kissed her, and she quivered as if she were being destroyed, shattered. The
5   lighted vessel vibrated, and broke in her soul, the light fell, struggled, and went dark. She was all dark, will-less, having only the receptive will.

He kissed her, with his soft, enveloping kisses, and she responded to them completely, her mind, her soul gone out. Darkness cleaving
10 to darkness, she hung close to him, pressed herself into soft flow of his kiss, pressed herself down, down to the source and core of his kiss, herself covered and enveloped in the warm, fecund flow of his kiss, that travelled over her, flowed over her, covered her, flowed over the last fibre of her, so they were one stream, one dark
15 fecundity, and she clung at the core of him, with her lips holding open the very bottommost source of him.

So they stood in the utter, dark kiss, that triumphed over them both, subjected them, knitted them into one fecund nucleus of the fluid darkness.
20 It was bliss, it was the nucleolating* of the fecund darkness.* Once the vessel had vibrated till it was shattered, the light of consciousness gone, then the darkness reigned, and the unutterable satisfaction.

They stood enjoying the unmitigated kiss, taking it, given to it endlessly, and still it was not exhausted. Their veins fluttered, their
25 blood ran together as one stream.

Till gradually a sleep, a heaviness settled on them, a drowse, and out of the drowse, a small light of consciousness woke up. Ursula became aware of the night around her, the water lapping and running full just near, the trees roaring and soughing in gusts of wind.
30 She kept near to him, in contact with him, but she became ever more and more herself. And she knew she must go to catch her train. But she did not want to draw away from contact with him.

At length they roused and set out. No longer they existed in the unblemished darkness. There was the glitter of a bridge, the twinkle
35 of lights across the river, the big flare of the town in front and on their right.

But still, dark and soft and incontestable, their bodies walked untouched by the lights, darkness supreme and arrogant.

"The stupid lights," Ursula said to herself, in her dark, sensual
40 arrogance. "The stupid, artificial, exaggerated town, fuming its

lights. It docs not exist really. It rests upon the unlimited darkness, like a gleam of coloured oil on dark water, but what is it?—nothing, nothing."*

In the tram, in the train, she felt the same. The lights, the civic uniform was a trick played, the people as they moved or sat were only 5 dummies exposed. She could see, beneath their pale, wooden pretence of composure and civic purposefulness, the dark stream that contained them all. They were like little paper ships in their motion. But in reality each one was a dark, blind, eager wave urging blindly forward, dark with the same homogeneous desire. And all 10 their talk and all their behaviour was sham, they were dressed-up creatures. She was reminded of the Invisible Man,* who was a piece of darkness made visible only by his clothes.

During the next weeks, all the time she went about in the same dark richness, her eyes dilated and shining like the eyes of a wild 15 animal, a curious half-smile on her darkly lighted face, a half-smile which seemed to be gibing at the civic pretence of all the human life about her.

"What are you, you pale citizens?" her face seemed to say, gleaming. "You subdued beast in sheep's clothing, you primeval 20 darkness falsified to a social mechanism."

She went about in the sensual subconsciousness all the time, mocking at the ready-made, artificial daylight of the rest.

"They assume selves as they assume suits of clothing," she said to herself, looking in mocking contempt at the stiffened, neutralised 25 men. "They think it better to be clerks or professors than to be the dark, fertile beings that exist in the potential darkness.—What do you think you are?" her soul asked of the professor as she sat opposite him in class. "What do you think you are, as you sit there in your gown and your spectacles? You are a lurking, blood-sniffing 30 creature with eyes peering out of the jungle darkness, snuffing for your desires. That is what you *are*, though nobody would believe it, and you would be the very last to allow it."

Her soul mocked at all this pretence. Herself, she kept on pretending. She dressed herself and made herself fine, she attended 35 her lectures and scribbled her notes. But all in a mood of superficial, mocking facility. She understood well enough their two-and-two-make-four tricks. She was as clever as they were. But care!—did she care about their monkey tricks of knowledge or learning or civic deportment? She did not care in the least. 40

There was Skrebensky, there was her dark, vital self. Outside her college, the other darkness, Skrebensky, was waiting. On the edge of the night, he was attentive. Did he care?

She was free as a leopard that sends up its raucous cry in the night.
5 She had the potent, dark stream of her own blood, she had the glimmering core of fecundity, she had her mate, her complement, her sharer in fruition. So, she had all, everything.

Skrebensky was staying in Nottingham all this time. He too was free. He knew no-one in this town, he had no civic self to maintain.
10 He was free. Their trams and markets and theatres and public meetings were a shaken kaleidoscope to him, he watched as a lion or a tiger may lie with narrowed eyes watching the people pass before its cage, the kaleidoscopic unreality of people, or a leopard lie blinking, watching the incomprehensible feats of the keepers. He despised it
15 all—it was all non-existent. Their good professors, their good clergymen, their good political speakers, their good, earnest women—all the time he felt his soul was grinning, grinning at the sight of them. So many performing puppets, all wood and rag for the performance!
20 He watched the citizen, a pillar of society, a model, saw the stiff goat's legs, which have become almost stiffened to wood in the desire to make them puppet in their action, he saw the trousers formed to the puppet-action: man's legs, but man's legs become rigid and deformed, ugly, mechanical.
25 He was curiously happy, being alone, now. The glimmering grin was on his face. He had no longer any necessity to take part in the performing tricks of the rest. He had discovered the clue to himself, he had escaped from the show, like a wild beast escaped straight back into its jungle. Having a room in a quiet hôtel, he hired a horse and
30 rode out into the country, staying sometimes for the night in some village, and returning the next day.

He felt rich and abundant in himself. Everything he did was a voluptuous pleasure to him—either to ride on horse-back, or to walk, or to lie in the sun, or to drink in a public-house. He had no use
35 for people, nor for words. He had an amused pleasure in everything, a great sense of voluptuous richness in himself, and of the fecundity of the universal night he inhabited. The puppet-shapes of people, their wood-mechanical voices, he was remote from them.

For there were always his meetings with Ursula. Very often, she
40 did not go to college in the afternoon, but walked with him instead.

Or he took a motor-car or a dog-cart and they drove into the country, leaving the car and going away by themselves into the woods. He had not taken her yet. With subtle, instinctive economy, they went to the end of each kiss, each embrace, each pleasure in intimate contact, knowing, subconsciously, that the last was coming. It was to be their 5 final entry into the source of creation.

She took him home, and he stayed a week-end at Beldover with her family. She loved having him in the house. Strange, how he seemed to come into the atmosphere of her family, with his laughing, insidious grace. They all loved him, he was kin to them. His raillery, 10 his warm, voluptuous mocking presence was meat and joy to the Brangwen household. For this house was always quivering with darkness, they put off their puppet-form when they came home, to lie and drowse in the sun.

There was a sense of freedom among them all, of the under- 15 current of darkness among them all. Yet here, at home, Ursula resented it. It became distasteful to her. And she knew that, if they understood the real relationship between her and Skrebensky, her parents, her father in particular, would go mad with rage. So subtly, she seemed to be like any other girl who is more or less courted by a 20 man. And she *was* like any other girl. But in her, the antagonism to the social imposition was for the time complete and final.

She waited, every moment of the day, for his next kiss. She admitted it to herself in shame and bliss. Almost consciously, she waited. He waited, but, until the time came, more unconsciously. 25 When the time came that he should kiss her again, a prevention was an annihilation to him. He felt his flesh go grey, he was heavy with a corpse-like inanition, he did not exist, if the time passed unfulfilled.

He came to her finally in a superb consummation. It was very dark, and again a windy, heavy night. They had come down the lane 30 towards Beldover, down to the valley. They were at the end of their kisses, and there was the silence between them. They stood as at the edge of a cliff, with a great darkness beneath.

Coming out of the lane along the darkness, with the dark space spreading down to the wind, and the twinkling lights of the station 35 below, the far-off windy chuff of a shunting train, the tiny clink-clink-clink of the wagons blown between the wind, the lights of Beldover-edge twinkling upon the blackness of the hill opposite, the glow of the furnaces along the railway to the right, their steps began to falter. They would soon come out of the darkness into the lights. It 40

was like turning back. It was unfulfilment. Two quivering, unwilling
creatures, they lingered on the edge of the darkness, peering out at
the lights and the machine glimmer beyond. They could not turn
back to the world—they could not.

5   So lingering along, they came to a great oak-tree by the path. In all
its budding mass it roared to the wind, and its trunk vibrated in every
fibre, powerful, indomitable.

"We will sit down," he said.

And in the roaring circle under the tree, that was almost invisible
10   yet whose powerful presence received them, they lay a moment
looking at the twinkling lights on the darkness opposite, saw the
sweeping brand of a train past the edge of their darkened field.

Then he turned and kissed her, and she waited for him. The pain
to her was the pain she wanted, the agony was the agony she wanted.
15   She was caught up, entangled in the powerful vibration of the night.
The man, what was he?—a dark, powerful vibration that encompassed her. She passed away as on a dark wind, far, far away, into the
pristine darkness of paradise, into the original immortality. She
entered the dark fields of immortality.

20   When she rose, she felt strangely free, strong. She was not
ashamed—why should she be? He was walking beside her, the man
who had been with her. She had taken him, they had been together.
Whither they had gone, she did not know. But it was as if she had
received another nature. She belonged to the eternal, changeless
25   place into which they had leapt together.*

Her soul was sure and indifferent of the opinion of the world of
artificial light. As they went up the steps of the foot-bridge over the
railway, and met the train-passengers, she felt herself belonging to
another world, she walked past them immune, a whole darkness
30   dividing her from them. When she went into the lighted dining-room
at home, she was impervious to the lights and the eyes of her parents.
Her everyday self was just the same. She merely had another,
stronger self that knew the darkness.

This curious separate strength, that existed in darkness and pride
35   of night, never forsook her. She had never been more herself. It
could not occur to her that anybody, not even the young man of the
world, Skrebensky, should have anything at all to do with her
permanent self. As for her temporal, social self, she let it look after
itself.

40   Her whole soul was implicated with Skrebensky—not the young

man of the world, but the undifferentiated man he was. She was perfectly sure of herself, perfectly strong, stronger than all the world. The world was not strong—she was strong. The world existed only in a secondary sense:—she existed supremely.

She continued at college, in her ordinary routine, merely as a cover to her dark, powerful under-life. The fact of herself, and with her Skrebensky, was so powerful, that she took rest in the other. She went to college in the morning, and attended her classes, flowering, and remote.

She had lunch with him in his hôtel; every evening she spent with him, either in town, at his rooms, or in the country. She made the excuse at home of evening study for her degree. But she paid not the slightest attention to her study.

They were both absolute and happy and calm. The fact of their own consummate being made everything else so entirely subordinate that they were free. The only thing they wanted, as the days went by, was more time to themselves. They wanted the time to be absolutely their own.

The Easter vacation was approaching. They agreed to go right away. It would not matter if they did not come back. They were indifferent to the actual facts.

"I suppose we ought to get married," he said, rather wistfully. It *was* so magnificently free and in a deeper world, as it was. To make public their connection would be to put it in range with all the things which nullified him, and from which he was for the moment entirely dissociated. If he married he would have to assume his social self. And the thought of assuming his social self made him at once diffident and abstract. If she were his social wife, if she were part of that complication of dead reality, then what had his under-life to do with her? One's social wife was almost a material symbol. Whereas now she was something more vivid to him than anything in conventional life could be, she gave the complete lie to all conventional life, he and she stood together, dark, fluid, infinitely potent, giving the living lie to the dead whole which contained them.

He watched her pensive, puzzled face.

"I don't think I want to marry you," she said, her brow clouded.

It piqued him rather.

"Why not?" he asked.

"Let's think about it afterwards, shall we?" she said.

He was crossed, yet he loved her violently.

"You've got a *museau*,* not a face," he said.

"Have I?" she cried, her face lighting up like a pure flame. She thought she had escaped. Yet he returned—he was not satisfied.

"Why?" he asked, "Why don't you want to marry me?"

5   "I don't want to be with other people," she said. "I want to be like this. I'll tell you if ever I want to marry you."

"All right," he said.

He would rather the thing was left indefinite, and that she took the responsibility.

10   They talked of the Easter vacation. She thought only of complete enjoyment.

They went to an hôtel in Piccadilly. She was supposed to be his wife. They bought a wedding-ring for a shilling, from a shop in a poor quarter.

15   They had revoked altogether the ordinary mortal world. Their confidence was like a possession upon them. They were possessed. Perfectly and supremely free they felt, proud beyond all question, and surpassing mortal conditions.

They were perfect, therefore nothing else existed. The world was 20 a world of servants whom one civilly ignored. Wherever they went, they were the sensuous aristocrats, warm, bright, glancing with pure pride of the senses.

The effect upon other people was extraordinary. The glamour was cast from the young couple upon all they came into contact with, 25 waiters or chance acquaintances.

"*Oui Monsieur le baron*," she would reply with a mocking curtsey to her husband.

So they came to be treated as titled people. He was an officer in the engineers. They were just married, going to India immediately.

30   Thus a tissue of romance was round them. She believed she was a young wife of a titled husband on the eve of departure for India. This, the social fact, was a delicious make-belief. The living fact was that he and she were man and woman, absolute and beyond all limitation.

35   The days went by—they were to have three weeks together—in perfect success. All the time, they themselves were reality, all outside was tribute to them. They were quite careless about money, but they did nothing very extravagant. He was rather surprised when he found that he had spent twenty pounds in a little under a week, but it 40 was only the irritation of having to go to the bank. The machinery of

the old system lasted for him, not the system. The money simply did not exist.

Neither did any of the old obligations. They came home from the theatre, had supper, undressed,* then flitted about in their dressing-gowns. They had a large bedroom and a corner sitting-room high up, remote and very cosy. They ate all their meals in their own rooms, attended by a young German called Hans, who thought them both wonderful, and answered assiduously:

"Gewiss, Herr Baron—bitte sehr, Frau Baronin."*

Often, they saw the pink of dawn away across the park. The tower of Westminster Cathedral* was emerging, the lamps of Piccadilly, stringing away beside the trees of the park, were becoming pale and moth-like, the morning traffic was clock-clocking down the shadowy road, which had gleamed all night like metal, down below, running far ahead into the night, beneath the lamps, and which was now vague, as in a mist, because of the dawn.

Then, as the flush of dawn became stronger, they opened the glass doors and went out on to the giddy balcony, feeling triumphant as two angels in bliss, looking down at the still sleeping world, which would wake to a dutiful, rumbling, sluggish turmoil of unreality.

But the air was cold. They went into their bedroom, and bathed before going to bed, leaving the partition doors of the bath-room open, so that the vapour came into the bedroom and faintly dimmed the mirror. She was always in bed first. She watched him as he bathed, his quick, unconscious movements, the electric light glinting on his wet shoulders. He stood out of the bath, his hair all washed flat over his forehead, and pressed the water out of his eyes. He was slender and, to her, perfect, a clean, straight-cut youth, without a grain of superfluous body. The brown hair on his body was soft and fine and adorable, he was all beautifully flushed, as he stood in the white bath-apartment.

He saw her warm, dark, lit-up face watching him from the pillow—yet he did not see it—it was always present, and was to him as his own eyes. He was never aware of the separate being of her. She was like his own eyes and his own heart beating to him.

So he went across to her, to get his sleeping suit. It was always a passionate adventure to go near to her. She put her arms round him, round his loins, and snuffed his warm, softened skin.

"Scent," she said.

"Soap," he answered.

"Soap," she repeated, looking up with bright eyes. They were both laughing, always laughing.*

Soon they were fast asleep, asleep till midday, close together, sleeping one sleep. Then they awoke to the ever-changing reality of their state. They alone inhabited the world of reality. All the rest lived on a lower sphere.

Whatever they wanted to do, they did. They saw a few people—Dorothy, whose guest she was supposed to be, and a couple of friends of Skrebensky, young Oxford men, who called her Mrs Skrebensky with entire simplicity. They treated her, indeed, with such respect, that she began to think she was really queen of the whole universe, of the old world as well as of the new. She forgot she was outside the pale of the old world. She thought she had brought it under the spell of her own, real world. And so she had.

In such ever-changing reality the weeks went by. All the time, they were an unknown world to each other. Every movement made by the one was a reality and an adventure to the other. They did not want outside excitements. They went to very few theatres, they were often in their sitting-room high up over Piccadilly, with windows open on two sides, and the door open on to the balcony, looking over the Green Park, or down upon the minute travelling of the traffic.

Then suddenly, looking at a sunset, she wanted to go. She must be gone. She must be gone at once. And in two hours' time, they were at Charing Cross taking train for Paris. Paris was his suggestion. She did not care where it was. The great joy was in setting out. And for a few days she was happy in the novelty of Paris.

Then, for some reason, she must call in Rouen on the way back to London. He had an instinctive mistrust of her desire for the place. But, perversely, she wanted to go there. It was as if she wanted to try its effect on her.

For the first time, in Rouen, he had a cold feeling of death: not afraid of any other man, but of her. She seemed to leave him. She followed after something that was not him. She did not want him. The old streets, the cathedral, the age and the monumental peace of the town took her away from him. She turned to it as if to something she had forgotten, and wanted. This was now the reality: this great stone cathedral slumbering there in its mass, which knew no transience nor heard any denial. It was majestic in its stability, its splendid absoluteness.

Her soul began to run by itself. He did not realise, nor did she. Yet in Rouen he had the first deadly anguish, the first sense of the death towards which they were wandering. And she felt the first heavy yearning, heavy, heavy hopeless warning, almost like a deep, uneasy sinking into apathy, hopelessness.

They returned to London. But still they had two days. He began to tremble, he grew feverish with the fear of her departure. She had in her some fatal prescience, that made her calm. What would be, would be.

He remained fairly easy, however, still in his state of heightened glamour, till she had gone, and he had turned away from St Pancras, and sat on the tram-car going up Pimlico to the Angel, to Moorgate Street on Sunday evening.

Then the cold horror gradually soaked into him. He saw the horror of the City Road, he realised the ghastly cold sordidness of the tram-car in which he sat. Cold, stark, ashen sterility* had him surrounded. Where then was the luminous, wonderful world he belonged to by rights? How did he come to be thrown on this refuse-heap where he was?

He was as if mad. The horror of the brick buildings, of the tram-car, of the ashen-grey people in the street made him reeling and blind as if drunk. He went mad. He had lived with her in a close, living, pulsing world, where everything pulsed with rich being. Now he found himself struggling amid an ashen-dry, cold world of rigidity, dead walls and mechanical traffic, and creeping, spectre-like people. The life was extinct, only ash moved and stirred or stood rigid, there was a horrible, clattering activity, a rattle like the falling of dry slag, cold and sterile. It was as if the sunshine that fell were unnatural light exposing the ash of the town, as if the lights at night were the sinister gleam of decomposition.

Quite mad, beside himself, he went to his club and sat with a glass of whiskey, motionless, as if turned to clay. He felt like a corpse that is inhabited with just enough life to make it appear as any other of the spectral, unliving beings which we call people in our dead language. Her absence was worse than pain to him. It destroyed his being.

Dead, he went on from lunch to tea. His face was all the time fixed and stiff and colourless, his life was a dry, mechanical movement. Yet even he wondered slightly at the awful misery that had overcome him. How could he be so ash-like and extinct? He wrote her a letter.

"I have been thinking that we must get married before long. My pay will be more when I get out to India, we shall be able to get along.

Or if you don't want to go to India, I could very probably stay here in
England. But I think you would like India. You could ride, and you
would know just everybody out there. Perhaps if you stay on to take
your degree, we might marry immediately after that. I will write to
5 your father as soon as I hear from you— —"

He went on, disposing of her. If only he could be with her! All he
wanted now was to marry her, to be sure of her. Yet all the time he
was perfectly, perfectly hopeless, cold, extinct, without emotion or
connection.

10 He felt as if his life were dead. His soul was extinct. The whole
being of him had become sterile, he was a spectre, divorced from life.
He had no fulness, he was just a flat shape. Day by day the madness
accumulated in him. The horror of not-being possessed him.

He went here, there, and everywhere. But whatever he did, he
15 knew that only the cypher of him was there, nothing was filled in. He
went to the theatre: what he heard and saw fell upon a cold surface of
consciousness, which was now all that he was, there was nothing
behind it, he could have no experience of any sort. Mechanical
registering took place in him, no more. He had no being, no
20 contents. Neither had the people he came into contact with. They
were mere permutations of known quantitites. There was no
roundness or fulness in this world he now inhabited, everything was
a dead shape mental arrangement, without life or being.

Much of the time, he was with friends and comrades. Then he
25 forgot everything. Their activities made up for his own negation,
they engaged his negative horror.

He only became happy when he drank, and he drank a good deal.
Then he was just the opposite of what he had been. He became a
warm, diffuse, glowing cloud, in a warm, diffuse, aërial world. He
30 was one with everything, in a diffuse formless fashion. Everything
melted down into a rosy glow, and he was the glow, and everything
was the glow, everybody else was the glow, and it was very nice, very
nice. He would sing songs, it was so nice.

Ursula went back to Beldover shut and firm. She loved
35 Skrebensky, of that she was resolved. She would allow nothing else.

She read his long, obsessed letter about getting married and going
to India, without any particular response. She seemed to ignore what
he said about marriage. It did not come home to her. He seemed,
throughout the greater part of his letter, to be talking without much
40 meaning.

She replied to him pleasantly and easily. She rarely wrote long letters.

"India sounds lovely. I can just see myself on an elephant swaying between lanes of obsequious natives. But I don't know if father would let me go. We must see.

"I keep living over again the lovely times we have had. But I don't think you liked me quite so much towards the end, did you? You did not like me when we left Paris. Why didn't you?

"I love you very much. I love your body. It is so clear and fine. I am glad you do not go naked, or all the women would fall in love with you. I am very jealous of it, I love it so much."

He was more or less satisfied with this letter. But day after day he was walking about, dead, non-existent.

He could not come again to Nottingham until the end of April. Then he persuaded her to go with him for a week-end to a friend's house near Oxford. By this time they were engaged. He had written to her father, and the thing was settled. He brought her an emerald ring, of which she was very proud.

Her people treated her now with a little distance, as if she had already left them. They left her very much alone.

She went with him for the three days in the country house near Oxford. It was delicious, and she was very happy. But the thing she remembered most was when, getting up in the morning after he had gone back quietly to his own room, having spent the night with her, she found herself very rich in being alone; and enjoying to the full her solitary room, she drew up her blind and saw the plum-trees in the garden below all glittering and snowy and delighted with the sunshine, in full bloom under a blue sky. They threw out their blossom, they flung it about under the blue heavens, the whitest blossom! How excited it made her.

She had to hurry through her dressing to go and walk in the garden under the plum-trees, before anyone should come and talk to her. Out she slipped, and paced like a queen in fairy pleasaunces. The blossom was silver-shadowy when she looked up from under the tree at the blue sky. There was a faint scent, a faint noise of bees, a wonderful quickness of happy morning.

She heard the breakfast gong and went indoors.

"Where have you been?" asked the others.

"I had to go out under the plum-trees," she said, her face glowing like a flower. "It is so lovely."

A shadow of anger crossed Skrebensky's soul. She had not wanted him to be there. He hardened his will.

At night there was a moon, and the blossom glistened ghostly, they went together to look at it. She saw the moonlight on his face as he
5 waited near her, and his features were like silver, and his eyes in shadow were unfathomable. She was in love with him. He was very quiet.

They went indoors and she pretended to be tired. So she went quickly to bed.

10 "Don't be long coming to me," she whispered as she was supposed to be kissing him goodnight.

.And he waited, intent, obsessed, for the moment when he could come to her.

She enjoyed him, she made much of him. She liked to put her
15 fingers on the soft skin of his sides, or on the softness of his back, when he made the muscles hard underneath, the muscles developed very strong through riding; and she had a great thrill of excitement and passion, because of the unimpressible hardness of his body, that was so soft and smooth under her fingers, that came to her with such
20 absolute service.

She owned his body and enjoyed it with all the delight and carelessness of a possessor. But he had become gradually afraid of her body. He wanted her, he wanted her endlessly. But there had come a tension into his desire, a constraint which prevented his
25 enjoying the delicious approach and the lovable close of the endless embrace. He was afraid. His will was always tense, fixed.

Her final examination was at midsummer. She insisted on sitting for it, although she had neglected her work during the past months. He also wanted her to go in for the degree. Then, he thought, she
30 would be satisfied. Secretly he hoped she would fail, so that she would be more glad of him.

"Would you rather live in India or in England, when we are married?" he asked her.

"Oh in India, by far," she said, with a careless lack of consider-
35 ation which annoyed him.

Once she said, with heat:

"I shall be glad to leave England. Everything is so meagre and paltry, it is so unspiritual—I hate democracy."

He became angry to hear her talk like this, he did not know why.

Somehow he could not bear it, when she attacked things. It was as if she were attacking him.

"What do you mean;" he asked her, hostile, "why do you hate democracy?"

"Only the greedy and ugly people come to the top in a democ- 5
racy," she said, "because they're the only people who will push themselves there. Only degenerate races are democratic."

"What do you want then—an aristocracy?" he asked, secretly moved. He always felt that by rights, he belonged to the ruling aristocracy. Yet to hear her speak for his class pained him with a 10
curious, painful pleasure. He felt he was acquiescing in something illegal, taking to himself some wrong, reprehensible advantage.

"I *do* want an aristocracy," she cried. "And I'd far rather have an aristocracy of birth than of money.* Who are the aristocrats now—who are chosen as the best to rule? Those who have money 15
and the brains for money. It doesn't matter what else they have: but they must have money-brains;—because they are ruling in the name of money."

"The people elect the government," he said.

"I know they do. But what are the people? Each one of them is a 20
money-interest. I hate it, that anybody is my equal who has the same amount of money as I have. I *know* I am better than all of them. I hate them. They are not my equals. I hate equality on a money-basis. It is the equality of dirt."

Her eyes blazed at him, he felt as if she wanted to destroy him. She 25
had gripped him and was trying to break him. His anger sprang up, against her. At least he would fight for his existence with her. A hard, blind resistance possessed him.

"*I* don't care about money," he said, "neither do I want to put my finger in the pie. I am too sensitive about my finger." 30

"What is your finger to me!" she cried, in a passion. "You with your dainty fingers, and your going to India because you will be one of the somebodies there! It's a mere dodge, your going to India."

"In what way a dodge?" he cried, white with anger and fear. 35

"You think the Indians are simpler than us, and so you'll enjoy being near them and being a lord over them," she said. "And you'll feel so righteous, governing them for their own good. Who are you, to feel righteous. What are you righteous about, in your governing.

Your governing stinks. What do you govern for, but to make things there as dead and mean as they are here?"

"I don't feel righteous in the least," he said.

"Then what *do* you feel. It's all such a nothingness, what you feel
5   and what you don't feel."

"What do you feel yourself?" he asked. "Aren't you righteous in your own mind?"

"Yes I am, because I'm against you, and all your old, dead things," she cried.

10 She seemed, with the last words, uttered in hard knowledge, to strike down the flag that he kept flying.* He felt cut off at the knees, a figure made worthless. A horrible sickness gripped him, as if his legs were really cut away, and he could not move, but remained a crippled trunk, dependent, worthless. The ghastly sense of helplessness, as if
15 he were a mere figure that did not exist vitally, made him mad, beside himself.

Now, even whilst he was with her, this death of himself came over him, when he walked about like a body from which all individual life is gone. In this state he neither heard nor saw nor felt, only the
20 mechanism of his life continued.

He hated her, as far as, in this state, he could hate. His cunning suggested to him all the ways of making her esteem him. For she did not esteem him. He left her and did not write to her. He flirted with other women, with Gudrun.

25 This last made her very fierce. She was still fiercely jealous of his body. In passionate anger she upbraided him because, not being man enough to satisfy one woman, he hung round others.

"Don't I satisfy you?" he asked of her, again going white to the throat.

30 "No," she said. "You've never satisfied me since the first weeks in London. You never satisfy me now. What does it mean to me, your having me—"*

She lifted her shoulders and turned aside her face in a motion of cold, indifferent worthlessness. He felt he would kill her.

35 When she had roused him to a pitch of madness, when she saw his eyes all dark and mad with suffering, then a great suffering overcame her soul, a great, inconquerable suffering. And she loved him. For Oh, she wanted to love him. Stronger than life or death was her craving to be able to love him.

40 And at such moments, when he was mad with her destroying him,

when all his complacency was destroyed, all his everyday self was broken, and only the stripped, rudimentary, primal man remained, demented with torture, her passion to love him became love, she took him again, they came together in an overwhelming passion, in which he knew he satisfied her. 5

But it all contained a developing germ of death. After each contact, her anguished desire for him or for that which she never had from him was stronger, her love was more hopeless. After each contact, his mad dependence on her was deepened, his hope of standing strong and taking her in his own strength was weakened. 10 He felt himself a mere attribute of her.

Whitsuntide* came, just before her examination. She was to have a few days of rest. Dorothy had inherited her patrimony, and had taken a cottage in Sussex. She invited them to stay with her.

They went down to Dorothy's neat, low cottage at the foot of the 15 downs.* Here they could do as they liked. Ursula was always yearning to go to the top of the downs. The white track wound up to the rounded summit. And she must go.

Up there, she could see the Channel a few miles away, the sea raised up and faintly glittering in the sky, the Isle of Wight a shadow 20 lifted on the far distance, the river winding bright through the patterned plain to seaward, Arundel Castle a shadowy bulk, and then the rolling of the high, smooth downs, making a high, smooth land under heaven, acknowledging only the heavens in their great, sun-glowing strength, and suffering only a few bushes to trespass on 25 the intercourse between their great, unabateable body and the changeful body of the sky.

Below she saw the villages and the woods of the weald, and the train running bravely,* a gallant little thing, running with all the importance of the world over the water-meadows and into the gap of 30 the downs, waving its white steam, yet all the while so little. So little, yet its courage carried it from end to end of the earth, till there was no place where it did not go. Yet the downs, in magnificent indifference, baring limbs and body to the sun, drinking sunshine and sea-wind and sea-wet cloud into its golden skin, with superb 35 stillness and calm of being, was not the downs still more wonderful? The blind, pathetic, energetic courage of the train as it steamed tinily away through the patterned levels to the sea's dimness, so fast and so energetic, made her weep. Where was it going? It was going nowhere, it was just going. So blind, so without goal or aim, yet so 40

hasty! She sat on an old prehistoric earth-work and cried, and the
tears ran down her face. The train had tunnelled all the earth,
blindly, and uglily. And she lay face downward on the downs, that
were so strong, that cared only for their intercourse with the
everlasting skies, and she wished she could become a strong mound
smooth under the sky, bosom and limbs bared to all winds and
clouds and bursts of sunshine.

But she must get up again and look down from her foothold of
sunshine, down and away at the patterned, level earth, with its
villages and its smoke and its energy. So shortsighted the train
seemed, running to the distance, so terrifying in their littleness the
villages, with such pettiness in their activity.

Skrebensky wandered dazed, not knowing where he was or what
he was doing with her. All her passion seemed to be, to wander up
there on the downs, and when she must descend, to earth, she was
heavy. Up there she was exhilarated and free.

She would not love him in a house any more. She said she hated
houses, and particularly she hated beds. There was something
distasteful in his coming to her bed.

She would stay the night on the downs. Up there, he with her.
It was midsummer, the days were glamorously long. At about half
past ten, when the bluey-black darkness had at last fallen, they took
rugs and climbed the steep track to the summit of the downs, he and
she.

Up there, the stars were big, the earth below was gone into
darkness. She was free up there with the stars. Far out they saw tiny
yellow lights—but it was very far out, at sea, or on land. She was free
up among the stars.

She took off all her clothes, and made him take off all his, and they
ran over the smooth, moonless turf, a long way, more than a mile
from where they had left their clothing, running in the dark, soft
wind, utterly naked, as naked as the downs themselves. Her hair was
loose and blew about her shoulders, she ran swiftly, wearing sandals
when she set off on the long run to the dew-pond.

In the round dew-pond the stars were untroubled. She ventured
softly into the water, grasping at the stars with her hands.

And then suddenly she started back, running swiftly. He was
there, beside her, but only on sufferance. He was a screen for her
fears. He served her. She took him, she clasped him, clenched him
close, but her eyes were open looking at the stars, it was as if the stars

were lying with her and entering the unfathomable darkness of her womb, fathoming her at last. It was not him.

The dawn came. They stood together on a high place, an earth-work of the stone-age men, watching for the light. It came over the land. But the land was dark. She watched a pale rim on the sky, away against the darkened land. The darkness became bluer. A little wind was running in from the sea behind. It seemed to be running to the pale rift of the dawn. And she and he darkly, on an outpost of the darkness, stood watching for the dawn.

The light grew stronger, gushing up against the dark sapphire of the transparent night. The light grew stronger, whiter, then over it hovered a flush of rose. A flush of rose, and then yellow, pale, new-created yellow, the whole quivering and poising momentarily over the fountain of the sky's rim.

The rose hovered and quivered, burned, fused to flame, to a transient red, whilst the yellow urged out in great waves, thrown from the ever-increasing fountain, great waves of yellow flinging into the sky, scattering its spray over the darkness, which became bluer and bluer, paler, till soon it would itself be a radiance, which had been darkness.

The sun was coming. There was a quivering, a powerful, terrifying swim of molten light. Then the molten source itself surged forth, revealing itself. The sun was in the sky, too powerful to look at.

And the ground beneath lay so still, so peaceful. Only now and again a cock crew. Otherwise, from the distant, yellow hills to the pine trees at the foot of the downs, everything was newly washed into being, in a flood of new, golden creation.

It was so unutterably still and perfect with promise, the golden-lighted, distinct land, that Ursula's soul rocked and wept. Suddenly he glanced at her. The tears were running over her cheeks, her mouth was working strangely.

"What is the matter?" he asked.

After a moment's struggle with her voice,

"It is so beautiful," she said, looking at the glowing, beautiful land. It was so beautiful, so perfect, and so unsullied.

He too realised what England would be in a few hours' time—a blind, sordid, strenuous activity, all for nothing, fuming with dirty smoke and running trains and groping in the bowels of the earth, all for nothing. A ghastliness came over him.

He looked at Ursula. Her face was wet with tears, very bright, like a transfiguration in the refulgent light. Nor was his the hand to wipe away the burning, bright tears. He stood apart, overcome by a cruel ineffectuality.

Gradually, a great, helpless sorrow was rising in him. But as yet, 5 he was fighting it away, he was struggling for his own life. He became very quiet and unaware of the things about him, awaiting, as it were, her judgment on him.

They returned to Nottingham, the time of her examination came. She must go to London.* But she would not stay with him in 10 an hôtel. She would go to a quiet little pension near the British Museum.

Those quiet residential squares of London made a great impression on her mind. They were very complete. Her mind seemed imprisoned in their quietness. Who was going to liberate her?

15 In the evening, her practical examination being over, he went with her to dinner at one of the hôtels down the river, near Richmond. It was golden and beautiful, with yellow water and white and scarlet-striped boat-awnings, and blue shadows under the trees.

"When shall we be married?" he asked her, quietly, simply, as if it 20 were a mere question of comfort.

She watched the changing pleasure-traffic of the river. He looked at her golden, puzzled *museau*. The knot gathered in his throat.

"I don't know," she said.

A hot grief gripped his throat.

25 "Why don't you know—don't you want to be married?" he asked her.

Her head turned slowly, her face, puzzled, like a boy's face, expressionless because she was trying to think, looked towards his face. She did not see him, because she was pre-occupied. She did 30 not quite know what she was going to say.

"I don't think I want to be married," she said, and her naïve, troubled, puzzled eyes rested a moment on his, then travelled away, pre-occupied.

"Do you mean never, or not just yet?" he asked.

35 The knot in his throat grew harder, his face was drawn as if he were being strangled.

"I mean never," she said, out of some far self which spoke for once beyond her.

His drawn, strangled face watched her blankly for a few moments, 40 then a strange sound took place in his throat. She started, came to herself, and, horrified, saw him. His head made a queer motion, the chin jerked back against the throat, the curious crowing, hiccupping sound came again, his face twisted like insanity, and he was crying, crying blind and twisted as if something were broken which kept him in control. 5

"Tony—don't," she cried, starting up.

It tore every one of her nerves, to see him. He made groping movements to get out of his chair. But he was crying uncontrollably, noiselessly, with his face twisted like a mask, contorted, and the tears running down the amazing grooves in his cheeks. Blindly, his face 10 always this horrible working mask, he groped for his hat, for his way down from the terrace. It was eight o'clock, but still brightly light. The other people were staring. In great agitation, part of which was exasperation, she stayed behind, paid the waiter with a half sovereign, took her yellow silk coat, then followed Skrebensky. 15

She saw him walking with brittle, blind steps along the path by the river. She could tell by the strange stiffness and brittleness of his figure that he was still crying. Hurrying after him, running, she took his arm.

"Tony," she cried, "don't! Why are you like this? What are you 20 doing this for? Don't! It's not necessary."

He heard, and his manhood was cruelly, coldly defaced. Yet it was no good. He could not gain control of his face. His face, his breast, were weeping violently, as if automatically. His will, his knowledge had nothing to do with it. He simply could not stop. 25

She walked holding his arm, silent with exasperation and perplexity and pain. He took the uncertain steps of a blind man, because his mind was blind with weeping.

"Shall we go home? Shall we have a taxi?" she said.

He could pay no attention. Very flustered, very agitated, she 30 signalled indefinitely to a taxi-cab* that was going slowly by. The driver saluted and drew up. She opened the door and pushed Skrebensky in, then took her own place. Her face was uplifted, the mouth closed down, she looked hard and cold and ashamed. She winced as the driver's dark, red face was thrust round upon her, a 35 full-blooded, animal face with black eyebrows and a thick, short-cut moustache.

"Where to, lady?" he said, his white teeth showing.

Again for a moment she was flustered.

"Forty Rutland Square," she said. 40

He touched his cap and stolidly set the car in motion. He seemed to have a league with her to ignore Skrebensky.

The latter sat as if trapped within the taxi-cab, his face still working, whilst occasionally he made quick slight movements of the head, to shake away his tears. He never moved his hands. She could not bear to look at him. She sat with face uplifted and averted to the window.

At length, when she had regained some control over herself, she turned again to him. He was much quieter. His face was wet, and twitched occasionally, his hands still lay motionless. But his eyes were quite still, like a washed sky after rain, full of a wan light, and quite steady, almost ghost-like.

A pain flamed in her womb, for him.

"I didn't think I should hurt you," she said, laying her hand very lightly, tentatively, on his arm. "The words came without my knowing. They didn't mean anything, really."

He remained quite still, hearing, but washed all wan and without feeling. She waited, looking at him, as if he were some curious, not-understandable creature.

"You won't cry again, will you, Tony?"

Some shame and bitterness against her burned him in the question. She noticed how his moustache was soddened wet with tears. Taking her handkerchief, she wiped his face. The driver's heavy, stolid back remained always turned to them, as if conscious but indifferent. Skrebensky sat motionless whilst Ursula wiped his face, softly, carefully, and yet clumsily, not as well as he would have wiped it himself.

Her handkerchief was too small. It was soon wet through. She groped in his pocket for his own. Then, with its more ample capacity, she carefully dried his face. He remained motionless all the while. Then she drew his cheek to hers, and kissed him. His face was cold. Her heart was hurt. She saw the tears welling quickly to his eyes again. As if he were a child, she again wiped away his tears. By now she herself was on the point of weeping. Her underlip was caught between her teeth.

So she sat still, for fear of her own tears, sitting close by him, holding his hand warm and close and loving. Meanwhile the car ran on, and a soft, midsummer dusk began to gather. For a long while they sat motionless. Only now and again her hand closed more closely, lovingly, over his hand, then gradually relaxed.

The dusk began to fall. One or two lights appeared. The driver drew up to light his lamps. Skrebensky moved for the first time, leaning forward to watch the driver. His face had always the same still, clarified, almost childlike look, impersonal.

They saw the driver's strange, full, dark face peering into the lamps under drawn brows. Ursula shuddered. It was the face almost of an animal, yet of a quick, strong, wary animal that had them within its knowledge, almost within its power. She clung closer to Skrebensky.

"My love?" she said to him, questioningly, when the car was again running in full motion.

He made no movement or sound. He let her hold his hand, he let her reach forward, in the gathering darkness, and kiss his still cheek. The crying had gone by—he would not cry any more. He was whole and himself again.

"My love," she repeated, trying to make him notice her.

But as yet, he could not.

He watched the road. They were running by Kensington Gardens. For the first time, his lips opened.

"Shall we get out and go into the park?" he asked.

"Yes," she said, quietly, not sure what was coming.

After a moment he took the tube from its peg. She saw the stout, strong, self-contained driver lean his head.

"Stop at Hyde Park Corner."

The dark head nodded, the car ran on just the same.

Presently they pulled up. Skrebensky paid the man. Ursula stood back. She saw the driver salute as he received his tip, and then, before he set the car in motion, turn and look at her, with his quick, powerful, animal's look, his eyes very concentrated and the whites of his eyes flickering. Then he drove away into the crowd. He had let her go. She had been afraid.

Skrebensky turned with her into the park. A band was still playing and the place was thronged with people. They listened to the ebbing music, then went aside to a dark seat, where they sat closely, hand in hand.

Then at length, as out of the silence, she said to him, wondering: "What hurt you so?"

She really did not know, at this moment.

"When you said you wanted never to marry me," he replied, with a childish simplicity.

"But why did that hurt you so?" she said. "You needn't mind everything I say, so particularly."

"I don't know—I didn't want to do it," he said, humbly, ashamed.

She pressed his hand warmly. They sat close together, watching
5 the soldiers go by with their sweethearts, the lights trailing in myriads down the great thoroughfares that beat on the edge of the park.

"I didn't know you cared so much," she said, also humbly.

"I didn't," he said. "I was knocked over myself.—But I care—all the world."

10 His voice was so quiet and colourless, it made her heart go pale with fear.

"My love!" she said, drawing near to him. But she spoke out of fear, not out of love.

"I care all the world—I care for nothing else—neither in life nor
15 death," he said, in the same steady, colourless voice of essential truth.

"Than for what?" she murmured duskly.

"Than for you—to be with me."

And again she was afraid. Was she to be conquered by this? She
20 cowered close to him, very close to him. They sat perfectly still, listening to the great, heavy, beating sound of the town, the murmur of lovers going by, the footsteps of soldiers.

She shivered against him.

"You are cold?" he said.

25 "A little."

"We will go and have some supper."

He was now always quiet and decided and remote, very beautiful. He seemed to have some strange, cold power over her.

They went to a restaurant, and drank chianti. But his pale, wan
30 look did not go away.

"Don't leave me tonight," he said at length, looking at her, pleading. He was so strange and impersonal, she was afraid.

"But the people of my place," she said, quivering.

"I will explain to them—they know we are engaged."

35 She sat pale and mute. He waited.

"Shall we go?" he said at length.

"Where?"

"To an hôtel."

Her heart was hardened. Without answering, she rose to acquiesce. But she was now cold and unreal. Yet she could not refuse him. It seemed like fate, a fate she did not want.

They went to an Italian hôtel somewhere, and had a sombre bedroom with a very large bed, clean, but sombre. The ceiling was painted with a bunch of flowers in a big medallion over the bed. She thought it was pretty.

He came to her, and cleaved to her very close, like steel cleaving and clinching on to her. Her passion was roused, it was fierce but cold. But it was fierce, and extreme, and good, their passion this night. He slept with her fast in his arms. All night long he held her fast against him. She was passive, acquiescent. But her sleep was not very deep nor very real.

She woke in the morning to a sound of water dashed on a courtyard, to sunlight streaming through a lattice. She thought she was in a foreign country. And Skrebensky was there an incubus upon her.

She lay still, thinking, whilst his arm was round her, his head against her shoulders, his body against hers, just behind her. He was still asleep.

She watched the sunshine coming in bars through the *persiennes*, and her immediate surroundings again melted away.

She was in some other land, some other world, where the old restraints had dissolved and vanished, where one moved freely, not afraid of one's fellow men, nor wary, nor on the defensive, but calm, indifferent, at one's ease. Vaguely, in a sort of silver light, she wandered at large and at ease. The bonds of the world were broken. This world of England had vanished away. She heard a voice in the yard below calling:

"O' Giovann'—O'-O'-O' Giovann'—!"

And she knew she was in a new country, in a new life. It was very delicious to lie thus still, with one's soul wandering freely and simply in the silver light of some other, simpler, more finely natural world.

But always there was a foreboding waiting to command her. She became more aware of Skrebensky. She knew he was waking up. She must modify her soul, depart from her further world, for him.

She knew he was awake. He lay still, with a concrete stillness, not as when he slept. Then his arm tightened almost convulsively upon her, and he said, half timidly:

"Did you sleep well?"

"Very well."

"So did I."

There was a pause.

"And do you love me?" he asked.

5   She turned and looked at him, searchingly. He seemed outside her.

"I do," she said.

But she said it out of complacency and a desire not to be harried. There was a curious breach of silence between them, which

10 frightened him.

They lay rather late, then he rang for breakfast. She wanted to be able to go straight downstairs and away from the place, when she got up. She was happy in this room, but the thought of the publicity of the hall downstairs rather troubled her.

15   A young Italian, a Sicilian, dark and slightly pock-marked, buttoned up in a sort of grey tunic, appeared with the tray. His face had an almost African imperturbability, impassive, incomprehensible.

"One might be in Italy," Skrebensky said to him, genially.

20   A vacant look, almost like fear, came on the fellow's face. He did not understand.

"This is like Italy," Skrebensky explained.

The face of the Italian flashed with a non-comprehending smile, he finished setting out the tray, and was gone. He did not under-

25 stand: he would understand nothing: he disappeared from the door like a half-domesticated wild animal. It made Ursula shudder slightly, the quick, sharp-sighted, intent animality of the man.

Skrebensky was beautiful to her this morning, his face softened and transfused with suffering and with love, his movements very still

30 and gentle. He was beautiful to her, but she was detached from him by a chill distance. Always she seemed to be bearing up against the distance that separated them. But he was unaware. This morning he was transfused and beautiful. She admired his movements, the way he spread honey on his roll, or poured out the coffee.

35   When breakfast was over she lay still again on the pillows, whilst he went through his toilet. She watched him, as he sponged himself and quickly dried himself with the towel. His body was beautiful, his movements intent and quick, she admired him and she appreciated him without reserve. He seemed completed now. He roused no

40 fruitful fecundity in her. He seemed added up, finished. She knew

him all round, not on any side did he lead into the unknown. Poignant, almost passionate appreciation she felt for him, but none of the dreadful wonder, none of the rich fear, the connection with the unknown, or the reverence of love. He was, however, unaware this morning. His body was quiet and fulfilled, his veins complete 5 with satisfaction, he was happy, finished.

Again she went home. But this time he went with her. He wanted to stay by her. He wanted her to marry him. It was already July. In early September he must sail for India. He could not bear to think of going alone. She must come with him. Nervously, he kept beside 10 her.

Her examination was finished, her college career was over. There remained for her now to marry or to work again. She applied for no post. It was concluded she would marry. India tempted her—the strange, strange land. But with the thought of Calcutta, or Bombay, 15 or of Simla, and of the European population, India was no more attractive to her than Nottingham.

She had failed in her examination: she had gone down: she had not taken her degree. It was a blow to her. It hardened her soul.

"It doesn't matter," he said. "What are the odds, whether you are 20 a Bachelor of Arts or not, according to the London University? All you know, you know, and if you are Mrs Skrebensky, the B.A. is meaningless."

Instead of consoling her, this made her harder, more ruthless. She was now up against her own fate. It was for her to choose between 25 being Mrs Skrebensky, even Baroness Skrebensky, wife of a lieutenant in the Royal Engineers, the Sappers, as he called them, living with the European population in India—or being Ursula Brangwen, spinster, school-mistress. She was qualified by her Intermediate Arts examination. She would probably even now get a post quite 30 easily as assistant in one of the higher grade schools, or even in Willey Green Grammar School. Which was she to do?

She hated most of all entering the bondage of teaching once more. Very heartily she detested it. Yet at the thought of marriage and living with Skrebensky amid the European population in India, her 35 soul was locked and would not budge. She had very little feeling about it: only there was a dead-lock.

Skrebensky waited, she waited, everybody waited for the decision. When Anton talked to her, and seemed insidiously to suggest himself as a husband to her, she knew how utterly locked out he was. On the 40 other hand, when she saw Dorothy, and discussed the matter, she felt she would marry him promptly, at once, as a sharp disavowal of adherence with Dorothy's views.

The situation was almost ridiculous.

5 "But do you love him?" asked Dorothy.

"It isn't a question of loving him," said Ursula. "I love him well enough—certainly more than I love anybody else in the world. And I shall never love anybody else the same again. We have had the flower of each other. But I don't *care* about love. I don't value it. I don't care

10 whether I love or whether I don't, whether I have love or whether I haven't. What is it to me?"

And she shrugged her shoulders in fierce, cruel contempt.

Dorothy pondered, rather angry and afraid.

"Then what *do* you care about?" she asked, exasperated.

15 "I don't know," said Ursula. "But something impersonal. Love —love—love—what does it mean—what does it amount to? So much personal gratification. It doesn't lead anywhere."

"It isn't supposed to lead anywhere, is it?" said Dorothy satirically. "I thought it was the one thing which is an end in itself."

20 "Then what does it matter to me?" cried Ursula. "As an end in itself, I could love a hundred men, one after the other. Why should I end with a Skrebensky? Why should I not go on, and love all the types I fancy, one after another, if love is an end in itself? There are plenty of men who aren't Anton, whom I could love—whom I would like to

25 love."

"Then you don't love *him*," said Dorothy.

"I tell you I do;—quite as much, and perhaps more than I should love any of the others. Only there are plenty of things that aren't in Anton that I would love in the other men."

30 "What, for instance?"

"It doesn't matter. But a sort of strong understanding, in some men, and then a dignity, a directness, something unquestioned that there is in working men, and then a jolly, reckless passionateness that you see—a man who could really let go—"

35 Dorothy could feel that Ursula was already hankering after something else, something that this man did not give her.

"The question is, what *do* you want," propounded Dorothy. "Is it just other men?"

Ursula was silenced. This was her own dread. Was she just

40 promiscuous?

"Because if it is," continued Dorothy, "you'd better marry Anton. The other can only end badly."

So out of fear of herself, Ursula was to marry Skrebensky.

He was very busy now, preparing to go to India. He must visit relatives and contract business. He was almost sure of Ursula now. She seemed to have given in. And he seemed to become again an important, self-assured man.

It was the first week in August, and he was one of a large party in a bungalow on the Lincolnshire coast. It was a tennis, golf, motor-car, motor-boat party, given by his great-aunt, a lady of social pretensions. Ursula was invited to spend the week with the party.

She went rather reluctantly. Her marriage was more or less fixed for the twenty eighth of the month. They were to sail for India on September the fifth. One thing she knew, in her subconsciousness, and that was, she would never sail for India.

She and Anton, being important guests on account of the coming marriage, had rooms in the large bungalow. It was a big place, with a great central hall, two smaller writing-rooms, and then two corridors from which opened eight or nine bedrooms. Skrebensky was put on one corridor, Ursula on the other. They felt very lost, in the crowd.

Being lovers, however, they were allowed to be out alone together as much as they liked. Yet she felt very strange, in this crowd of strange people, uneasy, as if she had no privacy. She was not used to these homogeneous crowds. She was afraid.

She felt different from the rest of them, with their hard, easy, shallow intimacy, that seemed to cost them so little. She felt she was not pronounced enough. It was a kind of hold-your-own unconventional atmosphere. She did not like it. In crowds, in assemblies of people, she liked formality. She felt she did not produce the right effect. She was not effective: she was not beautiful: she was nothing. Even before Skrebensky she felt unimportant, almost inferior. He could take his part very well with the rest.

He and she went out into the night. There was a moon behind clouds, shedding a diffused light, gleaming now and again in bits of smoky mother-of-pearl. So they walked together on the wet, ribbed sands near the sea, hearing the run of the long, heavy waves, that made a ghostly whiteness and a whisper.

He was sure of himself. As she walked, the soft silk of her dress—she wore a blue shantung, full-skirted—blew away from the sea and flapped and clung to his legs. She wished it would not.

Everything seemed to give her away, and she could not rouse herself
to deny, she was so confused.

He would lead her away to a pocket in the sand-hills, secret amid
the grey thorn-bushes and the grey, glassy grass. He held her close
5 against him, felt all her firm, unutterably desirable mould of body
through the fine fire of the silk that fell about her limbs. The silk,
slipping fierily on the hidden, yet revealed roundness and firmness of
her body, her loins, seemed to run in him like fire, make his brain
burn like brimstone. She liked it, the electric fire of the silk under his
10 hands upon her limbs, the fire flew over her, as he drew nearer and
nearer to discovery. She vibrated like a jet of electric, firm fluid in
response. Yet she did not feel beautiful. All the time, she felt she was
not beautiful to him, only exciting. She let him take her, and he
seemed mad, mad with excited passion. But she, as she lay after-
15 wards on the cold, soft sand, looking up at the blotted, faintly
luminous sky, felt that she was as cold now as she had been before.
Yet he, breathing heavily, seemed almost savagely satisfied. He
seemed revenged.

A little wind wafted the sea grass and passed over her face. Where
20 was the supreme fulfilment she would never enjoy? Why was she so
cold, so unroused, so indifferent?

As they went home, and she saw the many, hateful lights of the
bungalow, of several bungalows in a group, he said softly:

"Don't lock your door."

25 "I'd rather, here," she said.

"No, don't. We belong to each other. Don't let us deny it."

She did not answer. He took her silence for consent.

He shared his room with another man.

"I suppose," he said, "it won't alarm the house if I go across to
30 happier regions."

"So long as you don't make a great row going, and don't try the
wrong door," said the other man, turning in to sleep.

Skrebensky went out in his wide-striped cotton sleeping suit. He
crossed the big dining hall, whose low firelight smelled of cigars and
35 whiskey and coffee, entered the other corridor and found Ursula's
room. She was lying awake, wide-eyed and suffering. She was glad
he had come, if only for consolation. It was consolation to be held in
his arms, to feel his body against hers. Yet how foreign his arms and
body were! Yet still, not so horribly foreign and hostile as the rest of
40 the house felt to her.*

She did not know how she suffered in this house. She was healthy and exorbitantly full of interest. So she played tennis and learned golf, she rowed out and swam in the deep sea, and enjoyed it very much indeed, full of zest. Yet all the time, among those others, she felt shocked and wincing, as if her violently-sensitive nakedness were exposed to the hard, brutal, material impact of the rest of the people.

The days went by unmarked, in a full, almost strenuous enjoyment of one's own physique. Skrebensky was one among the others, till evening came, and he took her for himself. She was allowed a great deal of freedom and was treated with a good deal of respect, as a girl on the eve of marriage, about to depart for another continent.

The trouble began at evening. Then a yearning for something unknown came over her, a passion for something she knew not what. She would walk the foreshore alone after dusk, expecting, expecting something, as if she had gone to a *rendez-vous*. The salt, bitter passion of the sea, its indifference to the earth, its swinging, definite motion, its strength, its attack, and its salt burning, seemed to provoke her to a pitch of madness, tantalising her with vast suggestions of fulfilment. And then, for personification, would come Skrebensky, Skrebensky, whom she knew, whom she was fond of, who was attractive, but whose soul could not contain her in its waves of strength, nor his breast compel her in burning, salty passion.

One evening they went out after dinner, across the low golf links to the dunes and the sea. The sky had small, faint stars, all was still and faintly dark. They walked together in silence, then ploughed, labouring, through the heavy loose sand of the gap between the dunes. They went in silence under the even, faint darkness, in the darker shadow of the sand-hills.

Suddenly, cresting the heavy, sandy pass, Ursula lifted her head and shrank back, momentarily frightened. There was a great whiteness confronting her, the moon was incandescent as a round furnace door,* out of which came the high blast of moonlight, over the sea-ward half of the world, a dazzling, terrifying glare of white light. They shrank back for a moment into shadow, uttering a cry. He felt his chest laid bare, where the secret was heavily hidden. He felt himself fusing down to nothingness, like a bead that rapidly disappears in an incandescent flame.

"How wonderful!" cried Ursula, in low, calling tones. "How wonderful!"

And she went forward, plunging into it. He followed behind. She
too seemed to melt into the white glare, towards the moon.

The sands were as ground silver, the sea moved in solid brightness, coming towards them, and she went to meet the advance of the
5 flashing, buoyant water. She gave her breast to the moon, her belly to
the flashing, heaving water.* He stood behind, encompassed, a
shadow ever dissolving.

She stood on the edge of the water, at the edge of the solid,
flashing body of the sea, and the wave rushed over her feet.

10 "I want to go," she cried, in a strong, dominant voice. "I want to
go."

He saw the moonlight on her face, so she was like metal, he heard
her ringing, metallic voice, like the voice of a harpy* to him.

She prowled, ranging on the edge of the water like a possessed
15 creature, and he followed her. He saw the froth of the wave followed
by the hard, bright water swirl over her feet and her ankles, she
swung out her arms, to balance, he expected every moment to see
her walk in to the sea, dressed as she was, and be carried swimming
out.

20 But she turned, she walked to him.

"I want to go," she cried again, in the high, hard voice, like the
scream of gulls.

"Where?" he asked.

"I don't know."

25 And she seized hold of his arm, held him fast, as if captive, and
walked him a little way by the edge of the dazzling, dazing water.

Then there, in the great flare of light, she clinched hold of him,
hard, as if suddenly she had the strength of destruction, she fastened
her arms round him and tightened him in her grip, whilst her mouth
30 sought his in a hard, rending, ever-increasing kiss, till his body was
powerless in her grip, his heart melted in fear from the fierce,
beaked, harpy's kiss. The water washed again over their feet, but she
took no notice. She seemed unaware, she seemed to be pressing in
her beaked mouth till she had the heart of him. Then, at last, she
35 drew away and looked at him—looked at him. He knew what she
wanted. He took her by the hand and led her across the foreshore
back to the sand-hills. She went silently. He felt as if the ordeal of
proof was upon him, for life or death. He led her to a dark hollow.

"No, here," she said, going out to the slope full under the
40 moonshine. She lay motionless, with wide-open eyes looking at the

moon. He came direct to her, without preliminaries. She held him
pinned down at the chest, awful. The fight, the struggle for
consummation was terrible. It lasted till it was agony to his soul, till
he succumbed, till he gave way as if dead, and lay with his face buried
partly in her hair partly in the sand, motionless, as if he would be   5
motionless now for ever, hidden away in the dark, buried, only
buried, he only wanted to be buried in the goodly darkness, only that,
no more.

He seemed to swoon. It was a long time before he came to himself.
He was aware of an unusual motion of her breast. He looked up. Her   10
face lay like an image in the moonlight, the eyes wide open, rigid. But
out of the eyes, slowly, there rolled a tear, that glittered in the
moonlight as it ran down her cheek.

He felt as if the knife were being pushed into his already dead
body. With head strained back, he watched, drawn tense, for some   15
minutes, watched the unaltering, rigid face like metal in the moonlight, the fixed, unseeing eyes, in which slowly the water gathered,
shook with glittering moonlight, then, surcharged, brimmed over
and ran trickling, a tear with its burden of moonlight, into the
darkness, to fall in the sand.   20

He drew gradually away as if afraid, drew away—she did not
move. He glanced at her—she lay the same. Could he break away.
He turned, saw the open foreshore, clear in front of him, and he
plunged away, on and on, ever further from the horrible figure that
lay stretched in the moonlight on the sands with the tears gathering   25
and travelling on the motionless, eternal face.

He felt, if ever he must see her again, his bones must be broken,
his body crushed, obliterated for ever. And as yet, he had the love of
his own living body. He wandered on a long, long way, till his brain
grew dark and he was unconscious with weariness. Then he curled   30
in the deepest darkness he could find, under the sea grass, and lay
there without consciousness.

She broke from her tense cramp of agony gradually, though each
movement was a goad of heavy pain. Gradually, she lifted her dead
body from the sands, and rose at last. There was now no moon for   35
her, no sea. All had passed away. She trailed her dead body to the
house, to her room, where she lay down, inert.

Morning brought her a new access of superficial life. But all
within her was cold, dead, inert. Skrebensky appeared at breakfast.
He was white and obliterated. They did not look at each other nor   40

speak to each other. Apart from the ordinary, trivial talk of civil people, they were separate, they did not speak of what was between them during the remaining two days of their stay. They were like two dead people who dare not recognise, dare not see each other.

5   Then she packed her bags and put on her things. There were several guests leaving together, for the same train. He would have no opportunity to speak to her.

He tapped at her bedroom door, at the last minute. She stood with her umbrella in her hand. He closed the door. He did not know what
10   to say.

"Have you done with me?" he asked her at length, lifting his head.

"It isn't me," she said. "You have done with me—we have done with each other."

He looked at her, at the closed face, which he thought so cruel.
15   And he knew he could never touch her again. His will was broken, he was seared, but he clung to the life of his body.

"Well, what have I done?" he asked, in a rather querulous voice.

"I don't know," she said, in the same dull, feelingless voice. "It is finished. It has been a failure."

20   He was silent. The words still burned his bowels.

"Is it my fault?" he said, looking up at length, challenging the last stroke.

"You couldn't—" she began. But she broke down.

He turned away, afraid to hear more. She began to gather her bag,
25   her handkerchief, her umbrella. She must be gone now. He was waiting for her to be gone.

At length the carriage came and she drove away with the rest. When she was out of sight, a great relief came over him, a pleasant banality. In an instant, everything was obliterated. He was childishly
30   amiable and companionable all the day long. He was astonished that life could be so nice. It was better than it had been before. What a simple thing it was to be rid of her! How friendly and simple everything felt to him! What false thing had she been forcing on him?

35   But at night, he dared not be alone. His room-mate had gone, and the hours of darkness were an agony to him. He watched the window in suffering and terror. When would this horrible darkness be lifted off him? Setting all his nerves, he endured it. He went to sleep with the dawn.

40   He never thought of her. Only his terror of the hours of night grew

on him, obsessed him like a mania. He slept fitfully, with constant wakings of anguish. The fear wore away the core of him.

His plan was, to sit up very late: to drink in company until one or half past one in the morning: then he would get three hours of sleep, of oblivion. It was light by five o'clock. But he was shocked almost to madness if he opened his eyes on the darkness.

In the daytime he was all right, always occupied with the thing of the moment, adhering to the trivial present, which seemed to him ample and satisfying. No matter how little and futile his occupations were, he gave himself to them entirely, and felt normal and fulfilled. He was always active, cheerful, gay, charming, trivial. Only he dreaded the darkness and silence of his own bedroom, when the darkness should challenge him upon his own soul. That he could not bear, as he could not bear to think about Ursula. He had no soul, no background. He never thought of Ursula, not once, he gave her no sign. She was the darkness, the challenge, the horror. He turned to immediate things. He wanted to marry, quickly, to screen himself from the darkness, the challenge for his own soul. He would marry his Colonel's daughter. Quickly, without hesitation, pursued by his obsession for activity, he wrote to this girl, telling her his engagement was broken—it had been a temporary infatuation which he less than anyone else could understand now it was over—and could he see his very dear friend soon. He would not be happy till he had an answer.

He received a rather surprised reply from the girl, but she would be glad to see him. She was living with her aunt. He went down to her at once, and proposed to her the first evening. He was accepted. The marriage took place quietly within fourteen days' time. Ursula was not notified of the event. In another week, Skrebensky sailed with his new wife to India.

Chapter XVI

The Rainbow

Ursula went home to Beldover faint, dim, closed up. She could scarcely speak or notice. It was as if her energy were frozen. Her
5 people asked her what was the matter. She told them, she had broken off the engagement with Skrebensky. They looked blank and angry. But she could not feel any more.

The weeks crawled by in apathy. He would have sailed for India now. She was scarcely interested. She was inert, without strength or
10 interest.

Suddenly a shock ran through her, so violent that she thought she was struck down. Was she with child? She had been so stricken under the pain of herself and of him, this had never occurred to her. Now like a flame it took hold of her limbs and body. Was she with
15 child?

In the first flaming hours of wonder, she did not know what she felt. She was as if tied to the stake. The flames were licking her and devouring her. But the flames were also good. They seemed to wear her away to rest. She let the flames wrap her and destroy her to rest.
20 What she felt in her heart and her womb she did not know. It was a kind of swoon.

Then gradually the heaviness of her heart pressed and pressed into consciousness. What was she doing? Was she bearing a child? Bearing a child? To what?
25 Her flesh thrilled, but her soul was sick. It seemed, this child, like the seal set on her own nullity. Yet she was glad in her flesh that she was with child. She began to think, that she would write to Skrebensky, that she would go out to him, and marry him, and live simply as a good wife to him. What did the self, the form of life,
30 matter? Only the living from day to day mattered, the beloved existence in the body, rich, peaceful, complete, with no beyond, no further trouble, no further complication. She had been wrong, she had been arrogant and wicked, wanting that other thing, that fantastic freedom, that illusory, conceited fulfilment which she had
35 imagined she could not have with Skrebensky. Who was she to be

448

wanting some fantastic fulfilment in her life? Was it not enough that she had her man, her children, her place of shelter under the sun? Was it not enough for her, as it had been enough for her mother? She would marry and love her husband and fill her place simply. That was the ideal.

Suddenly she saw her mother in a just and true light. Her mother was simple and radically true. She had taken the life that was given. She had not, in her arrogant conceit, insisted on creating life to fit herself. Her mother was right, profoundly right, and she herself had been false, trashy, conceited.

A great mood of humility came over her, and in this humility a bondaged sort of peace. She gave her limbs to the bondage, she loved the bondage, she called it peace. In this state she sat down to write to Skrebensky.

"Since you left me I have suffered a great deal, and so have come to myself. I cannot tell you the remorse I feel for my wicked, perverse behaviour. It was given to me to love you, and to know your love for me. But instead of thankfully, on my knees, taking what God had given, I must have the moon in my keeping, I must insist on having the moon for my own. Because I could not have it, everything else must go.

"I do not know if you can ever forgive me. I could die with shame to think of my behaviour with you during our last times, and I don't know if I could ever bear to look you in the face again. Truly the best thing for me would be to die, and cover my fantasies for ever. But I find I am with child, so that cannot be.

"It is your child, and for that reason I must revere it and submit my body entirely to its welfare, entertaining no thought of death, which once more is largely conceit. Therefore, because you once loved me, and because this child is your child, I ask you to have me back. If you will cable me one word, I will come to you as soon as I can. I swear to you to be a dutiful wife, and to serve you in all things. For now I only hate myself and my own conceited foolishness. I love you—I love the thought of you—you were natural and decent all through, whilst I was so false. Once I am with you again, I shall ask no more than to rest in your shelter all my life—."

This letter she wrote, sentence by sentence, as if from her deepest, sincerest heart. She felt that now, now, she was at the depths of herself. This was her true self, for ever. With this document she would appear before God at the Judgment Day.

For what had a woman but to submit? What was her flesh but for childbearing, her strength for her children and her husband, the giver of life? At last she was a woman.

5   She posted her letter to his club, to be forwarded to him in Calcutta. He would receive it soon after his arrival in India—within three weeks of his arrival there. In a month's time she would receive word from him. Then she would go.

She was quite sure of him. She thought only of preparing her garments and of living quietly, peacefully, till the time when she
10 should join him again and her history would be concluded for ever. The peace held like an unnatural calm for a long time. She was aware, however, of a gathering restiveness, a tumult impending within her. She tried to run away from it. She wished she could hear from Skrebensky, in answer to her letter, so that her course should
15 be resolved, she should be engaged in fulfilling her fate. It was this inactivity which made her liable to the revulsion she dreaded.

It was curious how little she cared about his not having written to her before. It was enough that she had sent her letter. She would get the required answer, that was all.

20 One afternoon in early October, feeling the seething rising to madness within her, she slipped out in the rain, to walk abroad, lest the house should suffocate her. Everywhere was drenched wet and deserted, the grimed houses glowed dull red, the butt house* burned scarlet in a gleam of light, under the glistening, blackish purple
25 slates. Ursula went on towards Willey Green. She lifted her face and walked swiftly, seeing the passage of light across the shallow valley, seeing the colliery and its clouds of steam for a moment visionary in dim brilliance, away in the chaos of rain. Then the veils closed again. She was glad of the rain's privacy and intimacy.

30 Making on towards the wood, she saw the pale gleam of Willey Water* through the cloud below, she walked the open space where hawthorn trees streamed like hair on the wind and round bushes were presences showing through the atmosphere. It was very splendid, free and chaotic.

35 Yet she hurried to the wood, for shelter. There, the vast booming overhead vibrated down and encircled her, tree-trunks spanned the circle of tremendous sound, myriads of tree-trunks, enormous and streaked black with water, thrust like stanchions upright between the roaring overhead and the sweeping of the circle underfoot. She

glided between the tree-trunks, afraid of them. They might turn and shut her in as she went through their marshalled silence.

So she flitted along, keeping an illusion that she was unnoticed. She felt like a bird that has flown in through the window of a hall where vast warriors sit at the board.* Between their grave, booming ranks she was hastening, assuming she was unnoticed, till she emerged, with beating heart, through the far window and out into the open, upon the vivid green, marshy meadow.

She turned under the shelter of the common, seeing the great veils of rain swinging with slow, floating waves across the landscape. She was very wet and a long way from home, far enveloped in the rain and the waving landscape. She must beat her way back through all this fluctuation, back to stability and security.

A solitary thing,* she took the track straight across the wilderness, going back. The path was a narrow groove in the turf between high, sere, tussocky grass; it was scarcely more than a rabbit run. So she moved swiftly along, watching her footing, going like a bird on the wind, with no thought, contained in motion. But her heart had a small, living seed of fear, as she went through the wash of hollow space.

Suddenly she knew there was something else. Some horses were looming in the rain, not near yet. But they were going to be near. She continued her path, inevitably. They were horses in the lee of a clump of trees beyond, above her. She pursued her way with bent head. She did not want to lift her face to them. She did not want to know they were there. She went on in the wild track.

She knew the heaviness on her heart. It was the weight of the horses. But she would circumvent them. She would bear the weight steadily, and so escape. She would go straight on, and on, and be gone by.

Suddenly the weight deepened and her heart grew tense to bear it. Her breathing was laboured. But this weight also she could bear. She knew without looking that the horses were moving nearer. What were they? She felt the thud of their heavy hoofs on the ground. What was it that was drawing near her, what weight oppressing her heart? She did not know, she did not look.

Yet now her way was cut off. They were blocking her back. She knew they had gathered on a log bridge over the sedgy dike, a dark, heavy, powerfully heavy knot. Yet her feet went on and on. They would burst before her. They would burst before her. Her feet went on and on. And tense, and more tense became her nerves and her veins, they ran hot, they ran white hot, they must fuse and she must die.*

5   But the horses had burst before her. In a sort of lightning of knowledge their movement travelled through her, the quiver and strain and thrust of their powerful flanks, as they burst before her and drew on, beyond.

She knew they had not gone, she knew they awaited her still. But
10 she went on over the log bridge that their hoofs had churned and drummed, she went on, knowing things about them. She was aware of their breasts gripped, clenched narrow in a hold that never relaxed, she was aware of their red nostrils flaming with long endurance, and of their haunches, so rounded, so massive, pressing,
15 pressing, pressing to burst the grip upon their breasts, pressing forever till they went mad, running against the walls of time, and never bursting free. Their great haunches were smoothed and darkened with rain. But the darkness and wetness of rain could not put out the hard, urgent, massive fire that was locked within these
20 flanks, never, never.

She went on, drawing near. She was aware of the great flash of hoofs, a bluish, iridescent flash surrounding a hollow of darkness. Large, large seemed the bluish, incandescent flash of the hoof-iron, large as a halo of lightning round the knotted darkness of the flanks.
25 Like circles of lightning came the flash of hoofs from out of the powerful flanks.

They were awaiting her again. They had gathered under an oak-tree, knotting their awful, blind, triumphing flanks together, and waiting, waiting. They were waiting for her approach. As if from a far
30 distance she was drawing near, towards the line of twiggy oak-trees where they made their intense darkness, gathered on a slight bank.

She must draw near. But they broke away, they cantered round, making a wide circle to avoid noticing her, and cantered back into the open hillside behind her.

35 They were behind her. The way was open before her, to the gate in the high hedge in the near distance, so she could pass into the smaller, cultivated field, and so out to the high-road and the ordered world of man. Her way was clear. She lulled her heart. Yet her heart was couched with fear, couched with fear all along.

40 Suddenly she hesitated as if seized by lightning. She seemed to

fall, yet found herself faltering forward with small steps. The thunder of horses galloping down the path behind her shook her, the weight came down upon her, down, to the moment of extinction. She could not look round, so the horses thundered upon her.

Cruelly, they swerved and crashed by her on her left hand. She 5 saw the fierce flanks crinkled and as yet inadequate, the great hoofs flashing bright as yet only brandished about her, and one by one the horses crashed by, intent, working themselves up.

They had gone by, brandishing themselves thunderously about her, enclosing her. They slackened their burst transport, they slowed 10 down, and cantered together into a knot once more, in the corner by the gate and the trees ahead of her. They stirred, they moved uneasily, they settled their uneasy flanks into one group, one purpose. They were up against her.

Her heart was gone, she had no more heart. She knew she dare 15 not draw near. That concentrated, knitted flank of the horse-group had conquered. It stirred uneasily, awaiting her, knowing its triumph. It stirred uneasily, with the uneasiness of awaited triumph. Her heart was gone, her limbs were dissolved, she was dissolved like water. All the hardness and looming power was in the massive body 20 of the horse-group.

Her feet faltered, she came to a standstill. It was the crisis. The horses stirred their flanks uneasily. She looked away, failing. On her left, two hundred yards down the slope, the thick hedge ran parallel. At one point there was an oak-tree. She might climb into the boughs 25 of that oak-tree, and so round and drop on the other side of the hedge.

Shuddering, with limbs like water, dreading every moment to fall, she began to work her way as if making a wide detour round the horse-mass. The horses stirred their flanks in a knot against her. She 30 trembled forward as if in a trance.

Then suddenly, in a flame of agony, she darted, seized the rugged knots of the oak-tree and began to climb. Her body was weak but her hands were as hard as steel. She knew she was strong. She struggled in a great effort till she hung on the bough. She knew the horses were 35 aware. She gained her foot-hold on the bough. The horses were loosening their knot, stirring, trying to realise. She was working her way round to the other side of the tree. As they started to canter towards her, she fell in a heap on the other side of the hedge.

For some moments she could not move. Then she saw through 40

the rabbit-cleared bottom of the hedge the great, working hoofs of
the horses as they cantered near. She could not bear it. She rose and
walked swiftly, diagonally across the field. The horses galloped along
the other side of the hedge to the corner, where they were held up.
5   She could feel them there in their huddled group all the while she
hastened across the bare field. They were almost pathetic, now. Her
will alone carried her, till, trembling, she climbed the fence under a
leaning thorn-tree that overhung the grass by the high-road. The
use went from her, she sat on the fence leaning back against the
10 trunk of the thorn-tree, motionless.

As she sat there, spent, time and the flux of change passed away
from her, she lay as if unconscious upon the bed of the stream,* like a
stone, unconscious, unchanging, unchangeable, whilst everything
rolled by in transience, leaving her there, a stone at rest on the bed of
15 the stream, inalterable and passive, sunk to the bottom of all change.

She lay still a long time, with her back against the thorn-tree trunk
in her final isolation. Some colliers passed, tramping heavily up the
wet road, their voices sounding out, their shoulders up to their ears,
their figures blotched and spectral in the rain. Some did not see her.
20 She opened her eyes languidly as they passed by. Then one man
going alone saw her. The whites of his eyes showed in his black face
as he looked in wonderment at her. He hesitated in his walk, as if to
speak to her, out of frightened concern for her. How she dreaded his
speaking to her, dreaded his questioning her.

25 She slipped from her seat and went vaguely along the path—
vaguely. It was a long way home. She had an idea that she must walk
for the rest of her life, wearily, wearily. Step after step, step after
step, and always along the wet, rainy road between the hedges. Step
after step, step after step, the monotony produced a deep, cold sense
30 of nausea in her. How profound was her cold nausea, how profound!
That too plumbed the bottom. She seemed destined to find the
bottom of all things today: the bottom of all things. Well, at any rate
she was walking along the bottommost bed—she was quite safe:
quite safe, if she had to go on and on for ever, seeing this was the very
35 bottom, and there was nothing deeper. There was nothing deeper,
you see, so one could not but feel certain, passive.

She arrived home at last. The climb up the hill to Beldover had
been very trying. Why must one climb up the hill?* Why must one
climb? Why not stay below? Why force one's way up the slope? Why
40 force one's way up and up, when one is at the bottom? Oh, it was very

trying, very wearying, very burdensome! Always burdens, always, always burdens. Still, she must get to the top and go home to bed. She must go to bed.

She got in and went upstairs in the dusk without its being noticed she was in such a sodden condition. She was too tired to go downstairs again. She got into bed and lay shuddering with cold, yet too apathetic to get up or to call for relief. Then gradually she became more ill.

She was very ill for a fortnight, delirious, shaken and racked. But always, amid the ache of delirium, she had a dull firmness of being, a sense of permanency. She was in some way like the stone at the bottom of the river, inviolable and unalterable, no matter what storm raged in her body. He soul lay still and permanent, full of pain, but itself for ever. Under all her illness persisted a deep, inalterable knowledge.

She knew, and she cared no more. Throughout her illness, distorted into vague forms, persisted the question of herself and Skrebensky, like a gnawing ache that was still superficial, and did not touch her isolated, impregnable core of reality. But the corrosion of him burned in her till it burned itself out.

Must she belong to him, must she adhere to him? Something compelled her, and yet it was not real. Always the ache, the ache of unreality, of her belonging to Skrebensky. What bound her to him when she was not bound to him? Why did the falsity persist? Why did the falsity gnaw, gnaw, gnaw at her, why could she not wake up to clarity, to reality? If she could but wake up, if she could but wake up, the falsity of the dream, of her connection with Skrebensky, would be gone. But the sleep, the delirium pinned her down. Even when she was calm and sober she was in its spell.

Yet she was never in its spell. What extraneous thing bound her to him? There was some bond put upon her. Why could she not break it through? What was it? What was it?

In her delirium she beat and beat at the question. And at last her weariness gave her the answer—it was the child. The child bound her to him. The child was like a bond round her brain, tightened on her brain. It bound her to Skrebensky.

But why, why did it bind her to Skrebensky? Could she not have a child of herself? Was not the child her own affair, all her own affair? What had it to do with him? Why must she be bound, aching and cramped with the bondage, to Skrebensky and Skrebensky's world?

Anton's world: it became in her feverish brain a compression which enclosed her. If she could not get out of the compression she would go mad. The compression was Anton and Anton's world: not the Anton she possessed, but the Anton she did not possess, that which
5 was owned by some other influence, by the world.

She fought and fought and fought all through her illness to be free of him and his world, to put it aside, to put it aside, into its place. Yet ever anew it gained ascendancy over her, it laid new hold on her. Oh the unutterable weariness of her flesh, which she could not cast off,
10 nor yet extricate. If she could but extricate herself, if she could but disengage herself from feeling, from her body, from all the vast encumbrance of the world that was in contact with her, from her father, and her mother, and her lover, and all her acquaintance.

Repeatedly, in an ache of utter weariness she repeated: "I have no
15 father nor mother nor lover, I have no allocated place in the world of things, I do not belong to Beldover nor to Nottingham nor to England nor to this world, they none of them exist, I am trammelled and entangled in them, but they are all unreal. I must break out of it, like a nut from its shell which is an unreality."

20 And again, to her feverish brain, came the vivid reality of acorns in February* lying on the floor of a wood with their shells burst and discarded and the kernel issued naked, to put itself forth. She was the naked, clear kernel thrusting forth the clear, powerful shoot, and the world was a bygone winter, discarded, her mother and father and
25 Anton, and college and all her friends, all cast off like a year that has gone by, whilst the kernel was free and naked and striving to take new root, to create a new knowledge of Eternity in the flux of Time.* And the kernel was the only reality: the rest was cast off into oblivion.

This grew and grew upon her. When she opened her eyes in the
30 afternoon and saw the window of her room and the faint, smoky landscape beyond, this was all husk and shell lying by, all husk and shell, she could see nothing else, she was enclosed still, but loosely enclosed. There was a space between her and the shell. It was burst, there was a rift in it. Soon she would have her root fixed in a new
35 Day, her nakedness would take itself the bed of a new sky and a new air, this old, decaying, fibrous husk would be gone.

Gradually she began really to sleep. She slept in the confidence of her new reality. She slept breathing with her soul the new air of a new world. The peace was very deep and enrichening. She had her
40 root in new ground, she was gradually absorbed into growth.

When she woke at last it seemed as if a new day had come on the earth. How long, how long had she fought through the dust and obscurity, for this new dawn? How frail and fine and clear she felt, like the most fragile flower that opens in the end of winter. But the pole of night was turned and the dawn was coming in. 5

Very far off was her old experience—Skrebensky, her parting with him—very far off. Some things were real: those first glamorous weeks. Before, these had seemed like hallucination. Now they seemed like common reality. The rest was unreal. She knew that Skrebensky had never become finally real. In the weeks of passionate 10 ecstasy he had been with her in her desire, she had created him for the time being. But in the end he had failed and broken down.

Strange, what a void separated him and her. She liked him now, as she liked a memory, some bygone self. He was something of the past, finite. He was that which is known. She felt a poignant affection for 15 him, as for that which is past. But, when she looked with her face forward, he was not. Nay, when she looked ahead, into the undiscovered land before her, what was there she could recognise but a fresh glow of light and inscrutable trees going up from the earth like smoke.* It was the unknown, the unexplored, the undiscovered upon 20 whose shore she had landed, alone, after crossing the void, the darkness which washed the New World and the Old.

There would be no child: she was glad. If there had been a child, it would have made little difference, however. She would have kept the child and herself, she would not have gone to Skrebensky. Anton 25 belonged to the past.

There came the cablegram from Skrebensky: "I am married." An old pain and anger and contempt stirred in her. Did he belong so utterly to the cast-off past? She repudiated him. He was as he was. It was good that he was as he was. Who was she to have a man 30 according to her own desire? It was not for her to create, but to recognise a man created by God. The man should come from the Infinite and she should hail him. She was glad she could not create her man. She was glad she had nothing to do with his creation. She was glad that this lay within the scope of that vaster power in which 35 she rested at last. The man would come out of Eternity to which she herself belonged.

As she grew better, she sat to watch a new creation. As she sat at her window, she saw the people go by in the street below, colliers, women, children, walking each in the husk of an old fruition, but 40

visible through the husk, the swelling and the heaving contour of the
new germination. In the still, silenced forms of the colliers she saw a
sort of suspense, a waiting in pain for the new liberation: she saw the
same in the false hard confidence of the women. The confidence of
5 the women was brittle. It would break quickly to reveal the strength
and patient effort of the new germination.

In everything she saw she grasped and groped to find the creation
of the living God, instead of the old, hard barren form of bygone
living. Sometimes great terror possessed her. Sometimes she lost
10 touch, she lost her feeling, she could only know the old horror of the
husk which bound in her and all mankind. They were all in prison,*
they were all going mad.

She saw the stiffened bodies of the colliers, which seemed already
enclosed in a coffin, she saw their unchanging eyes, the eyes of those
15 who are buried alive: she saw the hard, cutting edges of the new
houses, which seemed to spread over the hillside in their insentient
triumph, the triumph of horrible, amorphous angles and straight
lines, the expression of corruption triumphant and unopposed,
corruption so pure that it is hard and brittle: she saw the dun
20 atmosphere over the blackened hill opposite, the dark blotches of
houses, slate roofed and amorphous, the old church-tower standing
up in hideous obsoleteness above raw new houses on the crest of the
hill, the amorphous, brittle, hard-edged new houses advancing from
Beldover to meet the corrupt new houses from Lethley, the houses
25 of Lethley advancing to mix with the houses of Hainor, a dry, brittle,
terrible corruption spreading over the face of the land, and she was
sick with a nausea* so deep that she perished as she sat. And then, in
the blowing clouds, she saw a band of faint iridescence colouring in
faint colours a portion of the hill. And forgetting, startled, she looked
30 for the hovering colour and saw a rainbow forming itself. In one
place it gleamed fiercely, and, her heart anguished with hope, she
sought the shadow of iris where the bow should be. Steadily the
colour gathered, mysteriously, from nowhere, it took presence upon
itself, there was a faint, vast rainbow. The arc bended and strength-
35 ened itself till it arched indomitable, making great architecture of
light and colour and the space of heaven, its pedestals luminous in
the corruption of new houses on the low hill, its arch the top of
heaven.

And the rainbow stood on the earth.* She knew that the sordid
40 people who crept hard-scaled and separate on the face of the world's

corruption were living still, that the rainbow was arched in their blood and would quiver to life in their spirit, that they would cast off their horny covering of disintegration, that new, clean, naked bodies would issue to a new germination, to a new growth, rising to the light and the wind and the clean rain of heaven. She saw in the rainbow 5 the earth's new architecture, the old, brittle corruption of houses and factories swept away, the world built up in a living fabric of Truth, fitting to the over-arching heaven.

APPENDIX I

Fragment of 'The Sisters'

Note on the text

This manuscript fragment (numbered pp. 291–6) is located at UT (Roberts E441a). DHL's paragraphing is reproduced; see Introduction, p. xiv.

Fragment of 'The Sisters'

barbaric. The womanliness, the care was missing from her.* She had almost lost her touch with conventional life, but lived alone, a blind, unconscious existence. For the most part she just lay passive. Her children, those that were at home, called on her once a day. Occasionally she appeared at meals, or even drove out. But more and more she kept to her rooms, where she lay passive, or where she read, or, very occasionally, wrote letters. Her letters were works of art. She re-wrote them, she balanced her sentences and shaped her paragraphs, all this quite without consideration of the recipient of the letter. It was the one output of her life, now.

Gerald* had set some of her energy free. Her lethargy, her apathy came partly from the sense that she was out of place, born into the wrong age. She had let society bind her down, and had gone half paralysed in bondage.—She began to write, or rather to compose, her various letters on the subject of her eldest son's marriage. The world outside did not really exist for her. She might as well have written letters to some mythological place of her own creation. But she wrote fictitiously, taking the tone of the usual, correct British matron.

4.

Gerald had braced himself for his task of informing those whom it was necessary to tell, and this included Winifred. He went to find her in the schoolroom, now her work-room. She was just washing her hands to go to Miss Brangwen. She was a reserved maiden, in her black dress with white lace collar and cuffs. Gerald, also in black, sat down. There was a curious distance about him, as if he were moving according to some instinct to which he yielded himself with pleasure, and yet in which he felt lost. Winifred looked at him.

"I am going down to Miss Brangwen's," he said. "I think she and I are going to marry."

Winifred's grey eyes watched him. Something about him, his queer abstraction, the faintly surprised look, as at some grateful sensation he felt but could not make out, rather fascinated her. Then she realised, and a flush crept into her dark face.

"Miss Brangwen marry *you?*" she said.

"I think so," he answered.

And for a second Winifred was angry.

"But why?" she said.

He remained not quite realising her.

"I must go and speak to her now. Will you come a little later?" he
5 asked.

Winifred did not answer. When he had gone, she stood and beat her
hand on the window sill hard, and cried tears of bewilderment and
grief and anger. When she came to, she was astonished and
displeased with herself.

10 He went down to Gudrun's lodging.

"The German gentleman is upstairs," said Mrs Bates.

"So!" he answered, and he went up.

Gudrun and the sculptor were seated on either side of the fire. He
shook hands with both. The German looked at his black-clothed,
15 well-groomed figure.

"The English are always too well-dressed," he said to himself.
"They are tailored out of temperament. This man has no Temperament at all—or where does he keep it?"

"You came this morning?" Gerald asked the sculptor.

20 "Half an hour ago," said the German, glancing at him with brown
eyes suspicious as a faun that will vanish at a movement. Gerald still
retained the queer, unseeing look in his eyes, as of a creature that
follows its instinct blindly, thoughtlessly as a leopard running on in
the sunshine, for the sake of running. There was a long pause.
25 Gudrun had not spoken. She sat impassive, regarding neither of
them.

"You know why I came?" asked the German, rather bitingly.
Gerald Crich looked at him.

"Yes," he answered, non-committal.

30 And the look about him, the dither of unconscious pleasure, as if,
without knowing it, he were pleased to be himself, irritated the
sculptor.

"I think," he said, "we place Miss Brangwen in a rather awkward
position[."] Gerald turned and looked at her. She was still and
35 impassive, regarding neither man. The sculptor fretted on his chair.

"Yes," said Gerald Crich, mildly, constrained also to wait. There
was a long pause.

"If we were in Germany," said the sculptor, with an agitated
smile, "we might settle it with pistols."

40 "We are not in Germany, are we?" said Gerald Crich.

"No," said the sculptor, his head bowed. Then he looked up at Gerald Crich, an anger blazing in his eyes. "That is the pity," he said.

The other man went pale, and looked aside. Gudrun sat aloof.

"Well," said the sculptor, with a sudden jerk, "what are we going to do?—You sent for me, Miss Brangwen—?"

"Yes," she said.

"Ecco!*—Here I am!"

He flung his hands apart in a gesture of exasperation and rage.

"But," said Gerald Crich, remonstrating, "it's not done like that."

"What isn't?" flashed the sculptor.

"Well—anything," deprecated Gerald.

The sculptor looked at him, bursting with rage and contempt. Then he turned to Gudrun.

"Shall I go back to Germany as I came?" he asked, in real bitterness.

"I don't know," replied Gudrun, very low, and still rather aloof.

"Why don't you know?" asked Gerald Crich.

Suddenly she burst into life.

"How *should* I know! You pretend *now* you want to marry me——"

"I *do* want to marry you," he said, going white to the gills, and his insouciance disappearing.

"You pretend it now," she said, "but why?—why now rather than at any other time these last six weeks?"

"I don't know why," he said doggedly.

"And *I* don't know why," she said, She was pale too, and her eyes were flashing. "And I want to know—so tell me."

"I can't tell you those things in public," he said.

"Ha!" she laughed; "there are plenty of other things you could do in public.—Why should I marry you, when you have treated me like the cheapest thing. I don't trust you. I want to know why this sudden change."

"You have no business to talk to me like this before other people," he said, beginning to twist his moustache, as he did when he was upset.

"Then you may go away," she answered, pale with anger, her eyes burning dark as she looked at him.

"I shan't go away," he said.

"Then let us hear why you have come," she said.

He was silent, stubborn in anger.

"I came to ask you again to marry me," he said at length, swallowing his anger.

"And I want to know why—why now—and not before?" she
5 asked. There was a ring of pathos in her voice.

"Because he can't bear that anyone else should have you," said the sculptor harshly. "He could leave you to waste in ruin, but—"

"I didn't know before," Gerald interrupted, lamely, but doggedly.

"What didn't you know before?" she cried.
10 "Whether it was to his advantage," said the sculptor, in hate.

"Yes," flashed Gerald Crich, looking back at him in hate. "I didn't know that—I didn't know—anything.—I didn't *know*." He nodded his head in stubborn emphasis on the last word.

"And in the interval no one else knew," said the sculptor
15 sarcastically.

Then he turned in a rage on Gudrun:

"I came to offer myself—you have no right to—to let me in for this."

"I didn't let you in," said Gudrun; "you came."
20 "And what were you willing to let *her* in for?" cried the sculptor.

"If you say any more," said Gerald Crich, turning at bay, "I'll break your neck." He sat leaning forward, staring at the other man. His fists were clenched and he breathed hard.

"One of your noble English threats, because you know you are a
25 little bigger, physically," said the sculptor, his face twisted with pain. He looked back into the other's eyes. He was too much moved to be afraid. "You trust to your position to play with *her*, you trust to your muscles to threaten me, just as you would threaten an unarmed man with your loaded gun—and shoot him righteously—that is what you
30 would do."

The sculptor was showing all his teeth, like an animal, with suffering and passion. Gerald Crich flinched, then shrank. He sat crumpled upon the chair. Somehow he felt the old shame of his murdered brother, of his miserable father, of his own falsity. He seemed
35 choked in the mud of his shame. Suddenly he flung up his face blindly, crying stubborn with misery:

"I didn't know."

The sculptor rose.

"I'll go before I am asked to go," he said, wretchedly, rising. And
40 suddenly, before he knew, his face had broken into lines of real

agony, all distorted, and he hurried to the stairs. Gerald Crich hung his head.

"He ought *never* to have been allowed to come," said Gudrun, passionately. Then she turned to Gerald "I shall always hate you a bit, for this," she said.

He sat bowed down, remembering, and suffering from the memory of the other man's distorted face, like a face from hell. She was silent, her lower lip between her teeth, thinking of Loerke. At that juncture Winifred came. She hesitated at the head of the stairs, looking at the two.

"Did I see Herr Loerke going up the road?" she asked.

"Yes," said her brother.

"Go and catch him up and talk to him," Gudrun begged. And in a second she was gone, and the silence had fallen again. After a time Gerald looked at Gudrun. He did not know what to say. She sat mute.

"He is a decent fellow, really," he said.

"Ha!" she cried. "Decent! He is decent. I loved him."
Again he was struck silent. It made him tired, and he felt a desire to wriggle somewhere out of sight, into a hole in the ground like a rat.

"But you didn't want to marry him," he persisted, at length.

"How *could* I marry him!" she cried.

"Why?" he asked, naïvely.

"You know why."

"Because of the child?—Without that, would you have preferred him to me."

"Oh, leave me alone," she cried, with an air of utter weariness.

He sat with his arms on his knees, his head down. He wanted to go to her and comfort her, but he dared not. She might not want him. He sat mustering his courage. Then at last he rose, and very hesitating, laid his hand on her shoulder. He trembled with fear. But she did not draw away.

"Gudrun!" he said, softly, and he put his hand on her cheek, and drew her face to him, and held it with his two hands against his chest. He bent down over her. She merely submitted. But the position, and the emotion, made him tremble. He sat down beside her in the big chair, and put his arms round her. She buried her face in his shoulder. And the love went through him like hard flame, love for her, for the movement, like a wild thing hiding itself from fear and misery against him. He had once seen one of Winifred's rabbits, attacked by a cat, hurl itself at a young groom, screaming, for protection, and the tenderness with which the youth had protected the thing, caressed it, soothed it, had hurt him deeply. For nothing would come to him to be sheltered and loved—nothing—never. And now she did turn to him so. He had two tears working painfully forward into his eyes, and he was thankful she did not look up, so that he would have time to blink them away. She lay against him with her face pressed on him, hiding, and she was panting. His arms clutched her involuntarily, closer, and he held her fast, and the little pain, of the coming of tears, began again near his eyes. He had not known it, scarcely in his life, and it gave him joy. He did not want to speak. It was enough to hold her close, like this, whilst she pressed her face against him for shelter. And he felt himself giving her shelter, relief, and ease, and his heart grew hot with a trembling joy. He was something he had feared he never could be: he had got something he had pretended to disbelieve in. And, breathing hard, he knew this was his life's fulfilment, and a wave of faith, warm, strong, religious faith went over him.

At last she raised her face to him, to be kissed. And again, afraid, he kissed her. It was something he thought he could never know, this complete tenderness of love. And still he was afraid, for fear he might not be good enough or solid enough, to keep it. But the fear vanished in a moment, as again she crept in against him, for protection. And she put her arms round him and held herself to him. And he felt he would empty every drop of blood out of his veins, to warm her and comfort her.

"Are you glad we're going to have a child, Gerald?" she asked at last.

"I'm so glad of you," he replied, unable to realise anything else than just her, warm and soft, and clinging to him.

"I knew you didn't understand—and I thought you never would," she said, plaintively. It cut him to be reminded.

"Don't tell me about it," he said clinging to her. "It is gone."

"Yes," she whispered. But he knew it had *not* really gone, and he should still have to do penance. He did not mind very much. In fact, he was glad if she made him suffer for that wherein he had made her suffer, for if she did, it was because she loved him, and she wanted them to be level. For if she had forgiven him anything, that left him in the position of the forgiven: which he could not bear, for it left him in bondage. He would rather she took an eye for an eye:* and he could trust her to do it: and for that he loved her, it made him feel free, in an open atmosphere. He had such a horror of the indoor, dark atmosphere of women, who forgive a man because they know his weakness. Gudrun knew his weakness, and hated him for it, and made him suffer for it till he was level with her. And that was fair. And so he could be open with her, and himself. 5

"Why did you come and ask me to marry you?" she said, looking at him quietly and earnestly. He jerked his head up, in a way he had when he was trying to get away from something.

"I didn't know," he said, helplessly.

"That you loved me?" she asked. 10

"No, I didn't know that I loved you—not—not fully," he said slowly.

"Even all that time, and when we went away?—you never loved me?"

"I did love you—only—it is different now." 15

She sat quiet, and he knew she was remembering. A little bitterness came into her face.

"I knew," she said. "And I knew what you thought. Sometimes I could have strangled you as you lay asleep—and then I thought, better strangle myself, for it was my fault." 20

A chill went through him. Something in her had shut up, or had gone frozen, during that time, and was now unresponsive to him, dead to him. It made a silence fall darkly inside him. There were enough shadows over them both, to start with. But he would get it all right. He knew he would be able to submit to suffering. In his new 25 conversion, he had almost a passion for submission: it was so new a thing to him. But he would never submit to fail in getting her love. That he made up his mind to.

"Are you glad I'm going to have a child?" she asked again, turning to look full in his face while he answered. He gave a queer little 30 laugh, in which she saw he was content enough that it was so.

"I'm glad," he said. "But it's you I want most."

"Do you want a boy or a girl?"

"I don't care—why—" he considered—"a boy—a girl—I don't mind." 35

"I want a boy," she said, and she fell to dreaming.
He sat silent awhile. Again something gnawed at him.

"Gudrun," he said, "you won't think more of the child than of me?"

She did not answer for some moments. How plainly he could see 40 things were not right between them.

"I have had only that to think of for so long, now," she said.

"For how long?—when did you know?"

"I thought it was so when we left Switzerland—but I wasn't sure."

"And then you thought only of the child?"

5 "When I saw how you were."

He was silent for a time.

"And Loerke, whom you were going to marry?" he asked.

"He would have come afterwards."

"But you *really* cared for me all along."

10 "I *did* care for you."

"And now?" he asked, pained.

She did not answer for some moments.

"I do love you," she said slowly. "But you killed a lot of it."

He sat holding her hand. He had this to suffer.

15 "But would you have married Loerke?"

"Oh yes—what else was there to do?"

"Even without loving him?"

"I did love him—in a way. And of you I had the child. That you could not take back, as you seemed to be able to take everything

20 else."

"But I wasn't able, Gudrun," he pleaded.

"No, but it looked like it," she said.

"But I couldn't, Gudrun," he pleaded, reminding her.

She sat still, quite still for a little time. Then, without looking at him,

25 she gave him her other hand.

"No," she said softly.

"And you'll care for me more than for the child."

She sat considering. Then she looked him full in the eyes.

"I shouldn't have cared for any other man's child," she said,

30 slowly.

He kissed her hands, and they sat still. There was a good deal that hurt still, between them. But he was humble to her. Only, she must love him—she must love him, or else everything was barren. This aloofness of hers—she came to him as the father of her child, not as

35 to a lover, a husband. Well he had had a chance, and lost it. He had been a fool. Now he must make the best of it, and get her again. But it hurt that she did not seem to want him very much. It hurt keenly.

Then while he was thinking, with his forehead hard with pain, she kissed him, drawing him to her [,? murmuring,]* "My love!"

[end of manuscript]

APPENDIX II
Fragment of 'The Sisters II'

Note on the text

This manuscript fragment (numbered pp. 373–80) is located at UT (Roberts E441a). DHL's paragraphing is reproduced; see Introduction, p. lxiv.

trembling, flushed, ashamed. And he sat passive, but in opposition to her going. Every movement she made, every breath she took, seemed made or taken in spite of him. So that she trembled as she fastened her boots. It seemed to her cruel.

When she was ready, he rose politely to see her to the door.

"Don't come out of the room," she said. "Is there any commission I could take for you?—No?—sure?—Goodbye."

She had got away, leaving him silent, impassive, but inside himself raging, only denying it all, because he was a gentleman. She hurried through the wet afternoon, as if running away from something. She was as yet free of him.

August came, when the family, all but Ella and Gudrun, went away to Scarborough, as was usual.* The eldest two girls preferred to stay at home. For them, it would be a great treat to have the house to themselves. Besides, neither of them wanted very much to go away from Willey Green at this time.

Ella enjoyed being alone, and doing little. She felt lethargic. A curious, rich lassitude kept her lying late in bed. She felt her life was going on inside her, she could not concern herself with outside things. Gudrun, on the other hand, was very active. So Ella lounged, dreamed, meditated, thinking, thinking about Mr Birkin. She did not know if she loved him. She did not want to kiss him. She did not want him to go away. What was it? She read absorbedly without quite taking in what she read. Then she caught herself up. She was reading Le Rouge et le Noir,* and the hero fascinated her. She wanted to understand him: she wanted to understand men: she wanted to understand Rupert Birkin. She hunted everywhere for understanding of herself and him, quite happy to be alone doing little or nothing, because her soul was so busy, even if her body were indolent.

The second day after the family had gone, Gudrun went out to a tennis party. Ella refused the invitation. People were a strain upon her. Her soul was too deeply occupied in itself. She wanted to be alone. Gudrun would come back to supper. It was a golden afternoon. Ella sat in the sunshine, read, sewed, mused, and was happy.

With the twilight a restlessness and a yearning come over her. She went into the drawing-room, and there, in the half light, she sat singing to herself, singing the sentimental songs like "Ich weiss nicht was soll es bedeuten."* Her idea of time was sketchy, but she had a strong, rather beautiful voice. And sitting alone in the house, with the twilight dying golden about her, the end of the hot summer day

5 sinking down, she sang from a full heart, her voice going on wings of yearning and sadness.

She started at the end of one verse, hearing the bell tingling down in the kitchen. Resentfully, she got up and left the piano. People, whoever it was, must have heard her, and she did not wish to be

10 heard. She did not wish to answer the door.

It was Birkin, standing rather hesitating on the threshold.

"I wondered if you would be at home," he said.

"I am alone," she said, half to keep him from coming in, half inviting him.

15 "Your people have gone away?" he answered, entering, "I did not know you sang so well—you have a beautiful voice."

"I didn't know anyone would hear," she replied.

"I like to hear you," he said, "Will you sing again?"

"No."

20 The house seemed very silent and ghostly about them, in the twilight, with doors and windows open.

"I am lucky in finding you in," he said.

He sat in the shadow near the door. He was wearing grey, and was almost invisible. She could see the shape of his finely modelled head

25 faintly and yet distinctly, in the grey clair-obscur.

"I am glad you were not out," he said, unconsciously repeating himself.

Ella felt embarrassed. Her heart was beating fast.

"Where is your sister?" he asked.

30 "I am expecting her," she replied.

They spoke quietly, because of the still house.

"When do you go away?" she asked at length.

"In two days," he said.

"You will have a good time up there," she said, making conver-

35 sation. "What will you do, shoot, golf—?"

"More or less," he replied.

There ensued an awkward silence. It was getting dark in the room. Suddenly, with a jerk, she got up, saying:

"I'll get some matches."

40 He rose also quickly, insidiously.

"I have some," he replied, shaking the box between his fingers. She was thwarted.

"Oh!" she said.

And hesitating, she held out her hand for the matches. Her fingers touched his, and she shrank away, quickly.

"Let me light it," he said quietly.

He went to the mantel-piece. The light leaped out, and fell on his upturned face. Ella was fascinated and half-terrified by it. It was intent, hard, without expression. The steady hardness of the eyes was dreadful to her. He threw the burnt match in the fireplace, adjusted the light, then turned to her.

"One lamp is enough?" he said.

His voice had a hard, vibrating quality, his eyes held hers with a hard look. She felt herself powerless against him, and yet not with him. She turned aside her face as she answered. Outside, on the lawn, she could see the bushes standing darkly. He stood near to her. Neither moved. Then he seemed to be coming to her. Summoning all her self-restraint, she put her hand on his arm and said, pleadingly, pathetically:

"No—no."

He stood still, silent. She felt his living arm beneath his sleeve. It was torture to her. Suddenly she caught him to her, and hid her face on his breast, crying, in a muffled, tortured voice:

"Do you love me?"

She clung to him. But his breast was strange to her. His arms were around her tight, hard, compressing her, he was quivering, rigid, holding her against him. But he was strange to her. He was strange to her, and it was almost agony. He was cold to her, however he held her hard in his power and quivered. She felt he was cold to her. And the quivering man stiffened with desire was strange and horrible to her. She got free again, and, with her hands to her temples, she slid away to the floor at his feet, unable to stand, unable to hold her body erect. She must double up, for she could not bear it. But she got up again to go away. And before she reached the door, she was crouching on the floor again, holding her temples in agony. Her womb, her belly, her heart were all in agony. She crouched together on the floor, crying like some wild animal in pain, with a kind of mooing noise, very dreadful to hear, a sound she was unaware of, that came from her unproduced, out of the depths of her body in torture. For some wild moments the paroxysms continued, when she crouched on the ground with her head down, mad, crying with an inarticulate, animal noise. Then suddenly it all stopped. It was gone. Her head was clear. And then she was confused with shame. She found herself crouching on the floor, her face running wet with tears,

5   a sobbing going on involuntarily. A moment longer she crouched so, giving little, sniffing sobs.

Then, very quiet, almost too quiet, too far gone for shame, she dried her face on the end of her skirts, like an animal wiping its face, and she got up.

10   His power, her pain, nay, all her emotion, was gone. She was tremulous, but quiet and almost still in herself.

"I am sorry" she said, turning to him but not looking at him. "I'm sorry. It isn't fair for you.—But I couldn't help it."
She was sorry for him, that he had been subjected to this outburst.

15   And her pride also rose against him—for his coldness.

He stood white to the gills, with wide, dark eyes staring blankly. His heart inside him felt red-hot, so that he panted as he breathed. His mind was blank. He knew she did not feel him any more. He knew he had no part in her, that he was out of place. And he had

20   nothing to say.—But gradually he grew a little calmer, his eyes lost their wide, dark, hollow look. He was coming to himself.

"What did I do?" he asked.

"You—it was nothing you did—I couldn't help it—I'm sorry."
Her simple, faltering answer, so devoid of any feeling for him, sent a

25   wave like flame over his heart, so that his brain seemed to swoon. He stood in a curious, motionless position of recoil. For a long time neither spoke. She stood averted by the mantel-piece.

"Hadn't you better go?" she asked, cruelly.
But he still stood staring, wide-eyed, motionless.

30   "Do you really care for me?" he asked, in a strange, changed voice. It seemed to her even now, he only wanted to know, he did not care.

"I don't know," she said. "Don't ask me now. You'd better go and leave me."

35   But he stood motionless, staring with dark, wide eyes.

And suddenly she caught her lip between her teeth. The hurt, the grief was rising again. In spite of all her efforts, her tears rose, and fell over her dark lashes onto her cheeks. But she kept her face still, her lower lip clenched between her teeth, and let the tears fall. He

40   watched, wide-eyed, for some moments. It was agony to him.

"Don't," he said, "don't—don't cry—don't cry—"
But the sound of his lost, helpless voice only made the tears come
faster, as from a touched wound. And as they came, and as they fell,
they seemed to him to come upon his breast bone eating into it like
fire. 5

She took her handkerchief and wiped her face and blew her nose
loudly. As she fumbled blindly for her handkerchief, it hurt him so
much, he felt he would die for her.

"I," he stammered, blanched with the struggle to speak—"I love
you." 10
Her tears came again. She felt no response, only the cruel, hurting,
yet easing surge up of her tears. He had not moved. Still he stood
with wide, unblinking eyes.

Again she was wiping her face, and blowing her nose, when they
heard the gate. 15

"That's Gudrun," she said, dully.
And she went out of the room.

Birkin stood motionless. He heard Gudrun's quick footstep come
freely up the path and through the open door. Another instant and
her white, beautiful form started with surprise in the doorway. 20

"Oh!" she cried, and for a moment could not speak.

"Well," she said, "it did surprise me—"
She was hiding her eyes from the light. She was flushed and bright
from the party.

"Did you have a good time?" he asked. 25

"Oh very," she replied, rather off-hand. "Where is Ella."

"She went upstairs," he said.
There was an awkward pause. Evidently Gudrun was not quite at
ease with him.

"Are you still staying at Wamsley Mill?"* she asked, stiffly. 30
They kept up a little desultory small talk, till Ella at last came down,
showing traces of weeping.

"You're late, Prune,* aren't you?" she said.

"It isn't eight yet," said Gudrun.
Ella did not look at Birkin, as she asked him: 35

"Will you stay to supper, Mr Birkin?"

"No thank you," he replied. "Perhaps you will come down to tea
on the island again, à la Robinson Crusoe, tomorrow."

"Thanks," said Ella, looking at Gudrun. "I don't know—"

"Oh, thank you," said Gudrun, vaguely. 40

He walked away, feeling as if the heavens had fallen, and he were not himself, he were somebody else, walking in a different life. In one crash, the whole form of his life, the whole conception of himself, which he had, was gone: he did not know what he was, who he was:
5 he did not know what he knew or what he did not know. Reduced to an elementary chaos, he drifted to his rooms, to sit till dawn by the fire, stunned, motionless.

"What is the matter, Ella?" Gudrun asked sharply.

"He proposed to me," said Ella.

10 "Proposed to you!" cried Gudrun in amazement.

Ella went to bed, very still after her outburst. She felt ashamed, but only superficially. Underneath she was not ashamed of having showed her deepest feelings to him. But it was a big responsibility, to have been quite so naked before another person. She felt a responsi-
15 bility coming upon her, that almost silenced her. She must wait and go slowly. She did not yet know quite where she was. She only knew that her fate was bringing her closer and closer into connection with this man, that something was taking place, implicating her with him, which she could never revoke or escape. And blindly, almost
20 shrinking, she lapsed forward.

The next day, she did not want to go to Wamsley Mill. It was too soon, she was too uncertain. Even the fact that he would be hurt did not influence her. She must stay away yet awhile.

Then there came a letter, the next morning, saying that the three
25 little children were all ill, and that the eldest girls must come to look after them. Ella was angry, Gudrun was disgusted. There never was any illness in the family, so they did not believe in it. But they began to prepare immediately to depart. They would catch the ten oclock train to Nottingham.

30 In the train Ella wrote to Birkin.

"I am sorry I've had to go away," she said. "You mustn't mind the scene I made you the other evening. I don't know how it is. But I think it takes us a long time to get rid of the old things. It is like the man who foamed at the mouth when the devils were cast out of him.
35 In a way I love you because I can make a fool of myself before you, and you don't mind. But you mustn't despise me. I am really not hysterical—not naturally. One gets so strained. And it is working the old strain off that makes one so upset. I am sorry I have to go away. Today I wanted to see you. It makes me miserable that the train
40 threads out all this distance behind me. But you will write to me, won't you?"

3

The children were not very ill. In a few days' time they were running about. The third day after her arrival in Scarborough, Ella had a letter from Birkin.

"I don't know why you should think I despise you," he said. "I 5 despise myself hard enough, that my own feelings are always so mixed, and I can never get them straight. I am a little afraid of you, and for you. I will do anything you want me to do. It seems that everything has come toppling down, like an earthquake, since I have known you, and here I am entangled in the ruins and fragments of 10 my old life, and struggling to get out. You seem to me some land beyond—somewhere where I have never attained, a shore upon which I have never yet climbed out. As I say, I am a little afraid of you. Already so much has gone smash because of you. But I want to see more of you. I want you to come back soon. I shall go to Scotland 15 immediately, but intend to stay only a few days. Perhaps I shall call in Scarborough on my way home. . ."

Ella puzzled over this letter. He always seemed so queer and abstract. It was as if he stated his love in algebraic terms.

When the children got better, she and Ella set out to walk to Filey. 20 It was a bright day, but windy, and the sea was breaking over Filey Brigg. The two girls wandered out along the causeway of rock. Green water heaved and smote on either side, the spray was in their hair. All the open space was fretted with restless water. A little steamer was rolling along, pitching, labouring, by Flamborough 25 Head,* where the water was smoking white.

The two girls were exhilarated and laughing with the wind and motion. They clung to their hats, the refreshing, strong coldness of the sea penetrated their clothing. Soon it got too cold.

As they returned, and were almost at the shore, they noticed two 30 other people, a man and a woman, coming, turning from the wind embarassed with their clothing.

"Ella," cried Gudrun. "There's Ben Templeman."

Ella felt the blood rush from her heart. For a second she seemed to lose consciousness. A wave of terror, deep, annihilating, went over 35 her. She knew him without looking: his peculiar, straying walk, the odd, separate look about him which filled her with dread. He had still power over her: he was still Man to her. She knew he would not see her, because he was rather short-sighted.

[end of manuscript]

APPENDIX III

Report and Letter on 'The Wedding Ring'

Report and Letter on 'The Wedding Ring'

501 West 113th Street.
November 10, 1914.

Dear Mr. Kennerley:

Reading the "Wedding Ring" has been a great treat. Here are my impressions.

I feel rather definitely that though we have here again some very fine writing and in parts a more mature character delineation (Birkin) the novel as a whole does not show much advance upon "Sons and Lovers". It lacks the artistic unity and singleness of purpose of that story as well as the kind of urgent passion which made "Sons and Lovers" so remarkable as a sheer piece of writing.

Plot. The real story is concentrated in the lives of Ella and Gudrun and the novel does not strike its best pace until we deal with them. But that does not become clear until we are almost half way through the novel so that the first part of the plot has a rambling quality which greatly contributes to the feeling of over-lengthiness. Mr. Lawrence takes us through practically three generations but our real interest lies only in the third. The story of Anna's childhood, charming as it is, acts as a kind of false start because she is dropped so sharply as soon as she is converted into a baby machine, nor does she exert any influence upon the later development of the novel. It seems to me that the whole story of Tom Brangwen's courtship of the Polish woman as well as Anna's marriage could be told in retrospect in much less space if the novel began with Ella's childhood. You will remember with what skill the time element was handled in "Sons and Lovers".

Psychology: Here I confess to a certain feeling of monotony and of repetition. You may remember my saying that Mr. Lawrence might turn out to be a one novel man. "The Wedding Ring" contains simply chunks and chunks of psychological motivation almost literally transferred from "Sons and Lovers". This is particularly notic[e]able in the men. The Brangwens, Skrebensky, Birkin, all take what is practically Paul's attitude towards love and marriage. "And all the while his heart beat tight with pain, a sort of constraint or fear, or an insufficiency. . ." (Skrebensky). They all have that same feeling of insufficiency, of failure and of being "half in love with death". They are all minor Pauls. Anna and Ella and Gudrun often echo Miriam and Clara in the same way. "She fretted in her soul" (Anna) "It was the madness of all desire that desired beyond him, beyond him". Here Ella echoes Paul again. If you will take the time to reread pages 410 to 458 of the Ms. and compare to the chapter called Derelict in "Sons and Lovers" you will find repetitions almost word for word. Mr. Lawrence has not been able to get away from himself. "I am so tired at the core of me. . .Because one is always exposed, exposed to space". Birkin is simply an older Paul, more wretched and more pitiless, with consumption to add to the sense of disintegration. "The physical side was a failure, no it was a failure all around". . ."Why must she rise up and take him instead of his taking her?" The difference is that in "Sons and Lovers" this psychology was beautifully and logically motivated while in "The Wedding Ring" it is merely transferred. That is why I feel that the novel shows little advance.

The complete breakdown of artistic restraint will also have to enter into your consideration. The trouble is that Mr Lawrence hovers between the artist and the neurotic and often falls a victim to his morbid subjectivism to such an extent that his writing loses artistic validity and becomes merely the expression of a symptom. "With what an agony of relief he poured himself into her" (Gerald Crich raping Gudrun in the boathouse)[.] That is a finely naked description of repressed sexual desire breaking through but it defeats its own end by its lack of restraint. The same thing must be said of Mr Lawrence's use of the word "belly" and other innovations in his vocabulary. They rob his love scenes of their artistic innocence by which alone his sexual realism can be carried through.

I have dwelt entirely on defects. But I do not want you to think that this novel has not stirred me to admiration or that I would be against publishing it. But in the interest of Mr. Lawrence's own reputation it must be condensed and foreshortened and it must also be expurgated, not for moral reasons but for artistic effect. Mr. Lawrence sees sex too obsessively. You may find it a difficult task to persuade him of this because it bites so deeply into his own character. That he is labouring under terrible sexual morbidities is hardly to be doubted after reading his "Honor and Arms".

Mr. Lipmann tells me that he has your permission to read the Ms. I have accordingly turned it over to him with his promise to deliver it to you shortly. I trust that this meets with your approval.

Thank you again for the privilege of reading it.

Yours sincerely,
Alfred Kuttner

501 WEST 113TH STREET

Thursday

Dear Mr. Kennerley –

Of course I should not have written my criticism in just that way if I had intended it for Mr. Lawrence's ears but as I am probably quite anonymous to him I don't mind your sending it on to him.

I realize your difficulties in dealing with Mr. Lawrence without a personal interview. Almost any criticism, and especially the kind of analytical criticism which I have used, must seem merely bewildering to Mr. Lawrence because his productivity is conditioned by such extreme subjectivism. It is painful to see such deterioration, and that is really the only word for it, going on in a gifted writer, knowing as I do that it is of neurotic origin. A rigorous Freudian analysis would make Mr. Lawrence both a happier man and a greater artist. But as mere strangers we have no business to invade his personality to that extent.

Yours sincerely
Alfred Kuttner

(See Introduction, pp. xxvii, lxvi; MSS at LC.)

APPENDIX IV

Chronology of *The Rainbow*

Chronology of *The Rainbow*

1823–36	New route for Nottingham canal, after Cossall Marsh embankment collapsed
1830	Paul Lensky born; died at 34 in 1864; 238:6
Late 1832	Lydia Lensky born ['just fifty' in late 1882, still 34 in Spring 1867; 120:5, 45:39]
Spring 1838	Tom Brangwen born [still 28 in Spring 1867, but 'a man of forty five' on 23 December 1882 (actually 44⅔); 45:40, 125:37]
'about' 1840	*Rainbow* begins
1840	London & Midland railway at foot of Ilkeston hill opened; Erewash spur, 1847
1850–?1855	Tom to Derby Grammar School [at 12, father's accident at hay-harvest when 17, Tom takes over farm completely at 18; 16:32, 19:20, 37]
?March 1862	Will Brangwen born [20 in Spring 1882, 22 in 1884; 99:40, 199:7]
January–Autumn 1863	INSURRECTION IN POLAND; the Lenskys possibly flee to London in the Autumn before the final suppression, since Anna is born in London and yet must be at least 3 when Lydia comes to the Marsh in Winter 1866 [see note at 49:14 and note 1 below]
October/November 1863	Anna Lensky born in London; 50:1–12, 239:27–36 ['nearly forty' in Summer 1902 though in a loose context, 18 when she meets Will in Spring 1882 and after corn-harvest; 388:1, 99:37, 117:38]
Late 1864	Paul Lensky dies, shortly after Anna's first birthday; 37:39, 50:13–32, 238:6–7
Spring 1865	Lydia to Yorkshire as housekeeper to dying vicar, who dies shortly after the end of the year; 51:8–52:26
February/March 1866	Lydia to vicarage in Cossethay, seen on the hill in the Spring by Tom (nearly 28), and for the season; 29:1ff., 52:37–54:1
March 1867	Betrothal of Tom (28) and Lydia (34); 40:32, 45:39–40
?May 1867	Tom marries Lydia

489

January 1868	Tom Brangwen, Jnr born; 70:10
?1869/70	Fred Brangwen born
1872	Anna Brangwen (9) to dame school in Cossethay; 92:3–4
?1873	Anna ('about ten') taken on first visit to Baron Skrebensky when his first wife alive; 93:1 (She has just died according to the MS version)
?late 1873/4	Anna and Lydia visit Baron Skrebensky; 183:8–10 [see note 2]
?1875/6	Anna to Nottingham High School for Girls, founded 1875 ['a tall, awkward girl' sounds post-puberty, perhaps 13, ?1876; 93:37, 40; enough time after the second visit to the Skrebenskys for the impression to be fading into memory]
?late 1876/7	Tom and Lydia visit 'Three years later' than the second visit, after the Baron has remarried in late 1876; 183:19–28
August 1877	Anton Skrebensky born [21 in July 1899, birth month; 184:7, 269:21–2, 285:5]
Autumn 1882	Betrothal of Will and Anna [she is 18 when they meet in Spring, he is 20; 99:37–40, 117:38–9]
Saturday 23 December 1882	Will marries Anna ['the Saturday before Christmas ... December the twenty third'; 120:38–121:1; Lydia is 50, Tom '45' but actually 44⅔; 120:5, 125:37]
October/November 1883	Anna and Will visit the Skrebenskys and Lincoln Cathedral; 183:3–4 [Anton a 'curly-headed little lad' and 'well-mannered'; 268:27, 30; old enough to remember Anna many years later]
November/December 1883	Ursula Brangwen born ['month-old' Ursula held up to see bluecaps in snow; 180:9–19, and Anna is pregnant early Spring; 165:33]
December 1884/January 1885	Gudrun Brangwen born [spoken of as just over a year younger than Ursula, Will still 22; 197:28, 199:7; but see note 3]
1886	Theresa Brangwen born [3 years younger than Ursula, leaves High School 1902, aged ?16; 204:3, 398:23]

by January 1888	Catherine ('Kate') Brangwen born [Will 26 after she is born, Ursula spoken of as a child of 4 so Catherine probably born between October 1887 and January 1888; 204:32–6]
Late 1891	William ('Billy') Brangwen born [8 years younger than Ursula, Will 'about' 28 when begins going to Nottingham in the football season of 1890–1, after 7 years of marriage and 4 girls; 243:4–7, 210:19; by early 1892, when Will about 30 Billy has been born; 221:17–18] Will starts carving class [Ursula 8, Will 30; 221:17, 25 – actually would be just short of these ages if classes began in Autumn]
1892–1901	Four more children: Cassandra, Tom, Margaret and one died in infancy; 243:7–8, 394:27, 395:7, 328:14–15 [all nine born before mid–1901, since Anna pregnant with the last when Ursula leaves school in mid–1900, Tom is old enough to walk 10 miles to Beldover in 1902; 328:4–14, 394:27–9]
Spring 1892	Tom Brangwen drowned (53 or 54) [Ursula 'about eight', Tom Jnr about 24 since 23 when he broke with his chief, 25 years after marriage with Lydia; 226:10, 225:28, 21. After Tom's death, Lydia spoken of as 60, i.e. late 1892/3, and 4 children younger than Ursula; 236:2, 4]
Autumn 1895/6	Ursula to Nottingham High School for Girls (12); 245:26–9 [she leaves in June 1900; if after 5 school-years would have gone in September 1895, aged not quite 12, Gudrun only 10⅔; if 'was twelve' means 1896, Ursula would only have had 4 years at High School]
1898	Lydia Brangwen dies ['two years' before September 1900; 341:37, 342:10]
July 1899	Skrebensky comes to the Marsh [Ursula 'nearly sixteen', Anton 21; 267:31, 269:22; 'It was summer': must be July because he only has a month's leave and has gone before his birthday; 272:26, 269:25, 285:5]
Late Summer 1899	The wedding dance at the Marsh, talk about Khartoum, recaptured by Kitchener in 1898; 288:17–19

October 1899	WAR DECLARED AGAINST BOERS IN SOUTH AFRICA: 'He wrote that he might have to go', and the 'constant bad news' in 1900; 303:18–20, 309:10. Skrebensky leaves for South Africa; 306:8–9 [deleted sentence on MS p. 486 says he is 22: in fact, not quite]
June 1900	London Matriculation and Ursula leaves school; 335:18
September 1900–July 1902	Ursula teaches at St Philips School, Brinsley Street, Ilkeston [she is 17 for most of the first year, teaches for 2 school years, ending in July; 341:37, 357:10–11, 365:26, 378:15–16, 391:38]
Summer 1902	Brangwens move from Cossethay to Beldover; 397:24–8 [Anna 'nearly' 40, Tom Jnr old enough to walk 'ten miles or more'; 394:10ff., 388:1, 394:28–9]
October 1902–June 1905	Ursula at University College, Nottingham
March 1905	Skrebensky returns from South Africa; 415:31 [Ursula is 22 (actually 21½; see note 4), 'about six years' from the dance; 406:21, 407:14–15]
Easter 1905	Ursula and Skrebensky spend the vacation in a London hotel, and in Paris and Rouen
June 1905	Ursula fails her examinations [after weekend in Dorothy's cottage at Whitsun, news of failure in July; 429:12ff., 439:8, 18]
August 1905	Beach-party in Lincolnshire, 'first week in August', Ursula breaks with Skrebensky, and he marries in late August; 441:8, 447:27
Early October 1905	Ursula encounters the horses and miscarries; 450:20ff.

Italics indicate fixed dates mentioned in *The Rainbow*.

Notes

1. Lydia gives Anna's age as 'four years' when she first visits Tom at the Marsh (37:37), but this must be wrong. Anna is 1 when Lensky dies in late 1864; Lydia goes to Yorkshire in the Spring of 1865 (51:8ff.), and the following February–March (1866) to Cossethay, and is seen by Tom on the road in the Spring (52:37–54:1). Her first visit to the Marsh occurs sometime between May 1866 and the winter of that year, so that Anna could be just 3 when Lydia says she is 4; DHL has perhaps forgotten that Anna was not born in Poland but in London.

2. Anna's age is also wrong for the second visit to the Skrebenskys (183:8–10) since if she is 14 it must be late 1877. DHL has become muddled among the four visits paid by the Brangwens to the Skrebenskys. The first visit is when Anna is 'about ten' (93:1) and the visit is therefore probably in 1873, when the first Baroness is still alive. The second visit, after her death, comes three years before the Baron remarries, and the third visit when Tom and Lydia call on the new Baroness (?1876/7, 183:28). The fourth visit, by the newly-wed Anna and Will, is in 1883: Anton (born in August 1877) is a 'curly-headed little lad' (268:27). Working backwards from the date of Anton's birth, the Baron would had to have remarried no later than November 1876; and that suggests that his first wife must have died around December 1873 or January 1874. Anna would have been 11 at the time of the second visit. This would make the third visit December 1876 or January 1877; and *then* Anna would have been 13. DHL seems to have confused the date of the second visit with that of the third.

3. At one point, DHL says that Ursula is 'not much more than a year old' (197:28) when her sister Gudrun is born. A little earlier, however, he had implied that Ursula is 16–18 months older than her sister: Anna knows she is pregnant for the second time before Ursula is 'ten months old' (192:39–40). However, since Ursula was born around October 1883, and Will is still 22 when Gudrun is born (he becomes 23 around March 1885), Gudrun cannot be 16–18 months younger than her sister. It is perhaps a little precocious of Ursula to be climbing stiles while Will is still only 22 (198:40–199:7), though this anecdote may have been added a bit later in composition.

4. Since Ursula is born towards the end of October 1883, she cannot be 22 just 'before Easter' 1905 (406:20–1) – she is 21½. DHL has simply calculated from the *years* (1905 minus 1883 equals 22), forgetting that Ursula – like her mother – is born late in the year.

A small number of anachronisms in the text are listed in Explanatory notes at 210:37, 342:6 and 400:34.

EXPLANATORY NOTES

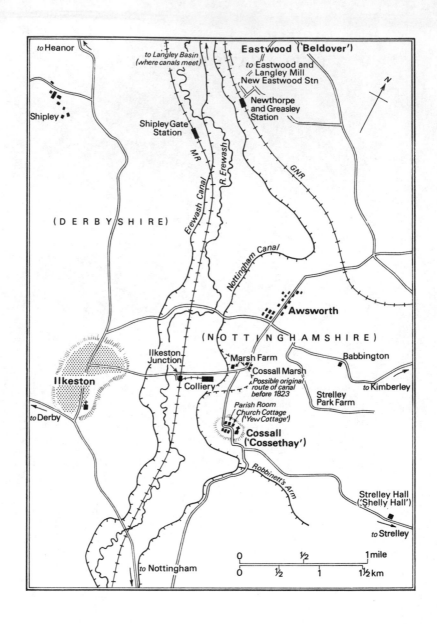

to Heanor

to Langley Basin
(where canals meet)

Eastwood ('Beldover')

to Eastwood and
Langley Mill
New Eastwood Stn

Shipley

Shipley Gate
Station

Newthorpe
and Greasley
Station

MR

Erewash Canal

R. Erewash

GNR

(D E R B Y S H I R E)

Nottingham Canal

Awsworth

(N O T T I N G H A M S H I R E)

Ilkeston
Junction

Marsh Farm

Cossall Marsh

Babbington

Ilkeston

Colliery

*Possible original
route of canal
before 1823*

Strelley
Park Farm

to Kimberley

to Derby

Parish Room
Church Cottage
('Yew Cottage')

Cossall
('Cossethay')

Robbinett's Arm

Strelley Hall
('Shelly Hall')

to Strelley

to Nottingham

| 0 | | ½ | | 1 mile |
| 0 | ½ | | 1 | 1½ km |

496

EXPLANATORY NOTES

5:1   **TO ELSE**   The dedication to Frieda's elder sister Else Jaffe, née von Richthofen (1874–1973) may have had several motivations. The first will have been gratitude for her help, in the early months of the elopement to Germany in 1912. A novel, moreover, which from the beginning had been about 'woman becoming individual, self-responsible, taking her own initiative' (*Letters*, ii. 165), would be appropriately dedicated to a remarkable 'New Woman', whose career had run parallel with Ursula's in many ways, only more successfully. Else too had become a teacher at seventeen; had not only studied at university but taken a doctorate; and as well as becoming a sexually and intellectually emancipated woman, had made her way in 'The Man's World' as an Inspector of Factories. Thirdly, however, for all her readiness to help, Else had been by no means convinced that Frieda ought to stay with DHL, and there may have been a point in presenting her with a book about the meaning of marriage as he saw it, and one very much the product of the experience and success of his own marriage to her sister. The idea of having the dedication in German, and in Gothic script, however, was disastrous unworldliness in 1915, and it was as well that Pinker talked him out of it (*Letters*, ii. 349, 354).

9:7   **the Marsh Farm ... little country town**   See map. Cossethay is based on the village of Cossall, near Ilkeston. The Marsh Farm-house used to be beside the embankment at Cossall Marsh, where the road from Eastwood to Ilkeston passes under the modern aqueduct of the old Nottingham Canal, a little beyond the turning to Cossall.

9:22   **a growing town,**   Ilkeston grew only from 4,446 in 1831 to 5,326 in 1846, but had expanded to 19,774 by 1881. See note on 13:20.

9:31   **heaven and earth was**   DHL often has a collective plural with a singular verb (e.g. 363:19, 400:6, 429:36) and singular collective nouns (see note on 74:39)

9:34   **and falling back,**   TS (p. 2) has a comma in pencil after 'and'. Since DHL revised in ink, this, and the pencil correction of typing errors, were by the typist. At 35:9 for example (TS p. 47), the mistake 'The the' for 'Then the' is compounded by deleting 'the' in pencil; the 's' in 'stranger' is pencilled in; and 'spole' is corrected to 'spoke'. At 52:34 (TS p. 77) the 'd' in 'gold' is pencilled in, where the carbon had not reached to the margin; and at 52:38 there are pencil commas again after 'moved' and 'oblivious'. Whereas DHL punctuated and phrased as he heard his prose, his typists often inserted commas where they thought them more 'correct'. In such cases, pencil and type, this edition reverts to MS unless the insertion was clearly necessary.

10:25   **The women were different.**   In chapters VI and VII of 'Hardy', DHL had developed the theory that the basis of life and creativity lay in the conflict, and

497

the marriage, of two universal and opposite impulses, one towards unification and stability, and the other towards differentiation, individuation and change. Both impulses exist and conflict within as well as between all persons, however, and *The Rainbow* reverses the quasi-gender attributions of 'Hardy'.

11:19 **knowledge,** See 'Hardy' 40–5, for the distinction between 'being' and 'knowing', and for the relation of 'knowledge' to the evolutionary process of increasing differentiation.

12:22 **Shelly Hall,** DHL was probably thinking of Strelley Hall, about 2 miles e. of Cossall.

12:35 **Odyssey** In Homer's Greek epic poem, about the long journey of Odysseus (Latin, Ulysses) home to Ithaca, after the sack of Troy, the hero was delayed for a year by the enchantress Circe, who turned men into animals. His wife Penelope evaded the suitors who pressed her to re-marry, by promising to decide as soon as her weaving was finished. At night she unravelled all she had woven by day.

13:20 **About 1840,** The conjunction where canal, colliery and railway used to be, can still be located and re-imagined from the canal embankment, beside the aqueduct (see note on 9:7). DHL's approximate date is short-hand for a longer and more complicated process, but may also be more accurate than appears at first sight. 1840 is nearer the end of the canal-building age than the beginning, and the Nottingham Canal had opened in 1796. There had been a colliery near Cossall from at least 1739. But when a meeting of Erewash Valley coal-owners, in the 'Sun' inn at Eastwood, resulted in the opening of the Midland Counties (later the Midland) Railway, in 1840 (with an Erewash valley spur in 1847), vast new markets for coal became available, and an extraordinary industrial, trading and population expansion began. (See note on 9:22.) New canal arms were cut, and new coal seams opened in the district, 'about 1840'. Barber Walker & Co. had taken over Cossall Colliery by 1844; and it seems that a new, shorter, but also steeper embankment-route for the Canal, involving a narrow-arched aqueduct across the road, may have been built between 1823 – when the old embankment on the other side of Cossall Marsh collapsed – and 1836, closing off the Marsh from Ilkeston for the first time. That aqueduct was demolished in 1957, in order to widen the road.

14:34 **whimsical,** The TS reading (p. 10), although a typist's mistake, has been preferred to MS 'yet rather whimsical' – as with all cases where DHL's subsequent revision, incorporating the mistake, has so altered the context as to make a return to MS inadvisable. Here (see Textual apparatus) he has cut the previous 'rather', and removed the 'direct' against which 'whimsical' originally contrasted, as 'quaint in her speech', now, would not.

15:25 **a lace-factory in Nottingham.** The Nottingham lace-curtain, that central feature of Victorian respectability, first went into factory production in 1846, and the city became the centre for factory-made lace of all kinds.

15:30 **to pedgill** To pick over and examine, to work minutely (dialect).

16:11 **crew-yard,** The straw-yard, 'the yard in which cattle are kept, especially during the winter, for fattening and for producing dung' (Richard Scollins and John Titford, *Ey Up, Mi Duck! An Affectionate Look at the Speech, History and Folklore of Ilkeston, Derbyshire and the Erewash Valley*, Ilkeston, 1976, ii. 45).

16:31 **a Grammar School** Derby Grammar School, an old foundation, dating from the mid-sixteenth century; 'grammar' because it offered the classical education in Latin and Greek.

17:35 **Tennyson's "Ulysses" or Shelley's "Ode to the West Wind."** 'Ulysses' (1842) and 'Ode to the West Wind' (1820) were probably chosen because they embody the impulse towards the unknown and the beyond. They were also among DHL's favourites; see E. T. [Jessie Chambers], *D. H. Lawrence: A Personal Record* (1935; reprinted Cambridge, 1980), pp. 95 and 99.

18:19 **over five foot eight."** This was the case until October 1914 when, in the interests of wartime recruitment, the height was reduced to five foot five inches, and in November to five foot three.

19:5 **David and Jonathan,** 1 Samuel xviii. 1–4, xix. 2–7, xx. Central figures in DHL's play *David* (1926).

19:14 **at his work** Here the section of MS in DHL's typing ends (p. 7), to be followed by autograph.

19:25 **mardy** Soft, spoiled (dialect).

19:34 **Prometheus Bound,** Greek tragedy by Aeschylus (525–456 B.C.). Prometheus, a Titan, outwitted the God Zeus and stole fire for men from the chariot of the sun, for which he was condemned to eternal torture, chained to a rock and torn by Zeus's eagle. In December 1914 and January 1915, DHL regarded him as a type of Egotism and of modern man needing to be Unbound; cf. *Letters*, ii. 248 and 283.

20:3 **little travelling theatres.** For DHL's memories of Teddy Rayner's, see Harry T. Moore, *The Priest of Love* (New York, 1974), p. 19 and *Letters*, i. 508 n. 3.

20:12 **my conscience-keeper, be the angel at the doorway** Cf. 'The Angel in the House' (1854, 1856) by Coventry Patmore (1823–96), close friend of Alice Meynell, in whose daughter's cottage at Greatham *The Rainbow* was written. See also the story of the angels entertained unawares, Genesis xviii. 1–22.

20:13 **my outgoing and my incoming."** Cf. 2 Samuel iii. 25, 2 Kings xix. 27, Psalm cxxi. 8, Isaiah xxxvii. 28, Ezekiel xliii. 11.

22:28 **Matlock ... Bakewell.** In the late eighteenth century, when the French Revolutionary Wars cut the English off from Continental tours and holidays, fashionable gentry began to visit the Derbyshire Peak District, and particularly to 'take the waters'. There were thermal springs at both Matlock (on the river Derwent) and Bakewell (on the river Wye); and at Matlock John Smedley later created a 'Hydro' for more elaborate hydropathic cures. From the turn of the century the romantic interest in landscape brought greater numbers of visitors to crags, woods and rivers – J. Hutchinson wrote a *Guide to the Romantic Beauties of Matlock* in 1818. The opening of the Manchester, Buxton and Midland Railway in 1849 (with a chalet-style station at Matlock for 'the English Switzerland') opened the resort to a much larger group of visitors. In 1862 when Tom was twenty-four (see Appendix IV), he and the 'little foreigner' (who may have been taking the waters) would probably have stayed in the Old Bath Hotel.

24:1   **this road,"**   In this fashion (dialect).

24:21   **By Jove … the night.**   The first American edition (A1) cut these sentences, and substituted 'That was a different experience. He wanted to see more of the girl.' Subsequent editions followed A1.

27:3   **gorping**   Yawning, gaping, gazing in astonishment (dialect).

27:35   **What the Hanover!,**   Mild expletive substitute for 'hell', presumably from the unpopularity of the Hanoverian Kings of England.

29:12   **britching**   From the 'breeching', the harness round the hindquarters of a carthorse, against which it bears backwards to take the strain when going downhill (dialect).

31:14   **menagerie confabulation?"**   Gossip about exotic creatures, or perhaps the 'menagerie' is the collection of henbirds gossiping.

31:18   **summat."**   Something (dialect).

31:25   **fuzz-ball."**   A dandelion head.

31:31   **axed**   Asked (dialect).

33:10   **land vivid**   The typist's misreading ('man vivid', TS p. 44) produced nonsense, which DHL attempted to make more sensible by revising (see Textual apparatus), but without reference back to the clear sense of MS (p. 41), which has therefore been restored; as at l. 13 where MS 'daze' replaces the typist's error 'days'. At l. 11, however, DHL has changed his mind, so the later reading 'also' has been preferred to MS 'not so completely'.

35:37   **Sluther up**   Hurry up, variant of 'slither' (dialect); cf. 'slippy' at 68:21.

37:12   ***two hundred years,"***   The same phrase is used in Edwin Trueman, *History of Ilkeston* (1880) about the Fritchley family of Cossall, and is repeated in Kelly's *Directories* from 1881.

37:33   **a large leaf**   Probably a cabbage leaf, often used for wrapping butter before the advent of 'grease-proof' paper.

37:37   **Four years,"**   See Appendix IV and note 1.

38:37   **that**   DHL originally wrote 'so that there was no active change or development' (MS p. 50); he replaced the last two words with 'took place.', but failed to delete 'there was' (see Textual apparatus and similarly at 219:13, etc.).

39:6   **the wedding-ring**   The title of the penultimate version of *The Rainbow*, a motif taken up with Anna's wedding-ring 126:22, the two wedding-rings 237:15, the false wedding-ring bought by Ursula and Skrebensky 420:13 and the rings in the 'Excurse' chapter of *Women in Love* (ed. David Farmer, Lindeth Vasey and John Worthen, Cambridge, 1987, pp. 302–11).

41:14   **clutterin'**   Working awkwardly or dirtily (dialect), so here, 'at the nipple', suckling messily.

43:2   **fleece**   The clear reading of MS (p. 58) replaces the typist's error 'flux' and DHL's subsequent attempt to make sense of it without reference to MS. 'Wisps' hardly does justice to the 'wild, flamy pieces' (32:17) or the fierce abundance of the 'lamb's wool' (84:20), and he would probably not have made the change if he had been presented with what he had written (cf. 63:39).

44:13   at her, for the truth of her.   The MS distinction ('at her, and not alone for the truth of her', p. 60) is perhaps more clearly personal than the E1 shortening, which requires accenting of the first 'her' to make itself clear. Without evidence of interference, however, E1 must have the benefit of the doubt.

45:17   a trespass.   A death, also (French, trépasser) a self-transcendence and an offence ('forgive us our trespasses', 147:19 and note); cf. the title of DHL's *The Trespasser*, which plays on the same senses.

45:40   thirty four ... twenty eight,"   The ages are those of Frieda and DHL in 1913 when 'The Sisters' was begun.

46:34   a contradiction in her.   The change from MS (p. 63; see Textual apparatus) may have been self-censorship in response to pressure from Methuen, see Introduction, p. lxvii; though it is also possible that DHL himself decided to make Tom's discomfort psychological rather than physical.

49:3   daughter of a Polish landowner   DHL gave Lydia his mother's first name, but probably drew for her background on that of Frieda's paternal grandmother, who was Polish; Amalie Louise v. Laschowski – Frieda's 'a Polish Countess Lashowska' – daughter of Karl v. Laschowski and Amalie Skrbensky, thus the *Genealogisches Handbuch des Adels* (Limburg, 1978), p. 372; the 'Skrbensky' spelling possibly in error. Frieda's grandfather and great grandfather had speculated ruinously, and there had been rows over her father's gambling.

49:7   a patriot.   I.e. determined to secure Polish independence.

49:13   "European."   I.e. belonging to Western Europe not the Slavic world, especially not Russo-Slavic.

49:14   the great rebellion.   Poland was partitioned in 1772, 1793 and 1795, the greater part going to Russia. Rebellions in 1831 and 1836 were brutally repressed. The Polish nobility hoped to redress grievances by petitioning the Tsar, but the professional classes and impoverished landed gentry were much more radical and anti-Russian, and formed a National Central Committee to direct resistance. In January 1863, seething discontent broke into open rebellion over the introduction of conscription. The peasantry did not, however, support the revolt, because the Russian government held out promises of land; and the struggle was fought out by small bands, under divided leadership. It was repressed with great severity, especially when rebels crossed the border of the old Polish kingdom, 'into the south of Russia', and it was virtually over by the Autumn, although resistance went on until the arrest of the National Committee in April 1864. English public opinion was very sympathetic to the Poles. In Nottinghamshire, Baron Rodolph von Hube (?1834–1910) who claimed to have evaded the Russians by swimming the Vistula, was installed as Vicar of Greasley in October 1866. He provided a model for Baron Skrebensky, see note on 183:22; and also figured as Baron Rudolf von Ruge in DHL's play *The Merry-Go-Round* (written 1910; published 1940).

49:20   **Jewish village ... Muscovite.** Ironic, since the Jews were no less oppressed by the Russians.

50:9   **like a brandished weapon,** Perhaps DHL was thinking of the angelic sword 'which turned every way', Genesis iii. 24.

50:16   **the dark, savage, mystic ride of dread, of death,** Either the Horsemen of the Apocalypse (Revelation vi. 2–8) or the Ride of the Valkyries, the nymphs of Valhalla who selected those about to die.

53:16   **mezereon tree,** A rare botanical inaccuracy by DHL, since Daphnis mezereum is not properly a tree but a deciduous bush with scented flowers.

53:19   **pea-flour** Pease-meal, flour made from peas; put in early crocuses as an addition to the pollen required for the rearing of young bees, when a colony was in danger of exhausting food supplies before the full flowering of Spring. The MS (p. 75) inadvertence 'pea-flower' has been repeated in all editions.

56:19   **his trial ... Gethsemane ... Triumphal Entry** Cf. the trial before Pilate, the agony in the garden and the entry into Jerusalem: Mark xv, xiv, xi; Matthew xxvii, xxvi, xxi.

57:32   **And** Here DHL cut a vivid MS passage (pp. 82–4) in which Tom disturbs a peewit while he is ploughing; see Textual apparatus.

59:11   *filles,* Specifically prostitutes, not merely 'girls' (jeunes filles).

59:17   **plainly beat** A phrase characteristic of DHL's Russian-born friend Samuel Solomonovich Koteliansky (1880–1955); cf. *Letters*, ii. 261, 290.

60:31   **lost himself.** Cf. 'Hardy' 103–4.

61:2   **deposition and toiling at the mill with slaves** Cf. *Samson Agonistes* i. 41 (?1647), by John Milton, for 'the mill with slaves'. The reference of 'deposition' is almost certainly not to the Deposition of Christ from the Cross, but to the dethronement of a king, or the loss of the 'stupendous power' (60:28), like Samson after Delilah's betrayal, Judges xvi.

61:5   **outer darkness,** A Biblical phrase (cf. Matthew viii. 12, xxii. 13, xxv. 30) whose destructive associations DHL reverses.

62:24   **the upper millstone** A Biblical phrase become proverbial ('between the upper and the nether millstone'); cf. Deuteronomy xxiv. 6, Job xli. 24.

66:17   **slipper.** DHL may have deleted MS (p. 100) 'patent' because about 1867 might be rather early for a Nottinghamshire child to be wearing American 'patent leather', though it had first become available in America in the 1850s.

67:21   **thysen** Yourself (dialect).

67:25   **a bomakle."** Perhaps mere nonsense, but possibly a childish mistake for 'abominable' which Tom turns against her with 'a comical'.

68:5   **Topsy,** The little black girl ('I 'spect I growed') in *Uncle Tom's Cabin* (1852) by Harriet Beecher Stowe (1811–52).

68:21   **Slippy!"** I.e. be quick (dialect).

69:8   **nobbut** Not but, i.e. only (dialect).

69:15 **ter** Thou – the intimate usage (dialect).

69:25 **turnips were pitted** I.e. buried for storage.

71:33 **one flesh.** Cf. Mark x. 8, where Christ refers to Genesis ii. 24. see Michael Black, *D. H. Lawrence: The Early Fiction* (1986), pp. 55, 244 *passim*.

71:38 **broken rock** Moses brought life-giving water out of rock, when he smote it at the Lord's command, Numbers xx. 11; correspondingly in the New Testament, the life-giving blood and water from Christ's side, pierced by the soldier's spear on the cross, John xix. 34. Cf. the hymn 'Rock of Ages, cleft for me'. See also 121:24.

74:39 **beast."** A collective singular, perhaps dialect, though cf. fowl (111:29), beast (301:35) and face (350:4); and see also 'two beast' in 'A Prelude', *Love Among the Haystacks and Other Stories*, ed. John Worthen (Cambridge, 1987), 6:22, and *Letters*, iii. 328 ('Two men ... carrying hay to the beast'). See also 75:39 and Textual apparatus; 76:6; 82:40.

75:22 **brewer's grains** Malted barley left over after beer-making.

76:16 **paisley shawl.** It reminds him of his mother (l. 17) because the Paisley design, from the manufacturing town of Paisley in Renfrewshire, Scotland, was newly fashionable in the 1830s.

77:20 **What had she to do with him?** A recurrent question in DHL, based on Christ's question to his mother, John ii. 4. See also 233:10.

79:6 **kicking against the pricks.** Rebelling against superior power or adverse circumstances, like a beast of burden when goaded (proverbial); cf. Acts ix. 5 and xxvi. 14.

80:18 **When the pie ... a king?"** From the nursery rhyme 'Sing a song of sixpence'. Anna goes on to muddle this (ll. 25–7) with 'Ring a ring 'o roses', which originally had the refrain 'Ash-a, ash-a', imitating a sneeze, but is now often sung 'A-tishoo, A-tishoo'.

81:13 **rarely,** Especially well or fine (dialect).

81:17 **great joy** Because 'off out a bit' has connotations of courtship, comical in this context.

81:30 **fawce** Shrewd, sharp-witted (dialect).

81:37 **sharp-shins."** Keen witted, sharp; perhaps from 'sharp-shinned', i.e. slender-shanked, used diminutively of a hawk, so 'little and skinny, but fierce' (dialect).

82:5 **"Black Swan."** In Goose Gate, Nottingham.

82:26 **stirks.** Bullcalves or heifers, but in Nottinghamshire usually the original Anglo-Saxon sense of cow-calf.

82:30 **met** Might (dialect).

83:32 **covered-in market ... "George Inn,"** Then recently constructed, in 1864 ... in Midland Road, Derby.

84:1 **apple-blossom face** Cf. the description of Hilda Mary Jones in *Letters*, i. 253.

84:25 It's hair." Cf. Frieda in E. W. Tedlock, ed., *Frieda Lawrence: The Memoirs and Correspondence* (1961), p. 45: ' "This isn't hair," he would tell her, stroking her head, "it's fluff like a young sparrow's." . . . she was aware of her light hair sticking out in all directions.' But cf. note on 43:2.

85:5 that road ... wambling In that way ... walking unsteadily (dialect).

86:8 Spencer ... Browning Herbert Spencer (1820–1903), positivist and philosopher of evolution, criticised as too unitary in 'Hardy' 98 ... Robert Browning (1812–89), poet, probably here as a 'progressive'.

90:31 baptism ... confirmation. Successive sacramental rites in Christian churches, each implying the acceptance of a covenant of grace, and initiation into a new state of being.

90:35 lost, and ... found. Cf. Matthew x. 39; Luke ix. 24.

90:39 bonds ... complete liberty. Cf. 'whose service is perfect freedom', the Collect for Peace in the Order for Morning Prayer of the Book of Common Prayer.

91:3 transfiguration ... glorification ... admission. Cf. Luke ix. 28–36. See also 284:20.

91:24 house was finished ... His abode. Cf. the creation of the Temple, 2 Chronicles v. 1 and 1 Kings viii. 13. Christ, however, created a temple 'made without hands', in the souls and bodies of believers; cf. Mark xiv. 58, Acts xvii. 24 and 1 Corinthians vi. 19.

91:35 pillar of fire ... pillar of cloud Cf. Exodus xiii. 21–2; also the discussion of pillar and arch in 'Hardy' 72, 74. See also 263:29.

92:4 dame's school I.e. a dame-school, a private school for young children, kept by a woman.

92:15 in fee. By heritable right or feudal obligation, as opposed to 'free'.

92:33 Baron Skrebensky, See notes on 49:14 and 183:22; and for the name Skrebensky, note on 49:3.

92:34 Mr Gladstone William Ewart Gladstone (1809–98), statesman, Prime Minister 1868–74 and again in 1880, 1886 and 1892.

93:28 knight of Malta. I.e. a knight of the famous Order of St John, dating back to the Crusades but, in the nineteenth century, devoted to charitable work.

93:40 a young ladies' school in Nottingham. It later becomes clear (146:15) that this is the Nottingham High School for Girls, very recently founded in 1875, only the sixth to be started by the Girls Public Day School Trust and among the earliest outside London.

94:22 bagatelle," A trifle (French); also a game involving the propelling of balls into holes at the semicircular end of a board, hence Tom's wordplay.

95:19 "As You Like It." Ursula responds differently to Shakespeare's play (310:33).

95:33 Alexandra, Princess Alexandra (1844–1925), wife to the Prince of Wales, the future King Edward VII, and a noted beauty, accompanied her husband to Nottingham when he opened the Castle Museum and Gallery in 1878.

96:20 **Goose Fair.** The annual Nottingham Fair, originally in September, dating back to the thirteenth century. In the 1870s it began on the first Tuesday in October. It provides the title for an early story, collected in *The Prussian Officer and Other Stories*, ed. John Worthen (Cambridge, 1983).

97:23 **great Separator** Christ is seen in 'Hardy' 63–5 as the opposite God to the great Unifier of the Old Testament (but in the reversed terms of the novel, the God appropriate to the 'Women', therefore).

98:3 **Ave Maria ... Pater Noster,** Originally the words of the Angel at the Annunciation, in the Latin of the Vulgate; thence an intercession in the Roman Catholic Church. DHL's Latin translates: 'Hail Mary, full of grace, the Lord is with thee, blessed art thou among women and blessed is the fruit of thy womb, Jesus. Hail Mary, Holy Mary, pray for us sinners now, and in the hour of our death, Amen.' But DHL misquotes; 'Ave Maria, Sancta Maria' should be 'Sancta Maria, Mater Dei' (Holy Mary, Mother of God) ... 'Our Father' (Latin), first words of the Lord's Prayer, cf. Matthew vi. 9, Luke xi. 2.

99:11 **stretched** Typed in TS (p. 159) as 'stretched', but 'ed' printed very faintly at the end of the line (and the page), probably because the carbon did not reach, or curled. Someone – it does not look like DHL – then wrote 'ing' in ink. Since the MS (p. 155) reading is clearly his, it has been preferred. Here there is also a change-over between typewriters, see Introduction, p. liii. On MS p. 153, near the foot, a tiny '159' marks the beginning of TS p. 159, and at 'stretched' in MS DHL has written 'start here, number the page 160'. TS p. 160 duly begins 'itself', with a change of typewriter, ribbon and paper. On the back of TS p. 159 appears 'Rainbow', possibly in Viola Meynell's hand.

99:32 **a certain Bishop of France,** Bishop la Balue, imprisoned in the Chateau of Loches in the reign of Louis XI. There is a similar cell in the Tower of London, known as 'Little Ease'.

101:3 **intimate,** DHL meant to delete 'strangely' before 'intimate' in MS (p. 158), but did so with a wavy line which left it quite legible and deceived the typist; see Textual apparatus.

104:17 **snirt** A smothered laugh, snicker, snort (dialect).

105:40 **Ruskin ... mediæval forms.** John Ruskin (1819–1900), critic of art and architecture, and essayist on social reform; key figure in the Gothic revival. (MS p. 167 goes on to suggest that Will is not an uncritical disciple; see Textual apparatus.)

106:18 **a hymn.** See the 'Excurse' chapter in *Women in Love*, ed. Farmer, Vasey and Worthen, 312:15–20, where Birkin and Ursula hear the bells of Southwell play a hymn. In 1884 the Minster became the cathedral for the diocese in which Nottingham is situated.

106:22 **sedilia** Seats in the chancel near the altar, for the officiating clergy (Latin), hence properly plural. The confusion about Latin number is probably meant to be Will's, who is largely self-educated.

108:12 **like the Devil looking over Lincoln,** A semi-proverbial phrase, used e.g. by Scott in *Kenilworth* but according to A. F. Kendrick, *The Cathedral Church of Lincoln* (1902), p. 57, of unknown origin. The famous grotesque on the South exterior of the cathedral is in the gable of the Consistory Court chapel, appropriately for Tom's attitude, since that was the Court for sexual offences.

108:36 **favorite work was wood-carving.** In this, and several other respects, DHL modelled Will on Alfred Burrows, father of his fiancée Louie, see also notes on 122:3, 221:5 and 388:14.

108:38 **a phœnix,** DHL found this symbol, which he was to make so much his own, in Mrs Henry Jenner's *Christian Symbolism* which he was reading in late 1914; cf. *Letters*, ii. 250 and 252 where n. 5 quotes Mrs Jenner. DHL's first drawing of the phoenix, copying Mrs Jenner's illustration from a thirteenth-century Bestiary, is reproduced in Keith Sagar, *The Life of D. H. Lawrence* (1980), p. 93. Chap. 1 of 'Hardy' 7–9 is called 'Of Poppies and Phoenixes and the beginning of the argument'.

111:24 **blur** E1's 'blurr' (p. 107) is an old-fashioned spelling still used in the late nineteenth century by Browning (*OED*), so this might be DHL – but the MS reading (p. 177), though mistaken by the typist as 'blue', is 'blur'.

112:11 **The veils had ripped** Cf. Matthew xxvii. 51, Mark xv. 38, Luke xxiii. 45. When the Veil of the Temple was rent at the Crucifixion, in the Christian interpretation, all men could freely come to God.

112:32 **the Creation of Eve.** Cf. Genesis ii. 21–5.

113:7 **covering their faces with their wings.** Cf. Isaiah vi. 2.

113:13 **puther** A cloud as of smoke or dust (dialect). The typist did not recognise the word in MS (p. 180) and guessed 'paths'.

117:15 **irritation.** There was no such feeling in MS (p. 186). It was created by the typist (TS p. 190) at 116:27, but noticed and repeated by DHL here, see Textual apparatus.

120:27 **the be-all and the end-all.** Cf. *Macbeth* I. vii. 5; also 'Hardy' 10.

120:32 **long, marital embrace [120:23] ... creative life** Cf. 'Hardy' 75.

121:15 **voice ... trembled,** 'Voice' does not make sense, and should be 'ears', but the MS reading is clear (p. 193) ... above 'trembled,' in MS (p. 193) appears 'out', in small writing, as though DHL contemplated some change but had been distracted.

122:3 **the cottage next the church,** Church Cottage was well known to DHL as the home (until 1908) of his fiancée Louisa ('Louie') Burrows (1888–1962). Her parents, Alfred (1864–1948) and Louisa Ann (1865–1954) Burrows, like Anna and Will, had five daughters and two sons; and the family provided so many recognisable details for the second and third generation of Brangwens that Louie was moved in later life (trying to protect her parents from further gossip) to ask DHL's sister Ada to cut, from her memoir *Young Lorenzo* (1932), 'all references to me and my family. You know how clearly Cossall has been identified with the scene of *The Rainbow* – and how very personally Bert used the characters of members of my family ... I never made such requests of Bert – because after all he was a genius, & I could not contemplate making it more difficult for him to earn a livelihood. I know there is no such need in your case' (letter from Ada Clarke to Laurence Pollinger, UT).

123:26 **dolly-tub,** Wash-tub, from the shafted disk with projecting arms, used for stirring the washing.

124:3 **the wedding,** DHL had written this chapter by 23 December 1914, when Frieda told Murry 'it had Marlowe and Fielding in an account of a genuine English wedding' (John Middleton Murry, *Reminiscences of D. H. Lawrence*, 1933, p. 48).

124:4 **cabs ... vehicles.** These would of course be horse-drawn.

128:32 **no marriage in heaven,"** Cf. Matthew xxii. 30: 'in the resurrection they neither marry, nor are given in marriage, but are as the angels' (A.V.; all quotations are from this version). For DHL's theory of two-in-one, see 'Hardy' 54–5, 127–8.

129:24 **uneasy.** This concludes TS p. 211. On the back, along with sundry doodlings in Frieda's hand of 'Frieda von Richthofen' and 'Sablon bei Metz', is a note in ink, 'Rainbow' in what looks like DHL's hand. Since this is only part of the first batch sent to Lady Ottoline, and of a section typed on typewriter no. 2, it is not clear why the note was made.

129:27 **one angel."** Tom was originally conclusive in MS (p. 209), and the typist's dash instead of the full stop in TS (p. 212) was an uncalled-for weakening. It seems unlikely that DHL would have altered his original if it had been presented to him with its confident two-in-one point, see note on 128:32, and 'Hardy' chap. v title and p. 43. Moreover, E1's 'an angel' (p. 126) may well be a typesetter's inadvertence. Therefore MS is restored. Cf. *The Trespasser*, ed. Elizabeth Mansfield (Cambridge, 1981), pp. 59–64.

130:19 **the wake** A group of minstrels and singers visiting homes and hostelries at the time of a 'wake' (dialect) or 'the wakes', an annual church or village festival – here Christmas; the Ilkeston Wakes were in October.

130:25 **guysers** Or 'guisers' (dialect), men and boys visiting houses in disguise (if only paper hats and blackened faces), mummers of the old Christmas plays, cf. 'A Prelude' in *Love Among the Haystacks*, ed. Worthen, pp. 8–11.

130:28 **club and dripping pan.** The attributes of Beelzebub in the traditional mummers' play of St George: 'In come I, old Beelzebub / Over my shoulders I carries my club, / In my hand a dripping pan, / Don't you think I'm a jolly old man?' (Alan Brody, *The English Mummers and the Plays* [n.d.], p. 60). Beelzebub does not usually fight St George but comes in as an extra character after the main combat. An account of 1800 describes Beelzebub 'with a frying pan upon his shoulder and a great flail in his hand threshing about him on friends and foes' (ibid., p. 11). Tom as Beelzebub playing 'Old Johnny Roger' suggests the wildness of Fools like Johnny Jack in the mumming plays, and also related folk games like 'Johnny Rover', and 'Johnny Ningo' which 'usually ends in a general scrimmage' (Joseph Wright's *English Dialect Dictionary*, 6 vols., 1898–1905.) See also 'A Prelude' in *Love Among* *the Haystacks*, ed. Worthen, pp. 5–15; and the mumming episode in Bk II, chap. V of Thomas Hardy's *Return of the Native* (1878); and 259:36.

130:39 **blanket fair ... Strike a daisy,** Fun and games in bed (dialect) ... slang imprecation, probably short for 'strike me a daisy', cf. 'strike me lucky' in Textual apparatus at 126:36.

131:15 **boz-eyed** Cross-eyed, squinting (dialect).

132:2 **a servant in,"** I.e. living in the house.

133:15 **"In the fields with their flocks abiding."** A carol by Frederick William Farrar (1831–1904) ['... field ...']; cf. Luke ii. 8.

134:2 **Anna Victrix** Anna the conquering female (Latin).

134:14 **under the flood.** The first of many references to the Biblical story (Genesis vii–ix) which generates the rainbow symbolism. See also notes on 136:38 and 173:21.

135:13 **the rim ... the great wheel** Chap. VI of 'Hardy' (52–5) is called 'The Axle and the Wheel of Eternity'.

136:38 **the Ark in the flood,** Cf. Genesis vii. 7.

137:20 **put off ... on, and** Cut from A1 (p. 137), and subsequent editions.

139:27 **Tablets of Stone** Cf. Exodus xxxi. 18 and 'Hardy' 62–3 (remembering that *The Rainbow* reverses the 'sexes').

140:12 **the Lord ... not consumed.** Cf. Exodus iii. 2. See also 188:40 and 263:29–30.

140:29 **king ... herd:** The particular story has not been identified, but in the mediæval 'Feast of Fools' a 'king' was crowned for a single day; cf. Enid Welsford, *The Fool* (1935), pp. 192–203.

141:23 **uncreated.** I.e. de-created, robbed of distinguishing identity (as opposed to 'not yet created').

147:20 **"And forgive ... against us—"** From the Lord's Prayer in the version of the Book of Common Prayer ['... trespass, ...']; cf. Matthew vi. 9–15, Luke xi. 1–4.

148:20 **lamb holding the banner,** The Agnus Dei (Latin, Lamb of God), symbol of the resurrected Christ, both sacrificial victim and Lord of Heaven, comes from Revelation v. (cf. John i. 29). In Christian iconography of the resurrection, Christ emerging from the grave is often shown carrying the banner of victory with the sign of the cross. The Lamb and Flag, in painting and carving, combines these symbolisms.

149:36 **Pietà** A representation of the Virgin holding the dead body of Christ, hence symbolically the 'body of Christ' eaten in the Eucharist.

153:10 **Bamberg Cathedral.** The cathedral of St Peter and St George is noted for an extraordinary Last Judgement above the West Door; for 'statues of women' such as the Elizabeth, Mary, Ecclesia and Synagogue; and for later sculptures and carvings by the sixteenth-century Bavarians Veit Stoss and Tilman

Riemenschneider. The Christmas Altar by Veit Stoss is in wood, and so are fine stall carvings such as the Queen of Sheba, who wears a crown and has her hair in long braids down her back. Ecclesia is also crowned.

154:16 **the outside being** DHL originally changed 'outsider' (MS p. 247) to this reading, which is therefore preferred to the 'outsider' which reappears, its 'r' added in pencil, as DHL and the typist attempt to make sense of the TS mistyping; see Textual apparatus.

155:36 **rejoiced in the way he crossed the floor,** In 'A Modern Lover' DHL recalls *Evelyn Innes* (1898): 'one of the men, as George Moore says, whom his wife would hate after a few years for the very way he walked across the floor' (*Love Among the Haystacks*, ed. Worthen, p. 40). (Moore wrote: 'Marry them, and they came to hate the way you walked across the room...', 1898 edn, p. 69.)

156:22 **full-butt** In point-blank meeting or violent collision, like a butting animal.

157:5 **Passion.** I.e. the Crucifixion and Resurrection, recalled in the Eucharist service.

157:34 **opposites, not complements.** This is the essence of DHL's concept of the marriage of opposites as the source of creativity in 'Hardy', and the essential difference between his 'two-in-one' and the idea of marriage as complementary meeting and merging into 'one flesh', which he associated with Christianity.

158:22 **six wings of bliss** Like the Seraphim in Isaiah vi. 2, or the Evangelists, closest to the Throne in Revelation iv. 8; or Milton's description of Raphael, *Paradise Lost* v. 277–85. DHL, in December 1914, described the Cherubim and Seraphim as '*absorbed in praise eternally*' (*Letters*, ii. 249).

158:28 **Annunciation** Cf. Luke i. 26–38.

158:30 **Angel of the Presence.** Cf. Luke i. 19 ('I am Gabriel, that stand in the presence of God'); cf. also Isaiah vi. 1–3; and Revelation iv. 11, viii. 2–3, etc. DHL listed the traditional orders of angels: Cherubim, Seraphim, Dominions, Powers, Principalities, Archangels, Angels (leaving out Thrones, *Letters*, ii. 249).

159:19 **Cana?** The first miracle of Jesus, a 'sign' of the transformation of marriage by the presence in it of the Holy Spirit; cf. John ii. 1–11 of which Will quotes from verses 4, 5 and 10 ['... thee? mine ... servants, Whatsoever ... it.'].

160:4 **went out, dark** At 'dark' TS begins a new page (though on the same machine), re-aligns the margins and begins to go further to the right than before. At the top, a numbering '250?' is crossed out, and the corrected numbering '264' substituted in the top right corner. DHL had sent TS pp. 1–263 to Lady Ottoline, see Introduction, p. xli, and had forgotten to note the number of the last page, so began the next batch '250 at random' (*Letters*, ii. 326).

160:5 **tasted of death.** I.e. tasted death; cf. Matthew xvi. 28.

160:40 **the brotherhood of man.** Cf. Mark xii. 31, John xiii. 34 and xv. 12–13; whence St Paul (Hebrews xiii. 1) and St Peter (1 Peter ii. 17).

161:12 **You've a right** It is right for you (?dialect); cf. also 265:19 and note.

161:20   **captain of the ship.**   Cf. DHL's comic parody of this idea in *Kangaroo* (1923), chap. XIX.

162:10   **Woman was made out of Man's body,"**   DHL had already over-turned the primogeniture of Genesis ii. 21–3 in his 'Foreword' to *Sons and Lovers*; see Aldous Huxley, ed., *The Letters of D. H. Lawrence* (1932), p. 99. For 'man is born of woman', cf. Job xiv. 1.

165:38   **along opposite horizons,**   Cf. the dance of men and women in 'Hardy' 61.

166:18   **"Magnificat."**   The song of the Virgin, 'My soul doth magnify the Lord', Luke i. 46–55, thence the canticle called the Magnificat (from the first word of the canticle in the Latin Vulgate) in the Evensong service of the Book of Common Prayer.

166:38   **Fra Angelico's "Entry of the Blessed into Paradise."**   I.e. the left side of the 'Last Judgement' in the Museo di S. Marco in Florence, painted 1430–1 by Fra Angelico (1387–1455). But cf. 'Hardy' 69, on its excess of the impulse to stability. See also Ursula, 259:4–24 below.

168:3   **his will upon her,**   The proof DHL was revising (see Textual appara-tus) read, on the evidence of the E1 spacing (p. 167), 'force her into / something'. DHL probably crossed out 'her into', and wrote 'his will upon her' above; but then left the original 'something' at the beginning of the next line undeleted, which produced E1's: 'force his will upon her something, there was something he wanted'. (If DHL had wanted that repetition, he would probably have needed to set it off by restoring the MS semicolon, without which E1 reads awkwardly.) This edition assumes, rather, that he simply failed to notice the 'something' from the discarded reading, and would have deleted it too, had he seen it.

170:11   **David ... Michal,**   Cf. 2 Samuel vi. 14–23.

170:15   **"Thou comest ... our hands."**   David's words to the giant Philistine, Goliath, 1 Samuel xvii. 45, 47 ['... sword, and with a spear, and with a shield: but ... of the Lord ... for ...'].

170:20   **Saul proclaiming his own kingship.**   Saul's presumption was not so much to proclaim his own kingship, as to take it upon himself, in his impatience, to offer the celebratory sacrifice to the Lord, instead of the high priest Samuel; cf. 1 Samuel x. 8 and xiii. 7–14. For this, and another act of disobedience, the favour of the Lord was transferred to David.

170:29   **was exalted over him, before**   DHL's revision was produced by the typist of TS (p. 281) mistaking 'exalted' for 'exulted', so there is a case for returning to MS 'exulted over him with' (p. 272). However, DHL might have made the change anyway. Apart from the question of repetition, the revision has produced a mounting scale, in relation to Will, from 'exemption' to 'his nullifi-cation' to 'exalted over him, before the Lord', which is therefore retained.

172:7   **outgoings ... prevented her.**   The Biblical echo in 'outgoings' and 'incomings' – cf. note on 20:13 – might suggest that 'prevented' carries, along with its normal meaning, that of the Book of Common Prayer – 'Prevent us, O Lord, in all our doings' – i.e. to go before.

173:21 **ark ... flood.** Genesis vii. 6–24. This story, like that of Adam and Eve in the Garden, and the journeying Israelites in search of the Promised Land, is referred to in the narrative of each generation of Brangwens.

174:4 **the old man of the seas,** Who begged to be carried, but once mounted refused to let go; from the story of Sindbad in the Arabian Nights ['. . . of the Sea'].

174:21 **a fury** In Greek mythology, one of the avenging spirits (also Eumenides or Erinnyes), usually female, who pursued criminals and carried out curses and punishments, as Orestes was pursued to punish his matricide in the *Oresteia* of Aeschylus.

176:36 **born for a second time,** Cf. 'Hardy' 65, 83. DHL is re-interpreting Christ's teaching in John iii. 3–7.

177:15 **him [almost dev]otionally,** MS (p. 284) is torn, though the tops of the ascenders are visible. The typist (TS p. 192) left a blank with a pencil question mark in the margin, so MS must have been torn by then. DHL seems never to have referred back to MS; but 177:21 supports the conjecture of the original reading, and the restoration. (The square brackets in the Textual apparatus indicate the defect in MS.)

177:30 **the lion lay down with the lamb** A semi-proverbial misquotation of Isaiah xi. 6. Cf. 317:39–40.

179:2 **Ursula because of the picture of the saint.** The legendary daughter of a Breton King, said to have been martyred along with eleven thousand virgins by the Huns at Cologne. The most famous pictures are by Memling, in Bruges, and Carpaccio, in Venice.

181:13 **Pisgah mount,** The mountain from which Moses saw the Promised Land, but where he died without entering it; cf. Deuteronomy xxxiv. 1–5.

181:16 **and a rainbow ... above it.** This, the first explicit reference to the title – though there had been implicit allusion at the end of chap. III – was added in MS (p. 291).

181:27 **Dawn and sunset were** For the cadence, cf. Genesis i. 5, etc.

181:40 **the three witnesses ... in the fire.** Shadrach, Meshach and Abednego in the burning fiery furnace of Daniel iii. 23–8.

182:17 **builded house,** A common Biblical expression, cf. 1 Kings viii. 27, 43, and similarly in 1 Chronicles, Ezra, Job, Proverbs, Ecclesiastes, Hebrews, etc.

183:10 **fourteen years old.** Cf. Appendix IV and note 2.

183:22 **"The History ... of Briswell."** Cf. Rodolph, Baron von Hube, *Griseleia in Snotinghscire* (Nottingham, 1901), his history of Greasley, which is however dedicated otherwise.

187:12 **outside of time!** A major revision within the MS begins here (p. 300), making it unlikely that the Cathedral scene was in 'The Wedding Ring'.

187:15 **transitation** The action of passing, passage (*OED*). DHL had a fondness at this time for unusually expanding words, cf. 'enrichened' (271:27) and 'enrichening' (317:3) and 'nucleolating' (414:20).

187:26 **all was contained in oneness.** The Cathedral scene as a whole is clarified by DHL's argument in 'Hardy' 56–76. At this point cf. particularly 63–6.

188:2 **the apex of the arch,** Cf. 'Hardy' 72.

188:10 **arch.** At this point in TS (p. 309) DHL began a radical re-casting in five autograph pages (310–14). This TSR now becomes the base-text from which E1 divergences are noted in the Textual apparatus; the original MS is given first in continuous transcription.

188:13 **and ecstasies.** TS (p. 310) is torn here, but probably after typesetting. Only 'and' – or probably '&' – is missing.

189:17 **little faces** Cf. 'Hardy' 66, on the opposition in mediæval cathedrals between monism and multiplicity.

189:21 **imps** DHL may be thinking particularly of the 'Lincoln Imp' in the Angel Choir.

189:28 **separate knowledge,** Cf. note on 11:19, and 'Hardy' 66, on the tension between the 'God' of aspiration and the 'God' of knowledge.

191:6 **jewel** The 's' in TS (p. 313) is pencil, and probably not DHL but the typesetter, worried by the unusual.

191:23 **rotonda** Variant of 'rotunda' (*OED*), a round building, especially one with a dome, like the Pantheon in Rome, but here the 'dome' of the sky.

196:11 **flesh and blood** A Biblical phrase, cf. Matthew xvi. 17, 1 Corinthians xv. 50.

196:18 **human cause** In TS (p. 320) 'human' is smudged, but is visible under magnification and light, and hence is restored here.

197:29 **She his** DHL occasionally used a 'hanging' phrase like this, with a kind of emphasis; cf. 113:30, 430:20.

197:33 **Gudrun.** In Norse mythology, and in the Nibelung story, the grand-daughter of Hagen and the daughter of Hilde; cf. also William Morris *The Lovers of Gudrun* (1868–70), a translation from the Laxdaela saga. In Wagner she is Hagen's half-sister, and married to Siegfried by deception.

199:7 **twenty two.** See Appendix IV.

199:33 **glassie** A glass marble (dialect).

204:34 **the ruddiest lilies of the field,** Cf. the poppy in 'Hardy' 7ff., recalling Matthew vi. 28–9.

205:8 **quivering needle.** I.e. of a compass.

205:34 **one of her earliest memories.** On the back of pp. [8–9] of the manuscript of DHL's 'The Prussian Officer' (Roberts E326.5), UT, Frieda drafted two versions of a similar childhood memory of gardening with her father.

206:3   **Ursula**   The presence of 'Ella' in MS, as here (p. 335) – see Textual apparatus – is probably evidence that the episode was in 'The Wedding Ring'.

206:7   **grip**   A shallow open furrow (dialect).

206:13   **taters ... sprits**   Potatoes which have sprouted (dialect).

210:22   **After a long bout of hostility,**   Here begins another major revision in TS (p. 343–55), inserting the episode with the girl in Nottingham and the new relation with Anna that follows. The final state of this revision (TSR) now effectively becomes the base-text from which E1 divergence is noted in the Textual apparatus; MS is given first.

210:32   **the football match**   Notts County Football Club, probably the oldest in the Football League, was founded in 1862. Nottingham Forest F.C. was founded three years later.

210:37   **the Empire**   The Empire Theatre of Varieties, opened 1898 – a rare anachronism. DHL might have confused it with the Palace of Varieties, which had flourished throughout the 1880s.

214:19   **together.**   E1 (p. 215) mistook the full stop for an exclamation and heightening. The top half of what the typesetter took to be an exclamation mark, however, is the comma after 'shut' in the line above. (Cf., similarly, Textual apparatus at 217:38, and at 218:33, the dot from an 'i' below is mistaken for a comma.) The cut, in proof, of the previous two sentences (see Textual apparatus) could conceivably have been self-censorship in response to pressure from the publisher, but the retention of this sentence might suggest otherwise; see Introduction, pp. lxvii–lxviii.

217:11   **Tom Cooper."**   Thomas Cooper was a neighbour of the Lawrence family when they moved to Lynn Croft, and provided some of the characteristics of the protagonist in *Aaron's Rod* (1922).

219:26   **He wished he were ... her flesh.**   These sentences were cut from A1 (p. 222), and subsequent editions. The reference to a tigercat takes up a motif, announced at 171:39, and originally made explicit in a long passage in MS (pp. 634–8) cut in TS (p. 660) (see Textual apparatus at 408:40), about how the full human being incorporates all evolution, so is and should be tiger and ape as well as homo sapiens in touch with Paradise. The cut in proof at 219:24 (see Textual apparatus) may be one of those made by DHL in response to pressure from the publisher; see Introduction, p. lxviii.

219:34   **Absolute Beauty,**   The capitals indicate what is almost a technical term, anticipated at several points in the previous pages. This kind of Beauty, as opposed to the relative kind produced by the marriage of opposites, is wholly self-contained, and separate from personality or any kind of human relationship or even other beauties – a thing-in-itself. It occupies only one extreme in the Lawrentian dialectic; which makes it in one sense infinite (since the opposed absolutes are outside time and change), and in another, deathly (since fullness of life comes from the clash of opposites in flux, momentary flowerings and consummations subject to mutability). See 'Hardy' 123ff.

220:14 Gothic ... round arch. DHL had used the contrast before, in *Sons and Lovers*, chap. VII, to set Miriam's spiritual aspirations and ecstasies against Paul's dogged will. Here the primary contrast is obviously spirit/flesh; but in the physical connotations of the images and the suggestion of something 'immoral and against mankind' there may be implied a further contrast between kinds of sexuality. This seems to be confirmed later in the language of 'shameful', 'sinister', 'unnatural', 'heavy, fundamental gratification'. Yet since Anna is no longer 'victrix' and both abandon themselves (albeit only in their 'dark' aspects), it is a liberating relationship creating new freedoms, especially for Will.

221:5 new Swedish methods, In 1890, woodwork was approved by the Department of Education as a subject for elementary schools. 'Sloyd' was a new method, originating in Sweden, of teaching manual dexterity through carpentry and carving. In 1891 it became possible to claim government grants for evening classes for boys, and in that year Alfred Burrows, who provided so much of the outer detail for Will Brangwen, started a woodwork class in Cossall which carved a new reredos for the village Church, of which he was organist.

221:26 parish room This is frequently mentioned in the *Ilkeston Pioneer* as the venue for concerts and readings.

221:33 an inspector Nottinghamshire, at this period, was fortunate to have W. J. Abel, a pioneer of great energy and drive.

223:8 High School I.e. Nottingham High School (for boys), previously known as the Free Grammar School (for 'grammar' see note on 16:31), in existence since the thirteenth century and re-founded in 1513. In 1866 it moved from Stoney Street to its present position near the Arboretum (the Botanical tree-garden), and became known as the High School. DHL won a county scholarship there and enrolled three days after his thirteenth birthday in September 1898, leaving three years later.

223:19 pupil of an engineer, Probably at the Royal School of Mines which, with the Royal School of Science, became Imperial College, London. There, in the 1880s, 'some of the most energetic scientific and mathematical people' were indeed to be found, including Thomas Huxley (cf. note on 224:15). When the Lawrences first met the young David Garnett, he was training as a botanist at the Royal College of Science.

224:13 gentlemen; Contrast their cousin Will who followed his father into the factory. The prosperity of the farming branch, as a result of the growing food-needs of Ilkeston, has turned the modest land-owner into a 'gentleman-farmer' (224:35) and almost a squire, as the MS (p. 345) says, except that he does not own a Manor. He is able to buy a gentleman's education for his sons, whereas their cousin Will is largely self-educated.

224:15 Ruskin and then the Agnostic writings. For Ruskin see also note on 105:40; but whereas Will read his writings on architecture, the context here suggests Ruskin's social criticism. DHL may have altered MS 'Fabian' (p. 344), as not merely more radical (since the Fabian Society founded in 1884 believed in socialism, albeit not by revolution), but also a little anachronistic, since the Fabian Essays were first issued in 1889, when Fred would be about thirty, whereas the references here are to 'young' men. The 'Agnostic writings' were those of Thomas Huxley (1825–95) who invented the word, especially the *Lay Sermons* (1870); and of Matthew Arnold (1822–81), such as *Literature and Dogma* (1872).

225:24 **a stranger within the gates,** Cf. the Fourth Commandment, on keeping the sabbath, Exodus xx. 8–10. The phrase also has a semi-proverbial force, since it was applied to Jewish writers who accepted some (e.g. the fourth) but not all of the Laws of Moses.

226:26 **suppering up ... slew** Feeding the animals; cf. 74:39 (dialect) ... a mining term (*OED* quotes William S. Gresley, *A Glossary of coal mining*, 1883) for a basin or natural swamp in a coal seam, often running several hundred yards.

226:37 **"Angel,"** The Old Angel Inn on the corner of Stoney Street and Woolpack Lane, dating from 1671.

227:5 **Noah ... dove an' olive branch** Cf. Genesis viii. 11.

227:38 **takes its hook** Cf. sling one's hook, or hook it: to make off, decamp (slang).

227:39 **falleth as rain on the just and unjust.** Matthew v. 45 ['sendeth rain ... and on the unjust'].

230:31 **The cut's** I.e. the canal (has) (dialect). DHL seems to have combined biblical myth with local history. The old embankment at Cossall Marsh had collapsed in 1823, and the Marsh Farm was inundated again, probably in the floods of 1875 (when Louie Burrows's grandmother was alone in the house with young children).

233:4 **laid in line, inviolable,** 'Laid in line': tidied up (dialect); but cf. ll. 9–10 'laid in line with the infinite', which suggests 'adjusted to, aligned with'; for 'inviolable', cf. 'Odour of Chrysanthemums' in *The Prussian Officer*, ed. Worthen, p. 196. The two scenes are closely parallel.

233:11 **Abstraction,** (Cf. 'Absolute', 219:34); an eternal verity limited by no opposite or otherness, cf. 'Hardy' 87; hence both infinite and a condition of death. Representing the Old World before the Flood, Tom is now seen as an Absolute revelation of what 'Hardy' called the Law of God the Father. The Biblical story is turned inside out; the antediluvian world is not wicked, though in the Lawrentian dialectic it must give way to its antithesis if there is to be growth; Noah the Just perishes in the Flood; but when he is seen naked he is not disgraced but magnificent (see Genesis vi–ix).

235:27 **She** DHL wrote 'She/She wanted' in MS (pp. 365–6), and he mistakenly deleted 'wanted' as well as the duplicated word, but the typist restored the reading.

236:13 **kindergarten** Infant school or class run on the principles laid down by Friedrich Froebel in 1826, in which object lessons and games figure largely. In Nottinghamshire, Inspector Abel took a keen interest in the kindergarten movement, opening classes for infant-teachers in 1883, and organising a model kindergarten at Bluebell Hill. The contrast here is with Anna, going to a dame-school at the age of nine (92:3), about 1872.

236:18 **bobby-dazzlin'** Lively and brightly coloured (slang or dialect), cf. bob (*OED*) or bobbish. See also *Sons and Lovers*, chap. VI.

236:38 **made them you."** A dialect formation 'made them for you'; cf. 'buy it you' (237:28).

237:35 **flushed** The next sentence, omitted in TS (p. 380), shows the reason for 'flushed', so both are restored, removing the interference and DHL's weak remedy (cf. Textual apparatus).

240:14 **In my ... many mansions.'** John xiv. 2 ['... Father's ...'].

241:18 **the beginning and the end.'** Cf Revelation i. 8, xxi. 6, xxii. 13.

243:1 **Chapter X** TS (p. 389) begins another series of arbitrary pagination '357(?)', being the beginning of the third batch of TS DHL sent to Lady Ottoline before receiving back the previous batch – itself misnumbered '250–374'; cf. note on 160:4. (The typist on machine no. 2 had taken, in order to keep track, to sub-numbering pages at the top left as well, in chaps V, VII–IX). All this mis-numbering was only sorted out in Pinker's office, see *Letters*, ii. 349.

243:10 **the little church school just near the Marsh.** This may still be seen between Cossall Marsh and Ilkeston. By this time, *c.* 1894, primary education had become compulsory (from 1880 in Notts) and – fortunately for Will and Anna with six children already – had been free since 1891. A 'church school' was one run by the Anglican National Society for the Education of the Poor in the Principles of the Established Church, and was often referred to as a 'National' school as opposed to the 'British Schools' founded by the Non-conformist Voluntary Society, in one of which DHL was a pupil-teacher in Eastwood.

244:6 **Clem** DHL used the name of a boy who had been at Beauvale School with him.

244:31 **raking** Wandering about, roaming (dialect).

244:37 **was out of taste** Had lost the taste (for), rather than 'unable to distinguish flavours' (*OED*).

245:29 **the Grammar School in Nottingham.** Cf. note on 93:40. By now, about 1895/6, it was a much more academically established school than when Anna was there in its earliest days, and had moved up into a large lace-manufac-turer's house (250:24) on the hill near the Arboretum and the boys' High School.

245:35 **equals: but not by diminishing herself.** Cf. 'Hardy' 18.

246:29 **a Rubens picture ... called "Fecundity,"** The Flemish painter Peter Paul Rubens (1577–1640) does not seem to have painted a picture with this title, but babies swarm in his 'Sacrifice to Venus' in Stockholm; and there are other candidates in 'The Garden of Love' in the Prado, Madrid, or 'The Feast of Venus' in the Kunsthistorisches Museum, Vienna.

247:11 **Andersen and Grimm ... "Idylls of the King"** The collections of fairy tales by Hans Christian Andersen (1805–75) and the brothers Jacob Ludwig (1785–1863) and Wilhelm Karl Grimm (1786–1859) ... by Tennyson; the quotation is from 'Elaine' (1859) ll. 1–4 ['... the loveable ... Elaine, the lily ... up a tower ... Lancelot'].

247:19   **castell,**   The deliberately mediæval and 'romantic' spelling of MS (p. 384) is recovered from what is almost certainly a typesetter's 'correction'.

248:17   **Venetian lace.**   I.e. Venetian point, a particular pattern of hand-made lace.

249:30   **before**   At the top of MS p. 390 DHL has written in pencil: 'I dont know if this is duplicate or if I merely omitted it on the last sending'. He may have sent a 'cleaner' transcript since this page, unlike the surrounding ones, is quite heavily revised – an interesting example, if so, of the amount of revision that may lie behind even the apparently 'clean' pages of MS. The presence of 'Ella', even though in a line of revision, might suggest by unconscious influence that the episode had been in 'The Wedding Ring'.

250:13   **High School.**   See notes on 93:40, 245:29. It is known as the 'High' (i.e. advanced) School for Girls, and is of the 'grammar' type, modelled on the old foundations offering a classical education (see note on 16:31). When at 250:32 DHL alters 'High' to 'Grammar' in E1 it is to express a greater and classical elevation: all Grammar Schools are High, but not all High Schools are Grammar Schools.

250:17   **without spot or blemish,**   Cf. Numbers xix. 2, etc.

250:37   **another hill-slope,**   For this motif see pp. 9, 181, 343, 429, 454, 458.

251:7   **"J'ai donné ... petit frère."**   'I have given the bread to my little brother' (French).

251:10   **"Longman's First French Grammar," ... "Via Latina"**   Edited by T. H. Bertenshaw in the widely-used series of Educational Books, published by Longman, Green & Co ... (The Latin Way) by William C. Collar (1897). The 'little grey Algebra' is *Algebra Part I* in Blackie's Elementary Text Books. 'H.' Lawrence's copy is at UN.

254:6   **sluthered**   Slithered, slipped (dialect).

254:32   **"Il était ... petit patapon,"**   A well-known French folksong: 'There was a little shepherdess, / And purr purr purr, little pussy-paw' ('patapon', although invented for the rhyme, suggesting the cat and its paw which appear later in the song). Some versions are risqué, pointing up Theresa's comment.

255:1   **Christ passed between olive trees.**   As, originally, in the garden of Gethsemane on the mount of Olives, Mark xiv, Matthew xxvi, etc. Returning from a wedding in the hills behind Fiascherino in 1913, DHL exclaimed 'Perché non ritorna Christo fra questi ulivi' (Why does Christ not return among these olive trees'). This is recorded in the form of a free-verse poem beside the figure of DHL in a fresco in the Albergo delle Palme. See also *Letters,* ii. 122.

255:3   **Samuel, Samuel!"**   Cf. 1 Samuel iii. 3–10.

255:8   **Sin, the serpent ... Judas with the money and the kiss.**   Genesis iii. 1–22 ... Mark xiv. 10–11, 44–5, Matthew xxvi. 14–16, 47–9, xxvii. 3–5.

255:24   **democratic Christian.**   For the point made by the MS reading, cf. 'Hardy' 18; for the sharper antagonism to the Christian–democratic in revision, see *Letters,* ii. 364–8, 370–1, of July 1915.

255:27   evangelical teachings.   Strictly, those which insist on the total depravity of human nature, justification of the sinner by faith alone, the free offer of the gospel to all and the plenary inspiration and exclusive authority of the Bible. However DHL seems to have in mind rather more the distinction he was to make in 'Hymns in a Man's Life', of how the Congregational tradition 'avoided the personal emotionalism which one found among the Methodists when I was a boy', *Phoenix II: Uncollected, Unpublished and Other Prose Works by D. H. Lawrence*, ed. Warren Roberts and Harry T. Moore (1968), p. 600. The evangelical children's hymn 'there is a green hill far away' insists on the personal application of the Crucifixion: 'We may not know, we cannot tell / What pains He had to bear, / But we believe it was for us / He hung and suffered there'.

255:33   Stigmata ... finger into His wounds,   The marks of the wounds in Christ's hands, feet and side (Greek) ... cf. John xx. 27.

255:40   the revivalists   Cf. 'Hymns in a Man's Life', *Phoenix II*, ed. Roberts and Moore, p. 600: 'the Primitive Methodists, when I was a boy, were always having "revivals" and being "saved," and I always had a horror of being saved.'

256:7   the mother ... vulgar clamour.   MS (p. 401) is consistent about Anna's conformity with 'the vulgar' (see Textual apparatus); but the revision in TS (p. 409), however self-contradictory, is clearly DHL's and must stand.

256:14   throng   Busy (dialect).

256:19   fettling   Arranging, tidying up, providing (Wright, *English Dialect Dictionary*).

256:31   Calvary,   The place where Jesus was crucified.

257:6   Sons of God [256:38] ... men of renown."   Genesis vi. 2–4 ['... sons ... man ... flesh: ... sons ... children to them ...']; see also DHL on 1 February 1915 when he was working on the next chap. (*Letters*, ii. 273). See also 271:17.

257:11   the only begotten Son?   Words of the Nicene Creed: '... and in one Lord Jesus Christ, the only-begotten Son of God, Begotten of his Father before all worlds'.

257:23   comparison of myths   DHL saw comparative religion as a significant factor in the decline of religious sensibility; cf. 317:8–24.

257:25   Jove had become a bull ... a giant, a hero.   The offspring of Europa, to whom Zeus (Jove, Jupiter) came in the form of a bull, were Minos King of Crete, Rhadamanthys the Judge and Sarpedon King of Lycia, though none was gigantic. But Jove also came to Alcmene disguised as her husband, and fathered Heracles (Hercules).

258:2   "It is ... enter into heaven."   Matthew xix. 24 ['... into the kingdom of God'], cf. Luke xviii. 25.

258:25   unless he ... the poor,   Matthew xix. 16–22, Luke xviii. 18–23.

258:33   we'll forego that heaven,   Ursula echoes DHL's argument in 'Hardy' 17–19.

259:4   Raphael's "Dispute of the Sacrament" or Fra Angelico's "Last Judgment"   Raphael (1483–1520) painted the 'Dispute' (1509–11) for the Stanze della Segnatura in the Vatican. For Fra Angelico's painting, see note on

166:38. DHL discusses both painters in 'Hardy' 68–70; and writes of Fra Angelico's concept of the 'whole', in very similar terms, on 27 and 28 January and 3 February 1915 (*Letters*, ii. 263, 265–6, 275). (Like Ursula he rejects Pan, as insufficiently 'differentiated', *Letters*, ii. 275.)

259:5   **renderings of the Adoration of the Magi,**   The visit of the Wise Men to the infant Christ was too popular a subject to make identification confident, but (since DHL mentions Fra Lippo Lippi, 1406–69) he may have had in mind the famous Tondo, now in the National Gallery, Washington, which is thought to be partly also by Fra Angelico. There are two versions by Giotto (*c.* 1266–1377), one in the Arena Chapel, Padua, and the other in the Metropolitan Museum, New York. Other 'beautiful, complicated' renderings abound.

260:11   **The star was risen**   Cf. Matthew ii. 1–10.

260:18   **Peace of the World**   Luke ii. 13–14.

260:21   **bank holiday,**   I.e. a day on which banks are closed, a secular and commercial holiday.

260:33   **the Magis' transport,**   Cf. Matthew ii. 10–11.

261:1   **the great light,**   Cf. Isaiah ix. 2, 42 and Matthew xiv. 16.

261:4   **The veil of the temple ... the ghost,**   Cf. the account of the crucifixion Mark xv. 37–8, Matthew xxvii. 50–1, Luke xxiii. 45–6.

261:8   **the Comforter was given.**   I.e. the coming of the Holy Spirit, celebrated by the Church on the Feast of Pentecost seven weeks after Easter; see John xiv. 16–17, 26 and Acts ii. 1–42.

261:24   **the Ascension**   Luke xxiv. 51–3 and Acts i. 9–11.

261:34   **'Touch me not ... my father.'**   Cf. John xx. 17 ['... Father:'].

262:1   **thirty three;**   The traditional age of Christ when he was crucified. Luke states (iii. 23) that he began his ministry at thirty.

262:6   **when Mary says: Rabboni,**   I.e. 'Master' (John xx. 16).

262:9   **The Resurrection is to life, not to death.**   Cf. DHL's letters on 20 December 1914 and 31 January 1915 (*Letters*, ii. 248–50, 267–9). His late story *The Escaped Cock* (1929) is the final expression of his quarrel with orthodox Christianity, as he saw it, on this point.

262:17   **walk this earth in gladness,**   A phrase from a poem by Ernest Collings ['... the Earth ...'] (*Letters*, i. 472).

263:17   **climbing the tree ... like the Lord,**   For Zacchaeus, see Luke xix. 1–8; for Peter on the sea, Matthew xiv. 28–31; the feeding of the five thousand, Mark vi. 34–44, John vi. 5–14.

263:28   **walking upon ... the Lord,**   Mark vi. 48, Matthew xiv. 25; for Paul on the road to Damascus, Acts ix. 3–9.

264:26   **"Sell all ... the poor,"**   Conflated from Luke xviii. 22 and Matthew xix. 21; cf. 258:24–5.

265:3   **turn the other cheek.**   Matthew v. 39.

265:19 **What right have *I*** I.e. How would it be right for me.

265:38 **"Oh Jerusalem ... would not—"** Matthew xxiii. 37 ['O Jerusalem, Jerusalem, ... how ... together, even as ... not!'].

266:7 **He** E1's capitalisation is almost certainly DHL's, wishing to distinguish these spiritual persons from the 'week-day' ones of the previous paragraph. A house-styling typesetter would have capitalised throughout.

266:17 **the Son of Man,** The Lord's address to Ezekiel (ii. 1); adopted as a title by Christ, e.g. Matthew viii. 20, Mark ii. 10.

266:27 **lift up the lambs in his arms!** Cf. the good shepherd, Psalm xxiii, Luke xv. 4–5, John x. 11 and xxi. 15.

267:10 **"Come unto ... you rest."** Matthew xi. 28.

268:5 **a serpent or a captured bird.** These images from nature are also part of DHL's symbolism of the genesis of selfhood from the garden of 'God the Father'; cf. Will's panel (112:32ff.), Anna's reaction to the cathedral (189:10, 32) and Ursula in the tree (385:15–23).

269:32 **in the Engineers** See Introduction, p. xxxvii.

271:15 **the nature of an aristocrat.** Cf. DHL's conception of 'the aristocrat' in 'Hardy' 45–9, taken up again pp. 95–100 in relation to Tess and Alec d'Urberville.

271:19 **Adam been driven cringing** Genesis iii. 23–4.

271:26 **three angels stood in Abraham's doorway,** Genesis xviii. 1–2; cf. 20:12 and note.

272:20 **a bird blown ... latitude?"** This, if a quotation, has not been identified.

273:29 ***perpetuum mobile.*"** I.e. perpetual motion (Latin).

274:13 **the sappers.** Nickname for the Royal Engineers; cf. 439:27.

274:15 **"Wuthering Heights"** DHL thought Emily Bronte's novel (1847) 'a great book', *Phoenix: The Posthumous Papers of D. H. Lawrence*, ed. Edward D. McDonald (New York, 1936), p. 226. He would see Skrebensky as belonging to the 'social' world of Thrushcross Grange, so there may be irony here.

275:8 **the large church,** St Peter's, the only mediæval church in Derby, but heavily restored and partly rebuilt in 1898: the West Tower was rebuilt and the nave extended.

282:39 **this last *coup*.** Since this is 1899, it is indeed a coup. There were only three suppliers in Nottingham then, and only 125 motor-cars in the whole shire three years later. The car can clearly only be hired with a driver (284:12). But Nottingham, like Derby, was a pioneering city in the development of the automobile, and several had been locally manufactured before the Automobile Club's expedition to popularise the motor-car came to town in 1900. DHL's awareness of date is shown at 282:36, by the change from MS 'taxi-cab' (p. 449); it is too early for taxis in Nottingham though there was a De Dion motor-car for hire in 1903.

283:19 **the Hemlock Stone** In *Sons and Lovers*, chap. VII, Paul and his friends walk to the 'little, gnarled, twisted stump of rock, something like a decayed mushroom, standing out pathetically on the side of a field'; it is near Stapleford, Notts.

285:23 **Salisbury Plain.** A military training area.

286:1 **the cynical Bacchus in the picture.** Probably Caravaggio's, in the Uffizi in Florence.

286:7 **Salisbury Training College,** Possibly chosen because Sue Bridehead had studied there in Hardy's *Jude the Obscure*.

286:22 **slip** A garment worn under another, usually an underskirt but here, in masculine usage, a waistcoat (or vest in USA).

288:14 **it is serious enough, killing."** DHL saw the seriousness rather differently in 'Hardy' 15–17.

288:19 **settle the Mahdi ... Khartoum."** In his revision of TS (p. 460) in April/May 1915, DHL substituted this for a less 'topical' argument about the Zulu wars, over by 1887, twelve years before. The followers in the Sudan of the Mahdi, Abdullah Sejjid Mohammed, having overrun Khartoum and killed General Gordon, were defeated by Kitchener at the battle of Omdurman in 1898. This conversation takes place in Summer 1899; but Ursula's antagonism to imperialist doctrines of 'Lebensraum', and her lack of belief in 'the nation' would be particularly pointed in the context of the publication of the novel in late 1915.

288:31 **I should still be myself,"** Cf. DHL's insistence that the individual is more important than the state in 'Hardy' 38–9.

289:38 **'Appen** Happen, i.e. maybe (dialect).

290:2 **Loughborough.** On the river Soar in Leicestershire, a mile from Quorn to which the Burrows family removed from Cassall in 1908. Directly linked to the Nottingham Canal. See also note on 314:32.

295:27 **glaucous,** Sea-green, the underwater effect of interrupted lantern-light on grass.

297:23 **as a pillar of salt.** Cf. Lot's wife in Genesis xix. 26; turned into a pillar of salt because she looked back, hankering after a form of life turned destructive in the Cities of the Plain. The symbolism of this episode transforms into sterile and destructive terms the earlier imagery of flood, the pillars of fire and cloud, moonlit harvest and the fertile marriage of opposites. Fierce Diana/Moon and salt water have power altogether to dissolve darkness and the apparent 'strength' of iron.

298:10 **moon-conflagration** Ironically reminiscent of the Exile in Babylon (as opposed to the journey to the Promised Land) as at 181:39–40, where Anna was confident that Ursula could walk in the fiery furnace like the witnesses of the Lord.

298:40 **"Let me come—let me come."** Cut from A1 (p. 303), and subsequent editions.

299:12 **She had triumphed:** Cf. Anna dancing Will's non-existence (170:28) and Victrix (179:10).

301:31 **"And God [301:24] ... all things."** Genesis ix. 1–3 ['... fruitful, and multiply, ... fishes of the ...'].

302:9 **"And you [301:36] all flesh."** Genesis ix. 7, 12–15 ['fruitful, and multiply; ... said, This ... be for a token ... that the bow ...'].

302:20 **Noah and ... and Japheth,** Genesis vii. 10ff.

302:29 **What was** At this point in revising TS (pp. 478–9), Lawrence cut three pages and revised the transition (302:29–38). See Textual apparatus for the original MS, given first, and then the further revision in E1 of TSR.

302:29 **maggots in a dead dog** Cf. *Hamlet* II. ii. 181: 'For if the sun breed maggots in a dead dog, being a good kissing carrion ... let [your daughter] not walk i' th' sun'. Some editors emend to 'God kissing'. Hamlet is horror-struck by the source of light and life breeding corruption; Ursula thinks dismissively that if God is 'in' everything including maggots there is no need to worry about the just or the unjust, or commandments or covenants.

302:35 **"The very ... all numbered."** Matthew x. 30.

303:18 **war was declared ... in South Africa,** I.e. 11 October 1899. The war between Britain and the Boer republics of the Transvaal and Orange Free State ended in May 1902.

303:26 **ate them all herself,** Frieda remembered doing the same, when in love at fifteen, *Memoirs and Correspondence*, ed. Tedlock, p. 62.

304:15 **snowdrops** Cf. *The White Peacock*, ed. Andrew Robertson (Cambridge, 1983), pp. 128–30. Louie Burrows sent DHL snowdrops in 1909 (*Letters*, i. 121–2).

305:4 **always with a view to preserving it intact.** The full measure of DHL's disagreement with Skrebensky's view may be gauged from 'Hardy' chaps. I, II and IV, and from his letter on 12 February 1915, while he was busy on *The Rainbow* (*Letters*, ii. 282–6).

305:20 **the highest good of the greatest number** Cf. 'Hardy' 17–19, and see Textual apparatus (305:28) for an overt attack on the Benthamism of all shades of English opinion, and the consequent need for 'the frame of this society' to be 'smashed', which DHL cut from TS. The cut begins on TS p. 484; the next page of TS was removed; and the following page (p. 485) resumes with 'It was anguish' (305:39).

306:1 **one rook ... ill-omen.** Cf. *The White Peacock*, ed. Robertson, 81:21 and n.; also *Letters*, i. 253 and n. 2.

307:13 **like the angel before Balaam,** Numbers xxii. 22–35.

307:25 **crush hat** An opera hat made so that it can be collapsed flat.

308:39 **"If I were the moon,** Frieda recalled writing at fifteen in her diary: 'If I were the moon ... I know where I would shine', *Memoirs and Correspondence*, ed. Tedlock, p. 62.

309:11 **the constant bad news of the war.** In the first six months of the Boer war, the fighting went against the British on every front. Mafeking, Kimberley and Ladysmith were besieged, and in a single week the Boers defeated three British armies, most alarmingly Buller's at Colenso. Again, the phrase would be pointed in late 1915 by the constant bad news of that year.

309:25 **nerves.** On the back of this page, which ends chap. XI, are the addresses of Viola Meynell in ink, and of Miss K. Lee in pencil. For the possibility that Miss Lee may have been involved in the typing of TS, see Introduction, pp. liii–liv. The page also ends, at '466', the arbitrary numbering which began as '357' on TS p. 389, see note on 243:1. There was an interval in the typing here, since chap. XII begins with yet another arbitrary misnumbering, '500', and a change of paper, though not of typist. This meant that p. 490 had finally to be numbered '490–9', to avoid having to renumber to the end of TS.

310:2 **Shame** See Introduction, pp. l and n. 53, lv.

310:4 **her matriculation examination.** I.e. the matriculation examination of the University of London (see 335:18), which Nottingham High School girls were able to take at the end of their studies. This was an entrance-qualification to degree courses at Colleges of the University and at those, such as the new University College of Nottingham (founded 1881) which were in special relationship with it. Matriculation was also a qualification for employment as an uncertificated teacher in the state school system.

311:23 **farouche** Shy, sullen, repellent in manner (French, literally 'wild').

311:28 **stand-back** I.e. support, someone to stand back to back with.

312:32 **Newnham.** One of two pioneering Colleges for women at Cambridge, founded 1871. Constance Garnett (1861–1946), wife of Edward Garnett, went there in 1878.

313:23 **Diana.** The virgin hunter-goddess, rejecter of men, associated with the moon.

314:1 **If she ... small breasts!** Cut from A1 (p. 319), and subsequent editions.

314:10 **heaved against ... were separate.** Cut from A1 (p. 319), and subsequent editions.

314:32 **a lovely little bungalow on the Soar,** It seems likely that the episode at the waterside cottage may have some relation to an early experience of Katherine Mansfield, see Claire Tomalin, *Katherine Mansfield: A Secret Life* (1987), pp. 35–8. The Soar rises in s. Leicestershire and runs n.w. to join the Trent.

314:38 **Sawley,** The railway junction (between Nottingham and Derby) for Loughborough and Leicester.

315:24 **remove** Here begins the section of typescript which was typed from E1 (see Introduction, p. liv) and in which there is consequently no authority. The only variations noted in the Textual apparatus therefore, to 347:6, are between E1 and MS.

316:4   **Ursula lay still ... her mistress.**   Cut from A1 (p. 321), and subsequent editions.

317:14   **Buddhists a royal prince, the Egyptians their Osiris.**   Gautama (560–480 B.C.) or Sakya Mundi, who became the Buddha or Enlightened One, was the son of a ruler of the Sakyas in north India. Osiris, brother and husband of Isis, was worshipped by the Egyptians as the Sun God whose death and resurrection brought about the cycle of days and seasons. The new 'comparative religion' may be contrasted with Anna's rationalism.

317:31   **Moloch.**   A Semitic deity mentioned in the Bible as the God of the Ammonites, whose worship demanded acts of cruelty and human sacrifice. Milton in *Paradise Lost* shows him as the fiercest and most bloodthirsty of the fallen angels.

317:34   **neither Lamb nor Dove ... the lion and the eagle.**   Cf. John i. 29, 32; cf. also Anna's attitude to the Lamb ... the lion and the eagle are symbols of royalty in the animal and the bird kingdoms, and of the evangelists St Mark and St John. DHL developed the contrast between the churches of the Eagle and the Dove in 'The Spinner and the Monks' in *Twilight in Italy* (1916).

318:15   **the Women's Movement.**   A collective term for all those campaigning in the second half of the nineteenth century for women's rights, especially the right to vote. See below notes on 377:19 and 400:34, and DHL's discussion of the suffragists in 'Hardy' 14–15. Louie Burrows, and DHL's friends Alice Dax and Blanche Jennings, the last two keen socialists and suffragists (see *Letters*, i. 44 n. 3 and 43 n. 2), were all active in the Movement (see *Letters*, i. 2). He had made Clara Dawes a suffragist in *Sons and Lovers*, chap. x.

318:20   **embrace themselves.**   Cf. DHL on 12 February 1915, *Letters*, ii. 284–5.

318:26   **serpents trying to swallow themselves**   An ancient symbol of eternity, but for Winifred an image of solipsistic intellect. (DHL, too, would attack the idea of 'Him With His Tail in His Mouth' in *Reflections on the Death of a Porcupine and Other Essays*, ed. Michael Herbert, Cambridge, 1988, pp. 309–17.)

319:28   **a big new colliery in Yorkshire.**   Barber Walker & Co. sank their new colliery in Bentley, Yorkshire, 48 miles n. of Eastwood, 1906–8.

321:19   **unliving shell ... hard, horny**   See the letter on 12 February 1915 (*Letters*, ii. 285). The revision in proof (see Textual apparatus) also bears the impress of DHL's visit to Cambridge in early March 1915; his sense of 'a form of inward corruption' (ibid., ii. 320) gave him nightmares of beetles – living creatures enclosed in horny unliving shell and associated with squalor; see Introduction, pp. xxxix–xl. The whole Wiggiston episode is darkened in revision by a new sense of 'evil' and 'corruption'; see the letters of March and April *passim*, but especially those on 19 and 24 March, 8 and 19 April and above all the letter to David Garnett on 19 April (ibid., ii. 309–11, 314–15, 318–21).

321:28   **the great, mathematical colliery**   'Mathematical' because the product of abstraction, a kind of knowing wholly separate from the unified world of organic nature, which the colliery however acts on, imposing human will. In the

Wiggiston episode DHL diagnoses both atrophy of the impulse to natural organic unity, and consequent hypertrophy of the impulse to separation and abstraction.

322:24 alter themselves to fit the pits Cf. Thomas Carlyle in *Signs of the Times* (1829): 'not the external and physical alone is now managed by machinery, but the inner and spiritual also'.

322:34 Zolaesque tragedy. As in *Germinal* (1885), the novel in which Emile Zola (1840–1902) traced the disastrous effects of the coal mining industry on miners and their families, see *Letters*, iii. 38.

324:7 *vogue la galère.*" Let come what may (French, literally 'let the galley row where it will').

325:31 nauseating effect of a marsh, See the letter of 19 March 1915 (*Letters*, ii. 309).

326:25 his thick thighs—" Cut from A1 (p. 332), and subsequent editions.

327:6 mate. On the back of MS p. 523, the numbers '502–523' are noted twice, in pencil. This is not, though it is nearly, the MS section of 'Shame' – actually 505–23 – that corresponds to the lost TS, which, along with a section from 'The Man's World', was replaced by typing from E1. It may have indicated the section of 'Shame' which was causing anxiety, since the first of the passages to be bowdlerised by A1 occurs on MS p. 502; see note on 314:1, and also notes on 314:10, 316:4 and 326:25 (the last is on MS p. 522, the penultimate page of the chap.).

330:20 the Donatello manner. Donato di Niccolo di Betto Bardi, Florentine sculptor (1386–1466). His best-known female head in high relief is the gilded stone 'Annunciation' in Santa Croce, Florence. See also note on 391:28.

330:24 the Della Robbia A family of Florentine sculptors and modellers in ceramic and enamel, of whom the best known are Luca (1400–82) and his nephew Andrea (1435–1525). See also note on 391:28.

330:36 Benvenuto Cellini, Florentine sculptor, metalworker, jeweller (1500–71), whose *Autobiography* DHL had read by 1907.

334:18 patience of a Jack-gnat Either ('jack' as diminutive) the tiniest gnat-sized amount; or (combining the gnat's tormenting agility with jumping-jack) no patience at all.

334:20 board-school I.e. after the Education Act of 1870, a state school administered by a School Board.

335:5 "Schoolmistress," A weekly newspaper (1881–1935) costing one penny.

335:18 June 1900." It is possible that DHL, on second thoughts in proof, did not wish to be too specific, although he evidently took care over the chronology. It seems as likely, however, that the reading was uncertain because of DHL's tiny terminal 's' in 'Dates' and 'Examinations' (see Textual apparatus); and DHL may have mistaken a query beside the typesetter's 'Date', as a question mark against the inclusion of the date itself. It would seem odd that Ursula should answer half the question and not the other half, when DHL had a specific date in mind, so MS (p. 536) is restored.

335:36 **"Gillingham" was such a lovely name,** Ursula's imaginings are ironic, since Gillingham by Chatham (near where DHL's mother had been a pupil teacher while her father worked in the Naval Dockyard at Sheerness) was in the most rapidly industrialising part of Kent; and Kingston on Thames is part of Greater London. It includes Richmond Park, and Hampton Court Palace (hence the references to Henry VIII, Cardinal Wolsey and Queen Elizabeth), but it is not there that teachers are wanted, but at Wellingborough Green, not far from Croydon where DHL himself had taught, in less than glamorous surroundings. Conversely, the school by the church and the green at Swanwick, (about 10 miles n. of Cossall), would have been much more attractive, but too close to home to set the imagination working.

337:11 **"Sweet Thames ... my song—."** The refrain of 'Prothalamion' (1595) by Edmund Spenser ['... softly, till ...'].

340:32 **"C'est la ... lui rendra—"** French children's song: 'It's mother Michel who has lost her cat, and who cries from the window "Who'll give it back"'.

342:6 **the tram.** DHL's memory accurately reconstructs his own familiar tram journeys from the terminus in front of Ilkeston station to Bath Street, changing to another tram up the hill to the Pupil Teacher Centre in the Gladstone Street School; the Centre later moved to Wilmot Street, and then to the new Carnegie Library near Ilkeston Church. St Mary's School, Hallcroft Place, was a little beyond the churchyard. Ursula's journey is a little anachronistic in 1900, since the Ilkeston tram service did not begin until 1903, but DHL would have known this very well, so the licence is deliberate.

342:7 **Behind her** E1 'Before her' might be either a typesetter's error, or a revising author spoiling, for syntactical balance, an accuracy he has failed to remember. Since MS 'Behind' (p. 546) is accurate both in space and time, it has been restored.

342:26 **swinging round the pole.** Since they ran on rails, trams were constructed so that they could simply reverse direction, with controls at both ends, reversible seats and a sprung pole conducting power from an overhead line, which could be lowered, swung through 180 degrees and released upward into contact again.

343:23 **She saw** From this point MS (pp. 549–604 and 608–13) is the typescript of 'The Wedding Ring', fairly heavily revised, see Introduction, p. lii.

343:31 **a jelly-tray.** An early method of duplicating documents. The master copy was handwritten or typed on special paper with special ink or ribbon. This master-sheet was then pressed face down against a prepared moist gelatin surface (i.e. the 'jelly-tray'), and its mirror-image transferred to the gelatin. An ordinary sheet of paper, placed against this impregnated gelatin and rubbed evenly, received the original image.

344:22 **"Why aren't they?"** Ursula is about to discover that three huge classes, each of over fifty children, have to be taught in the same 'big room', divided merely by glass partitions through which the goings-on are clearly visible and audible. The coming of universal free education between 1870 and 1891 was followed by legislation steadily increasing the age up to which attendance was compulsory. It was 10 in 1880 provided pupils passed the Standard Five exam, failing which they had to stay till 13. Hence the particular difficulty of Ursula's class. The minimum became 12 by 1899 and 13, by bylaw, in Nottinghamshire. There were not enough schools to cope in 1900, so severe overcrowding was inevitable.

345:1 **stuff hat,** Made from a mixture of fur and wool (*OED*).

346:7 **a caution,** Something extraordinary or astonishing (slang), often said in a tone of wry amusement.

346:38 **dread,** MS originally read 'dread and dislike,' (p. 553), but DHL deleted 'and dislike'. E1 restored, either because (in the missing TS) the typist failed to notice the single deleting line, or because DHL remembered and put back what he had originally written. Since the MS crossing out is the only firm evidence, however, it has been followed.

351:7 **bull** E1's 'wheel' (p. 353) must be a typesetter's aberration, as the rest of the sentence confirms that TSR 'bull' (p. 565) is right.

351:34 **Greuze ... Reynolds's "Age of Innocence,"** Jean Baptiste Greuze (1725–1805), known for genre scenes and portraits, especially of children – cf. *The White Peacock*, ed. Robertson, 334:8 – or of girls such as 'Girl with Doves' in the Wallace Collection, London ... Sir Joshua Reynolds (1723–92), portrait painter, first President of the Royal Academy and author of the *Discourses*. His 'Age of Innocence' is in the National Gallery, and he is mentioned sympathetically in 'Hardy' 105–6.

354:5 **monthly roses** The Indian or China rose, erroneously thought to flower once a month.

357:11 **St Philips** The name appears only once in DHL's hand, as 'St Phillips' (p. 596) – but the standard form of the typescript of 'The Wedding Ring' has been followed, as probably DHL's majority usage, as well as a less idiosyncratic form of the saint's name, which might also suggest a sardonic and private derivation from DHL's headmaster at Croydon, Philip Smith.

362:12 **the gold** A mixture of sovereigns and half-sovereigns (since Ursula pays her mother fifty shillings). For their value, see the note on 'Pounds, shillings and pence', pp. 671–2.)

362:34 **"Board of Education" ... Whitehall** I.e. at County level ... the location, in London, of the central government Ministry of Education.

365:26 **seventeen** MS (p. 574) corrects 'eighteen' to 'seventeen,' – in Frieda's handwriting. Her hand can be seen quite often in this part of MS, which is a section of the duplicate typescript of 'The Wedding Ring', into which she was transcribing DHL's revisions. Since the other copy has disappeared, there is usually no way of checking Frieda's corrections, which are therefore normally accepted, although she is known to have been haphazard and inventive in a similar task for *Women in Love* (ed. Farmer, Vasey and Worthen, pp. xxxii, lix–lxi). In this case however, MS originally had no punctuation, and TS dropped the unnecessary comma, as this edition does. The alteration of the age is however correct (see Appendix IV and also note on 7:1) and is retained. For the rare instances of Frieda's hand in TS, see notes on 380:36 and 415:3.

367:8 Proud-arse."   *OED* does cite one instance of 'arce' dated 1400, but the spelling of MS (p. 575) is probably a mistake rather than deliberate archaism (cf. ''arce' in *A Collier's Friday Night*, 1934, written 1909, I. i.), unrecognised by the lady-typists of 'The Wedding Ring' and *The Rainbow*, and amusingly compounded by A1 which tried to make sense of it as 'proud-acre' (p. 73), followed by later editions.

367:39 All else she would forsake.   In this 'man's world' decision, an ironic echo of the Marriage Service, 'and forsaking all other, cleave only ...'.

372:18 she saw   MS p. 583 is torn, but this must have happened after TS was prepared.

376:11 So   In the original typescript of 'The Wedding Ring', this began Section 4 of its chap. 10 (MS p. 588). At the beginning of Section 5, DHL decided in MS (p. 596) to make a new chapter in *The Rainbow*, 'The Widening Circle'. Chap. 11 of 'The Wedding Ring', 'Ella tries her wings', began at 387:12 with 'She was wearing', (MS p. 601). Section 2 was replaced by the new autograph pages, because of DHL's change of mind about the new house in Beldover (see Introduction, p. lii). Section 3, returning to 'The Wedding Ring' typescript, began with Ursula leaving school at 391:38 (MS p. 608), and Section 4 with the day of the removal at 394:10 (MS p. 611).

377:19 a great suffragette, trusting in the vote.   DHL's own view was nearer to Ursula's, see 'Hardy' 14–15. Maggie, Winifred and Dorothy Russell (cf. 400:34) are all committed to the Suffragist movement which had begun with a petition to the House of Commons in 1866, demanding that enfranchisement should be irrespective of gender.

378:7 a bicycle,   This is historically apt for the 'craze' which developed after the invention of the 'safety-bicycle', and because Nottingham had become the major centre of cycle-manufacture. For women particularly, the advent of this new freedom was a 'widening circle'.

379:28 some work about "Woman and Labour."   There were several, such as the Women's Co-Operative Guild's *Why Working Women Need the Vote* (1897), or Josephine Butler's *Women's Work and Women's Culture* (1869). But the combination of indefiniteness with quotation marks is probably because DHL had specifically in mind Olive Schreiner's *Woman and Labour*, but knew it was not published until 1911. He sent it to Louie Burrows in July that year, see *Letters*, i. 287–9.

380:7 "She shall ... mountain springs."   From 'Three years she grew in sun and shower' (1799) by William Wordsworth ['... the fawn ...'].

380:36 it was all a barren nothing.   'The Wedding Ring' had originally read (MS p. 594): 'what dry, barren stupidity in contrast with the corncrake in the summer grass, and the moon that shed down' – on which Frieda commented in the margin 'commonplace this!!' (and presumably too reminiscent of *Sons and Lovers*).

381:29 **to classes in Ilkeston,** I.e. to the Pupil Teacher Centre, which DHL attended for two and Louie Burrows for three years from 1903.

382:11 **He had denied her.** This is hardly true of Skrebensky (though see 306:16); and may therefore be a relic of the affair with 'Ben Templeman' which Garnett had criticised in 'The Sisters II'; cf. *Letters*, ii. 142, and see the end of Appendix II; or the relationship with 'Charles' Skrebensky (see MS p. 596), which replaced it in 'The Wedding Ring'.

382:34 **enclosure.** DHL in MS (p. 596) seems to have written 'enclosure' over 'enclosuress' but not to have deleted 'ess' (see Textual apparatus); he had originally written 'insecurity'.

383:4 **Belcote Hall.** Probably modelled on Annesley Hall and its old walled kitchen gardens – cf. *The White Peacock*, ed. Robertson, pp. 147–8 – though there DHL imagined the Hall (now ruined) still in use.

383:22 **the eyes of a satyr** The description of Anthony is close to that of 'Il Duro' in *Twilight in Italy*. It is not certain whether there was an earlier version of that essay, as well as those published as 'Italian Sketches' in 1913 in the *English Review* (and rewritten for *Twilight in Italy*).

385:16 **Coleridge's "Christabel."** The unfinished narrative poem (1797–1800) about the spell cast on Christabel by the demonic Geraldine, by Samuel Taylor Coleridge. See also E.T., *D. H. Lawrence: A Personal Record*, pp. 114–15, for the memory on which DHL was drawing in this scene.

385:23 **"You're like a bird in there!"** This scene is a marker for the 'development' of the third generation beyond the second, cf. Will's panel of the Creation and Anna's objections to it. See also note on 268:5.

386:23 **an infant crying in the night.** From Tennyson's *In Memoriam* (1850), lv.

386:29 **He did not see ... infinitely.** Another exact measure of the distance between the 'new woman' and the Brangwen Men of the Beginning; and of the relation between self-consciousness and separation from the natural world. It is not simply an advance ('He was the cleaner', l. 24).

388:14 **Art and Handwork Instructor for the County of Nottingham.** Alfred Burrows was appointed to such a post for the County of Leicestershire. Will, imprisoned in the lace factory and largely self-educated, has nevertheless, through his passion for early Italian art, Gothic architecture and Arts and Crafts, aligned himself with some of the major currents of the age, as represented by Ruskin, the pre-Raphaelites and William Morris; and through his involvement with evening classes and summer schools has become a pioneer in the new movement of adult education. As he rides into Beldover on his motor-cycle (see note on 394:31) he has moved from the margin into the mainstream of the times.

390:9 **other being.** This concludes MS p. 604, on the back of which, in pencil, is a note '548–604'. These are the new page numbers of the 'Wedding Ring' typescript (originally 219–75) – now to be interrupted by three autograph pages before recommencing as MS pp. 608–13 (originally 279–84), ending chap. XIV of *The Rainbow*.

390:25 **near Willey Green,** Moorgreen, near Eastwood (Beldover). The house in Beldover is modelled on that of William Edward ('Willie') Hopkin (1862–1951), long-time friend of DHL (see *Letters*, i, 176 n. 2), in Devonshire Drive 'near the large church' (391:1–2), though the removal draws on the move of the Burrows family from Cossall to Quorn. A cancelled passage in MS p. 608 (p. 279 in 'The Wedding Ring') suggests that the earlier version did place the Brangwens in a country village rather than in town, and Ursula still hankers after living 'in' rather than 'near' Willey Green.

391:20 **chesterfield** The widow's furniture is also up-to-date. The first reference in *OED* to this large and tightly-stuffed kind of sofa is from 1900.

391:24 **And as** This concludes TS p. 631, on the back of which is written '*Rainbow*' in DHL's hand. This may represent the end of the TS sent to Lady Ottoline, see Introduction, p. xlii.

391:28 **their Della Robbia, beautiful Madonna ... reliefs from Donatello,** Perhaps after the 'Madonna of the Cushion' by Andrea Della Robbia in the Bargello Museum, Florence ... After the 'Annunciation', perhaps the best known reliefs are 'St George freeing the Princess' in the church of Orsanmichele, Florence, and the 'Banquet of Herod' in the baptistery, Siena. See also notes on 330:20, 24.

391:29 **the Primavera and the Aphrodite and the Nativity** By Sandro Botticelli (1444–1510), the Florentine painter. 'La Primavera' and 'The Birth of Venus' (Aphrodite) are in the Uffizi Gallery, Florence; and the 'Mystic Nativity', one of DHL's favourite pictures, is in the National Gallery, London. All three are discussed in 'Hardy' 66–9.

392:23 **fought a good fight** Reminiscent of 'Fight the good fight with all thy might', which DHL mentions in 'Hymns in a Man's Life', *Phoenix II*, ed. Roberts and Moore, p. 600.

393:6 **Swinburne's ... Meredith's.** DHL discussed both with Louie Burrows (*Letters*, i. 241–2) but had begun to be disappointed in Meredith's poetry by 1914, see *Letters*, ii. 180; and is critical of Swinburne's one-sidedness in 'Hardy' 91. He may have meant the choice to be one of romantic youth.

394:31 **motor bicycle.** Will is very up-to-date for 1902; there were only 40 registered in Nottinghamshire in 1903, but several of those were locally manufactured. Campion were in production from 1901.

395:8 **The whole family** See Appendix IV for their names and ages.

396:3 **they ... wanted ... home, with** MS (p. 613) is torn (see Textual apparatus), but this is likely to have been after the typing, and the readings are clear.

397:2 **The Bitterness of Ecstasy** The decision to make a new chap. xv was made after the typing. The new chapter number and title are inserted in purple pencil, in Viola Meynell's hand, at the top of TS p. 640.

398:2 **some Latin and some Botany ... university course.** DHL himself did not enter the three-year university degree course, but did the two-year Teacher's Certificate, offering French and Botany as special options.

398:16   **the Art School in Nottingham.**   In contrast with her father, and his, though the Municipal School of Art and Design had been founded in 1843.

398:19   **Students' Exhibition in the Castle,**   Mounted every two years by the Art School. DHL describes a visit with Louie Burrows in *Letters*, i. 365–6.

398:29   **Chemist's … chemists',**   The typist ruined (TS p. 642) the carefully placed apostrophes, corresponding to the carefully observed social hierarchy in the small town, where one Chemist is the 'leading' one.

398:38   **The big college built of stone,**   The University College of Nottingham, founded 1881, was originally housed in a Victorian 'gothic' building in Shakespeare Street, not far from the Victoria Station.

400:10   **moved and lived and had its being.**   Cf. Actx xvii. 28: 'for in him we live, and move, and have our being'.

400:10   **Racine**   Jean Racine (1639–99), French dramatist, who is discussed by Clifford and Constance Chatterley in chap. x of *Lady Chatterley's Lover* (1928).

400:13   **Livy and Horace.**   Titus Livius (59 B.C.–17 A.D.), Roman historian, and Quintus Horatius Flaccus (65–8 B.C.), poet and satirist, wrote in the reign of the Emperor Augustus. The slight preference for Livy is presumably because, as admirer of the Republic, he is nearer the old stern 'Roman Spirit'.

400:34   **Women's Social and Political Union.**   Founded in October 1903 by Emmeline Pankhurst (thus by a year or two anachronistic here), and the most militant wing of the Women's Suffrage movement.

400:38   **Cassandra.**   Daughter of King Priam of Troy; she foretold its fate. Apollo loved her and endowed her with prophecy, but because she refused him, ensured that nobody would believe her. DHL discusses her in 'Hardy' 109.

401:29   **the handicraft holiday school**   The Rev. J. B. Paton, President of the Congregational Institute in Nottingham, founded the National Home Reading Union in 1889, which merged in 1897 with the Co-Operative Holidays Association, and held 'summer assemblies' in seaside resorts and the Lake district. The Burrows family holidayed in Scarborough in 1908, just after the move to Quorn.

401:36   **"There are … yet risen."**   From the Indian *Rigveda*, almost certainly via the citation on the title-page of Nietzsche's *Morgenröte (The Dawn)*: 'Es gibt so viele Morgenröten, die noch nicht geleuchtet haben'. See too *Letters*, ii. 315, 317.

402:7   **the sea was rough.**   For the source of this episode in memory, see *Lawrence in Love*, ed. James T. Boulton (Nottingham, 1968), pp. xiii–xiv.

402:39   **the glamour began to depart from college.**   As happened to DHL, see his letters of 4 May and 1 September 1908 (*Letters*, i. 49 and 72).

404:11   **the one study that lived**   According to Jessie Chambers DHL's nearest approach to a personal relationship was with 'a lecturer popularly known as "Botany" Smith' (*D. H. Lawrence: A Personal Record*, p. 76), and see also *Letters*, i. 146 n. 7.

404:37 **the shining doorway ... dirty and active and dead.** Ursula's experiences, seeming to lead always from promised land to wasteland, invert the Biblical sequences from the world destroyed by Flood to the Covenant of the rainbow, and from the Exile in Egypt to the Exodus guided by pillars of fire and cloud.

405:13 **In every phase ... always Ursula Brangwen.** Cf. 'You mustn't look in my novel for the old stable ego of the character. There is another ego, according to whose action the individual is unrecognisable, and passes through, as it were, allotropic states which it needs a deeper sense than any we've been used to exercise, to discover are states of the same radically-unchanged element ...' (*Letters*, ii. 183).

405:25 **the eyes of wild beasts,** When the Lawrences stayed with the Waterfields in their 'castle' near Fiascherino in 1913, DHL 'described his first impression when he walked in the roof-garden one evening and looked at the mountains. It seemed to him as though wild beasts were circling round a fire and he was filled with a feeling of apprehension' (*Letters*, ii. 122).

405:30 **area under an arc-lamp,** Cf. *Sons and Lovers*, chap. IV.

408:9 **special stuff** In TSR p. 660 it is simply cambium, 'a viscid substance, consisting of cellular tissue, lying immediately under the bark of exogens, in which the annual growth of the wood and the bark takes place' (*OED*). Appropriately for the timing here, it is inactive in winter but very active in spring.

408:13 **Dr. Frankstone,** The name may be an ironic reminiscence of the scientific presumption of Frankenstein in Mary Shelley's novel (1818).

408:39 **Suddenly in her mind** At this point (TS pp. 659–60), DHL began a major revision, excising a long passage about the evolution of the soul, which is seen as 'one continuous stream' stretching back into pre-humanity (so that man is still tiger, and ape) but also with its tip touching paradise, so that all potentialities are co-present; see Textual apparatus.

414:20 **nucleolating** A Lawrentian nonce-formation from 'nucleolated' given by *OED* as 'furnished with a nucleolus, a minute rounded body within the nucleus of a cell'. It seems to mean 'proliferating as the centres of nuclei do'.

414:20 **fecund darkness.** Lady Ottoline complained in her *Memoirs* of 'the habit which he then first began of repeating the same word about ten times in a paragraph. ... there were also passages of such intensity and such passionate beauty that they never leave one's memory' (Robert Gathorne-Hardy, ed., *Ottoline: The Early Memoirs of Lady Ottoline Morrell*, 1963, p. 283); see also Introduction, p. xlii.

415:3 **nothing."** To this, on TS p. 669, 'just' is added in Frieda's handwriting before the second 'nothing'. Since she has clearly not been transcribing DHL revisions into *The Rainbow* TS, as she had done with 'The Wedding Ring', this change may well be her own idea. As MS is demonstrably DHL, it is preferred. The possibility then also arises that the deletion at 415:1 may be hers too; but since in that case the further revision in proof (see Textual apparatus) may represent an endorsement of the change of emphasis by DHL, which he might have made in any case, the E1 reading is accepted there.

415:12   **the Invisible Man,**   In the novel of that title (1897) by H. G. Wells (1866–1946).

418:25   **leapt together.**   Cf. 'the act, called the sexual act ... is for leaping off into the unknown, as from a cliff's edge' ('Hardy' 53).

420:1   *museau,*   Muzzle (French) – hence face.

421:4   **undressed,**   Cut by A1 (p. 429), and subsequent editions.

421:9   **"Gewiss, Herr ... Frau Baronin."**   'Certainly, Baron – don't mention it, Baroness' (German).

421:11   **Westminster Cathedral**   I.e. the brand-new cathedral (1895–1903) in the Byzantine style, of the Roman Catholic Church, near Victoria Station, and hence a new landmark viewed from Piccadilly across Green Park (422:20–1); as opposed to Westminster Abbey, the thirteenth-century collegiate church of St Peter.

422:2   **But the [421:21] ... always laughing.**   Cut from A1 (p. 429), and subsequent editions.

423:15   **the City Road ... ashen sterility**   The imagery, which may have influenced T. S. Eliot's *The Waste Land* (1922) and F. Scott Fitzgerald's *The Great Gatsby* (New York, 1925), is of a City of the Plain which has altogether severed itself from the force called 'God the Father' in 'Hardy', and primary to the Brangwen Men in the opening pages of *The Rainbow*. See Genesis xix. 24. The irony is that Skrebensky, having become a Man of the City, now only knows that impulse through his relation with Ursula, and sees her attraction to the 'stability' of Rouen Cathedral and the orchard near Oxford as a turning away from him.

427:14   **aristocracy of birth than of money.**   Cf. DHL's argument in 'Hardy' chaps. iv and v, about the money-appetite, and the true aristocrat who instead of conforming to society 'must act in his own particular way to fulfil his own individual nature' (p. 49). Compare also the attack on democracy in the letters to Bertrand Russell in July 1915 (*Letters*, ii. 364–5), after DHL had submitted the novel to Methuen.

428:11   **the flag that he kept flying.**   Contrast 'Hardy' 18–19.

428:32   **"Don't I satisfy ... having me—"**   Cut from A1 (p. 436), and subsequent editions.

429:12   **Whitsuntide**   The Festival of the coming of the Holy Ghost at Pentecost. The timing is ironic, given DHL's concept of the Comforter and Reconciler ('Hardy' 125–8).

429:16   **low cottage at the foot of the downs.**   The cottage and downs landscape are based on Viola Meynell's cottage near Greatham, Sussex (in which *The Rainbow* was completed), and the walk over 'the camel's hump' nearby.

429:29   **the train running bravely,**   See DHL's letter of 11 February 1915 (*Letters*, ii. 282).

432:9   **must go to London.**   Like most university colleges, Nottingham prepared its students for the External degrees of the University of London until the grant of its own charter in 1948.

433:31   **taxi-cab**   London's taxis were first licensed in 1903 and were still rare before 1906. There is a powerful contrast, within and without, to the 'romance' of the car journey in 1899.

442:40   **She let** [442:13] ... **to her.**   Cut from A1 (p. 450), and subsequent editions.

443:33   **furnace door,**   Cf. Daniel iii. 23–8 and the ironic reminiscence of Anna's hopes, 181:39–40.

444:6   **She gave ... heaving water.**   Cut from A1 (p. 451), and subsequent editions.

444:13   **a harpy**   In Greek mythology, a horrible winged predatory monster, like those which preyed on Aeneas, or Phineus until rescued by the Argonauts.

450:23   **butt house**   The house on the corner, at the end of the row.

450:31   **Willey Water**   I.e. Moorgreen Reservoir, scene of the Water-Party in *Women in Love.*

451:5   **She felt like a bird ... the board.**   E. L. Nicholes in 'The simile of the Sparrow', *The Achievement of D. H. Lawrence*, ed. Frederick J. Hoffman and Harry T. Moore (Norman, Oklahoma, 1953), pp. 159–62, points to the ultimate source of this in Bede's account of the conversion of Edwin (*History of the English Church*, Harmondsworth, 1955, p. 125). See also Wordsworth, *Ecclesiastical Sonnets* (1822), xvi.

451:14   **solitary thing,**   Perhaps an unconscious reminiscence of Oliver Goldsmith's *Deserted Village*, l. 129.

452:4   **they must fuse and she must die.**   Contrast her grandfather 90:25–7 and compare Skrebensky, 443:36–8. The marriage of opposites has come in the third generation to seem destructive of the self; the elemental water and fire seem, in exile, annihilating rather than guides through the wilderness to a promised land. The imagery is also related to that of the phoenix.

454:12   **unconscious upon the bed of the stream,**   I.e. the 'Flood' in the Ursula story.

454:38   **Why must one climb up the hill?**   Cf. the opening paragraph, and the Brangwen Women, p. 9, and see also note on 250:37.

456:21   **acorns in February**   The MS of *The Rainbow* was completed on 2 March 1915.

456:27   **a new knowledge ... of Time.**   Cf. this proof revision with the letter of 20 June 1915 (*Letters*, ii. 358–9).

457:20   **inscrutable trees ... like smoke.**   Cf. Genesis. ii. 6: 'there went up a mist from the earth'.

458:11   **all in prison,**   Cf. the letter of 31 July 1915 (*Letters*, ii. 373–4).

458:27   **sick with a nausea**   Cf. the letter of 3 August 1915 (*Letters*, ii. 375.)

458:39   **the rainbow stood on the earth.**   Cf. Genesis ix. 11–17. This paragraph was considerably revised in proof, see Textual apparatus. Emile Delavenay prints another revision written by DHL into his sister Ada's copy: 'She knew that the fight was to the good. It was not to annihilation but at last to newness. She knew in the rainbow that the fight was to the good' (*D. H. Lawrence: The Man and His Work*, 1972, p. 381).

Fragment of 'The Sisters'

463:2 **her.** I.e. Mrs Crich, Gerald's mother.

463:12 **Gerald** Gerald Crich, Gudrun Brangwen and other characters in Appendixes I and II also appear in *Women in Love* where the Gerald–Gudrun–Loerke confrontation takes place in Austria and ends with Gerald's death (*Women in Love*, ed. Farmer, Vasey and Worthen, pp. 467–74). In a deleted ending dating from 1916, Gudrun is bringing up Gerald's son (p. xxxi). See also *Women in Love* Explanatory notes on 7:3, 12:38, 26:10 and 405:21.

465:8 **Ecco!** Behold! (Italian).

468:40 **eye for an eye:** Cf. Exodus xxi. 23–4.

470:39 **[?, murmuring,]** The manuscript (p. 296) is badly damaged at this point: the comma is likely, and 'murmuring' probable.

Fragment of 'The Sisters II'

473:14 **Scarborough, as was usual.** North Yorkshire seaside town and resort; the Burrows family holidayed there (see note on 401:29).

473:26 **Le Rouge et le Noir,** Novel (1831) by Stendhal (Henri Beyle) (1783–1842); DHL read it in 1911 (see *Letters*, i. 251, 255 and 262–3).

474:2 **"Ich weiss ... es bedeuten."** 'Lorelei' (1827) by Heinrich Heine (1797–1856), l. 1 ['. . . nicht, was . . .'] ('I do not know what it should mean'). There are musical settings by Schumann and Liszt as well as a folksong version.

477:30 **Wamsley Mill?"** DHL's recreation of Felley Mill, 2 miles n.e. of Eastwood; cf. 'Ramsley Mill' in 'A Prelude', *Love Among the Haystacks*, ed. Worthen, 8:27.

477:33 **Prune,** Early twentieth-century upper or upper-middle class slang: a slightly disparaging, affectionate endearment for either sex.

479:26 **Filey ... Filey Brigg ... Flamborough Head,** Yorkshire holiday resort, 7 miles s.e. of Scarborough ... n. boundary of Filey bay, a ridge of rocks extending nearly ½ mile into the sea ... headland at Flamborough, 10 miles s.e. of Filey. DHL (with his mother and friends) holidayed at Flamborough in 1908, and met members of the Burrows family at Filey on 13 August (see *Letters*, i. 70).

TEXTUAL APPARATUS

TEXTUAL APPARATUS

The following symbols are used to distinguish states of the text:

MS = Autograph manuscript
TS = Typescript
E1 = First English edition

Whenever the *MS* reading is adopted, it appears within the square bracket with no symbol. Other variants appear in chronological order as given above. In the absence of information to the contrary, the reader should assume that a variant recurs in subsequent states.

When a reading from a source other than *MS* has been preferred or coincides with the adopted reading, it appears with its source-symbol within the square bracket; the *MS* reading follows the bracket along with further variants from later states.

Entries for 315:29 to 347:5 record only *MS* and *E1* because this section of *TS* was typed from *E1*; see Introduction, p. liv and Explanatory note to 315:24. See also notes to 210:22, 376:11 and 390:9 and Introduction, pp. xxxviii–xxxix and lii for other peculiarities in *MS* and *TS*.

The following symbols are used editorially:

Ed. = Editor
Om. = Omitted
~ = Substitution for a word in recording a punctuation or capitalisation error
/ = Line or page break resulting in punctuation error
P = New paragraph
R = Autograph corrections by DHL to a state of the text, i.e. *TSR*
C = Autograph corrections by someone other than DHL, i.e. *TSC*
{ } = Partial variant reading

In order to reduce the difficulty of tracing DHL's revisions, some passages rejected in *TS* or *E1* (e.g. 22:18) are printed with variants internally recorded inside braces and, for an entry of more than 300 words, in a column extending to the left-hand margin. When variants occur in revisions which replace these passages, they are indicated by the note '*see also following entries to...*'.

7:1	TO ELSE *E1*] *Om. MS*	9:19	laughter, *TSR*] laughter, that shook its lights easily *MS*
9:5	alder trees *TSR*] willow stumps *MS* willowy stumps *TS*	9:19	hard,] ~ *TS*
9:11	something standing *TSR*] that which stood *MS*	9:30	not waste *TSR*] unwilling to waste even *MS*
9:18	plainly *E1*] with complete openness *MS*	9:31	it would ... the cattle. *TSR*] the cattle would be glad of it. *MS*

9:31 was *TSR*] were *MS see notes*
9:33 rush *E1*] ponderous rush *MS*
9:33 they knew the wave *E1*] the ebb and flow gave them being; they knew the massive wave of blood, *MS* they knew the massive wave of the purpose *TSR*
9:34 and] ~, *TSC see notes*
10:3 daytime, *TSR*] roots, the *MS*
10:5 such; *TSR*] ~: *MS*
10:7 after *E1*] after labour of *MS*
10:10 lustre *TSR*] silk *MS*
10:11 milk and pulse against *E1*] down their milk and their blood through *MS* milk and blood against *TSR*
10:12 men, the ... the hands *TSR*] men, into the blood and being *MS*
10:22 the men *TSR*] they *MS*
10:27 whilst] while the *TS*
10:30 mind *TSR*] mouth *MS*
10:30 giving utterance *TSR*] obtaining obedience *MS*
10:31 sound *TSR*] sound of voices *MS*
10:35 freshly *TSR*] freely *MS*
10:35 enough *TSR*] enough for the men *MS*
10:38 know in *TSR*] take into *MS*
10:39 blood, earth *E1*] blood from earth *MS* blood earth *TSR*
10:40 exchange and ... with these *TSR*] was the exchange and the interchange with them *MS*
11:1 surcharged, their ... turn round. *TSR*] satisfied, without knowing. *MS*
11:5 faced out from the *TSR*] stood midway between *MS*
11:6 fields, looked out to the road *TSR*] fields on the one hand, *MS*
11:7 and the world ... the far-off *TSR*] on the other. She stood facing out towards the *MS*
11:8 scope *TSR*] mind *MS*

11:9 secrets were ... desires fulfilled *TSR*] knowledge abounded and gave power *MS*
11:10 men moved dominant ... beyond, to ... and freedom *E1*] man moved in liberty, having overcome all the immediate claims and restraints of bodily life, in order to enjoy the pride of understanding and the satisfaction of the spirit *MS* men moved dominant ... beyond, set out to ... freedom *TSR*
11:17 activity *TSR*] vivid activity *MS*
11:19 had done ... to knowledge *TSR*] would do when he revealed himself in liberty *MS*
11:20 conquest *TSR*] clarity *MS*
11:21 battle that ... the unknown *TSR*] lips that uttered and the eyes that knew *MS*
11:22 of the fighting host *TSR*] supreme *MS*
11:26 moved in worlds *TSR*] had being *MS*
11:29 outwardness and range *TSR*] vividness *MS*
11:31 range of being *TSR*] concentrated force *MS*
11:32 dull and ... over her husband *TSR*] secondary and of lesser intensity, like a larger, ruddy flame beside a white light. The power was the vicar's, though Brangwen was twice the man in bulk *MS*
11:36 beast? She ... [12:4] of knowledge. *TSR*] earth? What was it that a man might raise out of his fellows as the labourer raises harvest out of the ground? How was it the vicar could stride over the common men as a labourer strides over the earth? She did not know. Yet she knew it was so. And she knew it was a question neither of money nor of physical

strength. Neither her husband's comfortable means nor his strong limbs, nor even his health and vigorous humour availed him here. There was a potency beyond him. *MS*

12:5 and not ... rank with *TSR*] but he was one of *MS*

12:12 education and experience, she decided *TSR*] some higher degree of life *MS*

12:14 education *TSR*] refinement *MS*

12:17 take place ... living, vital people ... land *E1*] flower on a leading twig *MS* take place ... living, primary people ... land *TSR*

12:19 laborers *TSR*] foliage *MS* labourers *E1*

12:27 common *TSR*] many *MS*

12:31 her life was the epic *TSR*] the epic and the lyric *MS*

12:32 in *TSR*] *Om. MS*

12:35 Odyssey enacting ... endless web *TSR*] Iliad, Agamemnon and Paris before them, and Achilles and Cassandra *MS*

12:38 fulfilment *TSR*] aspiration *MS*

12:39 Brangwen wife at *TSR*] women of *MS* Brangwen wife of *E1*

12:39 aspired beyond ... further life *TSR*] lived beyond themselves, towards the completeness *MS*

13:1 extended being ... [13:5] same thing. *TSR*] light she held up to them, of fine clear individuality that shaped their fates. Luckily Mrs {Mrs. *TS*} Hardy knew by instinct her own significance, and bore herself as became her responsibility. *MS*

13:7 strange movements ... great extent *TSR*] swift movements that should lay bare the very quick of life *MS*

13:10 wonderful *TSR*] watchful *MS*

13:10 comprehension *TSR*] penetration *MS*

13:11 be much fonder ... [13:18] their motion. *TSR*] like better Mr {Mr. *TS*} Hardy, the squire, who was warm and full of sensous {sensuous *TS*} life like their own men, yet was a gentleman as undeniable as Lord William. They felt more at home with him than with his lady or with the lean aristocrat, her friend. But they knew the squire in their own men, it was not in him the unknown quality, the quickening they looked for. *MS*

13:21 newly opened] newly-opened *TS*

13:22 travelled *TSR*] rose *MS*

13:25 Ilkeston *TSR*] the Ilkeston side *MS*

13:26 a *TSR*] the *MS*

13:30 Railway *E1*] railway *MS*

13:37 stiff alders *TSR*] willow stumps *MS*

14:7 bare *TSR*] bare and exposed *MS*

14:8 at *TSR*] in *MS*

14:10 farm-buildings *Ed.*] farm buildings *MS*

14:11 confusion of *TSR*] wilderness of jumbled *MS*

14:14 stray,] ~ *TS*

14:14 grass *TSR*] wild grass *MS*

14:15 canal *TSR*] great canal *MS*

14:18 astonished *E1*] astounded *MS*

14:20 raw *TSR*] great raw *MS*

14:23 a *TSR*] almost a *MS*

14:33 dark woman, quaint *TSR*] rather quaint woman, curiously direct *MS*

14:34 whimsical *TS*] yet rather whimsical *MS see notes*

14:34 sharp *TSR*] biting *MS*

14:35 did not hurt *E1*] only made people laugh *MS* never hurt *TSR*

14:35 oddly *TSR*] curiously *MS*

14:36 intrinsically separate and

14:39 her,] ~ *TS*
14:39 wonder and ... towards her *TSR*] laugh and feel warm *MS*
15:1 with a balanced ... she said *TSR*] in a tone of voice as if she liked him better with his shortcomings than if he had been without them *MS*
15:5 had *TSR*] had always *MS*
15:5 humorous *E1*] humourous *MS*
15:7 lord of ... calmly did *TSR*] good-natured, healthy firstling. He did just *MS*
15:8 natural *TSR*] healthy *MS*
15:9 frightened and broke her *TSR*] shook her to the depths of her nature *MS*
15:10 which seemed ... and which *TSR*] that *MS*
15:12 very separate beings, vitally connected *TSR*] curiously separate beings, curiously attached *MS*
15:13 root. *TSR*] root. He, in his goodnatured {good-natured *TS*} maleness, was just a little too blind and selfish. *MS*
15:19 yearning *TSR*] bitter *MS*
16:2 inscrutable *TSR*] intent *MS*
16:10 As a child *E1*] From the first *MS*
16:17 readily *TSR*] shallowly *MS*
16:23 public-house *Ed.*] public house *MS*
16:24 a noisy *TSR*] an empty *MS*
16:25 elder, *TS*] ~ *MS*
16:30 favorite *Ed.*] favourite *MS*
16:30 determination *TSR*] a strong effort *MS*
16:31 Grammar School *Ed.*] grammar-school *MS*
16:34 tightly covered] tightly-covered *TS*
16:34 now *TSR*] *Om. MS*
17:12 inability *TSR*] repulsion *MS*
17:15 got *TSR*] gave himself *MS*

indifferent, so *TSR*] at bottom so amiable and tolerant, *MS*
17:15 went very little *TSR*] got no *MS*
17:16 deliberately. His mind ... work. *TSR*] through the mind. *MS*
17:18 at the ... of himself *TSR*] wholesome. He was like a well-grown plant in his clarity *MS*
17:20 that *TSR*] he was unequally developed, that *MS*
17:20 hopeless good-for-nothing. So *TSR*] one. And on this score *MS*
17:22 time *TSR*] time he knew that *MS*
17:23 boys, and he was confused. *TSR*] boys. *MS*
17:24 they. For their mechanical stupidity he ... for them *E1*] they: he knew it, in his instinct *MS* they. For their coarseness and brutal crudeness he ... them *TSR*
17:27 He was at their mercy. *TSR*] *Om. MS*
17:33 betrayed *TSR*] tense *MS*
17:34 Ulysses"] ~," *E1*
17:37 his power ... moved by *TSR*] the strong, wholesale response in the boy. And Tom Brangwen valued *MS*
17:38 calculation *TSR*] others *MS*
17:38 was *TSR*] went *MS*
17:39 when, almost secretly and shamefully, *TSR*] when *MS*
18:1 prickly sensation ... [18:6] any person. *TSR*] flash of revulsion to strike over his flesh, and he could not go on. What came to him must come through feeling, not through the mind, the reason. *MS*
18:8 habits to ... start from *TSR*] knowledge to go by, no set of values, no working standard *MS*
18:9 palpable, nothing ... to begin *TSR*] tangible, nothing fixed in

himself, except perhaps some instinct that controlled him *MS*

18:11 understanding *TSR*] thinking *MS*

18:17 did at ... he knew *TSR*] could only think of a few facts *MS*

18:19 living conviction ... that his *TSR*] lurking suspicion that these *MS*

18:29 honest *TSR*] independent *MS*

18:39 this *TSR*] a *MS*

19:2 Yet his ... to hopelessness. *TSR*] *Om. MS*

19:3 clever *TSR*] brilliant *MS*

19:10 a fine experience to remember *TSR*] to see by and to believe in *MS*

19:11 Tom *TSR*] So Tom *MS*

19:12 I've] I have *TS*

19:13 He *TSR*] He was humble about it, he *MS*

19:16 having the ... own shortcomings, *TSR*] *Om. MS*

19:22 loud-mouthed,] ~ *E1*

19:32 didn't live ... a gentleman *TSR*] had a town wife who kept a fancy servant *MS*

19:39 centre *TSR*] central pillar *MS*

20:2 tipsy *E1*] drunk *MS*

20:4 public-house *Ed.*] public house *MS*

20:23 public-house] public house *TS*

20:24 him,] ~ *E1*

20:27 anger, *E1*] anguish *MS* anguish, *TS*

20:27 ash and of cold *TSR*] dreariness and of *MS*

20:28 that would happen *TSR*] he would accomplish *MS*

20:28 with *TSR*] with a *MS*

20:29 no more than this nothingness *TSR*] so paltry *MS*

20:30 slight sense of *TSR*] sense of anger and *MS*

20:30 fear that *TSR*] thinking *MS*

20:31 cold *TSR*] burning *MS*

20:35 very much ... no disease. *TSR*] all that much. *MS*

20:36 really *TSR*] knew that really *MS*

20:37 much. *TSR*] much. That was part of the disillusion. *MS*

20:38 mistrust *TSR*] weight of mistrust *MS*

20:39 emphasized] emphasised *TS*

20:39 fear of what was *TSR*] sense of isolation *MS*

20:39 in a few days *TSR*] very soon *MS*

20:40 happy-go-lucky *TSR*] zestful, strongblooded *MS*

21:1 face just ... as keen. *TSR*] being just as fresh. *MS*

21:4 hindered his outgoing *TSR*] left a dirty thumb-print on his nakedness. He felt some mistrust of himself, as a concrete person *MS*

21:8 inarticulate, powerful *TSR*] *Om. MS*

21:12 and terrifying ... to him. *TSR*] of all. *MS*

21:25 days *E1*] days and days *MS*

21:27 slow *TSR*] blind *MS*

21:36 knew *E1*] felt *MS*

21:40 inflamed *TSR*] hatred and *MS*

22:1 paucity which ... and bitterly *TSR*] nasty failure, that for very shame he had to make haste to forget *MS*

22:8 come *TSR*] destroy one *MS*

22:8 unawares, *MS*, *TSR*] unaware, *TS* unawares *E1*

22:18 very hearty ... very respectful. *TSR*] self-repressed; or again boisterously teasing and full of humour, laughing till his eyes were all water, going {teasing and going *TS*} quiet again and shutting his heavy jowl slightly surprised at it all. *MS*

22:22 bewilderment *TSR*] pleading *MS*

22:23 When he ... tipsy confusion *E1*] Then *MS* When he ... tipsy *égarement TSR*

22:26 light-o'love] light-o'-love *TS*

22:33 neglected for an afternoon by *TSR*] just wanting to throw over *MS*

22:35 the innate delicacy *TSR*] a certain sense of delicacy innate *MS*

22:36 But *TSR*] And *MS*

22:37 roused and ... dared anything *TSR*] throwing over a bully who outmatched her, so she dared to take on this one *MS*

22:40 hair,] ~ *E1*

23:1 easy laughter, flushed *TSR*] laughter, warm *MS*

23:1 inclined *TSR*] inclined to perspire and *MS*

23:2 manner. *E1*] manner. She was also quite direct and simple in her nature. It was mere recklessness that had led her to her form of life. *MS* manner. She was direct and forceful in her nature. It was dissatisfaction and anger that ... life. Yet she had always seemed jolly. *TSR*

23:3 in a state of wonder *TSR*] on tiptoe *MS*

23:4 roused, *E1*] warm with delight *MS* roused with delight *TSR*

23:5 too forward ... thought backward, *TSR*] backward, or too forward, *MS*

23:6 regard for women *TSR*] high regard for women altogether *MS*

23:8 and flushing deep with confusion *TSR*] that of a ninny *MS*

23:9 however, *TS*] ~ *MS*

23:9 became hard ... come on. *TSR*] sunned herself with him, and let him go on, giving him a little help. *MS*

23:12 said. *TSR*] said. "When I'm out I stop out if I feel like it." *MS*

23:15 commin'] ~', *E1*

23:16 an angry *TSR*] a deep *MS*

23:18 full, almost taunting look *TSR*] soft, almost offended eyes *MS*

23:18 trembled with unusedness *TSR*] felt she wanted him to stay. His heart halted *MS*

23:20 Shall you ... look at *TSR*] Come an' see what you think of *MS*

23:24 riding gaiters] riding-gaiters *E1*

23:27 like to if I could *TSR*] love to *MS*

23:27 I've] I have *TS*

23:28 said. *E1*] said, in his almost fatherly kindliness. *MS* said, in his almost brotherly gentleness and courtliness. *TSR*

23:33 And he ... beside her. *TSR*] But he held her distantly, ashamed to clasp her with an embrace, although he was almost weak with desire to do so. *MS*

23:37 said. *P* It *TS*] ~. / It *MS*

23:38 managed *TS*] ~, *MS*

23:39 an intent *TSR*] a great *MS*

24:7 went red with anger *TSR*] exchanged a look with the girl *MS*

24:8 Ay—don't worry, *E1*] What's your hurry? *MS* Ay—don't worry? *TSR*

24:8 back. *TSR*] back, almost callously. *MS*

24:10 said. *P* And *TS*] ~. / And *MS*

24:12 by-bye! *E1*] see yer afore then, *MS* by-bye!, *TSR*

24:12 friends. *TSR*] friends. "Don't get stuck i' th' mud. Dunna fa' in if yer canna swim—" *MS*

24:13 flushed *E1*] straight faced *MS* strait-faced *TS* dark-faced *TSR*

24:15 given his ... gone off *TSR*] taken the one remaining attic and had gone up *MS*

24:16 girl,] ~ *E1*

24:16 into the ... was or *TSR*] even now not believing *MS*

24:17 glorious *TSR*] astonishing *MS*

24:18 mad with ... the girl. *E1*] not sure whether he liked it or not. *MS* madly in love with the girl. By gad, she was a tanger. He admired her to extremity, he almost loved her. But he did admire her, and it *was* a success. *TSR*

24:19 glowed with ... something like! *TSR*] was very proud of himself. By Crimey, but that was a knock-out. *MS*

24:25 confused and gratified. *E1*] that nothing but himself and his own special quality of manliness would have won from her that interlude between her own proper affair. What was between him and her was *the* thing, the real thing, let her other man be what he might. *MS* that what was between himself and her was the right sort of thing, and what was between the other man and her was not the right sort of thing. So he wanted her to come with him. But she was too fair, and she wanted her hard, brutal freedom. She would be no man's woman. She wanted her price only. He was dark with anger. *TSR*

24:27 He could ... the girl *TSR*] So Brangwen was very pleased with himself *MS*

24:28 over-night. *Ed.*] over-night, why, he did not know, except that he had taken a room and that something held him. *MS* over night, why ... him. *TS* over night, because he could not go away. *TSR* over night. *E1*

24:29 meal; *TSR*] ~: *MS, E1*

25:4 old *TSR*] curious *MS*

25:8 It was an old, ageless face. *TSR*] *Om. MS*

25:9 The *TSR*] Yet the *MS*

25:14 cigarette *E1*] box of cigarettes *MS*

25:16 the one offered *E1*] one of these *MS*

25:19 lidded *TSR*] unlidded *MS*

25:21 other man *TSR*] foreigner *MS*

25:22 reserve, and ... self-surety *TSR*] delicacy, and for his quaint, monkey-like self-containedness *MS*

25:25 was excited *E1*] lived poignantly *MS* was roused powerfully *TSR*

25:25 was transported at meeting *TSR*] loved to meet *MS*

25:27 manner, the fine *TSR*] *Om. MS*

25:33 *voyage." P* Then *TS*] ~." / Then *MS*

25:36 There was a life *TSR*] Life was *MS*

25:40 that which he knew *TSR*] him *MS*

26:4 excitement *E1*] astonishment *MS*

26:5 set fire ... of cover *TSR*] fired all his imagination *MS*

26:8 significant *TSR*] wonderful *MS*

26:12 absorbedly *TSR*] eagerly *MS*

26:12 meeting with ... ancient breeding *TSR*] exquisite contact with a little, finely-bred {little finely-bred *TS*} gentleman *MS*

26:14 began *TSR*] began, eagerly, *MS*

26:15 subtle-mannered *TSR*] fascinating *MS*

26:16 foreigner *TSR*] man *MS*

26:16 subtle intimacy ... the satisfaction *TSR*] fine-textured fascination were always the limbs and body *MS*

26:18 absorbed in ... the actuality *TSR*] burdened with the intensity and the ever-present heat

MS bewildered with … heat *TS*

26:19 full of … the desire for the girl *E1*] and his strong chest thrust forward, his face closed and intent *MS* full of … the memory of the girl *TSR*

26:24 enclosure of … well-known pound of his own life *TSR*] face of reality, turned aside his head, looked for any turning to avoid it *MS* enclosure … well-known round of his own life *E1*

26:28 set *TSR*] ground *MS*

26:28 to which he would not submit *TSR*] which he *did* not want *MS*

26:29 before him *TSR*] out of the morning-glow *MS*

26:33 a nightmare … of impotency *TSR*] the seed of a nightmare to him. Now he felt in the same state *MS*

26:38 a life … was ridiculous *TSR*] finding a friend such as the foreigner was futile *MS*

26:39 dreamed of … sat stubbornly *TSR*] stuck to his fancies, feeling all the while in the greatest perplexity man was ever in, like a bird that was limed. There he would sit *MS*

27:1 musing *TSR*] staring *MS*

27:3 gorping farm-laborer *Ed.*] village idiot, a barm-pot *MS* gorping farm-laborer, who blorts if his mouth opens *TSR* gorping farm-labourer *E1*

27:4 restless anger *TSR*] restlessness *MS*

27:10 close. All … do something. *TSR*] climax. He felt something accumulating in him, accumulating to burst. He knew a break would come. *MS*

27:14 sensitive and emotional, his nausea prevented *TSR*] very healthy, a sort of nausea saved *MS*

27:15 much. *TSR*] much. He felt, when he had drunk a certain amount, that his stomach was full enough, and the thought of further drinking nauseated him. *MS*

27:16 in futile anger *TSR*] almost deliberately *MS*

27:16 determination and … he began *TSR*] good-humour and apparent sanity, he began at twenty six {twenty-six *TS*} *MS*

27:22 rose *TSR*] rose in a manly {in manly *TS*} fashion *MS*

27:22 rather awkwardly took his place amongst *E1*] saluted *MS* rather reluctantly took … amongst *TSR*

27:24 discovered he … quite well *E1*] proceeded to get drunk on brandy *MS* discovered he could quite pleasantly get drunk on brandy *TSR*

27:25 everybody in … alarm told *TSR*] he talked very cleverly. As a matter of fact, when the others in alarm kept telling *MS*

27:28 blissful *TSR*] shining *MS*

27:28 iss-a'-ri-ight] iss-al'-ri-ight *TS*]

27:28 it's a' right——let … be— *TSR*] don't yer bother—why, what's it matter?, {matter? *TS*} *MS* it's a'right—let … be—— *E1*

27:29 he laughed … the others *TSR*] was seriously indignant that anyone *MS*

27:31 it was the happiest and *TSR*] *Om. MS*

27:35 What *TSR*] what *MS*

27:35 Hanover!, *TSR*] ~, *MS* ~! *E1*

28:3 this was … glorious evening *TSR*] the only way to get out of it would be to drink again *MS*

28:4 And *TSR*] But *MS*

28:4 any more *TSR*] *Om. MS*

28:8 stubbornly waited … happen

next *TSR*] let his feelings resolve themselves out, giving himself up to his instincts, to let them, if only they would, tell him what to do. But they were very slow *MS*

28:10 he belonged to this world ... [28:15] any question, and were satisfied. *E1*] his dream might be fulfilled, that the object of his unexpressed desire existed? That was the question he wanted to ask himself. And he might have answered, that, since the little foreigner at Matlock, he did believe his dream, whatever it might be, might be fulfilled. He had not, however, the wit either to put or to answer the question. *MS* he belonged to this known meagre world ... any question. *TSR*

28:16 stubbornly *TSR*] decently *MS*

28:16 strain *TSR*] stress *MS*

28:17 him *TSR*] him again *MS*

28:17 consciousness was always awake *TSR*] feeling weighed *MS*

28:19 images, his ... remain normal *TSR*] images. He hated himself for it furiously, that he could not escape *MS*

28:20 woman. *TSR*] woman, to give himself outlet. *MS*

28:21 as if ... the wall *TSR*] till he became half mad *MS*

28:23 went deliberately ... o'clock ... [28:36] and develop. *E1*] rushed to Ilkeston, to escape the grinding millstones grinding so endlessly upon one another, with nothing in the mill. This time he knew the second day that it was not finished, so he continued the bout. And after three days {days' *TS*} heavy brandy-

drinking, he had at last burnt out his surplus accumulation, had consumed the vitality of his blood, and so purged himself of the intolerable, bursting agony of desire, and the torture of inflamed images. *MS* went ... oclock ... develop. *TSR*

28:38 brandy-drinking *TS*] brandy drinking *MS*

28:40 women, antagonistic. *TSR*] women. *MS*

29:6 aware of ... early in *TSR*] heeding nothing. It was the young of *MS*

29:17 motion, as ... by everybody, *TSR*] motion *MS*

29:21 the air ... was suspended *TSR*] his breast. It seemed to him perfectly beautiful. As a matter of fact it was almost ugly. He had not met her eyes *MS*

29:24 involuntarily *TSR*] in his heart *MS*

29:24 passed by *TSR*] drew near *MS*

29:27 a pain ... through him *E1*] feeling a pain like a flame run up his arms *MS* his face going white and a pain running through him *TSR*

29:28 of anything. *E1*] even of the touch between them as their eyes recognised each other. *MS* of anything after their eyes had met. *TSR*

29:32 passed by ... fixed motion. *TSR*] seen him. He felt as if she had recognised him, looked at him and recognised him in his innermost soul. He went on, afraid and elated almost to madness by this strange feeling, that they had exchanged recognition. *MS* seen ... she had recognised him in his innermost ... recognition. *TS*

29:36 face. He moved ... beyond

reality. *E1*] face, it was so poignant to him. How clearly he could see her shape in the cloak, the set of the back, the movement of the skirts! *MS* face, it was so poignant to him. He moved ... beyond reality. *TSR*

29:39 torment. *TSR*] surety. *MS* torment, *E1*

29:40 a nothingness *TSR*] engulfing *MS*

30:1 will to *TSR*] light of *MS*

30:3 state *TSR*] dream *MS*

30:3 again like ... the common, barren world *E1*] this dream began to waver *MS* again ... the reality *TSR*

30:7 As *TSR*] Then, as *MS*

30:8 later *TSR*] afterwards *MS*

30:8 woman *E1*] same figure *MS*

30:8 wanted to ... that there *TSR*] knew that she knew him, he knew that he existed for her as she for him. There *MS*

30:10 So he ... road. He *TSR*] As {So *TS*} he stood anxiously affirming it, looking at her for response, as she went down the road, he *MS*

30:17 why—"] ~"— *E1*

30:18 eyes— *E1*] eyes, that he was so used to and so fond of— *MS*

30:20 hen-bird, *TSR*] hen-bird stretchin' your neck, *MS*

30:23 the new *TSR*] his *MS*

30:26 housekeeper or ... a name? *TSR*] she's not nowt but a housekeeper, like a chest o' drawers, she's got more to her name than that, hasn't she? *MS*

30:30 What's her name? *TSR*] What *is* her name then? *MS*

30:33 vicarage? *TS*] ~. *MS*

31:2 keep it in their head *E1*] say it twice *MS*

31:4 What *E1*] Say what *MS*

31:8 Who told you that *TSR*] How do you know *MS*

31:10 reckon she's from, then *TSR*] make out it is *MS*

31:13 Who's] Who *TS*

31:14 confabulation *TSR*] confublation *MS* confuglation *TS*

31:16 Who says *TSR*] An' *what* do they say *MS*

31:17 Mrs Bentley—says as *TSR*] As *MS* Mrs. Bentley says as *E1*

31:18 summat." *P* Tilly *TS*] ~."/ Tilly *MS*

31:19 afraid *TSR*] terrified for fear *MS*

31:19 now. *E1*] now, as the Irishism goes. *MS*

31:21 They all say so *TSR*] Why everybody *MS*

31:22 brought her to these parts *TSR*] she doin' here *MS*

31:27 fair *TSR*] hair fair *MS*

31:28 Is there a father, then *E1*] Has she got a husband *MS*

31:30 brought her *TSR*] is she doing *MS*

31:36 You'd have ... went past. *E1*] And you know no more about her?" *P* "No—nobody knows no more about her, so far as I know of. *MS* And that's all you know about her, is it?" *P* "Nobody ... know of. *TSR*

31:38 half with ... hearing more. *E1*] to gather further particulars, if possible. He wondered if she could speak English all right. *MS* half ... hearing more. He was shy of asking about her. *TSR*

32:1 foreign like] foreign-like *TS*

32:2 girl,] ~ *TS*

32:4 the unreality established *TSR*] his desire made concrete *MS*

32:6 was to him a profound satisfaction *TSR*] gave him a mad joy *MS*

32:6   foreigner. *TSR*] foreigner. That would satisfy a deep craving in him. *MS*

32:9   stark *E1*] shadowy *MS*

32:9   barren, mere nullities *E1*] portentous, mere potencies *MS*

32:10   handle. *E1*] handle. He was like a fixed star in the universe now, whereas before he had been a nebulous, incandescent, uncertain quantity. *MS* handle. He ... quantity. The other reality had fallen back like the stones of the road, over which came the traffic of the new reality. *TSR*

32:12   not far off *TSR*] in the world *MS*

32:12   in *TSR*] to *MS*

32:14   her. *E1*] her. He waited for chance. *MS*

32:17   in *TSR*] in a *MS*

32:21   inflamed *E1*] was pregnant with acceptance of *MS*

32:21   grey-brown *TSR*] grey *MS*

32:25   The world ... its transformation *TSR*] His heart was big with pregnancy *MS*

32:30   fineness *TSR*] fineness of mould *MS*

32:31   She was strange ... his soul *E1*] Yet she was unaware *MS* She was so strange, yet so intimate. She was far away, like a ghost, a presence ... soul *TSR*

32:35   belonged to *E1*] was *MS*

32:36   fear for ... was only *TSR*] jealousy for her far-away life, that was beyond *MS*

33:2   absence. *E1*] absence. And a sharp flame ran through him, feeling it. *MS*

33:6   defense *TSR*] defensive *MS* defence *E1*

33:10   land vivid] man vivid *TS* air completely *TSR* air *E1 see notes*

33:11   also *TSR*] not so completely *MS see notes*

33:13   daze] days *TS* way *TSR see note on* 33:10

33:25   Mother—," *TS*] ~—", *MS* ~——," *E1*

33:25   was gone *TSR*] flitted *MS*

33:26   The mother had *E1*] Her mother *MS*

33:27   Brangwen. *E1*] Brangwen, whose blue eyes were puzzled. *MS*

33:28   isolated *E1*] so isolated *MS*

33:28   dominant *E1*] so dominant *MS*

33:29   existence. *E1*] existence. What was it, this unknown in her? *MS*

33:30   wide grey ... moving, held *E1*] wide, deep, grey eyes, so impersonal and yet {impersonal yet *TS*} so deeply penetrating, made *MS* wide, deep ... eyes, impersonal yet ... penetrating, held *TSR*

33:34   Mother—"] mother—" *TS* mother"— *E1*

33:34   continue,] ~ *TS*

33:35   Yes my child *E1*] Yes dear *MS* yes dear *TS*

33:37   abstract *E1*] quiet, strong toned *MS* quiet, strong-toned *TS*

34:4   like *TSR*] fair like *MS*

34:5   how *TSR*] why *MS*

34:6   The mother's ... She'd be *E1*] —Isn't {Isn't *TS*} the mother ugly?—but taking, somehow. She's *MS* The mother's plain, I must say—but the child is taking, somehow. She'd be *TSR*

34:8   But *TSR*] Effie also was fired by the strange woman. But *MS*

34:9   There's your *E1*] She's about the sort of *MS* There's a *TSR*

34:9   "You'd better marry *her.*" *TSR*] *Om. MS*

34:16   the] a *TS*

34:17   detached *E1*] proud *MS*

34:18   tried *TSR*] struggled *MS*

34:18   question. *E1*] question. They

34:20 stood near together, facing each other. *MS* question. They stood facing each other. *TSR*

34:20 affected *TSR*] overpowered *MS*

34:27 kitchen. *P* "Tilly *TS*] ∼. / "Tilly *MS*

34:29 like *TSR*] dark like *MS*

34:30 distance. *P* He *TS*] ∼. / He *MS*

34:32 on t' *TS*] on't *MS*

34:33 dairy. *P* Brangwen *TS*] ∼. / Brangwen *MS*

34:37 you're *TS*] you *MS*

35:1 cross eyes] cross-eyes *TS*

35:3 impatiently, *TSR*] *Om. MS*

35:5 on t' *E1*] on't *MS*

35:9 Then the] The the *TS* The *TSC*

35:9 spoke *TSR*] spoke for the first time *MS*

35:9 detached *TSR*] proud *MS*

35:11 come to trouble *TSR*] troubled *MS*

35:13 could not understand *TSR*] was non-plussed by *MS*

35:13 was *TSR*] *Om. MS*

35:14 politeness *TSR*] formal system of politeness *MS*

35:15 impersonal *E1*] insignificant *MS*

35:15 wills *TSR*] direct wills *MS*

35:15 Brangwen flushed ... Still he *E1*] And Brangwen *MS* Brangwen flushed as if her polite speech were almost an insult. Still he *TSR*

35:22 woman,] ∼ *TS*

35:22 angered *TSR*] bewildered *MS*

35:26 Yes,] yes, *TS*

35:33 Brown's] Browns *E1*

35:39 should not *TSR*] ought not to *MS*

36:1 inquiringly] enquiringly *TS*

36:3 confused *TSR*] troubled *MS*

36:4 How's that ... only protective. *TSR*] Why?" he said. *MS*

36:7 Her eyes ... the language. *TSR*] *Om. MS*

36:13 language,] ∼ *TS*

36:14 said. *P* And *TS*] ∼. / And *MS*

36:18 hearthrug *E1*] hearth-rug *MS*

36:19 Her *E1*] Her perfect *MS*

36:20 inspired him, *TSR*] baffled him, but *MS*

36:21 master of ... the situation. *TSR*] free of himself. *MS*

36:25 it middlin' rough *E1*] us a rough lot *MS*

36:26 "—a— —"] *Om. TS*

36:27 Our *E1*] A rough lot—our *MS*

36:30 said, "it's *E1*] said, relieved, "we're *MS* said, "we're *TSR*

36:30 here than what *E1*] than *MS* than what *TSR*

36:31 there." *P* She *TS*] ∼. / She *MS*

36:33 intimacy *E1*] utter deference *MS* lack of formality *TSR*

36:33 If he ... without formality? *TSR*] *Om. MS*

36:35 him. *P* She *TS*] ∼. / She *MS*

36:36 uncouth, almost ... he was *E1*] but difficult to understand, *MS* but foreign, almost ... was *TSR*

36:37 fair *E1*] ruffled fair *MS*

36:38 energy *E1*] latent confidence and light *MS* generosity and light *TSR*

36:38 healthy body ... with her *E1*] attractive body that he wanted to give away *MS* healthy body that seemed to glow to her *TSR*

36:40 uncouth, and confident *E1*] childish, and curiously proud *MS* childish, and confident *TSR*

37:5 old people *TSR*] garments *MS*

37:6 kin *TSR*] familiar *MS*

37:12 said. *P* Her *Ed.*] ∼. / Her *MS* ∼. Her *TS*

37:16 said. *P* He] ∼. He *TS*

37:17 and *E1*] with his blue eyes, and *MS*

37:17 It disturbed ... of him. He was so strangely confident and direct. *E1*] Curious, how it disturbed them both, how they

could not bear it, yet. {it yet.
TS} *MS* It disturbed ... of him.
TSR

37:22 you *E1*] you can *MS*

37:22 alone." *P* She *TS*] ~." / She
MS

37:24 meaning *TSR*] secret *MS*

37:26 heat beating *TSR*] flame
leaping *MS*

37:27 in conflict *TSR*] bewildered
MS

37:29 young, *E1*] blue, young, beautifully *MS* blue, young, generous, *TSR*

37:30 assume *TSR*] assert *MS*

37:30 her, to speak ... his protection.
E1] her. *MS* her, to speak to
her. *TSR*

37:31 Why did ... to her! *TSR*] How
could it be? *MS*

37:31 Why were ... nor signal *E1*]
Yet his eyes were {were as *TS*}
certain as daybreak, as full of
light and as confident, somewhere *MS* Yet his eyes were as
certain as ... confident, waiting
for no permission nor signal
TSR

37:33 At once *TSR*] But *MS*

37:34 speak, *E1*] ~ *MS*

37:36 asked *TSR*] asked suddenly
MS

38:1 yes." *P* Curiously *TS*] ~." /
Curiously *MS*

38:2 abstracted *E1*] indifferent *MS*

38:3 questions. *E1*] questions. It was
as if none of it were true to her.
Her life had gone on unreal
from some point before her
husband's death. She was there
still arrested. But, as if his
looks, the presence of his body
sent a warmth into her, her
heart began to stir like roots
underground heaving to return
back to the sun. *MS* questions.
It ... none of this present circumstance was real to her ...

on untrue from ... stir underground heaving in return to his
sun. *TSR*

38:3 again *E1*] in wonder *MS* in pain
TSR

38:4 could not ... away from *TSR*]
must go near to *MS*

38:5 him, till ... He saw *TSR*] him
with passion, till he was almost
mad with tenderness for her,
for *MS*

38:6 rise *E1*] *Om. MS*

38:7 butter,] ~ *TS*

38:9 of it *TSR*] o' that *MS*

38:12 your *TSR*] th' *MS*

38:13 You'd have to put in, shouldn't
E1] You'll have to know all
about it, won't *MS* You'll have
to put in, won't *TSR*

38:14 Tilly. *P* Brangwen stood by and
let be *Ed.*] Tilly. / Brangwen
{Tilly. Brangwen *TS*} lifted his
hand. *P* "You're not paying for
a broken bit of butter," he said.
/ She {said. *P* She *TS*} heard
the decision in his tone, and
knew it was no use gainsaying
him. He would not hear anything once his mind was made
up *MS* Tilly. Brangwen stood
... let be *TSR*

38:18 said; "—if] ~,—"~ *TS*

38:20 stood dimmed *E1*] felt stunned
MS felt dimmed *TSR*

38:21 was *E1*] stood *MS*

38:23 invisible *E1*] *Om. MS*

38:23 woman. *E1*] woman, as if there
were some unknown connec-
tion from him to her, almost
like a navel-string. He suffered
with a deep gladness. *MS*
woman, as ... her, invisible,
but more real than actuality.
He ... gladness. *TSR*

38:27 unable *E1*] stunned, unable
MS

38:28 between him and *E1*] from him
to *MS*

38:29 secret power. *E1*] navel string. *MS* navel-string. *TS* secret power, which was against the outward power of the world. *TSR*

38:30 come to the house *E1*] looked at him wondering and new like a girl, *MS*

38:37 that *Ed.*] that there was *MS see notes*

38:38 by his native good-humour *Ed.*] with his native genuineness *MS* with his native generosity *TSR* by ... good humour *E1*

39:6 It excluded ... wedding-ring, *E1*] And it stood for all that he must pass by on his way to the goal. It was not his, the wedding ring, {wedding-ring, *TS*} and *MS* It stood for his denial and suffering. Her hands were silent and alien, remote from him. It bound her life, the wedding-ring, *TSR*

39:7 for her *TSR*] for a *MS*

39:8 part. *TSR*] part, but which was her life. *MS*

39:8 herself and ... should meet. *E1*] the point where he and she met and joined to make a new life. Had she not looked at him, a girl? *MS* herself and himself which should meet and join to make one, joyfully. She had looked at him as a girl looks. *TSR*

39:10 As *E1*] Nevertheless, the other wedding-ring on her finger, and the wornness of her hands, was anguish to him, anguish that he must submit to, and must let pass over him, leaving him changed, ready to begin the new life with her, the life of him and her. And as *MS*

39:11 some *E1*] no *MS*

39:11 hands. *TSR*] hands—not yet. *MS*

39:12 But he ... be neglected. *E1*] He must not intrude, not yet. It were {It was *TS*} sacrilege. How could he break in to the sacred precincts of her life with another man? She must come out to him, he must wait for her. *MS* He ... It was ... break in upon the ... her. *TSR*

39:14 angry, made him *TSR*] want to *MS*

39:16 enraged *TSR*] bewildered *MS*

39:19 escape her *E1*] drink *MS* forget her *TSR*

39:25 stranger who ... her life *E1*] small, male head and the indomitable, yet lovable forehead *MS* small ... the low, indomitable ... forehead *TSR*

39:27 veins to *TSR*] veins into *MS*

39:27 again, to ... to respond *E1*] to live again, and to live in a new form, *MS* again ... to correspond *TSR*

39:31 skin. *E1*] skin, and licked over her. As it would be it would be. *MS*

39:33 destruction. *E1*] destruction. Her old self must die before there could be the new. And it fought against dying. *MS*

39:35 time, *E1*] time, he felt *MS*

39:35 fell *E1*] fall *MS*

39:35 leaving the ... his purpose *E1*] all the sheath and bracts and husk fall off, leaving the kernel of himself *MS*

39:36 then it ... his life. *E1*] then, in that hour of knowledge and weariness, it came upon him that he must ask her soon to marry him, that he must take the responsibility. Blindly, unconsciously, his feelings worked themselves out and gave him the inevitable conclusion. *MS* then, in ... knowledge and starkness, it ... him that he would marry her and she would be his life. Blindly ... gave him to the inevitable action. *TSR*

40:1 this pleasant ... the case *TSR*] his high view of himself *MS*

40:2 besides, he ... of her *TSR*] what then, what did he care if any woman in the world refused him? He was sufficient unto himself *MS*

40:4 did not belong to himself. *E1*] was not sufficient unto himself, and never would be. *MS*

40:5 that *E1*] that without her *MS* that without addition *TSR*

40:6 subject *E1*] useless *MS*

40:6 were *E1*] were all *MS*

40:7 travelling, the ... eternal voyage *E1*] wandering outside him, other than himself, the whole host passing him by and ignoring him *MS*

40:8 submissive to the greater ordering *E1*] poor and helpless, like a forgotten, impotent beggar as the procession goes by *MS*

40:9 Unless *E1*] And unless *MS*

40:9 a nothingness *E1*] nothing *MS*

40:10 hard experience *E1*] bitter lesson for his pride of self to learn *MS* hard lesson ... learn *TSR*

40:12 tried to escape *E1*] revolted *MS*

40:12 good enough by *TSR*] sufficient unto *MS*

40:14 the *TSR*] this *MS*

40:16 would be real *E1*] was everything *MS* would be everything *TSR*

40:16 were *TSR*] came *MS*

40:17 near *TSR*] to *MS*

40:18 she would ... and perfection. *E1*] then would not all the unknown come trooping after her, led to him, stars and dark sky and all the unknown wandering towards him to take part in him? *MS* she would lead all the unknown trooping after her, stars ... all the hosts wandering in her train, dependent on her? *TSR*

40:19 if it should *TSR*] should it not *MS*

40:20 him! *TSR*] ~? *MS*

40:20 was ordained *TSR*] must be *MS*

40:25 hard *TSR*] bad *MS*

40:26 landowner's *E1*] land-owner's *MS*

40:27 were only words to him *E1*] he had to get over *MS*

40:29 way of ... with him. *E1*] way. But he had his intrinsic manhood, that were nothing without her. *MS* way of distinction. But ... her. *TSR*

40:32 One *E1*] It came to him one *MS* It came one *TSR*

40:32 came the ... ask her *E1*] that the moment had come *MS* the moment to ask her *TSR*

40:33 him] ~, *E1*

40:34 fire. *E1*] fire, the great veins swollen in his wrists and down the backs of his hands, under the {his *TS*} thick skin. *MS* fire, the veins ... his thick skin. *TSR*

40:38 one." *P* Tilly *TS*] ~." / Tilly *MS*

41:2 absorbed *TSR*] beautiful *MS*

41:5 house *E1*] house from him *MS*

41:15 whosoever *TSR*] me if *MS*

41:15 likes." *P* This *TS*] ~." / This *MS*

41:20 scissors." *P* She *TS*] ~." / She *MS*

41:25 He *E1*] Slowly and scrupulously, as if preparing for some ritual, he *MS*

41:30 flowers *E1*] daffodils *MS*

41:33 Brangwen. *P* And *TS*] ~. / And *MS*

41:37 up *TSR*] straight up *MS*

42:9 rocking chair] rocking-chair *TS*

42:30 to hear *E1*] Om. *MS*

42:30 it." *P* The *TS*] ~." / The *MS*

42:32 mother. *P* He *TS*] ~. / He *MS*

42:34 child *E1*] drowning child *MS*

42:38 outside, suspended *TSR*] outside patiently *MS*

42:40 fate to ... the threshold *TSR*] ordeal to undergo, and he had to wait his time *MS*

43:2 fleece] flux *TS* wisps *TSR* *see notes*

43:3 curled up] curled-up *E1*

43:5 outside seeing the night fall *TSR*] and let be *MS*

43:6 fixed and *E1*] Om. *MS*

43:8 strong *E1*] fairly strong *MS*

43:15 beautiful *TSR*] easy *MS*

43:19 knocked *E1*] shut his jaw, gave his breast up to the ordeal, and knocked *MS*

43:21 I'll just *TSR*] Should I *MS*

43:21 minute." *P A TS*] ~." / A *MS*

43:25 again *TSR*] Om. *MS*

43:25 him, she] ~. She *TS*

43:29 towards *TSR*] full towards *MS*

43:32 only she ... come for *TSR*] and she knew him with a shock that possessed *MS*

43:33 man's figure *TSR*] figure of the man *MS*

43:34 face *TSR*] head *MS*

43:35 eyes *TSR*] face *MS*

43:36 knowing *TSR*] seeing *MS*

44:3 He *E1*] With an effort he lifted his face and looked at her. He *MS*

44:3 unknown, dread ... to him *E1*] like the other, unknown, dread half of life which was to be embraced *MS*

44:5 came up *TSR*] come *MS*

44:6 ask *E1*] see *MS*

44:10 length:] ~. *TS*

44:11 Yes. I am free to marry. *TSR*] Yes. *MS* Yes, I ... marry. *E1*

44:12 less impersonal *TSR*] nearer *MS*

44:13 her, *E1*] her, and not alone *MS* *see notes*

44:14 eternal *E1*] blue *MS*

44:14 change. *E1*] change, never. *MS*

44:15 created *E1*] giving way *MS*

44:17 said. *P A TS*] ~. / A *MS*

44:18 over his face *E1*] round his mouth and nostrils *MS*

44:19 Yes, *E1*] Yes, if you'll have me, *MS* Yes, it's what I came for, *TSR*

44:19 said. *P* Still *TS*] ~. / Still *MS*

44:20 suspense *E1*] a space of suspense *MS*

44:21 No ... No, I don't know *TSR*] Yes ... I want you *MS*

44:22 his fists slackened, he was *TSR*] and gripped his fists harder, *MS*

44:23 stood *TSR*] stood rigid, *MS*

44:23 vague collapse ... him. Then ... her come *E1*] effort of resistance to himself. She came *MS* vague ... him. She had not spoken to him. Then ... her come *TSR*

44:26 to *E1*] on *MS*

44:27 Yes I ... said, impersonally *E1*] Do you want me?" she said again *MS* Yes I want you?" she said, impersonally *TSR*

44:28 with supreme truth *TSR*] for the first time *MS*

44:36 He *TSR*] But he *MS*

44:36 obliterated *TSR*] white with pain *MS*

44:37 him, to ... from himself. *TSR*] him. *MS*

44:39 yet *E1*] yet, dear God, *MS*

45:4 sleep, utter, extreme oblivion *E1*] essence of sleep, in the densest, most fecund oblivion *MS* anguish of sleep, in which he merged into her, mingled with her, and was lost *TSR*

45:5   gradually, *E1*] gradually with her, *MS*

45:8   returned gradually ... of darkness *E1*] came to gradually, but new and refreshed as from a resurrection, a new bath of birth, in the womb *MS* came ... refreshed, renascent, as after a new gestation, from a ... womb *TSR*

45:9   Aërial *Ed.*] Aerial *MS*

45:10 morning, *E1*] morning among dew, so *MS*

45:10 newly begun] newly-begun *TS*

45:14 the dawn ... to pass *TSR*] it was good, it was very good *MS*

45:17 close] closer *TS*

45:18 soon *TSR*] now *MS*

45:19 sank, *TSR*] sank, so *MS*

45:19 him *TSR*] his breast *MS*

45:20 effaced *TSR*] resting *MS*

45:20 And in ... certain negation of him. *E1*] *Om. MS* And ... certain dreariness. *TSR*

45:22 silence. *P* He *Ed.*] ~. / He *MS* ~. He *TS*

45:23 a voice ... the wind *TSR*] the wind. Now he heard it *MS*

45:29 said. *P* The *TS*] ~. / The *MS*

45:30 again. *E1*] again. She was not with him. She was thinking apart from him. *MS* again. She would insist on that which was not between him and her alone. She would bid him remember the alien past. *TSR*

45:31 love her now," he said. *P* She *TSR*] should hope so," he said, almost huffed. / She *MS* should ... huffed. *P* She *TS*

45:32 lay still against him *TSR*] sat still on his knee *MS*

45:33 confirmation *TSR*] bliss *MS*

45:35 seemed so absent *E1*] took no notice of him *MS*

45:36 He did not know her. *TSR*] *Om. MS*

45:38 asked. *E1*] asked, indifferent. *MS*

46:1   years." *P* She *TS*] ~." / She *MS*

46:2   oddly concerned *E1*] so curiously unconcerned *MS* so curiously concerned *TSR*

46:5   so he ... power. He *E1*] like a wealth suddenly come. He troubled with no questions, he *MS* so ... power. He troubled ... questions, he *TSR*

46:6   He did not even know her. *TSR*] *Om. MS*

46:7   so strange *E1*] enough *MS*

46:7   there *TSR*] *Om. MS*

46:8   him. *E1*] his body, as he sat in the chair. *MS* him, as ... chair, it was enough that they two were one weight. *TSR*

46:9   The strange ... God. Amused *TSR*] And again *MS*

46:14 like it also, here *TSR*] did not mind it much *MS*

46:14 been in ... nice here *TSR*] lost so much, truly, then one does not mind so much what one does *MS*

46:17 But he did not mind. *E1*] *Om. MS* But ... mind what had been. He was too proud in what *was*. *TSR*

46:18 What was ... he asked. *TSR*] Was you a grand lady in your own parts?" he asked, thrilled with the idea. *MS*

46:19 replied. "It was near a river." *P* This *E1*] replied. / The term *MS* replied. *P* The term *TS* replied. "It was in the country." *P* This *TSR*

46:20 All was as vague as before *TSR*] He did not know whether to think of himself, who was a landowner, or of the Duke of Devonshire, who owned some of the land contiguous to his *MS*

46:21 care, whilst she was *TSR*] care very much, whilst he had her *MS*

46:22 "I *E1*] "And your husband was a doctor?" *P* "Yes. He was of good family. But he was an intellectual type." / Strange {type." *P* Strange *TS*} and foreign it all sounded! If it had not been that all sounds happened on the edge of a sphere of silence and intense bliss which enclosed him, he would have suffered. *P* "I *MS* "And ... family, but ... intellectual." *P* Meaningless and ... that nothing could encroach upon the strong centre of silence and fulfilment which he was, he would have suffered. *P* "I *TSR*

46:22 said *E1*] laughed *MS*

46:23 said. *P* He *TS*] ~. / He *MS*

46:25 breathing *TSR*] strong breathing *MS*

46:27 flame *TSR*] flame of bliss *MS*

46:29 But it ... She rose, *E1*] Then she rose, quietly, *MS* Then she rose, passed away, *TSR*

46:33 a contradiction in her *E1*] the liveness of the front of his body where she had reclined on him *MS see notes*

46:34 inscrutably *TSR*] with her head down *MS*

46:35 unused] mused *TS*

46:39 eyes, strained ... with unusedness, *TSR*] blue eyes, strained with unusedness and roused with strong light, *MS*

46:40 obedient, and as if] *Om. TS*

47:2 too strong ... got her. *E1*] strong in him, and an overwhelming desire for her, and a desire for real response. He had not roused her. *MS* strong in ... response. Again he had not got her. *TSR*

47:6 remoteness *TSR*] fineness *MS*

47:6 in touch with him *TSR*] incomprehensible *MS*

47:10 puzzled *TSR*] open *MS*

47:13 memory struggling with passion *TSR*] misery and of darkness *MS*

47:14 rejected him ... at once. *TSR*] received him and almost absorbed him. *MS*

47:15 He breathed with difficulty *TSR*] His chest heaved *MS*

47:17 slowly, always uncertain. *P* He *TSR*] slowly. / He *MS* slowly. *P* He *TS*

47:20 do." *P* Then *TS*] ~." / Then *MS*

47:23 held *E1*] showed *MS*

47:32 turned *TSR*] passed *MS*

47:34 hat. *P* She *TS*] ~. / She *MS*

47:40 Goodnight." *P* He *TS*] ~." / He *MS*

48:6 They were ... forever ... [48:10] each other. *TSR*] *Om. MS* They ... for ever ... other. *E1*

48:11 blown into *TSR*] blown in *MS*

48:17 darknesses] darkness *TS*

48:20 under *TSR*] into the merciful *MS*

49:2 They Live at the Marsh *TSR*] The First Year of Married Life *MS*

49:3 who, *E1*] who was *MS*

49:4 Jews, *E1*] Jews, who *MS*

49:4 had died *E1*] died *MS*

49:6 Berlin *E1*] Moscow *MS*

49:16 Poles *E1*] Poles, the size of sixpence, *MS*

49:23 along in *TSR*] away by *MS*

49:25 talk *TSR*] vaunting *MS*

49:33 her desire was *TSR*] a desire *MS*

49:34 nunnery *TSR*] monastery *MS*

49:34 her] ~, *E1*

50:2 locked into a resistance *E1*] into his eyes *MS*

50:4 fractious *TSR*] insolent *MS*

50:4 as *TSR*] as an *MS*

50:5   beggars *E1*] like beggars *MS*
50:9   brandished weapon *E1*] little flame *MS*
50:13   fixed idea *E1*] foolish fire *MS*
50:19   aloofness *E1*] darkness *MS*
50:22   these *TSR*] it *MS*
50:24   intelligibly *TSR*] unintelligibly *MS*
50:25   hostile host *TSR*] evil brood *MS*
50:26   isolated *E1*] a complete stranger *MS*
50:33   as *TSR*] whilst *MS*
50:34   unrolled beside *TSR*] moved round *MS*
50:38   looming *TSR*] looming but *MS*
51:4   then, she was *TSR*] almost mechanically, she asked to be *MS*
51:4   There *TSR*] For there *MS*
51:5   now *TSR*] nowadays *MS* now-a-days *TS*
51:6   land *TSR*] fields *MS*
51:7   village *TSR*] villages *MS*
51:11   it forced ... potency of *TSR*] somehow she associated it with her old home, it had some connection with *MS*
51:24   hurt her *TSR*] hurt *MS*
51:26   glitter *E1*] blue glitter *MS*
52:17   back *E1*] Om. *MS*
52:21   leaden,] ~ *TS*
52:23   half-submerged] half submerged *TS*
52:38   moved oblivious] ~, ~, *TSC*
53:12   hostile *TSR*] cruel *MS*
53:19   pea-flour *E1*] pea-flower *MS* *see notes*
53:26   felt] was *E1*
53:32   moved *TSR*] hurt *MS*
53:35   here? *E1*] ~. *MS*
53:39   owned *TSR*] admired *MS*
54:5   for *TSR*] on *MS*
54:7   indifference,] ~ *E1*
54:7   her,] ~ *TS*
54:12   her own sort *E1*] noble family *MS* higher degree *TSR*
54:15   life *E1*] passion *MS*

54:16   livingness *E1*] honesty *MS*
54:21   flat] ~, *TS*
54:23   uncouth fear ... bigger than *TSR*] himself, and driven by *MS*
54:26   new *TSR*] blind *MS*
54:28   himself, through ... an adherence to the line *TSR*] himself in the line of his understanding, his conception *MS* himself, through ... the adherence to the line *E1*
54:29   honorable] honourable *E1*
54:33   chaos *TSR*] madness *MS*
54:36   of self-fear ... honor ... of chaos *TSR*] his conception of how a man married. So in torture he refused her silent demand and offer, and turned away, his bones all turned to water *MS* of self-fear ... honour ... chaos *E1*
55:1   became real to *TSR*] stood on *MS*
55:3   her, *E1*] her, with the genuine female, *MS*
55:3   misery *TSR*] heavy misery *MS*
55:4   unliving *TSR*] silent *MS*
55:6   moved with *TSR*] sat before *MS*
55:7   violent, gloomy, wordless *TSR*] violent *MS*
55:10   waited,] ~ *TS*
55:15   open] opened *TS*
55:28   and fear of the unknown *TSR*] Om. *MS*
55:30   physical *TSR*] carnal *MS*
55:35   get rid ... forethought and *TSR*] drink away all forethought and all *MS*
55:36   moment *TSR*] moment triumphantly, riotously *MS*
55:38   only coiled him more. *TSR*] scarcely touched him. *MS*
56:5   more! *TSR*] ~. *MS*
56:9   elated by *E1*] afraid of *MS* glad with *TSR*
56:9   they served *TSR*] subdued before *MS*

56:17   tormented *TSR*] tortured *MS*

56:21   painful *E1*] darkness and *MS*
fecund *TSR*

56:23   give himself ... to him? *TSR*]
say "I know her." *MS*

56:25   all. And ... into an unknown
power! *TSR*] all. *MS* all, and ...
into the unknown power! *E1*

56:28   and be ... could conquer *TSR*]
when he would have *MS*

56:29   What *TSR*] Who *MS*

56:29   to which ... embrace, contain
TSR] and what was the darkness of her *MS*

56:32   He *TSR*] Yet he *MS*

56:32   established *TSR*] finished *MS*

56:34   at him, *Ed.*] ~ ~. *MS* ~ ~ *TS*

56:38   said. *P* He *TS*] ~. / He *MS*

56:40   half past] half-past *E1*

57:6   said. *P* Her *Ed.*] ~. / Her *MS*
~. Her *TS*

57:7   order *TSR*] orders *MS*

57:11   you?" *P* She *TS*] ~?" / She *MS*

57:13   him, in ... and desire, *TSR*]
him hot for her, *MS* him, hot
... her *TS*

57:15   want to *E1*] hope I shall *MS*

57:15   said,] ~ *TS*

57:17   let himself go from *TSR*] lost
himself, *MS*

57:18   moment *TSR*] naked moment
MS

57:20   together in ... superficial
foreignness *TSR*] only fulfilment *MS*

57:21   She was ... to him. *TSR*] *Om.*
MS

57:22   belief in ... for her *TSR*] gladness *MS*

57:26   became so ... his life *TSR*]
came so near and so poignantly
to him *MS*

57:28   on a new universe *TSR*]
nakedly *MS*

57:28   wondered in *TSR*] was conceited, *MS* was conceited in *TS*

57:29   triviality *E1*] crassness *MS*
unreality *TSR*

57:29   calm relationship *TSR*] poignant tenderness *MS*

57:32   And *E1*] As he was ploughing, a
pee-wit wheeled and screamed round
his head, troubling him. Then, as he
returned again down the next furrow,
there she was, pitching before him,
striking at him: and then, staggering to
earth, she was running away trailing her
wing as if wounded, running in a wild
zigzag to attract attention, a daring,
frantic thing with all her wits about her.
P "Why what's all that bustle about?"
he said to her, and looking round, saw
her four blotched, pointed eggs on the
ground, where he must pass with the
plough. He stooped to them. His heart
tightened as {heart knew them as *TSR*}
he felt their warmth. He carried them
carefully across {them across *TSR*} to a
furrow and found a place for them. He
did not like putting them on the cold
earth, so he tried to warm with the back
of his hand, pressing a hollow. {earth,
he pressed a little hollow with the warm
back of his hand. *TSR*} Then he laid
the four eggs in, points together. The
bird swooped on the air, crying sharply.
She dazed his head and his heart
{dazed his heart *TSR*} with her cries
and her sobbing flight. He looked at her
anxiously, pointing to the eggs. *P*
"Don't make such a to-do," he said;
"settle yourself. Get down to them and
see after them." *P* He jerked his head at
the eggs, indicating them to her. Then,
tormented by {fretted by *TSR*} her
frantic crying, the flash of black and
white above the cold earth, the sob of
her flight to ground, and up again, the
pathetic wheeling on the air, he went on
with his work. The next length, and still
she was crying sharply, poignantly. The
next, and she was swooping up and
down, protesting in her dread and pain
and anxiety. The next, she was swinging above the newly deposited eggs.
And then, to his infinite relief, {his

relief, *TSR*} as he passed again with the plough, he saw her settled, sitting there almost invisible, her wings drooped beautifully, for anxious love, her head sharp and keen among the newly turned clods of earth, watching him, as he watched her. *P* "Well I'm glad you've got back," he said to her. / She {her. *P* She *TS*} jerked her head sharply at the sound. He passed on behind the plough, his heart glad, praising. {glad, confident. He had known all along she would be all right. He understood her. The relationship between them was natural. *TSR*} *P* And *MS*

57:32   steadily *TSR*] eagerly *MS*

57:33   a profound, unknown satisfaction *TSR*] count his precious belongings *MS*

57:37   close-banded] closed-banded *E1*

57:38   Somehow,] ~ *TS*

57:39   woman to him. As *TSR*] naked woman to him, with rich, strong loins and strong rounded legs, even as *MS*

57:40   apron, her *TSR*] ~. Her *MS*

58:1   revealed itself to him *TSR*] revealing itself *MS*

58:1   intrinsic *TSR*] unclothed *MS*

58:2   woman, he ... her essence, that ... to possess *E1*] woman to him, he knew her body *MS* woman, he ... her body, that ... possess *TSR*

58:4   unaccountable *TSR*] uncountable *MS*

58:5   other, consciously. *TSR*] other. *MS*

58:7   answered. *P* He *TS*] ~. / He *MS*

58:11   forgetting, *TS*] ~ *MS*

58:13   wife, as, in *TSR*] wife with *MS*

58:14   fichu, she was *TSR*] fichu *MS*

58:15   him, and ... go away? *TSR*] him. He felt beside himself. He could not believe it, he did not feel like a possessor. *MS*

58:17   a real ... go away *TSR*] established, this marriage of theirs *MS*

58:24   satisfied, never ... go away. *TSR*] satisfied. *MS*

58:29   him, and ... till morning. *TSR*] him. *MS*

58:30   self-sufficient,] ~ *TS*

59:5   remember, *E1*] know *MS* know, *TSR*

59:11   know, *filles E1*] know such girls *MS* know, filles *TSR*

59:11   wagon full] wagon-full *TS*

59:15   things'— — —] ~.' *TS*

59:19   said,] ~ *TS*

59:20   say] ~, *TS*

59:22   know— —] ~. *TS*

59:26   him— —] ~—— *E1*

59:29   "I ... know"; *E1*] '~ ... ~'; *MS* '~ ... ~;' *TS*

59:30   "Don't ... it," *E1*] '~ ... ~,' *MS*

59:33   convent—.] ~— *TS* ~. *E1*

59:38   shocked *TSR*] aghast *MS*

60:2   a lover, a *E1*] an inferior *MS*

60:11   hostility *E1*] wrath *MS*

60:12   unchanged *E1*] the same *MS*

60:22   rush *TSR*] world *MS*

60:23   create the world afresh *E1*] throw the cattle across the field, and push a clear gap in the clouds with his hand as he went home *MS*

60:27   passionate servants to him, *TSR*] solid flame, so *MS*

60:28   power *TSR*] wealth *MS*

60:31   lost *TSR*] forgot *MS*

60:32   went to take *TSR*] took possession *MS*

60:33   mad to ... the while *TSR*] revelling in her, and she *MS*

60:35   secrets aside ... delight. *P* What *E1*] secrets, her deepest secrets, into the air and caught them again with a laugh, and she laughed to see them tossed and caught and played with. *P* So he strode and laughed in the bowels of the earth, and struck the stars across the sky in his amusement. What *MS* secrets aside ... delight. *P* So he moved excited in the bowels of the earth, and amongst the stars in the sky in his exploration. What *TSR*

60:38 they were ... or not? *E1*] he was, and who she was, in particular? They were man and woman stripped together, and who cared about anything else? They were man and woman, complete in lordship, they had themselves and each other and the universe to kick about and to take pleasure of. And during their hour, they took their pleasure. *MS* they ... or not? They were thrusting into the outer darkness, away from the lights and the camp fires, into the outer darkness to explore the unknown, and add it on to them. What should they remember, of the camp-fires and the talking at the tent-doors, that should detain them. During their hour, they left the world and took their fill of the beyond. *TSR*

60:40 again, there ... between them, *TSR*] again into anger *MS*

61:1 for her, *TSR*] *Om. MS*

61:2 for him *TSR*] *Om. MS*

61:3 for it ... [61:7] the adventure. *TSR*] to get hold of it on the instant, seize another hour as full, when the secrets of the woman are playthings for the man, tossed about, when the secrets of the man are the woman's huge game, and they both enjoy themselves: when a man can play at marbles with the moon and the stars, using the moon for the dob-taw,

{dob-tau, *TS*} squandering the pleiades out of their hole, and pitching on the three straight stars of Orion's belt, to make them hop. *MS*

61:8 silence *TSR*] eternal silence *MS*

61:10 cast out. He seethed *TSR*] sent to school. He boiled *MS*

61:15 off, anywhere. *TSR*] hulking off. *MS*

61:18 receive him back again, *TSR*] come back to him, *MS*

61:25 foreigner with a bad *TSR*] nasty foreigner with a nasty *MS*

61:37 absent as ... in indifference *E1*] strange as any foreign woman from the sea *MS*

61:38 home. *E1*] home. There he felt himself in a wire cage, looking through at her. *MS*

61:40 forfeited *TSR*] outraged *MS*

62:13 acknowledgment] acknowledgement *TS*

62:17 withheld *TS*] with-held *MS*

62:20 Anna. *E1*] Anna, for her response and love. *MS*

62:22 or reading *TSR*] *Om. MS*

62:30 mad, and] mad, *TS*

63:12 his heart *E1*] he *MS*

63:16 pain *TSR*] cruel pain *MS*

63:23 somnambulant *E1*] somnambule *MS*

63:29 solace *E1*] solace, his chief stay now *MS*

63:38 nightdress *Ed.*] night-dress *MS*

64:4 on." *P* The *TS*] ~." / The *MS*

64:9 dear." *P* The *TS*] ~." / The *MS*

64:11 voice. *P* The *Ed.*] ~. / The *MS* ~. The *TS*

64:19 stillness] silence *TS*

64:33 bird *E1*] rabbit *MS*

64:34 mother, pleasantly. *P* The *TSR*] mother. / The *MS* mother. *P* The *TS*

64:36 bed,] ~ *TS*

64:36 enough. *E1*] enough. You don't

want to turn me out, do you?
MS

64:39 day,] ~ *TS*

65:6 now." *P* And *TS*] ~." / And *MS*

65:15 Brangwen. *P* Anna *TS*] ~. / Anna *MS*

65:17 *want*." *P* And *Ed.*] ~." / And *MS* ~."And *TS*

65:20 easy *E1*] gentle *MS*

65:26 her *E1*] her mother *MS*

65:31 gone, gone *E1*] gone, gone, gone *MS*

65:36 active, *E1*] active and *MS*

66:5 them. *P* Brangwen] ~. Brangwen *TS*

66:9 *not*] not *TS*

66:17 slipper *TSR*] patent slipper *MS*

66:19 flushed] flashed *E1*

66:25 said. *P* She *TS*] ~. / She *MS*

66:31 is. *E1*] is, and ask 'em if they don't mind you playing here. *MS*

66:34 imperiously: *TS*] ~. *MS*

66:37 This *E1*] She *MS*

67:21 door. *P* The] ~. The *TS*

67:22 him, pale with fear. *TSR*] him. *MS*

67:23 her] up *TS*

67:23 courage, seeing him become patient. *E1*] courage. *MS* courage ... become still. *TS*

67:25 him:] ~. *TS*

67:26 shouted. *P* Her *TS*] ~. / Her *MS*

67:27 came—] ~. *TS*

67:29 comakle." *P* She *TS*] ~." / She *MS*

67:30 forward] forwards *TS*

67:34 bomakle." *P* He was *E1*] bomakle." / They were both *MS* bomakle." *P* They were both *TS*

67:38 ay? *TSR*] ~! *MS* ~. *TS*

67:40 replied,] ~ *TS*

68:2 came *TSR*] would come *MS*

68:3 peaceful *E1*] empty *MS*

68:10 little,] ~ *TS*

68:17 it'll pass wi' *TSR*] it only calls for *MS*

68:26 shrill] shrill laugh *TS*

68:30 unhappy,] ~. *TS*

68:36 elvish] elfish *TS*

69:6 carelessly *E1*] endlessly *MS*

69:13 home." *P* There *TS*] ~." / There *MS*

69:15 then?" *P* And *TS*] ~?" / And *MS*

69:16 intent] ~, *TS*

69:18 gateway *Ed.*] gate-way *MS*

69:29 Mother!" *P* Mrs *Ed.*] ~!" / Mrs *MS* ~!" *P* Mrs. *TS*

69:33 cowsheds *Ed.*] cow-sheds *MS*

70:3 earth *E1*] earth under his normal attention *MS*

70:5 with the *E1*] where there was so much *MS*

70:7 emptiness *TSR*] stark emptiness *MS*

70:13 sudden *TSR*] coloured *MS*

70:20 The birds pecked *TSR*] Did not the birds peck *MS*

70:20 the horses were *TSR*] were not the horses *MS*

70:21 the bare *TSR*] did not the bare *MS*

70:21 flung *TSR*] fling *MS*

70:22 radiated *TSR*] radiate *MS*

70:22 light. He ... it all. *TSR*] light? Was he not keen, keen for it all? *MS*

70:24 separated from ... then let ... would be. *TSR*] sombre, extinguished, then, for a little while, she was not real. She would be real again, later. *MS* separated ... then, let ... be. *E1*

70:28 to the ... was happy. *TSR*] with zest to the horses. *MS*

70:30 reined in *E1*] pulled up *MS*

70:36 She suffered, but he *E1*] One suffered with her, but one *MS*

70:37 indecent *TSR*] a sort of showing off *MS*

70:40 Well,] ~ *TS*

71:5 lavender] ~, *TS*

71:10   light *E1*] moon *MS*
71:10   journey. *P* The] ~? The *TS*
71:12   stopped. *E1*] stopped. Who can escape his hour? *MS*
71:15   loaf *TSR*] huge loaf *MS*
71:15   tea-pot] tea- / pot *TS* teapot *E1*
71:18   remote *E1*] lone *MS*
71:27   dust-coloured   *E1*]   dusty-coloured *MS*
71:31   fundamental   *E1*]   imminent *MS*
71:33   she, *TSR*] she were *MS*
71:33   put forth *TSR*] torn *MS*
71:39   one *TSR*] one creative *MS*
72:3   asked. *P* She *TS*] ~. / She *MS*
72:11   downstairs] down-stairs *E1*
72:14   unheeding. *P* She *TSR*] but unheeding. / She *MS* but unheeding. *P* She *TS*
72:17   baby." *P* The *TS*] ~." / The *MS*
72:21   tired." *P* There *TS*] ~." / There *MS*
72:24   desolation. *P* Tilly *TS*] ~. / Tilly *MS*
72:28   duckie; *TSR*] ~, *MS*
72:29   angel." *P* But *TS*] ~." / But *MS*
72:35   doesn't." *P* Tilly *TS*] ~." / Tilly *MS*
72:38   me.—] ~— *E1*
72:38   mother—",] ~,"— *TS*
72:39   child's *E1*] little *MS*
73:1   wilful *TSR*] a naughty *MS*
73:5   undressed] ~, *E1*
73:18   crying. *TSR*] crying, its maddening insistence, mechanical. *MS*
73:20   thin *TSR*] cold *MS*
73:20   anger. *P* And *TS*] ~. / And *MS*
73:29   while,] ~ *TS*
73:32   unheedingly *E1*] grimly *MS*
73:34   body   convulsed   *TSR*]   face steady *MS*
73:36   herself.   *P*   Brangwen]   ~. Brangwen *TS*
73:39   Wheer's] Where's *TS*
73:40   Anna *E1*] She *MS*

74:2   small, convulsed, *TSR*] small, *MS* small *TS*
74:18   new degree of anger *TSR*] weariness *MS*
74:20   crying? Why ... to heart *TSR*] crying. Why should he bother *MS*
74:24   offering *TSR*] miserable but offering *MS*
74:27   little,] ~ *TS*
74:27   bit *TSR*] little bit *MS*
74:34   that. *E1*] that. It'll be better. *MS*
74:36   beside herself *TSR*] impervious *MS*
74:38   We'll] we'll *E1*
75:8   close *E1*] very safe *MS*
75:15   nail,] ~ *TS*
75:15   in *TSR*] safe in *MS*
75:19   rain, inside, *TSR*] ~. Inside *MS*
75:19   softly-illuminated *TSR*] softly illuminated *MS*
75:20   barn *TSR*] big barn *MS*
75:36   running *TSR*] chocking *MS*
75:37   sharply; *TSR*] ~, *MS*
75:39   beast *TSR*] creatures *MS see note on* 74:39
76:1   returned,] ~ *TS*
76:11   stuff *TSR*] food *MS*
76:13   still,] ~ *E1*
76:15   outside *TSR*] the farm *MS*
76:31   open. *E1*] open. Poor little mite! His heart was hot with an anguish of pity and tenderness for her. *MS* open. Poor creature! His ... with pity ... her. *TSR*
76:32   quietly] quickly *TS*
77:2   water-butts *TSR*] water butts *MS*
77:9   young man, untouched. *E1*] bachelor. What a change had come over him! Well, he was glad. *MS* young man, untouched. Things were changed now! Well ... glad. *TSR*

77:10 fists *E1*] fist *MS*
77:11 the woman *TSR*] his wife *MS*
77:11 asleep. *E1*] asleep. He felt virtuous. *MS*
77:13 the woman *TSR*] his wife *MS*
77:21 himself. *E1*] him. She was not human, she did not belong to him. She was as remote, as alien, as the angels, or demons, or such beings that do not share our feelings. Her feelings were not his feelings. He {our feelings. He *TS*} stood in dread of woman, and of what she represented. It was not to be denied. *MS* himself. She was not for him, she ... our feelings. He ... dread of her, and of her terrible impersonality. Yet she was ... denied. *TSR*
77:23 brown-grey *TSR*] grey *MS*
77:24 the *TSR*] a *MS*
77:26 her;] ~: *TS*
77:27 male. *E1*] male. He was her husband. *MS*
77:31 bowels *E1*] bowels burnt in the fire *MS*
77:35 There was ... of life. *E1*] The hands of joy were thrusting forward her pain, and he must not believe only in the horror. He sat by the fire enduring the slow procession of pain, footstep after footstep, moment after moment, stride after stride, and never nearing the end. *MS* The ... slow procreation of ... end. *TSR*
78:3 as *TSR*] so much as *MS*
78:3 his step-child *TSR*] the little *MS*
78:9 she were transplanted *TSR*] all her energy were used up for the time being *MS*
78:12 seemed *TSR*] was *MS*
78:21 robust, mortal exchange *E1*] same robust, fierce, full-blooded tourney *MS* robust, wholesale exchange *TSR*
78:23 intensity *TSR*] thing *MS*
78:24 experience *TSR*] experience in his life *MS*
78:24 it, *TSR*] it again, again, *MS*
78:28 delirious in *TSR*] shouting in him for mad *MS*
78:29 almost *TSR*] Om. *MS*
78:30 made him ... eternal knowledge *E1*] was enough to make him hail the whole world with welcome, till the nights rang with clear stars, and day chimed like a bell, and the weeks clashed in peals and carillons, and everybody was a gladness *MS* was ... hail his whole world with acclamation, when the nights rang their clear ... and everything was triumphal *TSR*
78:33 finished *E1*] exhausted *MS*
79:5 ugly scenes *E1*] a ghastly storm *MS* horrible scenes *TSR*
79:8 was,] ~ *TS*
79:9 to *TSR*] Om. *MS*
79:10 spent *TSR*] spilled *MS*
79:12 given him *MS, E1*] given him some *TSR*
79:14 essential *TSR*] intrinsic *MS*
79:16 close *TSR*] mild *MS*
79:19 troublesome *TSR*] turbulent *MS*
79:22 Also *TSR*] And *MS*
79:25 delighted and serene and secure, *E1*] mild and glowing and serene, *MS* delighted and glowing and secure, *TSR*
79:31 elsewhere than on her *TSR*] on Brangwen *MS*
79:32 freed, she] ~. She *TS*
79:32 independent, forgetful *TSR*] independent *MS*
79:36 activity *E1*] life *MS*
79:40 Old King Cole *MS, E1*] "~ ~ ~" *TSR*
80:1 Brangwen,] ~. *TS*

80:5 soul *E1*] little soul *MS*
80:10 black-bird *Ed.*] blackbird *MS*
80:13 black-bird *Ed.*] black bird *MS* blackbird *TS*
80:13 tuning-up] tuning up *TS*
80:14 black-bird's] blackbird's *TS*
80:15 black-bird's] blackbird's *TS*
80:15 singing *TSR*] singing four an' twenty *MS* singing four-and-twenty *TS*
80:16 shouted *TSR*] sang *MS*
80:22 Sing *E1*] Art singin' a song o' sixpence, tha thripenny-bit? Sing *MS* Art ... sixpence, thripenny-bit? Sing *TSR*
80:22 up." *P* And *TS*] ~." / And *MS*
80:23 loudly *TSR*] *Om. MS*
80:25 "'Sing] ~ *TS* "~ *TSR*
80:27 Ascha!'—] ~! *TS* ~!—— *E1*
80:31 What] what *TS*
80:31 racket!" *P* Brangwen *TS*] ~!" / Brangwen *MS*
80:36 extremely *E1*] infinitely *MS*
80:37 to her *TSR*] she could not understand that *MS*
80:37 people, they ... her equals *TSR*] people in themselves *MS*
80:39 whirling] whir-/ing *TS* whirring *E1*
81:7 them] him *TS*
81:9 chuckling *TSR*] little chuckling *MS*
81:14 father: *TS*] ~ *MS*
81:18 him ... her *TSR*] her ... him *MS*
81:19 into *TSR*] in *MS*
81:20 beer *E1*] glass of beer *MS*
81:24 Brangwin] Brangwen *E1*
81:27 inanities. *P* She *Ed.*] ~. / She *MS* ~. She *TS*
81:28 touch-me-not *TSR*] noli-me-tangere *MS*
81:28 inquiries *E1*] attitude *MS*
81:29 people *E1*] people towards her *MS*
81:32 comment] comments *TS*
81:32 child. *P* Then *Ed.*] ~. / Then *MS* ~. Then *TS*

81:37 sharp-shins." *P* Anna *TSR*] sharp-shins." / Anna *MS* sharp-skins." *P* Anna *TS*
81:40 him. *P* "I] ~. "I *TS*
82:3 gentleman-farmer] gentleman farmer *TS*
82:5 in to] into *TS*
82:7 his *TSR*] all his *MS*
82:9 bewilderment *E1*] amazement *MS*
82:16 refreshment booth] refreshment-booth *TS*
82:21 didna *Ed.*] did na *MS* did-na *TSR*
82:25 bar-man] barman *E1*
82:29 unabated *TSR*] unmoderated *MS* immoderated *TS*
82:31 Brangwen." *P* The *TS*] ~." / The *MS*
82:35 them. A] ~. *P* A *TS*
82:38 timeless,] ~ *TS*
83:7 question] questions *TS*
83:9 Missis." *P* Anna *Ed.*] missis." / Anna *MS* missis." *P* Anna *TS*
83:13 little,] ~ *TS*
83:14 cow's-tail *Ed.*] cows-tail *MS* cows's-tail *TS*
83:15 people] ~, *TS*
83:25 all the *E1*] all *MS*
83:27 cattle-market *TS*] cattle market *MS*
83:28 best *E1*] very much *MS*
83:32 "George Inn," *Ed.*] "~" ~, *MS* "~" inn, *TS* ~ Inn, *E1*
83:36 o'clock, *Ed.*] oclock, *MS* oclock *TS* o'clock *E1*
83:40 fierce] ~, *E1*
84:1 round her ... her] round the ... her *TS* round the ... the *TSR*
84:2 the men *TSR*] they *MS*
84:3 gentleman-farmer *TS*] gentleman farmer *MS*
84:4 pole-cat *TSR*] pole cat *MS*
84:7 goes." *P* She *TS*] ~." / She *MS*
84:10 what?" *P* She *TS*] ~?" / What *MS*

84:12 man." *P* Which *TS*] ~." /
Which *MS*
84:16 flamed. *P* There *TS*] ~. /
There *MS*
84:19 ma] me *TS*
84:20 wool?" *P* He *TS*] ~?" / He *MS*
84:28 her. *P* Instead *TS*] ~. / Instead
MS
84:32 crétin] cretin *TS*
84:39 tha'] th' *TS*
85:13 an educated *E1*] a well-
educated *MS*
85:14 Alfred *Ed.*] Arthur *MS*
85:26 woman,] ~ *TS*
85:31 woman *E1*] lady *MS*
85:38 he] that he *TS*
85:39 in,] ~? *E1*
86:1 drawing room] drawing-room
TS
86:7 Spencer—and] ~. And *TS*
86:8 Browning *TSR*] Byron *MS*
86:9 deep,] ~ *E1*
86:12 this way inclined *TSR*] one o'
this sort *MS*
86:13 an unusual *TSR*] a remarkable
MS
86:14 new idea of *E1*] sense of
possession of *MS* sense of connection with *TSR*
86:17 separate *TSR*] solitary *MS*
86:17 her. There] ~, there *TS*
86:20 tea-time,] ~ *TS*
86:22 courtly,] ~ *TS*
86:23 strange *E1*] astounding *MS*
86:28 well-off ... well-off *Ed.*] well
off ... well off *MS*
86:28 Alfred *Ed.*] Arthur *MS*
86:33 beyond him, *E1*] extraneous
MS extraneous, *TS*
86:33 regretted,] ~ *TS*
86:34 time,] ~ *TS*
86:34 a prisoner, *E1*] like a coward
for *MS* a skulker, *TSR*
86:35 sitting *TSR*] sitting so *MS*
86:35 unadventurous *TSR*] meagre
MS
86:35 risk *TSR*] suffering
86:36 Browning *TSR*] Byron *MS*

86:37 Forbes'] Forbes's *TS*
87:7 figure] ~, *TS*
87:7 quiet,] ~ *TS*
87:15 woman-haunt *TSR*] woman
haunt *MS*
87:19 gave *TSR*] held *MS*
87:20 defensive *E1*] hostile *MS*
87:21 said. *P* She *TS*] ~. / She *MS*
87:23 Why do you go? *TSR*] I don't
want you to go, *MS*
87:23 said. *P* His *TS*] ~. / His *MS*
87:25 No reason ... said *TSR*] Why
don't you?" he asked *MS*
87:27 go away *TSR*] leave me now *MS*
87:28 replied. *P* She *TS*] ~. / She
MS
87:30 said. *P* It *TS*] ~. / It *MS*
87:34 said. *P* He *TS*] ~. / He *MS*
87:35 Did he?, *Ed.*] '~ ~?', *MS*
'~ ~?' *TS*
87:38 Yet he knew he was. *TSR*] He
was asking for nothing. *MS*
88:1 me? *TSR*] ~! *MS*
88:2 you?" *P* He *TS*] ~?" / He *MS*
88:5 making to *TSR*] me to make
you *MS*
88:6 don't *TSR*] do not *MS*
88:7 interested *TSR*] eager *MS*
88:8 *you*—] ~, *TS*
88:8 now?" *P* There *Ed.*] ~?" /
There *MS* ~?" There *TS*
88:10 asked. *P* His *TS*] ~. / His *MS*
88:12 there] ~, *TS*
88:13 separate *TSR*] distinct *MS*
88:17 said,] ~ *TS*
88:18 said. *P* He *TS*] ~. / He *MS*
88:19 for *E1*] in astonishment for *MS*
88:19 ashamed *TSR*] indignant *MS*
88:20 like *TSR*] care for *MS*
88:21 liked her *TSR*] would like to
MS
88:21 persistently. *P* He *TS*] ~. / He
MS
88:22 wife] own wife *TS*
88:24 these things *TSR*] off *MS*
88:24 his wife *TSR*] a stranger *MS*
88:25 this, as ... a stranger. *TSR*]
this? *MS*

88:26 didn't *E1*] shouldn't *MS*

88:27 Alfred." *P* His *TS*] ~." / His *MS*

88:29 told *TSR*] not even told *MS*

88:29 Wirksworth, but ... he thought *TSR*] Wirksworth. Now he hid it as a guilty thing *MS*

88:32 oppose her *TSR*] boil *MS*

88:33 her? *TSR*] ~. *MS*

88:36 said. *P* The *TS*] ~. / The *MS*

88:39 me?" *P* Suddenly *TS*] ~?" / Suddenly *MS*

89:5 alone,] ~ *TS*

89:5 come to] take *TS*

89:7 What am ... about you *TSR*] Well what do you want me to do *MS*

89:10 was for ... or nothing— *TSR*] were for nothing, for nothing. Paul came for something, it *was* something when he came to me—a real man I had. *MS* was ... nothing—— *E1*

89:13 said. *P* They *TS*] ~. / They *MS*

89:15 seething and chaotic *TSR*] blind and troubled *MS*

89:16 held *TSR*] dogged *MS*

89:17 dominant *TSR*] hounding *MS*

89:18 hard *TSR*] handsome *MS*

89:30 said. *P* And *TS*] ~. / And *MS*

89:32 him against *TSR*] his loins against *MS*

89:34 her. *TSR*] her. He wanted himself. *MS*

89:35 said. He ... heart. He *TSR*] said. / He *MS* said. *P* He *TS*

89:38 compulsion to ... awful unknown *TSR*] contact with her *MS*

90:1 go *TSR*] go to her *MS*

90:2 himself,] ~ *TS*

90:2 ashamed] too ashamed *TS*

90:3 waited for *TSR*] wanted *MS*

90:4 before her,] ~ ~ *TS*

90:5 submission. *P* She *Ed.*] humble response. *P* She *MS* humble response. She *TS* reverent submission. She *TSR*

90:6 And it ... in her *TSR*] Oh, and the anguish, that he must become active, participant *MS*

90:8 embrace and know *TSR*] mingle with *MS*

90:9 shrank from *TSR*] resisted *MS*

90:17 began to *TSR*] would *MS*

90:18 to draw near. *TSR*] he would draw near. He would draw near her, in the way of love, nearer, as close as a man might come, to see if he could really come to her, if he could reach her and at last embrace her. She waited for him, and he trembled. *MS*

90:19 desire *E1*] pure desire *MS* absolute desire *TSR*

90:20 meet *TSR*] come to *MS*

90:20 reality *TSR*] glistening reality *MS*

90:21 just beyond ... him. Blind *TSR*] shining just beyond him dazzled him, blinded him. The light of the transfiguration was on his face, he was blind *MS*

90:22 consummation of *TSR*] transfiguration *MS*

90:23 darkness *TSR*] incandescence *MS*

90:23 swallow *TSR*] destroy *MS*

90:25 of darkness *TSR*] *Om. MS*

90:26 till *TSR*] into flame, till *MS*

90:26 consummation *TSR*] radiance *MS*

90:31 trod strange ground of *TSR*] were bright with *MS*

90:32 with discovery *TSR*] with surety *MS*

90:33 re-echoed *TSR*] chimed *MS*

90:34 in discovery *TSR*] in knowledge *MS*

90:34 gladly and forgetful. Everything *TSR*] glad, like masters, along the roads, like inheritors. Nothing *MS*

90:35 The new ... be explored. *TSR*] All was found, it remained only to be discovered. The inheritance was indescribable, it was unfathomably rich, the wealth could never be told, neither in this generation nor in the next, nor in many that would come after. Could it ever be counted out? *MS*

91:6 world,] ~ *TS*

91:12 meaning, *E1*] utterance *MS*

91:14 strong *TSR*] bright *MS*

91:17 of] to *TS*

91:17 reality *E1*] conclusion *MS*

91:19 He *TSR*] he *MS*

91:20 fully making Himself *TSR*] ever making himself *MS*

91:22 He was declared *TSR*] he had made himself known *MS*

91:23 joined *TSR*] linked *MS*

91:24 His *Ed.*] his *MS*

91:24 abode *TSR*] abode in the house *MS*

91:27 they? *TSR*] they? One does not think of the daylight one lives by, nor of the darkness that nourishes one. *MS*

91:32 asked *TSR*] cried out *MS*

91:32 length. *TSR*] length, and he knew whither to direct his way. *MS*

91:34 she saw *TSR*] as it were a pillar to the east, and a pillar to the west, far away under the sky, she saw *MS*

91:36 assurance ... assurance *TSR*] sign ... sign *MS*

91:37 more] longer *TS*

91:39 met to *TSR*] like pillars supported fixedly *MS*

92:3 dame's] dames' *TS*

92:8 patronised *TSR*] pitied *MS*

92:17 arrogance *TSR*] impudence *MS*

92:23 Very *TSR*] For very *MS*

92:24 parts] part *TS*

92:28 Fred *TSR*] Peter *MS*

92:31 real] ~, *TS*

93:3 He *TSR*] Although he *MS*

93:4 but *TSR*] *Om. MS*

93:12 a tall ... with pride *E1*] just dead, and he was mourning for her *MS*

93:23 responded,] ~ *TS*

93:34 when *TSR*] *Om. MS*

94:13 contemptuously,] ~; *TS*

94:14 could] would *TS*

94:31 She wanted to respect them. *TSR*] *Om. MS*

94:34 falsities *TSR*] bonds *MS*

94:35 home,] ~ *TS*

94:35 leave] leaving *TS*

94:37 no mean *TSR*] nor mean *MS*

94:37 care for *TSR*] *Om. MS*

94:39 could *TSR*] could now *MS*

94:40 were too separate *E1*] had taken an independent order *MS* had an ... order *TSR*

95:1 common *TSR*] strong *MS*

95:2 supreme relation *E1*] powerful feeling *MS* profound feeling *TSR*

95:4 dignity *E1*] dignity and ease *MS* dignity and subtlety of instinct *TSR*

95:6 begrudge her her very *TSR*] have no independent *MS*

95:7 go *TSR*] go out *MS*

95:10 usually at *TSR*] always at *MS*

95:11 She was] She *E1*

95:15 school-mistresses *Ed.*] schoolmistresses *MS*

95:17 Good? *E1*] ~. *MS*

95:21 Because she ... the mistress. *TSR*] *Om. MS*

95:23 authority. *TSR*] authority, always. *MS*

95:25 to be always] always to be *TS*

95:26 really *TSR*] quite *MS*

95:34 indifferently over all *TSR*] on the necks of *MS*

95:39 indifferent to *TSR*] absolved from *MS*

96:5 hearty, warm. *TSR*] still hearty. *MS*

96:6 respect *E1*] court *MS*

96:8 open-handed *TSR*] open handed *MS*

96:9 so long as *TSR*] because *MS*

96:11 sons,] ~ *E1*

96:15 all. *E1*] all. She simply was not aware that outside comment might be passed on her. *MS* all. She ... comment existed. *TSR*

96:21 insignificant. *P* It] ~. It *TS*

96:29 pleased *TSR*] quiet *MS*

96:37 an anger *TSR*] a flame *MS*

97:2 Il'son?" *P* She *TS*] ~?" / She *MS*

97:3 eyes, yet ... flouted him. *TSR*] eyes. *MS*

97:5 a law to themselves *TSR*] lawless *MS*

97:6 a small republic ... invisible bounds *E1*] and quite unaware of it *MS* a small, fine republic ... bounds *TSR*

97:7 Ilkeston *TSR*] all Ilkeston *MS*

97:7 claims *TSR*] individual claims *MS*

97:8 from outside *TSR*] *Om. MS*

97:13 lacked *TSR*] yielded *MS*

97:14 beliefs *E1*] ideals *MS*

97:18 Mystery] mystery *TS*

97:20 Absolute *E1*] Mystery *TSR*

97:23 the great Separator ... His ... Great Mystery *E1*] her own Mystic Saviour and Bridegroom, something gleaming, imminent, terrible, rejoiceful, something private *MS* the great Lawgiver ... his ... great Mystery *TSR*

97:24 telling. *TSR*] telling, something exclusive, that had no relation with other people. *MS*

97:25 Whom she ... her senses, *TSR*] *Om. MS*

97:28 within a ... her destiny *TSR*] her real inner language being a sort of symbolism, a code of mystic images *MS*

97:30 To *TSR*] And to *MS*

97:30 reduced *E1*] initiated *MS*

97:31 the general ... the world *TSR*] intellectual criticism *MS*

97:32 symbols and indication *E1*] ritualistic *MS* symbols and ritual *TSR*

97:33 mystery *TSR*] ritual *MS*

97:34 profound *TSR*] thrilling *MS*

97:36 apart *TSR*] strange *MS*

97:36 village, for ... well-to-do. *TSR*] village. *MS*

97:39 own *E1*] *Om. MS*

98:6 ora *TSR*] Ora *MS*

98:6 peccatoribus, *TSR*] ~ *MS*

98:7 nostrae, *TSR*] ~ *MS*

98:8 when translated *TSR*] *Om. MS*

98:10 irritated *TSR*] bored *MS*

98:11 She *TSR*] It savoured of cant phrase. She *MS*

98:12 Maria":] ~;" *TS*

98:14 not satisfactory, somehow *TSR*] too special, too specified *MS*

98:23 surety and confidence, *TSR*] lack of mind, and yet *MS*

98:24 things,] ~ *TS*

98:25 silent overriding *E1*] blithe ignoring *MS*

98:37 wordless, *TSR*] almost wordless, but *MS*

99:1 interchange *TSR*] intercourse *MS*

99:3 nor] or *TS*

99:4 went *TSR*] turned *MS*

99:11 stretched] stretching *TSC see notes*

99:24 the religious feelings *TSR*] they *MS*

99:24 her,] ~ *TS*

99:29 nothingness *TSR*] frippery *MS*

99:40 lace-factory *Ed.*] lace factory *MS*

100:9 she was a lady. *E1*] there was something of a lady about her. *MS*

100:12 her. *E1*] her. She had never looked at a young man to know him. She knew vaguely that men *were* human beings, but not very important, a species of cattle having separate existence. *MS* her. She ... beings, but they were a species ... existence. *TSR*

100:13 pleasant *TSR*] dashing *MS*

100:19 incidental. *E1*] shapes, not filled out. They were all figures in the flat to her, like cardboard shapes, comical, strange, even rather thrilling, but not seriously alive. *MS* shapes, not ... all external to her ... rather exciting, but not partaking of her life. *TSR*

100:28 among *TSR*] among all *MS*

100:29 unawareness of *E1*] indifference to *MS*

100:32 conventionally *E1*] naturally *MS*

100:35 repelled *E1*] surprised *MS*

100:36 something strange *TSR*] nothing else *MS*

100:39 it. *E1*] it. How odd young men were! *MS*

101:3 intimate] strangely intimate *TS* *see notes*

101:10 this? *TSR*] this? Is somebody bad? *MS*

101:11 month." *P* Anna *TS*] ~." / Anna *MS*

101:12 making her ... this stranger! *TSR*] putting her off before this stranger of whom he was making so much fuss! *MS*

101:14 re-asserted] reasserted *E1*

101:17 went *TSR*] went quickly *MS*

101:21 twinkling *TSR*] flashing and twinkling *MS*

101:23 silver *TSR*] much silver *MS*

101:26 half a sovereign] half-a-sovereign *TS*

101:28 startled. *E1*] startled. Who was this? *MS*

101:30 half a sovereign] half-a-sovereign *TS*

101:39 Give it here *TSR*] Put it wheer tha got it from *MS*

101:39 father. *P* Hastily *TS*] ~. / Hastily *MS*

101:40 the purse *TSR*] it *MS*

102:4 bird's ... hawk's *E1*] wild creature's ... bird's *MS*

102:5 'll *TSR*] 'ull *MS*

102:5 father. *P* Anna *TS*] ~. / Anna *MS*

102:7 hovering *TSR*] hovering there *MS*

102:8 him: she] ~. She *TS*

102:9 was antagonistic to *E1*] did not want to be aware of *MS* was not ready to ... of *TSR*

102:10 waited *E1*] waited graciously *MS*

102:11 Fred *TSR*] Peter *MS*

102:14 high-road *Ed.*] highroad *MS*

102:14 a strangeness in her being. *E1*] somebody walking beside her, expecting her to speak to him. *MS* a strangeness walking beside her. *TSR*

102:16 her brother's *TSR*] Peter's *MS*

102:17 Fred *TSR*] Peter *MS*

102:18 church." *P* Fred *TSR*] church." / Peter *MS* church." *P* Peter *TS*

102:25 self-possessed *TSR*] well-mannered *MS*

102:28 Fred *TSR*] Peter *MS*

102:35 the small boy's *TSR*] Peter's *MS*

103:4 fool's-parsley *Ed.*] fools parsley *MS* fools-parsley *TSR*

103:4 foamy, *TS*] ~ *MS*

103:4 number *E1*] coloured number *MS*

103:7 Fred *TSR*] Peter *MS*

103:9 the] *Om. TS*

103:17 conscious of ... she knew. *TSR*] watching the glow of the two hands of her cousin. They were brown and thin and alive. They lay quite still on the thighs, two separate hands, brown-skinned, glowing red and yellow, very luminous. Each had a life of its own. Each might fly up, like a bird, any {bird any *TS*} moment. She watched them as they lay unconsciously resting in the stillness, glowing and unaware. It was as if she were watching two wild creatures that would slip away if her shadow touched them. *MS*

103:22 a strange influence entering in to *TSR*] some influence there beside *MS*

103:23 dark,] ~ *TS*

103:23 she had not known before *TSR*] not connected with any person *MS*

103:25 hands moved. *TSR*] glowing hands moved, almost afraid. *MS*

103:26 *wished*] wished *TS*

103:31 over-riding *E1*] baritone *MS*

103:31 tenor *E1*] alto *MS*

103:31 Her soul opened in amazement. *TSR*] But it was amazing! *MS*

103:33 She *E1*] From sheer amazement she *MS*

103:34 Up and down rang his *E1*] Volumes of sound were produced from him. Out they came—up and down went his alto *MS* Volumes ... down boomed his alto *TSR*

103:35 helplessly shocked into laughter *TSR*] irresistably tickled *MS*

103:38 into] in *TS*

103:38 was amazed, and *TSR*] *Om. MS*

104:2 Fred *TSR*] Peter *MS*

104:6 knelt *E1*] sat *MS*

104:6 giggling *TSR*] amusement *MS*

104:13 pregnant *TSR*] rich *MS*

104:13 peace. Her] ~. *P* Her *TS*

104:14 pocket handkerchief] pocket-handkerchief *TS*

104:21 Fred *TSR*] Peter *MS*

104:26 Fred *TSR*] Peter *MS*

104:29 The whole church heard it.] *Om. TS*

104:33 exhausted,] ~ *TS*

104:37 arrived,] ~ *TS*

104:38 resoundingly *E1*] with gusto at the alto *MS*

105:2 tinkling] twinkling *TS*

105:5 Fred *TSR*] Peter *MS*

105:7 half mocking] half-mocking *TS*

105:10 said. *P* They *TS*] ~. / They *MS*

105:13 o'laughing] o' laughing *TS* and laughing *E1*

105:15 choir. *P* She *TS*] ~. / She *MS*

105:18 Cousin *TS*] cousin *MS*

105:18 said. *P* At *TS*] ~. / At *MS*

105:25 why." *P* And *TS*] ~." / And *MS*

105:26 table. Will] ~. *P* Will *TS*

105:27 dark *E1*] eager, bright *MS*

105:27 said *E1*] opening his wide mouth, said *MS*

105:28 choir *E1*] Choir *MS*

105:28 of *E1*] at *MS*

105:28 Nicholas'.] ~' *TS* ~. *TSC*

105:29 Oh,] ~ *TS*

105:29 then?] ~! *TS*

105:30 youth. *P* It *TS*] ~. / It *MS*

105:36 they *TSR*] *Om. MS*

105:37 drawn out *TSR*] really roused *MS*

105:39 mediæval *E1*] mediaeval *MS*

105:40 forms. *TSR*] forms which by no means accorded {accord *TS*} with the Ruskin dogmas. *MS*

106:3 close *TSR*] *Om. MS*

106:6 dim coloured] dim-coloured *TS*

106:6 something took place *TSR*] heavy pillars rose *MS*

106:8 altar *TSR*] altar under the window of jewels *MS*

106:10 be covered with *TSR*] make with the sky *MS*

106:10 mystic *E1*] hushed *MS*

106:14 talked of ... thrilled her *TSR*] did not talk much of Gothic or Renaissance, or of Perpendicular *MS*

106:17 o'clock, *Ed.*] oclock, *MS* o'clock *TS*

106:17 churchyard *TS*] church yard *MS* church-/yard *E1*

106:21 forward. *E1*] forward, so steady. *MS* forward so steady. *TS*

106:23 porch—] ~.— *TS* ~—— *E1*

106:24 afternoon. *E1*] afternoon. He had never been so fired. *MS* afternoon. He came fully into his own. *TSR*

106:25 kindled round *TSR*] seemed to have swept *MS*

106:27 half moved] half-moved *TS*

106:28 half moved] half-moved *TS*

106:30 lodgings] lodging *TS*

106:31 glittering] ~, *TS*

106:32 vital *TSR*] spiritual *MS*

106:34 his unknown *TSR*] fiercely *MS*

106:35 ready *TSR*] eager *MS*

106:36 wanting *TSR*] eager for *MS*

106:38 sunshine *TSR*] magic sunshine *MS*

106:39 an outside world *TSR*] a symbolic earth *MS*

107:1 recurred the ... before it *TSR*] came the burning, fiery interest which carried everything up into flame *MS*

107:2 Sometimes] ~, *TS*

107:3 loved] ~, *TS*

107:4 revolt *TSR*] dislike *MS*

107:8 cat-like] cat-/ like *TS* catlike *E1*

107:10 was taken by *TSR*] loved *MS*

107:12 separate *TSR*] real *MS*

107:12 life. *TSR*] life. She had so very few real people in her life. *MS*

107:13 youth *TSR*] boy *MS*

107:14 glowing *TSR*] shining *MS*

107:19 without cognisance of the other person *TSR*] for his own pleasure *MS*

107:24 older] elder *TS*

107:28 special *E1*] narrow *MS*

107:29 abstracted *E1*] particularised *MS*

107:29 separate *E1*] narrow *MS*

107:30 nature. *E1*] nature. There was,

Brangwen thought, so much left out of the youth. He was so complete by virtue of this very omission, this blindness to other people. *MS*

107:31 agony *E1*] misery or agony *MS*

107:32 people's affairs. *TSR*] people's affairs. And his nephew was like this, said Tom Brangwen. *MS*

107:33 instinctive affairs *E1*] secret desires *MS* instinctive desires *TSR*

107:38 the *E1*] his *MS*

107:40 create a new thing *TSR*] find full, unhampered enjoyment *MS*

108:1 talked churches *E1*] churned in the dairy *MS*

108:3 he *TSR*] the young devil *MS*

108:11 cousin,] ~; *TS*

108:14 own wonder *TSR*] amazement *MS*

108:15 wonder *TSR*] amazement *MS*

108:19 acutely angry *E1*] blazingly indignant *MS*

108:21 or look elsewhere *E1*] the two intruders *MS*

108:23 of *TSR*] over *MS*

108:24 insistent *TSR*] exultant *MS*

108:24 balking] baulking *TS*

108:25 smash *TSR*] smash his way *MS*

108:29 absorbed *TSR*] in the trance *MS*

108:36 favorite] favourite *TS*

108:37 butter stamper] butter-stamper *TS*

108:37 a phœnix, *E1*] *Om. MS*

108:39 rose upwards *TSR*] pointed inwards *MS*

108:40 of the cup *TSR*] *Om. MS*

109:6 smooth *TSR*] scalloped *MS*

109:10 Every *TSR*] On every *MS*

109:10 became *TSR*] was *MS*

109:14 Why] ~, *E1*

109:20 him. *TSR*] him. He had a ruddy

face, that shone in the candle-light. *MS*

109:22 strange, re-echoing ... her being *TSR*] glad, or angry, always meant something or other *MS*

109:26 large *TSR*] great *MS*

109:33 near him *TSR*] rounded *MS*

109:35 quick, *TSR*] so quick, so *MS*

109:39 purpose *E1*] pride *MS*

109:40 hawk. *E1*] hawk. She lifted her mouth and they kissed. *MS*

110:2 hawk *TSR*] golden hawk *MS*

110:8 constant *TSR*] reddish *MS*

110:14 definite *E1*] young *MS*

110:21 for a moment *E1*] and shrink back *MS* and shrink for a moment *TSR*

110:26 retorted *TSR*] flashed *MS*

110:26 father. *P* She *Ed.*] ~. / She *MS* ~. She *TS*

110:28 stared *E1*] flared *MS*

110:39 loft,] ~ *TS*

111:6 sound:] ~. *TS*

111:7 you." *P* It *Ed.*] ~." / It *MS* ~." It *TS*

111:12 gulf of *TSR*] gulfing *MS*

111:14 oscillations, *TSR*] oscillations, a great pendulum-stroke, *MS*

111:24 blur] blue, *TS* blurr, *E1 see notes*

111:26 them] ~, *TS*

111:29 fowl] fowls *TS*

111:30 floor. *TSR*] floor. It was a vision up there in the falling rain. *MS*

111:31 of anger *TSR*] *Om. MS*

111:31 of self-effacement *TSR*] *Om. MS*

111:34 how much of herself *E1*] the priceless self *MS*

111:37 thoughtless fellow *E1*] grinning tom-cat *MS*

111:37 arms] ~, *E1*

112:3 Now she ... was finished *TSR*] And she was not his *MS*

112:11 endless] the endless *TS*

112:12 out,] ~ *TS*

112:14 Almighty *E1*] Father *MS*

112:15 thrusting *TSR*] drawing *MS*

112:18 transfigured *E1*] agonised *MS*

112:18 Almighty, *E1*] God, all *MS*

112:20 subject,] ~ *TS*

112:21 touch *TSR*] touch of the Almighty God *MS*

112:24 sombre *E1*] glittered *MS*

112:32 Creation *E1*] creation *MS*

112:34 His *E1*] his *MS*

112:35 small,] ~ *TS*

112:35 issuing *TSR*] leaping *MS*

112:40 lines, in ... her creation. *TSR*] lines. *MS*

113:6 angels *Ed.*] Angels *MS*

113:8 angels] Angels, *TS*

113:9 faces] ~, *TSR*

113:11 canal] Canal *TS*

113:13 puther] paths *TS*

113:15 glow of light *TSR*] darkness *MS*

113:15 his *TSR*] her *MS*

113:17 Corn-harvest *Ed.*] Corn harvest *MS*

113:18 farm-buildings *Ed.*] farm buildings *MS*

113:18 nightfall *TS*] night-fall *MS*

113:18 hung *TSR*] swung *MS*

113:29 Anna. *P* So *Ed.*] ~. / So *MS* ~. So *TS*

113:35 waiting,] ~ *TS*

114:8 glowingly to uncover *TSR*] to thrust a glowing hand in *MS*

114:13 pent-house] pent house *TS*

114:22 heaving *TSR*] the sea heaving *MS*

114:22 moonlight.—] ~. *TS*

114:23 had fallen *TSR*] fell *MS*

114:30 turn,] ~ *TS*

114:35 nearer and *TSR*] weaving nearer and *MS*

114:38 meet? Gradually a *TSR*] ~. A *MS*

114:40 her gradually *E1*] her, gradually, at length, *MS* her, gradually *TSR*

115:16 darkly *E1*] heavily *MS*

115:18 purpose *E1*] passion *MS*

115:33 turn." *P* His *Ed.*] ~." / His *MS* ~." His *TS*

115:36 he trembled as *E1*] his heart laughed and *MS*

115:37 arms *E1*] arms for the pleasure of kissing her *MS*

115:38 privilege *E1*] right *MS* intention *TSR*

115:38 She *E1*] And she *MS*

116:1 He wondered over *E1*] Marvellous, *MS*

116:8 afar. *P* The *Ed.*] ~. / The *MS* ~. The *TS*

116:15 love." *P* And *TS*] ~." / And *MS*

116:17 birthpain of love *TSR*] rapture *MS*

116:18 rapturous. *P* And *Ed.*] ~. / And *MS* ~. And *TS*

116:27 before. *TSR*] before. She had a face, she had hands and feet and soft dresses, but one could not want her. Yet now he did want her. *MS*

116:27 initiation] irritation *TS*

116:29 The conflict was gone by. *E1*] *Om. MS*

116:31 He was hers *E1*] In his heart she was his wife *MS* She was his *TSR*

116:31 glad,] ~ *TS*

116:32 fields] field *TS*

116:35 up. Then] ~ then *TS* ~, then *TSC*

116:37 chagrin. Why ... from him? *E1*] bitter grief. In his heart she was his wife. Yet she drew away from him. *MS* bitter ... his wife, yet ... him. *TS* bitter ... his own, yet ... him. *TSR*

116:39 said, *TSR*] said, pathetically, and *MS* said pathetically, and *TS*

117:1 dazed *TSR*] hurt *MS*

117:2 move. *TSR*] move. He was neutralised with an irresoluteness. *MS*

117:6 Anna." *P* She *TS*] ~." / She *MS*

117:8 Anna *E1*] my love *MS*

117:8 we?" *P* She *TS*] ~?" / She *MS*

117:13 own for ever *TSR*] wife *MS*

117:14 accomplishment. But ... irritation. *P* He *E1*] accomplishment. / He *MS* accomplishment. *P* He *TS*

117:19 money,] ~? *E1*

117:19 mother. *P* The *TS*] ~. / The *MS*

117:20 He hated these words *TSR*] Already he was up against opposition *MS*

117:25 I s'll] I'll *TS*

117:27 Yes." *P* There *TS*] ~." / There *MS*

117:29 week?" *P* Again *TS*] ~?" / Again *MS*

117:30 spirit were ... in him. *E1*] blood were being taken out of him, the life. *MS* blood were being injured in him. *TSR*

117:32 bright,] ~ *TS*

117:33 hawk's. *P* Brangwen *TS*] ~. / Brangwen *MS*

117:36 money] the money *TS*

117:36 later on *TSR*] when I'm older *MS*

117:36 raise *TSR*] borrow *MS*

117:39 boy *TSR*] child *MS*

118:2 bright,] ~ *TS*

118:3 am,] ~? *E1*

118:5 let us *E1*] I *MS*

118:9 boy. *P* And *TS*] ~. / And *MS*

118:12 strange and untouched *TSR*] white and clinched *MS*

118:12 felt he could not *E1*] felt, if he had to *MS* felt, he could not *TSR*

118:13 he was *E1*] he had *MS*

118:13 his will ... not be destroyed. He *TSR*] if he could not marry her soon, he would have to be broken. And he would not be broken. And he *MS*

118:15 get some ... not matter *TSR*] ask everybody he knew for some money, till he had fifty pounds, and he would marry her *MS*

118:19 it] it *TS*
118:22 said. *P* She *TS*] ~. / She *MS*
118:26 unconsciousness. *P* His *TS*] ~. / His *MS*
118:28 contempt. *P* The *Ed.*] ~. / The *MS* ~. The *TS*
118:34 father." *P* She *TS*] ~." / She *MS*
118:36 her. *E1*] her. He was white as if bled. *MS*
118:37 said. *P* But *E1*] ~. / But *MS*
118:40 bemused *E1*] dazed *MS*
119:2 and position *TSR*] *Om. MS*
119:7 obstinate *TSR*] pig-headed *MS*
119:9 had had] had *TS*
119:13 purely *E1*] merely *MS*
119:19 daddy—"] ~." *TS*
119:22 heart] head *TS*
119:33 child-husband, as] ~. As *TS*
120:3 himself. *E1*] himself for wanting what was not his, and put his foot on his own heart. *MS*
120:5 How poignantly he saw her! *E1*] He thought her beautiful. *MS*
120:9 poignant *E1*] beautiful *MS*
120:11 the control, *E1*] *Om. MS*
120:12 ugly, *E1*] so ugly, so *MS*
120:12 yield place *E1*] belong to his own time *MS*
120:13 must stand ... large demon. *E1*] should be all giving, all mellowness! *MS*
120:15 was missing in his *E1*] had he had in *MS*
120:15 was not ... had that *E1*] counted. That *MS* counted. What *TS*
120:17 Anna.] ~? *TSR*
120:18 but *TSR*] ah, but *MS*
120:19 Yet he ... know it. *E1*] *Om. MS*
120:21 nothing? *E1*] nothing but the woman? *MS*
120:21 to *E1*] else to *MS*
120:21 work? *TSR*] ~. *MS*
120:22 known *E1*] to show *MS*

120:23 long, marital embrace *TSR*] supreme embraces *MS*
120:23 wife?] ~! *TS*
120:24 his life *TSR*] a man's life *MS*
120:24 to! *TSR*] ~. *MS*
120:24 something, it was eternal *E1*] what *his* {his *TS*} life amounted to *MS* something ... was sufficient *TSR*
120:26 and she was still his fulfilment, *E1*] *Om. MS* and ... still the unknown, *TSR*
120:32 further *E1*] *intimate MS*
120:32 creative *E1*] dual *MS* adventurous *TSR*
120:33 himself,] ~ *TS*
120:35 It was ... the girl. *E1*] *Om. MS*
120:40 she was ... day should *E1*] he waited tense and hard for the day to *MS* she was his, he waited suspended for the day to *TSR*
121:1 twenty third *Ed.*] twenty-third *MS*
121:2 He lived in it *E1*] Just as one must wait for Christmas Day to have Christmas, so he must wait for his wedding day to have her *MS*
121:3 in a ship ... to port *E1*] by the Pole Star, he travelled by his coming wedding day. All that went before was preparation *MS* in a ship, he waited for the coming to port *TSR*
121:6 her:] ~; *TS*
121:11 life: she] ~. She *TS*
121:15 trembled, *TS*] trembled, out *MS* *see notes*
121:20 reality *E1*] male body *MS*
121:21 unreal *E1*] shadowy *MS*
121:21 him] ~, *TS*
121:38 thick *TSR*] pitch *MS*
121:38 darkness,] ~ *TS*
121:39 its *TSR*] his *MS*
122:2 twenty one *Ed.*] twenty-one *MS*
122:2 years] ~' *E1*
122:7 whitewashed *E1*] heavy *MS*

122:11 churchyard *E1*] church-yard *MS*

122:20 god-father] godfather *E1*

122:22 He was *TSR*] These things were his interest: {interest; *TS*} dress, furniture, architecture, either of cottage or cathedral. So he had to be *MS*

122:23 dressers] the dressers *E1*

122:32 doubtful *E1*] quite cold *MS*

122:33 days *E1*] ~, *MS*

122:38 resounding *E1*] ringing *MS*

123:7 said,] ~ *TS*

123:16 Why,] ~ *TS*

123:18 it] ~, *TS*

123:20 wash-tub." *P* He *Ed.*] ~." / He *MS* ~." He *TS*

123:25 in to] into *TS*

123:33 nip *TSR*] fair nip *MS*

123:33 onto] on to *TS*

124:1 V *TSR*] IV *MS*

124:2 Wedding at the Marsh *TSR*] Haste to the Wedding *MS*

124:9 peacock blue] peacock-blue *E1*

124:19 down,] ~· *TS*

124:19 shy, *E1*] ~ *MS*

124:19 viewed *TSR*] seen *MS*

124:21 veil,] ~ *TS*

125:3 floating,] ~ *TS*

125:9 lilies of the valley] lilies-of-the-valley *E1*

125:10 tuberoses *Ed.*] tube roses *MS* tube-roses *TSR*

125:10 maiden-hair] maidenhair *E1*

125:13 dark *E1*] very dark and rich *MS* dark and rich *TSR*

125:22 flowers,] ~ *TS*

125:25 man?" *P* He *Ed.*] ~?" / He *MS* ~?" He *TS*

125:27 were *TSR*] *Om. MS*

125:28 hastily. *P* Anna *TS*] ~. / Anna *MS*

125:30 was! *E1*] was! What a funny voice Will said the responses in! *MS*

125:32 *should*] should *TS*

125:33 arrived *E1*] mature *MS*

125:37 uncertainties *E1*] children *MS*

125:38 years,] ~ *TS*

125:39 unestablished *E1*] young *MS*

125:40 confident *E1*] old *MS*

126:2 completed *E1*] experienced *MS*

126:10 strangely, with torture. *E1*] strangely. *MS*

126:12 endless *E1*] earth and the endless *MS*

126:12 that was *E1*] they were *MS*

126:15 life *TSR*] blood *MS*

126:17 burned dark *E1*] burned *MS*

126:17 Always it … and unformed! *E1*] *Om. MS*

126:24 Lensky." *P* "Anna *E1*] ~." / "Anna *MS*

126:28 Brangwen." *P* That *E1*] ~." / That *MS*

126:30 sign] ~, *TSC*

126:31 "'Thomas Brangwen'] "~ ~ *TS*

126:36 How *E1*] Strike me lucky, how *MS*

126:36 Brangwens? *TS*] ~?, *MS*

126:37 family name *TSR*] patronymic *MS*

126:40 yew-trees *E1*] yew trees *MS*, *E1* Yew trees *TS*

127:18 they *E1*] you *MS*

127:19 Night an' day *E1*] Kettle an' th' oven *MS* Kettle an' teapot *TSR*

127:19 they *E1*] you *MS*

127:21 Hammer an' tongs *E1*] Bed and bedding *MS* Bed and blessing *TSR*

127:21 they *E1*] you *MS*

127:25 ye *E1*] we *MS*

127:25 it." *P* There *E1*] ~." / There *MS*

127:27 Bed an' blessin' *E1*] Oven an' pantry *MS* Pig-sty an' pantry *TSR*

127:27 ye *E1*] we *MS*

127:27 Brangwen. *P* There *E1*] ~. / There *MS*

127:29 Comin' and goin' *E1*] Bed an' beauty *MS*

127:29 ye *E1*] we *MS*

127:31 now!" *P* There *E1*] ~!" / There *MS*

127:34 a large *E1*] an enormous *MS*

128:4 fashion,] ~ *TS*

128:5 dominated *TSR*] ran *MS*

128:9 time;] ~, *TS*

128:11 is what we're made for *E1*] was made for enjoyment *MS*

128:16 That's a true word," said *Ed.*] Hear-hear," shouted *MS* That a ... said *E1*

128:17 likewise *E1*] I hope *MS*

128:17 a *E1*] that a *MS*

128:18 at least we surmise *E1*] we'll believe *MS*

128:19 bother—" *Ed.*] ~—," *MS* ~——" *E1*

128:20 they'd be summisin' *E1*] *he* knows *MS*

128:21 be *E1*] enjoy being *MS*

128:24 be *E1*] enjoy bein' *MS*

128:28 Don't run ... our legs *E1*] Let's have a drink betweenwhiles *MS* Let's ... between whiles *TS*

128:33 *is*] is *TS*

128:33 marriage. *E1*] marriage.—And there's very little else. *MS*

128:34 That's the ... 'em," said *E1*] Hell!" shouted *MS* What about Hell?" shouted *TSR*

128:34 Brangwen, mocking. *TSR*] Brangwen. *MS*

128:37 thank you for *TSR*] listen to *MS*

128:39 soul] own soul *TS*

128:40 gnawin', gnawin', gnawin' *TSR*] gnawgin', gnawgin', gnawgin' *MS*

129:7 man nor ... amongst them *E1*] male and a female angel *MS*

129:9 *one*] one *TS*

129:12 *less*] less *TS*

129:14 being—] ~. *TS*

129:18 *got*] got *TS*

129:20 one *E1*] a whole *MS*

129:23 jeering *TSR*] bitingly *MS*

129:27 one angel.] one angel— *TS* an Angel—— *E1 see notes*

129:28 I know ... three, sometimes *TSR*] Summat happens when their bodies meets together *MS*

129:33 I am *E1*] my soul is *MS*

129:33 angel *Ed.*] Angel *MS*

129:38 angel.'] ~?' *TS* ~!' *E1*

130:8 angels,' *Ed.*] ~', *MS* ~' *TS*

130:13 candles,' *E1*] ~' *MS* ~', *TSR*

130:13 work! *TSR*] ~. *MS*

130:15 of *TSR*] o' *MS*

130:16 we got ... know what——— *Ed.*] what work——— *MS* we ... what ... *E1*

130:17 inspiration *E1*] inspiration, when he had solved the riddle of the universe for himself, *MS*

130:29 Jove *E1*] Christ *MS*

130:36 red-faced,] ~ *TS*

131:15 boz-eyed] boss-eyed *TS*

131:17 boz-eyed] boss-eyed *TS*

131:17 And] and *E1*

131:20 half way] half-way *E1*

131:22 Why] ~, *TS*

131:23 It's plain ... th' looks *TSR*] I can tell by th' look *MS*

131:23 some *E1*] some of yer *MS*

131:26 anything, *E1*] ~ *MS*

131:28 day dress *TSR*] coat and skirt *MS*

131:34 lights] light *E1*

131:38 half past *Ed.*] half-past *MS*

132:9 'Cock] ~ *E1*

132:9 Robin.'" *Ed.*] ~'." *MS* ~.' *TS* ~." *E1*

132:16 brother] ~, *TS*

132:25 oldish *E1*] tired *MS*

132:28 Most folks ... with me *E1*] Everybody I've come into contact with—as I've wanted to run with me *MS* Everybody ... as has attempted to run with me *TSR*

132:30 alongside *E1*] your road *MS*

132:35 it. *E1*] it. And in the same instant, in anger, he despised his elder brother a little, for a fool. *MS*

132:40 brother. *P* And *Ed.*] ~. / And
MS ~. And *TS*
133:3 to,] to go *TS*
133:9 Nay] ~, *TS*
133:9 for th' last time *E1*] they
deserve it *MS*
133:11 wall *E1*] church-yard wall *MS*
133:11 by *E1*] of *MS*
133:12 glowed] glowered *TS*
133:15 commotion *E1*] strong body
MS
133:19 whispered. *P* She *TS*] ~. / She
MS
133:23 voice. *P* They *Ed.*] ~. / They
MS ~. They *TS*
133:25 said. *P* She *TS*] ~. / She *MS*
133:32 silly?] ~, *TS*
133:32 whispered. *P* And *TS*] ~. /
And *MS*
134:1 VI *TSR*] V *MS* Five *TS*
134:3 some weeks of *E1*] a fortnight's
MS
134:3 after *E1*] for *MS*
134:7 in a new world, *E1*] *Om. MS*
134:16 gods *E1*] Gods *MS*
134:18 lane:] ~; *TS*
134:20 breakfast:] ~, *TS*
134:26 peacefully] ~, *TS*
134:29 satisfying *E1*] so peaceful *MS*
134:30 not *TSR*] *Om. MS*
134:31 church clock *Ed.*] church-clock
MS
135:6 There it ... worldly experience.] *Om. TS*
135:8 like] all like *TS*
135:8 hard] ~, *TS*
135:11 eternity *E1*] peace *MS*
135:12 distraction] destruction *TS*
135:17 close *E1*] clasped *MS*
135:21 steady *TSR*] clinched *MS*
135:29 reality *E1*] fire *MS*
136:3 significance *E1*] importance
MS
136:6 said. *P* It *TS*] ~. / It *MS*
136:8 unmoving. *P* And *TS*] ~. / And
MS
136:33 kettle *TSR*] kettle and cut the
bacon into slices *MS*

136:36 half dressed] half-dressed *TS*
137:1 accused *E1*] dejected, miserable *MS* dejected, accused
TSR
137:2 it *TSR*] her *MS*
137:2 unnoticed? *TSR*] ~. *MS*
137:9 unspent,] ~ *TS*
137:10 when *E1*] as *MS*
137:17 held] stretched *TS*
137:17 plate.—] ~— *TS*
137:20 on *TSR*] *Om. MS*
137:23 said. *P* She *TS*] ~. / She *MS*
137:25 unseen,] ~. *E1*
137:27 unacknowledged *TSR*] unrecognised *MS*
137:27 recusant *E1*] unalive *MS*
137:28 fact *TSR*] knowledge *MS*
138:4 pillows] pillow *TS*
138:9 answered. *P* He *TS*] ~. / He
MS
138:17 him, *TS*] ~ *MS*
138:19 his responsibility *E1*] some of
his uneasiness *MS*
138:29 How he ... back to *TSR*] But
he was a little bit out of faith
now. If he had to do *MS*
138:29 Creation-panel *TSR*] Creation
panel *MS*
138:30 finish his Eve, tender *TSR*]
would not make Eve leap forth
so live *MS*
138:31 yet *TSR*] any more *MS*
138:32 of immortality *E1*] that hurt
him *MS* that beyond death
TSR
138:33 glimmeringly *TSR*] slowly *MS*
138:34 her, yet ... a radiance. *TSR*]
her. *MS*
138:36 asked. *P* He *TS*] ~. / He *MS*
138:37 shy *TSR*] blank *MS*
138:39 hard and *TSR*] *Om. MS*
139:1 know. She ... more—," ...
tenderness. *P* There *TSR*]
know." / There *MS* know." *P*
There *TS* know. She ...
more——," ... tenderness. *P*
There *E1*
139:3 joy *TSR*] pain *MS*

139:5 She went to him. *TSR*] *Om. MS*
139:6 an open flower *TSR*] open flowers *MS*
139:9 lit up ... other-world, so *E1*] so exceedingly themselves *MS*
139:11 troubled *E1*] fretted *MS*
139:14 Instead, *E1*] And there *MS*
139:15 then] and then *TS*
139:15 up; *Ed.*] ~, *MS*
139:18 half past] half-past *TS*
139:19 gladly and perfectly *E1*] easy and matter-of-course *MS* pleasantly and naturally *TSR*
139:20 strange *TSR*] ultimate *MS*
139:28 Indeed *E1*] My word *MS*
139:31 discarded *TSR*] mere broken *MS*
139:33 the surface *TSR*] great chunks *MS*
139:33 broken *TSR*] blown *MS*
139:35 peeled *TSR*] blown *MS*
139:36 strange *TSR*] one's own *MS*
139:38 woman *E1*] Woman *MS*
139:39 confounding *E1*] too amazing *MS*
139:39 seem! *TSR*] ~. *MS*
140:6 tea-time] teatime *TS*
140:9 supremely absolved *E1*] delightedly criminal *MS*
140:12 were not consumed *E1*] burned not away *MS*
140:13 the *E1*] a *MS*
140:20 timeless *E1*] Titanic *MS*
140:20 perfect *E1*] unclothed *MS*
140:20 immortal breast *E1*] glistening breasts *MS* glistening breast *TS*
140:21 old,] ~ *TS*
140:21 finished. The *E1*] finished and the *MS* finished. And the *TS*
140:23 gleaming core, to action, *TSR*] surface to the gleaming core, *MS*
140:24 dead *E1*] *Om. MS*
140:26 frightened *E1*] so frightened *MS*
140:26 miserable *E1*] so miserable *MS*
140:27 unto] into *TS*

140:30 sullen. *E1*] apprehensive and suffering. *MS* apprehensive. *TSR*
140:31 His fear ... he hated *TSR*] And underneath, he was furious, he hated her for *MS*
140:32 joy *TSR*] gusto *MS*
140:33 all that was *TSR*] something *MS*
140:33 carelessly taking off *TSR*] gladly throwing away *MS*
140:34 an artificial figure ... artificial *E1*] a tea-party woman ... worthless *MS* a vulgar woman ... vulgar *TSR*
140:35 perfect ... perfect *E1*] a queen ... king *MS*
140:36 intimate connection? *E1*] passionate desire. *MS* intimate knowledge? *TSR*
140:37 deposed, his ... be destroyed *TSR*] cast out, his glory must be taken from him *MS*
140:37 vulgar, shallow death of an outward existence *E1*] sordid, everyday {sordid everyday *TS*} clothes and walk forth under a common, manufactured guise *MS* vulgar ... of common existence *TSR*
140:39 uneasiness and fear *TSR*] rage *MS*
140:40 housework] house-work *TS*
140:40 turning him away *TSR*] throwing him aside *MS*
141:1 miserably] miserable *TS*
141:2 Dread] ~, *E1*
141:2 him] ~, *E1*
141:3 dependence on her *TSR*] weak dependence *MS*
141:3 anger *TSR*] rage *MS*
141:4 The wonder ... away again *TSR*] It had all been a lie—it had been illusion *MS*
141:5 going to ... the outside things ... her departure ... helplessness, almost ... [141:9] the house *E1*] illusory, no more

than the dressed up Christmas tree which gets dusty and must be undressed and thrown away. It was all a lie. He was beside himself with frantic rage. The time had come for disillusion. This magnificent, gleaming Tree of Life, this bush blazing with the Presence of God, was only a Christmas tree decked up, with the candles now gone out, and sordid dust upon it, waiting to be untrimmed and thrown on the rubbish heap. In a ghastly, gathering access of despair he wandered comfortless round the house. His mouth was full of dust, his soul gathering rage and destructiveness. *MS* going to ... the worthless things ... her shallowness ... paralysis, almost ... house. *TSR*

141:12 said. *P* And *TS*] ~. / And *MS*
141:13 fretting with resentment *TSR*] burning with fury *MS*
141:15 anything? *E1*] ~, *MS*
141:17 harsh with pain *TSR*] miserable and ashy *MS*
141:18 Anywhere." *P* How *TS*] ~." / How *MS*
141:22 He winced and hated it *TSR*] How he hated her *MS*
141:23 flayed and uncreated. *E1*] ashy and comfortless. The {He *TS*} felt as if he were in one of those raw, cold parlours where a white dust settles out of a dead air. He sat with mind and body a grey, ashy blank. *MS* stark and comfortless. *TSR*
141:24 must come *TSR*] came *MS*
141:25 wanting ... with him, *TSR*] *Om. MS*
141:26 irritated her ... was fiendish in his thwarted soul. *E1*] stung her, maddened her against him. He wouldn't do anything,

he wouldn't go anywhere, he just hung on to her like an idiot. Her soul clinched against him. She would not have cared what became of him, so long as he were removed from her. *MS* irritated ... was the devil to her. *TSR*

141:31 violent underworld *TSR*] damp hole underground *MS*
141:33 thing] ~, *TS*
141:33 pursuing her, *E1*] pursuing her like a shadow, *MS* pursuing her like a devil, *TSR*
141:36 something? *TS*] ~. *MS*
142:2 existed in its own power *TSR*] ran its own dark way *MS*
142:4 His will ... upon her. *TSR*] *Om. MS*
142:5 She retreated *TSR*] But she was not really, in the last issue, afraid. She retreated *MS*
142:6 her parents' *TSR*] their *MS*
142:16 capable *E1*] masterly *MS*
142:18 path. *P* But *TS*] ~. / But *MS*
142:20 plaintively. *P* He *TS*] ~. / He *MS*
142:21 fixed *TSR*] wooden *MS*
142:22 which *TSR*] that *MS*
142:22 dazed *E1*] hard *MS*
142:28 evil *TSR*] ugly *MS*
142:29 cruel *E1*] evil *MS*
142:30 to take ... torturing her *TSR*] callously *MS*
142:32 in to *Ed.*] in *MS* into *E1*
142:33 malignant *TSR*] vicious *MS*
142:37 femaleness *TSR*] womanliness *MS*
142:38 lacerate *TSR*] trample on *MS*
143:4 coming?" *P* She *TS*] ~?" / She *MS*
143:7 anguish. Fear ... a child *TSR*] anguish of desolation. It was so desolate, so desolate, and she was so hurt *MS*
143:9 father; she ... taken her. *TSR*] father. *MS*
143:12 in to] into *TS*

143:14 exacerbating *TSR*] so nerve-jarring *MS*

143:14 cruel! *E1*} ~. *MS*

143:15 upon her! *E1*] ~ ~. *MS*

143:17 lifeless, fixed, persistent *E1*] blind, like a rat's face going its course *MS*

143:21 negative insensitiveness to her *E1*] horrible insensitiveness *MS*

143:22 clayey and ugly *E1*] horny and gross *MS*

143:22 was *E1*] was cunning and *MS*

143:23 unnatural *E1*] horrible *MS*

143:23 something negative ensconced opposite one *E1*] an invertebrate in a horny, invulnerable shell *MS* something evil esconced in an invulnerable shell *TSR*

143:25 self *E1*] unlovely self *MS* malignant self *TSR*

143:28 unchanging as a bird of prey *TSR*] selfish as a rat's *MS*

143:29 voice. *P* She *TS*] ~. / She *MS*

143:34 glittered evilly, and ... desire. *TSR*] glittered evilly. *MS* glittered, and ... desire. *E1*

143:35 being beaten down *E1*] when a rat watches her evilly *MS*

143:38 influence *E1*] evil influence *MS*

144:1 Suddenly he ... was hurt. He ... of compassion. *E1*] His heart became quiveringly alive again. *MS* Suddenly ... was lonely. He ... compassion. *TSR*

144:4 tears—he ... bear it. *TSR*] tears. *MS*

144:5 out his ... her, utterly. *TSR*] himself over her like the oil of healing. But he could not, not yet. *MS*

144:10 grief. He trembled *TSR*] tears. He quivered *MS*

144:12 hesitating, burdened ... offering. *TSR*] hesitating. *MS*

144:27 hesitating, in ... self-offering. *TSR*] hesitating. *MS*

144:35 relaxed] relapsed *TS*

144:36 suffering for her. *E1*] pain. *MS* pain for her. *TSR*

145:4 calm and numb *E1*] heavy and dumb *MS* calm and dumb *TSR*

145:4 a sort ... love, now *TSR*] tears *MS*

145:11 he *E1*] *Om. MS*

145:13 He was ... touch her. *TSR*] *Om. MS*

145:13 her face *TSR*] it *MS*

145:14 He loved ... restore her. *TSR*] *Om. MS*

145:19 His blood ... enveloping her. *TSR*] *Om. MS*

145:21 His limbs ... in flames *TSR*] The passion began to beat up his limbs in flame *MS*

145:23 The flames *TSR*] The passion *MS*

145:27 upon her *TSR*] *Om. MS*

145:31 happily *TSR*] *Om. MS*

145:34 wonder of consummation *E1*] faith glad in last issue *MS* honour of consummation *TSR*

146:1 immune *TSR*] together *MS*

146:1 there was ... no time. *TSR*] cut off from the world. *MS*

146:3 The snow ... the Sunday *TSR*] But *MS*

146:4 foot-prints] footprints *E1*

146:5 snow-print] snowprint *E1*

146:6 churchyard *E1*] church-yard *MS*

146:6 For three ... perfect love. *TSR*] *Om. MS*

146:11 any *E1*] a thrill of *MS*

146:11 Today *TSR*] It was a case of the "regular-churchgoer." Now *MS* To-day *E1*

146:12 after such consummation of love, *TSR*] *Om. MS*

146:13 delighted *TSR*] thrilled *MS*

146:13 She was ... eternal world. *E1*]. *Om. MS*

146:15 School] ~, *TS*

146:20 quickly this palled *E1*] after a while it began to pall *MS*

146:20 short *E1*] certain *MS*

146:21 something *E1*] [?S]omething *MS* Something *TS*

146:23 ready-made *E1*] *business* or *MS*

146:24 social duty *E1*] her *business MS* her outside *business TSR*

146:26 As *E1*] And *MS*

146:30 help it *TSR*] support *MS*

146:30 it counted *E1*] she counted it *MS*

146:30 life. *E1*] life. She went her own way. *MS*

146:33 became hostile ... ostensible Church, she hated *Ed.*] was angry with the living part church, she despised *MS* was became hostile to the living part church, she hated *TSR* became ... ostensible church, she hated *E1*

146:35 had no ... what it *TSR*] believed It to be right in what It *MS*

146:36 and] *Om. TS*

146:37 performing certain acts conducive *TSR*] contributing *MS*

146:38 Very good ... of mankind.] *Om. TS*

146:40 so, *TSR*] not so very difficult *MS*

147:2 doing this thing ... doing that, *E1*] contributing to the welfare of mankind *MS* doing this simple thing ... that, *TSR*

147:17 powerful *TSR*] woolly *MS*

147:18 Church *E1*] Christian *MS*

147:20 us—"] ~"— *E1*

147:24 week-days *Ed.*] weekdays *MS*

147:26 stuff. *TSR*] stuff. Church had nothing to do with it. *MS*

147:27 good natured] good-natured *TS*

147:30 or of her *TSR*] *Om. MS*

147:36 verity *E1*] lettering *MS*

147:37 Church, his ... the Absolute. *E1*] church. *MS* Church. *TS*

147:38 great,] ~ *TS*

148:2 self ... self *E1*] Ego ... Ego *MS*

148:4 self *E1*] Ego *MS*

148:7 thing, abstract. *E1*] thing. *MS*

148:21 interior,] ~ *TS*

148:22 this] the *TS*

148:23 fore-paw] forepaw *E1*

148:26 creature *E1*] lamb *MS*

148:28 toys *E1*] lambs *MS*

148:35 in correspondence with *TSR*] transfigured by *MS*

148:37 faint] ~, *TS*

148:39 glass? *TS*] ~. *MS*

148:40 dominant *E1*] almost dominant *MS*

149:1 Suddenly she ... another world *E1*] It seemed set up, powerful, compelling *MS* It ... powerful, triumphant *TSR*

149:4 Instantly *E1*] But instantly *MS*

149:18 hear *TSR*] know *MS*

149:18 word." *P* He *TS*] ~." / He *MS*

149:20 an underworld refuge *E1*] a subterfuge *MS*

149:28 churches;] ~: *TS*

149:32 whose eyes ... his chest *E1*] without ears *MS*

149:33 later. *E1*] later, who could only see, and could not take in what he heard. *MS*

149:35 puzzled, interested, and antagonistic *E1*] puzzled but interested in the devils: she despised a reproduction of St. Veronica's Kerchief, {kerchief, *TS*} but she said nothing *MS*

149:36 Pietà *E1*] Sacred Heart and the Seven Wounds *MS*

149:37 loathsome *E1*] ridiculous things *MS*

149:39 bodies with ... be worshipped *E1*] sacred hearts. It seems to me horrid to show hearts in bodies, as if the chest were open. I think it *is* nasty *MS*

149:40 the Sacraments, the Bread *E1*] Love *MS*

150:1   it's worse *E1*] never say you love me, at that rate *MS*

150:2   slit, nor ... it me *E1*] opened and your red heart there *MS*

150:3   horrible? *E1*] horrible? You'd be mutilated and dead. *MS*

150:4   It isn't me, it's Christ. *E1*] Well, wasn't Christ dead? *MS*

150:5   What if ... the Sacrament *E1*] Not like that. Besides, he's pretending to be alive. I think it's abominable *MS*

150:8   your *E1*] a *MS*

150:8   put up ... then worshipped *E1*] pulled open *MS*

150:9   else?" *P* They *TS*] ~?" / They *MS*

150:12 parish—" *P* She *TS*] ~—" / She *MS* ~——" *P* She *E1*

150:18 no—" *P* And *TS*] ~——" / And *MS* ~——" *P* And *E1*

150:24 mean?" *P* He *TS*] ~?" / He *MS*

150:27 Resurrection." *P* She *TS*] ~." / She *MS*

150:28 baffled. A *Ed.*] ~, A *MS* ~, a *TS*

150:33 toy-lamb *TSR*] toy lamb *MS*

150:33 Christmas-tree *TS*] christmas-tree *MS*

150:33 paw *TSR*] foot *MS*

150:38 symbols *E1*] uncouth symbols *MS*

150:38 Lamb] lamb *E1*

150:39 mystic *E1*] *Om. MS*

150:39 Eucharist *E1*] Sacred Heart *MS*

151:4   previous gloom *TSR*] yesterday *MS*

151:7   of *E1*] *Om. MS*

151:9   all *E1*] some of *MS*

151:17 proud *TSR*] haughtily proud *MS*

151:18 inhuman *E1*] native *MS*

151:21 He was ... his prey. *E1*] *Om. MS*

151:28 existence] ~, *E1*

151:34 unperturbed *TSR*] imperturbed *MS*

151:38 she struck ... got rusty. *TSR*] with a snarl, because she threw aside his tools, she struck back. *MS*

152:2   cried *TSR*] cried fiercely *MS*

152:3   like." *P* They *TS*] ~." / They *MS*

152:5   with victory *E1*] as a knife. And they quivered at daggers drawn *MS* as a knife. So they stood at ... drawn *TSR*

152:12 stop *TSR*] stop making *MS*

152:12 row.] ~? *TS*

152:13 daytime?" *P* She *TS*] ~?" / She *MS*

152:25 rage—] ~ *TS*

152:32 same, *E1*] same: be damned, *MS*

152:37 with rage *E1*] and cold and unconcerned *MS* and black with rage *TSR*

153:1   mind *E1*] soul *MS*

153:7   more agreeable *TSR*] very satisfactory *MS*

153:8   mad restlessness *TSR*] hunter's pleasure *MS*

153:8   running amok *TSR*] discovering them *MS*

153:9   bookshop] book-shop *TS*

153:11 restaurant *E1*] public house *MS* public-house *TS*

153:17 inclosure] enclosure *TS*

153:17 room. *TSR*] room, with a storied, drab wall-paper. *MS*

153:18 finely wrought] finely-wrought *TS*

153:20 woman-faces. *P* He] ~. He *TS*

153:24 intensely *TSR*] with rapture *MS*

153:24 statues!] ~ *TS* ~, *TSC*

153:27 to *E1*] of *MS*

153:28 make the world his own *TSR*] fulfil him *MS*

154:3   couldn't *TSR*] didn't *MS*

154:6   considered,] ~ *TS*

154:10 That would ... leave her?] *Om. TS*

154:16 outside] outsider *TS* outsider, the *TSR see notes*

154:18 own *TSR*] Om. *MS*

154:22 resounding, *TS*] ~ *MS*

154:32 him. *P* But *Ed.*] ~. / But *MS* ~. But *TS*

155:1 go." *P* He *TS*] ~." / He *MS*

155:2 so clear and shining *TSR*] open towards her *MS*

155:9 irritably. *P* She *TS*] ~. / She *MS*

155:12 women] ~, *TS*

155:16 roused and glad. *P* Her *Ed.*] intimate and caressing. / Her *MS* intimate ... caressing. Her *TS* roused ... glad. Her *TSR*

155:18 In spite ... was strange, attractive, exerting ... over her. *E1*] Om. *MS* In ... was the wonderful, attractive unknown, exerting ... her. *TSR*

155:26 newly-opened *Ed.*] newly opened *MS*

155:27 He was ... abstracted. *TSR*] Om. *MS*

156:19 hers, in connection with her *TSR*] hers to inherit *MS*

156:21 joyfully *TSR*] wildly *MS*

156:25 solitary *TSR*] fierce *MS*

156:27 doorway,] ~ *TS*

156:31 the passion was consumed in *E1*] passion is *MS* the passion was in *TSR*

156:34 clothes and ... new, primal *TSR*] drab clothes and glistened with new *MS*

156:38 cottages *TSR*] cottages all *MS*

156:39 tense] intense *TS*

157:1 a universe to her *E1*] important, a goal *MS*

157:7 regained *E1*] plunged into *MS*

157:23 mercy.] ~? *TS*

158:24 upright *E1*] circle of the Presence, six-winged, an upright *MS*

158:25 Creation *E1*] Glory *MS*

158:29 burning *E1*] flaming *MS*

158:30 resisted *E1*] worshipped *MS*

158:31 in his service *E1*] with honor *MS*

159:3 was,] ~ *TS*

159:4 honor] honour *E1*

159:13 But *E1*] Well, *MS*

159:13 judgments *Ed.*] judgements *MS*

159:16 soul *E1*] religion *MS*

159:18 soon in a white *E1*] in a towering *MS*

159:27 red *TSR*] red, glowing *MS*

159:28 mother: *P* "Woman] ~: "Woman *TS*

159:30 come." *P* And *TS*] ~." / And *MS*

159:37 could it ... was wrong. *E1*] hydrogen and oxygen, H_2O, the stuff he had seen decomposed in chemical experiments, could it, could it turn into wine, could the alcohol,—Anna did not remember the chemical formula for alcohol,—but {alcohol—but *TS*} could the alcohol appear out of nowhere, and take its place among the water, suddenly spring in between the molecules: alcohol, and {alcohol and *TS*} the special acid, and the dozen other things wine contained? Wine—what was wine? It was no element. One must call up its ingredients. *MS* hydrogen ... alcohol—but ... appear instead of water, suddenly have place without birth or conveyance; alcohol and ... ingredients. *TSR*

160:6 formed *E1*] founded *MS*

160:14 "The best wine!" *E1*] Jesus had made the best wine from the water. *MS*

160:17 denial] ~, *TS*

160:21 in his soul *E1*] and act *MS*

160:27 Bible *TS*] bible *MS*

160:27 said. *P* That *TS*] ~. / That *MS*

160:29 Bible *E1*] bible *MS*

160:29 drove her to contempt *E1*]
almost drove her to do so *MS*

160:30 Bible *E1*] bible *MS*

160:40 brotherhood of man *E1*]
supremacy of the mind *MS*

161:2 knowledge. *E1*] mind. *MS*

161:2 but in ... was immortal *E1*] and
know resurrection in the mind
MS

161:4 mind. *E1*] mind. True, it was
only omnipotent when it
accorded with God. But she
tended to conceive God as the
Whole Human Mind. *MS*

161:9 frantic in sensual *E1*] in horror
and *MS*

161:16 them *E1*] you *MS*

161:17 are.] ~! *TSC*

161:28 hard *E1*] very, very hard *MS*

161:32 collapses *TSR*] horrible collapses *MS*

161:34 being to fulfil the *E1*] body to
fulfil some *MS*

161:38 her it was enough that *E1*] she
knew *MS*

162:6 saying: *P* "She *Ed.*] ~ "She
MS

162:9 "It is ... what arrogance!" *E1*]
Om. MS

162:17 Burnt." *P* She *TS*] ~." / She
MS

162:21 When?" *P* She *TS*] ~?" / She
MS

162:26 She said no more *E1*] "It's like
you, to do such a thing out of
jealousy, when I'm away," she
answered coldly *MS* "It's ... of
spite, when ... coldly *TSR*

162:29 pain *E1*] misery, like the brittle
{brittle, *TS*} fine bulb-flowers
at spring *MS*

162:33 touched by *TSR*] indeed fond
of *MS*

163:2 sensitive *TSR*] sensitive as a
violet *MS*

163:8 glance;] ~, *TS*

163:8 now?" *P* The *TS*] ~?" / The
MS

163:9 came *TSR*] came in her breast
MS

163:14 father. *P* She *TS*] ~. / She
MS

163:16 make *TSR*] go an' make *MS*

163:16 father:] ~; *E1*

163:19 else, *TSR*] ~ *MS*

163:20 You'd be *TSR*] You're *MS*

163:22 are." *P* She *TS*] ~." / She
MS

163:26 pond." *P* This *TS*] ~." / This
MS

163:32 Between two ... your way. *E1*]
Om. MS

163:35 did,] ~ *TS*

164:15 tense *E1*] black *MS*

164:16 administered,] ~ *TS*

164:17 calm *E1*] happiness *MS*

164:23 voice. *P* He *TS*] ~. / He *MS*

164:24 destruction *E1*] vengeance *MS*

164:27 length *TSR*] length o' days *MS*

164:30 sharp *E1*] far *MS*

164:33 am?" *P* And *TS*] ~?" / And *MS*

164:34 warm *TSR*] genial *MS*

165:10 father—"] ~"— *E1*

165:20 was—"] ~"— *E1*

165:21 alive *TSR*] all alive *MS*

165:22 steady *TSR*] like a statue *MS*

165:31 other? *E1*] ~. *MS*

165:37 the *TSR*] the far *MS*

165:39 dark-blue] dark blue *E1*

165:40 off. *P* He *TS*] ~. / He *MS*

166:2 know? *TSR*] ~. *MS*

166:3 said. *P* They *E1*] said. "I'm
sure." / They *MS* said. "I'm
sure." *P* They *TS*

166:5 intervening space, two separate
people. *TSR*] vast, intervening
space. *MS*

166:6 wind *TSR*] dark wind *MS*

166:10 always one with her? *E1*] all, all.
MS all, all? *TSR*

166:12 separateness *E1*] great isolation
MS

166:13 him? *TSR*] ~. *MS*

166:18 far-off] ~, *TS*

166:25 limitation *TSR*] incompleteness *MS*

166:25 uncompleted, as yet uncreated *E1*] raw-edged *MS*
166:26 liberate him into the *TSR*] seal him *MS*
166:29 weighed on ... a madness *TSR*] almost drove him mad *MS*
166:36 glad. *P* He *E1*] glad. Her husband *MS* glad. He *TSR*
167:1 melody *E1*] simplicity of concord *MS*
167:2 floweriness, the ... too inno-cent *E1*] vision of innocence fascinated her, the innocence of knowledge become perfect, of perfect gladness *MS*
167:6 beam *TSR*] ray *MS*
167:11 were *E1*] were all *MS*
167:13 loveliness] loneliness *TS*
167:20 sisters *TSR*] children *MS*
167:21 apple-blossoms *Ed.*] appleblossoms *MS*
167:30 other-world *E1*] savage lust *MS*
168:3 his will upon her, *Ed.*] her into something; *MS* her into some-thing, *TSR* his will upon her, something, *E1 see notes*
168:6 lovely *E1*] unreal *MS*
168:7 hostile *E1*] angular *MS*
168:7 drew back in *TSR*] writhed with *MS*
168:13 it? *TSR*] ∼. *MS*
168:16 constraint *E1*] whip *MS*
168:16 will *TSR*] desire *MS*
168:17 yew-trees *E1*] yew trees *MS*
168:21 tense *E1*] wistful *MS*
169:9 her own paradise *E1*] Paradise *MS*
169:10 And *E1*] Only the satisfied, the fulfilled, could come to Para-dise. And *MS*
169:12 throw these ... trample the flowers to ... He would *E1*] dash these aside and trample them out. He would smash and *MS* throw ... trample them to ... would *TSR*
169:15 all *TSR*] one *MS*

169:15 a *TSR*] one *MS*
169:34 off. *E1*] off, with David. She had always loved David. It had haunted her, how he danced naked before the Ark, and the wife had taunted him. And David had said "It was before the Lord: the Lord hath chosen me, therefore will I play before him." *MS*
169:35 pride and curious pleasure *E1*] the pride and the ecstasy of this *MS*
169:36 exult *E1*] dance *MS*
169:37 Unknown *E1*] Lord *MS*
170:1 Unseen *E1*] Lord *MS*
170:1 Creator who ... she belonged *E1*] Lover whose name was unutterable *MS*
170:4 Creator *E1*] Lord *MS*
170:9 herself. *TSR*] herself, being David. *MS*
170:9 liked the story of *E1*] was in love with *MS*
170:10 exultingly *E1*] shamelessly *MS*
170:11 common *E1*] vulgar *MS*
170:16 rang *E1*] was like a trumpet sounding *MS*
170:17 was her own *E1*] she declared as the *MS*
170:17 over *E1*] into her hands *MS*
170:18 to come against her? *E1*] hung about with Armour. *MS*
170:20 like *E1*] Saul, with the old offi-cious armour and the old official weapons. He was *MS*
170:20 kingship. *E1*] kingship. Let him brandish the old weapons and mouth the old cry. *MS*
170:20 heart. *E1*] heart with scorn. *MS*
170:21 proclaiming his *E1*] strutting, proclaiming his own *MS*
170:22 pride *E1*] scorn *MS*
170:23 exultation beyond *E1*] scorn of *MS*
170:23 Because *TSR*] Even when *MS*
170:24 her Creator ... from the *E1*] the Lord in contempt of *MS*

170:25 her] the *TS*
170:28 nullification *E1*] annulling *MS* deposition *TSR*
170:29 her unseen *E1*] the *MS*
170:29 was exalted over him, before *TSR*] exulted over him, with *MS* exalted over him, with *TS*
170:36 to annul him, *E1*] *Om. MS*
170:40 movements,] ~ *TS*
171:6 was *E1*] *Om. MS*
171:8 her *E1*] the *MS*
171:9 at the stake *TSR*] on some rack of torture *MS*
171:10 burned alive *TSR*] racked *MS*
171:11 consumed *TSR*] annulled *MS*
171:11 burned *TSR*] dead *MS*
171:19 said, "you] ~. "You *TS*
171:21 his presence a violation *E1*] her expelling him *MS*
171:32 brow *E1*] dark muzzle *MS* dark brow *TSR*
171:33 were suspended *TSR*] to do *MS*
171:34 beast *E1*] beast of prey *MS*
171:35 working *E1*] potent *MS*
171:38 exerts its will to *E1*] wills the subjection, *MS* contains the subjection, *TSR*
171:40 steadily enforces *TSR*] wills, steadily wills *MS*
171:40 the death] death *TS*
172:1 light *E1*] fleet *MS*
172:3 for her *TSR*] to spring *MS*
172:5 obscure *E1*] hidden *MS*
172:8 heavy *E1*] savage *MS*
172:12 in his power *TSR*] body for his own *MS*
172:13 at leisure *TSR*] *Om. MS*
172:16 beside *E1*] clinched beside *MS*
172:18 suspension *TSR*] neutrality *MS*
172:22 kill her spirit? *TSR*] ~ ~ ~. *MS*
172:24 body *TSR*] carcase *MS*
172:26 darkness *E1*] inertia *MS*
172:36 He *TSR*] For he *MS*
172:39 that he *TSR*] and that he *MS*
172:40 fire went black in *E1*] bitter fire

corroded *MS* fire went black *TSR*
173:11 unable] was unable *TS*
173:13 great,] ~ *TS*
173:14 The *E1*] Night after night he dreamed he was swimming in a big, dark sea, and the moment was coming when he could swim no more. The *MS*
173:18 sea] ~, *TS*
173:22 the *E1*] a *MS*
173:24 woman? *TSR*] ~. *MS*
173:28 life? *TSR*] ~. *MS*
173:30 had no desire for death *E1*] wanted to live *MS*
174:8 grasping *E1*] octopus *MS*
174:17 He *E1*] Pity, he *MS*
174:21 without *E1*] haggard, stony, without *MS*
174:22 bright *E1*] stony *MS*
174:40 and belly] *Om. E1*
175:4 falling *E1*] falling, falling *MS*
175:11 answered. *P* He *TS*] ~. / He *MS*
175:19 bed-time] bedtime *E1*
175:20 Goodnight *Ed.*] Good night *MS* Good-night *TS*
175:20 or *E1*] or die *MS*
175:23 a long time *E1*] two hours *MS* some time *TSR*
175:25 He *E1*] And he *MS*
175:29 you?" *P* And *TS*] ~?" / And *MS*
175:37 sleep—!] ~—— *E1*
175:40 *must E1*] must *MS*
175:40 now, now] now *TS*
176:16 was desolate as *E1*] blubbered like *MS*
176:27 subdued *E1*] gentle *MS*
176:29 and distinct ... as before *E1*] like two children *MS*
176:31 not alive *TSR*] silenced *MS*
176:32 and *E1*] and love her, and still *MS*
176:34 peaceful *TSR*] beautiful *MS*
176:38 not *TSR*] *Om. MS*
176:39 Before,] ~ *TS*
176:40 self,] ~—— *TS*

177:2 quiet] ~, *TS*
177:2 He had *TSR*] But he had *MS*
177:3 last, free, separate, independent. *TSR*] last. *MS*
177:6 husband. *E1*] husband. She had faith. *MS*
177:9 rested *E1*] rested safe *MS*
177:11 looked,] ~ *TS*
177:14 hold *E1*] uncover *MS*
177:15 him [almost dev]otionally, *Ed.*]
        him [   ]otionally, *MS*
        him   *TS* him, *TSR see notes*
177:25 now from the *E1*] at a decent *MS*
177:25 flower-like *E1*] mystic *MS*
177:26 off, a stranger. *E1*] off. *MS*
177:28 delicately *E1*] exquisitely *MS*
177:29 lay down *TSR*] went *MS*
177:32 precious, remote *E1*] gleaming, mysterious *MS*
178:9 OO] Oh *E1*
178:13 bad enough. *TSR*] pretty bad. *MS*
178:16 a masterly force of *TSR*] masterly life, always *MS*
178:16 bottommost *Ed.*] bottom-most *MS*
178:17 She knew she was winning *TSR*] Winning *MS*
178:23 great,] ~ *TS*
179:2 Ursula *TS*] ~, *MS*
179:2 because of ... the saint. *E1*] which they said meant "the little bear." *MS*
179:11 was out ... with her *E1*] no longer adhered to the great scheme of man's world *MS*
179:15 river-side] river-/ side *TS* riverside *E1*
179:16 rear up *E1*] conceive *MS*
179:16 ugly *E1*] powerful *MS*
179:17 nature?] ~! *TS*
179:19 himself, almost monstrous. *E1*] himself. *MS*
179:20 felt that *TSR*] would forfeit *MS*
179:21 was exterior ... own real *TSR*] rather than his mere *MS*
179:22 monstrous *E1*] massive *MS*

179:25 and the new ... his soul *E1*] *Om. MS*
179:35 attended by *TSR*] goaded with *MS*
179:35 more, something ... might. What *E1*] outside, that he did not attain. And yet, what *MS* outside, that ... attain. But as yet, he was so warm and fulfilled. What *TSR*
179:38 fabricated *TSR*] man's *MS*
180:1 troubled *TSR*] ashamed *MS*
180:1 acquiescence. She ... with him. *E1*] acquiescence. *MS* acquiescence and his satisfaction. *TSR*
180:2 Infinite *E1*] world *MS*
180:4 oblivion, he ... was unsure. *E1*] oblivion. If she would kiss him, if she would love his body, he asked no more. And this, to have her love his body and bear him children, he would live for and die for in his age. *MS* oblivion. If ... would love his body and bear him children, he asked no more. And this ... age. *TS*
180:7 uncertainty *E1*] beyond *MS*
180:7 which *TSR*] *Om. MS*
180:11 singsong] sing-song *TS*
180:12 claim from ... the voice *E1*] far-off sound of a bell, a summons from the distance, or the summons *MS* summons from ... summons *TSR*
180:13 claim on him *TSR*] dawn *MS*
180:14 submit *E1*] go forth, to take place in the new dawn *MS*
180:14 back,] ~ *TS*
180:15 aloof *E1*] at home *MS*
180:16 deny *E1*] burst forth from *MS*
180:16 be himself *E1*] stay at home *MS*
180:20 bird;— *Ed.*] cherub;— *MS* cherub— *TS* bird— *TSR*
180:26 them!" *P* Suddenly *Ed.*] ~!" / Suddenly *MS* ~!" Suddenly *TS*

180:29 it!" *P* She *Ed.*] ~!" / She *MS* ~!" She *TS*

180:33 they've] they're *E1*

181:7 own light *E1*] hand for help *MS*

181:8 yet. *E1*] yet, not yet. *MS*

181:10 a slight *E1*] an awaiting, *MS* an awaiting *TS*

181:16 Must she be *E1*] Was there no *MS*

187:17 did *E1*] could *MS*

181:18 at. There ... She stood *E1*] at, she knew was through the door. Why could her feet not start on the journey? They remained *MS*

181:19 this] the *TS*

181:24 light *E1*] flame *MS*

181:24 It *E1*] it *MS*

181:26 It *E1*] it *MS*

181:28 Why should ... further *E1*] How could she get beyond *MS*

181:33 making this *TSR*] all you *MS*

181:34 so busy about *TSR*] secret *MS*

181:34 alone *E1*] come to share *MS*

181:35 apart from ... of him *E1*] behind her, close behind her, her rear-guard, not her advance-guard *MS*

181:39 witnesses *E1*] brave ones *MS* brave witnesses *TSR*

182:1 sure of *E1*] she knew *MS*

182:3 denying her *E1*] more to be said *MS*

182:5 satisfied *TSR*] content *MS*

182:6 took away *E1*] robbed her of *MS*

182:6 She forgot that she had *TSR*] For had she not *MS*

182:7 forward. *TS*] ~? *MS*

182:8 She forgot ... moon had *TSR*] Had not the moon *MS*

182:10 follow. *E1*] ~? *MS*

182:13 satisfaction *E1*] a pang *MS*

182:13 She was bearing her children. *E1*] The sun knew, and the moon knew, that she could not go alone, save the man took her, as Joseph took Mary to Egypt. He would not take her. He could not rise up and quit his home. His feet clung to the beloved earth of his home, he could not depart. So she must stay. *MS* She was bearing her children. And she knew that she could ... rise up and depart for the unknown. His ... stay. *TSR*

182:15 There *E1*] But there *MS*

182:17 arrived now, *E1*] reached now, at her journeys {journey's *TS*} limit, *MS*

182:19 passing *E1*] beckoning *MS*

182:20 journeying *TSR*] journeying hosts of nights and suns *MS*

182:23 direction to take *TSR*] journey *MS*

183:1 VII *TSR*] VI *MS*

183:5 Skrebensky *TSR*] Skrebenski *MS*

183:6 Anna's mother *E1*] the Polish woman *MS* the Anna's mother *TSR*

183:7 girl *TSR*] Anna *MS*

183:8 Skrebensky *TS*] Skrebenski *MS*

183:9 raving] ~, *TS*

183:11 small,] ~ *TS*

183:11 sharp *E1*] soldierly-looking *MS* militant *TSR*

183:16 heavy,] ~ *TS*

183:21 Briswell—] ~, *TS*

183:22 Skrebensky *TSR*] Skrebenski *MS*

183:23 incoherent, *TSR*] incoherent yet *MS*

183:23 interesting exhumations. *TSR*] fascinating exhumations from unknown sources. *MS*

183:27 Brangwen, *TS*] ~ *MS*

183:31 strange *TSR*] attractive *MS*

183:31 exposed *TSR*] left *MS*

183:33 under her spell. *TSR*] smitten by her. *MS*

183:33 snuggle like a kitten *TSR*] imply that she sheltered *MS*

183:34 elusive and ... her claws *TSR*]
the most elusive little creature,
suggesting exquisite and secret
refinements of nature *MS*

184:1 was almost ... quite happy
TSR] doted on her. She, perfectly happily *MS*

184:3 elusive *E1*] subtle *MS*

184:5 as if ... elderly Baron *TSR*]
over it *MS*

184:7 Skrebensky was loud *TSR*]
Skrebenski was mad *MS*

184:10 half Venetian, *TSR*] *Om. MS*

184:12 satisfied his maddened pride
E1] satisfied him *MS* placated
his ... pride *TSR*

184:15 Skrebenskys *TSR*] Skrebenskis
MS

184:16 Skrebensky *TSR*] Skrebenski
MS

184:16 having *E1*] having inherited
MS

184:16 fortune of her own *TSR*] three
hundred pounds a year when
she came of age *MS*

184:21 a kind ... some weasel *E1*] the
charm of naïveté {naiveté *TS*}
born of sang-froid and subtlety
MS a kind ... some sea-
creature *TSR*

184:22 respected her ... by the *TSR*]
loved her, and envied her her
MS

184:24 surety of ... it, fascinated *TSR*]
surety, that was not devoid of
pretty cunning *MS*

184:24 Baron *Ed.*] baron *MS*

184:29 concentrated *TSR*] wise *MS*

184:29 informed *TSR*] instructed *MS*

184:29 faculty *TSR*] amazing faculty
MS

184:29 deliberate *TSR*] accurate *MS*

184:32 fine, deliberate *E1*] subtle,
intricate *MS* hard, deliberate
TSR

184:33 He was ... death-like ... so
distinct in ... to him. *E1*]
There was something statu-

esque and remote about him: a
small, fine statue, removed
infinitely from any spiritual
contact with a woman, yet so
marvellously active on his own
part, so fine and intricate. *MS*
He was ... deathlike ... so
isolated in ... him. *TSR*

184:37 hard *TSR*] sharp *MS*

184:37 fascinated *TSR*] half fascinated
MS

184:38 diffuse *TSR*] close, intermingling *MS*

184:39 She seemed ... high, sharp air
... [185:3] to her? *E1*] *Om. MS*
She seemed ... high, cold air
... her? *TSR*

185:4 Baroness *Ed.*] baroness *MS*

185:6 see all ... irritated. Yet *TSR*]
take her. He was the wrong sort
for her, not subtle enough. She
was rather bored. And yet *MS*

185:9 face, *TSR*] ~ *MS*

185:10 despised him ... his uncritical,
unironical ... with deferential
interest ... was different in
kind. She ... fire glowing steadily ... not object. He ...
[185:17] too different. *E1*]
wished she were like him, easy
and unconscious as a full fire
burning, burning without
flickering. Herself, she was
uneasy, twisting and restless as
a ferret, stirring with the same
chill, uneasy, restless flame.
MS despised ... his steady,
warm, unironical ... with naïve
interest ... was too stupid. She
... fire burning steadily ... not
understand. He ... too stupid.
TSR

185:18 quick, slight ... his interest
TSR] quick little thing, with
sharp, perceptive instincts *MS*

185:20 outsider. *TSR*] outsider. They
were of alien breed. *MS*

185:20 stayed by *E1*] ran to *MS*

185:21 acknowledged her, *TSR*] *Om.*
MS
185:21 observant *TSR*] changeable
MS
185:22 glance *TSR*] sort of sparkle
MS
185:22 at *TSR*] in *MS*
185:24 aristocratic *TSR*] aristocratic,
commanding *MS*
185:24 distance in their relationship,
the *TSR*] detachment between
them, the extraordinary *MS*
distance ... the relationship,
the *E1*
185:25 on the ... filial subordination
on *E1*] of the one, son-ship of
MS on the ... filial detachment
on *TSR*
185:26 in their different degrees *TSR*]
sharp and graceful and *MS*
185:27 differing as ... in relationship
E1] male man and innocent
child, unchangeable *MS* original father and derivative child,
separate *TSR*
185:28 Baroness] barones *TS* baroness
E1
185:29 having *TSR*] yet having *MS*
185:30 attraction *TSR*] life *MS*
185:31 lot] life *TS*
185:32 being] living *TS*
185:36 blood-relation, was annulled.
TSR] blood-relation. *MS*
185:37 one *TSR*] one flesh *MS*
186:1 being, his hot life, *E1*] hot
blood, his only wealth, *MS* hot
being, his hot physical life, his
only form of life, *TSR*
186:3 in a world ... cool outside *TSR*]
to produce a new, third self, as
which she must henceforth
exist *MS*
186:8 partly *E1*] too *MS*
186:10 Skrebenskys' *Ed.*] Skrebenskis'
MS Skrebenskis', *TS*
Skrebenskys', *TSR*
186:10 Will Brangwen's *TSR*] his *MS*
186:16 Skrebenskys *MS*, *TSR*]

Skrebenskis *TS* Skrebenskys'
E1
186:18 ran ahead *E1*] left Anna's side
and flew its own flight *MS* left
Anna's side and ran ahead *TSR*
186:21 the Spirit *E1*] heaven *MS* the
Unseen *TSR*
186:24 said. P The *TS*] ~. / The *MS*
186:28 pressed] passed *TS*
186:31 transported *MS*, *E1*] transfigured *TSR*
187:1 leapt, *TS*] ~ *MS*
187:2 absorbed by *TSR*] tiny,
swooned under *MS*
187:6 awe. *TSR*] awe, but hostile
rather than attuned. *MS*
187:7 his progress. *TSR*] the progress
of his possession. He had
passed out of the light, into the
darkness beyond, and nearer,
nearer to the mystery. *MS*
187:7 essence *TSR*] core *MS*
187:10 day *E1*] eternity *MS*
187:11 profound,] ~ *TS*
187:16 seed] ~, *TS*
187:18 were the circle ... with the *E1*]
lay in the two extremes of
silence. Like a shadowy *MS* lay
within the circle ... the *TSR*
187:19 folded music ... hushing up
TSR] spanned from silence to
silence, darkness to darkness,
fecundity to fecundity, as a
seed spans from life to life and
death to death, containing *MS*
187:22 between *TSR*] folded between
MS
187:22 parts, the ... it involves, and ...
embrace again. *E1*] parts. *MS*
parts, the ... it will achieve, and
... again. *TSR*
187:25 Here in ... his consummation.
TSR] So, silence folding {fol-
lowing *TS*} on silence, death
upon what shall be, and time
obliterated, even eternity made
meaningless, Brangwen was set
free. Here was no before and

after. All *was*. Here, all was immemorial ecstasy. From ecstasy through ecstasy to ecstasy, on, on to the final, the ecstasy of ecstasies {ecstasies, *TS*} it was all here, in One! *MS*

187:28 womb] ~, *TS*

187:29 after knowledge] ~ ~, *TS*

187:31 betweenwhiles] between-/while *TS* between-while *E1*

187:36 horizontal *TSR*] plain clear *MS*

187:38 ah, to *TSR*] and ah, *MS*

187:39 consummation, *TS*] ~. *MS*

187:40 neutrality *TSR*] interlocking *MS*

188:3 only this ... [188:8] leaped, leaped *E1*] all was there, all present at once, and past and future were made one. Till again from his body awakening, every jet strained and leaped, leaped, gathered itself, leaped *MS* only this ... leaped, leaped, leaped *TSR*

188:10 arch. *TSR*] arch. *P* The illusion of time was destroyed, the flagrancy of day after day. Not day after day, nor night after night took place. But the soul in passion gathering itself together, and passion taking the spring, and leaping, leaping upwards, to declension, and thus, ah, reaching the clasp, and swooning forever, locked there in the swooning, upper ecstasy, forever in the clasp of consummation. And so, to escape from Time, to the timeless All. And again, the gathering together, the great, heart-shattering leap from earth, up, up, to the climax, the eternal embrace fixed unthinkably aloft without support. It must recur again, and again. And ever the immemorial ecstasy, recurrent, the same. So the progression. So, arch after arch, leap after leap from earth, up, up, and too far, and the clash in the midst of declension, the meeting, the ecstatic clasp, the swoon at consummation, in the utter mystery, the consummate ecstasy, studded aloft, and perfect:—so the progression was pointed out, the point fixed; yet on, on, and on, surging always upward, yet, through the embrace and the climax, swinging ever one step forward, and one stride forward, and one stride forward, up the unthinkable progress, to the Altar, and the Holy of Holies, and the Surpassing Ecstasy. *MS*

188:11 but silenced ... [189:19] little faces ... [191:21] life outside ... [192:24] abide. She *TSR*] and silenced, lifted up. But something in her was uneasy, unsure. Though she was lifted up, she was not fulfilled. *P* Yet again the power of the cathedral swept her up and carried her out of herself. She could not think or look or notice, only dimly around her the great shadow resounded: "Take off your shoes, this is holy ground—take off your shoes, for this is holy ground." And in fear, her soul stooped to the latchet of its sandals. *P* She had come from the busy, rattling town of people and vehicles, she had come through the hills and valleys of the country, many many places there were under the sky she belonged to. She felt them all going, falling back forever to extinction. The living, mystical stone was leaping up around her, the world was falling asunder. It was gone, and the leaping stone met and clinched about her, it was finished, this was the conclusion. This was the end. The great arches had leapt to their conclusion, the shadow was united forever in the roof overhead, the jewelled windows shone like memorials. It was stupendous, and final. *P* She looked towards her husband. His face glowed. "Divesting is all he needs," she said in herself. She had seen in one of his pictures a soul, leaving a saint's mouth, being lifted up to heaven by two angels;—and the soul was a naked little man, standing very stiff. She stood away from him. *P* Willingly, cravingly, she turned again to the cathedral, a postulant. She wanted to give herself. The wonderful, soaring height, it would lift her up! Her soul yearned and swung. But her desire was not satisfied. She stood far back and looked down the nave, yearning with her whole soul. Down there, far down there, should be the altar. But it was dark confusion. Down there should be the altar flickering with the angels of the Presence, or lofty with the Shadow. And it was not so. There was no altar. *P* There was only the awful, shadowy height, and shadowy recurrence in height. And she was in trouble. She was taken up each moment, she was lifted and consummated there in the height, in the upper shadow where the stone met and clinched. But her soul yearned after the stately, mystic march of the pillars down the nave. She wanted to follow the pillars. Whither? Ah, there was no goal, and every time she was caught up and carried to the great, clinched rapture above. She was lost, lost. *P* For she knew the goal was missing, even in her rapture of her holy, awful height. Her soul leapt up. It leapt to the ecstasy and the isolation and the agony up there, lifted out of itself. And ah, the stud of ecstasy overhead! Let it be enough. *P* So the first day she was carried out of herself, with the darkness. *P* But at night she was sad, uneasy. Not this, ah not this! She ached away from it. Why this agony and isolation of ecstasy each time? How could one go on and on, if one were nailed in high ecstasy? Why must she be tortured with exaltation, with this height of ecstasy? Why must she leap to her soul's supreme altitude of self-knowledge, in the search of God? Why surpass these hands and feet, to know one's greatest leap, the utmost of the soul. Why agonise one's body with the awful altitude of the soul? Why these repeated full-stops of ecstasy! *P* Was this all the knowledge of God, to know the utmost, immemorial "I"? Could she know no more, than this ecstatic consummation of herself, of her own soul? Could she not yearn forwards, forwards? Was there nothing else? Whither could she follow the moving pillars, the silent, marching pillars of shadow? Would they not lead her forward, forward, on to the threshold of the Unknown, to the brink of the Mystery, the altar steps, and there cast her down. *P* She dreamed of the angels, who went in shadow by day, at night in flickering flames. They flickered on the outer circle of the Most High like altar flames, they quivered in flames of praise. And she knew in her dream, that beyond these were the fiery, stately Archangels, and beyond these the fiercely bright circle of the Cherubim, the Innermost, palpitating to the awful brightness of the Presence, absorbed in their wonder of praise. *P* When she woke, her face was still sheer brightness, her heart was as dead in the fear of her dream. *P* She went gladly to the cathedral in the morning, hoping to see, down the vista of shadowy, progressive ecstasies, the flickering lights of the angels, who should use the altar as an alighting-stone, as they descended from the beyond. *P* And they were not there. Only the columns soared up in all their power, only the myriad points of ecstasy overhead. But where were the altar-flames, where was the tempered brightness of God, which at length should transfigure the face and the hands and the feet of the postulant, remove the uncleanness of the stigmata. For she had known her height of ecstasy, her hands and feet had been nailed at the summit of self-realisation, she had died in the common body, and her single soul had risen supreme, immortal, the eternal "I", her own consummated soul. *P* And whither now, after the resurrection? Ah now, to be absorbed in praise, the hands and the feet made whole and clean, the body bright with adoration! Was it at an end? Was it indeed at an end, her journey. *P* She wanted to go on a long, far journey, with hands lifted exulting towards the Mystery, and feet beating to bliss, and soul quivering like a flame that leaps higher, higher, higher, in the Outermost Service of the Most High. *P* Where were the messengers of praise, the Angels? What were they calling outside the closed door? And where was the door, that she might open it? For the cathedral had no flickering altar and no door. She was shut in. *P* There was the sky outside. Outside, above the cathedral arches, the sky was infinitely high. The tallest leap of man's self-realisation was but a sparrow's flight. Even the rooks went higher. What could his ecstasies do for him, how carry him to a zenith, save he had a heavy roof above him, that should make him seem so high, he was the zenith, should fix his consummate "I" forever, in immemorial ecstasy, culminated under the roof. *P* Remembering the sky above the cathedral, how tiny was man's stud of ecstasy in his immortal soul, how little and partial his passion for God! Could man with his Ego occupy the whole rotonda of Day, or the dome of night? *P* Let him have done now. Let him turn from the shame of the Cross,

and know the healing of the Most High upon his wounds. Let him be aware of the angels awaiting him. *P* Yet, if the sky were a blue rotonda, what then? She did not know whither to move, nor where to look, and there was nothing to say. If the sky were a great dome hung with twinkling lamps, which star should she choose? *P* For her heart asked whither, whither? And there was no reply. If she turned her round in the great, noble rotonda of the day, she could only know its completeness. And she knew her own incompleteness. Therefore whither? The blue rotonda of the day made no answer, nor the twinkling dome of night. *P* In the cathedral, once, there had been the surge forward, wave after wave, leap after leap, towards the altar, and the flickering flames that announced the Mystery. But the altar was a dragged nest, the Mystery was gone, the candle-flames were shed away, leaving the sacred bush exposed, common, fireless, with a dragged nest. *P* She wanted to rise like a bird from the builded earth and find a low, stern wind in her wings that would carry her somewhere. She wanted to rise as a bird rises with wet, limp feet from the sea, to lift herself, thrust herself as a bird thrusts its body from the heave and pulse of the water that bears it forward, tear itself away like a bird on wings, and in the open space where there is clarity, risen up above the motion, a separate speck hanging suspended, moving this way and that, give herself to the pulling of the goal, feel the touch of summons, and answer, swinging on, falling back into the heaving motion of the days, but never forgetting, remembering always whither. *P* She wanted to rise into the gladness of light, to make sure of the angels standing all round the rotonda of day, brightening the horizon, and announcing the All-High. And which would beckon to her? In her dream she struggled with anticipation. *P* She wanted to escape from the builded earth, from man's day after day. Was man and his present measure to be forever the measure of the universe? *P* But she must grasp at some resistance, before she could thrust off. It was so difficult. *P* In the cathedral, she caught at the little human faces carved in stone across the screen. The very humanness of the features made her aware that somehow, these [189:19] little faces with their nice and nasty traits, as they peered out from the big tide of the cathedral, made sly little mockery of the church's grand impulse of goodness. They knew better, these little faces. Their little human features retorted on the grand scheme of goodness. It was a scheme so complete only because it excluded so much. And these little faces belonged to the things that the passionate will of man's conception of goodness would have excluded. But would he exclude them? They winked and jeered. *P* These little faces, with their separate wills, separate motions, rippled back in defiance of the tide, and laughed in the triumph of their very littleness. *P* "Look!" she cried: it was a face plump and sly, at once scolding and genial. "Look, that's the wife of the man who carved her. He liked her, for all that." *P* Brangwen was irritated by her interrupting him in his passionate intercourse with the cathedral. For some time, she had been making friction in his soul. *P* "That's a man," he said. *P* "It isn't!" she cried. "Look— anyone can see it's his wife. A man—!" *P* He laughed shortly, and moved on. Yet he was aware of her loitering, hanging behind him. Why would she not come along, and be with him? His brows began to gather. He was being put out of connection with the cathedral that fulfilled him. Why would the woman not *know* what a good thing this

was? *P* "Now then," she said, "now tell me who she is? Now say if it's a man! It's his wife, and he hated her too. He's paying her back. Look at her thin eyelids!" She stopped before another little face. *P* "It's a man!" he said harshly, and he turned away. *P* He was very angry. He went away from her. She let him go. But it spoiled it all for him. They were still lovers, and he could not be whole-hearted unless she were there. He was aware of her hostility, he could not see the church. She had put him out of connection. His soul was out of joint, and stiff with rage and pain. He wanted to be with his cathedral, he wanted to satisfy his passion. And he could not. She, accursed, had come in between, and dislocated his soul. In torment, he girded and writhed, trying to love the cathedral. It was as meaningless and soulless to him as a cardboard place. But he *would* have it for his soul, he *would* enjoy it. None the less, it was a meaningless, sterile. *P* Black with disappointment, and rage, and a sort of girding despair, he went home with her. And they fought again. It was as if devils of rage possessed him, and blackly tortured his soul. Then she jeered at his gothic ecstasies and his cathedral religion! Pure selfishness it was, she said. *P* He went about for days in torture of raging misery and hatred. His cathedrals, which had brooded over the earth like Eagles, like the Holy Spirit crouching there supreme and transcendent on the high places of the world, what had they become? Mere architecture, museum things, relics of bygone history: mere historical things. He could not bear it. His cathedrals! Till now, he had but to think himself at their doors for his soul to leap up, he had but to imagine himself in the great, singing gloom of the pillars, and he was fulfilled. The choir-stalls were there like fixed music, with myriad dark points pricking up, the windows hung round in tablets of jewel emanating their own glory. And when he came to service, in the choir, he came into his own. His soul went up like a flame on the chanting and the ritual; it strove like a flame, rising higher, till it touched the reality and the satisfaction. *P* And now, and now, bitterly, he knew he would never reach his culmination again in this way. Where was the reality his soul had yearned up to in flame? It was not here, in the singing and the arching of the cathedral. *P* The gloom of the church, the soaring of the clustered columns, what were these to the thrushes in the garden? He listened to the call, call, call of the thrushes and the blackbirds. It had nothing to do with churches. It was a life outside. And a field-ful of dandelions broadspread in the sun: this had nothing to do with the mystery of the church. It was another, freer note. It was larger. *P* There was a great [191:21] life outside the church, that the church must needs exclude. Why must the church invest itself with shadow? Why not give way to the light and a blossoming world? Was a temple then never fully a temple, till it was broken and roofless, and birds built in its capitals and wall-flowers grew on its altars? *P* He could not bear it, for he clung to the shadow and the mystery. He would rather give up the morning sun and the dandelions than the church. If his church were exclusive rather than inclusive, as he had imagined, let it be so. It was still his Via media. He was made that way. The lark liked the early morning and a straight rise to the sun. He loved the pillars and arches and wonderful tracery, the roof overhead, the gloom, the mystery, the ritual. Let it be so. *P* But he was almost apologetic. Anna did not believe in his church. Her spirit would not be sifted through the jewelled gloom, it would

not take its flight among the leaping stone. His spirit would. They had different ways. He went his way, because it was the road of his nature. She found no way. She went to church as a matter of form. She found no way of her own. Yet he deferred to her. She had the lead. *P* The little church drew him across his garden wall. He entered the choir—he became choir-master. Anna was pleased for his sake. She had the child now. Let it all wait, this unresolved desire. She was occupied now. Let it abide, the adventure of her soul, let the quest for the hidden door be put off. If she did not go, the child might go, this child, another child. If her soul should not find utterance and fulfilment, her womb should. He too should wait in the shadow of the church. It was no way, she thought, the church: but when the door was under the foot of the rainbow, it was the soul's desire that mattered, more than the direction; at least for the time being; and he would breed children in her, she would have the children. *P* The church that neighboured with his house became little by little more poignantly his home than the cottage where Anna was. She was apart from him: he believed in her, he did not know her. The church he knew. In its shadowy atmosphere he came into being. He loved to sink himself into its hush as a stone sinks satisfied into deep water. And there, at the depth of shadow and its dim, waiting silence, his heart put forth like a water-lily root, stirred towards flowering. *P* He wanted to go secretly across his garden, climb the wall by the little steps, and enter alone into the church. When the heavy door was closed behind him, and his foot re-echoed up the aisle, his heart filled with a passion of elation; even the fear he needed. He loved to light the candles at the organ, and then seat himself, at the core of his desire, and begin to practise for the service. He loved to have the church, the darkness, the music, and himself, all one. The whitewashed arches retreated into the darkness, there were faint, ghostly noises in the tower, and the music swelled out, his heart gave out paens of praise. *P* Why should he fret any more about his life? The office where he worked was gone into unreality. His wife was with him, really. She hovered on the shadow of the church: she waited to be with him: she *MS see also following entries to* 192:23

188:13 and *E1*] [   ] *TSR see notes*
188:18 far-off *E1*] far-up *TSR*
188:29 meeting, ecstasy *E1*] mating, recurrence *TSR*
188:32 altar, recurrence of ecstasy. *E1*] altar. *TSR*
188:34 Eternity *E1*] the Unknown *TSR*
188:36 flights *E1*] undulation *TSR*
189:4 leaps *E1*] flows *TSR*
189:5 Infinite *E1*] unknown *TSR*
189:5 flinging *E1*] sullenly swinging *TSR*
189:6 leaping, forward-travelling *E1*] undulating, forward-thrusting *TSR*
189:11 surcharged *E1*] dogged *TSR*
189:22 suggestion *E1*] cognisance *TSR*
189:26 spring *E1*] swell *TSR*
189:39 face." *P* Her *E1*] ~." / Her *TSR*
190:2 waited, *TSR*] ~ *E1*
190:5 good *E1*] lovely *TSR*
190:8 He must ... a nice *E1*] Oh what a lovely *TSR*
190:10 he. *TSR*] ~? *E1*
190:22 dead, dead *E1*] dead, dead, dead *TSR*
190:25 stand *E1*] shelter *TSR*
190:28 perfect *E1*] grand perfect *TSR*
190:32 cathedral, *TSR*] ~; *E1*
190:36 felt *E1*] feeling *TSR*
190:37 be *E1*] be as real *TSR*

190:40 a sort of side show, *E1*] *Om. TSR*
191:6 jewel *TSR*] jewels *TSC see notes*
191:15 garden, *TSR*] gardens *E1*
191:24 it seemed, *E1*] wondered, if *TSR*
191:25 perfectly *E1*] fully *TSR*
191:27 symbol *E1*] ruin *TSR*
191:31 sacred *E1*] fragile *TSR*
191:32 wood-work *TSR*] woodwork *E1*
191:35 superficial *E1*] isolated *TSR*
191:37 uncreated *E1*] elsewhere *TSR*
191:39 into unknown realities *E1*] for truth or freedom *TSR*
192:7 sank back *E1*] came *TSR*
192:11 aisle *E1*] little aisle *TSR*
192:12 He was ... his fulfilment. *E1*] *Om. TSR*
192:22 go. *E1*] go. What would be, would be. *TSR*
192:23 had conquered *E1*] and he were together *TSR*
192:24 one *E1*] together *MS*
192:25 protestation *TSR*] gratefulness *MS*
192:25 lay in *E1*] went up into *MS*
192:25 darkness,] ~ *TS*
192:27 a complete bliss and fulfilment *TSR*] like a narcotic *MS*
192:28 sank into abeyance *TSR*] ceased to torment her *MS*
192:29 She *TSR*] Yet / *MS*
192:32 everything *TSR*] all *MS*
192:32 all occupied here. *TSR*] drugged, *MS* dragged. *TS*
192:33 was a *TSR*] was purely a *MS*
192:33 It was ... and powerful ... And before ... [192:40] she was *E1* She had few dreams for her child: it was a girl, and it did not excite her imagination. All she wanted, was its complete animal well-being. To this, her nature was roused. And before six months had gone by, she had almost succeeded. By that time she was herself *MS* It ...

and beautiful. And before ...
she was *TSR*
192:40 child. She ... fecund storm of
life ... of everything. *Ed.*] child.
P Gradually, in the second year
of his marriage, Brangwen's
life settled to its course. Anna
had very little time to give him,
she could not notice him very
much. He must thrown {throw
TS} out his own line. *MS* child.
She ... fecund storm of life ...
to her. *TSR* child. She ...
fecund of storm life ... to her.
She felt ... everything. *E1*
193:3 Brangwen occupied himself
with *E1*] So, he gave himself to
MS Brangwen gave himself to
TSR
193:4 Sunday School *Ed.*] Sunday-
School *MS* Sunday-school *TS*
193:5 He was happy enough. There
... time exciting himself with
the proximity of some ... yet
fathomed. *E1*] Anna let him be.
He never wanted to dogmatise
or theorise. Only, the bible had
a great, mystic {great mystic
TS} glamour for him, and
some of this {the *TS*} glamour
of the bible stories he trans-
mitted to those around him.
Even she herself lived in the
spell. *MS* He was happy. There
... time trying to find out for
himself some ... fathomed.
TSR
193:9 his wife ... [193:24] the outer
E1] her and shared the work
with her, making very little
manly distinction. This was
new to her. Her father had
always kept the man's position.
It was not in his nature to nurse
a baby or prepare its food. Her
husband shared this with her,
he did the nursing and the
menial little things as they

came or as was necessary. At
first she was afraid of what
other people might think, she
was afraid for his dignity. But
he was ignorant of any dero-
gation. So she became used to
him. *P* Judging from the men
she knew, she did not consider
him manly. But then why
should he be? He never sought
the company of other men, he
served the new, tiny matriarchy
at home, he served the church
outside his home, he did his
work in the office, alone and
single always. At first she could
not get used to him, the *MS* his
wife ... of the children ...
importance. He was too simple
and direct, too indifferent of
his own dignity, he made too
little of his own importance.
But it was his very abandoning
... upon his own activity, that
made him really attractive,
remarkable. *P* Anna ... set her
in another world ... and single
always ... outer *TSR*
193:25 her sneer ... and completely
E1] sharply the shame hit her
back! She loved him *MS*
sharply her sneer changed to a
sort of reverence. She did not
understand everything about
him: he was also beyond her
TSR
193:28 be *E1*] be with him as *MS*
193:29 She *E1*] And she *MS*
193:30 devotion *E1*] intense devotion
MS
193:30 for; and ... for something *TSR*]
for, not the Church of Christ
MS
193:32 wood-work *Ed.*] woodwork *MS*
193:34 business *TSR*] craving *MS*
193:34 intimate,] ~ *TS*
193:38 still loves *TSR*] will not know
MS

193:39 Church] church *TS*

193:39 was false *E1*] betrayed him *MS* had betrayed him *TSR*

193:39 attentively. *TSR*] passionately. His soul, in a little anguish, followed his will. *MS*

193:40 kept himself *TSR*] made himself blanched, *MS*

194:4 waited *TSR*] waited, waited *MS*

194:5 its darkness. His hour would come *TSR*] hot germination. He would have love too from his infant *MS*

194:8 her laws ... his own. *E1*] his own laws, whilst his nature adhered to the letter. *MS*

194:13 by *TSR*] from *MS*

194:16 said] ~, *TS*

194:18 in?" *P* He *TS*] ~?" / He *MS*

194:22 with inchoate ... to disintegrate. *TSR*] and torn with bitter misery and rage. *MS*

194:24 occasionally came ... and awful *TSR*] this was the outcome. At last he got up. She could see the torture in his ugly, dark muzzle. She revolted from him, he was repulsive *MS*

194:30 ignore him ... her own *TSR*] put her arm round him and try to love him and comfort him *MS*

194:31 come back ... the ugly strain in ... Then he *E1*] submit to her. But at last he learned, and he yielded to her, and *MS* come back ... the yellow dancing light in ... Then he *TSR*

194:36 wood-work *Ed.*] woodwork *MS*

194:37 he had *TSR*] there was *MS*

194:38 wood-work] woodwork *E1*

195:1 limitation *E1*] imperfection *MS*

195:1 He even ... became quieter. *TSR*] *Om. MS*

196:1 VIII *TSR*] VII *MS*

196:6 unfathomed *TSR*] far, dark *MS*

196:8 perilous and imminent? *TSR*] far back and dark? Was he not as he had conceived himself, spun out of the daylight of today. Was Today only the surf, breaking on the unknown, but rolling in from unthinkable distances behind? And he was one with the distances behind, these distances were himself, he was these also? *MS* far back ... to-day. Was To-day only the breaking ... also? *TS*

196:12 distances *E1*] far distances *MS* savage distances *TSR*

196:13 Sometimes,] ~ *TS*

196:15 face,] ~ *TS*

196:17 impersonal *TSR*] inhuman *MS*

196:18 human *TSR*] *Om. MS*, *E1* see notes

196:19 its madness *TSR*] in tune *MS*

196:19 frenzy. *E1*] frenzy. The unknown quality of the infant was the disremembered quality of himself, that he could not bear to have made known. For was he not pure stuff of today?— {to-day?— *TS*} and to know the presence of illimitable yesterdays was a horror to him. *MS* frenzy. The ... stuff of the present?—and to hear the voice of his dark and savage origins, still insistent and powerful, was ... him. *TSR*

196:20 obliterated sources *TSR*] forgotten yesterdays *MS*

196:21 were the origin of *E1*] still formed *MS*

196:21 He *TSR*] Ah, how he *MS*

196:22 Then he ... potent, dark *TSR*] And the conceptions {conception *TS*} must go *MS*

196:34 tiny] ~, *TS*

197:11 become his *TSR*] arrive *MS*

197:14 infant *E1*] baby *MS*

197:15 newly opened] newly-opened *TSR*

197:15 newly dawned] newly-dawned *TS*

197:18 laugh. *TSR*] laugh. The child knew him and loved him. *MS*
197:19 child *E1*] baby *MS*
197:22 ecstasy *TSR*] ecstasy in the eyes *MS*
197:27 red hot] red-hot *TS*
197:28 not much more than *TSR*] only about *MS*
197:29 She *TSR*] *He* was for *MS*
197:29 He had ... on her. *TSR*] This was the one he had placed in his heart. *MS*
197:36 Oh, Oh] ~, oh *TS*
197:36 life *TSR*] mouth *MS*
197:37 Oh, Oh, Oh] ~, oh, oh *TS*
197:38 yet passionately at her *TSR*] at the *MS*
197:39 seeking her ... vital knowledge *TSR*] opening avidly and blindly *MS*
197:40 consummate peace *TSR*] silence *MS*
197:40 sank, the mouth and throat *TSR*] sank still, *MS* sank, still *TS*
198:1 drinking life ... own existence, *E1*] almost sobbing for breath with eagerness, and *MS* drinking ... own being, *TS*
198:4 back, not to be gainsaid. *TSR*] back. *MS*
198:7 the weaned child; *TSR*] *Om. MS* the weaned child, *E1*
198:8 wondering,] ~ *E1*
198:9 who had waited ... was for *E1*] a little ecstasy shone from them to *MS* who waited ... for *TSR*
198:10 still *TSR*] already *MS*
198:11 entirely hers *TSR*] impotent *MS*
198:11 direct upon her *TSR*] more absolute *MS*
198:13 So Ursula became *TSR*] And Ursula was *MS*
198:16 extravagant *TSR*] brilliant *MS*
198:18 housework,] ~. *E1*
198:20 her children *E1*] they *MS*

198:25 lifted Ursula over into *TSR*] and set Ursula in *MS*
198:25 with a *TSR*] saying *MS*
198:27 tottering, wind-blown *TSR*] ~ ~ *MS* ~ ~, *TS*
198:29 windmill *TSR*] uncertain *MS*
198:30 up and down *E1*] *Om. MS*
198:38 had] *Om. TS*
199:6 a child along with her *TSR*] like a child himself *MS*
199:7 unsettled *TSR*] active *MS*
199:7 twenty two *Ed.*] twenty-two *MS*
199:10 who would make *TSR*] suddenly start to make *MS*
199:10 doll *TSR*] little doll *MS*
199:12 eyes!" *P* And *TS*] ~!" / And *MS*
199:15 underneath *TSR*] *Om. MS*
199:18 took *TSR*] would quickly take *MS*
199:18 said *TSR*] say *MS*
199:19 ear-rings] ~, *TS*
199:21 to see the queen? *TSR*] out to see the queen, then? *MS*
199:24 You won't dirty ... white frock *E1*] Your father's late tonight *MS* You mustn't dirty ... frock *TSR*
199:25 He *TSR*] It was he who *MS*
199:26 And he *TSR*] It was he who *MS*
199:29 helped *TSR*] was present, taking part *MS*
199:31 And he ... deep moralities. *TSR*] *Om. MS*
199:35 waiting *TSR*] in the playful threatening command *MS*
199:35 taking *TSR*] pretending to take *MS*
199:37 on *TSR*] back here, Miss *MS*
199:37 repeated, with ... command. *P* An *TSR*] repeated sternly. / An *MS* repeated sternly. *P* An *TS*
199:40 Milady!" *P* She *Ed.*] ~!" / She *MS* ~?" *P* She *TS*
200:1 fleeting *TSR*] frightened *MS*
200:1 her] ~, *TS*
200:2 up. *TSR*] up. She was given into his hands. *MS*

200:3 Who was ... he said, *E1*]
Milday, Milady!" he said
grimly, *MS* Who was ... said,
grimly, *TSR*
200:5 that *TSR*] when *MS*
200:5 his *TSR*] unswerving *MS*
200:19 vital, physical *E1*] warm *MS*
200:27 it *E1*] and yet *MS* and yet, *TS*
200:28 intent *TSR*] animal *MS*
200:30 slight,] ~ *TS*
200:33 cat *E1*] tom-cat *MS*
200:37 were *TSR*] were abandoned *MS*
201:2 penetrating *TSR*] cat-like *MS*
201:5 other:] ~; *TS*
201:6 potent with ... voluptuousness *TSR*] omnipotent *MS*
201:9 sensual *TSR*] magnificent *MS*
201:14 in the light ... thick darkness, *TSR*] as night and day, and as *MS*
201:17 close *E1*] lustrous *MS*
201:18 All his ... life, was *TSR*] Usually, however, he was busy, in *MS*
201:22 original form. *TSR*] true form and beauty. *MS*
201:23 She was ... his darkness. *TSR*] *Om. MS*
201:26 second *TSR*] feline *MS*
201:27 was at rest *TSR*] took no notice *MS*
201:28 unthinking *E1*] in the dark *MS*
201:29 flickering upon him *TSR*] *Om. MS*
201:32 hung *TSR*] always hung *MS*
201:32 carelessly, *TSR*] *Om. MS*
201:33 concentrated, with ... own, isolated *TSR*] flexible, soft, and {soft and *TS*} had a gradual, soft insistence like flexible steel *MS* concentrated with ... isolated *E1*
201:34 child,] ~ *TS*
201:35 fore-arm] forearm *E1*
201:35 electric flexibility *TSR*] soft rigidity *MS*
201:36 through *TSR*] with *MS*

201:37 ambushed in a sort *TSR*] creating an impression *MS*
201:39 black, curved eyebrows arching *TSR*] eyes gleaming *MS*
201:40 Twittermiss!" *P* And *TS*] ~!" / And *MS*
202:1 Then *TSR*] And then *MS*
202:1 happy,] ~ *TS*
202:2 that smelled *TSR*] smelling *MS*
202:2 wood and resounded *TSR*] wood, resounding *MS*
202:3 was charged with *TSR*] full of *MS*
202:4 absorbed *TSR*] full of zest *MS*
202:6 she did not approach them *TSR*] that was enough *MS*
202:10 Again,] ~ *E1*
202:10 transported *E1*] happy and proud *MS*
202:11 pale, void *TSR*] cold, silent *MS*
202:12 practising,] ~ *E1*
202:13 by *TSR*] with *MS*
202:14 darkness,] ~ *TS*
202:16 rope-grips *TSR*] rope grips *MS*
202:19 seized with ... mother's superficial *TSR*] sullen, full of resentment. She objected to her mother's common, day-time *MS* sullen ... common day-time *TS*
202:20 assert her own detachment *TSR*] stay with her father *MS*
202:24 weeks *TSR*] time *MS*
202:24 char-woman] char-/ woman *TS* charwoman *E1*
202:26 harpy *E1*] vulgar harpy *MS*
202:29 Ursula:] ~. *TS*
202:31 bits?" *P* His *TS*] ~?" / His *MS*
202:38 destroying." *P* The wife *TSR*] destroying." / Anna *MS* destroying." *P* Anna *TS*
202:39 rolled *TSR*] turned *MS*
202:40 then?" *P* He *TS*] ~?" / He *MS*
203:3 done." *P* Ursula *TS*] ~." / Ursula *MS*
203:4 anger *TSR*] ignominy *MS*
203:4 she," *TS*] ~", *MS*
203:8 "It's not ... out so much, it's ...

that old woman ... rage here."
E1] *Om. MS* "It's ... out like it,
it's ... that grimy woman ...
here." *TSR*

203:12 In the ... There she *TSR*] And
her heart was very heavy and
desolate. She *MS*

203:16 right, in ... underworld. *TSR*]
right. *MS*

203:16 angry *E1*] rebuked *MS* savage
TSR

203:17 blackness and brutal silence
TSR] silence and darkness *MS*

203:18 amusement *TSR*] intent
amusement *MS*

203:19 not changes] nor changes *E1*

203:20 day apple-blossom] day,
apple-blossoms *TS*

203:25 what had ... was accidental.
TSR] and hope and long for
things, every day she was born
anew full into that which was
there. *MS*

203:27 accidental to ... to endure. *E1*]
the same: a condition {creation
TS} of the moment. *MS* accidental to her: a momentary
existence, that happened to
endure as a condition. *TSR*

203:30 back,] ~ *TS*

203:31 away: ... away,] ~, ... ~ *TS*

203:33 merely *E1*] suddenly *MS*

203:33 reason for *TSR*] effort at *MS*

203:37 out of joint *TSR*] sad *MS*

204:2 strength and her greater self.
TSR] trust and her shield and
her strength. *MS*

204:3 three *TSR*] only three *MS*

204:3 another *TSR*] still another *MS*

204:6 brown haired, fair skinned]
brown-haired, fair-skinned *TS*

204:8 was a *TSR*] was such a *MS*

204:8 so *TSR*] *Om. MS*

204:10 other *E1*] other at all *MS*

204:11 favorite] favourite *TS*

204:15 barren *E1*] broken *MS* unfruit-
ful *TSR*

204:18 to the *TSR*] his *MS*

204:19 came into being *TSR*] seemed
MS

204:20 alliance *E1*] consciousness *MS*

204:20 was *TSR*] was aware of him,
and *MS*

204:21 But in ... for nothing *TSR*] It
was a great stay for him *MS*

204:22 He took ... her accord *TSR*]
And even when she was a baby,
she counted with her parents,
her attitude, her choice, were
important *MS*

204:25 violent *TSR*] *Om. MS*

204:26 but always contained *TSR*] but,
MS

204:26 motherhood. *TSR*] motherhood, really content. *MS*

204:27 violent *TSR*] *Om. MS*

204:28 tropically *TSR*] *Om. MS*

204:29 a fecund gloom *E1*] slumbering
light *MS* a fecund light *TSR*

204:31 The outside ... her, really.
TSR] *Om. MS*

204:32 twenty six *Ed.*] twenty-six *MS*

204:33 intrinsically like the ruddiest
E1] as much like the *MS* intrinsically like the flamboyant *TSR*

204:33 field *TSR*] field as possible *MS*

204:34 drag him *TSR*] drag him down
MS

204:35 to be with *TSR*] towards *MS*

204:35 was with *TSR*] sympathised
with *MS*

204:37 suffered from *E1*] hated *MS*

204:38 really *TSR*] connected with *MS*

204:38 wanted it ... she wanted *E1*]
merely waited for it to have
gone by, *MS* passionately
wanted ... wanted *TSR*

204:39 normal *TSR*] *Om. MS*

204:40 echoed to ... in him *E1*] felt in
him some need *MS* felt in him
the crying of some need *TSR*

205:1 responded blindly *TSR*] loved
him *MS*

205:1 tie with her ... love which *E1*]
message for her *MS* need for
her ... which *TSR*

205:3   its love *E1*] his service. In spirit she was with him, his child *MS* his love *TSR*

205:6   inadequacy, a ... of worthlessness. *TSR*] inadequacy. *MS*

205:6   enough *TSR*] big enough *MS*

205:7   This knowledge ... the first *TSR*] The knowledge pained her childish susceptibility *MS*

205:8   Still *TSR*] Yet *MS*

205:9   directed by her *TSR*] tinged with *MS*

205:9   her wakefulness *TSR*] a wakefulness *MS*

205:16   power *E1*] yearning *MS*

205:20   breast, *TSR*] breast, and *MS*

205:21   striving *E1*] clamour *MS* yearning *TSR*

205:22   body *TSR*] heart *MS*

205:22   fulfilment *TSR*] relief *MS*

205:30   half past] half-past *TS*

205:31   usually *E1*] sure to be *MS*

205:31   garden with him *E1*] garden, if he was *MS*

205:32   year] ~, *TS*

205:33   The occasion ... earliest memories. *TSR*] She always remembered the occasion. *MS*

205:39   a line *E1*] his line *MS*

206:3   Ursula *TS*] Ella *MS see notes*

206:6   clear *TSR*] fascinating *MS*

206:6   sharp,] ~ *TS*

206:15   separate *TSR*] solitary *MS*

206:19   unused *TSR*] fluttered *MS*

206:21   The responsibility ... her up. *TSR*] *Om. MS*

206:22   dread *TSR*] awe *MS*

206:24   overcome by *TSR*] afraid of *MS*

206:27   Not *E1*] Not quite *MS*

206:28   rearranging *TS*] re-arranging *MS*

206:29   terrified *TSR*] *Om. MS*

206:29   unseeing *TSR*] swift *MS*

206:30   wanted *TSR*] wanted so hard *MS*

206:33   sharp *TSR*] next *MS*

206:33   spade cuts] spade-cuts *E1*

206:36   helplessly, stranded on his world *TSR*] balancing on the sides of her feet *MS* helplessly stranded ... world *E1*

206:38   him, as ... his work. *TSR*] him. *MS*

207:1   presence, *TSR*] presence, as he would miss a warmth, *MS*

207:11   breach *TSR*] breach in power *MS*

207:12   The grown-up ... to her. *E1*] So she dreaded work. *MS*

207:17   things? *TSR*] ~. *MS*

207:23   seed *E1*] seed for *MS*

207:23   nuisance! *TSR*] you little nuisance. *MS*

207:24   over my seed beds? *TSR*] where I've made a seed bed. *MS*

207:24   no heed ... own greedy nose *E1*] undo a man's hours' work as leave as look *MS* no heed ... own blind nose *TSR*

207:26   in his intent world *E1*] into anger *MS* in his dark world *TSR*

207:28   trampled *TSR*] destroyed *MS*

207:30   and unreality *TSR*] *Om. MS*

207:31   shut off and senseless, *TSR*] in her misery shut off, *MS*

207:33   unreality *TSR*] separate existence *MS*

207:35   superior with self-asserting *TSR*] blind with obstinate *MS*

207:40   of *TSR*] of fixed *MS*

208:1   glancing *TSR*] fixed *MS*

208:2   fixed *E1*] imperturbable *MS*

208:4   lie *TSR*] lay *MS*

208:5   the *TSR*] *Om. MS*

208:8   She asserted her self ... to believe *TSR*] And very early, she believed *MS* She asserted herself ... believe *E1*

208:12   was *TSR*] might be *MS*

208:12   carly,] ~ *TS*

208:16   to her] ~ ~, *TS*

208:16   Why, Ursula, did you trample *E1*] Oh {Oh, *TS*} Ursula, you've trampled *MS* Why Ursula, did you trampled *TSP*

208:17 bed? *E1*] ~, *MS*
208:18 she was ... seed bed. It ... [208:24] violent will. *Ed.*] when he bullied her she only became hard. She became a little separate world by herself, in which she played on, ignoring all the rest. *MS* she was ... seed-bed. It ... will. *TSR* she was ... seed-bed? It ... will. *E1*
208:25 As *E1*] Yet as *MS*
208:26 Yet it ... universe, impregnable. *TSR*] He wanted her with him, she gave him a sense of real companionship. *MS*
208:35 taught *TSR*] tried to teach *MS*
208:36 fearless *MS, E1*] devilish *TSR*
208:36 he dared her *TSR*] dared *MS*
209:1 There was ... wills. He *TSR*] Carefully he *MS*
209:3 a deliberate will set upon his ... herself fixed *E1*] complete confidence in him. She merely held close *MS* a daredevil will set against his ... fixed *TSR*
209:5 The *TSR*] Only the *MS*
209:6 body, with ... remained fixed *TSR*] body. She just held still *MS*
209:10 darkly, *TSR*] *Om. MS*
209:11 yet reserved and unfathomable, so *TSR*] and *MS*
209:15 born. They ... daringly, almost wickedly. Till ... fought for a few ... [209:25] them. When *E1*] born. *P* When *MS* born. They ... daringly, devilishly. Till ... fought with a few ... them. When *TSR*
209:26 swingboats *TSR*] swing-boats *MS*
209:26 and, *TSR*] ~ *MS*
209:26 holding on ... higher, perilously *TSR*] held on to the irons and began to drive the thing *MS*
209:28 her *TSR*] the *MS*

209:29 Do you want to go any *TSR*] Dare you go *MS*
209:29 said to her *E1*] called *MS* taunted her *TSR*
209:32 "Yes," she ... and melt away. The ... up again. *E1*] *Om. MS* "Yes ... and die The ... again *TSR*
209:35 shoulder, his ... to her. *TSR*] shoulder. *MS*
209:37 She laughed with white lips *E1*] If he dared her she would have said yes had it killed her. She nodded *MS* "Yes, higher," she said, laughing with white lips *TSR*
209:40 The jerk ... attracting censure *TSR*] His paroxysm passed, he was satisfied *MS*
210:8 said. *P* There *Ed.*] ~. / There *MS* ~. There *TS*
210:12 passionately angry and contemptuous of *TSR*] coldly furious with *MS*
210:14 for *TSR*] she was for *MS*
210:15 a disillusion ... her sick. *E1*] afraid of him, she would not trust him. She believed more in her mother. He was not good. She almost saw him ugly. *MS* she disliked him, she was separate and cold to him, she had nothing to do with him. She went over to her mother. He was evil and enjoyed giving pain. It made her sick. *TSR*
210:18 forgot and ... more coldly. *TSR*] loved him. *MS*
210:20 sensual *E1*] almost sensual *MS* strongly sensual *TSR*
210:22 After *TSR*] Anna watched him with some astonishment and dread. She had four children, all girls. It seemed as though, having so many children, she had almost regained some freedom to attend to her husband again. She watched him, feeling that it was critical with him, the way he should

choose now. *P* But she exerted, almost voluntarily, all her power over him, to keep him, to keep him good. Her will rose in a struggle with his, she fought his passion to its ends. Almost it terrified her, that she and he, parents of four young children, should find themselves delivered over to an extreme of physical passion that seemed always on the point of shattering everything. *P* But for some months she let herself go, she gave him also his full measure, she considered nothing. Children and everything she let go, and gave way to her last desires, till she and he had gone all the devious and never-to-be-recorded ways of desire and satisfaction, to the very end, till they had had everything, and knew no more. Whatever their secret imagination had wanted, they had. And they came through it all at last cleared, resolved, freed. They were not ashamed of any of it. They were now resolved into satisfaction. They had taken every liberty, were prisoners to no more lurking desires. The marriage between them was complete and entire. *P* She found herself again with child. But now she had a new liberty, she was more free of herself. Even with a child coming, she was interested as well in things outside herself, she wanted to see what her husband would next do. He seemed ripening for a new departure. He seemed to be moving outwards. *P* Nothing very important happened, and yet the sense of adventure, of moving to another life, continued. This was the time when night schools and night classes were beginning in the villages. Brangwen, catching at the notion, suggested to the vicar that they should start a woodwork and carpentry class. *P* So the parish room was fitted up as a workshop. It was a high, stone, barn-like place standing isolated in an old garden near the Brangwen's cottage. There was a good deal of

excitement in its preparation. The government grant was obtained, eleven boys enrolled their names, Brangwen felt at last he was doing something in the world, for the world. *P* And in the Yew Tree Cottage, for the first time was heard the lap-lapping of the sea of outer life, over the threshold. The household was caught in the outer tide of the Education movement, and carried a little out of itself. *P* To Ursula, the magic was continuous, and the creator of magic, her father. Whether he came in from Ilkeston with news of the town, whether he went across to the church with his tools on a sunny evening, and she flitted after him, whether he sat in his white surplice on Sundays at the organ, leading the singing with his strong baritone voice, or whether he were in the work-shop teaching the boys, his strong voice sounding out in command, cheerful, indifferent, yet with a peculiar twang in it that sent a thrill over her like hypnotism, he was always in the midst of magic, there was always the gleam of another life about him. He represented change and the unknown to the child, that which was beyond her, taking place in gleam and mystery. *P* After *MS*

211:6 unadmitted *E1*] underworld *TSR*

211:9 not enough *E1*] extinct *TSR*

211:12 It was so vulnerable. *E1*] *Om. TSR*

211:16 Her childishness ... his hands *E1*] There would be pretty little places in her body, that he wanted to discover. He wanted to know them and enjoy them. He wanted to have his fill of them *TSR*

211:21 He was himself ... the object *E1*] There was himself, the reality, and then all the rest of the world, the object, *TSR*

211:29 cheek *TSR*] cheeks *E1*

211:30 sensation. *E1*] sensation. He was agreeably stimulated. *TSR*

211:31 her, she ... and palpitating *E1*] her zestfully, with a hunter's appreciation *TSR*

211:32 said. *P* Again *E1*] ~. / Again *TSR*

211:36 week." *P* He *E1*] ~." / He *TSR*

211:37 him. *E1*] him to note everything. *TSR*

211:38 He was ... common girl *E1*] Very good *TSR*

212:4 vulnerably *E1*] attractively *TSR*

212:7 purposive *E1*] made-up *TSR*

212:8 a fine ... He was *E1*] athletics. His sentences were ready, he was as it were *TSR*

212:9 so full of strength *E1*] every stroke told *TSR*

212:12 wilful. He would press *E1*] attentive. He would watch press *TSR*

212:18 mercy. *P* There *Ed.*] ~. / There *TSR* ~. There *E1*

212:20 Rollins, *TSR*] ~? *E1*

212:22 Carson's *E1*] Carswells *TSR*

212:22 then?" *P* There *E1*] ~?" / There *TSR*

212:25 well?" *P* There *E1*] ~?" / There *TSR*

212:29 Another time, then *E1*] Sure you haven't time *TSR*

212:30 Oh, *E1*] No *TSR*

212:40 distinct attractions *E1*] real beauties *TSR*

213:1 keen æsthetic *E1*] profound sensual *TSR*

213:2 know *E1*] enjoy *TSR*

213:3 That he reserved as yet *E1*] Out of that he would get his chief pleasure *TSR*

213:4 estimating and ... young softness *E1*] feeling and handling with sensual pleasure her several features *TSR*

213:6 unaware that ... his attention *E1*] callous. But the features in which he felt an impersonal

beauty he relished thoroughly. He wanted to come closer *TSR*

213:8 said. *P* She *E1*] ~. / She *TSR*

213:10 seemed to ... his will *E1*] liked it, he liked it very much *TSR*

213:11 walk *E1*] little walk *TSR*

213:12 said. *P* He *E1*] ~. / He *TSR*

213:14 transfused *E1*] amused. The whole thing gratified him peculiarly *TSR*

213:16 a world *E1*] *Om. TSR*

213:18 insignificant *E1*] opposite *TSR*

213:19 properties *E1*] beauties *TSR*

213:27 made him ... muscular self *E1*] delighted him, in the rainy night *TSR*

213:30 like a star *E1*] very good, supreme *TSR*

213:32 being *TSR*] ~, *E1*

213:33 upon. *E1*] upon. He forgot all time and space, as in the cathedral. *TSR*

213:34 dark *E1*] quite dark *TSR*

214:1 her. *E1*] her, in full appreciativeness. *TSR*

214:2 discover *E1*] know the touch of *TSR*

214:3 through *E1*] my God, through *TSR*

214:3 touched *E1*] touched and revelled in *TSR*

214:8 pleasure, in the dark! *E1*] pleasure! *TSR*

214:14 knowledge *E1*] mention *TSR*

214:18 knowledge. *E1*] knowledge. Only as if mechanically she kept her knees closely shut together. And however absolutely she gave herself to his touch and discovery, she kept her knees tight shut, as if this were the reflex movement. *TSR*

214:19 together. *TSR*] ~! *E1 see notes*

214:30 yet *E1*] soft *TSR*

214:34 her. *P* With *TSR*] ~. With *E1*

214:35 sudden, *TSR*] ~ *E1*

214:37 don't!" *P* It *E1*] ~!" / It *TSR*

215:2 noise. *E1*] noise. It reminded

him of the sudden terrified shriek of a rabbit in the night, when a weasel has got it. *TSR*

215:3   calmly, *TSR*] ~. *E1*

215:3   matter?" *P* She *E1*] ~?" / She *TSR*

215:9   manage *E1*] manage the job *TSR*

215:10 And *E1*] But *TSR*

215:10 But another ... him and *E1*] Still, something *TSR*

215:11 in contempt *E1*] *Om. TSR*

215:19 don't." *P* His *Ed.*] ~." / His *TSR* ~!" *P* His *E1*

215:26 fondling *E1*] cold fondling *TSR*

215:26 living desire despising her, *E1*] sensual desire prompting him *TSR*

215:36 said *E1*] said suavely *TSR*

215:39 irony *E1*] suave irony *TSR*

216:7   goodnight *E1*] Goodnight *TSR*

216:15 well *E1*] *Om. TSR*

216:19 her? *E1*] her? What did *she* matter? *TSR*

216:22 said. *E1*] said. That pleased him too. *TSR*

216:29 coldly. *TSR*] ~? *E1*

216:32 town. *P* She *Ed.*] ~. / She *TSR* ~. She *E1*

216:39 asked. *P* But *E1*] ~. / But *TSR*

217:7   sinister *E1*] ironical, cruel *TSR*

217:11 Cooper." *P* She *E1*] ~." / She *TSR*

217:18 her. *E1*] her. Things of his own home had no influence over him. *TSR*

217:20 since he was *E1*] as if he were *TSR*

217:21 affect *E1*] exist for *TSR*

217:28 instant, *TSR*] ~ *E1*

217:30 her *E1*] their *TSR*

217:30 supremacy *E1*] tenderness *MS*

217:31 But *TSR*] And *E1*

217:32 This *E1*] So-ho! this *TSR*

217:34 new. *E1*] new. Very good, she too would take the new turn of affairs. *TSR*

217:35 up. *E1*] up. She too absolved herself: she absolved herself from her "goodness," from her connection with the Ten Commandments of our ordered life. *TSR*

217:38 indeed. *TSR*] ~! *E1*

217:40 smile *E1*] smile of gratification aforethought *TSR*

217:40 challenge *E1*] indifference *TSR*

218:1   keep *E1*] play the moral game, to keep *TSR*

218:8   inscrutability *E1*] recklessness *TSR*

218:12 sensual *E1*] *Om. TSR*

218:12 pleasure *E1*] satisfaction *TSR*

218:14 She adhered ... moral world *E1*] Goodbye moral responsibilities *TSR*

218:15 nothing *E1*] a feather *TSR*

218:17 good. *E1*] good. She was far more interested in him as a self-seeking stranger than in the aforetime good, responsible husband. *TSR*

218:24 They abandoned ... and simple *E1*] Down went the moral fortress, the good knight was a free lance flying the banner of his own sensual desires, the good maiden was out in the wilderness enjoying herself *TSR*

218:29 come in *E1*] carried her off *TSR*

218:33 beauty *TSR*] ~, *E1*

218:36 that which he discovered *E1*] the beauties he unfolded *TSR*

218:39 in *E1*] of *TSR*

219:3   discovery *E1*] gratification *TSR*

219:4   it was a duel *E1*] pure sensuality *TSR*

219:13 hollow *E1*] hollow in *TSR*

219:15 a thick darkness of *E1*] his skin roll with *TSR*

219:17 give *E1*] go give *TSR*

219:18 hidden resources *E1*] endless wealth *TSR*

219:19 undiscovered *E1*] inexhaustible *TSR*
219:24 tongue. *E1*] tongue: a tiger-cat, to lick till the blood came, so he could lap it up till it ran from the corners of his mouth: so he could tear her flesh with his mouth. *TSR see note on* 219:26
219:27 dangerous *E1*] cat-like *TSR*
219:29 him *E1*] more *TSR*
219:30 perish *E1*] murder her *TSR*
219:32 offspring *E1*] swarming animals *TSR*
219:33 darkness and death *E1*] extravagances *TSR*
220:1 right even *E1*] right, for example, *TSR*
220:3 folded *E1*] delirious, folded *TSR*
220:5 a sensuality ... as death *E1*] and this was what it remained: a sensual voluptuousness *TSR*
220:8 senses, a passion of death *E1*] flesh *TSR*
220:9 Absolute *E1*] absolute *TSR*
220:10 fear *E1*] hate *TSR*
220:12 broken desire *E1*] will *TSR*
220:15 violence *E1*] delight *TSR*
220:22 It was pure darkness, *E1*] And shameful *TSR*
220:28 extreme *E1*] rich *TSR*
220:31 accepted *E1*] blotted out *TSR*
220:31 one with it *E1*] free of it, even *TSR*
220:32 It was incorporated *E1*] The shame simply did not exist *TSR*
220:38 violently *E1*] profoundly *TSR*
220:39 set another *E1*] left a superficial *TSR*
220:39 free *E1*] disengaged *TSR*
220:39 new *E1*] superficial *TSR*
221:1 created *E1*] ripened *TSR*
221:2 He wanted ... purposive mankind. *E1*] *Om. TSR*
221:9 purposive *E1*] public *TSR*
221:11 wood-work *Ed.*] woodwork *TSR*

221:17 wood-work *Ed.*] woodwork *TSR*
221:23 yew-trees *Ed.*] yew trees *TSR*
221:24 human endeavour *E1*] public movement *TSR*
221:28 Brangwens' *Ed.*] Brangwen's *MS*
221:40 tenor *E1*] baritone *TSR*
222:7 mind. *E1*] mind. It was the secret of the passion between her father and her mother. But all her limbs vibrated to it. *MS*
223:1 IX *TSR*] VIII *MS*
223:8 possessed *TSR*] not very human *MS*
223:9 London,] ~ *TS*
223:9 attracting *E1*] making friendship with *MS*
223:10 energy *E1*] importance *MS*
223:10 gave place *TSR*] responded *MS*
223:11 independent *E1*] detached *MS*
223:12 was unresolved *E1*] seemed to have no being *MS*
223:14 almost] *Om. TS*
223:18 balance *E1*] measure *MS*
223:19 been *TSR*] become *MS*
223:19 favorite] favourite *E1*
223:20 well-known *E1*] very famous *MS* famous *TSR*
223:21 master *E1*] leader *MS*
223:21 kept acquaintance *E1*] became acquainted *MS* was acquainted *TSR*
223:22 various *TSR*] vigorous, *MS* vigorous *TS*
223:22 individual, outstanding *TSR*] individual *MS*
223:24 rest. He ... being. So *TSR*] rest. *P* So *MS* rest. So *TS*
223:25 while still ... some of *E1*] in touch and almost closely in touch {touch, *TS*} with *MS* while still young welcomed by some of *TSR*
223:26 energetic *E1*] famous *MS* advanced *TSR*
223:26 people in London ... an equal *E1*] world of London, when

{London when *TS*} he was still young *MS* people London ... equal *TSR*

223:27 impersonal *TSR*] reserved *MS*

223:28 place and ... a judgment *TSR*] stand by giving value to exceptional character *MS* place ... judgement *E1*

223:30 stature] ~, *TS*

223:34 curiously attractive, *TSR*] exceedingly *MS*

223:34 well dressed] well-dressed *E1*

224:1 reserved *TSR*] unobtrusive *MS*

224:9 as to *TSR*] as *MS*

224:13 rare *E1*] subtle *MS*

224:13 nature,] ~ *TS*

224:14 high,] ~. *TS*

224:15 Agnostic *E1*] Fabian *MS*

224:16 though *TSR*] whilst being *MS*

224:17 indulgent to them, *TSR*] *Om. MS*

224:22 soft *E1*] subtle *MS*

224:22 strange *TSR*] astonishing *MS*

224:22 repose and ... to his *E1*] good breeding, and then his really remarkable *MS* repose and air of good breeding, added to his *TSR*

224:24 emphasize *TSR*] bring out *MS* emphasise *E1*

224:24 superior,] ~ *TS*

224:25 as if soft *E1*] simple *MS* as if naïve *TSR*

224:25 affable *Ed.*] ~. *MS* ~, *TSC*

224:27 reserved *TSR*] connected *MS*

224:27 to *TSR*] with *MS*

224:28 different *E1*] higher *MS*

224:30 distant *TSR*] crude *MS*

224:34 Brangwen,] ~ *TS*

224:35 gentleman-farmer. *E1*] gentleman-farmer, a sort of squire. *MS*

224:39 very much *TSR*] a great deal *MS*

225:1 Yet he ... in life. *TSR*] *Om. MS*

225:5 him:—who *TSR*] ~. Who *MS*

225:10 puzzled *TSR*] still sensitive *MS*

225:10 himself,] ~ *TS*

225:15 his *TSR*] a good *MS*

225:16 well-to-do *TSR*] good *MS*

225:17 But one ... than another. *E1*] *Om. MS* But somehow, one ... another. *TSR*

225:21 twenty five *Ed.*] twenty-five *MS*

225:24 fixed *E1*] barbaric *MS*

225:28 twenty three *Ed.*] twenty-three *MS*

225:31 Germany; *TSR*] ~, *MS*

225:31 same *TS*] ~, *MS*

225:32 carefully-dressed, attractive young man, *E1*] perfectly-dressed, aimiable, {amiable, *TS*} *MS* perfectly-dressed, amiable young man, *TSR*

225:33 outside of everything *TSR*] rootless *MS*

225:37 sweets] ~, *TS*

225:38 her *TSR*] Ursula *MS*

225:38 long,] ~ *TS*

225:40 rough *TSR*] unevenly cut *MS*

226:3 was undefinably *TSR*] ~, ~, *MS* ~ ~, *TS*

226:3 outsider. He ... no society. *TSR*] inferior. *MS*

226:6 marriage. At ... and she *TSR*] marriage, in abeyance. They *MS*

226:9 the father died. *E1*] Tom Brangwen, the father, was removed. He drove very frequently to town, and very frequently did not return home till rather late. *MS* the father, died. *TSR*

226:10 spring-time] springtime *E1*

226:11 he, *TSR*] *Om. MS*

226:11 Brangwen, *TSR*] ~ *MS*

226:17 fidgeted *E1*] fidgetted *MS*

226:25 laborers] labourers *E1*

226:27 He heard in indifference. But *TSR*] And *MS*

226:28 in the world *TSR*] soaked in everything *MS*

226:37 "Angel," *TSR*] "~" *MS* ~, *E1*

226:37 in Nottingham, *TSR*] *Om. MS*

226:39 Jack] ~, *TS*

226:39 Tha'rt *TSR*] tha'rt *MS*
226:39 cock, Jacky-boy . . . if not *TSR*] bird, thou art, Jack, tha does credit *MS*
227:1 homestead *TSR*] Ark *MS*
227:1 heart, what . . . the night *TSR*] God, what weather *MS*
227:3 young slender feller *TSR*] old boy *MS*
227:3 Noah *TSR*] Noah in this little outfit *MS*
227:3 It seems . . . is bursted. *TSR*] *Om. MS*
227:4 'll *TSR*] 'ull *MS*
227:5 at this . . . an' all. *E1*] presently. *MS* at this rate—yi, an' dove an' olive branch. *TSR*
227:6 up, we're . . . they was *TSR*] up. "Into the cold an' driving sleet—blind drunk!" By God, it's the jumping rain as 'ud make anybody *MS*
227:8 does rain-water . . . it out?" *P And Ed.*] hast iver been drunk on rain-watter?" *P And MS* hast . . . rain water?" And *TS* does . . . out?" And *TSR*
227:10 laughed to himself *TSR*] sniggered *MS*
227:11 ashamed *TSR*] anxious *MS*
227:12 drinking, always . . . the horse. *TSR*] drinking. *MS*
227:12 apologetic frame *TSR*] anxiety *MS*
227:14 stiff *TSR*] firm *MS*
227:17 rode *TSR*] sat *MS*
227:17 attention was . . . burning *TSR*] consciousness remained burning clearly *MS*
227:18 last *TSR*] *Om. MS*
227:19 fact *TSR*] mere fact *MS*
227:21 himself, sententious in his anxiety, *TSR*] himself *MS*
227:23 gleaming *TSR*] steaming *MS*
227:28 to kingdom-come *TSR*] a yard deep into th' mud *MS*
227:31 and back again *TSR*] *Om. MS*

227:31 they *would TSR*] they'd *MS* they would *E1*
227:33 mount *TSR*] go *MS*
227:38 hook, *MS, E1*] departure *TSR*
227:38 it *TSR*] and *MS*
228:5 several *E1*] four *MS*
228:8 slop." *P And TS*] ~." / And *MS*
228:15 consciousness,] ~ *E1*
228:18 sleep-walker, *TSR*] ~; *MS*
228:20 She *E1*] The horse *MS*
228:20 backed. *E1*] backed. {bucked. *TS*} He did not really believe it. *MS* bucked. *TSR*
228:23 thickly *E1*] utterly *MS*
228:28 cart-shed *E1*] cart shed *MS*
228:30 He laughed . . . hurt you!" *TSR*] *Om. MS*
229:2 from, though . . . his feet. *E1*] from. *MS*
229:3 shakily *E1*] adventurously *MS*
229:4 now knee deep] knee deep *TS* knee-deep *E1*
229:4 He stumbled, reeled sickeningly. *TSR*] *Om. MS*
229:7 his feet *E1*] him *MS*
229:8 He did . . . to turn. *TSR*] *Om. MS*
229:9 swayed *TSR*] stood *MS*
229:10 attack, reeling *TSR*] dark attack, swaying *MS*
229:11 fall *E1*] go with it *MS* be carried away *TSR*
229:12 staggered,] ~ *TS*
229:13 turmoil *TSR*] black horror *MS*
229:13 fought *TSR*] fought, gone mad *MS*
229:14 borne down, borne *TSR*] weighed down, weighed *MS*
229:16 struggle of *TSR*] / of *MS* of *TS*
229:20 waters *E1*] strong waters *MS*
229:20 pouring *TSR*] rushing *MS*
229:25 swirled outside *TSR*] should swirl her away *MS*
229:27 deep *TSR*] great *MS*
229:28 outside *TSR*] lost *MS*
229:29 Fred!" *P Away* . . . a mass of

water rushing downwards. *E1*]
Fred!" *MS* Fred!" / Away ... a
heavy mass of water falling
downwards. *TSR*

229:40 cushions] cushion *TS*

229:40 parcels] parcel *TS*

230:3 She *E1*] Then she *MS*

230:4 sound of waters *TSR*] roar of
water *MS*

230:7 Tom!" *P* And *TS*] ~!" / And
MS

230:9 asked. *P* He *TS*] ~. / He *MS*

230:11 uncanny, elvish *TSR*] childish
MS

230:13 To—om! To—om] To-om!
To-om *TS*

230:13 unnatural, *TSR*] *Om. MS*

230:17 shrill, unearthly *TSR*] shrill *MS*

230:18 small *TSR*] *Om. MS*

230:18 There was only *TSR*] For
answer was *MS*

230:18 mooing *TSR*] calling *MS*

230:19 cattle, and ... the darkness
TSR] cattle. *MS*

230:23 water, water, running *TSR*]
water, water everywhere *MS*
water, water, everywhere *TS*

230:25 night. It *TSR*] night, that *MS*

230:37 blazed *TSR*] white *MS*

230:38 into the house *TSR*] *Om. MS*

230:40 in?" *P* Mrs *Ed.*] ~?" / Mrs *MS*
~?" *P* Mrs. *TS*

231:5 loo—ok] loo-ok *E1*

231:5 him." *P* His *TS*] ~." / His *MS*

231:12 To—om—Tо—о—om]
To—om, To—о—om *TS*
To-om, To-o-om *E1*

231:13 gripped his ... a frenzy *TSR*]
wanted to be normal *MS*

231:14 this? He ... and horrible. *TSR*]
this! *MS* this. *TS*

231:17 said, growling ... be normal.
TSR] said. *MS*

231:19 sank into *TSR*] was wading in
MS

231:20 rushing *TSR*] roaring *MS*

231:20 distance, *TS*] ~ *MS*

231:24 drew *TSR*] went *MS*

231:25 the—e—ere] the-e-ere *E1*

231:27 To—om—To—о—om] To-
om—To-o-om *E1*

231:27 free, unearthly *TSR*] desolate
MS

231:28 seemed high ... almost pure
TSR] had a note of despair *MS*

231:29 nearly drove ... a song *TSR*]
seemed to say his father was
dead *MS*

231:31 Beeby's,] ~ *TS*

231:32 Tilly. *P* He] ~. He *TS*

231:38 They were ... for her. *TSR*]
Om. MS

231:40 clucking and trickling *TSR*]
silence *MS*

232:3 Birds began ... grew brighter.
TSR] *Om. MS*

232:5 raw *TSR*] desolate *MS*

232:9 gleam was gone *TSR*] glamour
passed *MS*

232:11 unrelaxing, *E1*] ~ *MS*

232:11 pallid *TSR*] glowing *MS*

232:12 glimpse *TSR*] gleam *MS*

232:12 in the floods, *TSR*] for a
moment *MS*

232:13 hedge. She *TSR*] hedge, and
she *MS*

232:13 She was ... was found. *TSR*]
Om. MS

232:14 dragged him out of *TSR*] found
him in *MS*

232:21 came. *TSR*] came, and restoration was tried. *MS*

232:25 back,] ~ *TS*

232:27 forgotten *TSR*] neglected *MS*

232:33 sodden *TSR*] wet *MS*

232:35 the *TSR*] always the *MS*

232:38 vicarage] Vicarage *TS*

233:3 calm *TSR*] placid *MS*

233:4 and, *TSR*] but, *MS*

233:4 in line, *TSR*] straight in line, he
was *MS*

233:5 inaccessible *TSR*] unseizable
MS

233:8 seeing death. *TSR*] knowing
her own death not far off. *MS*

233:8 He was ... [233:15] inaccessibly himself. *E1*] Death was another kingdom from Life. He was now a subject of death as he had been before a subject of life. Who should lay claim to him, {him *TS*} seeing that now he was this majestic, inviolable son of death, as he had been before the warm son of life? Life could not claim him, nor death even. Who was he, that went from the one to the other? And who could lay claim to him, in the stripped moment of transit, {transit *TS*} as he stepped from life into death? Neither the living nor the dead could claim him, he went from one to the other, inviolable. There was no claim to be made, only a choice of companionship, {companionship *TS*} in life and death. *MS* Death was ... subject of death. Ought she to be with him, also? Not with him, but in death. She laid no claim on him now, the majestic ... of death. Could she ever lay claim on him? They had met, and now he had taken his place apart from her. Life and death were separate. Who was ... lay claim to him, who could speak of him, of the him who stepped in the stripped moment of transit from life ... inviolable, inaccessibly himself. There ... only a remembrance of companionship in life. *TSR*

233:16 belong in ... to eternity, *E1*] shall now know death, *MS* shall know death apart from you, *TSR*

233:17 knowing *TSR*] foreknowing *MS*

233:17 singleness *TSR*] transmission *MS*

233:18 did not ... life. You ... me,

supreme *E1*] knew life in you, and I see you majestic *MS* did not ... life, [?Y]ou ... me majestic *TSR*

233:21 blanched *TSR*] sullen *MS*

233:21 shut *TSR*] clenched *MS*

233:21 hatred and rage *TSR*] vengeance *MS*

233:22 father, bleeding ... bear it. *TSR*] father. *MS*

233:26 still,] ~ *TS*

233:29 name-plate] ~, *TS*

233:30 Born— Died—."] ~— ~—" *TS* ~——, ~——." *E1*

233:37 somehow pleasant *E1*] meaningless *MS*

234:7 fixed *TSR*] rolled up *MS*

234:11 And] But *TS*

234:14 bestial, almost corrupt. *E1*] bestial. *MS*

234:17 good-bye] Good-bye *TS*

234:25 she wanted him *TSR*] he came to her, and the passion was terrible upon them, life and death concentrated together upon them. Afterwards they were still *MS*

234:29 there] ~, *TS*

234:30 the more inevitably *TSR*] inviolably *MS*

234:34 Unknown *TSR*] unknown *MS*

234:37 day,] ~ *E1*

235:2 town, *TSR*] ~ *MS*

235:3 candid, uncanny *TSR*] candid *MS*

235:4 Ursula *E1*] Ella *MS*

235:9 passion *E1*] power of passion *MS*

235:17 disintegration *TSR*] misery *MS*

235:21 her against] against *TS*

235:23 forever] for ever *TS*

235:25 old,] ~ *TS*

235:26 story,] ~ *TS*

235:30 garden gate] garden-gate *E1*

235:38 lie] lie down *TS*

235:40 an unsifted *TSR*] a rich *MS*

236:8 hushed, paradisal land *E1*] wonderland *MS*

236:13 in *E1*] at *MS*
236:14 lesson *E1*] school *MS*
236:19 spirit *TSR*] tone *MS*
236:20 with *TSR*] with the ghost of *MS*
236:22 nosegay *E1*] nose-gay *MS*
236:29 a *E1*] the *MS*
236:37 saying: *P* "I] ~, "I *TS*
236:40 finger] fingers *TS*
237:4 story-land *E1*] wonderland *MS*
237:12 all special and wonderful *TSR*] very delicious *MS*
237:13 little,] ~ *TS*
237:15 must] Must *TS*
237:18 child." *P* Ursula *TS*] ~." / Ursula *MS*
237:20 must you] you must *TS*
237:20 the] *Om. TS*
237:22 ring?" *P* The *E1*] ~?" / The *MS* ~? *P* The *TS*
237:25 grandfather's,] ~ *E1*
237:31 grandfather." *P* Ursula *TS*] ~." / Ursula *MS*
237:34 brows,] ~ *TS*
237:34 think." *P* Ursula *TS*] ~." / Ursula *MS*
237:35 flushed] ceased *TSR see notes*
237:35 She wanted ... the mirror.] *Om. TS*
237:39 was never still *E1*] always had ideas *MS*
238:2 twenty five *Ed.*] twenty-five *MS*
238:6 thirty four *Ed.*] thirty-four *MS*
238:13 house *E1*] family *MS*
238:16 important *E1*] grave *MS*
238:22 in German *TSR*] *Om. MS*
238:35 girl-bride *TS*] girl bride *MS*
238:36 honor *Ed.*] honour *MS*
238:39 for him] ~ ~, *E1*
239:2 liberty, of science. *E1*] liberty. *MS*
239:4 consider *TSR*] think of *MS*
239:9 attentions] attention *TS*
239:12 and *TSR*] *Om. MS*
239:13 nurse] a nurse *TS*
239:15 separate *TSR*] narrow *MS*
239:16 ideas—] ~,— *TS*
239:19 thought] ~, *TS*
239:25 really *TSR*] were it not that this

made him a better instrument *MS*
239:29 her] ~, *TS*
239:31 himself] *Om. TS*
239:34 joy ... joy *TSR*] effort ... effort *MS*
239:36 died,] ~ *TS*
239:36 there was *TSR*] he had given her *MS*
239:37 grandchild *TSR*] child *MS*
239:38 honored] honoured *TS*
239:40 her, *TSR*] her, for his needs, *MS*
240:3 Yet there ... in him. *TSR*] *Om. MS*
240:9 served *E1*] known *MS*
240:10 made himself immortal in *TSR*] taken into death *MS*
240:11 with *E1*] of *MS*
240:12 immortality *TSR*] death *MS*
240:13 'In ... mansions.'] "~ ... ~." *E1*
240:17 fulfilment, *E1*] knowledge, *MS* knowledge *TS*
240:17 had given her being *E1*] would give her {him her *TS*} recognition *MS*
240:18 served *E1*] acknowledged *MS*
240:18 honorably] honourably *TS*
240:18 one with her *E1*] of his own choice *MS*
240:19 established in *E1*] glad she had known *MS*
240:19 she *E1*] and *MS*
240:22 own *E1*] real *MS*
240:24 heart,] ~ *TS*
240:24 vague *E1*] keen, poignant *MS*
240:25 wrong *E1*] young *MS* young and unfulfilled *TSR*
240:26 really become himself. *E1*] known another soul. *MS* really become himself, fully. *TSR*
240:27 And he ... on her. *E1*] Ah, if she could have known, and opened his eyes to her, and given him being, instead of leaving him to his cold instrumentality! But then she was

only a girl, younger than he.
How could she know? And he
had gone his way, unquickened. Something in her soul
was cold to him. *MS* Ah, if ...
his fierce instrumentality ...
him. *TSR*

240:33 married *E1*] liked *MS*
240:35 difference." *P* They *TS*] ~." /
They *MS*
240:37 asked. *P* Lydia *TS*] ~. / Lydia
MS
240:39 he was ... of anybody *E1*] it was
as if something was eating him
up inside *MS*
241:2 wasn't *TSR*] wasn't a bit *MS*
241:3 in the world *E1*] *Om. MS*
241:5 almost as if he hated me, *E1*]
Om. MS
241:6 said] ~, *TS*
241:7 London *E1*] hellish London
MS
241:12 failure *E1*] good-for-nothing
MS
241:13 child.] ~! *TS*
241:21 have *TSR*] become mother of
MS
241:22 ourselves—] ~. *TS*
241:37 will somebody *E1*] shall I have
to love somebody, and will they
MS
241:38 some man will love you *E1*]
you'll have to love somebody
MS you'll have to love a man
TSR
241:39 for what ... we want. *E1*] and
know you for what you are.
Don't betray yourself, even for
love's sake. *MS* and give you
what you want. Because we
have a right to what we want.
Our own natures are our own
righteousness. *TSR*
242:3 security *E1*] fulfilment *MS*
242:4 the past, *E1*] *Om. MS*
242:5 tiny,] ~; *TS*
242:8 past *E1*] whole *MS*
243:1 X *TSR*] IX *MS*

243:12 Ursula "Urtler," *E1*] ~, "~"
MS
243:12 Gudrun "Good-runner *E1*]
Gudrun, "Good-un *MS*
243:22 existences] existence *TS*
243:26 warfare *E1*] war-fare *MS*
243:29 nothing." *P* Then *TS*] ~." /
Then *MS*
243:31 Phillipses *E1*] Phillips *MS*
243:32 You *TSR*] Yah, you *MS*
243:33 and looking superbly *TSR*]
putting her tongue out *MS*
243:35 Why shan't I *TSR*] Who says I
shonna *MS*
244:1 sang] said *TS*
244:2 You come *TSR*] Come *MS*
244:2 dursna." *P* Up *TS*] ~." / Up
MS
244:4 In a rage *TSR*] Immediately
MS
244:5 Phillipses *E1*] Phillips *MS*
244:6 fray *TSR*] wild fray *MS*
244:9 lugged *TSR*] mightily lugged
MS
244:9 torn *TSR*] in rags *MS*
244:17 pinafore.] ~? *E1*
244:19 etc. etc.] etc., etc. *TS*
244:23 Phillips's *E1*] Phillips' *MS*
244:25 moment,] ~ *TS*
244:31 *will* not] will *not TS*
245:7 Ugly-Mug,— *TSR*] Ugly-
Mug— *MS* Ugly Mug,— *E1*
245:9 her. *P* Then] ~. Then *TS*
245:11 Phillipses *E1*] Phillips *MS*
245:14 caring *TSR*] considering *MS*
245:22 down,] - *E1*
245:29 Grammar *E1*] High *MS*
245:32 Phillipses *E1*] Phillips *MS*
245:36 when he was ... her, he *E1*] he
was always mean. He *MS* he
was ... her. He *TSR*
245:40 circumstance *TSR*] circumstances *MS*
245:40 Grammar *E1*] High *MS*
246:12 indifferent to *TSR*] fearless of
MS
246:20 school *E1*] the High School *MS*
246:21 half past] half-past *E1*

246:22 overfull] overful *TSR*
246:29 Fecundity," *E1*] ~" *MS* ~",
　　　TS
246:31 welter] swelter *TS*
246:32 mother;] ~, *TS*
246:33 spirituality *TSR*] serenity *MS*
246:35 yew-trees *E1*] yew trees *MS*
246:36 cleaning-woman *TSR*] clean-
　　　ing woman *MS*
246:38 bee-hive] beehive *E1*
247:1 out *TSR*] *Om. MS*
247:2 Ursula!" "Ursula] ~! ~ *E1*
247:5 Then] These *TS*
247:16 bedroom *TS*] bed-room *MS*
247:17 warm *E1*] dark, warm *MS*
247:19 castell] castle *E1*
247:24 high *TSR*] solitary *MS*
247:26 high-pitched] light-pitched *TS*
247:28 locked." *P* Then *E1*] ~." /
　　　Then *MS*
247:31 Ursula?" *P* No *E1*] ~?" / No
　　　MS
247:33 now. *P* Still *Ed.*] ~. / Still *MS*
　　　~. Still *TS*
247:38 cry. *P* It] ~. It *TS*
248:4 for?" *P* Then] ~?" Then *TS*
248:5 parish room *E1*] parish-room
　　　MS
248:8 she was gifted with *E1*] who
　　　{she *TS*} was a student of *MS*
248:24 with] with her *TS*
248:27 she *E1*] her father *MS*
248:29 of the parish room *E1*] *Om. MS*
　　　of the Parish Room *TSR*
248:34 considered *E1*] hoped *MS*
248:34 over. *E1*] over. But she waited
　　　trembling. *MS*
248:35 knitted] knotted *TS*
248:37 mother. *P* He *Ed.*] ~. / He *MS*
　　　~. He *TS*
248:38 and flapped the cloth hard *E1*]
　　　savagely and hit it *MS* like a
　　　beast and flapped ... hard *TSR*
249:10 a] the *TS*
249:10 said. *E1*] said, churlish. *MS*
249:22 fire *E1*] seed *MS*
249:39 winter; *E1*] ~, *MS*
250:3 this Ursula *TSR*] Ella *MS*

250:5 Grammar School *E1*] high
　　　school *MS* High School *TSR*
250:14 amongst] among *TS*
250:21 introduction] ~, *TS*
250:22 head-mistress *Ed.*]
　　　headmistress *MS*
250:32 Grammar *E1*] High *MS*
251:4 liberated into an intoxicating
　　　air ... unconditioned *E1*]
　　　increased *MS* liberated into the
　　　free air ... unconditioned *TSR*
251:9 perfect *TSR*] far off *MS*
251:10 "Longman's ... Grammar,"
　　　E1] 'Longmans ...~', *MS*
　　　"Longman's ...~", *TS*
251:10 "Via Latina" *TS*] '~ ~' *MS*
251:12 magic in *TSR*] grateful attach-
　　　ment to *MS*
251:13 learning,] ~ *TS*
251:14 intuitively] instinctively *TS*
251:16 school-mistresses *Ed.*]
　　　schoolmistresses *MS*
251:29 half formed] half-formed *TSR*
251:36 was safe now. *TSR*] had a posi-
　　　tion now that she could keep in
　　　peace. *MS*
251:37 twinge] tinge *TS*
252:7 Nevertheless] ~, *TS*
252:13 lost, destroyed *TSR*] irrepar-
　　　ably damaged *MS*
252:14 There was ... against her.
　　　TSR] *Om. MS*
252:15 cruelty and *TSR*] *Om. MS*
252:17 mob *TSR*] Average *MS*
252:17 exception *TSR*] exceptional
　　　MS
252:22 attacked *TSR*] and rent *MS*
252:22 resentment *TSR*] ruthlessness
　　　MS
252:23 Self *TSR*] *Om. MS*
252:32 remembered:—] ~ *TS*
252:34 twenty four *Ed.*] twenty-four
　　　MS
253:1 Saturday night's] Saturday's
　　　night *E1*
253:3 half naked *Ed.*] half-naked
　　　MS
253:10 voice; *TSR*] ~, *MS* ~: *E1*

253:11 it." *P* It *TS*] ∼." / It *MS*
253:18 half naked] half-naked *E1*
253:21 young ones *E1*] children *MS*
253:21 nightdresses *TS*] night-dresses *MS*
253:24 sheep-skin] sheepskin *E1*
253:26 bronze *TSR*] stentorian *MS*
253:27 sheep-skin] sheepskin *E1*
253:33 We say *TSR*] It's *MS*
253:34 I am ... your shirt *TSR*] You speak as if you knew no better *MS*
254:21 after church *TSR*] *Om. MS*
254:27 so that *E1*] and *MS*
254:29 Sabbath *E1*] sabbath *MS*
254:32 patapon," / Theresa] ∼," *P* Theresa *E1*
254:35 she wavered *TSR*] the eldest girl persisted in spite of her own heart *MS* the eldest ... own head *TS*
255:5 Sabbath *TS*] sabbath *MS*
255:8 kiss. *E1*] kiss. This was Sin, the vision. *MS*
255:9 *actual TSR*] *real MS*
255:17 mischievously *TSR*] joyfully *MS*
255:19 the eternal and immortal *E1*] grandeur and myth *MS* grandeur and mystery *TSR*
255:21 badly-behaved *TSR*] very badly-behaved *MS*
255:21 arrogant, though ... were generous. *TSR*] arrogant. *MS*
255:22 had] ∼, *E1*
255:24 jealous *TSR*] creeping *MS*
255:24 democratic Christian. *TSR*] humble Christian, nor with the jealous social ideal of equality in mediocrity. *MS*
255:28 He *E1*] he *MS*
255:30 dreariness *TSR*] nausea *MS*
255:30 His *E1*] his *MS*
255:31 was distasteful to her *TSR*] made her sick *MS*
255:33 His *E1*] his *MS*
255:34 like a villager ... his sores *E1*] and thenceforward to behave

according to certain rules of conduct, like a soldier showing his scars *MS* and thenceforward ... like a vulgar common villager gloating in his sores *TSR*
255:34 was enemy *E1*] hated *MS*
255:36 living in ordinary human life *TSR*] pulled down to the level of other men *MS*
255:36 indifferent. *E1*] godless. *MS* bored. People bored her. *TSR*
255:38 vulgar *E1*] vulgar, petty *MS*
255:40 revivalists *E1*] tax-payer *MS* jealous *TSR*
256:1 everyday *E1*] vulgar *MS*
256:1 dress Jesus up in *TSR*] force Jesus into *MS*
256:2 compel Him to *TSR*] exact from Him *MS*
256:3 ask, *E1*] ask, in its nasty accent *MS*
256:3 He *Ed.*] he *MS*
256:4 shoes? *TS*] ∼. *MS*
256:6 was caught ... careless of *TSR*] paid most heed, or who was most in accord with *MS see notes*
256:13 was *TSR*] was for *MS*
256:15 instinctively *TSR*] *Om. MS*
256:16 resented *TSR*] hated *MS*
256:17 hankering to worship an unseen *E1*] worship of the unrevealed *MS* worship of the mysterious *TSR*
256:22 her,] ∼ *E1*
256:23 He was *E1*] he ∼ *MS*
256:23 His *E1*] his *MS*
256:24 the] his *TS* His *E1*
256:25 Ursula *TSR*] Ella *MS*
256:30 sunset *E1*] sun-set *MS*
256:38 fair;] ∼: *TS*
257:7 stirred as ... far off *TSR*] roused to her depths *MS*
257:9 God? *TS*] ∼. *MS*
257:14 offspring *E1*] children *MS*
257:15 the *E1*] we *MS*
257:16 recognise *E1*] know *MS*

257:20 genuine *E1*] great, magnificent *MS*

257:21 essential *E1*] primeval *MS*

257:21 Sons *Ed.*] [?s]ons *MS* sons *TS*

257:33 the other *TSR*] one *MS*

257:34 eternal truth *E1*] verity of utter desire *MS* verity of utter truth *TSR*

258:4 foot-passengers] foot passengers *TS*

258:8 School teacher] school teachers *TS*

258:11 dwindled *E1*] diminished *MS*

258:20 Absolute World *E1*] unknown *MS*

258:21 relative world *E1*] known *MS*

258:26 tight] too tight *TS*

258:31 laborers] labourers *TS*

258:33 forego that *E1*] have another sort of *MS* do without *TSR*

258:33 at any rate *TSR*] not *MS*

258:37 scriptures. *P* Her] ~. Her *TS*

259:2 Filippo Lippi *E1*] Leonardo *MS*

259:3 "Dispute ... Sacrament" *TS*] '~ ... ~' *MS*

259:4 "Last Judgment" *TS*] '~ ~' *MS*

259:6 gradual fulfilment *TSR*] rich shock *MS*

259:7 establishment *TSR*] sumptuous building up *MS*

259:7 whole *TSR*] *Om. MS*

259:7 which used *TSR*] using *MS*

259:9 "Last Judgment." *TS*] '~ ~.' *MS*

259:10 arrayed] arranged *TS*

259:12 descent *TSR*] ladder *MS*

259:12 satisfied *E1*] fulfilled *MS*

259:23 banality for *E1*] neutral *MS* commonplace *TSR*

259:28 foot-steps *MS, TSC*] footsteps *TS, E1*

259:28 snow,] ~ *E1*

260:8 dress-rehearsal; *TSR*] ~, *MS*

260:28 dark-faced *TSR*] dark faced *MS*

260:30 Upon the ... her life. *TSR*] *Om. MS*

260:33 Magis'] Magi's *TS*

261:10 glad? *E1*] ~. *MS*

261:12 smell *TSR*] sadness *MS*

261:12 grave-cloths] grave-clothes *TS*

261:15 Christianity *Ed.*] christianity *MS*

261:17 fulness *TSR*] manhood *MS*

261:28 so long ... was dead. *TSR*] with the casting off of the body. *MS*

261:30 grave, after ... of anguish, *TSR*] grave *MS*

261:31 'Mary!'] "~!" *TS*

261:32 Him ... He *Ed.*] him ... he *MS*

261:33 'Touch ... father.'] "~ ... ~." *TS*

261:36 resurrection *E1*] cold, fleeting resurrection *MS* cold, dreary resurrection *TSR*

261:40 over; *E1*] over! Alas, *MS*

261:40 thirty three; *Ed.*] thirty three! *MS* thirty-three! *TS* thirty-three; *E1*

262:1 that the half of *E1*] Alas, that half *MS* Alas that the half of *TSR*

262:1 Alas] ~, *TS*

262:4 Resurrection! *E1*] ~. *MS*

262:7 breast? *E1*] ~. *MS*

262:13 ill-health? *TS*] ~. *MS*

262:14 Resurrection? *E1*] Resurrection and until the Ascension into Heaven? *MS* Resurrection. *TSR*

262:15 be shadowed by *E1*] remember the *MS*

262:16 mystic, perfect *E1*] triumphant *MS* mystic, glorious *TSR*

262:18 kiss *E1*] kiss the breasts of *MS*

262:20 fellows? *E1*] days. *MS* days? *TS*

262:22 off, or ... and untouched? *TSR*] off? *MS*

262:25 humus? *E1*] humus. {humus? *TS*} *P* Nay, but the body shall rise to live in the flesh, to celebrate and to enjoy its marriage in the flesh, to have pleasure in

its outgoings and its incomings,
to fulfil its heaven in the flesh,
to tread through the earthly
paradise in full, corporeal
being, before its translation
into the unknown. *MS* humus?
P Nay ... being, having its full
relation with death and the
unknown. *TSR*

263:1 XI *TSR*] X *MS*
263:9 undiscovered *E1*] unlived *MS*
263:10 oneself] herself *TS*
263:11 pathlessness,] ~ *TS*
263:18 fell away *E1*] dropped off *MS*
263:20 in] an *E1*
263:22 Five] the Five *TS*
263:24 daily life *TSR*] the flesh *MS*
263:25 week-day *Ed.*] weekday *MS*
263:27 of absolute ... living mystery
        TSR] visions *MS*
263:35 week-day *Ed.*] weekday *MS*
264:1 a week-day *Ed.*] week-day *MS*
        weekday *TS* a weekday *TSR*
264:10 one denied *TSR*] had become
        unreal *MS*
264:11 learn *E1*] conquer *MS*
264:13 oneself? *TS*] ~. *MS*
264:30 hast, *E1*] ~ *MS*
264:31 that? *TS*] ~. *MS*
264:33 unlovely,] ~ *TS*
264:34 "the poor"] ~ "~" *TS*
264:39 everybody!] ~. *E1*
264:40 hast, *E1*] ~ *MS*
264:40 poor." *P* One *TS*] ~." / One
        MS
265:1 it,] ~ *TS*
265:1 How dreary ... made her! *E1*]
        Om. MS
265:4 Christian *TS*] christian *MS*
265:8 anger] ~, *TS*
265:8 writhing *E1*] despicable *MS*
265:8 so *E1*] and *MS*
265:11 said] ~, *TS*
265:12 unChristian *Ed.*] unchristian
        MS
265:17 more? *TS*] ~. *MS*
265:19 Ursula.] ~? *E1*
265:19 poor,] ~? *TS*

265:20 rights,] ~ *TS*
265:22 inquire] enquire *TS*
265:28 locks,] ~ *TS*
265:30 horse: always ... course. *TSR*]
        horse. *MS*
265:33 Cossethay,] ~ *TS*
265:36 Oh Jerusalem] ~ ~, *TS* ~,
        ~— *E1*
265:39 her,] ~ *TS*
266:2 Oh] oh *TS*
266:4 Man] man *TS*
266:6 Vaguely,] ~ *TS*
266:7 vision world, *Ed.*] vision-world,
        MS vision-world *TS*
266:7 He *E1*] he *MS*
266:8 He ... His *E1*] he ... his *MS*
266:10 week-day *E1*] weekday *MS*
266:10 not] nor *TS*
266:11 week-day *Ed.*] weekday *MS*
266:12 week-day ... week-day *Ed.*]
        weekday ... weekday *MS*
266:15 this] the *TS*
266:19 week-day *Ed.*] weekday *MS*
266:36 Oh,] ~ *E1*
267:4 His *Ed.*] his *MS*
267:5 carnality *E1*] sensuousness *MS*
        temporality *TSR*
267:9 heavy laden] heavy-laden *TS*
267:11 temporal *TSR*] sensuous *MS*
267:12 yearning,] ~ *TS*
267:28 sensation *E1*] sensuousness
        MS triviality *TSR*
267:31 Skrebensky *E1*] Skrebenski
        MS
267:33 unreserved *TSR*] a wholesale
        MS
268:1 her,] ~ *TS*
268:1 antagonism *TSR*] cynicism *MS*
268:2 mistrust] distrust *TS*
268:20 savage misery *E1*] savagery *MS*
268:21 speaker, whose] ~? Whose *TS*
268:29 laugh *E1*] little laugh *MS*
268:32 Did] did *TS*
268:37 Now,] ~ *TS*
269:4 show *E1*] zest *MS*
269:15 proud,] ~— *TS*
269:21 readiness *E1*] warm readiness
        MS

269:28 strong *TSR*] strange *MS*
269:29 feel, vaguely,] ~ ~ *TS*
269:32 army] Army *TS*
269:35 quickly. *P* Skrebensky *E1*] ~. /
Skrebensky *MS* ~. *P*
Skrebenski *TS*
269:37 father. *P* But *Ed.*] ~. / But *MS*
~. But *TS*
270:4 grammar." *P* He *TS*] ~." / He
MS
270:10 quizzically and *E1*] almost *MS*
naïvely, as if he were talking to
himself, and *TSR*
270:11 Whether *E1*] She did not care
whether *MS* It piqued her,
whether *TSR*
270:12 independent *TSR*] incalculable
MS
270:18 have courage *E1*] care *MS*
270:19 Courage for *E1*] Care about
MS
270:20 For *E1*] About *MS*
270:20 everything." *P* Tom *TS*] ~." /
Tom *MS*
270:24 Everything's nothing *E1*]
That's a tall order *MS*
270:24 uncle. *P* She *TS*] ~. / She *MS*
270:25 moment. *E1*] moment. He
refused to take her meaning.
MS
270:27 has courage *E1*] cares *MS*
270:32 slight, *E1*] elegant, *MS*
270:33 full-blown *TSR*] coarse *MS*
270:35 finer, and ... be shining. *TSR*]
finer. *MS*
270:36 simply *TSR*] so simply *MS*
270:37 beyond any ... about him that
fascinated her. *E1*] aware that
he was no more and no less
than himself. *MS* beyond any
... about him. *TSR*
270:40 being. In ... for itself. *TSR*]
being, for it was susceptible to
no variation. *MS*
271:1 perfectly, even fatally established *E1*] to come out of
himself towards one *MS* to
perfectly ... established *TSR*

271:8 unsatisfactory flux *TSR*]
ungenuine thing *MS*
271:10 upon his ... about himself *E1*]
from the firm ground of his
own assured self *MS*
271:11 was irrevocable *E1*] *was* certain
MS was free *TSR*
271:11 isolation *TSR*] being *MS*
271:13 distinct, self-contained, self-
supporting *TSR*] sure *MS*
271:14 a nature like fate, the *TSR*] the
unquestioned *MS*
271:16 on] of *TS*
271:18 fair. *E1*] ~? *MS*
271:18 servile. *MS*, *E1*] servile, a pos-
tulate. *TSR*
271:19 been a beggar *TSR*] cringed
MS
271:20 since, seeking its own being.
TSR] since. *MS* since? *TS* since
... being? *E1*
271:21 could *E1*] did *MS*
271:21 beg *TSR*] cringe *MS*
271:21 He was ... stood alone. *TSR*]
His natural right to himself and
his own desires was
unquestionable. He was one of
a finer inheritance than
Adam's. *MS*
271:25 Visit] visit *TS*
271:27 enrichened] enriched *TS*
271:31 dog-cart] dogcart *E1*
271:31 up] ~, *TS*
271:33 her,] ~ *TS*
271:34 isolated within ... atmosphere,
and ... if fated. *E1*] a revelation
continually adding itself in
{itself to *TS*} her soul *MS* isolated within ... atmosphere.
TSR
271:36 resting in his own fate *TSR*]
unwavering sureness *MS*
272:2 Who?" *P* It *TS*] ~?" / It *MS*
272:5 them." *P* Ursula *TS*] ~." /
Ursula *MS*
272:7 Where is really *TSR*] What do
you really call *MS*
272:7 home,] ~ *TS*

272:11 own?" *P* His *TS*] ~?" / His *MS*

272:12 greenish grey] greenish-grey *TS*

272:15 wanted,] ~— *TS*

272:17 my *TSR*] poor *MS*

272:22 No—] ~, *TS*

272:22 very much *E1*] *Om. MS*

272:27 blue and white] blue-and-white *E1*

272:30 perceiving, critical fashion. *P* She *E1*] sort of manly fashion, but with real perception of her. / She *MS* sort ... fashion but ... her. *P* She *TS*

272:32 time,] ~ *TS*

272:40 rocking chair] rocking-chair *TS*

273:1 languidly] ~, *TS*

273:4 of my own *E1*] *Om. MS*

273:9 more though.] ~, ~? *TS*

273:12 mind] mind it *TS*

273:16 himself,] ~ *TS*

273:19 daughters." *P* But *TS*] ~." / But *MS*

273:23 in] [?o]n *TS* on *E1*

273:29 *perpetuum mobile TSR*] perpetuum mobile *MS*

273:33 misfortune." *P* And *TS*] ~." / And *MS*

274:3 fiercely. *P* Ursula *TS*] ~. / Ursula *MS*

274:4 sudden, steel-like start *E1*] sudden start of ferocity, *MS*

274:9 again. *P* Ursula *TS*] ~. / Ursula *MS*

274:16 progress,] ~ *E1*

274:16 said:] ~, *TS*

274:19 fine!] ~, *TS*

274:21 said, *TS*] ~ *MS*

274:22 too attractive for] attractive to *TS*

274:23 helped *E1*] laughing, helped *MS*

274:25 Other people ... to him. *TSR*] *Om. MS*

274:30 a roused light *TSR*] pleasure *MS*

274:34 flames *E1*] dancing fire *MS*

274:35 swingboats *E1*] swing-boats *MS*

274:36 steed,] ~ *TS*

274:37 at his ... antagonism to *E1*] happy. An element of outrage against *MS* at home, in his own element. A zest of outrage against *TSR*

274:39 carousel] carousal *E1*

275:3 higher] high *TS*

275:4 away, *E1*] away, however, *MS*

275:5 level, *E1*] level, having the sensation, therefore, of being less than ordinary size in stature, *MS*

275:10 crunched *TSR*] ground *MS*

275:17 plaster] ~, *TS*

275:25 come?" *P* There *TS*] ~?" / There *MS*

275:31 influence *E1*] trespass *MS*

275:33 urging her to something *E1*] pressing for advantage upon hers *MS*

275:35 voluptuous *TSR*] wonderful, voluptuous *MS*

275:36 swung *TSR*] was drawn *MS*

275:37 the wrap *E1*] his coat *MS*

275:37 his *TSR*] *Om. MS*

275:39 carefully,] ~ *TS*

275:40 subtlety *E1*] labour *MS* working *TS*

276:2 living creature *TSR*] mole *MS*

276:3 in the dark underworld *TSR*] the earth *MS*

276:5 thing,] ~ *TS*

276:7 steady *TSR*] acute *MS*

276:12 superficiality,] ~ *TS*

276:15 asked. *P* She *TS*] ~. / She *MS*

276:21 Well—] ~, *TS*

276:23 cried] ~, *TS*

276:23 impulsively. *P* They *E1*] ~. / They *MS*

276:25 disadvantages,] ~ *TS*

276:29 the girl *TSR*] Emily *MS*

276:31 cathedral." *P* She ... almost defiantly, in ... soul. *P* He *E1*] cathedral. *P* He *MS* cathedral." / She ... almost

flippantly, almost cruelly, in ...
soul. *P* He *TSR*

276:35 Who,] ~? *TS*

276:38 names,] ~ *TS*

276:38 a common tale *TSR*] all about
the place *MS*

277:6 eyebrows." *P* Ursula *TS*] ~." /
Ursula *MS*

277:9 lovers? *TS*] ~, *MS*

277:12 mentioning *E1*] talking about
MS

277:13 talk about *E1*] go to see *MS* go
and see *TS*

277:17 women] woman *TS*

277:22 toilet." *P* Ursula *TS*] ~." /
Ursula *MS*

277:23 quivered,] ~ *TS*

277:24 asked. *P* Her *TS*] ~. / Her *MS*

277:29 Her *TSR*] And she was coming
to knowledge of it, her *MS*

277:35 harder, more beautiful, less
personal *TSR*] more personal
MS

277:37 approach,] ~ *TS*

277:38 insidiously,] *Om. TS*

277:39 pressed in upon *E1*] grown in to
MS

277:39 her; *TSR*] ~, *MS*

278:9 on] to *TS*

278:16 lips. *TSR*] lips, at the gate.
MS

278:17 her mouth *TSR*] the gates *MS*

278:22 strangely, *TS*] ~ *MS*

278:33 hard] hand *TS*

278:36 same,] ~ *TS*

279:2 fragrant *TSR*] so fragrant *MS*

279:3 first,] ~ *TS*

279:4 nobody:] ~; *TS*

279:13 flirting? *TSR*] ~. *MS*

279:21 half past] half-past *E1*

279:21 nine." *P* There *TS*] ~." /
There *MS*

279:24 him." *P* She *TS*] ~." / She *MS*

279:26 Yes] ~, *TS*

279:27 friend." *P* But *TS*] ~." / But
MS

279:34 petulantly] ~, *TS*

279:37 *no*] no *TS*

279:38 mother. *P* And *TS*] ~. / And
MS

280:4 pleased *TSR*] exasperated *MS*

280:5 position *TSR*] tolerant sufficiency *MS*

280:6 could *TS*] would *MS*

280:6 be beneath ... public relation
TSR] trouble herself about
anyone *MS*

280:13 a spirit ... young vitality *TSR*]
pride and sufficiency of belief
in his own energy *MS*

280:16 courteous to *TSR*] aware of *MS*

280:17 and to *E1*] and of *MS*

280:18 as] and *E1*

280:22 even] ever *TS*

280:25 door. *P* And *TS*] ~. / And *MS*

280:28 said. *P* And *TS*] ~. / And *MS*

280:37 with enjoyment of the game
TSR] overbearing *MS*

280:39 enjoyment *TSR*] choice *MS*

280:40 they knew *TSR*] *Om. MS*

280:40 their *TSR*] that *MS*

281:2 just *TSR*] merely *MS*

281:2 dare-devilry *TSR*] rank dare-
devilry *MS*

281:3 cut at *TSR*] bitter denial of *MS*

281:6 wrongly] ~, *TS*

281:8 wide opened *Ed.*] wide-opened
MS

281:9 her] the *TS*

281:10 poignant, reckless, *Ed.*] poignant reckless *MS* poignant
recklessness *TS*

281:11 pain, *TS*] ~ *MS*

281:16 vivid] ~, *TS*

281:16 all,] ~ *TS*

281:17 poignant *E1*] great *MS*

281:17 transience *E1*] sadness *MS*
hopelessness *TSR*

281:20 desirable] ~, *TS*

281:22 self, in ... of life? *E1*] self? *MS*

281:26 begun,] ~ *TS*

281:30 in *TSR*] in its *MS*

281:31 in *TSR*] its *MS*

281:34 the parents *TSR*] they *MS*

281:35 in action *TSR*] *Om. MS*

282:1 *rendez-vous Ed.*] rendez-vous

MS rendezvous *TS* *rendezvous TSR*

282:4   chilled *TSR*] frightened *MS*

282:5   indomitable,] ~ *TS*

282:10 on his back, *TSR*] *Om. MS*

282:28 now *E1*] *Om. MS*

282:30 Saturday however] ~, ~, *TS*

282:32 go,] ~ *TS*

282:35 stay,] ~ *TS*

282:36 had a motor-car *E1*] called a taxi-cab *MS*

283:1   situation, she] ~. She *TS*

283:5   his *TSR*] Skrebensky's *MS*

283:6   But they ... two children.] *Om. TS*

283:12 troubled. *E1*] troubled, and the blood flamed in his belly. *MS*

283:16 motion *E1*] car *MS*

283:18 now *TS*] how *MS*

283:20 Strange,] ~ *TS*

283:20 looked,] ~ *TS*

284:4   old,] ~ *TS*

284:12 tapped,] ~ *TS*

284:13 goodbye] good-bye *TS*

284:14 school-girl] school-/ girl *TS* schoolgirl *E1*

284:18 him? *TSR*] ~. *MS*

284:22 there! If] ~, if *E1*

284:23 day,] ~ *TS*

284:28 no-one *Ed.*] no one *MS*

284:30 happiest] happier *TS*

284:34 garden *TSR*] nest *MS*

284:36 near,—] ~— *TS*

285:2   button] buttons *TS*

285:5   some *TSR*] infinite *MS*

285:11 Anton—] ~. *TS Anton. E1* [*E1* prints letter in italics]

285:13 I] "*I E1*

285:14 isn't *Ed.*] is n't *MS* is not *TS is not E1*

285:15 enough,] ~. *TS enough. E1*

285:16 I] "*I E1*

285:17 Your] "*Your E1*

285:17 friend] ~, *TS* friend, *E1*

285:18 Ursula] "*Ursula E1*

285:23 Plain *TS*] plain *MS*

285:27 school-mistress] schoolmistress *TS*

285:28 Ilkeston,] ~ *TS*

285:29 dim,] ~ *TS*

285:29 blue-and-gold *E1*] blue and gold *MS*

285:31 softest,] ~ *TS*

285:37 strong] ~, *E1*

285:39 cynical Bacchus *TSR*] faun *MS*

286:4   demurred *TSR*] demurred shyly *MS*

286:7   College, knew ... morris-dancing. *TSR*] College. *MS*

286:9   bon-fires] bonfires *TS*

286:10 feast *TSR*] great feast *MS*

286:13 clear,] ~ *TS*

286:19 wedding party] wedding-party *TS*

286:23 womanish *TSR*] fine *MS*

286:24 black,] ~ *TS*

286:25 him,] ~ *TS*

286:25 beauty:] ~; *TS*

286:26 nostrils,] ~ *TS*

286:29 brilliant] ~, *E1*

286:30 curious, *TSR*] ~ *MS*

286:38 wedding!" *P* There *Ed.*] ~!" / There *MS* ~?" *P* There *TS*

287:7   braggart *TSR*] timid, braggart *MS*

287:8   down,] ~. *TS*

287:10 out,] ~ *E1*

287:14 church-tower] church tower *TS*

287:17 evening, *E1*] ~ *MS*

287:18 alder trees *Ed.*] alder-trees *MS*

287:34 only do things *E1*] are only made *MS* only make things *TSR*

287:37 war,] ~ *TS*

287:38 go." *P* A *TS*] ~." / A *MS*

288:2   it would be genuine *E1*] not just making belief *MS*

288:3   toy-life,] ~ *TS*

288:10 fighting." *P* A *TS*] ~." / A *MS*

288:11 hard separateness *E1*] dreariness *MS* hard dreariness *TSR*

288:11 her. *TSR*] her. He was dreary. *MS*

288:12 more serious than anything else *E1*] serious *MS*

288:13 You *TSR*] Because you *MS*
288:14 killing *TSR*] getting killed *MS*
288:15 dead,] ~ *TS*
288:16 was silenced for a moment *TSR*] winced *MS*
288:17 It matters ... or not *TSR*] If we hadn't wiped out the Zulus, they'd {Zulus they'd *TS*} have wiped us out *MS*
288:19 to *TSR*] Om. *MS*
288:19 we don't care about Khartoum *E1*] because we didn't go to the Zulu's land *MS* because we don't want to go to Khartoum *TSR*
288:20 You want ... make room. *TSR*] Somebody must go to Zulu-land, or where are the colonies, {Colonies, *TS*} and how are we going to expand? *MS*
288:22 I *TSR*] *I MS*
288:22 live in ... of Sahara *TSR*] expand into a colony *MS*
288:26 nation,] ~ *TS*
288:29 *they TSR*] they *MS*
288:29 weren't,] ~ *TS*
288:31 asserted,] ~ *TS*
288:32 yourself,] ~ *TS*
288:34 or] and *TS*
288:36 you've] you'd *TS*
288:37 care what ... [289:3] stiff and wooden. What ... for, really?" *E1*] believe people are so vile. They're much viler in masses than by themselves. I think a man is much nastier when he thinks himself the nation than when he thinks himself just himself, as {himself as *TS*} he is." *P* "And what is going to become of us, if {us if *TS*} the nation goes to blazes?" *P* "And what is going to become of us if it doesn't? You only fight to remain as you are, not for any-thing, really." *MS* care ... stiff mannikins. What ... really?" *TSR*

289:8 I belong ... the nation. *TSR*] Serve the nation which shelters me. *MS*
289:14 Nothing. I ... needed." *P* The *TSR*] Nothing." / The *MS* Nothing." *P* The *TS*
289:16 "It seems ... nothing to me." *TSR*] Om. *MS*
289:19 reached] had reached *TS*
289:20 with a ... cabin hood, *TSR*] red and yellow over the cabin hood, at the end, *MS*
289:23 smoking, *E1*] ~ *MS*
289:25 water] ~, *TS*
289:30 Good-evening] Good evening *TS*
289:30 attracted. *P* He *Ed.*] ~. / He *MS* ~. He *TS*
289:32 Good-evening] Good evening *TS*
289:32 now!] ~? *TS*
289:33 very nice." *P* His *E1*] for them as thinks so." / His *MS* For them ... so." *P* His *TS*
289:34 moustache, his] ~. His *TS*
289:36 Oh] ~, *TS*
289:36 *is*. Why ... it weren't? *E1*] *is*, whether you think so or not. *MS*
289:38 'Appen for ... so rosy *E1*] Oh {Oh, *TS*} is it! You come down here an' mind this childt. Then we'll see who says it's nice or nasty *MS* Oh, is it? 'Appen ... rosy *TSR*
289:39 look inside your ... asked Ursula. *E1*] come?" *MS* come into your ... asked Ursula. *TSR*
289:40 you; you ... like." *P* The *TSR*] you." / The *MS* ~." *P* The *TS*
290:2 "Annabel," *TS*] "~", *MS* *Annabel, E1*
290:3 keen, twinkling *E1*] twinkling, blue *MS* keen, twinkling, blue *TSR*
290:4 appeared,] ~ *TS*
290:7 spurting and ... gloom beyond

TSR] running away below on the far side *MS*

290:8 bright water *TSR*] canal level *MS*

290:15 like." *P* She *TS*] ~." / She *MS*

290:18 sandy haired] sandy-haired *TS*

290:19 young, *TSR*] *Om. MS*

290:20 Oh] ~, *TS*

290:21 with a little wonder *TSR*] *Om. MS*

290:22 Isn't it lovely *E1*] Don't you love *MS*

290:23 altogether, *E1*] altogether, thank goodness, *MS*

290:24 Loughborough *TSR*] Loughborough right enough *MS*

290:25 husband,] ~ *TS*

290:28 blue-eyed *TS*] blue eyed *MS*

290:34 Ursula,] ~. *E1*

290:34 nice,] ~ *TS*

290:39 nothing,] ~? *E1*

290:39 baby. *P* The *Ed.*] ~. / The *MS* ~. The *TS*

291:8 Annabel,] ~ *TS*

291:9 defiant. *P* The *TS*] ~. / The *MS*

291:11 said. *P* And *TS*] ~. / And *MS*

291:16 that's heavy-laden if you like *TSR*] she'd go to th' bottom wi' a load like that *MS* that's heavy-laden, if . . . like *E1*

291:18 she hasn't even got *TSR*] they won't let her have *MS*

291:20 added. *P* He *TS*] ~. / He *MS*

291:27 dumb-founded] dumbfounded *TS*

291:30 called. *P* There *TS*] ~. / There *MS*

291:32 y' hear] y'hear *TS*

291:34 'Ursula'? *TSR*] ~? *MS*

291:36 combat *TSR*] tooth and nail combat *MS*

291:37 lass's *TS*] lasses *MS*

291:37 said] ~, *TS*

291:37 gently. *P* The *TS*] ~. / The *MS*

292:2 touched. *P* Ursula *Ed.*] ~. / Ursula *MS* ~. Ursula *TS*

292:8 Are you goin' to *TSR*] You'll *MS*

292:9 Annabel,] ~? *E1*

292:9 said, decisively. *TSR*] said. *MS*

292:11 silence.] ~, *E1*

292:13 vainly *TSR*] proudly *MS*

292:16 *awfully*] awfully *TS*

292:20 boldly] ~, *TS*

292:21 admiration *E1*] gentleness *MS*

292:22 necklace?" she . . . uncle Tom . . . [292:29] real: it . . . [292:32] bargee. *P* He . . . [293:3] careful reverence. *Ed.*] handkerchief?" she said. "It has 'U' {U *TS*} for Ursula on it." *P* She stretched out the bit of cambric. It was a very pretty handkerchief edged with real lace. She loved giving it. *P* "And I must give it something silver. Anton, have you got a shilling?" *P* He reached down to her from the wharf. She put the shilling into the baby's hand, which in a moment let the coin drop on to the coal-dusty floor. The father groped for it. *MS* necklace?" . . . uncle Tom . . . real: it . . . bargee. / He . . . reverence. *TSR* necklace?" . . . Uncle Tom . . . real; it . . . argee. *P* He . . . reverence. *E1*

293:4 fingers groping . . . jewelled heap. *TSR*] fingers. *MS*

293:6 He took . . . still and attentive . . . [293:10] said. *P* Ursula . . . said, "It . . . Ursula." *P* And . . . its warm . . . [293:22] Brangwen. *P* The . . . half gallant, half impudent . . . [293:25] knew, always. *Ed.*] *Om. MS* He . . . still and sad {still and attentive *E1*} . . . said. / Ursula {said. *P* Ursula *E1*} . . . said, "It {said. "It *E1*} . . . Ursula." / And {Ursula." *P* and *E1*} . . . its small, warm { its warm *E1*} . . . Brangwen. / The

{Brangwen. *P* The *E1*} ... half gallant, half impudent {half-gallant, half-impudent *E1*} ... always. *TSR*

293:26 She wanted ... ladder. Ursula ... lock above ... them go. *TSR*] But she wanted to go now. *P* "Goodbye," {*Good-bye," TS*} she said. *P* The woman came and said farewell, pleased as from a fairy visit. The man smiled, impudently, gallantly, and wistfully. There was a touch of pathos and wistfulness in him as he watched the white-clad, slim girl go away. His gallantry was not for her. *P* Ursula went hastily down the bank with Skrebensky. *MS* She ... ladder. *P* Ursula ... lock, above ... go. *E1*

293:34 Was he gentle? *TSR*] I don't call that gentle, *MS*

293:34 The woman ... that." *P* Ursula winced. *E1*] I should have thought he was pretty rough— {*rough,— TS*} and common at that." *MS* The woman ... that." / Ursula winced. *TSR*

293:37 underneath." *P* She *TS*] ~." / She *MS*

293:39 pleasant,] ~ *TS*

293:40 her own *TSR*] *Om. MS*

294:1 somehow *E1*] with his talk of nations *MS*

294:2 ashes *E1*] an ash-heap *MS*

294:4 impudent *TSR*] gallant *MS*

294:5 worship *TSR*] wistful worship *MS*

294:7 knew *TSR*] was so clean as to know *MS*

294:8 but was only glad *TSR*] and *MS*

294:8 that the ... of communion *TSR*] its own limit of range *MS*

294:10 did he ... wanted her. *TSR*] must he want either her body only, or her soul only, in a

soul-friendship? *MS*

294:14 desire *TSR*] passion *MS*

294:16 stiff-set *TSR*] strongly-built *MS*

294:16 half-educated *TSR*] advanced *MS*

294:17 secret *E1*] subtle *MS*

294:18 flame *TSR*] hot flame *MS*

294:19 another *TSR*] a *MS*

294:26 violins] ~, *TS*

294:28 unreached-for] unreached for *TS*

294:31 these,] ~ *TS*

294:36 background *TS*] back-/ ground *MS*

294:40 Ursula,] ~ *TS*

295:2 hay-stacks *Ed.*] hay-/ stacks *MS* haystacks *E1*

295:4 and be *TSR*] her hand up *MS*

295:5 and be *TSR*] *Om. MS*

295:6 It was ... hound were *TSR*] She was like a hound *MS*

295:8 quarry, into] ~ ~ *TS*

295:8 And she ... the hound. *TSR*] *Om. MS*

295:9 The darkness was *TSR*] The unknown, dark and *MS*

295:10 heaving. It *TSR*] heaving, *MS*

295:10 receive her in her flight *TSR*] be surprised *MS*

295:11 let go *TSR*] start *MS*

295:11 She must ... the unknown. *TSR*] *Om. MS*

295:12 hands and feet] feet and hands *E1*

295:14 began to slip *TSR*] were broken *MS*

295:15 dancing with ... the water. *TSR*] dancing, silent and transferred, with the bride. *MS*

295:17 with another *TSR*] with the *MS*

295:18 deep underwater *TSR*] whirlpool *MS*

295:22 as if into *TSR*] with *MS*

295:22 subtle power of his will *TSR*] near knowledge of the trance *MS*

295:25 It was ... in flux. *TSR*] *Om. MS*

295:29 profound *TSR*] great *MS*

295:29 deep *TSR*] great *MS*

295:30 fluid, underwater *TSR*] fluid, silent *MS* fluid silent *TS* fluid underwater *E1*

295:30 gave them unlimited strength *TSR*] carried them completely *MS*

295:31 waving ... flux of *TSR*] silent in the *MS*

295:32 re-passed] repassed *E1*

295:33 darkness, it ... great flood. *TSR*] darkness. MS darkness. It ... flood. *E1*

295:36 with the ... the surface *TSR*] making the music as an overtone *MS*

295:37 ecstatic] ~, *TS*

295:37 on *TSR*] of *MS*

295:38 flood heaving *TSR*] rocking, *MS*

295:39 oblivion *TSR*] equilibrium *MS*

296:1 crisis] crises *TS*

296:3 As *TSR*] And *MS*

296:3 heavily on, *TSR*] swooning on. And *MS*

296:3 some influence *TSR*] someone *MS*

296:4 looking-in upon her. *TSR*] looking. *MS* looking in upon her. *E1*

296:4 looking at ... glowing sight was *E1*] looking. Something very near was *MS* looking at ... glowing eyes were *TSR*

296:5 upon her, but ... upon her. *TSR*] at her, but through the very core of her. She quivered with submission and fulfilment. *MS*

296:10 ceased] ~, *TS*

296:11 like bits ... a shore *TSR*] exposed *MS*

296:13 was cleaved ... transparent jewel *TSR*] wanted to cleave *MS*

296:14 filled with *TSR*] offering herself to *MS*

296:14 moon, offering ... moon, consummation. *TSR*] moon. *MS*

296:19 her and *TSR*] ~, ~ *MS*

296:20 above *TSR*] on *MS*

296:22 She was ... breasts and ... her knees ... [296:27] and chaos of people to *Ed*.] And she wanted to run, she wanted to run. She wanted to fling away her cloak and her shoes and run barefoot, fleetfoot, to the trees and *MS* She ... breasts and her belly and her thighs and her knees ... and nothingness of people, to *TSR* She ... breasts and her knees ... and chaos of people to *E1*

296:28 the people ... like magnetic stones ... loadstone ... [296:35] down by dark, impure magnetism. He ... free moonlight. *E1*] Skrebensky, dark like a shadow beside her, kept her. He wanted to draw closer to her. She felt him, like a black shadow, wanting to draw close to her. Whilst she wanted the brightness and the brilliance of the moon! Ah, with the moon on her, she could kill him if she wanted to. She knew it. But he was bending nearer to her. *MS* the people ... like dead magnetic stones ... barren stone ... down with dark, impure dross. He ... moonlight. *TSR*

297:1 tonight? *Ed*.] ~, *MS* to-night? *TS*

297:1 voice. *P* And *TS*] ~. / And *MS*

297:2 that,] ~ *TS*

297:2 would die ... tear things ... felt destructive, like ... of destruction *E1*] could tear him to pieces, scatter his shadow in fragments under the moonlight *MS* would ... tear living things ... felt like knives, like ... destruction *TSR*

297:5 said. *P* A *TS*] ~. / A *MS*
297:6 darkness, an ... of inertia *TSR*]
hunter's madness and determination came over him too *MS*
297:7 inert *TSR*] dark *MS*
297:8 silver white] silver-white *TS*
297:9 again,] ~ *TS*
297:11 Always present ... her down,
TSR] Supple, supple, and
insinuating *MS*
297:13 the weight ... with him, *TSR*]
his breast, his belly, his legs
running warm and insinuating
upon her, *MS*
297:16 still in ... passion. She ...
[297:22] even wished he might
overcome her. She ... of salt
E1] between him her body was
firm with a fierce, cold passion.
Only she liked the supple run
of his movement upon her,
warm and dark and attached
like clothing to her. And he
exerted all his power to warm
her to him. She liked him, but
she remained scarcely softened
MS still ... passion, She ...
even triumphed in it. She ...
salt *TSR*
297:24 His will ... encompass her and
... [297:29] compel her! *TSR*]
He was mad with passion for
her firm, cool body, that was
compact of brilliance like the
moon itself. His muscles set in
tension upon her, he could not
relax. He must have her
entirely—entirely. *MS* His ...
encompass him and ... her! *E1*
297:30 will *TSR*] will and his body *MS*
297:31 his body ... playing *TSR*]
bending like iron *MS*
297:32 bright as ever, intact. *TSR*]
hard and compact as ever. *MS*
297:33 her in ... shadows, caught. *E1*]
her. *MS* her. in ... caught. *TSR*
297:35 her, he ... was caught. *TSR*]
her. *MS*

297:39 She was ... a blade that hurt
him. Yet ... killed him. *E1*]
Om. MS She ... a steel blade.
Yet ... him. *TSR*
298:5 present *TSR*] night-like *MS*
298:5 night-blue *TSR*] softened blue
MS
298:6 dimly present *TSR*] dimly-
woven *MS* dimly woven *TS*
298:7 burn *TSR*] flit *MS*
298:8 like cold fires *TSR*] faintly *MS*
298:8 All was ... whitish-steely fires
E1] But his heart burned hot
for the shadows, the real, actual
shadows *MS* All was ... bluish-
steely fires *TSR*
298:9 He was ... corn-stacks ...
would die *TSR*] He wanted to
lead her there *MS* He was ...
cornstacks ... die *E1*
298:13 She stood ... gleaming power.
She ... and make him into
nothing. Her ... dissipate,
destroy as the moonlight destroys a darkness, annihilate ...
and inspired. She ... [298:26]
held her. *E1*] But she put him
away, and stood in the terrible,
overwhelming luminosity of
the moon, looking this way, and
that. Again he followed her,
and put his arm round her, and
drew her to his warm, dark
body. *P* She submitted. He
drew her into the deep shadow
of a wheat-stack, leaned back
against the stack, holding her in
his arms, warm there, captured, netted, folded in the
warm iron of the shadow, of his
body. *MS* She ... gleaming
lust. She ... and scatter him to
the moonlight. Her ... dissipate, tear to pieces as the
moonlight tears a darkness,
scatter, annihilate ... and evil.
She ... held her. *TSR*
298:27 temerously, his ... own hands,

net ... [298:34] corroding, as
... [298:37] awful death. She
... upon her *E1*] again his
hands went over her, over the
firm, compact coolness of her
body. And he strained her to
him till he trembled to break, as
if he would crush her. And
blindly, avidly, in a frenzy of
will and of desire, he sought for
her mouth. Which she yielded.
So he pressed himself there
MS temerously ... own limbs,
net ... corroding, shrivelling
and burning like gum and
becoming less and less, as ...
awful acid. She ... her *TSR*

298:39 over *TSR*] over again *MS*
299:1 took *TSR*] clung to *MS*
299:1 seized *TSR*] came *MS*
299:2 burning corrosive *TSR*] cold
MS
299:3 summoning *TSR*] gathering
MS
299:3 keep ... keep himself in the
TSR] place ... place his *MS*
299:5 had fastened *TSR*] cleaved *MS*
299:6 a *TSR*] *Om. MS*
299:6 soft iron *TSR*] supple shadow
MS
299:7 corrosive, seething ... some
cruel, corrosive ... soul
crystallised with ... was dissolved with ... victim, consumed, annihilated. She ...
[299:13] any more. *E1*] blazing
fierce and hard and cold upon
him, and his heart was gone,
and his strength. Under her
hard, open-mouthed, coldly
fierce kiss he succumbed, and
she held him there, the victim.
MS corrosive ... some horrible, corrosive ... soul screamed
with ... was silent with ...
victim, shrivelled, bloodless,
like an infinitely shrivelled
corpse. She ... more. *TSR*

299:14 began to ... accustomed, mild
reality ... really there?—who
was he? He ... [299:21] had
happened? *E1*] realised that she
was on the earth. Gradually she
came to the fact of the common
reality of the night. A sort of
horror possessed her. Here she
was kissing Skrebensky. She
recognised her own little self.
But what of the big, fierce self
of the moonlight? *MS* began ...
accustomed, dead reality ...
really gone—was he really
nothing. He ... happened. *TSR*
299:22 mad. What ... [299:29] her
hand *TSR*] mad? Should she be
ashamed? What should she do?
Which was she? *P* She relaxed
herself and laid her head *MS*
mad: what ... hand *E1*
299:31 caressingly. *P* And *Ed.*] ~. /
And *MS* ~. And *TS*
299:32 dead. And ... warm self, *TSR*]
dead. *P* She became aware of
him, *MS*
299:38 She was his ... [300:4] be
subject now, reciprocal, never
... broken him. *E1*] But the
core would not return to his
courage. He was bolstered up
and male again, but there was
no vital, initiatory core to his
pride. The heart of his courage
would not beat again. *MS* She
... be automatic now, functional, never ... him *TSR*
300:10 knew he ... touch her *TSR*]
could not feel him *MS*
300:12 at all compelled by it *TSR*]
there *MS*
300:13 me." *P* And *TS*] ~." / And *MS*
300:15 empty and finished *E1*] hard
and fierce and proud *MS* hard
and cold and finished *TSR*
300:17 and quite ... She had been
proud ... she had been also ...
good girl. She ... and good.

E1] along with her. *MS* and quite ... She was proud ... she also ... good girl. *TSR*

300:30 bridegroom *E1*] bridegroom for her to take *MS*

300:31 shadows. *E1*] shadows, for bridal service. *MS*

300:32 yew-trees *E1*] yew trees *MS*

300:35 bliss, agony, *TS*] ~ / ~, *MS* ~, ~ *E1*

300:37 of sorrow ... in annihilating him *E1*] as of rejection, or only half-acceptance *MS* of sorrow ... in murdering him *TSR*

301:6 unreal *E1*] attentive *MS*

301:10 exudation *E1*] exudation of its flesh *MS*

301:10 exhausted *E1*] uninterrupted *MS*

301:12 subsiding transports *E1*] passionate yearnings *MS*

301:13 fulfilment *E1*] satisfaction *MS*

301:14 church bells *Ed.*] church-bells *MS*

301:18 lovely,] ~ *TS*

301:22 glanced at *E1*] read *MS*

301:23 favorite *Ed.*] favourite *MS*

301:23 Bible *TS*] bible *MS*

301:32 not moved by the *E1*] impatient with her beloved *MS* impatient with her the *TSR*

301:32 Multiplying and ... earth bored her ... and fishes. *E1*] It seemed such a mean business: {business; *TS*} man was to multiply in order to replenish the earth, to make the property more valuable, and beasts and fowls were provided for the belly of man, they were his stock. How sickening and greedy it all was. Always the inferior, material good! Shall the beasts and fowls and herbs have no existence, save as they are of use to man? How she *hated* the words: {words; *TS*} *MS* Multiplying ... earth irri-

tated her. Altogether the earth irritated her, with its multiplication and its timorous beasts. She was angry with the beasts and fishes for being afraid of her. She was almost ready to destroy them, because they were afraid of her. *TSR*

301:36 multiply:] ~; *TS*

301:38 In her ... ten turnips *E1*] It was like a farmer reckoning up how many sheep he could breed for the next season *MS* How she hated the earthly way of multiplying and reckoning up; more this year, and a few more next, and so on *TSR*

301:40 said:] ~; *TS*

302:2 generations:] ~; *TS*

302:6 cloud:] ~; *TS*

302:8 flesh;] ~, *TS*

302:10 "Destroy all flesh," why "flesh" in particular? Who ... of flesh? *E1*] Angry, it {Angry it *TS*} made her! What proprietor was this, pronouncing for his own particular property. *MS* 'Destroy all flesh, destroy all flesh,' why 'flesh' in particular? The talk was very big. *TSR*

302:11 Perhaps a few *TSR*] After all, the *MS*

302:13 frightened, but *TSR*] only a few had been even frightened, *MS*

302:20 Japheth, *Ed.*] Japeth *MS* Japeth, *TSR*

302:21 rain, *TSR*] rain and *MS*

302:23 themselves] ~, *TS*

302:23 thing *E1*] terrestral thing *MS* terrestrial thing *TS*

302:24 the great Proprietor *E1*] their particular Lord *MS* the Lord *TSR*

302:27 people who ... their Proprietor and their Flood *E1*] less self-important people *MS* people

... their God and their Flood *TSR*

302:29 What was ... [302:30] surfeited ... [302:32] He ... [302:33] Him ... numbered." He did ... [302:39] alone. *P* Ursula *Ed.*] So she turned to the New Testament, to the Sermon on the Mount. And she knew that Christ was sad, at first, because of the sufferings of the people. *P* But then some dignity and strength came out, some pride, that she was seeking for. *P* "Ye are the light of the world. A city that is set on a hill cannot be hid." *P* Yet she did not want to be the light of the world. It seemed conceited. The world was so vast. There were the sun and the moon in their places. And even the sun could only light half the world at once. *P* Always rights and wrongs, always considering mankind, always the public conscience! She was *not* a member of the human community, any more than a bird is a member of the bird community. *P* "For where your treasure is, there will your heart be also." *P* But why have a treasure? Why always possessions? Either one must *own* a good treasure or a bad treasure. Again, she wearied of ownership. What treasure had the dryads and the nymphs, except the things that no one owns, air and the free earth and water. *P* "And why take ye thought for raiment? Consider the lilies of the field, how they grow; they toil not, neither do they spin." *P* But why take thought for the kingdom of God and his righteousness either? That all these things may be added to us? But we don't *want* anything added to us. The earth itself is enough, we ourselves are so plenteous, by the wealth of infinite God. The lilies do not take thought for righteousness. They are themselves and that is the whole of righteousness to them. So with the nymphs and fauns. If we are to consider the lilies, why not consider this in them. *P* "Give not that which is holy unto the dogs, neither cast ye your pearls before swine." *P* Is not my body holy, and my flesh more precious than pearls? Shall I hire this out to dogs of money makers, or yield this over to the rabble to crucify? *P* "Do men gather grapes of thorns, or figs of thistles?" / But does man therefore wish every thorn-tree annihilated, and every thistle? Do men gather purple thistle blossoms off a fig-tree, or the may-blossom from a vine? Has a man only a belly, that he shall hew down all that is not food? *P* "And the rain descended and the floods came and the winds blew, and beat upon that house; and it fell; and great was the fall thereof." *P* Even so. But the rain descended and the floods came and the winds blew, and beat upon that house which the prudent man had builded upon a rock; and the house stood; and the man within that house rotted amidst his shelter and security and his having, and gradually he fell, and petty was the fall thereof. *P* How long shall we answer to the promise of possessions? For is not our kingdom of God a vested interest held out to us? What care I if I die tomorrow? God is the same yesterday and today and for ever. *P* It is enough, that God *is*. It is enough that in me He is manifest. If maggots in a dead dog be but God kissing carrion, then when the moon breeds dances and desires in me, are not these also offspring of the kisses of God. Did not God kiss the loins of man, so that he begot the Dryads, and the womb of woman, so that she conceived the faun? *P* Then make room, make room! Make room among all this private ownership of men and God, particular men and a particular God covering all with the notice: *P* "Private Property." / Remove the trivial notices of God and Man. There is no private property. The fauns shall run in your parks and the dryads shall play among the pews of your churches, and Jesus, whole and glad after the Resurrection, shall laugh when evening falls and the nightingale sings, and he shall give himself to the breasts of desire and shall twine his limbs with the nymphs and the oreads, putting off his raiment of wounds and sorrows, appearing naked and shining with life, the risen Christ, gladder, a more satisfying lover than Bacchus, a God more serene and ample than Apollo. And the proudest dryad of all shall sit in the shadows of the trees in the morning, twisting her hair round her breasts to make a bouquet of them, and saying from her radiant face: *P* "Jesus came starting through the leaves last night, and flung away his garments, and caught me with wonderful hands, more exquisite and lover-like than the hands of Bacchus, and kissed me, more poignant and far-reaching and clearer-ringing than the kiss of Iacchos, and folded me more gloriously than Apollo, and embraced me more mightily than Jove. I am the most mortal of nymphs, I am the most immortal. Because I lay with death as well, since Jesus has passed through this also. He is the only perfect lover, since he is risen from the grave, the only perfect lover in heaven or earth." *P* But Skrebensky heard only the old voice, the old words uttered in the monotonous voice. *P* "But the very hairs of your head are all numbered." / Nay, down to the most minute thought, everything was fixed and registered and ordered. There remained only to obey, to do as one was bid. Who should initiate even one single movement of soul, where all was ordered and laid down? Those that loved God obeyed the ordering. Those that did not obey, were the bringers of confusion. And he did not believe in confusion. *P* But Ursula *MS* What was ... weary ... he ... him ... numbered." Everything was

registered and regulated, everything was ordered. The divine law was, that the order should not be destroyed. The order must be kept, the form obeyed. Those that did not obey were the bringers of confusion. He would never willingly be a bringer-in of confusion. *P* Ursula *TSR* What was ... surfeited ... He ... him ... numbered." He did ... alone. *P* Ursula *E1*

302:40 wanted to react upon him ... his being. She ... life, gratified *E1*] refused the ordering and ignored his adhesion. His world and her world were not the same. But her world overlapped his at one place. And in so far, she had to do with *MS* wanted to disorder him ... his form. She ... gratified *TSR*

303:4 romantic *E1*] whimsical *MS*

303:6 in] at *TS*

303:9 photograph,] ~ *TS*

303:15 soul *E1*] pride *MS*

303:21 idea] thought *TS*

303:25 However] ~, *TS*

303:26 bed] ~, *TS*

303:36 organised *E1*] *Om. MS*

303:40 honor] honour *TS*

304:10 the hills in *E1*] back the hills from *MS*

304:17 Puzzled,] ~ *TS*

304:22 connections] connection *TS*

304:23 matter,] ~ *TS*

304:25 be ensured, not ruptured *E1*] never be broken, or betrayed *MS*

304:28 whole *E1*] scheme *MS*

304:32 left the girl out *TSR*] put the girl aside *MS*

304:32 serving what he had to serve *E1*] preserving his form of life intact *MS* preserving the form ... intact *TSR*

304:34 To his ... [304:38] beyond question. *TSR*] For he could not incorporate her into his form of life. He knew too well, he was so finely bred {bred, *TS*} as to know that she would never submit. Nor he could ever {never *TS*} depart from the corporate body of civilisation, {civilization, *TS*} this completed fabric of community in which he lived. And he knew she would never accept him as a diversion, she would demand the whole man; she would never accept a partial, superficial connection with him. She would demand him entire at the moment of meeting, and if he cheated her just for his gratification—ah, he could not do it. His mere personal, physical desire was not complete enough, could not be sufficiently strong. Because he must remain, with all his will, that was set rigid as a locked mechansim, he must remain always within the established form of the community, he must in his own being represent the rigid idea of the State, he must preserve it entire upon its established basis, as if it were himself; because {because, *TS*} in this, in the existing idea of the State, was vested the highest good, the good of the greatest number, for all mankind. *MS*

305:1 every man ... State ... State ... it intact *TSR*] within the framework of the State, one might labour for a still further benefit of this class of the community, or that class—but always from the great, established basis of the State as we find it now *MS* every ... state ... state ... intact *E1*

305:5 community would, however,]

community, however, would *TS*

305:6 fulfilment *E1*] self-effectuation *MS*

305:7 soul *E1*] self-effectuation of the soul *MS*

305:7 a man ... important in so far as he ... all humanity *E1*] in the effectuation of the social unit *MS* a man ... important only when he ... humanity *TSR*

305:9 to see, *TS*] ~ ~ *MS*

305:15 statement of ... all inspiration or value to ... general nuisance, representing ... low level. *E1*] abstraction from the many sinks in suggestive value below the average intelligence of the individual, then that abstraction becomes worthless, pernicious. *MS* statement ... all beauty or suggestiveness to ... general nuisance. *TSR*

305:20 chiefly *TSR*] now *MS*

305:24 giving up his life *TSR*] subscribing to the order *MS*

305:25 everybody else? *TSR*] the rest of the community? *TSR* everybody else! *E1*

305:26 worthy of ... behalf of *TSR*] of soul-vital importance for *MS*

305:28 oh, he ... [305:39] depressed, apprehensive. *TSR*] what was it? *P* But here he was like a donkey grinding in a circle. As soon as he conceived of himself as a serious, purposeful individual {individual, *TS*} he saw himself as an earnest member of the community. A sort of lid seemed to drop down on him. *P* The literal translation of "Thou shalt love thy neighbour as thyself," gradually reduced to practice during the course of ages, in the form of "Thou shalt consider the material well-fare of thy neighbour {neighbours *TS*} as important as thy own material welfare," had gradually taken on itself an arbitrary authority, the human constitution had become mechanised by it, so that Skrebensky worked automatically. Touch him on his deeper, more religious side, and instantly, automatically his will took the form of: {of,— *TS*} "Thou shalt support this great, and elaborate State, which has been brought to this highly complex & {and *TS*} efficient pitch by the effort of ages, and whose reason and whose sole purpose is the greatest good of the greatest number of people." *P* "What do you mean by the greatest good of the greatest number?" came the question sometimes. *P* "The highest pitch of material prosperity," came the automatic answer. *P* Everything, Christianity, the Church of England, the Roman Catholic Church, the great Nonconformity, Fabians, Socialists, Free-thinkers, Liberals and Conservatives, everybody hammered out the same formula, more or less elaborately: *P* "Thou shalt strive for the greatest degree of material prosperity for all men." *P* And some, the passionate souls, really trying to fulfil their religious passion, strove for the material welfare of others and were utterly indifferent to their own. Which was a pathetic religion at least. *P* The great text: *P* "Thou shalt love thy neighbour as thyself," admits of many renderings. But to Skrebensky as to the others only the one rendering was possible, and this was stamped upon him, he fought for its preservation. *P* "Thou shalt love thy neighbour as thyself." / If it be interpreted, "Thou shalt wish for thy neighbour's self-effectuation as for thine own self-effectuation," then the frame of this society must be smashed, the State must be burst asunder, a new unit must be taken, a new fabric slowly built up, using the material of the old. But he had only his own interpretation. *P* And Ursula felt she had to submit. She felt a great sense of impending loss. But as

yet it was all too vague. She could not disentangle fate and foreboding, nor desire, nor sorrow, nor resentment. She continued in the confused, wholesale suffering of youth. *MS*

306:2   extinguished *TSR*] demented *MS*

306:9   day *TSR*] couple of days *MS*

306:13 blindly:] ~, *TS*

306:18 hide? *TS*] ~. *MS*

306:19 day *TSR*] first day *MS*

306:25 church-tower   *TS*]   church tower *MS*

306:31 Here!] ~, *TS*

306:31 voice. *P* And *TS*] ~. / And *MS*

306:35 answered. *P* She *TS*] ~. / She *MS*

306:39 arms. *P* But *TS*] ~. / But *MS*

307:1   not under … rested in *TSR*] to be treated honorably, {honourably, *TS*} and by *MS*

307:4   was not … was a breach between … hostile worlds *E1*] excluded her, even whilst she clung to him. For he adhered to the other life, where the individual was never alone, never the single male meeting and answering the woman *MS* was … was an antagonism between … worlds *TSR*

307:11 him] ~, *TS*

307:12 her spirit *E1*] any woman *MS* such a woman *TSR*

307:12 she *TSR*] a woman *MS*

307:13 angel *TS*] Angel *MS*

307:13 drive him … going, into a wilderness *E1*] frustrate his going forth *MS* drive … going, the beaten, fixed road of his life *TSR*

307:22 station:] ~; *TS*

307:25 over-coat] overcoat *TS*

307:35 peculiar] ~, *TS*

307:38 Goodbye] Good-bye *TS*

307:38 again. *P* He *TS*] ~. / He *MS*

308:7   effeminately-dressed   *TSR*] loudly-dressed *MS*

308:23 still *E1*] calm *MS*
308:24 train] ~, *TS*
308:26 at the] at *TS*
308:39 down." *P* It *TS*] ~." / It *MS*
309:6 But who ... desire only. *TSR*] Om. *MS*
309:11 hurt, a hurt, a hurt] hurt, a hurt *TS*
309:21 woman] women *E1*
310:1 XII *TSR*] XI *MS*
310:8 was,] ~ *TS*
310:12 ransom *TS*] ransome *MS*
310:16 she had ... of freedom *E1*] and through this, indomitable *MS*
310:19 duty] ~, *TS*
310:23 giving herself, never *Ed.*] giving herself / never *MS* Om. *TS*
310:25 history *TS*] History *MS*
310:31 angered *E1*] bored *MS*
310:31 she hated ministers *E1*] dates were not interesting *MS*
310:32 enlarging,] ~ *TS*
310:33 studies:] ~; *TS*
310:35 body,] ~; *TS*
311:1 Romans,] ~ *TS*
311:1 contact; she] ~. She *E1*
311:12 triumph *E1*] tenderness *MS*
311:14 ash,] ~ *TS*
311:16 unformed *E1*] inorganic *MS*
311:19 trees] ~, *TS*
311:19 birds] ~, *TS*
311:20 fixed *E1*] free *MS*
311:21 a *E1*] was a *MS*
311:23 farouche] *farouche E1*
311:23 animal] ~, *TS*
311:24 petty secrecies and jealousies *TSR*] domesticated nullity *MS* domesticated nullities *TS*
311:25 school-girl] school-/ girl *TS* schoolgirl *E1*
311:25 intimacy *TSR*] intimacies *MS*
311:27 untrustworthy *E1*] cowardly *MS*
311:30 person] other person *TS*
311:30 *dislike*] dislike *TS*
311:35 her] ~, *TS*
311:38 twenty eight *Ed.*] twenty-eight *MS*

311:39 to] *Om. E1*
312:3 and,] ~ *TS*
312:3 thought,] ~ *TS*
312:11 person] ~, *TS*
312:18 classroom] class-room *TS*
312:32 Arts] ~, *TS*
312:34 bearing] ~, *TS*
312:40 clean] calm *TS*
313:1 craved ceaselessly *E1*] craved, ah craved *MS* craved, ah craved, *TS*
313:13 emerald-green] emerald green *TS*
313:14 whitish,] ~ *TS*
313:20 opened,] ~. *E1*
313:22 looked.] ~! *TS*
313:23 proud,] proud, and*TS*
313:26 shoulders] ~, *TS*
313:28 now] ~, *TS*
313:29 mistress *TSR*] friend *MS*
314:4 on,] ~ *TS*
314:6 bath—] ~, *TS*
314:7 waist,] ~ *TS*
314:15 Goodbye] Good-bye *TS*
314:23 Ursula,] Ursula, did you? *TS*
314:23 Inger. "Did you?" *P* The *Ed.*] Inger ... you?" / The *MS* Inger. *P* The *TS*
314:24 open, *TSR*] ~ *MS*
314:28 she *TSR*] Ursula *MS*
314:29 said,] ~ *TS*
314:29 difficulty:] ~, *TS*
314:32 we.] ~? *TS*
314:39 warm,] ~ *TS*
315:6 suffered:] ~; *TS*
315:10 Inger. *P* They *TS*] ~. / They *MS*
315:13 Ursula. *P* The *TS*] ~. / The *MS*
315:23 bungalow] ~, *TS*
315:29 moment." *P* Ursula *E1*] ~." / Ursula *MS*
315:39 saying softly:] ~, ~, *E1*
315:40 water." *P* Ursula *E1*] ~." / Ursula *MS*
316:1 mistress's *E1*] mistress' *MS*
316:3 Winifred. *P* But *E1*] ~. / But *MS*

316:5 a while] awhile *E1*
316:8 and her belly] *Om. E1*
316:10 her. *E1*] her, black, hopeless, dumb. *MS*
316:14 Above all ... natural surroundings. *E1*] *Om. MS*
316:25 time,] ~ *E1*
316:26 in an underworld *E1*] by the black waters *MS*
316:33 Cossethay,] ~ *E1*
316:34 elsewhere? *E1*] ~. *MS*
316:36 suddenly seemed] seemed suddenly *E1*
316:39 water—] ~,— *E1*
317:11 thing—] ~,— *E1*
317:17 religion,] ~ *E1*
317:19 fear:] ~; *E1*
317:19 do] Do *E1*
317:36 strong *E1*] positive *MS*
317:36 passive subjects *E1*] limp attributes *MS*
317:38 mild *E1*] limp *MS*
317:40 honor] honour *E1*
318:6 destructive *E1*] positive *MS*
318:7 greatest] ~, *E1*
318:12 fiercer *E1*] wiser *MS*
318:16 more—] ~,— *E1*
318:17 fuss,] ~ *E1*
318:18 fit into an old, inert *E1*] an *MS*
318:18 a dead *E1*] an *MS*
318:21 exist *E1*] am I *MS*
318:22 an instrument *E1*] a figurehead *MS*
318:23 apparatus *E1*] limb *MS*
318:23 dead theory. *E1*] own body! *MS*
318:24 act:] ~; *E1*
318:36 terrible] ~, *E1*
318:36 poisonous *E1*] leprous *MS*
318:37 anything] ~, *E1*
319:14 you—] ~,— *E1*
319:15 Ursula] ~, *E1*
319:19 perverted life *E1*] grosser, heavier flame *MS*
319:26 again,] ~ *E1*
319:28 big] ~, *E1*
319:33 remaining *E1*] more on earth *MS*
319:35 had wanted *E1*] wanted *MS*

319:36 disintegrated lifelessness ... good-humour *E1*] calm, good-humoured despair *MS*
319:38 woman] ~, *E1*
319:39 stability *E1*] certainty *MS*
319:39 He did *E1*] Therefore he did *MS*
319:40 Only he ... own life. *E1*] *Om. MS*
320:1 Only,] ~ *E1*
320:1 He was still healthy. *E1*] *Om. MS*
320:2 fill each moment *E1*] do as Rome did *MS*
320:3 It was ... his nature. *E1*] *Om. MS*
320:6 He believed ... by time. *E1*] *Om. MS*
320:9 red-brick] red brick, *E1*
320:10 red-brick *E1*] red-brick, new *MS*
320:10 dwellings] ~, *E1*
320:14 pinkish *E1*] red-brick *MS*
320:15 ugliness:] ~; *E1*
320:15 grey-black,] ~ *E1*
320:17 window] ~, *E1*
320:17 new-brick *E1*] red-brick *MS*
320:17 nowhere] ~, *E1*
320:18 amorphous, yet ... itself endlessly *E1*] homogeneous *MS*
320:19 house-windows,] ~ *E1*
320:22 market-place] ~, *E1*
320:22 black,] ~ *E1*
320:23 red-brick *E1*] red brick *MS*
320:24 windows] ~, *E1*
320:24 doors] ~, *E1*
320:25 public-house *Ed.*] public house *MS* public-/ house *E1*
320:25 on *E1*] in *MS*
320:31 amorphous *E1*] *Om. MS*
320:34 rapidly spreading ... skin-disease *E1*] suddenly crystallised into finality *MS*
320:37 red-brick *E1*] red brick *MS*
321:1 colliery *E1*] ~, *MS*
321:1 around *E1*] round *MS*
321:2 gorse, *E1*] ~ *MS*
321:3 heath, the *E1*] heath and *MS*

321:4 was just *E1*] was *MS*
321:6 dream, some ... become con-crete *E1*] joke in a nasty illus-trated paper *MS*
321:8 Winifred *E1*] Miss Inger *MS*
321:8 motor-car *Ed.*] motor car *MS*
321:8 raw *E1*] squalid *MS*
321:10 The place ... and rigid. *E1*] *Om. MS*
321:13 streets *E1*] street *MS*
321:17 within some utterly unliving shell, *E1*] *Om. MS*
321:18 It was ... them all. *E1*] *Om. MS*
321:21 simply] ~, *E1*
321:23 devoted *E1*] devoted all *MS*
321:24 handsome room, *E1*] ~ ~ *MS*
321:24 laboratory *E1*] great laboratory *MS*
321:25 but *E1*] and therefore *MS*
321:25 the same *E1*] a rare *MS*
321:25 hard, mechanical ... inchoate, and *E1*] leisure and holiday to the idlers who loitered before its windows, *MS*
321:27 country *E1*] county *MS*
321:28 mathematical *E1*] stately *MS*
321:29 curved drive. *E1*] curved/ *MS*
321:30 but,] ~ *E1*
321:35 fastened *E1*] buttoned *MS*
321:37 stand *E1*] run *MS*
321:38 ashamed *E1*] afraid *MS*
321:39 that it chilled the heart *E1*] as one might imagine the clasp of an octopus *MS*
322:6 nose] ~, *E1*
322:7 strange, repellent ... revealed itself *E1*] grosser mould of his features. Yet it was evident *MS*
322:10 servile, slightly cunning *E1*] servile *MS*
322:13 the young girl asked, *E1*] asked the young girl, *MS*
322:34 tragedy. *P* He *E1*] ~. / He *MS*
322:37 But ... good wages. *E1*] *Om. MS*
322:40 replied,] ~ *E1*
323:1 colliery-manager] colliery manager *E1*

323:4 summer house] summer-house *E1*
323:8 a sinister *E1*] an uneasy *MS*
323:10 his death *E1*] it *MS*
323:14 everybody.'—] ~.' *E1*
323:15 boy *E1*] little boy *MS*
323:16 yes Sir] ~, sir *E1*
323:17 bad—] ~,— *E1*
323:17 comfortable—] ~,— *E1*
323:17 oh yes—!] ~, ~,— *E1*
323:17 But you see—] but, ~ ~, *E1*
323:18 an'] and *E1*
323:22 still smiling *E1*] abstracted *MS*
323:23 doesn't] does not *E1*
323:25 Ursula, '—'they're] ~. "They're *E1*
323:25 colliers'?] ~? *E1*
323:26 as *E1*] as it is *MS*
323:28 knew he represented his job *E1*] reckoned him as a loader *MS*
323:32 side-shows *E1*] side shows *MS*
323:32 'em."—He] ~." *P* He *E1*
323:32 round *E1*] out *MS*
323:33 chaos, the rigid, amorphous *E1*] disarray, the unmanage-able small *MS*
323:33 Wiggiston.—"Every] ~. *P* "Every *E1*
323:34 side-show *E1*] side show *MS*
323:37 really *E1*] vitally *MS*
323:39 shop] ~, *E1*
323:40 the bit ... can't digest *E1*] prac-tically none of him *MS*
323:40 he,] ~ *E1*
324:1 a standing ... of work *E1*] usually a nuisance *MS*
324:5 man is] man's *E1*
324:9 Oh] ~, *E1*
324:12 it all ... end up. *E1*] too tired, I suppose. *MS*
324:20 with her ... the heavens *E1*] working grimly *MS*
324:21 mass *E1*] new mass *MS*
324:24 it—] ~,— *E1*
324:30 machine *E1*] mercenary machine *MS*

324:33 But it ... was meaningless. *E1*]
  Om. MS
324:38 mistress] ~, *E1*
324:38 who is in love *E1*] continues to
  live *MS*
325:2 freedom,] ~ *E1*
325:4 hatred *E1*] burden *MS*
325:4 wholely, without cynicism *E1*]
  without self-consciousness *MS*
325:8 impure *E1*] *Om. MS*
325:8 mechanisms of matter *E1*] pure
  inhumanity of the machine *MS*
325:9 machine, was *E1*] pure
  machine, was *MS*
325:10 mechanism *E1*] machine *MS*
325:11 matter, living or dead, *E1*] the
  children of the world *MS*
325:12 unison, her immortality *E1*]
  freedom *MS*
325:13 smash *E1*] smash some part of
  MS
325:19 summer house *Ed.*]
  summer-house *MS*
325:20 tidy] tiny *E1*
325:25 inert *E1*] dirty *MS*
325:27 sunshine,] ~ *E1*
325:31 marsh, where ... are one. *E1*]
  marsh. *MS*
325:32 repellent *E1*] repellant *MS*
325:33 her. *E1*] her, as if he were some
  lustful, meaningless dog. *MS*
325:35 All was ... and ugly. *E1*] *Om.
  MS*
325:36 stayed. She stayed also *E1*]
  stayed *MS*
325:37 her sense *E1*] sense *MS*
326:3 corruption *E1*] corrosion *MS*
326:5 soft *E1*] slimy *MS*
326:5 half corrupt] half-corrupt *E1*
326:7 of *E1*] of her *MS*
326:8 said:] ~, *E1*
326:9 dear—] ~,— *E1*
326:9 I?" *P* The *E1*] ~?" / The *MS*
326:10 muddy *E1*] slimy *MS*
326:16 Ursula. *P* The *E1*] ~. / The
  MS
326:25 thick *E1*] fat *MS*
326:25 thighs—" *P* Ursula *Ed.*]

~—" / Ursula *MS* ~——" *P*
  Ursula *E1*
326:32 an *E1*] a private *MS*
326:33 seemed to ... his validity. *E1*]
  never mentioned to the niece.
  Why should it be so secret,
  unmentionable? *MS*
326:35 Brangwen *E1*] The two people,
  Brangwen *MS*
326:35 Inger continued engaged *E1*]
  Inger, dragged on *MS*
326:36 married. *E1*] did marry. After
  all, *MS*
326:37 children. Neither marriage nor
  E1] children, and *MS*
326:38 establishment meant ... propagate himself *E1*] establishment.
  Since all adventure was over,
  he would retreat into a well-
  provided tomb *MS*
326:39 instinct *E1*] cunning *MS*
326:40 rest *E1*] safety *MS*
327:1 complete *E1*] brutal *MS*
327:2 him:] ~; *E1*
327:2 warm *E1*] unwilled *MS*
327:4 from which ... its motion *E1*]
  it depended on in its inertia
  MS
327:4 As for ... his mate. *E1*] *Om.
  MS*
328:1 XIII *E1*] X *MS* XI *TS* XII *TSC*
328:4 school-days] schooldays *E1*
328:8 blinded,] ~ *E1*
328:11 shortly,] ~ *E1*
328:13 There *E1*] They *MS*
328:14 borne *E1*] born *MS*
328:22 darkness *E1*] darkness that *MS*
328:24 physical considerations *E1*]
  material considerations
  immediately at hand *MS*
328:25 else, was horrible. *E1*] else. *MS*
328:26 house *E1*] money *MS*
328:30 thereby she] she thereby *E1*
328:34 years,] ~ *E1*
329:6 heat *E1*] fire *MS*
329:8 domesticity.] ~! *E1*
329:11 that *E1*] which *MS*
329:16 own *E1*] *Om. MS*

329:23 commonness, the triviality *E1*]
meanness, the sordidness *MS*
329:25 ideas *E1*] philosophy *MS*
329:31 scathingly] ~, *E1*
329:32 and *E1*] *Om. MS*
329:36 loop-hole] loophole *E1*
329:37 his] this *E1*
330:4 to *E1*] *Om. MS*
330:7 panel] ~, *E1*
330:8 But now ... [330:14] labours.
Now *E1*] He had become a
skilled worker in wood—
carpenter, joiner, carver—
during his years at Cossethay,
teaching the boys and working
by himself. He had built an
organ for the church, and made
the necessary furniture for his
home. Now at last *MS*
330:16 busy, too uncertain, confused
E1] obscured *MS*
330:19 set-to *E1*] set to *MS*
330:23 mouth,] ~ *E1*
330:24 the *E1*] *Om. MS*
330:26 His *E1*] All his *MS*
330:26 some of *E1*] *Om. MS*
330:26 naïve *E1*] some naïve *MS*
330:33 church-tower] church tower *E1*
330:35 meaning *E1*] outline *MS*
330:39 start *E1*] passion *MS*
331:1 women folk] womenfolk *E1*
331:6 time,] ~ *E1*
331:8 So that ... of education.] *Om.
E1*
331:10 oblivious] ~, *E1*
331:12 nationality] ~, *E1*
331:17 out-going] outgoing *E1*
331:19 had] *Om. E1*
331:22 revived *E1*] clung to *MS*
331:22 passion, after ... of Winifred
E1] tenacity *MS*
331:26 But even ... her imagination.
E1] *Om. MS*
331:31 her—] ~,— *E1*
331:32 diary:] ~; *E1*
331:33 down." *P* Ah *E1*] ~." / Ah *MS*
331:37 And the ... her imagination.
E1] *Om. MS*

332:1 No-one ... no-one *Ed.*] No one
... no one *MS*
332:13 nothing:] ~; *E1*
332:13 Brangwen,] ~ *E1*
332:15 seventeen] ~, *E1*
332:20 core-rotten *E1*] barren, core-
rotten *MS*
332:20 provided:] ~; *E1*
332:29 her. *E1*] her. But she still
valued herself too much. *MS*
332:30 High School *E1*] high-school
MS
332:31 should *E1*] can *MS*
332:32 school-teacher] school teacher
E1
332:36 you in *E1*] *Om. MS*
332:38 take *E1*] fill *MS*
332:38 at *E1*] in *MS*
332:39 task which ... to fulfil *E1*] effort
of humanity *MS*
333:3 quick,] ~ *E1*
333:18 being *E1*] feeling *MS*
333:19 animal estimation. *E1*] low estimation in her pride. *MS*
333:27 expressionless *E1*] strained *MS*
333:32 for?" *P* His *E1*]] ~?" / His *MS*
333:33 strong] ~, *E1*
333:33 ready] ~, *E1*
333:34 this." *P* A *E1*] ~." / A *MS*
333:36 life! *Ed.*] ~!, *MS* ~? *E1*
333:36 Why] ~, *E1*
333:37 want?" *P* She *E1*] ~?" / She
MS
334:5 matric." *P* He *E1*] ~." / He
MS
334:6 wished *E1*] devoutly wished
MS
334:7 earn,] ~ *E1*
334:7 matric?] ~.? *E1*
334:9 said. *P* He *E1*] ~. / He *MS*
334:12 own,] ~ *E1*
334:13 be,] ~ *E1*
334:19 'dirty ... brats.' *Ed.*] '~ ... ~'.
MS ~ ... ~. *E1*
334:23 work-shop] workshop *E1*
334:23 lamp-light] lamplight *E1*
334:25 chisels] chisel *E1*
334:34 contempt,] ~ *E1*

334:36 indifference:] ~, *E1*
335:3 belly] soul *E1*
335:3 bitterness. *E1*] bitterness. Then she went. *MS*
335:5 "Schoolmistress,"] *Schoolmistress, E1*
335:12 first): _____." *P* In *Ed.*] ~): _____." / In *MS* ~): ......" *P* In *E1* [*E1* has multiple dots to right margin (to 335:19) for the form-questions, and MS single quotation marks are here house-styled to *E1* doubles.]
335:13 wrote "Brangwen—] ~, "~,— *E1*
335:14 Date of ..." *P* After *Ed.*] Date of Birth: _____" / After *MS* date of birth: ......" *P* After *E1*
335:16 Dates of ..." *P* With] Dates of Examinations: _____' / With *MS* date of Examination: ......" *P* With *E1*
335:18 June 1900.] *Om. E1 see notes*
335:19 Experience and ..." *P* Her *Ed.*] Experience and Where Obtained: _____." / Her *MS* experience and where obtained: ......" *P* Her *E1*
335:28 letters,] ~ *E1*
335:28 post-office,] ~ *E1*
335:36 "Gillingham"] ~ *E1*
335:37 hop-fields] hopfields *E1*
336:1 corn-flowers] cornflowers *E1*
336:3 blossom,] ~ *E1*
336:5 and:] ~, *E1*
336:6 Oh] ~, *E1*
336:15 old,] ~ *E1*
336:16 well-born,] ~ *E1*
336:17 metropolis] ~, *E1*
336:18 girls,] ~ *E1*
336:18 large, old, Queen-Anne] ~ ~ Queen Anne *E1*
336:18 house] ~, *E1*
336:19 and,] ~ *E1*
336:19 peace,] ~ *E1*
336:24 There] Then *E1*

336:26 wanted—] ~, *E1*
336:32 Now,] ~ *E1*
336:34 underneath,] ~ *E1*
336:35 this] the *E1*
337:9 cloaks] ~, *E1*
337:10 side,] ~ *E1*
337:11 Thames] ~, *E1*
337:11 song—.] ~. *E1*
337:15 unconsciously,] ~ *E1*
337:15 an animal ... its food *E1*] which a dog gives to a bone *MS*
337:17 try *E1*] go over *MS*
337:17 tunes,] ~ *E1*
337:19 still, he] ~. He *E1*
337:21 music stool] music-stool *E1*
337:22 movement] movements *E1*
337:25 music,] ~ *E1*
337:26 said. *P* He *E1*] ~. / He *MS*
337:27 looked *E1*] started, and looked *MS*
337:29 earth. *P* It *E1*] ~. / It *MS*
337:34 to." *P* Then *E1*] ~." / Then *MS*
337:36 Oh, *E1*] And *MS*
337:40 Yes." *P* And *E1*] ~." / And *MS*
338:2 candles:] ~. *E1*
338:5 10th. *Ed.*] 10th *MS* 10th *E1*
338:5 a.m., *E1*] a.m. *MS*
338:6 referring *E1*] in regard *MS*
338:7 School] Schools *E1*
338:9 quiet *E1*] mystery *MS*
338:11 Well] ~, *E1*
338:15 emphatic,] ~ *E1*
338:16 organ] ~, *E1*
338:25 At length *E1*] Suddenly *MS*
338:25 asked:] ~. *E1*
338:27 to *E1*] *Om. MS*
338:29 herself,] ~ *E1*
338:30 social individual. *E1*] entity! *MS*
338:30 note] ~, *E1*
338:32 angry *E1*] cold *MS*
338:33 said] ~, *E1*
338:35 He was beaten. *E1*] *Om. MS*
338:36 said] ~, *E1*
338:36 try,' *E1*] ~', *MS*

338:36 retorted, almost apologising to him. *E1*] retorted. *MS*
338:39 Brangwen—] ~, *E1*
338:39 Cottage—] ~, *E1*
338:40 final *E1*] exclusive *MS*
339:3 going." *P* Ursula *E1*] ~." / Ursula *MS*
339:8 said. *P* And *E1*] ~. / And *MS*
339:10 letter. *P* She *E1*] ~. / She *MS*
339:12 curious] ~, *E1*
339:14 hard *E1*] dim *MS*
339:16 contents *E1*] contents of the letter *MS*
339:21 Oh] ~, *E1*
339:21 indeed." *P* The *E1*] ~." / The *MS*
339:23 callousness *E1*] sheer indifference *MS*
339:25 Her eldest ... way now. *E1*] *Om. MS*
339:27 *good*] good *E1*
339:31 calmly. *P* How *E1*] ~. / How *MS*
339:33 place,] ~ *E1*
339:37 asked *E1*] said *MS*
340:6 long,] ~ *E1*
340:6 yourself,] ~ *E1*
340:7 good." *P* Between *E1*] ~." / Between *MS*
340:8 her *E1*] the *MS*
340:12 said. *P* Again *E1*] ~. / Again *MS*
340:16 Well, you're ... away," he said. "I'll *E1*] Well," he said, "you're ... away. I'll *MS*
340:17 by yourself *E1*] on your own *MS*
340:21 said. *P* There *E1*] ~. / There *MS*
340:22 silence,] ~ *E1*
340:30 parlour:] ~. *E1*
340:31 chat] ~, *E1*
340:32 qu'est-ce qui *E1*] qu'est-ce-qui *MS*
340:35 said. *P* The] ~. The *E1*
340:37 father: *Ed.*] ~. *MS* ~, *E1*
341:7 hard,] ~ *E1*
341:12 her] ~, *E1*

341:13 application *E1*] applications *MS*
341:14 school in a poor quarter, *E1*] common school, *MS*
341:19 it *E1*] she felt it *MS*
341:23 relationship.] ~ *E1*
341:30 classrooms *Ed.*] class-rooms *MS*
341:32 common *E1*] stupid *MS*
341:33 esteem,] ~ *E1*
341:34 long; she] ~. She *E1*
342:2 dinner bag] dinner-bag *E1*
342:7 Behind] Before *E1 see notes*
342:8 before:] ~; *E1*
342:15 childhood:] ~; *E1*
342:15 grandfather *Ed.*] grand-father *MS* grandfather, *E1*
342:15 eyes] ~, *E1*
342:23 sidled *E1*] stumbled *MS*
342:30 char-woman] charwoman *E1*
342:33 down *E1*] forward down *MS*
342:37 grey,] ~ *E1*
343:10 been.] ~! *E1*
343:18 rain *E1*] water *MS*
343:18 building *E1*] school *MS*
343:20 place *E1*] school *MS*
343:21 threatening *E1*] bullying *MS*
343:22 architecture] ~, *E1*
343:22 domineering *E1*] self assertion *MS*
343:25 prison,] ~ *E1*
343:26 forward,] ~ *E1*
343:29 room,] ~ *E1*
343:30 table,] ~ *E1*
343:31 looked *E1*] glanced *MS*
343:32 morning," *E1*] -", *MS*
343:34 aside,] ~ *E1*
343:36 gas-light] gaslight *E1*
343:38 morning?] ~, *E1*
343:39 said. "It's] ~, "it's *E1*
343:39 weather." *P* But *E1*] ~." / But *MS*
343:40 here,] ~ *E1*
344:4 asked. *P* The *E1*] ~. / The *MS*
344:7 Twenty five *Ed.*] Twenty-five *MS*
344:8 morning." *P* Ursula *E1*] ~." / Ella *MS*

344:10 the paper *E1*] paper *MS*
344:12 curled, white and scribbled] ~ white-and-scribbled *E1*
344:14 Ursula. *P* Again *E1*] Ella. / ~ *MS*
344:21 they're not *E1*] they aren't *MS*
344:22 voice. Ursula *Ed.*] ~. Ella *MS* ~. *P* Ursula *E1*
344:23 mechanical *E1*] absolute *MS*
344:23 her] ~, *E1*
344:25 count, as ... a machine. *E1*] count. She disliked it. *MS*
344:27 many, *E1*] ~? *MS*
344:28 said. *P* That *E1*] ~. / That *MS*
344:32 cold, and against his nature. *E1*] cold. *MS*
344:34 twenty eight *Ed.*] twenty-eight *MS*
344:35 Oh] ~, *E1*
344:36 up.—] ~. *E1*
344:37 peg—] ~. *E1*
344:37 Teacher *Ed.*] teacher *MS*
344:38 off?" *P* Miss *E1*] ~?" / Miss *MS*
345:3 frizzed *E1*] own frizzed *MS*
345:4 morning!] ~, *E1*
345:5 another,] ~ *E1*
345:6 'em—" *P* She *Ed.*] 'em—" / She *MS* 'em——" *P* She *E1*
345:10 Ursula *E1*] Ella *MS*
345:11 half past] half-past *E1*
345:12 Well] ~, *E1*
345:12 Mamma's] mamma's *E1*
345:13 Ursula *E1*] Ella *MS*
345:14 yes *E1*] yea *MS*
345:14 send,] ~ *E1*
345:14 Harby. *P* Ursula's *E1*] ~. / Ella's *MS*
345:15 cock-sure,] cocksure *E1*
345:17 people.] ~? *E1*
345:18 Ursula *E1*] And Ella *MS*
345:18 callous,] ~ *E1*
345:26 Mamma] mamma *E1*
345:27 you?" *P* The *E1*] ~?" / The *MS*
345:30 Hey!] ~, *E1*
345:30 Now] now *E1*
345:31 for:—what] ~? What *E1*

345:31 Mamma] mamma *E1*
345:33 "'Please] "~ *E1*
345:36 Yes] ~, *E1*
345:39 Please] ~, *E1*
345:39 Brangwin *E1*] Branwen *MS*
346:1 him *E1*] the boy *MS*
346:2 minute." *P* The *E1*] ~." / The *MS*
346:5 Harby] ~, *E1*
346:6 Ursula *E1*] Ella *MS*
346:7 bad] ~, *E1*
346:8 weakly. *P* The *E1*] ~. / The *MS*
346:14 Five-Six-and-Seven *E1*] five six and seven *MS*
346:15 Five—" *P* She *Ed.*] ~—" / She *MS* ~——" *P* She *E1*
346:18 wall *E1*] thick wall *MS*
346:26 frowsy *E1*] frowsty *MS*
346:38 dread] dread and dislike *E1* *see notes*
346:39 reality—] ~, *E1*
347:5 bruised her ... her shrink *E1*] crystallised her sentiment into hard impersonality *MS*
347:6 anticipations. *TSR*] anticipations. This hard shell of a school was not meant for love and personal feeling: it had a hard purposiveness that she could not understand. *MS*
347:8 rebuffed *TSR*] rebuked *MS*
347:10 teachers'] teacher's *TS*
347:14 teachers'] teacher's *TS*
347:16 chalk] ~, *TS*
347:18 school-master *Ed.*] schoolmaster *MS*
347:34 go." *P* Ursula *TS*] ~." / Ursula *MS*
347:35 No-one *Ed.*] No one *MS*
347:39 papers. *P* The *TS*] ~. / The *MS*
348:2 moment,] ~ *TS*
348:3 school-master *Ed.*] schoolmaster *MS*
348:4 and domineering *TSR*] *Om.* *MS*
348:16 girls] ~, *TS*

348:23 Quiet] ~, *TS*
348:23 quiet!" *P* There *TS*] ~!" /
There *MS*
348:24 down,] ~ *TS*
348:25 Harby] ~, *TS*
348:25 shrilly. *P* There *TS*] ~. /
There *MS*
348:28 shrilly. *P* Pairs *TS*] ~. / Pairs
MS
348:31 Five] ~, *TS*
348:31 Harby. *P* There *TS*] ~. /
There *MS*
349:2 herself,] ~ *TS*
349:5 tune.] ~, *TS*
349:9 Ursula. *P* They *TS*] ~. / They
MS
349:11 continued. *P* The *TS*] ~. / The
MS
349:12 Harby, *TS*] ~ *MS*
349:15 Halt!" *P* There *TS*] ~!" /
There *MS*
349:20 that?" *P* Ursula *TS*] ~?" /
Ursula *MS*
349:21 her, *TS*] ~ *MS*
349:24 silence *E1*] respect *MS*
349:25 distance:] ~. *TS*
349:26 *back*] back *TS*
349:26 girls." *P* The *TS*] ~." / The
MS
349:31 fifty five *Ed.*] fifty-five *MS*
350:3 each?" *P* A *TS*] ~?" / A *MS*
350:4 face] faces *TS*
350:14 before *TSR*] she had *MS*
350:14 she was always at bay *TSR*]
depending on her *MS*
350:19 squadron *E1*] gang *MS*
350:21 collective] ~, *TS*
350:22 Dinner-time *Ed.*] Dinner time
MS
350:22 went *TSR*] went up *MS*
350:23 teachers' room *Ed.*] town *MS*
teacher's room *TSR*
350:26 malevolent system *E1*] drawn
will MS mechanical system
TSR
350:27 ahead] *Om. TS*
350:30 again] then *TS*
350:32 became neutral and non-

existent *TSR*] yielded her will
to him *MS*
350:33 listening-genial *TSR*] false-
genial *MS*
350:35 she had ... her body *TSR*] he
had her soul in his power *MS*
350:36 class. *TSR*] class and he
asserted it. *MS*
350:40 source *E1*] secret *MS*
351:1 school,] ~ *TS*
351:1 power] ~, *TS*
351:3 Soon *TSR*] So soon *MS*
351:4 hate, for ... of her. *TSR*] hate.
MS
351:7 bull *TSR*] rock *MS* wheel *E1 see
notes*
351:8 blind *TSR*] inviolable *MS*
351:9 subjects *TSR*] subordinates
MS
351:10 pupils] scholars *TS*
351:10 Only, because ... detest them.
TSR] *Om. MS*
351:12 favorite *Ed.*] favourite *MS*
351:13 also, even ... dislike her.] also.
TS
351:15 could *TS*] did *MS*
351:15 come to grips with *TSR*]
understand *MS*
351:16 too strong for her *TSR*] she
could not get in agreement with
MS
351:16 young] ~, *TS*
351:27 during *TSR*] in *MS*
351:28 Standard Three *TS*] Standard-
Three *MS*
351:28 classroom] class-room *TS*
351:33 Greuze] ~, *TS*
351:33 Innocence," *TS*] ~", *MS*
352:3 class-teaching] class teaching
TS
352:5 midday] mid-day *TS*
352:7 *laisser-aller TSR*] laisser-aller
MS
352:15 absorption. *P* She *TS*] ~. / She
MS
352:16 manner] ~, *TS*
352:23 hungry,] ~ *E1*
352:23 pot,] ~ *TS*

352:25 jolly,] ~ *TS*
352:28 a] the *TS*
352:31 pointed *TSR*] unpenetrating *MS*
352:34 class." *P* Ursula *TSR*] kids." / Ursula *MS* kids." *P* Ursula *TS*
352:36 you? *TS*] ~, *MS*
352:37 enough? *TS*] ~. *MS*
352:38 Because!] ~, *TS*
352:40 be ... you] ~. You *TS*
353:1 weeks—" *TS*] week—" *MS* weeks"— *E1*
353:2 'em,] 'em *TS*
353:3 Oh] ~, *TS*
353:7 out.—] ~. *TS*
353:8 with—] ~. *TS*
353:19 so—.] ~—— *TS* ~—— *E1*
353:24 trite. *P* Ursula *TSR*] impersonal. Ursula *MS* impersonal. *P* Ursula *TS*
353:27 Well] ~, *TS*
353:29 yourself," *TS*] ~" *MS*
353:31 helped." And *E1*] helped. There's help for those that want it," and *MS*
353:32 departed. *P* The *TS*] ~. / The *MS*
353:35 acid with shame *TSR*] ashamed, devouring his own vitals *MS*
353:38 newcomer] new-comer *TS*
353:39 unclean *E1*] angular *MS*
354:1 she asked *TSR*] asked Miss Schofield *MS*
354:6 different *E1*] restful *MS*
354:6 Ursula,] ~ *TS*
354:9 Schofield;] ~, *TS*
354:9 it!" *P* She *TSR*] ~." / She *MS* ~." *P* She *TS*
354:10 ignomious position ... class beneath. *TSR*] ignominy of handling a subordinate authority over unwilling individuals. She was, like any teacher, between two meannesses, the meanness of the jealous authorities who controlled her, the meanness of the resentment from the children and the children's parents. *MS*
354:15 authority *E1*] official *MS*
354:16 withholding *TS*] with-holding *MS*
354:17 big,] ~ *TS*
354:28 either." *P* And *TS*] ~." / And *MS*
354:35 School] ~, *TS*
354:36 poor,] ~ *TS*
354:38 to some *TS*] a *MS*
354:38 place *TSR*] post *MS*
355:5 Schofield] , *TS*
355:9 room.—] ~— *TS*
355:10 ah—" *P* She *TS*] ~—" / She *MS* ~——" *P* She *E1*
355:19 louts—" *P* She *Ed.*] louts—" / She *MS* louts—" *P* She *TS* louts——" *P* She *E1*
355:20 difficulty,] ~ *TS*
355:22 response *TSR*] keeping *MS*
355:24 *He's*] He's *TS*
355:25 side,] ~ *TS*
355:25 he sets the children *TSR*] the children are *MS*
355:31 rude *TSR*] relentless *MS*
356:1 teacher] ~, *TS*
356:2 head-master *TSR*] head master *MS* headmaster *E1*
356:4 head-master] headmaster *E1*
356:7 judgment] judgement *E1*
356:13 strain] strive *TS*
356:14 of a large class *TSR*] *Om. MS*
356:15 through] by *TS*
356:16 application of ... certain knowledge *TSR*] exertion of will to action, to achieve an object beyond his personal interest *MS*
356:19 teacher,] ~ *TS*
356:25 therefore against *E1*] ready to destroy *MS*
356:25 Secondly] ~, *TS*
356:26 fixed *E1*] brute *MS*
356:34 her] the *TS*
356:38 iron ... upon *TSR*] roof ... above *MS*
356:38 sky] sun *TS*

356:39 Often,] ~ *TS*
356:40 fantasy *TSR*] falsity *MS*
357:2 subjugate to a bad, destructive will *E1*] only an instrument, a horrible mechanism *MS* only ... a faulty mechanism *TSR*
357:5 and vicious *E1*] *Om. MS*
357:7 said] ~, *TS*
357:8 beyond] herself beyond *TS*
357:9 Sundays,] ~ *TS*
357:13 beech woods] beech-woods *TS*
357:16 oh] ~, *TS*
357:18 gone!] ~. *TS*
357:19 All the while, they pursued *E1*] Nevertheless they haunted *MS* All ... they haunted *TSR*
357:22 hands] ~, *TS*
357:24 aloud,] ~ *TS*
357:31 Teacher] teacher *TS*
357:33 on] over *TS*
357:34 was brought down *E1*] had fallen short *MS*
357:35 school-teacher *TS*] school teacher *MS*
357:36 accusation.—] ~. *E1*
357:38 recording *TSR*] dial *MS*
357:39 negation *E1*] deficiency *MS*
357:39 was incapable ... the knowledge. *TSR*] had fallen short as a school-teacher. Whatever she was in herself, in the task to which she had allowed herself to be set, she was almost a failure. *MS*
358:6 which was ... of her *TSR*] to which she had set herself *MS*
358:15 Her very ... at test *E1*] She could slip out of it like this *MS*
358:17 rather] *Om. TS*
358:18 Her dread ... larger. She *TSR*] He represented something she dreaded. And she *MS*
358:20 and destroy her *TSR*] brutally *MS*
358:23 offences *TS*] offenses *MS*
358:30 asked. *P* There *TS*] ~. / There *MS*

358:33 Please Miss] ~, ~ *TS* ~, miss *E1*
358:34 mockery. *P* At *TS*] ~. / At *MS*
358:36 up] ~, *TS*
358:36 voice. *P* Everybody *TS*] ~. / Everybody *MS*
359:1 Harby. *P* The *TS*] ~. / The *MS*
359:4 Please Sir] ~, ~ *TS* ~, sir *E1*
359:6 desk." *P* The *TS*] ~." / The *MS*
359:10 crawling,] ~ *E1*
359:13 leer,] ~ *TS*
359:14 head-master's *Ed.*] headmaster's *MS* head-/ master's *E1*
359:16 sideways,] ~ *E1*
359:23 down." *P* The *TS*] ~." / The *MS*
359:25 arms." *P* They *TS*] ~." / They *MS*
359:28 head-master *Ed.*] head master *MS* head-/ master *E1*
359:32 detestable *TSR*] petty *MS*
359:39 Five." *P* Ursula *TS*] ~." / Ursula *MS*
360:4 power, and ... blind, native beauty. *E1*] power. *MS* power ... blind, stupid beauty *TSR*
360:8 cruel, stubborn, evil spirit, he was imprisoned in ... a servile acquiescence, he ... had to earn his living. He ... would keep the job going, since he must. And ... "caution" ... suppressed hatred, always ... [360:16] Ursula suffered *E1*] devilish office, dealing all in pin-pricks and little blows and twisting the joints of weaker children, when fulfilling the law of the school. She was tormented by him *MS* sullen, stubborn, subdued will, that acquiesced in ... a blind, passionate fury, he ... had set himself to it. He ... would see the job through, whoever opposed him. And ... "cau-

tious" ... suppressed, clumsy force, always ... suffered *TSR*

360:16 handsome and powerful *TSR*] sturdy and like a bull dog {bull-dog *TS*} *MS*

360:17 class *TSR*] class for her *MS*

360:18 doing. He ... a decent, powerful ... soul. *E1*] doing, so unmanly and insulting to his own being. *MS* doing. He ... a manly, powerful ... soul. *TSR*

360:19 his will ... so little and vulgar, out of place. She ... fettered wickedness ... rage in the long run, so ... a persistent, strong creature tethered. It ... [360:25] to her. *E1*] he used all his force and passion in the doing. He seemed to become infinitely less, lower than himself. She saw the shamefulness of his position, and it jarred on her like torment. *MS* his will ... so much less and meaner than his own nature. She ... fettered passion ... rage at the slightest provocation, so ... a mad brute that had lost control over itself. It ... her. *TSR*

360:26 rigid, neutral *TSR*] attentive *MS*

360:27 had it ... [360:30] she must. *TSR*] did, which she could not do, and which she wished to do. *MS*

360:31 to see him *TSR*] that he *MS*

360:32 using *TSR*] should use *MS*

360:32 horrible *TSR*] indecent *MS*

360:33 The strange ... was really vicious, and ugly, his ... of torture. *E1*] *Om. MS* The strange ... was a vicious, cruel glint, his ... of torture. He was like a stallion kept up in a stall, fretted, and going mad. *TSR*

360:35 clear, pure purpose *E1*] purposive will *MS*

360:36 brute will. He did not believe in the least in the education he kept inflicting year after year upon the children. So ... and ugly and out of place. Ursula ... [361:2] bear it *E1*] personal influence, domination. He wanted to exercise his personal domination over her too. She despised him with detestation *MS* personal will. He was stupid, animal, clumsy in his nature, yet not unbeautiful, until he was in this degrading chafing position. And here ... and big and clumsy. Ursula ... it *TSR*

361:2 wrong and ugly *E1*] so improper and undignified *MS* wrong and hideous *TSR*

361:4 room,] ~ *TS*

361:4 thud] the thud *TS*

361:6 that *E1*] that, if she died, *MS*

361:7 school-master *Ed.*] schoolmaster *MS*

361:8 The brute ... should never be allowed to continue ... bullying cruelty. *E1*] The man and his job were one, loathsome, petty, bullying. *MS* The brute ... should commit suicide, rather than continue ... cruelty. *TSR*

361:13 out,] ~ *TS*

361:18 ashamed *TS*] like an ashamed *MS*

361:28 work] ~, *TS*

361:30 blackboard *E1*] black-board *MS*

361:37 misery *TSR*] mess *MS*

361:38 trouble *TSR*] muddle *MS*

362:12 tram-car *TS* tramcar *MS*

362:13 established and strong *TSR*] fine and free *MS*

362:13 home,] *TS*

362:15 today *Ed.*] to-day *MS*

362:16 coolly. *P* Then *TS*] ~. / Then *MS*

362:19 lie. *P* Ursula *TS*] ~. / Ursula *MS*
362:40 only] *Om. TS*
363:1 Teacher *Ed.*] teacher *MS*
363:2 Teacher *Ed.*] teacher *MS*
363:7 week-ends *TSR*] week ends *MS*
363:11 her!—this *Ed.*] ~! this *MS* ~. This *TS*
363:11 respite. As] ~, as *TS*
363:13 week-end *Ed.*] week end *MS*
363:17 it,] ~ *TS*
363:21 believe] believe that *TS*
363:28 Harby,] ~ *TS*
363:29 him;] ~: *TS*
363:29 alleys] valleys *TS*
363:31 disliked the reserved *TSR*] despised the creeping *MS*
363:32 school-master] schoolmaster *E1*
363:37 now he was] he was now *TS*
363:39 turbulent crowd *TSR*] nasty anarchy *MS*
363:40 school's work *TSR*] school *MS*
363:40 someone ... someone] some one ... some one *E1*
364:3 head-master had *TSR*] head-master *MS* headmaster had *E1*
364:3 an obsession ... against her. *TSR*] blind fury. *MS*
364:5 no good *TSR*] pernicious *MS*
364:6 very life ... bodily movement *TSR*] extension of himself, which was the machine working to his will *MS*
364:8 danger that ... a fall *TSR*] extraneous matter that must be cast forth *MS*
364:13 stroke *TSR*] *Om. MS*
364:14 allowed all ... to be *TSR*] was the cause of the abnormally bad state of the class *MS*
364:22 through the scholars *TSR*] *Om. MS*
364:27 class,] ~ *TS*
364:29 chagrin: *Ed.*] ~. *MS*
364:31 how *TSR*] what *MS*
364:31 let *TSR*] doing *MS*

364:33 there is ... are free *TSR*] I am not keeping an eye on you, you have unbridled licence *MS*
364:34 ever learnt] have ever learned, *TS* ever learned, *TSR*
364:34 go back ... Standard Three *TSR*] behave as if you were a herd of savages *MS*
364:35 all *TSR*] these *MS*
364:38 pale, quivering class, *TS*] class of pale, quivering class, *MS*
365:3 order,] ~ *TS*
365:9 judgment] judgement *E1*
365:14 Teacher *Ed.*] teacher *MS*
365:15 Teacher] teacher *E1*
365:20 task] ~, *TS*
365:26 seventeen *TS*] ~, *MS see notes*
365:27 official *TSR*] shut-off *MS*
365:38 today *Ed.*] to-day *MS*
365:39 Fifty two *Ed.*] Fifty-two *MS*
366:1 said.] ~, *E1*
366:1 Staples?" *P* Ursula *TS*] ~?" / Ursula *MS*
366:7 ago," the ... on, "there] ago there *TS*
366:8 forty eight ... forty eight *Ed.*] forty-eight ... forty-eight *MS*
366:11 Please] ~, *TS*
366:11 Sir *Ed.*] sir *MS*
366:13 eyes. *E1*] ~: *MS*
366:15 head-master *Ed.*] head master *MS* headmaster *E1*
366:19 Yes] ~, *TS*
366:20 again." *P* The *TS*] ~." / The *MS*
366:24 head-master *Ed.*] head master *MS* headmaster *E1*
366:25 worst-behaved *TSR*] worst behaved *MS*
366:26 into the bargain *TSR*] as well *MS*
366:28 them? *TS*] ~. *MS*
366:32 much upset *TSR*] miserable *MS*
366:32 felt almost mad *TSR*] scarcely felt any more *MS*
366:33 head-master *Ed.*] headmaster *MS*

366:36 indiarubbers] india-rubbers *TS*

367:8 Proud-arse." *P* When *Ed.*] Proud-arce." / ~ *MS* Proud-arce." *P* ~ *TS see notes*

367:9 Gudrun] ~, *E1*

367:11 Brangwen." *P* She *TS*] ~." / She *MS*

367:14 Cossethay, *TS*] ~ *MS*

367:14 Teacher] teacher *E1*

367:20 darkness,] ~ *TS*

367:23 Never more] Never *TS*

367:25 Teacher *TS*] teacher *MS, E1*

367:27 School *Ed.*] school *MS*

367:38 all,] ~ *TS*

368:1 stone-throwing] stone throwing *E1*

368:3 for mastery *E1*] as teacher *MS*

368:6 enough *TS*] enough as *MS*

368:10 inkwell *Ed.*] ink-well *MS*

368:14 the] *Om. TS*

368:20 Please] ~, *TS*

368:22 actor. He *Ed.*] ~, He *MS* ~, he *TS*

368:27 teacher. *P* This *TS*] ~. / This *MS*

368:29 o'clock,] ~ *TS*

368:30 said. *P* And *TS*] ~. / And *MS*

368:33 Please] ~, *TS*

368:33 Miss *TS*] miss *MS*

368:34 Ursula. *P* The *TS*] ~. / The *MS*

368:37 Ursula. *P* And *Ed.*] ~. / And *MS* ~. And *TS*

368:38 desk] ~, *TS*

369:2 evening." *P* The *TS*] ~." / The *MS*

369:11 doing?" *P* He *TS*] ~?" / He *MS*

369:18 said. *P* But *TS*] ~. / But *MS*

369:20 cringing] ~, *TS*

369:28 distress. *P* She *TS*] ~. / She *MS*

369:31 said. *P* She *TS*] ~. / She *MS*

370:1 said. *P* The *TS*] ~. / The *MS*

370:4 rat-like *E1*] ratlike *MS*

370:4 grinning. *P* Something *Ed.*] ~. / Something *MS* ~. Something *TS*

370:6 class,] ~ *TS*

370:17 white, *TS*] ~ *MS*

370:23 then,] ~ *TS*

370:34 roared. *P* Ursula *TS*] ~. / Ursula *MS*

370:37 head-master *Ed.*] head master *MS* headmaster *E1*

371:1 head-master *Ed.*] head master *MS* headmaster *E1*

371:3 dart,] ~ *TS*

371:5 said. *P* As *TS*] ~. / As *MS*

371:7 head-master *Ed.*] head master *MS* headmaster *E1*

371:10 as if ... to death *E1*] fighting her own battle *MS*

371:11 head-master *Ed.*] headmaster *MS*

371:12 mad] a mad *TS*

371:17 history] the history *TS*

371:17 monitors. *P* There *TS*] ~. / There *MS*

371:24 Ursula. *P* There *TS*] ~. / There *MS*

371:25 a *E1*] the *MS*

371:31 reading book] reading-book *TSC*

371:32 as *E1*] and as *MS*

371:35 felt] felt that *TS*

371:36 forever] for ever *TS*

372:3 said. *P* He *TS*] ~. / He *MS*

372:11 strange] a strange *TS*

372:17 she saw *TS*] [ ] saw *MS see notes*

372:18 it] that it *TS*

372:22 She could ... swollen hand *E1*] It was a hideous secret she must keep in her heart *MS*

372:25 much too] too much *TS*

372:27 ate the] the *TS* ate *TSR*

372:28 bread and butter] bread-and-butter *E1*

372:35 escape *E1*] comfort *MS*

373:4 instinct,] ~ *TS*

373:6 morning,] ~ *TS*

373:7 head-master *Ed.*] head master *MS* headmaster *TS*

373:11 boys.—] ~. *TS*
373:13 Brangwen." *P* He *TS*] ~." /
He *MS*
373:16 ill dressed] ill-dressed *TS*
373:19 cleanliness, *TS*] ~ *MS*
373:23 dress,] ~ *TS*
373:24 Ursula *TS*] Ella *MS*
373:25 well dressed] well-dressed *TS*
373:28 today *Ed.*] to-day *MS*
373:31 heart." *P* The *TS*] ~." / The
MS
373:33 know." *P* She *TS*] ~." / She
MS
373:36 ugly *E1*] handsome *MS* handsome, bitter *TSR*
373:37 human: *TSR*] ~. *MS*
373:38 yes. He *Ed.*] ~, He *MS* ~, he
TS
373:38 heart-disease] heart disease
TS
374:4 school-master *Ed.*]
schoolmaster *MS*
374:5 Oh] ~, *TS*
374:11 doctor." *P* Mr *Ed.*] ~." / Mr
MS ~." *P* Mr. *TS*
374:14 son,] ~ *TS*
374:14 money. *P* "I *TS*] ~. / "I *MS*
374:17 shamefully *TSR*] shockingly
MS
374:17 doctor. I'm … was known.
TSR] doctor— *MS*
374:20 because she … excusing
herself *TSR*] *Om. MS*
374:21 the dilemma … two women.
E1] it. *MS* it, malignantly. *TSR*
374:25 doctor—Is … Mr Harby?" *P*
The head-master *TSR*]
doctor—" / Ursula *MS*
doctor—" *P* Ursula *TS*
doctor.—Is … Mr. Harby?" *P*
The headmaster *E1*
374:27 Ursula *TSR*] She *MS*
374:28 loathed *TSR*] *Om. MS*
374:28 cunning and … occasion *E1*]
triumph in the scene *MS* brute
cunning and … occasion *TSR*
374:31 decent." *P* Ursula *TS*] ~." /
Ursula *MS*

374:32 on] at *TS*
374:35 delicate." *P* Ursula *TS*] ~." /
Ursula *MS*
374:39 marks." *P* Mr *Ed.*] ~." / Mr
MS ~." *P* Mr. *TS*
375:4 today *Ed.*] to-day *MS*
375:4 up." *P* Yet *TS*] ~." / Yet
MS
375:8 Oh] ~, *TS*
375:8 him,] ~ *TS*
375:9 triumph *E1*] gloating *MS*
375:13 head-master *Ed.*] head master
MS headmaster *TS*
375:14 troublesome,"—] ~," *TS*
375:16 delicate." *P* Ursula *TS*] ~." /
Ursula *MS*
375:17 superb *TSR*] bored *MS*
375:18 tickled *Ed.*] to tickled *MS* to
tickle *TS*
375:20 had to] had *TS*
375:21 understand." *P* She *TS*] ~." /
She *MS*
375:22 go, surprised and angry *TSR*]
go quickly *MS*
375:25 Ursula *TS*] Ella *MS*
375:25 ill looking] ill-looking *TS*
375:27 you." *P* The *TS*] ~." / The
MS
375:40 Ursula. *P* "It's *TS*] ~. / "It's
MS
376:5 trouble.—" *P* Ursula *Ed.*]
~.—" / Ursula *MS* ~." *P*
Ursula *TS*
376:6 scandal … brutality] brutality
… scandal *TS*
376:7 sordid *TSR*] horrid *MS*
376:10 nasty *TSR*] horrid *MS*
376:10 altogether. *P* So *TS*] ~. / 4. /
So *MS*
376:13 hated her … a man. *TSR*]
would not help her. *MS*
376:14 thrashing *E1*] good thrashing
MS
376:17 independence *TSR*] flighty
independence *MS*
376:18 Now] ~, *TS*
376:21 head-master *Ed.*] head master
MS headmaster *TS*

376:22 with fixed ... anger, she] *Om.*
TS
376:26 soul] ~, *TS*
376:28 She,] ~ *TS*
376:38 herself and *TSR*] *Om. MS*
377:2 evil *E1*] brutal *MS*
377:3 a school-teacher *Ed.*] an
impersonal brute *MS* a school
teacher *TSR*
377:5 the beatings *TSR*] it *MS*
377:8 as well as *TSR*] before *MS*
377:14 of] *Om. TS*
377:21 automatic *E1*] mechanical *MS*
377:23 utterance. *P* For] ~. For *TS*
377:26 She was in revolt. *E1*] *Om. MS*
377:30 freedom,] ~ *E1*
377:33 them; *E1*] ~: *MS*
377:34 there remained always *TSR*]
what was it, really, *MS*
377:35 to. *Ed.*] ~? *MS*
377:36 difficult!] ~. *TS*
378:3 these,] ~ *TS*
378:4 them,] ~ *TS*
378:4 them. *TSR*] them. *P* She was
finding freedom so. By putting
herself entirely within the
system which governed her as a
teacher, she knew what the
system was, and she could estimate herself with regard to it,
and be free of it. Much as it
cost her of her youth and sanguine carelessness, she still had
gained more than she had lost.
For she was stronger somewhere, and surer. She had rati-
fied her place in this, the
world's work and government
also. *MS*
378:7 her money *E1*] up *MS*
378:13 strength] the strength *TS*
378:18 rate,] ~ *TS*
378:21 destroying *TSR*] hateful to *MS*
378:22 manage *TSR*] manage fairly
well *MS*
378:22 spilling] spoiling *TS*
378:25 strain, always unnatural. *E1*]
strain. *MS*

378:30 almost *E1*] really almost *MS*
378:32 during the struggle *TSR*]
struggling *MS*
378:33 class-teaching *Ed.*] class
teaching *MS*
378:34 became hard and independent
E1] settled down to some
health and order *MS* became
firm and independent *TSR*
378:35 enough,] ~ *TS*
378:38 strenuous *E1*] splendid *MS*
379:6 was a violation *TSR*] seemed
wrong *MS*
379:13 fool's-parsley *E1*] fools parsley
MS
379:15 half submerged] half-submerged *TS*
379:18 unreality *E1*] unrealness *MS*
379:35 broad-cast *Ed.*] broad- / cast
MS broadcast *TS*
380:1 wrong—] ~, *TS*
380:4 was not difficult *E1*] they could
all do *MS*
380:7 springs." *P* She *TS*] ~." / She
MS
380:8 that,] ~ *TS*
380:9 away,] ~ *E1*
380:26 right till *TSR*] even at *MS*
380:29 the burden and shame of *E1*]
that she had not done well in
MS the burden and shame well
of *TSR*
380:33 it,] ~ *TS*
380:34 duty? *TS*] ~. *MS*
380:36 nothing.] ~! *TS*
381:7 world *TSR*] man-made world
MS
381:8 working *TSR*] man-made
MS
381:10 But she ... its enemy. *E1*] *Om.*
MS
381:15 school-teacher *TSR*] school
teacher *MS*
381:18 ever. And *Ed.*] ~. / and *MS* ~,
and *TS*
381:18 yet,] ~ *TS*
381:20 And] *Om. TS*
381:22 off] ~, *E1*

381:24 years] years' *E1*
381:25 applied,] ~ *E1*
381:32 subordinated *E1*] neglected *MS*
381:37 school-teacher *Ed.*] school teacher *MS*
382:4 know,] ~ *TS*
382:8 found, and ... its duration. *TSR*] found. *MS*
382:12 absolute? *TS*] ~. *MS*
382:14 And always ... it lead? *E1*] *Om. MS*
382:17 Ursula. *P* She *TS*] ~. / She *MS*
382:25 knows it] *Om. TS*
382:30 heavy,] ~ *E1*
382:32 St Philips *Ed.*] St Phillips *MS* St. Philips *TS* St. Philip's *E1* see note on 357:11
382:32 its] a *TS*
382:34 enclosure *Ed.*] enclos[uress] enclosedness *TS* see notes
383:1 XIV *TSR*] X *MS*
383:6 gardeners,] *Om. TS*
383:12 tall] ~, *TS*
383:13 well-made] well made *TS*
383:14 long,] ~ *TS*
383:15 Ursula *TS*] Ella *MS*
383:18 eldest, *TS*] ~ *MS*
383:22 satyr *TSR*] faun *MS* fawn *TS*
383:25 faun, *Ed.*] satyr, *MS* faun *E1*
383:25 pleased,] ~ *TS*
383:26 hot-houses] hothouses *TS*
383:27 cinerarias *Ed.*] cinararias *MS*
383:29 queer,] ~ *TS*
383:32 farm-yard] farmyard *E1*
383:33 already,] ~ *TS*
383:34 darkness,] ~ *TS*
384:1 upwards,] ~ *TS*
384:6 up] ~, *TS*
384:9 acquiescence *E1*] subjection *MS*
384:9 acceptance *E1*] the slave *MS*
384:14 and *TS*] *Om. MS*
384:23 stiff] ~, *TS*
384:30 cold, gleaming *TSR*] goats' cold, incalculable *MS*
384:33 Maggie. *P* She *TS*] ~. /

She *MS*
384:35 friend. *P* They *TS*] ~. / They *MS*
384:39 foot-prints *Ed.*] footprints *MS*
385:4 went] went on *TS*
385:5 brook] ~, *TS*
385:7 pertly-marked *TSR*] pertly marked *MS*
385:15 and,] ~ *TS*
385:15 trunk,] ~ *TS*
385:16 Christabel." *TS*] ~". *MS*
385:20 him. *P A TS*] ~. / *P A MS*
385:22 jerking *TSR*] triumphing *MS*
385:23 there!" *P* And *Ed.*] ~!" / And *MS* ~." *P* And *TS*
385:24 peculiar] ~, *TS*
385:30 it." *P* There *TS*] ~." / There *MS*
385:32 Oh] ~, *TS*
386:3 her. *P* They *TS*] ~. / They *MS*
386:6 coldly-gleaming,] ~ *TS*
386:7 chilled *E1*] melted *MS*
386:10 terror *E1*] horror *MS*
386:12 brown and hard] hard and brown *TS*
386:13 She seemed ... some insult. *E1*] *Om. MS*
386:14 answered] ~, *TS*
386:14 involuntarily. *P* He *TS*] ~. / He *MS*
386:19 anger *E1*] pain *MS*
386:21 sensation of *E1*] desire for *MS*
386:21 of the ... offered her, *E1*] *Om. MS* for the ... her, *TSR*
386:24 cleaner *E1*] nobler *MS*
386:36 felt she] *Om. TS*
386:36 pleasaunces] pleasances *TS*
387:2 him.—] ~. *E1*
387:3 But] ~, *TS*
387:5 liked *E1*] did love *MS*
387:5 life, at ... he offered. *E1*] life the thought of Anthony stirred in her a strong, impersonal passion, made her feel strong. *MS* life the ... strong, restive passion ... strong. *TSR*
387:8 isolated *E1*] aimless *MS*
387:8 senses *E1*] sensuous life *MS*

387:9 knew *E1*] loved *MS*
387:13 went,] ~ *TS*
387:21 also was] was also *TS*
387:30 handwork *Ed.*] hand-work *MS*
387:31 space *E1*] great light *MS*
387:33 enclosure *TSR*] twilight *MS*
387:36 ruddy, alert *E1*] bright, eager *MS*
388:7 fashion,] ~ *E1*
388:9 come *TS*] ~, *MS*
388:10 way,] ~ *TS*
388:31 'Ello *E1*] Ello *MS*
389:1 really] *Om. TS*
389:10 earth] ~, *TS*
389:18 voice,] ~ *TSC*
389:22 favorite *Ed.*] favourite *MS*
389:23 winter-darkened *TSR*] winterdarkened *MS* winter/ darkened *TS*
389:25 woods,] ~ *TS*
389:25 oak-tree *Ed.*] oak tree *MS*
389:30 Ursula *TS*] Ella *MS*
389:34 flowers] ~, *TS*
389:37 dusk] dark *TS*
390:5 suggestive *E1*] goodly *MS*
390:18 blue as *TSR*] like *MS*
390:20 pale green] pale-green *TS*
390:22 swiftly,] ~ *TS*
390:23 this year] *Om. TS*
390:25 near *TSR*] in *MS*
390:27 odd,] ~ *TS*
390:35 Green,] ~ *TS*
391:1 colliery-manager *Ed.*] colliery manager *MS*
391:3 distinction,] ~ *TS*
391:6 drawing room,] drawing-room *TS*
391:7 study,] ~ *TS*
391:9 bath-room] bathroom *E1*
391:12 substantial,"] ~" *TS*
391:14 chimney-pieces *E1*] chimney pieces *MS*
391:17 importance? *TSR*] ~. *MS*
391:18 amount, also,] ~ ~ *TS*
391:18 in common *TSR*] really in remarkable *MS* really in remarkably *TS*

391:20 chesterfield] Chesterfield *TS*
391:21 large *TSR*] great *MS*
391:24 *élite*] élite *TS*
391:25 no-one] no one *TS*
391:27 Robbia,] ~ *TS*
391:29 Primavera *E1*] ~, *MS*
391:29 Aphrodite *E1*] ~, *MS*
391:30 reception room] reception-room *E1*
391:31 Beldover. *P* and *E1*] Beldover as Simeon was made dumb. And *MS*
391:32 to be princess ... the country *E1*] to dwell in the tents of wickedness than to be a doorkeeper amid the host of the wicked *MS* to princess ... the county *TSR*
391:36 of school-term,] of school-term *TS* of the school-term *E1*
391:39 commenced *TSR*] began *MS*
391:40 school-room] schoolroom *E1*
392:2 Soon,] ~ *TS*
392:10 pride,] ~ *TS*
392:12 lesson] lessons *TS*
392:16 Goodbye] Good-bye *TS*
392:18 No] ~, *TS*
392:18 Miss *Ed.*] miss *MS*
392:18 faces. *P* She *TS*] ~. / She *MS*
392:25 harsh] hard *TS*
392:35 imperturbable,] ~ *TS*
392:36 goodbye] good-bye *TS*
392:40 you." *P* Then *TS*] ~." / Then *MS*
393:4 table: *E1*] ~; *MS*
393:4 them." *P* Ursula, *Ed.*] ~." / Ursula, *MS* ~." *P* Ursula *TS*
393:5 shy,] ~ *TS*
393:8 so—" *P* She *TS*] ~—" / She *MS* ~——" *P* She *E1*
393:10 nervously] eagerly *TS*
393:11 nothing. *P* Mr *Ed.*] ~. / Mr *MS* ~. *P* Mr. *TS*
393:17 choice—" *P* He *TS*] ~—" / He *MS* ~——" *P* He *E1*
393:18 peculiar] ~, *TS*
393:18 smile,] ~ *TS*
393:21 felt] felt that *TS*

393:28 day." *P* He *E1*] ~." / They *MS*
~." *P* They *TS*
393:31 tremulous] tremendous *TS*
393:38 future] ~, *TS*
393:39 School] school *TS*
393:40 head-master's] . headmaster's *E1*
394:4 all, they] ~. They *TS*
394:6 school] the school *TS*
394:10 Then the *TSR*] The *MS*
394:10 home *TSR*] *Om. MS*
394:11 The *TSR*] Then the *MS*
394:15 clean-scrubbed *TSR*] clean scrubbed *MS*
394:16 dining-room *E1*] dining room *MS*
394:16 thick *E1*] kind of thick, *MS* kind of thick *TSR*
394:16 hard *E1*] hard as iron *MS*
394:18 pale grey *TSR*] white *MS*
394:18 darker *TSR*] enamelled *MS*
394:21 road] ~, *TS*
394:23 No-one *Ed.*] No one *MS*
394:30 man] men *TS*
394:35 cheerful *E1*] so genial *MS* so laughing *TSR*
395:1 them *TS*] it *MS*
395:1 Dinner-time] Dinner time *TS*
395:3 Brangwen] ~, *TS*
395:7 uncle *Ed.*] the uncle *MS* Uncle *E1*
395:11 pleasantly. *P* And *TS*] ~. / And *MS*
395:16 hearthrug *Ed.*] hearth-rug *MS*
395:27 morning,] ~ *TS*
395:29 up,] ~ *TS*
395:29 was." *P* There *TS*] ~." There *MS*
395:32 windows,] ~ *TS*
395:33 houses,] ~ *TS*
395:34 space,] ~ *TS*
395:38 evening,] ~ *TS*
396:2 And they *TS*] And [ ] *MS see notes*
396:3 They wanted *TS*] The wan[ ] *MS*
396:3 home, with *TS*] hom[ ] *MS*

397:1 Chapter XV ... of Ecstasy *TSC*] *Om. MS see notes*
397:8 metal work] metal-work *TS*
397:8 hammered *TSR*] schemed *MS*
397:10 ready *E1*] quick *MS*
397:10 at work *TSR*] hammering away *MS*
397:12 drawing room] drawing-room *TS*
397:19 dining-room *TS*] dining room *MS*
397:23 hurting them *E1*] fear *MS*
397:25 proportion] proportions *TS*
397:27 servant's *Ed.*] servants *MS* servants' *TS*
397:32 under-manager *TS*] under manager *MS*
397:34 Botany] botany *TS*
398:4 ordinary *TSR*] vulgar *MS*
398:10 a *E1*] even a *MS*
398:11 train-fares] train fares *TS*
398:13 well-off *Ed.*] well off *MS*
398:15 enough *E1*] plenty *MS*
398:16 in] at *TS*
398:19 Exhibition *E1*] exhibition *MS*
398:21 School,] ~ *E1*
398:29 Chemist's] chemist's *TS see notes*
398:29 chemists'] chemist's *TS*
398:29 three] *Om. TS*
398:29 doctors' *TS*] doctors *MS* doctor's *E1*
398:30 under-manager's—] ~,— *TS*
398:31 people *TSR*] these people *MS*
398:31 wanted *E1*] pretended *MS*
398:39 lime-trees *E1*] lime trees *MS*
398:40 magic-land] magic land *TS*
399:4 Gothic *E1*] gothic *MS*
399:7 decoration, *TS*] ~ *MS*
399:10 amorphous *E1*] silly and amorphous *MS*
399:12 mediæval *E1*] mediaeval *MS*
399:19 genuine things *TSR*] meaning things of their souls *MS*
399:22 mean *E1*] mundane *MS* sordid *TSR*
399:24 hand] hands *TS*
399:34 echo *TSR*] timeless echo *MS*

399:34 timeless *TSR*] eternal *MS*
399:37 priest *TSR*] node *MS*
400:2 bacon] ~, *TS*
400:4 forever] for ever *TS*
400:5 were the *TSR*] were *MS*
400:5 end] the end *TS*
400:11 steady *E1*] cold *MS*
400:12 measured *TSR*] supreme *MS*
400:12 realm of the reality *E1*] stately company of kings *MS* realm of the Absolute *TSR*
400:14 cared for him *E1*] got the real Horace *MS* cared for Horace *TSR*
400:15 for Livy *E1*] the real Livy *MS* the for Livy *TSR*
400:16 gossipy *TSR*] cosy *MS*
400:16 classroom   *Ed.*]   class-room *MS*
400:17 Spirit] spirit *TS*
400:17 gossip-stuff ... and verbosities. *TSR*] examination-stuff to her, curiosities and verbosities. The study went dead. *MS*
400:23 Botany *Ed.*] botany *MS*
400:27 record her ... were good. *TSR*] call her neighbour to see the result, if it were good, laughing ruefully if it were bad. *MS*
400:29 college-friend] college friend *TS*
401:10 and *TSR*] and yet *MS*
401:11 half languid] half-languid *TS*
401:12 balanced and inalterable *E1*] hard and relentless *MS*
401:16 hopeless *TSR*] mad *MS*
401:17 purposes,] ~ *TS*
401:18 coat-and-skirt *TSR*] coat and skirt *MS*
401:30 could, *TSR*] ~ *MS*
402:3 beautiful, ... beautiful,] ~ ... ~ *TS*
402:5 no-one *Ed.*] no one *MS*
402:15 harbour-wall] ~, *TS*
402:30 A *TSR*] An egoist with a spoiled soul, he saved himself in his own eyes by being a devoted father. A *MS*

402:31 full of human feeling, *TSR*] *Om. MS*
402:33 sufficiently *TSR*] completely *MS*
402:34 glad to ... self-deception with *TSR*] taken in by *MS*
402:36 relieved *TSR*] glad *MS*
402:39 year,] ~ *TS*
403:1 handling *TSR*] retailing *MS*
403:2 had become ... of them *TSR*] did not care about nor appreciate *MS*
403:3 so much ... knowledge *TSR*] so many scraps of notes and scraps of labelled beauty *MS* So much ... knowledge *E1*
403:5 market value] market-value *TS*
403:5 curios:] ~; *TS*
403:5 dull *TSR*] dull, foolish *MS*
403:10 spurious:] ~; *TS*
403:16 was further equipped *TSR*] learned another dodge *MS*
403:17 little, *TSR*] ~ *MS*
403:17 slovenly laboratory for the *E1*] money-making *MS* confused laboratory for the *TSR*
403:19 harsh and ugly disillusion *TSR*] darkness and a bitterness *MS*
403:20 now, the ... under everything. *TSR*] now. *MS*
403:26 workshop *TSR*] seclusion *MS*
403:26 store *E1*] factory *MS*
403:27 single *E1*] sordid *MS*
403:27 gain, and *E1*] gain; and *MS* gain, and yet *TSR*
403:27 no productivity. It *TSR*] all the while, it *MS*
403:28 exist by ... of knowledge. *TSR*] be the religious retreat of learning. *MS*
403:28 But the ... was become a flunkey to the god of material success. *E1*] *Om. MS* But the ... was a form of flunkeydom to the God of Material Success. *TSR*
403:32 lecture,] ~ *TS*
403:33 word] ~, *TS*

403:35 pink *TSR*] white *MS*
403:36 white *TSR*] *Om. MS*
403:40 terricr *TSR*] terrier dog *MS* terrier-dog *TS*
404:1 In what ... what warehouse of ... confined? *E1*] Where was the root of the mystery? Where was the root of the mystery? And oh, who should lift the unrisen dawn over the horizon. *MS* In what ... what slag-heap of ... confined? *TSR*]
404:3 Anglo-Saxon ... long service at the inner commercial shrine. Yet ... this only? *E1*] it to make Anglo-Saxon a qualification for passing an examination, to enhance one's own commercial value? Where did one go to be pure in spirit? How should one get free to be pure in spirit? *MS* Anglo-Saxon ... long preparation for the commercial world. Yet ... only? *TSR*
404:8 the same *E1*] a mechanical *MS* a material *TSR*
404:9 produce vulgar ... material life *E1*] serve, to feed the ever-running machine which turns out all lives to a pattern *MS* produce material things, to add to material life *TSR*
404:10 honors] honours *TS*
404:12 life] lives *TS*
404:12 was fascinated ... human world. *TSR*] knew the pulse of the vacuoles and the quivering of the cambium tissue. She knew it. She {it, she *TS*} lived it. *MS*
404:15 cheap *E1*] false *MS*
404:15 converted *TSR*] turned *MS*
404:16 petty commerce *TSR*] swindling barter *MS*
404:16 come] gone *TSC*
404:18 barrenly, *E1*] slyly, *MS* callously, drily, barrenly, *TSR*
404:19 examination room; *E1*] market

of the world: *MS* market ... world; *TS*
404:20 ready-made *E1*] sham *MS* quack *TSR*
404:20 stuff,] ~ *TS*
404:20 really *TSR*] *Om. MS*
404:21 fetch;—] ~— *E1*
404:22 college,] ~ *TS*
404:23 Botany *Ed.*] botany *MS*
404:24 degrading herself ... of sham gewgaws. *Ed.*] putting off the dignity of living to perform foolish tricks wherewith to take people in. What was her Anglo-Saxon but a foolish trick? And how she hated it all. *MS* degrading herself ... of dead tricks of priestcraft. *TSR* degrading ... sham jewjaws. *E1*
404:25 Angry *TSR*] Grudging *MS*
404:25 terms] term *TS*
404:28 school] School *TS*
404:28 degradation *TSR*] tastelessness *MS*
404:29 Street,] ~ *TS*
404:29 either. She *TS*] ~, She *MS*
404:33 had the ... the same? *TSR*] would be glad to depart. Yet now some disillusion made her hesitate. *MS*
404:35 ahead:] ~; *TS*
404:36 gate *TSR*] mere gate *MS*
404:36 ugly yard ... active and dead. *E1*] enclosure! *MS* ugly yard ... active with greed. *TSR*
404:38 hill,] ~ *TS*
404:39 sordid *TSR*] confined, dusty *MS*
404:39 amorphous, squalid activity. *E1*] factories and smoke and disorder. *MS* the amorphous, squalid activity of material production. *TSR*
405:2 little church school *Ed.*] school *MS* little Church-school *TSR* little Church school *E1*
405:6 feeling] being *TS*
405:8 peacefulness;] ~, *TS*

405:10 college *TS*] College *MS*

405:10 France;] ~ *TS*

405:11 move,] ~ *TS*

405:14 was full ... [405:20] This world *TSR*] felt a confused, un-defined, vague thing, whose identity was never quite estab-lished. She was afraid of her own vagueness. What might be, and {be and *TS*} what might not be, in {be in *TS*} what might not be, in herself. The present, this accepted scheme *MS*

405:22 thought was ... was disclosed *TSR*] had thought was the *all*: {all: *TS*} that all was known *MS*

405:26 terror,] ~ *E1*

405:28 machine-produce *TSR*] machine produce *MS*

405:31 blinding *E1*] eternal *MS*

405:36 felt *TSR*] knew *MS*

405:37 "Beyond ... nothing," *TS*] '~ ... ~', *MS*

405:39 sinking fire *E1*] bonfire *MS* dying fire *TSR*

405:40 System of Righteousness *TSR*] Absolute System of Good and Evil *MS*

406:2 half-revealed *TSR*] half revealed *MS*

406:4 did,] ~ *TS*

406:4 jeered *TSR*] beaten *MS*

406:4 Fool, anti-social knave, why *TSR*] Fool and base knave, *MS*

406:9 belittle us with the darkness? *E1*] invent the bogey of dark-ness! *MS* introduce the dark-ness? *TSR*

406:10 grey shadow-shapes *E1*] ~ shadow shapes *MS*

406:11 beasts *TS*] beast *MS*

406:14 hyena] hyæna *E1*

406:14 wolf] the wolf *TS*

406:16 hyena *Ed.*] hyaena *MS* hyæna *E1*

406:19 denied, like ... of fangs. *TSR*] denied. *MS*

406:21 twenty two *Ed.*] twenty-two *MS*

406:24 post-card *E1*] post card *MS*

406:27 like the ... ashy day *TSR*] to have waked her into life *MS*

406:29 morning. And ... later daytime. *TSR*] a summer morning. *MS*

406:31 known the sunshine *TSR*] gone straight to fulfilment *MS*

406:32 of a spoiled day *TSR*] by the way *MS*

406:33 angel *TSR*] Saviour *MS* saviour *TS*

406:33 the sunshine *TSR*] her beauti-ful fate *MS*

406:34 delight *TSR*] enjoyment *MS*

406:36 sky *TSR*] prairie *MS*

406:37 Ah] ~, *TS*

406:38 illimitable,] ~ *TS*

406:40 in,] ~ *TS*

407:8 man *E1*] saviour *MS* angel *TSR*

407:9 all space *TSR*] her soul *MS*

407:10 did not believe *TSR*] was not sure *MS*

407:11 My dear Ursula] MY DEAR URSULA *E1*

407:15 am fully *TSR*] too am *MS*

407:15 older,] ~,— *TS*

407:15 I have ... at Cossethay: *TSR*] else sixteen. I seem to have lived through a long time since we kissed on the hill going up to your house. *MS*

407:17 come *TSR*] be coming *MS*

407:19 answer—Anton Skrebensky." *TSR*] answer by every post— Anton Skrebensky." *MS* answer. *P* "ANTON SKREBENSKY" *E1*

407:20 college *E1*] College *MS*

407:27 then] ~, *TS*

407:29 Dear Anton] DEAR ANTON *E1*

407:30 college *TS*] College *MS*

407:39 in] *Om. E1*

407:40 letter-rack,] ~ *E1*

408:4 Botany *E1*] botany *MS*

408:6 then,] ~ *TS*

408:13 before,] ago *TS*
408:15 No] ~, *TS*
408:23 for] of *TS*
408:23 alone — — — —] ~—— *TS*
408:25 purpose, what ... purpose
    TSR] soul, the soul *MS*
408:30 ciliary *E1*] cilliary *MS*
408:37 Was its ... itself? *TSR*] *Om. MS*
408:40 world gleamed ... knowledge.
She could ... not limited ... nor mere
purpose ... self-assertion. It was ...
[409:6] of infinity. *E1*] whole situation
was reversed. Instead of the chemical
and physical activities uniting to origi-
nate a unity, a will, she saw the will
itself, something indefinable, and unutterable, yet in its activity forever recognisable, moving in more or less habitual
ways, and its habits were the easily
recognised activities, chemical and
physical. It was the settled habits of the
unknown Will which science studied, as
a hunter studies the habits of his game.
But the hunter does not seek to know
the unfathomable secret of the tiger's
being: he wants the dead body of the
tiger. So with science. And the tiger's
body is only the tiger's most settled
habit. The tiger's being has established
a habit of muscles and striped skin, but
this habit is not the tiger. *P* What then
was the tiger? Was it something existent
but non-created? And what is creation?
Is it only the singling out still further of
that which is tiger from all that which is
not tiger? Is this the whole business—
this infinite singling out of that which *is*
from that which, for the particular
instance, is *not*? And so, through infinite
singling out, shall all things arrive at
Being? *P* Is this, then, immortality of
the soul? Is the soul of the individual
tiger immortal, or only the soul of the
race? Or is immortality only relative?
When we have killed all the tigers, will
the tiger's being continue to exist? Is the
tiger's being complete in the tiger, and
therefore almost non-existent? Or is the
tiger habit-bound, so that the striped
tiger must disappear from the face of
the earth, before the tiger's being can
continue further to liberate itself from
all that is not-tiger? *P* Can I continue
the singling out of my own being from
the matrix, regardless of the rest of
mankind? Or am I only as pure as the
race I belong to? Can a man himself be
free who knows his race habit-bound?
Am I not bound by the same habit as
binds all my race? In so far as I am one
of many, I am forced to live according to
the accepted habit. And if the accepted
habit is a prison to me, I am not free nor
pure. *P* But then why should I talk of my
purity? Am I not also beast and plant.
Have I not the habit of eating the flesh
of other beasts, like the tiger, of lusting
after satisfactions, like the ape. / "Every
man must crush within him / Moods of
tiger and of ape—" / Not only moods of
tiger, but real tiger: the living tiger is in
me, and the living ape. *P* Must I then
destroy myself, since I am tiger and
ape? Or what shall I do? Is there not
room for all, within me, so long as none
shall prevent me from becoming more
and more myself? I am tiger, I am ape, I
am savage man, I am monk and mediaeval swashbuckler, I am puritan, and
profligate, and scientist, I am myself in
the fullest of my knowledge, and I have
within me my unfulfilled being which
shall be fulfilled, singled out. *P* As a
stream I come out of the mountains,
through the rocks and the forest and the
deep jungle, through the marshes and
out to the plains, on and on through
cities, and beyond. Only that is against
me which stops my further progress, at
my extremest tip of travel. *P* Why must I
crush the tiger?—I am also the tiger. In
my hour, I am the tiger. Why must I
destroy the ape?—I am the ape also.
But the tiger is not *me*. The tiger is of
me. And the ape is of me. *P* Does the
ape or the tiger in me prevent my being?

Not so, for I am ape and tiger, I know, and still I am myself. Because the river flowed through the jungle, with crocodile and poisonous filth, shall it not water the plain and push on to the unknown? Because it must travel through strange and savage places, must it be cut off at the source? *P* I am all these beasts, I am all these shameful things, each in its hour. Within my body at this moment is the whole sequence of creation, from the start up to this moment. And every pulse of the sequence still beats in me. And at times, I am scarcely more than the amœba. And at times, I am a marsh beast, a clammy lizard. And at times I am a jungle beast with a cat's cry and a cat's lust. And at times I am a lurking, chattering ape, and at times a craven dog. *P* But none of these do contradict that I am I. For none of these *shall* contradict that I am I. For I am I, pushing on into the unknown. And all that is behind me, is of me. But nothing that is behind me, shall retain me. And nothing that I am, shall detain me. And nothing that I want to be shall make me deny that which in truth and in the proper hour, I am. For if I would be a God; yea, and if I become God, I am still at the same moment the ape and the tiger. The stream that flows into Paradise is flowing unbroken through the jungle and the plain, through filth and bloodiness and the greasy wharves of Commerce: it only arrives at Paradise, whilst {Paradise whilst *TS*} flowing in one continuous stream through all that is behind, existing at the same moment in all, but with its tip advancing into Paradise. *P* My care is, that none shall bar my tip from pushing on into paradise. {Paradise. *TS*} Not if commerce builds me round as if I were a dock, will I submit. The dock shall be washed away, I will go on, for I must go. *P* But I say, I am the river, and the greasy wharves are mine, are me, and the marshes where the beasts wallow and crawl, and the jungle where my water is red with cruel blood. I, who am all this at this moment, at this same moment beat with my waves at the gates of Paradise. *MS* world gleamed ... knowledge, she was transfigured within the bright world of complete transfiguration. She could ... not this limited ... nor this base purpose ... self-assertion. She was pushed with the growing tip onto the verge of Paradise. She felt the gleam of Paradise in the quivering cambium. She saw the light of Paradise in the nucleus under her slide. *TSR*

409:8   in the new ... new world, *TSR*] taking count of itself. *MS*

409:10 yet *TSR*] *Om. MS*

409:19 to depart *TSR*] for action *MS*

409:20 gone. She ... own transfiguration. *TSR*] out in the throng of them, oblivious, oblivious, active. She wanted to be active. *MS*

409:21 the new life, the reality *E1*] anything new—anything new *MS*

409:25 Skrebensky—] ~, *TS*

409:26 beginning *E1*] activity *MS*

409:32 frightened *TSR*] puzzled *MS*

409:34 She *TSR*] He had the knack. She *MS*

409:34 the chill ... new world. *TSR*] how alien he was to her. This was her beloved Anton. *MS*

409:37 white *TSR*] cream *MS*

409:38 and gleam ... unknown upon *TSR*] of college about *MS*

410:3   moment,] ~ *TS*

410:6   knew *TSR*] felt *MS*

410:7   It was ... had met *TSR*] The blood-relationship was the same, perhaps, but they were on opposite sides in the battle *MS*

410:10 were enemies ... a truce *TSR*]

would never be able to get near to each other *MS*

410:11 being *TSR*] intention *MS*

410:21 decision, also .. animal darkness. *TSR*] decision. *MS*

410:25 She could ... animal desire. *TSR*] *Om. MS*

410:27 This *TSR*] What *MS*

410:27 her. *Ed.*] ~? *MS*

410:28 hopeless fixity *E1*] tragic helplessness *MS* mechanical fixity *TSR*

410:29 cold *TSR*] *Om. MS*

410:29 His desires were so underground *TSR*] She was not God *MS*

410:30 admit *TSR*] help *MS*

410:31 that should be nameless *TSR*] *Om. MS*

410:32 she flashed ... [410:37] admit nothing. *TSR*] her will was fixed. He was her lover. This man was her lover, he, and {he and *TS*} no other. She was brilliant, proud, flashing. He leaned towards her as if drawn towards her strong influence. She would have him. *MS*

411:2 rigidity *E1*] deadness *MS*

411:9 There's a ... horse—and *TSR*] there is good hunting—polo, and so on. I shall be able to have one or two good horses—and there will be *MS*

411:11 work—] ~, *TS*

411:12 He was ... own soul *TSR*] It all seemed so final *MS*

411:22 But that ... her road. *TSR*] *Om. MS*

411:31 gold grey] gold-grey *TS*

411:32 He burned ... caught his *TSR*] They burned, he and she, to one flame, two brands to one flame. She had a *MS*

411:37 flower] ~, *E1*

412:4 individuality? *TSR*] ~. *MS*

412:6 away.] ~? *TS*

412:9 do?" *P* It *TS*] ~?" / It *MS*

412:11 said. *P* Which *TS*] ~. / Which *MS*

412:14 timidly. *P* In *TS*] ~. / In *MS*

412:20 he took ... and they *TSR*] they linked arms and *MS*

412:21 subtle *TSR*] glad *MS*

412:23 trees] ~, *TS*

412:24 powerful *TSR*] *Om. MS*

412:24 held her ... their universe. *TSR*] with the subtle, impulsive passion, as he had kissed her when she was a girl. *MS*

412:28 said. *P* Yet it *TSR*] ~. / The thought *MS* ~. *P* The thought *TS*

412:29 not in ... one thought. *TSR*] in his mind at the same moment. His heart seemed to answer her. The understanding was perfect. *MS*

412:31 length. *P* She *TS*] ~. / She *MS*

412:33 asked. *P* The *TS*] ~. / The *MS*

412:34 directness *TSR*] naïve directness *MS*

412:34 overcame him, submerged *TSR*] staggered *MS*

412:35 darkness travelled massively along *TSR*] wind blew over the full, mysterious river *MS*

412:36 said, as ... of everything." *P* She *TSR*] said. / She *MS* said. *P* She *TS*

412:39 always." *P* The dark ... in him. *TSR*] always." / His pride came up strong. *MS* always." *P* His ... strong. *TS*

412:40 himself. He must ... of himself *TSR*] himself. She wanted him *MS*

413:2 on *TSR*] *Om. MS*

413:6 wondering that ... was inhabited *TSR*] interested *MS*

413:8 said. *P* Then *TSR*] said, satisfied. *P* She loved him for the saying. / Then *MS* said, satisfied. *P* She ... saying. *P* Then *TS*

413:9 in a low, vibrating voice *TSR*] *Om. MS*

413:12 it is ... are here *TSR*] like the air *MS*

413:13 massive and fluid with *TSR*] to bristle with unknown *MS*

413:15 They worship ... the darkness. *TSR*] Their Gods {gods *TS*} are all fear, really. *MS*

413:24 night, heavy with fecundity *TSR*] earth, a heavy, moist quickness *MS*

413:26 desire, seemed ... to pass. *TSR*] desire. *MS*

413:28 walked *TSR*] walked in *MS*

413:29 massive *TSR*] hidden *MS*

413:29 rich and *TSR*] drawn *MS*

413:30 vibrating with a low, profound *TSR*] plucked into *MS*

413:31 The deep ... the darkness ... not heard. *E1*] *Om. MS* The ... the heavy darkness ... heard. *TSR*

413:37 you." *P* He *TS*] ~." / He *MS*

414:8 responded *E1*] replied *MS*

414:9 completely *E1*] spontaneously *MS*

414:14 were *TSR*] were laved in *MS*

414:14 dark fecundity *TSR*] bath *MS*

414:17 stood *TSR*] stood enveloped *MS*

414:18 knitted them *TSR*] blotted them out *MS*

414:19 fluid *TSR*] *Om. MS*

414:20 nucleolating of the fecund darkness *TSR*] drenching, complete torrent *MS*

414:21 vessel *E1*] vessel of light *MS* *Om. TSR*

414:21 of *E1*] of the *MS*

414:22 satisfaction *E1*] bliss *MS*

414:23 enjoying *E1*] enfolded in *MS*

414:23 given to *TSR*] taking *MS*

414:33 existed in *E1*] looked at *MS*

414:39 said to herself, *E1*] said *MS* said, *TS*

414:39 dark,] ~ *E1*

415:1 unlimited *E1*] great, un-

mitigated, sensual *MS* great, *TSR*

415:3 nothing.] just nothing. *TSC see notes*

415:5 trick played *TSR*] gewgaw *MS*

415:5 only dummies exposed *TSR*] gewgaws *MS*

415:6 wooden *TSR*] foolish *MS*

415:8 that contained *TSR*] running, bearing *MS*

415:10 homogeneous *E1*] *Om. MS*

415:11 they were ... creatures. She ... his clothes. *E1*] as if one dressed up a cat in a paper suit. *MS* they ... creatures of darkness. She ... clothes. *TSR*

415:16 animal *TSR*] beast *MS*

415:16 on her ... half-smile] *Om. TS*

415:19 pale *TSR*] prinking *MS*

415:20 gleaming. "You subdued beast *E1*] chuckling. "Wolves *MS* chuckling. "You darknesses *TSR*

415:20 you primeval ... social mechanism *TSR*] jungle beasts dressed up in a masquerade of united endeavour to be false *MS*

415:22 subconsciousness *Ed.*] sub-consciousness *MS*

415:23 mocking *TSR*] jeering *MS*

415:23 daylight *TSR*] consciousness *MS*

415:27 fertile *E1*] omnipotent *MS*

415:27 exist *TSR*] were conceived *MS*

415:27 potential *E1*] womb of *MS*

415:27 darkness.—What *TSR*] darkness. Yah—what *MS* darkness. What *E1*

415:28 her soul asked of *TSR*] she asked *MS*

415:29 are, *TSR*] ~ *MS*

415:30 lurking, blood-sniffing *TSR*] two legged, hairy *MS* two-legged, hairy *TS*

415:33 allow it *E1*] give it credence *MS*

415:34 Her soul *TSR*] She *MS*

415:34 mocked *E1*] was amused *MS*

416:1 there was ... vital self *TSR*] he was with her *MS*

416:1 her college] the college *TS*

416:2 the other darkness, Skrebensky, *TSR*] he *MS* the outer darkness, Skrebensky *E1*

416:3 attentive *TSR*] prowling *MS*

416:4 leopard *TSR*] wild panther *MS*

416:8 all this] all the *TS*

416:9 no-one *Ed.*] no one *MS*

416:11 shaken kaleidoscope ... of people *TSR*] spectacle to him, as a monkey may watch the chattering schools of birds in the jungle *MS*

416:14 incomprehensible *E1*] acrobatic *MS*

416:14 keepers *TSR*] monkeys *MS*

416:15 non-existent *TSR*] unnecessary *MS*

416:18 puppets ... and rag for the performance! *E1*] animals! Such a side-splitting, ridiculous menagerie. *MS* puppets ... and rag! *TSR*

416:20 He watched the citizen *TSR*] Look at this professor *MS*

416:20 model, saw the *TSR*] model. Look at his *MS*

416:21 the desire ... ugly, mechanical. *TSR*] his desire to hide them, to deny, by the make of his trousers, that they are there at all. Goat's legs—but goats {goat's *TS*} legs stiffened and deformed and made ridiculous, ugly! Pah! The menagerie is filthy. *MS*

416:28 he *E1*] and he *MS*

416:34 in a public-house ... for words. *E1*] and talk with country people in a public house. *MS* in a public house ... for words. *TSR*

416:36 voluptuous richness *TSR*] sufficiency *MS*

416:36 the fecundity ... universal night he ... puppet-shapes ... from them *Ed.*] pleasure in his own being *MS* the fecundity ... universal darkness he ... puppet-shapes {puppet shapes *E1*} ... them *TSR*

417:1 motor-car ... dog-cart *TSR*] taxi-cab *MS*

417:2 and *E1*] and the driver and *MS* *Om. TSR*

417:5 knowing, subconsciously,] ~ ~ *TS*

417:5 last *TSR*] other *MS*

417:5 to be ... of creation *E1*] their riches to come *MS* to be ... of darkness *TSR*

417:8 her family *TSR*] them *MS*

417:8 Strange,] ~ *E1*

417:11 warm, voluptuous *TSR*] *Om. MS*

417:11 presence *E1*] of other people *MS*

417:12 always quivering ... puppet-form ... and drowse in the sun. *Ed.*] like a jungle, and the performing tricks were clumsily done by them. They did not take naturally to civic being. *MS* always ... puppet-form {puppet form *E1*} ... and bask in {and drowse in *E1*} the sun. *TSR*

417:15 sense *TSR*] great sense *MS*

417:15 among] amongst *TS*

417:15 all, of ... And she *TSR*] all. And yet Ursula *MS*

417:17 that,] ~ *TS*

417:19 mad *E1*] blind mad *MS*

417:22 for the time *TSR*] *Om. MS*

417:22 complete and final *E1*] deep and thorough and triumphant *MS* deep and final *TSR*

417:23 She admitted ... and bliss. *TSR*] *Om. MS*

417:27 an *TSR*] like *MS*

417:28 exist, if the time passed unfulfilled. *E1*] exist. This feeling of not-existing, of grey, corpse-like deadness, was a cold suffering, absolute, deathly. *MS* exist. This ... not existing ... absolute, deadly. *TS* exist, if the time passed unfulfilled. This ... not-existing ... was annihilation, absolute and deadly. *TSR*

417:29 came to ... superb consummation *TSR*] took her one evening under an oak-tree *MS*

417:30 heavy *TSR*] boisterous *MS*

417:30 had come ... lane towards *TSR*] were walking back to *MS*

417:31 were at *TSR*] had come to *MS*

417:32 there was ... darkness beneath. *TSR*] the next step was to take. *MS*

417:34 darkness *TSR*] open darkness *MS*

417:34 space *TSR*] field *MS*

417:36 far-off *TSR*] *Om. MS*

417:36 tiny *TSR*] *Om. MS*

417:37 lights] light *E1*

417:39 glow *E1*] flare *MS*

417:40 It was like ... Two quivering, *TSR*] Like two *MS*

418:3 machine glimmer] machine-glimmer *E1*

418:3 They could ... could not. *TSR*] *Om. MS*

418:12 brand *TSR*] rush *MS*

418:13 waited for *TSR*] received *MS*

418:14 agony ... agony *TSR*] unhappiness ... unhappiness *MS*

418:16 vibration that *E1*] vibrating being that *MS*

418:17 passed away ... of immortality. *TSR*] was hurt, she was afraid, she was broken, she was satisfied. The man and she had met, finally. *MS*

418:21 ashamed—] ~,— *TS*

418:22 they had ... had received another nature. She ... leapt together. *E1*] the man. She knew herself, the woman. What more? *MS* they ... had become immortal. She ... to-

gether. *TSR*

418:26 sure and ... opinion of *TSR*] hard against all opinion from *MS*

418:33 knew *E1*] inhabited *MS*

418:34 separate *E1*] hard *MS*

418:38 let *TSR*] ignored it, let *MS*

418:40 implicated *E1*] taken up *MS*

419:4 secondary *E1*] subordinate *MS*

419:5 as a ... under-life *TSR*] acquiescent *MS*

419:7 powerful, that ... the other. *TSR*] vital, that she could let the other be. *MS*

419:8 flowering, and remote *TSR*] acquiescent, passive, because her being was so vital and confident in its activity *MS*

419:10 She had lunch *TSR*] Every lunch she had *MS*

419:12 But *TSR*] In fact *MS*

419:14 absolute and ... calm. The *TSR*] confidently happy and perfectly secure. The supreme *MS*

419:15 consummate being *TSR*] existence *MS*

419:15 entirely *TSR*] ridiculously *MS*

419:16 free *TSR*] really free *MS*

419:21 the actual facts *TSR*] all such material considerations *MS*

419:22 wistfully *TSR*] ruefully *MS*

419:23 deeper *TSR*] purer *MS*

419:23 make public *TSR*] legalise *MS*

419:25 nullified *TSR*] bullied *MS*

419:25 him, *TS*] ~ *MS*

419:25 moment *TS*] ~, *MS*

419:26 dissociated *TSR*] free *MS*

419:28 diffident and abstract *TSR*] indifferent to her *MS*

419:28 part of that complication of *TSR*] touched by that *MS*

419:29 his under-life *TSR*] he *MS*

419:30 One's *TSR*] One *MS*

419:30 almost a material symbol *E1*] as good as any other social wife *MS* almost an abstraction, a symbol *TSR*

419:32 be, she ... contained them. *TSR*] be. *MS*

419:36 think I ... brow clouded *TSR*] want to marry you and live in a house with you and have a servant," she said, plainly *MS*

419:38 "Why not ... her violently. *TSR*] *Om. MS*

420:2 "Have I ... not satisfied. *TSR*] "No," she said. "I never thought of *marrying* you." *P* It piqued his vanity. *MS*

420:4 asked, "Why ... marry me?" *TSR*] asked. *MS* asked, "why ... me?" *E1*

420:5 don't want ... other people *TSR*] hate married people living in houses *MS*

420:5 want to be like this *E1*] just want to love you, now {you now *TS*} *MS* want to be on my own *TSR*

420:7 said. *P* He *TS*] ~. / He *MS*

420:8 would rather *TSR*] was glad *MS*

420:10 complete enjoyment *E1*] becoming quite free *MS* complete fulfilment *TSR*

420:13 wedding-ring *TS*] wedding ring *MS*

420:15 They had revoked altogether ... mortal world *E1*] Everything they did seemed perfectly right and good *MS* They had surpassed altogether ... world *TSR*

420:17 free *TSR*] right *MS*

420:17 beyond all ... mortal conditions. *TSR*] of their own being beyond all question. *MS*

420:19 therefore nothing ... civilly ignored *TSR*] and they alone *MS*

420:21 were the sensuous aristocrats ... of the senses. *E1*] went like the elect glancing over their heritage, with a warm, bright glance of supreme wealth. *MS*

were the supreme aristocrats ... of immortality. *TSR*

420:26 *Oui Monsieur le baron Ed.*] Oui Monsieur le baron *MS* Oui, Monsieur le baron *TS Oui, Monsieur le baron TSR*

420:26 curtsey] curtesy *E1*

420:28 as *TSR*] more or less as *MS*

420:29 immediately *TSR*] very shortly *MS*

420:32 living *E1*] real *MS*

420:33 were *TSR*] were elect *MS*

420:33 absolute ... all limitation *E1*] elect beyond all others *MS* absolute ... all condition *TSR*

420:36 they themselves ... to them *TSR*] the amazing glamour continued as reality, the other meagre reality was gone *MS*

420:37 quite *TSR*] perfectly *MS*

420:37 money, but ... very extravagant. *TSR*] money. *MS*

420:39 it was ... irritation of *TSR*] he was only annoyed at *MS*

421:20 sluggish *TSR*] foolish *MS*

421:21 went *TSR*] fled *MS*

421:25 bathed, his ... electric light *TSR*] sat in the white bath, ducking his head, the electric light above *MS*

421:26 out of *TSR*] up in *MS*

421:28 slender] ~, *TS*

421:28 to her *TSR*] she thought *MS*

421:37 passionate] perfect *E1*

421:38 round his loins,] *Om. E1*

422:3 midday, close ... one sleep. *Ed.*] mid-day. *MS* mid-day, close ... sleep. *TSR*

422:4 ever-changing reality *TSR*] ever-perfect bliss *MS*

422:5 They alone ... lower sphere. *TSR*] Prince and princess of the whole realm of glamour they were. *MS*

422:11 queen] quite *TS*

422:13 she had ... she had. *TSR*] it would do her homage if she turned to it. *MS*

422:15 ever-changing reality *TSR*]
lordly delight *MS*

422:15 All the ... [422:18] were often
in ... sitting-room ... hours'
time, they ... [422:26] of Paris.
Ed.] Whatever they did was just
part of the fabric, the whole of
which was so vivid and brilliant
that no part stood out. Suddenly it occurred to them, they
would like to go to Paris. So
within an hour's time they were
driving to Charing Cross. They
spent five days in Paris, and
were as happy as ever there.
Paris, London— {London,—
TS} what did the place matter?
Place was accidental. They
themselves were the reality,
wherever they were. *MS* All
... were most of the time in
{were often in *E1*} ... sitting
room {sitting-room *E1*} ...
hours time, they {hours' time
they *E1*} ... Paris. *TSR*

422:28 her desire for *E1*] *Om. MS* the
dullness of *TSR*

422:30 on] upon *TS*

422:31 had a ... death: not afraid *TSR*]
was jealous: not *MS* had ...
death; not afraid *E1*

422:32 leave *TSR*] ignore *MS*

422:33 She did not want him. *TSR*]
Om. MS

422:35 took her away from him. *TSR*]
affected her. *MS*

422:35 something she ... and wanted.
E1] a sense of permanency. *MS*
something she had not, and
wanted. *TSR*

422:36 now the reality: this *TSR*] permanent. This *MS* now the
reality; this *E1*

422:37 which *TSR*] this *MS*

422:38 heard any denial *TSR*]
movement *MS*

422:38 stability, its splendid absoluteness. *TSR*] stability. *MS*

422:40 run by itself *TSR*] revert from
Skrebensky *MS*

423:1 deadly *TSR*] twinge of *MS*

423:1 death towards which ...
wandering *E1*] unsubstantiabi-
lity of their state *MS* death in
which ... wandering *TSR*

423:3 hopeless warning *TSR*] yearning *MS*

423:4 sinking into apathy, hopelessness *TSR*] slumber become
half conscious within her *MS*

423:12 on Sunday evening *E1*] *Om.*
MS

423:13 cold *TSR*] *Om. MS*

423:13 soaked into *TSR*] laid its grip
on *MS*

423:14 cold *TSR*] *Om. MS*

423:15 stark, *TS*] ~ *MS*

423:15 ashen sterility ... surrounded
TSR] sordidness ... in its grip
MS

423:17 rights? *TS*] ~. *MS*

423:17 this *E1*] this cold *MS*

423:19 mad.] ~? *E1*

423:20 tram-car *TS*] tram car *MS*

423:20 ashen-grey *TSR*] sordid *MS*

423:21 lived ... in *TSR*] driven ...
through *MS*

423:23 an ashen-dry ... spectre-like
TSR] a great world of ash, dead
walls and dead machine-traffic
and sordid, mechanical *MS*

423:25 only ash ... stood rigid, *TSR*]
buried in ash, *MS*

423:26 a rattle ... and sterile. *TSR*]
dry as dead bones, and as cold.
MS

423:27 the sunshine ... were unnatural ... the ash ... the sinister gleam of decomposition.
E1] dead ash settled down
instead of sunshine, upon the
town, on the ashen-bodied
people, as if cold ash settled
upon him himself, slowly
putting out his fires. *MS* the
sunshine ... were the un-

natural ... the extinct ash ... the gleam of decomposition. *TSR*

423:34 Her absence ... his being. *E1*] *Om. MS*

423:35 His face ... awful misery ... a letter. *E1*] Then he went into the writing room and wrote her a long, close letter, very close and reasoned. *MS* His ... awful deathliness ... letter. *TSR*

424:3 know just everybody *E1*] have a place among the best people *MS* mix with just everybody *TSR*

424:5 you— —] ~—— *E1*

424:6 on, *TSR*] on and on, *MS*

424:6 disposing of ... with her! *E1*] as if obsessed. *MS*

424:7 Yet all ... or connection *TSR*] He was demented, and this was his mania *MS*

424:10 extinct *TSR*] hollow *MS*

424:11 being of ... spectre, divorced from ... flat shape. *E1*] content had fallen out of him. He was not a complete, filled thing any more, but just an outline, a rim. *MS* being ... spectre, utterly cut off from ... shape. *TSR*

424:15 cypher *Ed.*] outline *MS* flat sterility *TSR* cipher *E1*

424:16 theatre:] ~; *E1*

424:16 cold surface of consciousness, *TSR*] recipient surface *MS*

424:17 there was nothing behind it, *TSR*] but he felt nothing, *MS*

424:19 registering *E1*] motion *MS*

424:21 permutations of known quantities *E1*] fronts, things in the flat *MS*

424:23 a dead shape mental arrangement, without ... being. *E1*] made in the flat, without further existence. *MS* a dead shape in the flat, without ... being. *TSR*

424:24 Much of *TSR*] All *MS*

424:24 Then he ... Their activities ... they engaged his negative horror. *E1*] He talked, he laughed, but it was all mere noise-making, like tapping on cardboard. There was nothing behind it. There was nothing at all, except the flat figure of himself. *MS* Then he ... Their existence ... they cancelled his negative horror. *TSR*

424:27 only became *TSR*] was only *MS*

424:27 and he *TSR*] and *MS*

424:28 he was ... opposite of what ... aërial world. *TSR*] just the opposite took place. He was a warm, vague, nebulous mass in a warm, vague whole. *MS* he was ... opposite to what ... aerial world. *E1*

424:30 in a diffuse *TSR*] vaguely in a maudlin, *MS*

424:31 a rosy glow *E1*] an amiable fog *MS* an rosy glow *TSR*

424:31 the glow ... glow ... glow *TSR*] the fog ... fog ... fog *MS*

424:33 songs *TSR*] maudlin songs *MS*

424:37 response *E1*] feeling *MS*

425:10 fall in love with *TSR*] be after *MS*

425:23 was when, *E1*] ~, ~ *MS*

425:25 alone; *Ed.*] ~, *MS*

425:26 plum-trees *E1*] plum trees *MS*

425:31 dressing *TSC*] dress *MS*

425:40 lovely." *P A TS*] ~." / A *MS*

426:1 anger *TSR*] wrath *MS*

426:5 silver, *TSR*] the silver blossom, *MS* silver *E1*

426:10 whispered] ~, *E1*

426:11 goodnight. *P* And *Ed.*] goodnight. / ~ *MS* good-night. *P* ~ *TS*

426:24 a constraint *TS*] an constraint *MS*

426:30 fail *TSR*] be plucked *MS*

426:32 England,] ~ *TS*

426:34 Oh in India,] ~, ~ ~ *TS*

426:38 I hate *TSR*] a false *MS*
426:39 became angry *TSR*] hated *MS*
426:39 this, he … know why. *TSR*] this. *MS*
427:1 things. It … attacking him. *TSR*] the existing State. *MS*
427:3 mean; *TSR*] ~, *MS* ~? *E1*
427:3 hostile, "why do you hate *TSR*] hostile, "by a false *MS* hostile. "Why do you hate *E1*
427:5 Only the … degenerate races are democratic. *E1*] Every pursy little man, as soon as he gets a bit of money, shoving himself forward and becoming a voice, putting his finger in the pie, no matter what voice of a fool he's got, nor what dirty finger. *MS* Only … degenerate people are democratic. *TSR*
427:9 rights,] ~ *TS*
427:11 acquiescing in … reprehensible advantage *TSR*] getting something he had no right to *MS*
427:17 money-brains;] ~, *TS*
427:21 money-interest] money interest *TS*
427:22 amount of … hate them. *TSR*] social position as we have: the same income. I hate it. *MS*
427:23 money-basis] money basis *TS*
427:24 dirt *TSR*] Circe's swine *MS*
427:27 against her *TSR*] cornered, helpless *MS*
427:31 me!] ~? *TS*
427:35 fear *TSR*] tense as a cornered rat *MS*
427:36 simpler than *E1*] different from *MS*
427:37 you'll feel … righteous. What … governing. Your … are here? *TSR*] all the time trying to make them like us. It's such a childish dodge, after all. If you don't believe in being as we are, how can you go and make the Indians like us, and feel you are

fulfilling a high mission in doing it. *MS* you'll … righteous? What … governing? Your … here! *E1*
428:3 righteous *TSR*] as if I were fulfilling a high mission *MS*
428:6 do you … own mind?" *TSR*] high mission do you think *you* are fulfilling?" he asked her, contemptuously. *MS*
428:8 Yes I … she cried. *TSR*] I don't feel I am fulfilling anything," she cried, "neither will *you* fulfil me." *MS*
428:11 he kept flying. *TSR*] was flying above them. *MS*
428:14 helplessness *TSR*] non-existence *MS*
428:27 round *TSR*] sniffing round *MS*
428:30 weeks] week *TS*
428:38 Oh] oh *TS*
429:7 desire for … had from *TSR*] pity for *MS*
429:9 contact,] ~ *TS*
429:9 deepened, *TSR*] deepened, strengthened, *MS*
429:10 in his own strength *TSR*] *Om. MS*
429:12 a few *E1*] three *MS*
429:15 low *TSR*] charming *MS*
429:21 on] in *TS*
429:23 a high, *E1*] a *MS*
429:30 water-meadows *Ed.*] water meadows *MS*
429:34 baring] bearing *TS*
429:35 with superb … of being, *TSR*] *Om. MS*
430:1 hasty *TSR*] potent *MS*
430:3 uglily. And] ~. *P* And *TS*
430:3 downward] downwards *TS*
430:9 and away *TSR*] *Om. MS*
430:9 patterned *TSR*] sunken *MS*
430:10 shortsighted the … to the … so terrifying in … such pettiness in … activity. *E1*] blind, such a pathetic energy of blindness. Again she had to cry. *MS* shortsighted the … to peer at

the ... so shortsighted in ... such shortsightedness in ... activity. *TSR*
430:14 be,] ~ *TS*
430:15 descend,] ~ *TS*
430:17 love *TSR*] take *MS*
430:19 distasteful *E1*] disgusting *MS*
430:20 downs. Up] ~, up *TS*
430:21 half past *Ed.*] half-past *MS*
430:27 out, at ... on land. *TSR*] out. *MS*
430:29 all her] her *TS*
430:34 dew-pond *TS*] dew pond *MS*
430:38 sufferance *TS*] suffrance *MS*
431:4 earth-work] earthwork *E1*
431:8 darkly *TSR*] stood erect *MS*
431:9 stood *E1*] *Om. MS*
431:16 waves,] wave , *E1*
431:25 distant,] ~ *TS*
431:26 pine trees] pine-trees *E1*
431:32 asked. P After *TS*] ~. / After *MS*
431:34 so beautiful *TSR*] England *MS*
431:35 It was ... so perfect, and so unsullied. *E1*] She meant the land was England. *MS* It was ... so dear, and so unlovely in its activity. *TSR*
431:36 He too *TSR*] Then he *MS*
431:37 fuming with dirty *TSR*] belching *MS*
432:2 apart, overcome by a cruel *E1*] apart. He knew his own *MS*
432:4 Gradually,] ~ *TS*
432:4 yet,] ~ *TS*
432:20 comfort. P She *TS*] ~. / She *MS*
432:23 said. P A *TS*] ~. / A *MS*
432:26 her. P Her *TS*] ~. / Her *MS*
432:34 asked. P The *TS*] ~. / The *MS*
432:38 her. P His *TS*] ~. / His *MS*
433:2 curious] ~, *TS*
433:6 up. P It *TS*] ~. / It *MS*
433:7 nerves,] ~ *TS*
433:9 with *TS*] but *MS*
433:9 contorted,] ~ *E1*
433:14 half sovereign] half-sovereign *E1*

433:15 silk *E1*] *Om. MS*
433:21 Don't!] ~. *TS*
433:22 cruelly, coldly defaced *E1*] deeply, utterly ashamed *MS* deeply, coldly ashamed *TSR*
433:27 uncertain *E1*] tottering *MS*
433:38 showing. P Again *Ed.*] ~. / Again *MS* ~. Again *TS*
433:40 Forty] ~, *E1*
433:40 said. P He *TS*] ~. / He *MS*
434:4 slight *TSR*] little involuntary shaking *MS*
434:16 really." P He *TS*] ~." / He *MS*
434:20 you,] ~ *TS*
434:20 Tony?" P Some *TS*] ~?" / Some *MS*
434:21 against her *TSR*] *Om. MS*
434:31 hers,] ~ *E1*
434:40 hand, then gradually relaxed. *E1*] hand. *MS*
435:10 love? *TSR*] ~, *MS*
435:11 motion. P He *TS*] ~. / He *MS*
435:16 her. P But *Ed.*] ~. / But *MS* ~. But *TS*
435:17 yet,] ~ *TS*
435:19 time,] ~ *TS*
435:21 coming. P After *TS*] ~. / After *MS*
435:24 Corner." P The *TS*] ~." / The *MS*
435:33 ebbing *E1*] glancing *MS*
435:37 so?" P She *TS*] ~?" / She *MS*
436:2 say,] ~ *TS*
436:9 world." P His *TS*] ~." / His *MS*
436:14 nor] nor in *TS*
436:17 duskly] duskily *E1*
436:18 me." P And *TS*] ~." / And *MS*
436:27 remote *E1*] restrained *MS*
436:34 engaged." P She *TS*] ~." / She *MS*
436:38 hôtel." P Her heart was hardened *Ed.*] hôtel." / She knew what he meant *MS* hotel." P She ... meant *TS* hotel." P Her ... hardened *E1*
437:20 *persiennes TSR*] persiennes *MS*
437:27 England *E1*] bonds *MS*

437:29 "O] "O *TS*
437:29 O'-O'-O' Giovann'—!" *P* And
　　　　Ed.] O'-O'-O' Giovann'—!" /
　　　　And　　*MS*　　O'-O'-O'-
　　　　Giovann'—!" *P* And *TS*
437:30 new country *E1*] foreign
　　　　country *MS*
437:35 further *TSR*] rarer *MS*
437:38 timidly: *MS*, *E1*] ~; *TS*
438:2 I." *P* There *TS*] ~." / There
　　　　MS
438:4 asked. *P* She *TS*] ~. / She *MS*
438:5 him,] ~ *TS*
438:7 said. *P* But *TS*] ~. / But *MS*
438:17 incomprehensible　　*TSR*]
　　　　incomprehensive *MS*
438:19 genially. *P* A *Ed.*] ~. / A *MS* ~.
　　　　A *TS*
438:22 explained. *P* The *TS*] ~. / The
　　　　MS
438:26 half-domesticated wild *TSR*]
　　　　trained *MS*
438:27 sharp-sighted　　*E1*]　　short-
　　　　sighted *MS*
438:31 chill *TSR*] weary *MS*
438:35 over] ~, *TS*
438:36 himself] ~, *TS*
438:39 reserve. He … now. He *E1*]
　　　　reserve, yet he *MS* reserve. But
　　　　he seemed known to her,
　　　　known. He *TSR*
438:39 roused] aroused *TS*
438:40 fecundity *E1*] fear *MS*
438:40 added up, finished. She *E1*] set
　　　　in her midst, she *MS* limited,
　　　　finite. She *TSR*
439:3 rich fear … the unknown *E1*]
　　　　potent fear, the sense of jeop-
　　　　ardy *MS*
439:5 quiet *E1*] warm *MS*
439:5 complete *E1*] drenched *MS*
439:6 finished *E1*] consummated *MS*
439:16 no more attractive *E1*] more
　　　　distasteful *MS*
439:32 Grammar] *Om. TS*
439:32 do? *TS*] ~. *MS*
439:35 Skrebensky amid *E1*] *Om. MS*
440:11 me?" *P* And *TS*] ~?" / And *MS*

440:12 cruel] angry *TS*
440:18 Dorothy] ~, *TS*
440:31 strong *E1*] spiritual *MS*
440:31 understanding *TSR*]
　　　　abstractness　　*MS*　　abstrac-
　　　　tedness *TS*
440:32 dignity *E1*] warmth *MS*
440:33 working *TSR*] common *MS*
440:33 men, and … go—" *P* Dorothy
　　　　Ed.] men." / Dorothy *MS*
　　　　men." *P* Dorothy *TS* men, and
　　　　… jolly, red … would give you
　　　　a really reckless time—" *P*
　　　　Dorothy *TSR* men, and …
　　　　jolly, reckless … could really
　　　　let go——" *P* Dorothy *E1*
440:38 men?" *P* Ursula *TS*] ~?" /
　　　　Ursula *MS*
441:2 badly." *P* So *TS*] ~." / So *MS*
441:3 herself,] ~ *TS*
441:8 party *E1*] party of relatives *MS*
441:10 given *E1*] given really *MS*
441:10 pretensions *E1*] instinct *MS*
441:13 twenty eighth *Ed.*] twenty-
　　　　eighth *MS*
441:18 two smaller writing-rooms *E1*]
　　　　a small breakfast or writing
　　　　room *MS*
441:24 homogeneous　　*E1*]　　hetero-
　　　　geneous *MS*
441:27 unconventional *E1*] anarchistic
　　　　MS
441:40 his] her *TS*
442:4 grey thorn-bushes *TSR*]
　　　　grey-thorn bushes *MS* grey
　　　　thorn bushes *TS*
442:17 He seemed revenged. *TSR*]
　　　　Om. MS
442:20 supreme fulfilment *E1*] endless
　　　　voluptuousness *MS* supreme
　　　　voluptuousness *TSR*
442:26 it." *P* She *TS*] ~." / She *MS*
442:33 cotton] *Om. TSC*
443:12 continent *E1*] Continent *MS*
443:15 foreshore *TS*] fore-shore *MS*
443:16 *rendez-vous Ed.*] rendez-vous
　　　　MS rendezvous *TS*
443:22 attractive *E1*] lovable *MS*

443:22 soul *E1*] arms *MS*
443:22 its *E1*] their *MS*
443:30 head] ~, *TS*
443:34 sea-ward] seaward *TS*
443:40 wonderful!" *P* And *TS*] ~!" /
And *MS*
444:2 white] *Om. TS*
444:9 rushed *E1*] washed *MS*
444:13 to him *TSR*] *Om. MS*
444:18 walk *TSR*] drop *MS* drop, *TS*
444:18 in to] into *TS*
444:24 know." *P* And *TS*] ~." / And
MS
444:27 there,] ~ *E1*
444:28 destruction *E1*] an octopus *MS*
444:37 sand-hills] sandhills *TS*
445:5 hair] ~, *TS*
445:8 no] and no *TS*
445:18 then,] ~ *TS*
445:28 love *E1*] fear *MS*
445:31 sea grass *Ed.*] sea-grass *MS*
445:33 gradually, *E1*] gradually, gradually, *MS*
445:37 down,] ~ *TS*
446:1 trivial talk … were separate *E1*]
abstract civilities {civilities,
TS} that the situation required
MS
446:2 of what was between them *E1*]
to each other *MS*
446:3 They were … each other. *E1*]
Om. MS
446:5 There were several guests *E1*]
They were several *MS*
446:8 door,] ~ *TS*
446:11 me? *TS*] ~. *MS*
446:18 same] ~, *TS*
446:19 has] had *E1*
446:19 failure." *P* He *TS*] ~." / He
MS
446:23 down. *P* He *TS*] ~. / He *MS*
446:24 away, afraid to hear more. *TSR*]
sullenly away. *MS*
446:26 waiting *E1*] anxious *MS*
446:28 pleasant banality *E1*] levity, a
gaiety *MS*
446:30 amiable and companionable
E1] gay and relieved *MS*

446:31 nice *E1*] good *MS*
446:31 had *E1*] had ever *MS*
446:31 a simple *E1*] a wonderful *MS*
446:32 How *E1*] How amazingly *MS*
446:33 him!] ~. *TS*
446:33 false *E1*] horrible *MS*
446:33 she been forcing on him *E1*]
been between them *MS*
446:35 night,] ~ *TS*
447:2 anguish *E1*] terror *MS*
447:3 sit up very late *E1*] begin rather
late to drink *MS*
447:3 in company *E1*] heavily *MS*
excitedly *TSR*
447:4 morning:] ~; *E1*
447:5 shocked *E1*] terrified *MS*
447:7 daytime *TS*] day-time *MS*
447:8 trivial present … and satisfying
E1] moment in refuge from the
darkness, the space *MS*
447:10 and felt normal and fulfilled
E1] driven by the fear behind
him *MS*
447:11 trivial *E1*] delightful *MS*
447:13 him upon *E1*] him, about *MS*
him about *TS*
447:17 marry,] ~ *TS*
447:18 for] of *TS*
447:19 Colonel's *TS*] colonel's *MS*
447:22 anyone *TS*] any one *MS*
448:1 XVI *TSR*] XII *MS*
448:9 inert *TSR*] inert as a dead
flower *MS*
448:19 She let … to rest.] *Om. TS*
448:26 own nullity *E1*] slavery *MS*
448:29 as a good wife to *E1*] in the
flesh, with *MS*
448:29 self *E1*] life *MS*
448:31 body *E1*] flesh *MS*
449:3 She would … the ideal. *E1*]
Om. MS
449:25 for me would be] would be for
me *TS*
449:25 my *E1*] my conceited *MS*
449:36 life—.] ~—— *TS*
450:23 house] houses *TS*
450:24 scarlet *E1*] in scarlet *MS*
450:35 wood,] ~ *TS*

450:36 tree-trunks *Ed.*] tree trunks *MS*
451:1 tree-trunks *TS*] treetrunks *MS*
451:2 shut her in *TSR*] enfold her *MS*
451:2 marshalled] martialled *TS*
451:21 Some horses were *E1*] It was horses *MS*
451:33 without *TS*] as without *MS*
452:19 massive fire *E1*] ever-restrained passion *MS*
452:28 awful *E1*] beautiful *MS*
452:28 triumphing *E1*] avenging *MS*
452:31 slight] single *TS*
453:9 thunderously *TSR*] fiendishly *MS*
453:14 up against her *E1*] ready *MS*
453:20 massive body ... horse-group *E1*] horse-knot *MS*
453:23 failing *E1*] helpless *MS*
453:25 oak-tree *Ed.*] oak tree *MS*
453:30 her *E1*] the gate *MS*
453:37 realise *E1*] adjust themselves *MS*
454:6 They were ... now. *E1*] *Om. MS*
454:8 by the *TS*] by *MS*
454:38 up] *Om. TS*
455:1 burdensome!] ~. *TS*
455:7 to call] call *TS*
455:10 dull *E1*] strange *MS*
455:14 illness] ~, *TS*
455:15 knowledge. *E1*] knowledge, in the possession of which she was glad. *MS*
455:16 knew *E1*] knew herself *MS*
455:24 him? *TSR*] ~. *MS*
455:26 reality? *Ed.*] ~. *MS*
455:38 affair,] ~? *TS*
456:1 became *E1*] ~, *MS*
456:1 a compression *E1*] like a packing case *MS*
456:2 compression ... compression *E1*] packing-case ... packing-case *MS* packing case ... packing-case *TS*
456:3 world:] ~, *E1*
456:8 Oh] ~, *TS*
456:11 feeling, from her body *E1*]

Anton's being, from his world *MS*
456:12 encumbrance] encumbrances *TS*
456:16 things *TSR*] unreason *MS*
456:17 they none of them exist, *E1*] *Om. MS* they are all unrealities, *TSR*
456:18 them, but they are all unreal *E1*] it, but I do not belong to it *MS* them, but I ... belong to them *TSR*
456:19 which is an unreality *E1*] when the nut must grow *MS*
456:22 naked,] ~ *E1*
456:24 bygone winter, *E1*] fibrous shell *MS*
456:25 year that has gone by *E1*] fibrous shell discarded *MS*
456:27 root, to create ... of Time. *E1*] root. *MS* root, to create a new world. *TSR*
456:28 reality:] ~; *E1*
456:34 rift in it. *TSR*] space between it and her. *MS*
456:35 Day *E1*] world *MS*
456:35 bed *E1*] wrapping *MS*
456:38 with *E1*] into *MS*
457:7 real:] ~; *E1*
457:10 never become finally real *E1*] always been unreal *MS*
457:11 ecstasy *E1*] glamour *MS*
457:11 with her in *E1*] the object of *MS*
457:11 him for ... broken down. *E1*] him, subjectively. All the while, he was of the old world, the cathedrals, the towns, the accomplished system: he was the shell, the husk. *MS* him, subjectively ... world, the falsities, the traffic, the ... was of the shell, the husk. *TSR*
457:13 void *E1*] Rubicon *MS*
457:14 a memory, some bygone self *E1*] an old book, or a picture by Turner *MS* an old ... a childish picture *TSR*

Pounds, shillings and pence

Before decimalisation in 1971, the pound sterling (£) was the equivalent of 20 shillings (20/- or 20s). The shilling was the equivalent of 12 pence (12d).

A price could therefore have three elements: pounds, shillings and pence (£., s., d.). (The apparently anomalous d. is an abbreviation of the Latin *denarius*; but the other two terms were also originally Latin; the pound was *Libra*; the shilling *solidus*.) Such a price might be written as £1. 2s. 6d. or £1/2/6; which was spoken as 'one pound two-and-six', or 'twenty-two and six'.

Prices below a pound were written as (for instance) 19s. 6d. or 19/6, and spoken as 'nineteen and six'. Prices up to £5 were sometimes spoken in terms of shillings: so 'ninety-nine and six' was £4/19/6.

The penny was divided into two half-pence and further into four farthings, but the farthing had minimal value and was mainly a tradesman's device for indicating a price fractionally below a shilling or a pound. So 19/11¾ (nineteen and elevenpence three farthings) produced a farthing's change from a pound, this change often given as a tiny item of trade, such as a packet of pins.

The guinea was £1/1/- (one pound, one shilling) and was a professional man's unit for fees. A doctor would charge in guineas (so £5/5/- = 5 gns). Half a guinea was 10s. 6d or 10/6 (ten and six).

The coins used were originally of silver (later cupro-nickel) and copper, though gold coins for £1 (sovereign) and 10s. (half-sovereign) were still in use in Lawrence's time. The largest silver coin in common use was the half-crown (two shillings and sixpence, or 2/6). A two-shilling piece was called a florin. Shillings, sixpences and (in Lawrence's time) threepences were the smaller sizes. The copper coins were pennies, half-pence (ha'penny) and farthings.

Common slang terms for money were 'quid' for pound, 'half a crown', 'two bob' for a florin, 'bob' for a shilling, 'tanner' for sixpence, 'threepenny-bit', 'copper' for a penny or half-penny.

The pound since 1971 has had 100 pence, distinguished from the old pennies by being abbreviated to p. instead of d.

An indication of wages, and some sense of the relative value of money during the period covered by *The Rainbow*, may be gleaned from John Burnett, *Plenty and Want* (1966), chap. VI. From 1850 to 1873 there was an improvement of wages 'which more than kept up with the increase in food prices', and then a levelling-off in the rate of increase until 1914. In 1885 an unskilled labourer earned 20s. to 22s. a week and a joiner 33s. 6d. Will Brangwen as a 20-year-old apprentice (and as such, paid little) earns 20s. a week in 1882 (117:29). The MS has him thinking (see Textual apparatus for 118:15) that he ought to have £50 in cash to get married. (Thirty years later, in 1911, DHL thought he himself needed twice as much and an income of £120 p.a., see *Letters*, i. 223.) Tom Brangwen makes about £400 a year (86:29–30) from the farm, in the early years of his marriage at the end of the 1860s – compared with a clergyman's £200 p.a. – but he 'could make more', and with the increased market because of the big increase of population in Ilkeston he obviously does, in addition to his investments which 'got better every day'. In 1882 he is able to hand £2,500 to Anna (119:10) – a very considerable sum.

671

In the third generation, at the turn of the century, Ursula earns £50 a year as a teacher qualified only by London matriculation, exactly what DHL himself earned as an uncertified teacher (with London matriculation) 1905–6, but that is 'enough for her to live on independently' albeit very modestly (334:15–16). (Louie Burrows with a college education started at £75 p.a. in 1908.) Skrebensky gets £150 p.a. as a subaltern in the Royal Engineers, to add to the further £150 p.a. of his private income (273:4–8). Will now has £400 p.a. 'with his wife's money and his own' (334:12); and when he gets his new County post his salary goes up to £200 (398:13–14), though that is spoken of as 'only' £200 and is obviously not over-generous. Ursula gives her mother 50s. a month which, she is quite sure, will pay for her keep (362:17); and indeed an agricultural labourer in 1900 only earned an average 58s. a month. Full board and lodging, with a landlady, would cost 45–60s. a month. Against this may be measured the extravagance of Ursula and Skrebensky in London, when they spend £20 in 'a little under a week' (420:39), i.e. more than a third of Ursula's annual salary as a teacher. An experienced shop-assistant received 28s. or 30s. for an eighty-hour week on the eve of the First World War.